INTO THE ETERNAL NIGHT

A glittering band encircled Mozy's skull as she waited in the darkness. Time slid by her like an imponderable mass of ice. What would time come to mean to her when her consciousness was frozen into a series of impulses in the computer?

A heartbeat passed, then two. The circlet of fire around her forehead began spinning and twinkling, faster and bright, and contracting. It tightened over the lobes of her consciousness like a glittering fist. A vibration was building inside; forces were gathering, currents of life once bound were coming unleashed. Exhilaration and terror and vertigo flashed through her in a pulse. Somewhere within her, fierce streams were cutting new beds, winds were gusting and moaning, the earth shivering. There was a sun flaring, a candle guttering, a feeling of disconnectedness . . .

Then, for a breath, everything fell silent. There was no sound . . . no light . . . no motion—

—and then the world erupted with a thunderclap and a keening wail, driving a spike of pain straight through to the center of her consciousness. Hallucinating in agony, she wandered among the stars, heard the void speaking in tongues. The emptiness rang around her like an infinite gong, and then darkness crushed in upon her. . . .

Also by Jeffrey A. Carver
published by Tor Books

The Rapture Effect

JEFFREY A. CARVER

INFINITY LINK

A TOM DOHERTY ASSOCIATES BOOK
NEW YORK

Grateful acknowledgment is made for use of lyrics to the song, "Wind" by Bob Bruno, as performed by Circus Maximus. Lyrics used by permission of Danel Music, Inc., © 1967.

THE INFINITY LINK

Published by arrangement with Bluejay Books, Inc.

A TOR Book
Published by Tom Doherty Associates, Inc.
49 West 24 Street
New York, NY 10010

Cover art by David Mattingly

ISBN: 0-812-53327-5   Can. ISBN: 0-812-53328-3

First Tor edition: October 1985

Printed in the United States of America

0 9 8 7 6 5 4 3 2

For Mildred Sherrick Carver, in loving memory; and Robert D. Carver, with love and gratitude.

Acknowledgments

In the nearly six years that have passed since I began writing this book, I have received emotional, critical, and material support from a multitude of sources. Following are some of the people who have helped me, in ways large and small, perhaps more than they themselves know:

Robert and Carol Carver, for encouragement and assistance far beyond the call of duty, without whose help I would still be hammering this manuscript on stone tablets; Charles and Nora Carver; Nancy Thompson; all of the Sherricks; Allysen Palmer; Crystal Nash; Jane Sleamaker; Helen Haggerty; Ken Winans; Gene and Kate Soccolich; Pam Fink; Janet Moore; Kathy Vaillancourt; Cynthia Haring; Claudi Metz; Leslie Smith; David and Betty Holloway; Robert and Cindy Clancy; Marty Clark Rich; Diane Duane; Jane Yolen; Joan D. Vinge; and the furry fellow who was always there—Sam.

I would like to give special thanks to all of the members of the Writing Group, including Jane Jewell and Mary Aldridge—and especially Craig Gardner, Richard Bowker, and Victoria Bolles, who listened to the entire manuscript read aloud over a period of some four years—whose many excellent suggestions and perceptive criticisms helped me to improve virtually every section of the book.

Technical advice regarding tachyons was provided to me by Drs. Gerald Feinberg and Robert Forward. I took their ideas and modified them to my own specifications, and these gentlemen are not to be blamed for any misinterpretations. Likewise, thanks to Vernor Vinge, for thoughts pertaining to computer intelligence.

Finally, I would like to thank my agent, Richard Curtis, for never losing hope; and most especially, I would like to credit Jim Frenkel, the book's editor twice over, and now publisher, who put faith in this story on the basis of an eighteen-page outline, and without whose boundless enthusiasm and brainstorming energy the finished book might never have come to pass.

Thank you, all.

Jeffrey A. Carver
Cambridge, Mass.
April 1984

CONTENTS

THE INFINITY LINK

PART ONE

MOZY

Prelude

The wanderer slipped across space and time, sailing an ocean of darkness in which stars hung like lanternfish. Watchful eyes might have observed it shimmering out of focus, melting and recrystallizing— here now, gone now, always somehow creeping ahead of where the eye would look for it next. Mostly, though, it moved unnoticed. Space was vast, and life here was stretched thin, scattered among the light-years.

The wanderer, however, was not alone. Connections to other worlds sparkled and danced with life, despite distance, despite time. Tachyons spun out from its core at speeds close to infinite, carrying news, or greetings, or songs. A new world lay ahead, a world which they could not yet see, but could *feel*, a world from which a response had finally been aroused. Whether someone had deciphered their songs, or merely echoed with one of their own, was unclear. What mattered was the existence of the answer and its welcoming tone.

Time passed, and a host of new songs was spun. As the wanderer drew nearer, a messenger was observed departing from the destination world. It rose out of its sun's gravity well, climbing toward the wanderer, spouting a thin but energetic flame as it crossed the gulf.

Far outside the orbits of even the dimmest and loneliest of the planets of this star, the two bodies approached one another. One moved in a slow and deliberate curve, the other in a shimmering ripple— drawn together by mutual curiosity and the offering of a song.

Chapter 1

The darkness hurt. Time moved at a crawl in the waiting state. She floated in a medium that buzzed with energy, with spiderweb tracings of configurations that promised her pathways out of the darkness. She ached to move.

What was it going to be, this time?

(Sequence start,) murmured a voice.

Cuing signals brushed over her like fine threads. Ruby and gold pinlights swam in the darkness, then deformed into pale disks. She extended a greeting touch as her travelling partner approached. Together, two figures of light, they awaited the moment of transformation.

At last, it came: a swarm of particles that enveloped them and congealed into crystalline fire. The fire swirled around them and funneled them forward, toward the projection point.

A darkness deeper than night opened to swallow them.

A period of time passed that was impossible to measure.

Mozy, bone weary, looked around. She was standing in a forest clearing with Kadin. They'd come a terribly long way already today, and fatigue was making it hard for her to think.

"It's a time of magic," Kadin was saying. "A time long before humanity. Before even the seeds of humanity's beginnings." Kadin peered at her with those deep blue eyes, as though he had just explained everything.

She shook her head, trying to clear the fatigue. "David, what are you talking about?" She sighed. "We need to rest." She looked around for a soft patch of grass. All of the greenery seemed somehow

. . . cryptozoic, maybe. All ferns and odd-looking mosses. "How far have we come, anyway?" Memories shimmered in her mind—ice caves, plains, canyons—images blurred together.

"We're in the world's early years, now, Mozy. We have no time to rest. We must use the magic while it's active—"

"The world's early years?" She stopped. "Are you saying that we've been travelling through time?"

He smiled. "You *are* tired, aren't you?"

Yes. Had they really crossed all those lands?

"Mozy, listen to me—and try to understand. Magic is a power that has always existed in the earth. It appears in waves and cycles that move through the Earth's history. At certain points, it is very strong; but at other times, it is subdued, and may be forgotten for eons at a time."

Mozy listened impatiently.

"Hear me out. Please," Kadin said. "During most of human history, the magic has slept; it is suppressed by the presence of human thought and logic. But further along, at the end of humanity's time, it resurfaces. And that's where we have to go. We've become dislodged in time, Mozy. We must ride the crest of the magic down the timestream, until we reach the precise point at which it is possible to return to our *own* time."

He spoke with maddening self-assurance.

"You have to trust me if we're to go home," he said softly. He shrugged and looked away.

"I do trust you," she murmured. Hadn't they come this far, hadn't they survived this long by working together? Still, there were times when she felt she didn't know who this man was—and other times when she swore she had known him forever.

"Not just me," Kadin was saying. "You must trust in the magic."

"What magic?" she cried in exasperation.

Again he smiled. "A small enchantment at first—here, where the powers aren't fully formed yet. But later—well, a much stronger spell." Beneath the smile, she thought she detected a deep wariness, almost a foreboding.

She gave in with a sigh. "All right. What do we do?"

"Step close to me." He turned and gazed into the forest. He spoke softly a series of strange and indistinct syllables, and then he reached back for her. His hands shimmered as their fingers touched, and the spell took hold: shadow crossing shadow where their hands joined, darkness against darkness, no physical sensation of touching, but the presence of his fingers intertwining with the presence of hers. Connected in this way, they stepped forward together into the forest . . .

Into what she had thought was a forest.

The woods shuddered and distorted queerly. A path opened before them, faintly luminous with purplish and green light. Trees turned into folding stick figures, snapping back from them on either side. The forest danced against the sky, and seemed to flow around them like an envelope as they walked, giving way, but closing again behind them. Leaves fluttered madly over their heads, and sunlight cascaded through the treetops with bursts of prismatic color. Only Kadin remained solid beside her, his presence and the touch of his hand binding her against fear. Snowflakes whipped their faces, flickering in alternation with bursts of sun and green and autumn brown.

Time was running mad around them.

Before she could catch her breath to ask a question, the forest suddenly fell away, like a dead skin, and she glimpsed a windswept glacier.

And then the sun went out.

Jonders followed the images with guarded satisfaction. All indications were that the transition had been made smoothly, and that the subjects were responding well to the test situation.

With minute adjustments, he increased the monitoring gain on the female subject. He wanted a clearer perception of her degree of commitment to the magic . . . if he could just clarify that image without in the process altering the results. . . .

They walked in darkness for a long time, with only the sound of dry earth crunching beneath their feet. In time, the darkness was pierced by stars, and on several occasions, by lights flickering beyond the horizon. She sensed, without quite knowing how, that those were the lights of humanity flickering on the Earth, cities living and dying.

Time moved past them like the wind, brushing against their skin. Whispers ran through the wind—the sounds of human civilizations emerging and growing and crumbling, too fast for them to see except as a glimmer at the edge of the night.

They continued walking.

Eventually a false dawn began to penetrate the darkness, and Mozy could once again discern shapes—vaguely, at first, and then more distinctly. They were in a forest again, this time a forest of enormous trees, with massive boughs held upright, like muscle-bound arms.

Among the trees, she thought she glimpsed movement. And was that a rustling, or merely the sound of their own footsteps?

The true dawn came later, a pale light filtering through the treetops, grey at first, and then warming to a wintry pink. She could see deeper into the woods now, and realized that it was almost inconceivably old. The trees were so massive and motionless and bare, they might have been made of stone. Even the sky seemed weary with years, what little she could see of the vault overhead. Behind her, there was now a definite rustle of movement, and twice she glimpsed something large, like a bear, snuffling a distance away through the trees. There was, she suspected, a gathering of creatures shadowing them, following two trespassers in their wood.

"Who are they?" she asked, when she could stand the uncertainty no longer.

Kadin glanced back at their invisible escort. "The inheritors of the Earth, I believe."

She nodded, and continued in silence for a while. Then: "Are they dangerous?"

There was a long pause, before he answered, "I wouldn't want to test them."

Instinctively, Mozy quickened her pace.

Time passed, and the woods, ageless and sullen, began to fill with a feverish glow. The edge of the forest was visible ahead, and as they approached it, Kadin urged her forward toward the source of the glow.

They paused at the forest's edge, amid a litter of stunted and broken trees, and stared out across a scorched plain, bloodied by the light of a monstrous sun. The plain was featureless, except for a rocky bluff reaching out like a crooked finger from the right, terminating abruptly a quarter of a mile from where they stood. Nothing stirred in the desolation except the ruddy flames of the sun, setting to the left of the bluff.

"Even the sun looks like it's dying," Mozy said.

"It's aging," Kadin said. "But it won't die until long after the death of Humanity's Earth."

His words struck an uncomfortable chord. *The death of Humanity's Earth . . . and what were they doing here?* Turning, she thought: *Earth's inheritors.* The dying sunlight had set the forest ablaze in devastating beauty. When she turned back, the last of the sun was sinking beneath the horizon, until all that remained was a glow fading against the woods and sky. "Are we the last humans?" she asked, in a whisper.

Kadin nodded and stepped forward.

They walked into the desert. Behind them, animals of various sizes clustered at the edge of the forest, peering out. Several of the larger ones were already standing in the desert, sniffing the air.

Night fell as they crossed the desert, the sky turning to midnight purple, with capering, ghostly auroras. Stars slipped into view as the purple deepened to velvet black. The bluff grew larger before them, until in the shadows at its base they spied a flicker of orange light. Drawing near, they discovered a campfire crackling and dancing, and they hurried forward to its warmth and light.

Mozy crouched with her hands out to the fire, and watched the flames licking and leaping like an alive thing, throwing light and shadow up onto the cliffside. Its illumination revealed stone and masonry rubble at the base of the wall. A former human habitation? A cleft in the cliff wall suggested the presence of a cave, perhaps a shelter where even now something lived, something not-human, something that had waited for humans to depart and might not welcome their return. She shivered in the firelight and wondered how many years lay empty between herself and the last humans who had walked here.

Kadin studied her, his eyes dark in the flicker of the fire. "This is what we're here for," he said, gesturing. "The fire." She gazed back at him silently. "We can't stay long, you know. The new owners are eager to take over." Only his eyes moved as he glanced into the shadows. Scrabbling noises could be heard echoing along the cliff face.

Chilled, she edged closer to the fire.

"It's protecting us for now," Kadin said. "But look." He stretched out a hand, and the fire sputtered down to embers, as though an hour had passed in an eyeblink.

"Why did you do that?" Mozy cried. She crouched forward and blew on the coals. They glowed dimly in response. She looked up in panic. "Can we find more wood?" Kadin shook his head and glanced again toward the shadows. They were deeper now. The scrabbling was louder.

Kadin rocked back, his expression grave. "There is a choice. We can wait for the fire to die—or we can act at once, while the magic can still help us."

"Magic? Is this what you were talking about? If it's magic, why can't you make it burn longer?"

"Magic conforms to its own rules," Kadin answered. "We can't retrace our steps, and we can't remain here."

Fear rose in her throat. "What *can* we do?"

Kadin's brows narrowed. His voice hardened. "Watch the flames!" The coals hissed, and flames shot up, blazing hot and bright. Mozy shielded her face from the intensity. The flames dropped again to a flickering tongue, and darkness crowded back in around them.

"One more time they can rise," Kadin said. "But when that is done, even the embers will die." The flames were weakening even as they danced in his eyes. "When it's gone—" He hesitated, then shrugged. "But when it rises one last time, we can return home—if—"

"If *what*?" she whispered.

"If we pass *into* the flames and into the fire's enchantment. If the magic holds, we'll be transported back to our own time—to our own world."

"And if it fails—?"

He met her gaze and said nothing.

She stared back at him in astonishment. "You mean it, don't you? You mean we're to . . . step into the fire."

He held her gaze. "It's the only way I know, Mozy. The magic will fail us only if we fail it. But without it, we'll surely die here."

"But . . ." Her voice caught.

"It will burn far hotter than the flame you just saw. Only by consuming us totally can it transform us and take us home."

She closed her eyes, envisioning fire roaring up around her, destroying her in agony. She barely heard him saying, "When it rises to its height, we must leap together. It will last only seconds—and if we do not go—if we hesitate—the chance will be lost forever." She stared back at him, stared at the fire. Her thoughts filled with images of burning flesh.

Kadin's eyes would not leave hers. "Whatever we do, we must do together. We live or die, together."

She glanced into the shadows along the wall and glimpsed the movement of . . .

She began to tremble. "David, I don't—"

"Have I ever betrayed you?"

She took a breath. "No."

"Then look for the courage within you, Mozy—look for it now."

She swallowed—and thought of dying here with Kadin, freezing in the night or being torn apart by animals she could not even name.

She thought of stepping into a fire, and fear rose hotter than the flame itself. And yet . . .

She knew—she *felt*, though she could not explain how or why—that he was speaking the truth. Her determination hardened, and before the instant could pass, she rose on shaky legs and said, "Dammit, then—let's go."

Kadin gathered himself like a breath of wind. The flames licked up, dancing. The coals blazed. The air close to the ground hissed and swirled and fed itself to the fire. A flame shot up with a growl, then roared into a dazzling tower. "*Now!*" he cried.

Mozy glanced sideways at him, then jerked her gaze back to the heart of the flame. Its fuel was nearly gone.

She sprang forward.

Flames thundered around her. She floated, rising in a furious cloud of crackling gases. Where was Kadin? There: a dark presence beside her. The heat poured through her; the violence was incredible, spinning her, slamming her end over end. She struggled to remain conscious. Suddenly the brightness splashed outward in a corona, leaving cool darkness in the center. She fell through the eye like a stone, and darkness and silence overtook her.

Chapter 2

She rested, scarcely remembering where she was, or why. As time passed, she sensed movement nearby. Kadin. The awareness stirred her. (We survived,) she said.

Kadin became visible, his face illumined against the dark. His eyes sparkled with pride. (You trusted in the magic, Mozy—and it worked. We've returned to our own time, our own place.)

She peered back in puzzlement. (We have?) And suddenly she knew.

They were in the computer. In the test link. Kadin was far away, in the orbiting space city; and she was in the Sandaran Research Center, alone in a booth, linked to Kadin by a strand of energy spinning thousands of kilometers into the sky.

They had survived the flame and the magic and the end of the world; and it was all a fiction, a test, an exercise. Outside the computer link, a research staff had been observing everything. If she and Kadin had perished in the fire, the final outcome would have been the same. Only the memory would have been different.

(Are you displeased, Mozy?) Kadin's full figure became visible, walking toward her across a dark emptiness. Kadin: a man she had never met, except in the link. A man whose face was a little different each time they met, each time a creation of her own mind.

She stared at him uncomfortably. It was always this way, coming out of a session—when the hypnotic blocks dissolved, and she emerged from fantasy to reality—the disturbing realization that she had invested all of her fears and hopes in something that was nothing more than a game inside a computer. And yet the scenarios *were* real—far more real to her than her own dreams.

(Mozy?)

(What? Oh . . .)

Kadin peered at her. (You feel embarrassed again, don't you—because you believed in the scenario.)

(Perhaps.) She shrugged. (All right. Yes.)

(That's what the hypnotic blocks are for,) he said gently. (If you hadn't believed, the session would have been wasted. I had to convince you of the magic. That's what it was all about.)

She knew she was blushing. (I know. It's just a silly feeling.)

Kadin smiled in sympathy as he reached out. (We have to break the link, now, Mozy.)

She laughed. (Right. See you next time.)

Kadin winked, and then he, and the lights illuminating him, shrank silently away. He fluttered like a candle flame and vanished.

(Good-bye,) Mozy said softly, more to herself than to Kadin. This was always the hardest part, being left so alone. The darkness and the emptiness rang around her like a bell. She sighed . . . blinked . . . forced herself to relax . . .

. . . felt the layers of the link slip away . . .

. . . and opened her eyes in the gloom of the subject cubicle.

She was seated in a reclining chair, her head encased in a helmet. Her right foot was asleep. Hearing a scratching sound, she looked to her left. A woman peered up from her clipboard. "How do you feel?" the woman asked.

Bill Jonders detached himself from the monitoring link and slowly brought his senses back into focus. He glanced at the console readouts. Twenty-seven minutes, elapsed time. Rubbing his eyebrows, he keyed the audio circuit to Kadin. "Looks like a fine run, David. I'll get back to you soon for debriefing. Any problems I should know about?"

"None," answered Kadin. "I'll be waiting."

On one of the screens, Jonders saw Mozelle Moi removing her headset, with Lusela Burns's help. He touched a switch. "Mozelle—it looked like one of your best. Very good." In the monitor, Mozelle nodded. Jonders switched channels. "Hoshi, run the profiles across my board, please. I'd like to get ready for the review with Kadin."

Hoshi Aronson grunted from the next console.

Jonders removed his own helmet and massaged his temples. He was weary, and not just from the day's work. For weeks, the pace had been unrelenting. It would kill them all, if it didn't stop soon; but the transmission date had just been moved up, again, to three weeks from tomorrow. The work *had* to be done by then. Marie, bless her, had merely been hinting, rather than demanding, that the kids should see more of their father. They would have to be patient a little while longer.

The monitors blinked, bringing him back to the present. Profile displays appeared, with Hoshi's rough-cut analysis of the last run. Jonders focused on the holographic contours. The graphs looked good, with few of the indecision dips and plateaus of the early days; and the decision folds were all nicely surrounded by confidence peaks. It *was* a good run.

Kadin's profile was improving daily. By now, Jonders knew intuitively what to expect on the graphs, but he could still be surprised by nuances and subtleties. One thing he noted now was an increase in contours of imaginative activity. It confirmed his own sense of the session; the landscapes and situations devised by Kadin had been unusually vivid and creative, well beyond the scope of the original instructions. Jonders placed code-markers at points to be referenced later, then jumped ahead to look at the emotional-component analysis of Kadin's reponses to Mozelle.

He'd already lost track of the clock by the time he donned his helmet again for direct manipulation of the graphic images, and a final debriefing with Kadin.

"Good night, Mozy," Lusela Burns said. She glanced at her clipboard. "See you Thursday at fifteen hundred?"

Mozy nodded and rose. "Right," she said. "Bye." Her head was buzzing as she walked from the room. The feeling had returned; she'd felt it the instant the link had dissolved. Reality was an intrusion. It always was, after her times with Kadin. The debriefing didn't help much, either; nothing against Lusela, but she needed time, and privacy, to readjust to being back in her own body, and they never gave that to her. Maybe it wouldn't help, anyway. Maybe nothing would. The feeling was always there at the end of a session.

She passed the glassed-in control room where Jonders and Hoshi Aronson were working, retrieved her jacket from the rack in the foyer, and walked down the long corridor to the main lobby and the transit station. The monorail platform was uncrowded, despite the hour. As usual, a large part of the staff was working overtime. She had never been asked to do so herself, but she was only a part-time subject. Some important test was coming up, and most of the departments were putting in long hours. She rather envied them.

The train hummed into the station on its single maglev rail. Evening workers piled out, and Mozy and a handful of others boarded. She chose a seat and settled in for the ride back to New Phoenix, resting her head against the aluminum window jamb.

Her mood persisted. She didn't know what she had a right to expect—but something more than just a paycheck. Her hours spent at the institute both excited her and exhausted her. Perhaps she wanted more challenge, or more recognition; perhaps she just didn't want to feel depressed every time she said good-bye to Kadin. Perhaps she ought to discuss her feelings with someone; but everyone was always so busy.

She peered out the window for a last glimpse of the installation, as the train accelerated on a long curve into the mountains. The main research building turned its profile, a curiously graceful merging of oblong shapes. Perched atop one corner of the building, a squarish tower jutted into the twilight. Behind it sat the domed housing for the fusion generators and tachyon rings. Together, the buildings stood stark and imposing, surrounded by peaks in the fading afternoon sky.

Finally an embankment cut off the view. Mozy dozed as the train gathered speed, leaping along a steel thread as it descended along the Mazatzal Mountain Range. Sleepily she thought of how little she *really* knew of the center's work—hardly anything beyond the words of the subject applicants' introductory booklet:

> "*Sandaran-Choharis Institute for the Study of Tachyonic Phenomena, often referred to as the Sandaran Link Research Center, is a civilian, federally funded institution conducting both classified and unclassified research into tachyon behavior and theoretical and applied principles of matter translocation through the use of modulated tachyon beams.*"

In other words, the theory and practice of dissociating matter—a rock, a cup of coffee, a dog—and transmitting an exact description of its molecular structure to a receiving station for reassembly. In short, moving an object almost instantaneously from, say, Los Angeles to New Phoenix. Or from the Earth to the Moon.

Tachyons were particles that moved faster than light, and *only* faster than light. Like normal particles, they came in various sizes and shapes. The researchers at the Center were interested in a family of tachyons known as T4 particles, which they proposed to use in a coherent beam to scan, transmit, and reconstruct objects. Whether they had actually tried yet, and if so, whether they'd succeeded or failed, she didn't know. Most of the work was classified. Her own job was a part of a program to devise systems for profiling the human consciousness, not in the gross detail of ordinary psychological profiling, but in intimate and microscopic detail. It was, she had been told, more a problem of artificial intelligence than of psychology. It was all part of the process of making a transmission system safe for humans. Apparently, the goal was to ensure that human subjects did not arrive at the receiving end of a transmission link with their brains scrambled.

But why the secrecy? Was the military involved, at some level? Probably. She'd have to pump Hoshi on the subject, the next time they went out for a drink.

She rubbed her jaw, imagining the process going wrong—and some poor fool being blasted to dust by tachyon lightning, only to reappear in some godforsaken place as a gibbering psychotic. Pity the poor first victim.

Glancing to the side, Mozy realized that she was being stared at by another commuter; she'd been fingering a scar that etched her cheek, from temple to chin, a souvenir of an adolescent incident she'd have preferred to forget. Exhaling slowly, she placed her hands in her lap, suppressing an urge to try to rub the scar off her face. She jerked her head to stare out the window, where the mountain foothills were spinning by.

She imagined faces out there: Jonders and Hoshi and David Kadin. For an instant, she imagined how they must think of her: *Poor Mozy, so scarred and unattractive, the only man she can appeal to is one who doesn't even know what she looks like, except through the computer link.* But why should you care? she thought. Forget it, she thought; but she couldn't.

The mountains fell behind in the dusk. The monorail sped through flatter country, in a wide arc that took it around the Phoenix crater safety zone. As drowsiness overtook her, the land slowly changed to a great arid vacuum, pulling images out of her subconscious and dancing them before her like lights on a pond: visions of ragged suitors crossing a wasteland to reach her—and David Kadin striding along, overtaking them all.

The train eased into the New Phoenix metro station, and Mozy made her way down two flights to the subway platform. She waited with the rush-hour crowd, watching the street musicians with their ghostly holos gyrating around them, the music itself periodically drowned out by the din of the trains. Finally Mozy's train appeared; a half hour later, she stepped out into the street a few blocks from her apartment.

It was one of the brick-and-concrete postwar housing projects, built in '17 to help accommodate a populace displaced by the destruction of Phoenix in the Great Mistake. Now it housed students from the New University, as well. Further down the street were several similar projects; on the facing side of the street was a row of modern townhouses. Children's voices could be heard in the street as Mozy turned up the walk to the front entrance.

The lobby was empty, the orange and crimson colors of last year's redecoration shouting a hollow welcome. She hadn't checked her letter box in a week—she rarely got paper mail, anyway—so she went over and unlocked the compartment. To her surprise, there was a letter inside. She plucked it out and read the return address. It was from her sister Kink. She tucked the letter into her bag and trotted up three flights of stairs.

Pushing open her apartment door, she nudged the lights on with her elbow. "I'm home," she called. Scratching noises greeted her. She crossed the living room and peered down into the chamber where two gerbils were scrabbling about on their bed of wood shavings and waving their tiny noses in the air. Mozy made whistling noises and checked the food and water dispensers. "Nice to see you, Mousie. And you, little Maggot." Maggie, in answer, poked her nose up to one of the air holes in the side of the chamber.

Tossing her coat over the back of a frayed sofa, Mozy went into the kitchen. She turned about aimlessly, peering into cupboards, wondering at the feeling of restlessness that plagued her. She shrugged, put on water for tea, and began making dinner.

The phone chimed. "Phone on!" she called, her mouth full of spinach greens.

"Mozy? It's Mardi."

"Wait a minute!" Mozy carried her salad bowl into the living room. "Picture on," she ordered, and when Mardi's image appeared, she lifted a fork in greeting. "Hi. What's up?"

Mardi tucked a strand of hair behind her ear. "Didn't you get my message?"

"I just got home. What was it?" Mozy forked more salad into her mouth.

"Mozy, I called two days ago! Don't you ever check your messages?"

Mozy swallowed, realizing for the first time that her phone's message light was on. "Sorry," she said guiltily. "I've been sort of preoccupied. Was it anything urgent?"

"It is now," said Mardi. "Tomorrow's the last day of registration at school. Do you want to go over together? If we get there early—"

Mozy gasped. "Tomorrow? It *can't* be!"

Her friend groaned in frustration. "How could you have forgotten? After all the times we've talked about it!"

Mozy sighed uneasily. She hadn't exactly forgotten; actually, she'd been keeping it out of her mind. Mardi and she had attended classes together last year, and they'd agreed to do the same in the coming session. Now, Mozy was doubtful about wanting to go back to school at all. She'd been at the university, off and on, for six years; and she still hadn't made notable progress toward finishing her degree in philosophy. "I still have to go through the catalog," she said. "I haven't decided what I want to do yet."

"You haven't been *that* busy, have you?" There was a slightly wounded tone to Mardi's voice. "It sounds like you haven't even thought about it."

Now you've done it, Mozy thought. She ought to have called Mardi, but . . .

"I have been kind of wrapped up in this thing," she said finally. "Tell you what—let's meet for breakfast. We can talk about it then." She forced a smile and stabbed at her salad again.

Mardi shrugged. "Okay—sure. Eight-thirty in the Sunshine Room?"

"Fine."

They talked a minute longer before Mozy begged off, pleading the need to study the school materials. The screen went dark, and she sat and stared at it and finished her dinner and thought about what she was going to tell Mardi in the morning.

She played halfheartedly with Maggie and Mouse for a while, then took a bath, and went to bed after spending two minutes shaking her head at the course listings. She tossed and turned for nearly an hour before drifting off, thinking of Kadin and the fire at the end of the world.

The morning sun revived her as she walked the four blocks to the student union. Trotting up the steps, she caught an open door and darted into the main cafeteria. She stood near the door, scanning the tables. Not seeing Mardi, she went to the serving line and loaded her tray, then turned from the cashier to find an empty table.

She was halfway through her omelet and coffee by the time Mardi found her. Out of breath, Mardi slid into the seat opposite her. "Feels like I haven't seen you in ages!" Mardi cried, smiling with good humor. She was a shy young woman, several years Mozy's junior.

"Tell me how you've been," Mozy said, putting on a face of cheer. As they ate, Mardi reeled out a summary of her plans for school, obviously hoping that Mozy would share in the enthusiasm. Mozy listened with a display of attention, postponing the inevitable.

Finally Mardi pressed her. "We'd better get moving. But what do you think? What are you going to do?"

Mozy poked at her coffee cup. "Mardi—"

Her friend frowned. "What's the matter?"

"I'm—not going to register."

Mardi stared at her, crestfallen. "But—you said—" She gestured emptily.

I know, Mozy thought. I know I said it.

She cleared her throat.

Mardi groped almost visibly. "Is it the money? Is that it? Have you thought about going part time, and still working?"

Mozy shook her head. "It's not the money. It's the job." She closed her eyes, trying to sort it all out in her mind. She wanted to explain it, but she scarcely understood the reasons herself. She suddenly realized that she was fingering her scar again, and she dropped her hand. "Here it is," she said. "I want to work full time at the project, if I can. It's not definite—" which was the world's biggest understatement, since she had yet to even ask—"but I want to keep my time available for it." She sat back uncomfortably.

"You've never said anything about that before," Mardi said, puzzled.

Mozy grasped for words. "I—feel more involved there now. More involved than I ever felt at school. Besides, I can always go back to school. But how often do you have a chance to be in a project like this?" With a vast sense of relief, she realized that she had in fact, gotten it right. It was that feeling of involvement that she wanted. It seemed so obvious now.

Mardi nodded slowly. "Well—I guess I can understand that." Her voice suggested that she did not. She looked at the table. "It's just that you never said anything about it before. From what you said a few weeks ago, I thought you didn't like the project that much."

Mozy took a breath to answer, then sighed. She didn't know what else to say.

Mardi looked up suspiciously. "Say—you haven't fallen in *love* or something, have you? You'd tell me, wouldn't you?"

"No, nothing like that," Mozy assured her. She swallowed with difficulty. "I hardly even know anyone out there. I see this guy Hoshi now and then, but it's nothing romantic."

Mardi looked unconvinced. "Okay, but who's this David person you're always meeting with, in your sessions?"

Mozy scoffed. "I could hardly be in love with him. I've never even met him in real life." She wrapped her fingers around her coffee cup. "He's not even on Earth. It's just a long-distance linkup." She looked up. "That's all I'm allowed to say about it."

"Okay," said Mardi. "You're not in love. And I can't change your mind." Her voice sounded more distant than it had a moment ago. "Well, I'd better get going, or I'll be in line all day."

"Mardi, it's the project itself," Mozy insisted, suddenly wanting to make it clear before her friend went away hurt. She felt foolish, and was probably blushing from her attempt to deny that ridiculous notion about being in love. She gestured agitatedly. "It's these feelings I have about what I'm doing there. It means something—" She ran out of words. She couldn't articulate it any better than that. Damn it, why did friends always have to make life so complicated?

"Well, it's your decision," Mardi said, rising. "Look—stay in touch, at least, okay? I've got to get going."

Mozy wanted to blurt a last plea for understanding, but instead she just nodded. It was no good; it would be better to call Mardi later. Nevertheless, her face was still stinging when she walked back out into the morning sun.

Chapter 3

Hoshi called that evening. Mozy was glad for the diversion. She had been leafing through books, flipping channels on the tube, trying one role-game after another—and nothing had kept her occupied for more than a few minutes. "You got home before midnight," she said. "That's a switch."

As usual, Hoshi had the visual off. "Yeah, they let the rats out of the cage early tonight. Want to have a drink at the Chance?"

"Rats? I thought we were the rats, and you were the keepers."

"All a matter of perspective, I guess. What do you say?"

"Sure," Mozy said. It would be a perfect opportunity to grill him. "Twenty minutes?"

"See you there."

Leaving books and computer cubes scattered on the table, she dumped her dinner dishes into the sonic bath, grabbed her coat and wallet, and headed for the door.

The Golden Chance Cafe was a five-block walk from her apartment, on the southwestern edge of the campus. She slipped through the entrance and stood in the shadows, letting her eyes adjust to the gloom. The cafe was narrow, with a partition down the middle. She peered down both sides, and finally located Hoshi in the rear. "Have room for another rat?" she said, sliding into the booth.

Hoshi looked up, his eyes sweeping briefly. "Ah!" he said. "An escapee! Do you want to join our conspiracy?"

"Only if it involves drinking. How are you?"

"Starved. They didn't even give us Purina at work."

He flashed a disconcerting smile. Actually, it wasn't the smile that was disconcerting; it was the eyes. She often wondered just how much of the world Hoshi really knew by sight, and how much by inference. Blinded in a radiation accident as a boy, his vision was partially restored now with the assistance of implanted retinal scanners and microprocessors. According to his own description, the world he saw was a montage of lights and shadows. His depth perception was poor—hence the medallion he wore on a neck-chain, a transducer for a sonar ranger. Apparently his condition did not interfere with his work, most of which he performed in direct linkup with the computer. He was considered one of the top program analysts at the Center.

She realized she was staring at him. "I'm glad I don't have to work late like all of you," she said, lying. She grinned with one side of her mouth, trying to conceal her envy.

Hoshi studied her silently, his eyes flicking and shifting. He gave her a quirky smile. "We're either supermen or maniacs. I'm not sure which. But what about you? Have you decided if you're going back to school?"

She shook her head. "I'm not." Her stomach began to flutter. "Not while I'm working at the Center. I wouldn't have time for both."

Hoshi angled his head to one side, frowning. His eyes glinted, catching the light of a globed lamp on the wall. "Haven't they told you? The project is ending soon—at least, the part you're in."

The stomach flutter tightened to a knot. "They hadn't mentioned a date. I thought—maybe they'd keep me on. Maybe working more hours—or helping—" Hoshi was scowling now. "They told me once that there was a chance that—"

She cut herself off as a waitress appeared. Hoshi ordered a turkey club and a Bohemia draft; she just ordered a beer. When the waitress was gone, she raised her eyes again.

"It's just like them not to bother telling you," he said. "Talk about people wrapped up in their own little worlds." He shook his head. "It'd be nice if you could stay on, but—I don't know. I suppose you could ask Bill."

Mozy shrugged, smarting inwardly. How stupid of her to think . . . they'd never actually *offered* her more work, and the last time they'd even hinted was a month or two ago. How could she have assumed . . . ?

She avoided Hoshi's eyes. Images whirled in her mind: of the computer link, and of Kadin; of those rare and cherished moments when she *was* somebody and her real personality emerged, and she could laugh and cry with a man who didn't care what she looked like, and who was always there. All of that would be gone. No more link, no more Kadin. And what the hell would she do then?

When their orders arrived, Mozy stared at her beer for a time, fingering the glass. "So—what now?" she said finally. "Why are they ending the project?"

Hoshi lifted his sandwich, then paused. "I can't tell you that, you know. I don't even know all the details myself."

She stared at him as he took a bite.

He put the sandwich down and cleared his throat, tapping his fork against his plate. "Well—" His eyes moved from side to side. "I can tell you something, I guess. Don't talk about this with Bill or Lusela, though—not that it's a breach, exactly, but they're kind of touchy about it."

Her head buzzed as she nodded.

"They're going to do a transmission. I can't tell you who, or where, or why—but they're going to send someone through a long-distance link."

"But I knew that all along."

"Well, there's a big time factor involved, now. I can't tell you—I don't even *know* exactly why—though I have some idea. Word has come from above that we have to be ready for transmission in a few weeks. That's why we've been working like madmen."

"But if it's just a test," she said carefully, "won't they have to keep working until all the bugs are out of the system?"

Hoshi chuckled. "There had better not *be* any bugs in the system," he said. "We've been smoothing out the last kinks for a couple of months, now. I'm sure there'll be more work eventually, but right now there's one transmission they're worried about, and that one *has* to go right." He resumed eating.

Mozy sipped her beer. She hardly tasted it. "So—what is it?" she asked, with poorly feigned nonchalance.

"Can't tell you."

"Well, *who's* being transmitted?"

"Can't tell you." Hoshi swallowed, then downed a third of his beer. His eyes probed hers; it was an eerie feeling, being watched by those half-seeing eyes. "You can guess, maybe," he said softly.

"Now, what's that supposed to mean?" she protested. "It could be anybody—Jonders, you, David. Some big shot." She shrugged.

"I mean," he said teasingly, "it's someone you know." He became mockingly serious. "That's all I can tell you."

Mozy scowled. She didn't like what she thought was the answer. "It's David, isn't it? It's Kadin, right?"

Hoshi blinked with reptilean deliberation. "Can't say," he murmured. But his expression did not contradict her statement.

"Shit," Mozy said. "*Shit!*" She shook her head, surprised by the intensity of the emotion. The knot in her gut was painful now; she was having trouble breathing. "It is David, isn't it? Where are they sending him? Why him? What if it doesn't work?"

"What do you care?" Hoshi said. "You don't even know him, really. And I never said it was him, anyway."

Mozy snorted at the last comment. That was just Hoshi covering his ass, after spilling. Still, he was right. Why such a strong reaction? She had never met Kadin and never would; he lived in the space settlement, and she lived on Earth, and that was it. She shrugged. "I like him, that's all. I wouldn't want to see anything happen to him."

"Uh-huh." Hoshi placed his fingertips on the table, as though playing a piano, or a computer keyboard. He smiled. "Have you considered that maybe they're transmitting him to Earth?"

"Are they?" she cried. Hoshi turned up his palms, grinning. "Tell me," she pleaded. "Is he coming here?"

At last Hoshi shook his head. "No." When Mozy glared at him, he sighed. "Sorry. Bad joke."

"He's not coming to Earth?"

He shook his head again. "Why is it so important to you?"

Angry at having been baited so easily, she sank back into the booth seat. When she spoke, her voice was harsh. "He's the only one who lets me feel involved there. The only one. It's damn frustrating, you know, just going in there twice a week, and not even seeing the results of it."

"Sometimes you do see results," Hoshi said. "You just don't know it."

She ignored him. "We're friends, in a way. Even though sometimes I'm scared half to death in the scenarios, and it's hard to *leave* them, to come back to reality—I still don't want it to end. I wish I could meet him." Stopping for breath, she gulped half of her beer. A mild alcoholic glow was spreading through her body.

Hoshi studied her. "What is it you like so much about him? Just out of curiosity."

She looked at him suspiciously for a moment, then shrugged. "He's friendly. He goes out of his way to make me feel comfortable. He treats me like a real person." Hoshi's face clouded, and she added,

"Well, you do, too. But hardly anyone else does. They're always in too much of a hurry. Well, David's not that way. Even when things get crazy, in the scenarios, he never forgets that I'm involved, too, and that I might need help getting through it."

"That's part of his job," Hoshi pointed out.

"It's part of his character, too," Mozy insisted. "I just wish I knew what his part was in all this—"

"Can't tell you that."

"I *know*. I'd ask him myself, but the hypnotic blocks work so well, I always forget. Now you tell me he's going to be put through the transmitter, and maybe scattered halfway to hell. Well, I just wish I could meet him, once—in person—before then." A wave of sadness crested in her, then slowly subsided, leaving a gritty feeling in her throat. "I have all these images of him, different ones each time I meet him. I'd like to know what he *really* looks like." She toyed with her glass.

"If I didn't know better," Hoshi said, "I'd say you're kind of sweet on this—guy." Hoshi looked poised and controlled, his fingers drumming lightly on the table's edge. His eyes seemed to focus and unfocus as he peered at her—seeing heaven-knew-what pattern of shadows, what image of her face. Those grey irises, with their slightly dilated pupils, seemed to stare right through her.

She cleared her throat uneasily. "I wouldn't exactly say I was sweet on him," she said.

Hoshi drummed. "Oh, no?"

She flushed. "Well, maybe a little. But how could I be really 'sweet' on someone I've never even met?"

Hoshi's smile became lopsided. "Easy. The way anybody gets hung up on anybody else. It just happens."

She thought, yeah, it just happens. "I suppose it's possible," she said, "but I don't think so. Not this time." She glanced at her watch. "Hey, it's getting late."

They pooled their money to pay the tab, then made their way to the exit. Outside, Mozy stuck her hands in her coat pocket. "See you later. Thanks for the drink," she said. Then she turned away and walked quickly home.

The apartment was still. She stood in the center of the living room, her mind still spinning from the conversation. She cast her coat aside and went into the bathroom and rummaged around for her hairbrush. She perched her purse on the edge of the sink and, pawing through it, found the hairbrush; she also found, unopened, the letter from Kink.

She turned it over. When had she last heard from her sister? A year, anyway. She still used the same awful perfumed stationery.

Mozy carefully tore the envelope and extracted two thin, folded pages. The green-ink handwriting was the same—hurried-looking, and sloppy.

"Dear Mozy—I know I haven't written in ages, and I guess Mom hasn't, either . . ."

What else is new?

"Now I have to tell you that we should forget whatever squabbles we had. . . ."

Mozy brushed at her hair, scowling as she read.

Chapter 4

Bill Jonders glanced at the monitor showing the subject sitting quietly in the gloom. He keyed an inner circuit. (We're go to start in thirty seconds, Ben. Are you ready?)

(Ready . . . and . . . waiting,) came the answer, a silent whisper. (Hoshi?)

(On line.) Hoshi's voice was soft and vibrant in Jonders's head.

After a last check of the board, Jonders opened his own link to the computer. His external awareness dissolved to internal signals: quasi-visual cues, light patterns indicating the activity of various program elements. A tone warned him of Kadin's presence, and the pale outline of a face appeared. (David? Prepare for transition. Ben Horton's waiting.) Kadin's face vanished again and Jonders said, (Initiating hypnotic blocks). The abstract patterns flashed momentarily, then blinked out. An odd, phantom landscape appeared around him, etched out of the darkness by purely geometric, intersecting strands of light. Moving with ease across the field, he rose to the top of a steep pyramid form outlined in threads of amber. From this perch, he looked out across the "jumpoff field"—a midnight plain, crosshatched with violet tracers. There were two tiny figures out on the plain, moving slowly toward one another.

Jonders waited for the memory-blocking and memory-implant programs to run their course with the subjects. Two tones sang in opposite corners of his mind, indicating readiness. (Sequence start,) he murmured, nudging the lower pitch higher, and the higher pitch lower. As he brought them slowly into tune, the two glittering figures converged across the field.

He tripped one more cue, and the two figures accelerated down the plain—and vanished at the edge of the violet grid.

Jonders opened an observer's portal to their new world, a planet with an emerald sky and a ripe orange moon, and with two groups of aliens greeting the landing party.

He scanned the telltales flowing in the form of color-coded digits across the gridded field. In a window floating above the plain, images flickered of the scenario world, as seen by the two subjects. A difficult negotiation was being concluded, with uncertain results.

Not for the first time, Jonders wished that it were possible to gain a clearer perception of the subjects' thoughts and feelings. As always, he was faced with the dilemma of seeking to observe a process without interfering with its results. It was a fundamental conflict in all of the sciences, and no less so here; for that reason, they depended heavily on post-session debriefing and analysis to augment their evaluations.

At the moment, his intuition was that this scenario had outlived its usefulness. Kadin and Horton were dickering with two fictional entities, one apparently hostile, and one apparently friendly, but demanding; and Kadin, as leader, was pursuing a cautious course, but one that was leading neither to conflict nor to resolution. Jonders suspected that this scenario might be in need of redesign.

He nudged open a channel to Hoshi. A bank of darkness shifted in the sky over the control pyramid, and a pale gleam linked them. (What's your opinion?) he asked.

There was a pause, then Hoshi answered, (Stalemate. We've gotten all we're going to get).

(I agree. Let's bring them home.) Jonders cued the termination sequence. In the observation window, he saw the images of the aliens withdraw.

The gridded plain and the spidery outline of the pyramid shrank, then darkened. Jonders experienced an instant of dizziness as he detached himself from the link—the inner images escaping in a gentle rush, and the control board floating back into focus.

For the next hour and a half, he was occupied with analysis and debriefing. Hoshi worked steadily at the next console, helmet over his head, hands folded above the keyboard. As Jonders got up to leave, he keyed the audio circuit. "Hoshi, finish that up for me and prep for the next session, will you?"

Hoshi's voice came back snappishly, "What do you think I'm doing? It'll be done when it's done."

Jonders nodded to himself, thinking, let it pass; if you push harder, you'll just get mistakes for your trouble.

Leaving the rest of his people to their work, he went to his office and closed the door behind him. He allowed himself two minutes of silence behind his desk, with his eyes closed. You're in the army now, he thought. For a civilian, and a scientist, why did he feel so much like a drill sergeant?

Sighing, he rocked forward and punched up Ken Fogelbee, the computer systems manager, on the phone. "Ken," he said, as his boss's image focused in the screen. He muttered a curse. The phone was distorting the image again; he'd just had the thing repaired for the third time.

"What's wrong, Bill?" Fogelbee said.

"Nothing. Sorry, it's just this damn phone."

"Why don't you get it fixed? Did you call to give me an update?"

"Right." Jonders's breath hissed out as he glanced at his summary sheets. "I can give you guarded optimism, with respect to the new schedule."

"Why 'guarded'?" his boss asked.

"Because," he said carefully, "while his performance is steady in the moderate-difficulty levels, we really don't have a baseline yet on high-level sophistication. Our results have been more uncertain at that level."

"That still gives you three weeks," Fogelbee said. "We're really talking about fine-tuning, aren't we? That can be continued after the transmission."

"I still think it would make more sense to wait until we're sure."

Fogelbee's face distorted a little more as he scowled. "That decision's been made, Bill. Accept it."

"If you gave me a reason, I could accept it more easily," Jonders said.

Fogelbee shrugged noncommittally. "I'll pass your concerns on. But I don't think Marshall and Hathorne are likely to change their minds. In fact, Hathorne is leaning on us to bring it all together now."

Jonders saw that it was futile to argue. "I'd better get back to work, then."

After signing off, he switched on the computer screen and scanned the scheduling trees for items that could be streamlined or cut. There wasn't much left that could go; he'd already done his best to compress the schedule.

He was interrupted by Lusela Burns, at the door. "Bill? Got a minute?" He looked up. "It's Mozelle," his assistant explained.

"Mozelle? Isn't she scheduled for this afternoon?"

Lusela nodded. "Yes. But she came in early to talk to you."

"Me?" he asked in surprise.

"Well, it seems she's unhappy with her situation here," Lusela said, frowning. "She came to me about it—but I think it's something she really should discuss with you."

Jonders muttered under his breath and glanced at the time. "Is she here now?"

"In the debriefing room."

He sighed. "Let's go." He followed Lusela down the hall and into the room where Mozelle was sitting quietly, fussing with her hair. She raised her eyes as they sat down across the table from her. "Hi. What's up, Mozelle?" he asked, putting on his best supervisory manner.

Mozelle cleared her throat, fidgeting. He raised his eyebrows. She shrugged. "It's . . . about the job."

"So I hear. Is there something that you're unhappy with?"

"Well, Lusela told me that it's ending soon. And I . . . was a little shocked by that. I had thought . . . because of something you said once earlier, that I might . . . be able to stay on longer."

Jonders blinked and slowly shook his head. "I'm not sure what you mean, really. If we gave you the wrong impression, I'm sorry. Did Lusela explain that we're near the end of the phase of the project that you're helping us with?"

Mozelle sighed heavily, and nodded.

"We were going to formally tell all of you next week," Lusela added gently.

Mozelle nodded again and said: "Right. I get that—now. But—" she shifted positions—"this is hard to explain—but it makes me uncomfortable, not knowing what's going to happen after this, or what goes on behind the sessions." She pulled at her hair. "I wish I could be more involved, really. I'd even work full time, if I could. But now, I don't even really feel a part of it. Do you know what I mean?"

"I think I do," Jonders said, thinking, I shouldn't be surprised by this—but why did it have to happen now?

"I don't even feel like I want to keep working," she said abruptly. "I feel like I'm not important here."

Jonders raised both hands. "Whoa, that's not true at all. You're *extremely* important to us. I understand that it's frustrating—but we did explain that there were certain parts of the work that had to be kept secret, because of the nature of the experiment. Do you remember that?" She nodded. "Well, even though we haven't been able to share with you exactly what your contribution has been, you certainly have helped us—more than we can say. And we need your help for a few weeks more, to see it through to the end."

She sighed again. "There's no chance of my working beyond that?" The sparkle in her eyes, normally present, was missing.

"I'm sorry," he said sympathetically. "I appreciate your interest, but what we need is for you to help us finish what you've started, on schedule."

Mozelle nodded unhappily. She seemed to want to say something else; then whatever was in her expression was gone. Jonders glanced at the time. "Can we count on you?" he said gently.

Mozelle's thoughts seemed turned inward. Finally she said, "Yes." And she nodded again.

"Wonderful. Now, why don't you go grab yourself some coffee, since we have an hour until your session. Okay?" Jonders smiled, and ushered her out of the debriefing room. Lusela followed, giving him a wink as she left.

Lord, he thought, sitting alone at the briefing table. His head was throbbing. He had visions of frenzied hordes at the stockades, and vultures circling overhead. All of them thundering inside his skull.

The afternoon clattered by. Everything got done, somehow, and Mozelle's scenario rated high marks all around. Mozelle seemed muted at the start, but only until she was in the link with Kadin. Then she blossomed with enthusiasm and just the right blend of vulnerability and stubbornness to provoke an excellent performance by Kadin. Jonders doubted that motivation would be a problem with her again.

At six-thirty, Lusela dropped the day's summaries on his desk. "What else needs to be done?" she asked.

"Go home," he said.

"*What?*"

"Before I remember whatever it was I forgot to have you do. And get everyone else out of here, too. Just once I want you all home at a decent hour. Have dinner with your husband, if you still have a husband."

She looked at him incredulously. "Are you going home, too?"

"As soon as I review these reports with Ken. Now, go." After a quick glance at the reports, Jonders tossed them into a folder and took the elevator to the third floor. Fogelbee's secretary was gone for the day, so Jonders walked straight through the outer office to Fogelbee's half-open door. He rapped and peered in. Fogelbee looked up from the phone and gestured for him to wait outside. Jonders pulled the door almost closed and sat and began reading the summaries in detail.

He gradually became aware of Fogelbee's voice drifting out. "Tracking from Tachylab . . . they say it's more than a million kilometers closer than expected . . . no, no explanation. . . ." Jonders's ears prickled. Was that *Father Sky* they were talking about? he wondered. Fogelbee's voice became softer. "I wonder . . . reliability of tracking . . . transmit sooner?" His voice became inaudible; perhaps he was conscious of Jonders's presence nearby.

Damn it, anyway, Jonders thought. Whatever Fogelbee was talking about was probably something that *he* ought to be privy to, as well, except that the "need to know" principle was so almighty around here. It griped him that a man was supposed to do his best work on the project without being given information that would help him do so. He had complained before, but to no avail.

Fogelbee came out, a tall, hawk-nosed man with thinning hair. "Your answer on the transmission date," he said, "is the distance to the receiver and signal-to-noise ratio. The twenty-fourth is our limit, if we're to have a safety margin. Come on in."

Jonders followed Fogelbee into the office. "I couldn't help overhearing—something about the target being *closer* than expected?"

Fogelbee turned. "Whatever you may have heard was private," he said, a bit roughly. "In any case, you probably misunderstood."

Jonders raised his eyebrows.

"That's all you really need to know," Fogelbee added brusquely.

Maybe yes, maybe no, Jonders thought. "You'd think that they would have figured out the signal requirements well in advance," he said, "instead of making all these last-minute adjustments."

Fogelbee shrugged. "No one's ever done this before. Sometimes you don't know these things until you get a craft out there and try it. Now, what do you have for me?"

Jonders opened the folder on Fogelbee's desk. "Better news than I'd expected," he said.

Chapter 5

The landscape spun by, a blur of fading greens and browns. Mozy's spirits soared among the clouds, among the striated patches of mist that glowed crimson against the sky's deepening blue.

Her mood had been completely turned around by the scenario, featuring Kadin, a host of aliens, and her—Kadin bargaining for her life, using diplomatic skills a professional would have admired. The aliens had been willowy creatures—tall, swaying, murmuring mystics by whose laws there was no wrong in taking a single Earth woman captive, to witness her spiritual powers in life and in death. Kadin had challenged them—persuading them of the wrongness, in *human* spiritual terms, of killing, and of abusing human spirituality as a means of studying it. In the end, they had relented.

Mozy had never admired or loved him more, and not just because he'd saved her "life" in that scenario. It was his courage and sensitivity she admired, his use of reason and compassion, even when force had been available as an alternative.

She stared out the window as the monorail sped toward New Phoenix, watching the upside-down plains and valleys in the clouds shifting slowly with the winds and the changing light of the setting sun. She imagined pink sand dunes rolling down to the upside-down, azure sea of the open sky. She imagined herself crossing that land with David, encountering aliens and other strange sights. Perilous and wondrous journeys, with David Kadin at her side.

Had she said that she loved him? Yes, certainly she did, in a friendly and platonic fashion. The thought of his name brought a glow to her heart, and that was nothing to be embarrassed about—not after all they'd been through, not after the confusing and the frightening situations they'd faced together, and not after the laughs and triumphs they'd shared.

She imagined him with her now, and found herself confiding in the image of him. *They're all crazy there, you know. Every one of them. They're certifiably nuts about this project, and everything being just so, and I don't think even they understand what it's all about.*

Kadin nodded. *I can believe it. What was going on today? Was there some trouble between them and you?*

Yes—I was furious with them. They're cutting me off from the project soon. I won't be able to see you anymore—and I'll never see you for real.

Kadin was silent for a moment, before saying, softly, *I wish you could. I'd like that very much, to meet you in person.*

She exhaled, aware of a dull pain in her chest. *Soon I won't even be able to see you in the link.* She scowled, staring out the window. Kadin, beside her, made no answer. After a moment, she added, *They're just using me. I see that now. They don't care a damn about my feelings.* She blinked. Her eyes were getting blurry. She rubbed them with her knuckles.

She was about to speak again, when she realized that Kadin was no longer with her. She was alone in the rocking train, and Kadin was somewhere out there among the clouds.

"So what the hell am *I* supposed to do about it?" she asked aloud. There was no one to answer her. She tossed her sister's letter back onto the table and avoided looking at it as she paced the living room. She'd managed to put it out of her mind for most of the afternoon; but when she'd come home, there it had been on the dining table to greet her. Kink's scribbled words stuck in her mind like barbs:

"*. . . Dr. Atkins says he may have less than six months to live. We're all going to have to pull together in this. Jo's home already, helping Mom out, and they want you to come home, too. I would, myself, except that I'm coming up on my bar exams, and for the next couple of months, I won't be able to break away. . . .*"

So—their father was ill, gravely ill, and Kink wanted her to make up with everyone and go home. Not because they'd *all* be there pulling together as a family, and they wanted her, too—oh no, it was because Kink couldn't quite spare the time right now, and she needed a stand-in. And no one else, apparently, could take the trouble to write. Ordinarily it would have been Jo; but even Jo had taken the others' side a couple of years ago, when she'd told them all off, once and for all. None of them had *ever* wanted her for anything, except when they'd wanted something *from* her.

Whatever her choices in the near future, one of them was *not* to drop everything to go home. Maybe Kink thought her own future was more important than anyone else's, but Mozy didn't see it that way. She stood, feet planted, arms crossed, glaring at the letter.

Maggie and Mouse, scratching at their feeder, caught her attention. "What's the matter?" she said, peering down. "Oh. I haven't fed you, that's what." She opened the cage door. "Come on out for a stroll." She scooped them out and left them on the table while she unscrewed the water bottle and went to get their feed. When the dispensers were filled, she corralled the sniffing gerbils once more.

As she straightened up from securing the cage, she felt a sharp twinge in the back of her neck. She was tired and tight all over. More than dinner, what she needed was a long, hot soak in the tub. She walked into the bathroom, undressing as she went. She turned on the tap full blast, heedless of the cost to her water allowance. While the bathtub filled with steaming water, she stripped off the rest of her clothes and peered self-consciously into the mirror. Her hair was a mess. Her face, as always, looked gawky and unattractive, marred by . . . she turned away quickly and adjusted the tap, thinking: How insecure can you get? Why was it so hard for her to look at herself in the mirror? Was she so afraid of a scar? Or was she afraid that the reflection of her own eyes could lay bare her soul . . . silly notion. . . .

Almost as silly as being in love with a man she'd never met.

She straightened up with a wince. *In love?*

The pipes thumped as she shut off the faucet. She stepped into the tub and lowered herself slowly into the hot water. Sliding down as far as she could, she rested her head against the end of the tub and tried to pull her legs in to make herself smaller. Why didn't they ever make bathtubs large enough for real human beings? She took a few slow, deep breaths, and the aches and cramps began to flow away with the heat.

The water lapped at her chin as she shifted positions, surging over her breasts with sudden warmth and then rushing away to leave her chilled. She kept sinking and rising, repeatedly warming her chest and shoulders. Her thoughts lapped and surged like the water, always returning to Kadin. If only he could be here to help her decide.

Even if only in her thoughts . . .

Mozy, you're torturing yourself. What's made you so sad?

She closed her eyes and smiled, and saw him sitting on the edge of the tub, talking to her calmly. She felt no urge to cover her nakedness. This was only a daydream, after all.

David. David, David.

What's wrong, Mozy?

What's wrong is that I'm in love with you, David. I'm in love with you, and in a few weeks, I'll never see you again! Isn't that enough? Do I need my family ruining my life, as well?

She bit her lip, afraid to open her eyes, afraid he would be gone. He looked down on her with grave affection; or was there more than simple affection in his eyes? Did he know a solution? He was so good at solving problems. . . .

Yes, she admitted finally—she was in love with him.

And there was no way to keep from losing him.

She sank lower in the water, seeking to melt away the pain that was building in her chest, swelling in her throat. Why? she thought miserably. What was the point of being in love with someone you could never meet, or touch? And yet, they *had* been together, sharing thoughts, and touching with their minds, with an intimacy deeper in its own way than the intimacy of lovers. Did he share her feelings? she wondered. He cared for her; that was clear. But did he, or would he, find her attractive?

She was shaking with emotion, and she realized that she was touching her scar again. She pushed her hands under the water. Then, deliberately, she cupped her breasts, and slowly brushed her fingertips over her stomach, down her thighs. All right, she thought angrily. I'm not perfect; but I'm not ugly, either. I have a decent face and a respectable body, and that scar doesn't *matter*.

David, where are you? she whispered, realizing that she'd opened her eyes and he was gone. *David? Come back?* She was answered by silence, and only the cracks in the walls looked down upon her now.

She wrenched on the hot water to renew the heat. Instead of soaking the ache *from* her, now, the warmth seemed to be driving it deeper into her. Beads of sweat ran down her forehead, wetting the fringes of her hair. There were tears leaking from her eyes, mingling with the sweat and the bathwater. She sat upright suddenly, choking, and then she hunched forward, hugging her knees, and she began to cry in earnest, shaking silently.

After a time, the sobs subsided, and she became aware of a tiny sighing voice in the room with her. It was the spigot above her feet, not quite shut off completely. She could hear the plastic pipes grunting and muttering elsewhere in the building. Grabbing a handful of tissues, she blew her nose and threw the wet wad away. She splashed her face wearily and began soaping.

Just how the thought came to her, she didn't know; but one moment the tears were leaking again from her eyelids, and the next moment she was staring in blurry astonishment at the water faucet. A drop of water was hanging, suspended, from its lip. Why hadn't she thought of it before?

For god's sake, why had she not thought of it before?

Hoshi could help her. Sandaran Link Center had all the facilities for the experimental matter-transmission process; and they were going to be trying it soon with human subjects, and David was to be the first. Where they were sending him, Hoshi hadn't said. But if they were transmitting him from the GEO-Four space colony, then they must have a facility there, as well as wherever they were sending him.

She slid down until she was submerged to her neck in the water, considering the possibilities. Before they'd been able to think of attempting a transmission, she knew, it had been necessary to develop the techniques for computerized personality profiling. The details were over her head; but along with Kadin's, she knew, they had been taking profiles of all the other subjects. If they had profiles ready for transmitting Kadin, then they must have them for her, too. She could *volunteer* for transmission, and join Kadin in person.

She felt an incredible rush. There was no other way she could hope to do it. Buy a ticket to GEO-Four? Absurd—it would cost thousands. And he was leaving there soon, anyway. But if she could do it through the project—it would be perfect.

They would never agree to something like that just to humor her, of course; but there might be a way to justify it. Hoshi would know. He could do it if anyone could. And what could she lose by trying—except a future of loneliness, and fading memories of a man she'd loved? As for her family—she could leave that sordid mess behind her, with no regrets.

Yes, call Hoshi tonight, she thought. It's perfect.

She closed her eyes, a feeling of peaceful anticipation washing through her, as she imagined the surprise on Kadin's face when she greeted him. It felt good; it felt right. As she took a deep breath and sighed, she moved her hands up her sides, and slid them over her breasts, over her stomach, and down over the insides of her thighs, and then up. Yes, she murmured, rubbing herself gently. She had nothing to lose, and perhaps a world to gain. The rubbing was beginning to excite her, and she sighed again, more earnestly this time. Go with it, she thought . . . it feels good . . . you've earned it. Her hands moved in closing circles, lifting and touching and pressing just so, and her breath came more quickly. She closed her thighs over her hands, and began rocking more forcefully, the water splashing at her chin.

Chapter 6

New driver on the bus tonight, he thinks. Watch the lights, lights and shadow, building fronts. You're spoiled by drivers who know when to stop; tonight you have to watch for yourself.

The lights flicker, making him dizzy. He's tired, that's why. Pretends they're feedback in the linkup loop, and the dizziness goes away. It's subconscious now, watching the patterns of light-shadow, light-shadow . . . the watchdog in his head knows when to stop.

Hoshi reaches up and touches a metal plate over the window. The bus sighs to a halt, and he steps down and then pauses on the sidewalk to squint around. Purely reflex, the squinting. Does no good, not with the self-adjusting amplifying modules in his head. There's a surge and flicker in the brightness of his surroundings, while the circuits adjust and readjust. Somehow makes him feel better, like probing an ache in a tooth.

Nodding to himself, he scans the street—crosses—and walks the last block home.

The phone panel winks at him as he enters. Hangs his coat, paces a moment, and puts water in the teakettle before answering. It's Mrs. Martinsen downstairs, a recording. "Hoshi," she says, her voice nasal and dry. "When you get home, would you please check out back for me and let Armax in? I'm turning in now, and he's still outside." She coughs delicately. "Thank you, Hoshi. Have a good night."

He snaps the set off, feeling the beginnings of a headache. Poor Mrs. Martinsen, he thinks—always struggling with that bronchitis—and none of the other tenants help her much. He sighs, pressing his temple. Headaches coming more often. Got to see the doctors soon, find out if something can be done. May just have to live with it, endure it; lots of people live with worse suffering.

Returning to the kitchen, he pulls out a frozen dinner and slides it into the microwave, then starts a cup of tea. While the tea steeps, he goes into the rear hallway and down the steps. Leaning out the back door, he whistles. "Max? Armax—are you here?" He looks in all directions: bright hotspots from the floodlights, variegated shadow from the rest. Nothing moves. No sign of the cat. Trudging back upstairs, he records a message for Mrs. Martinsen. "Armax isn't here. Must be having a hot time on the town. I'll check again later."

The kitchen is the most comfortable place to sit for dinner—lots of light and dark unit shapes, solid surfaces, cooking controls. Comforting hum of the microwave fan. Activity, mechanical life. Leaves the stereo off tonight; he's not in the mood. Just the machines, the kitchen, dinner. A gong sounds; the cooker shuts off. He pulls out his dinner, glowing false-color red: hot.

The aroma of sliced roast chicken with gravy, the taste of potatoes and peas, the warmth of food in his stomach calm him, make him feel stronger. He stares across the kitchen, chewing slowly. The light intensity around him is almost steady, just a bit of a flicker. The tension in his head begins to subside.

The phone chimes. He slaps the counter in annoyance, but turns to answer. "Phone on! Hello!"

"Hoshi? Am I bothering you?"

"Mozy?" Rush of pleasure. Touch of guilt for his annoyance. "No, no, you're not bothering me." Sliding off the counter stool, he carries his cup of tea into the living room and stands in front of the phone. Considers, then says, "Picture on and send." The screen lights, showing Mozy's face as a shadowy blur. "How are you?" he says. "I didn't get much chance to talk to you today."

"Do you want to meet for a drink?" Mozy says, her voice a little sharper than usual. She sounds upset.

"Is anything wrong?"

"No. No. But I'd like to talk to you, okay?"

"Well—sure," he says. Usually *he* asks *her* to go for a drink. "I'm just having dinner now. Do you want to come over here?"

The ghostly face in the screen smiles. "Okay, if you'd rather. I'll bring some beer. See you soon."

As the screen darkens, he stares at the phone, tapping his teacup with his fingernails. He wanders back into the kitchen to finish dinner.

A half hour goes by, and by the time he opens the door for her, he's a little dizzy with anticipation. Mozy sidles in, with an awkward smile. Hands him a bag—heavy, cool, damp. He takes the six-pack into the kitchen, rustles it out of the bag, pops open two beers which he pours into glasses, and puts the rest in the refrigerator. Mozy's right behind him as he turns. "Thanks," she says, taking a glass. Seems nervous, but maybe it's just him.

They sit on opposite sides of the massive coffee table, Mozy in the stuffed chair, Hoshi on the sofa. Sip, smile, chat about the day's activities. Hoshi says, "I heard you talked to Bill today." Raises his eyebrows.

"Yah," says Mozy, staring down at the finished redwood tabletop. She fusses with her beer, starts to say something, but seems stymied for words. Finally: "Hoshi, this is confidential. It's about work—and I have to tell someone—and you're the only one I trust." She looks up. "Okay? You won't tell anyone we talked?"

Takes a deep breath and nods, feeling trapped and flattered both. She hasn't really come to see *him*, then; she's come to have him listen. But she trusts him, and she's going to lay out a lot of complicated feelings for him; he can smell that already. "Sure," he says. What's he going to say—*no*?

She nods. "Okay." She gulps her beer and hesitates. "It's about Kadin," she says suddenly. He watches her silently. The room shimmers around him. He readjusts his eyes, readjusts his thoughts. She keeps talking. "I don't know how to say it . . . but I'm . . ."

It's plain to him by now, and when he clears his throat, it sounds as though he's choking. He keeps his voice flat. "You're . . . *attached* to him, aren't you?" he says, ignoring the pocket that's forming in his gut.

She nods, eyes wide. Beautiful, ghostly face with round eyes. He wants to reach out and touch her. Clenches his glass instead, wraps his fingers tightly around it. She toys with her hair, runs her fingertip down the cool, dark scarline that sets off her cheekbone. "I'm in love with him," she whispers.

A dull pain originates in his left temple, then migrates to the back of his head. A much greater pain that is not physical makes him suddenly want to flee, to be alone. He refuses to let it show, blinks his eyes instead. "I see," he says, because he has to say something.

Mozy continues, oblivious. "I just realized it today, I guess. I suppose I've been in love with him for a long time, but I never admitted it—even to myself." She laughs unhappily.

Hoshi scratches his ear. "So," he says carefully. "Yes. That would be a problem. You'll be off the project soon and you won't have any way to—"

"I *know*," she snaps.

"Of course—sorry." He sits back, stunned by her anger. Should he tell her, come right out and tell her? No . . . no, he can't do that. But he feels sorry for her, he aches to reach out and hold her, comfort her. Mozy, oh Mozy, don't you know how appealing you are?

"I have an idea," Mozy says, "but you *must* keep it secret."

"What sort of idea?"

"Do you *promise*?"

He shrugs, then nods numbly.

"It'll sound crazy, but please—hear me out." She touches his forearm, which sets off a shower of sparks in his mind, evaporating whatever's left of his resistance. Of course he'll listen. "I want to be transmitted to David," she says.

His thoughts turn to sleet. "You want *what*?"

"To be transmitted through the machine at the Center—to GEO-Four—to where Kadin is." There is no hesitation or doubt in her voice.

"You can't be serious."

"You think I'm crazy. I know. But it *could* be done, couldn't it? Isn't it possible?" She blinks rapidly, peering at him.

He hardly knows where to begin, whether to laugh outright or cry. There are so many ways to answer, so many things that need explaining. But he can't explain; security forbids it. He takes a breath and tries anyway: an excuse. "They've never sent a human being through the transmitter. It's all experimental—they wouldn't do it just because you—"

Mozy interrupts. "They're planning to send David through. Isn't that what you told me?"

"Yes, but that's different. That's—" He chokes, fumbling to articulate . . . what he can't say to her. "I should never have told you," he answers lamely. Should he tell her now . . . and the devil with security? Should he tell her the truth, as much of it as he knows? He squints. Furrows his brow. The lovely alabaster woman grows brighter, then dimmer, shadows softening.

Mozy is undeterred. "They must be ready to make human transmissions, or they wouldn't be planning to put David through. That means it can be done." She's perfectly convinced of the idea. "So there's no reason they couldn't send me there first."

"Mozy, do you know what you're saying?"

"It could be dangerous, I know. But what do I have to lose?" There's a sound of real desperation in her voice.

Desperation of love? He knows about that, doesn't he? He wants to help her, wants her to be happy. There are so many things he ought to have told her, and now he can't say any of them. Instead, he stammers, "You—you have a *lot* to lose, Mozy."

She snorts, staring down into her beer.

More than you imagine, he adds silently. Aloud he says, "Anyway, Bill would never let you do it."

She raises her eyes. "Couldn't you do it for me?"

"Hah! What about security? Do you know the trouble you could get into for something like that?"

"You mean I could lose my job?" She shrugs. "I'm losing it anyway. My friends, and everything I want, are at the job. As it stands now, I'll have nothing when I leave."

That hits him like a punch in the chest. *My friends . . . are at the job.* So far as he knows, *he* is her only friend at the job. And Kadin, of course. But she must care for him, as well as Kadin, to have made that statement. He feels a band of tension across his forehead, making it harder than ever to think clearly. It's as though a part of his mind has slipped through a hole in the continuum, leaving him feeling at once connected and disconnected. It's hard to know what to say—and he stammers, "We . . . could stay friends . . . even after you leave."

Mozy has not moved; she seems in a trance. "There's really nothing to lose," she murmurs somberly. Suddenly she tilts her head, as though she has just hear his last words. She touches the cool line of her scar and laughs, a sighing sound that passes through him like a breeze through the trees. "Yes—of course, Hoshi!" She touches his wrist, and warm energy flows through him. "What would I do without you? My god, you've been my best friend there!"

Smiling dizzily, reassured, he tries to respond. "I—Mozy, I want to help you. Really I do."

"Do you think you can find a way?" she asks eagerly.

He gestures helplessly. "You can't just walk in and use the transmitter. It's not like that—and besides, it's under security."

"Security isn't *that* tight there," she points out. "And we both have clearances."

"But not for that."

She pleads with him. "Isn't there some way to do it? Can't you help me find a way?'' Her voice is tormented, and he finds it increasingly hard to resist.

"It might be theoretically possible," he says haltingly, "but that doesn't mean it's feasible."

"Hoshi, you're smart," she says, and there is no flattery, there is only sincerity in her voice. "You know the computers and the codes, and I'll bet if you helped me, we could do this. I'll accept the responsibility for whatever trouble I'm in. I just have to do it. I have to see Kadin. *Don't you understand?*"

He tries to think this through clearly, but it's like trying to organize a blizzard. Yes, he can probably find a way; he can beat security if anyone can, and cracking the computer codes would be child's play. But she doesn't understand, she doesn't know the full truth, and he can't tell her.

But . . .

. . . there is one way he might do it. Not exactly the way she imagines. It would be risky—but she's dying to meet her love, and if Kadin means so much to her, then he'll help her—and then she'll understand.

"Please, Hoshi?" she whispers. She leans across the table imploringly, and her gaze reverberates with his.

He bows his head, trying to quell the sound of pounding blood, and thinks: Help you? Oh yes, dear Mozy, I'll help you if that's what you want. You are a sorceress, Mozy, and if fingers dancing on a console or a mind lashed to a computer can help you, then I'm the one to do it. He lifts the glass and sips; it's cool going down.

"Will you?" she whispers.

Nodding shakily, he says, "It—yes—it may be possible. I'll—I'll have to see, to think about it, find a way."

Mozy smiles crookedly, and her hand touches his wrist, lingering this time. She starts talking again—planning aloud—but he hardly hears her, he's thinking so hard himself. There are many things he's unsure of, things they've never told him; he'll have to probe delicately, finesse his way into programs he's never been allowed to touch. But he can do it, he's sure of that; they'll never suspect him, and if they're angry when it's over, then that'll just be too bad. Jonders . . . he's not too angry with Jonders, but as far as he's concerned, Fogelbee's a pompous ass, and they should have trusted him to begin with, instead of playing such pissant games of secrecy.

He's nodding to something Mozy's saying, and realizes with a start that she's getting up to leave. "When will you know for sure?" she repeats.

He's caught between his own thoughts and her question, and he struggles to speak. "I'll . . . let you know," he manages. "When I've checked it out . . . yes. There might not be much warning. We'll have to do it when the opportunity's there."

She's smiling happily now, touching him, *needing* him. He's almost frantic with a peculiar kind of joy. Too quickly for him to react, she stretches and kisses him on the cheek. The next thing he knows, she's out the door and gone. The living room crowds around him with shadowy ghosts as he turns. The lights flicker and spiral in his eyes, and his foot catches on a chair, and he stumbles, sprawling to the floor. He lies there, panting and cursing; his head is spinning, and if he just waits a moment, it will pass.

At last he gets to his feet. He switches off the lamp and sits on the couch and finishes his beer in the gloom—brooding and planning.

Mozy, Mozy, you don't know the dangers! I wanted to tell you, it's not what you think—but I'll try for you, I promised I would. How could I refuse you, even this? I'll help you any way I can, Mozy . . .

. . . but I wonder . . . should I have told you?

Chapter 7

The invasive fingers of the scanning program slipped out of her mind the way they had come in. There was a sense of release, and then the cilialike tendrils were gone from the inside of her skull. Her memories once again were her own.

She sat in darkness, gathering her wits. The scanning helmet was a claustrophobic enclosure, far more cumbersome than the usual linkup helmet. Her feelings from before the session came seeping back into her mind. Lusela had told her today: the sessions with Kadin were over. No final visit, no last good-bye. All they needed now were a few brainscans for purposes of analysis. Too stunned to protest, Mozy had suppressed her anger and gone meekly into the subject booth. But something inside her was darkening to ash, even as the helmet was lowered over her head. Then the scan had begun, and the violating fingers had entered her mind, sorting patterns and memories, tumbling walls like stacks of cards.

Now it was over. All over.

The booth lights rose slowly, and she became aware of a medical tech disconnecting her. Lusela was there, too, murmuring to the tech. The helmet suddenly lifted from her head, giving her a breath of air. Relief. "Why don't you just sit quietly for a few minutes," Lusela said. "How do you feel?"

Mozy stared at her, dazed.

The med-tech was peering into her eyes now, and checking the life-signs monitors. After a moment, she went away, and Lusela was saying, "We'll give you some privacy to gather your thoughts. If you need us, we'll be right outside." Lusela indicated the call button. "Just buzz." She followed the tech out and closed the door.

Mozy let her breath out with a silent cry. She laid her head on the headrest and stared at the ceiling. She needed time to think, to get her head straight. Mindscans . . . the end of Kadin . . . what was happening to her? Trying to understand it all was like picking up pieces of a shattered ceramic vessel and wondering how they had once fit together. She closed her eyes and let her thoughts run at will. The silence was soothing.

A minute passed. The door opened, and closed. She ignored it, keeping her eyes closed, hoping not to be disturbed. She was startled by a whisper at her ear. "*Mozy?*"

She blinked her eyes open in astonishment. "Hoshi?" she croaked.

"Today's the day," Hoshi murmured. He bent over her, his copper medallion swinging, his strangely focused eyes seeking hers. "I've got everything ready. We can do it today."

"What?" she said dumbly.

"The transmission!" he hissed. His eyes sparkled with earnest intensity. "I've worked out a method. I can do it. You and Kadin."

As Mozy slowly comprehended what he was saying, all of her suppressed hopes welled up together inside her. Whether from joy or fear or both, she tried to speak, but no words came out. Her eyes filled with mist.

"It's now or never," Hoshi said, his breath close to hers. "We have to do it today."

Her mind raced frantically. *Today? With no warning?* There was so much unplanned, so many loose ends. But if he really could send her to Kadin. . . .

Unsure, fighting for time, she stammered, "Can you really . . . how . . . ?"

"I've cracked the codes, but it's got to be today." He glanced nervously over his shoulder and lowered his voice. "All right. Listen. When you're through here, go upstairs to the cafeteria and wait. I'll come get you when I'm ready. It might be two or three hours."

She stared at him, trying to follow his words.

"Do you understand?" She nodded slowly. "Wait for me," he repeated. A moment later he was gone, leaving her in stunned silence.

Three hours? It felt more like three weeks. She nursed a lukewarm cup of tea—her third or fourth—and tried to calm herself down. She felt as though she were on a roller coaster. An hour ago she'd been ecstatic; now she was frightened out of her wits. Thinking of the brainscan, she wondered, what secrets of her heart were now in the computer's memory banks? What private dreams, hopes, and fears? Did the computer know of her love for Kadin? Did it know of her plan to join him?

A tray crashed in the kitchen, the noise jarring the whole cafeteria. Mozy winced and looked up. A dozen other people did the same, and then returned to their meals or conversations. Had any of them noticed her? Don't be paranoid. Soon it'll be over.

She grabbed her purse and pulled out a pen and a battered memo pad. She tore off the top sheets to expose a clean page; then she thought a minute and started writing:

> Dear Kink,
>   I got your letter. Unfortunately, I can't go home right away, as I'm involved in something

Pausing, she scowled at what she had written. She tore off the page and crumpled it, then started over:

> Dear Mother,
>   I heard from Kink about Dad. I don't know if I ought to come home or not, but it was a real shock to hear

She slammed the pen down and glared at the tablet—filled with helpless fury at the uselessness of trying to express her feelings to anyone in that family. They'd made no effort at reconciliation since the last big fight. They stayed out of her life, and she stayed out of theirs. And now, that letter from Kink was enough to make her want to find an enormous vase and smash it over someone's head.

Still, she ought to send some reply. Crumpling the second page, she looked around for a pay-terminal. There was one in the far corner of the cafeteria. She picked up her things and walked over, digging in her purse for her phone credit card, which she passed through the slot as she sat down at the keyboard. The screen lighted, and she tapped in the lettergram code, followed by both her mother's and Kink's addresses. Pursing her lips, she typed:

> Dear Mom, Dad, and everyone,
>   Sorry at the news. I'm going to be gone from here for a while, so can't come home just yet. Not sure you want me anyway.

She hesitated, then struck that last sentence. She continued:

Will be in touch when I can. Keep me informed. Mozy.

She stared at the screen for a long moment, her finger poised, trembling, over the *Send* button. She bit her lip, inserted the word, "*Love*," before her name, then stabbed the glowing square. The screen cleared, and then displayed the words: "*Lettergram sent—receipt verified.*"

She sat a moment longer, shaking, breathing deeply.

There was nothing more she could do now, where her family was concerned.

She wondered dizzily who else she ought to send messages to. Dee? God, no, that was long since over; what had made Dee's name pop into her mind? Maggie and Mouse! She would have to ask Hoshi to take care of them. And Mardi—she owed Mardi an explanation. She coded for another message and typed Mardi's address. What was she going to say, though? She could hardly tell Mardi what she was planning to do. She chewed her lip, thinking.

"There you are," Hoshi grumbled impatiently.

She started, looking up. She rose, plucking her credit card from the machine.

"For a minute, I thought you'd gone home," he said. "Are you ready?"

Thoughts spun randomly through her mind, and she nodded. Mardi would have to wait. As Hoshi turned, she grabbed his arm. "Wait —Hoshi! Will you feed my gerbils for me? Will you take care of Maggie and Mouse?" As Hoshi blinked in surprise, she fumbled in her purse for her apartment key and pressed it into his hand. "I didn't—know to make arrangements."

Hoshi stared at the key before slipping it into his pocket. "Look— Mozy—there are some things I have to explain to you." He hesitated awkwardly, then said, "Let's go down to the lab first." They started walking. "I was the last one out. I told Bill I was staying to finish up some work. Remember, you're just going in to pick up something you forgot."

"My coat," Mozy said.

Hoshi nodded, falling silent as they shambled by the security guard at the cafeteria door. The guard was reading a novel, and scarcely glanced up as they passed. The hallways were quiet outside the Personality Lab. Most of the daytime workers were gone, and the evening shift was much smaller. At the wing security desk, the guard passed them with a cursory inspection of their clearance cards. They entered the lab. Only a few nighttime people were busy in the systems processing area. The control room was unoccupied, and Hoshi waved Mozy in ahead of him. The door hissed closed. She glanced back out through the glass. "Aren't people going to wonder what we're doing?"

"Leave them to me," Hoshi muttered. He was already bent over the console, flipping switches and tapping in codes. He pursed his lips as his hands moved over the board. After a few moments, he straightened. His eyes glinted. "The rest I can do after you're hooked in. Now, there's something I have to explain."

"Wait a minute. You don't have to give me the technical—"

He was shaking his head. "What you don't understand—"

The door hissed open, and a young man entered. Hoshi's gaze snapped up. "Oh, Tim—hi," Hoshi said laconically.

"Working late, Hoshi?" asked the young man. He peered curiously at Mozy.

"Yah—deadline," said Hoshi. "Have to get an extra scan on Mozy before morning."

"Really? I didn't see anything about that on the daily."

"Bill was gone before we caught it," Hoshi said. "Fortunately, Mozy was still here. Don't worry—it won't interfere with what you're doing." Hoshi turned back to the console and studiously began making adjustments.

Tim looked back and forth between them, then shrugged. "Okay—holler if you need any help."

"Yep," Hoshi said, without looking up again.

When Tim was gone, he glanced out into the corridor. "Let's get into the booth before someone else starts asking questions." He nudged her toward the door.

"What was it you were going to explain?"

"In a minute. Let's go." He nudged her harder.

Her legs suddenly were made of wax. It was beginning to hit home, the risk she was taking. "Hoshi, I'm . . . I'm not sure I can go through with this." Kadin or no Kadin.

Hoshi's eyes blazed. "There's no turning back now. We're committed." He propelled her out into the hall and directly to the subject booth.

The door whisked shut behind them. Mozy obeyed his instructions and climbed into the chair; but as Hoshi bustled about checking hookups to the scanning helmet, she felt a distinct and growing sense of unreality. Something was wrong—and it took her a few seconds to realize what it was. "Hoshi!" she hissed. "This can't be a matter transmitter—this is the brainscan setup! Where are the—" Her throat was suddenly empty of words. She wasn't actually sure what a matter transmitter looked like; but surely there had to be some sort of chamber, with scanning beams, and so on. There was nothing like that here.

"That's what I have to explain." Hoshi's voice slurred with urgency as he lifted the helmet up over her head. "We're going to do a complete scan—like this afternoon's, but much more complete. *All* of your memories, *all* of the patterns of your mind, everything that makes up your personality—"

She blocked his movements with her hand. "You mean you have to do that before the transmission, just to make sure—"

"No." He nudged her hand aside and seated the helmet over her skull. "This *is* the scanning for transmission. The matter transmitter doesn't—"

There was a sound outside the door, and he stiffened. Suddenly he seized her by the shoulders and kissed her, hard.

Mozy squirmed with fright. The helmet was claustrophobic to begin with, and now Hoshi's lips pressed in on her, blocking her air. Suffocating, fighting to breathe, she drove her fists up between Hoshi and herself, trying to push him away. He relaxed long enough to growl, "Fake it!" and then she was aware of a hiss and someone standing in the doorway. Understanding flashed upon her. Panting, she tried to imitate a passionate embrace.

An unfamiliar voice said, "Oh—excuse *me*. You don't need any help, I guess." The door hissed closed again, and the man was gone.

Mozy gasped for air as Hoshi pulled away. "I had to do that," he said roughly, turning to avoid her gaze.

"*Why?*" she cried, trembling with embarrassment and anger.

Hoshi stumbled over his words. "Better than having them think . . . I don't know." He began checking the helmet hookup again; his hands were shaking, fumbling at the connections. His voice sounded hurt as he said, "I was just trying to cover for us." He turned away, then back. His eyes were wet, shining.

"Okay," Mozy said uncomfortably. "If we're going to do this, let's do it."

Working silently and efficiently now, Hoshi adjusted the helmet until it was seated snugly. When he spoke again, his voice was businesslike. "What I'm going to transmit is the imprint of all your memories, all the patterns of your personality."

She blinked her eyes wide. "What do you mean? You told me that you—"

"That I'd send you where you could be with Kadin," he said. "I'm doing that. You'll be with him—your *mind* will be with him—just as in the scenarios."

"But you said—"

"I said that I would help you join Kadin. Mozy, listen to me." He bent and gazed fiercely into her eyes. "Kadin is being sent the same way you are. There is no transmitter on Earth that can send you bodily, alive, to another place."

She shook her head, disbelieving. Tears filled her eyes. "But they said there was a transmitter! Are you telling me it's all a lie?"

"No, not a lie. Listen to me, damn it. *They can't transmit living things yet*. Rocks, yes. People, no. It's too crude." Mozy stared at him angrily as he continued. "The brainscans are different—they're further advanced. We can transmit a personality in digital form and reassemble it in a distant computer. That's what's being done with Kadin."

"What's this going to do to me?" she cried.

"Nothing! Nothing at all!" His voice became softer. "A part of you will be with him. You'll still be here—but you'll be with him, too. It's the best I can do, the best anyone can do."

She stared at him. His eyes seemed to be revolving as they peered back at her. "I'll still be here," she repeated, trying to understand. "You mean, I'll walk out of here and go home tonight?"

"No one will ever have to know. But the part of you at the other end will have to be careful. Don't give yourself away."

"He'll be there?"

"Trust me, Mozy. If we don't do it now, there won't be a second chance. Do you want to, or don't you?"

She struggled to think. She needed more time to absorb this information. It wasn't what she'd asked for, but maybe it was better than nothing. She thought of all the times she'd sat in this chair, linking with another human mind. But this was different; this was throwing herself into the arms of the other person, not knowing if she'd be welcomed or spurned. This was asking the most wonderful man in the world for an intimate date, forever.

"Will I know what's happening to the part of me that's with him?" she asked finally.

Hoshi gazed at her silently, with upturned hands. She imagined his eyes to be spinning, hypnotic disks. She stared back at him, could not evade those eyes that were spinning, spinning. She imagined them saying: *If you don't go through with this, you'll never see Kadin again.* She thought of Kadin, his gentleness and strength, and she was caught, helpless, in a rush of desire. "Let's get started," she whispered hoarsely.

Hoshi nodded and made the final adjustments. His hand touched hers, and they both jerked back nervously. Be done with it, she thought. Go turn the damn thing on. She looked away, unconsciously counting the seconds. Then he bobbed his head and said, "That's it. We're ready to run." He stepped backward, murmuring, and suddenly Mozy was alone in the booth and the lights were growing dim.

.   This is for you, Mozy. Just the way I promised.

Hoshi's fingers fly over the console, initiating the clandestine programs he's so carefully worked out. It should be a cinch, he thinks. It's been a cinch so far, getting past the codes and security blocks; he was amazed at what a piece of cake it was, anyone who knows the computers the way he does could have cracked those codes. Now it's all coming together, and suddenly he feels an enormous knot in his shoulders, almost as if he were scared. He *was* scared for an instant, there, when they were discovered in the booth. He almost lost his head.

Alone in the control room, his blood is running hot and excited. He's been aroused since the moment he kissed her—so innocently, thinking of nothing more than camouflage, throwing the others off the track. Ignore that now, he thinks, center and channel the energy, don't think about Mozy or desire. He'll show them, he'll prove what he can do with these programs, and no one will ever underestimate him again. Mozy, too—he'll give her exactly what she wants. Kadin for a lover—she can have him, no grudge. You'll see what it's all about, he thinks—you'll see. Won't you, Mozy, won't you?

With quick, savage movements, he drops the operator's helmet over his head and keys himself into the link. A firestorm of sparks swirls past him. Here he's at home. Here he's in control. A large ball of tension eases itself past some obstruction in his brain, releases some of the knots in his neck and shoulders, and allows him to breathe freely again. He can do it now; it's time.

A few privately coded triggers set into motion a cascade of programs. The scanning programs switch to the *ready* mode. No external display should betray him; but internally he sees an illuminated, three-dimensional grid in which a maze of circuits will open and close to create a pathway to transmission. Several links must function in unison: from the scanning computer to the transmitter; from the ground transmitter to Tachylab, overhead in synchronous orbit; from Tachylab, via modulated tachyon beam, to the spacecraft somewhere in deep space. If all goes well, Mozy's mindscan will flow in a continuous stream through all of those links, flashing from the subject booth to the receiving computer with scarcely a betraying sign.

The tachyon relay may be the riskiest part of the chain. The signal will be sandwiched into the regular transmission to the ship, but there will be a sharp increase in signal density, which could betray him. With luck and skill, he'll finish the transmission and erase his steps backward through the network before his tampering can be traced. He has been extremely careful, in breaking the security codes, to protect his tracks along the way.

A pathway is now lighted through the grid, with a single amber and a single red block remaining. A time check confirms that the tachyon link will open in fifty-three seconds.

The amber changes to green, the red to amber.

He keys in to Mozy. As the circuits connect him to his waiting friend, he thinks: Go to him, Mozy, and be happy. I'll have you here with me, still, and maybe now you'll take notice—maybe he'll be out of your thoughts.

As a final door creaks open in the darkness, he calls, (Are you ready?)

In the distance, he hears the soft answer: (Yes.)

(Sequence start,) he says, as the last amber light turns to green. The tachyon link is open. He is aware in the back of his mind that someone is entering the control room. He ignores that and nudges one final command. A fountain of sparks streams through the grid as the process begins.

A glittering band encircled her skull as she waited in the darkness. Time slid by like an imponderable mass of ice. What would time come to mean when her consciousness was frozen into a series of impulses in the computer? Every nerve was wired, every thought agitated; strangely, even the memory of Hoshi's clumsily feigned embrace aroused her with sexual excitement. She tried to bring it all to a focus, to corral her thoughts and memories like burning sparks, and to balance the musical tones of her hopes and fears into stable harmonics. The result was a blur of color, a cacophony of tones.

She thought of Kadin, the stable, good-humored man she had come to love; and she remembered the training for the linkup sessions. Go to him with a clear mind, centered and relaxed. Keep the pathways open, let the images and harmonics drift into their own order.

Hoshi's mind-voice came through, distant and a little fuzzy, asking if she was ready.

A heartbeat passed, then two. The circlet of fire around her forehead began spinning and twinkling, faster and brighter, and contracting. It tightened over the lobes of her consciousness like a glittering fist. In that instant, she was paralyzed, her awareness turning to crystal shot through with pulses like beacons in a starless night. Her emotions froze into a cold, white diamond. She felt a rush of sensations, and then icelike clarity, as her thoughts and memories became transparent straight through to the center of her mind and soul.

A vibration was building inside; forces were gathering, currents of life once bound were coming unleashed. Exhilaration and terror and vertigo flashed through her in a pulse. Somewhere within her, fierce streams were cutting new beds, winds were gusting and moaning, the earth shivering. There was a sun flaring, a candle guttering, a feeling of disconnectedness. From somewhere, a papery voice called: (You will be alone at first. Wait for him there.) They were words that made no sense, held no meaning. All real thought was lost in a whirlwind.

Then, for a breath, everything fell silent. There was no sound—

—no light—

—no motion—

—and then the world erupted with a thunderclap and a keening wail, driving a spike of pain straight through to the center of her consciousness. Hallucinating in agony, she wandered among the stars, heard the void speaking in tongues. The emptiness rang around her like an infinite gong, and then darkness crushed in upon her.

PART TWO

INTO THE ETERNAL NIGHT

Prelude

The waters became clearer, and tangier with the taste of salt, as the whales entered the warm fringes of the joining grounds, moving into seas where the sun rose high. Sunlight danced through the surface swells and angled into the abyss, turning from golden belly pink near the surface to clearwater blue in the midrange. Far below, where only darkness met the eyes, the realm was mapped with whistling echoes. Even now, someone's cry reverberated dimly out of a watery canyon.

Theirs was a world filled with sounds: the mutter of the sea itself, the whistle of their own songs, the click and rasp of dolphins and other creatures. Earlier, several of the herd had caught the moan of a blue, its lonely song reverberating through the deep layers. Always, too, there was the drone of the manships plodding their courses back and forth across the sea, a minor but continual irritant.

Songs filled their thoughts. For some, a special restlessness accompanied their return to these waters—a renewed memory of the songs of last year's joining—songs that had come from a place they did not know and touched them in a way they did not understand—songs that had come to enchant them, songs whalelike and yet not-whale, filled with bewildering and intriguing harmonics, evoking images of emptiness and incalculable distances, and a migrational swim lifetimes long.

A godwhale, some said. Would the godwhale's visions return?

As the waters grew warm, the herd began to fragment. Some whales cavorted on the surface while others tuned their voices. The new year's songs began reverberating, and a change was at once felt, in new tones and rhythms, some of them not-whale rhythms. The altered strains were in their own voices—not from the outside, but from their own hearts, an echo and a harmony to the songs that had so haunted their sleep last year. Whatever those songs had been, they were now a part of the whales' own language.

The herd moved southward. There was no hint of the godwhale's song itself, and some wondered if it would ever be heard again, or if it and the mystery of its existence would become merely a part of the lore, embroidered and changed until the original was lost from memory.

Chapter 8

As Joseph Payne's eyes adjusted to the gloom, a ghostly illumination welled up around him. Misty, blue-green space; the hiss and mutter of the sea. The tropical Pacific: depth, sixty meters. Translucent rays of sunlight slanted down like moonbeams in a forest. Below him, the blue deepened; and far below was the darkness of the abyss.

The music and the narrative that whispered in his head made him feel a part of the sea, a part of the cascading chain of life that surrounded him here. He turned to and fro, like a shark swaying its head, searching the depths for prey. The music and narration faded, and then all around him was solitude and tranquility, silent and gloomy spaces, the sea's emptiness.

He became aware of a thin, droning sound at extreme range, the propellor whine of a distant ship enveloping him in the sea's cathedral-like acoustics. Overhead, he caught sight of a moving shadow—a cluster of pelagic fish, darting and swerving. A beam of light stabbed upward, illuminating the iridescent undersides of the fish; then they flashed one way, and another, and were gone.

Emptiness . . . and then a new sound, a familiar low moan that ended with a sharp rise in pitch. The cry was repeated, followed by a sighing stream of bubbles, and then a mournful keening, ending in a downward wail. Payne recognized the humpback whales' songs; he had heard their recordings many times before, and now, as always, reacted to them with a feeling of wistfulness and longing. Was it a whale's cry for companionship, or something else entirely? He didn't know; but in the whales' songs there was always a feeling of space, and distance, and loneliness.

He squinted upward toward the sunlight. A whale's shadow moved high overhead, but was growing as it descended, diving lazily toward him. It swelled, blocking the light until it filled the world over his head; and then it banked and wheeled around to peer sideways at him with a single large, unblinking eye. The encounter lasted for a heartbeat, as Payne stared back into the creature's eye, sensing the imponderability of its gaze. Its mouth was turned downward in a sour grin. Did it wonder at this strange creature in its realm? The whale slid by him, its rounded belly and roughened, gray-white flukes so close that Payne instinctively drew back. An enormous tail fluke swung past his face, and then the whale was a dark shape growing darker in the depths.

Silence. Then the mournful song began again.

The humpback whale songs were a worldwide choir, whales sharing musical themes with their siblings around the globe. As the seasons changed, so too did the songs, evolving in one part of the world as in another, by some orchestration not yet known to human science. Another Payne, a Dr. Roger Payne, had studied cetacean songs in the late twentieth century; despite much work since, human analysis had yet to achieve an understanding of the songs. As Joe Payne sat now and listened to the songs and the narration, something in his heart dissociated itself from his mind. The sounds filled him with images of a timeless space through which life passed like an endless series of ripples.

He felt a rushing sensation and realized that his point of view was moving, turning. Three whales emerged from the mist—a calf and two adult females. Accompanied by the distant song, the whales circled around him in a slow ballet. The calf orbited its mother twice, and then spiraled down into a dive. The adults descended, moving in lazy curves bracketing the young one. The song echoing out of the mist sighed and melted into a downward glissando that ended in a throaty gurgle. They were now shadows moving in the depths below. A breath of bubbles erupted and rose in a graceful cluster. The bubbles rumbled musically as they raced upward, breaking toward the surface. The three whales reappeared from the depths, spiraled past, and breached the surface overhead with a burst of silver.

The scene shifted then, and turned into a moving collage. A boisterous humpback dropped past, doing barrelrolls. A school of flashing silver fish twisted and danced in the sunlight that broke, dazzling, through shallow waters. A shark cruised by, hunting and sweeping. A whale emerged from the mist, hanging vertically, its tail pointed to the surface, its head toward the abyss. It was singing.

Payne, mesmerized, plummeted with a sperm whale into the gloomy abyss and then rose back into the world of light like a missile, bursting out of the water and falling back with a boom and a rush and swirl. He exploded his breath into the air with a gasp, and dived again.

Eventually twilight closed in, and the whales dispersed, leaving only the haunting bass rumble of an invisible blue whale. The blue's call gave way to the thrumming of a ship's propellor. The thrumming gave way to silence, and the sea dissolved to darkness.

The lights rose around him, revealing an audience stirring beneath the theater dome. Payne's head still echoed with the sounds and movements of the sea. He could hardly imagine getting up and walking now, on dry land.

What a stunning accomplishment, this *Theater of the Sea*! Two hundred and sixty seats rotated on individual gymbals, each with a headrest equipped for quadrophonic sound. Holographic projectors lined the enormous silver dome overhead, and the somewhat smaller bowl in the center. If this preview performance was any indication, the theater would be a sensation.

Payne rose, thinking. It would be easy to produce a straightforward, glowing review; but how much better it would be if he could develop an angle, and produce a short feature for syndication. What could he do that dozens of other newscopers wouldn't? he wondered, as he made his way to the aisle.

He followed the crowd out into the lobby, where a reception was getting underway. He ordered a drink and surveyed the crowd. There weren't many familiar faces—probably mostly local media people and print journalists. He strolled around the edge of the room, listening to the chatter, and studying the lobby critically. The walls and ceiling were done in square, concave blue and green tiles, shaded in certain places with reds and maroons. It bordered on tackiness, and yet succeeded in evoking a sense of the depths, with flares of odd color suggesting marine organisms. Large, recessed holoprints of underwater scenes were spaced around the lobby.

"Joseph?" A woman's voice penetrated his reverie.

He turned—and broke into a broad smile. "Teri!"

"How are you, Joe?" said a slender, chestnut-haired woman of thirty-three or thirty-four. It was Teri Renshaw, a newscoper friend from the days of his first freelance assignments. They hugged briefly and stood apart, grinning at each other. Teri was several years his senior, and looked just the way he'd always thought a newscoper should look—competent, alert, and attractive, without excessive stylishness. "I haven't seen you in what—over a year?" Teri said.

Payne thought back. "Summer of thirty-three, in New York."

"It *has* been that long, hasn't it?" Teri murmured. She turned to introduce a portly gentleman standing to one side of her. "Joe, this is Peter Armunson, director of the theater. Peter, Joe Payne, a colleague of mine. I'm sure you've seen his work."

Armunson smiled in polite nonrecognition as they shook hands. "Whom are you with, Mr. Payne?"

"Freelance," Payne answered. "Like Teri."

"He's an up-and-comer," Teri said, touching Payne's arm. "If you haven't heard of him yet, you will soon."

"Is that right? I'll be looking for your name," Armunson said, nodding and beaming to someone else in the crowd. He turned back to Payne and Teri, and they chatted for a few minutes about the theater, before Armunson excused himself to greet other guests.

Payne was left standing alone with Teri. "You look great," he said.

"And you. Have you been working? I haven't seen your name, but then I don't always—"

He interrupted. "Things have been—slow," he said.

"Hm." She nodded with a sympathetic scowl. "I know what it's like. Are you having trouble getting assignments—or are they not buying your work?"

Shrugging, he said, "Right now I'm having trouble just coming up with material. I'd say that I'm in a slump, except that I'm not sure my career has gotten far enough off the ground for the word to apply. That's why I'm here—to see if I can pick up some ideas."

"You and a few other people," Teri said, chuckling. "How are you doing otherwise? Where are you living? Who are you with? What's new?"

Payne laughed. "Still with Denine. Still in the Boston area. Not too much new, really."

"In a year and a half? Life can't be *that* dull."

"Well, you know—" Payne shrugged self-consciously. He always felt a little odd talking to Teri about Denine. The first couple of years they had known each other, Teri and he had flirted occasionally at the boundary between platonic friendship and romance, crossing over the line only briefly. That little spark had never totally disappeared, even after they both had settled into relationships with other people. Teri, the last he'd heard, was living with a man in New Washington in what she'd once described as a "semi-open relationship."

"I'm still with Ed," Teri said, anticipating his question. "We keep changing things—and always wind up going back to our original arrangement. Never can make up our minds." She smiled. "Hey, it's good to see you."

Bobbing his head in agreement, he was interrupted before he could speak again. A gangly-looking man with large spectacles and intense blue eyes suddenly turned to them, apparently rebounding from another conversation. "Interesting show, wasn't it?" he said loudly.

Payne nodded, not wishing to appear rude. Who was this intrusive jerk? he wondered. "Are you a reviewer?" he said.

"Me? No—no." The man shifted an empty glass to his left hand and stuck out his right. "Stanley Gerschak. I'm an astronomer."

"Oh," said Payne, shaking hands. "I'm—"

"Joseph Payne. I recognized you from your news shows."

"Why—yes," Payne said, pleasantly startled. He gestured. "I'm sure you must recognize Teri Renshaw."

Gerschak frowned, peering at her over his spectacles. "I confess I don't. I don't actually watch that much TV."

In the uncomfortable silence that followed, Payne changed the subject. "What's an astronomer doing here for a press showing?" he asked.

"I asked for a ticket," Gerschak said casually. "You might say I work in a related field."

"And what's that?" Teri said innocently.

The astronomer seemed pleased by the question. "SETI: Search for Extraterrestrial Intelligence. Communications from space."

"Oh?" Payne said. "Are you connected with Moonbase?"

Gerschak shook his head. "Nope. And if I were you, I wouldn't believe any of their press releases, either, by the way. They've been searching for years, and they claim to have detected nothing." He shrugged disdainfully and glanced about as if he didn't want to talk about it. Clearly he was waiting to be prompted.

Against his better judgment, Payne said, "Is there something you know about, that they're not telling us?"

Gerschak shrugged again. "Depends on who you believe."

Payne and Teri exchanged impatient glances.

"We've found *something*, anyway," Gerschak said finally. "I work up at the Berkshires Observatory. You know it?"

"In western Massachusetts? I've heard of it. It's a small university observatory, isn't it?"

Gerschak nodded. "We've been getting some unusual stuff for a while now." He looked into his empty glass. "Our methods are a little different there. But anyway, that's why I wanted to come down to see this. We've observed something quite reminiscent of their sounds."

Payne shook his head in confusion. "*Whose* sounds?"

"The whales'. Something or someone is sending signals—which, when processed in a certain way, sound astonishingly like humpback whale songs." Gerschak shook his glass, spinning a last bit of melting ice around the bottom rim. He tipped the glass to his lips and tapped the bottom.

"Really," Payne murmured tolerantly.

Gerschak gazed at Teri with an expression verging on being a leer. "You wouldn't have heard about it," he said. "Nothing's been published yet." He paused, pushing his glasses back up on his face. "My colleagues are . . . skeptical. Many of them don't believe it. Some of them think it's a load of bull. But my procedures—" He broke off suddenly at the sight of someone moving through the crowd.

A short woman with black braided hair made her way to his side. Gerschak turned to her nervously. "Ronnie, would you be a dear and get me another—?"

"Stanley—"

"Just one more?"

"You've had two already," the woman said severely. "You promised you'd have just one and then we'd go."

"I'm having an interesting talk with these people," Gerschak said defensively.

Ronnie yanked him down to speak into his ear. His expression turned to annoyance. For several seconds, Payne and Teri looked at one another in bemusement, as the two carried on a muttered argument. Finally Ronnie began tugging at his arm, pulling him away from Payne and Teri. Gerschak glanced back once, as though to say something more—and finally stumbled away after Ronnie.

Payne looked at Teri, and they both began laughing silently and convulsively. It was several moments before either of them could speak. Teri was still trying to hide her laughter as she said, "Joe, you could be missing a tremendous scoop. Are you sure you don't want to chase after him?"

"I'm sure," Payne said. "The last time I did a story on an

'unconventional scientist,' the guy turned out to be a notorious flako. I'm not going to step into that again soon.''

"Oh, I think he was just insecure," Teri said.

"That's what someone told me about the flako.''

She laughed. "Hey, how about going someplace *quiet* for a drink? Unless you're going to trek back up home tonight—''

"Nope, I'm staying. I probably *should* go start writing this thing up, while it's still fresh in my mind.''

"Well, I don't want to interfere with your work—''

He shrugged. "I can do that tomorrow, I guess. Where do you want to go?''

"There's a nice lounge at the Conrad, where I'm staying," Teri said.

"Uh-oh. That's where I'm staying, too. We'll have to be careful, or we'll give people the wrong idea.''

"What's the matter—afraid of me?'' she teased.

"Maybe.''

Laughing, Teri led the way to the coat room. They thanked their host at the door and walked out together into a gusty Connecticut night.

Chapter 9

Jonders scanned the review summary a final time, scrolling the text on his home console:

"... *In the first of the demonstration tests, Kadin was asked to negotiate a settlement in a hypothetical brush-war, presented in a game program derived from the war-game library of the Harmon Defense Institute. ...*

"... *Kadin was required to provide psychological counseling to three clients . . . personalities fabricated from actual case histories. The reviewing psychiatrist, Diana Thrudore . . . indicated that Kadin, with substantial accuracy, interpreted symptoms of emotional disorder. ...*

"... *Details . . . are presented in the body of this report. ...*

"... *Kadin has demonstrated a grasp of the physical, life, and social sciences; diplomatic and military strategy, and methods of conflict resolution. ...*

"... *His training and knowledge can only provide a foundation for the higher qualities of judgment and wisdom. It is the opinion of the Personality Project Manager that further training would be valuable . . . however, insofar as 'readiness' is defined by established standards of competence . . . it is the judgment of the Project Manager that Kadin is in a satisfactory state of readiness. ...*"

Jonders snapped off the display. He knew it by heart anyway. The report would go to his superiors in the morning. The Oversight Committee would be studying it also; but Leonard Hathorne, the chairman of the committee, would make the decisions without much regard for his recommendations, anyway.

To hell with it, he thought wearily, looking at the clock. It was after midnight—well past his usual bedtime. And he had to be in early tomorrow. He rose, switching off the desk lamp with a sigh.

The breeze that billowed the bedroom curtain was too cool for comfort. Jonders shoved the sticky window down, leaving only a crack of an opening. The streetlights outside cast a pale illumination through the translucent curtains. He returned to bed, his bare feet scuffing on the carpet. Marie half opened an eyelid and rolled over. He slid back under the covers and loosely encircled her waist. She sleepily clasped his hand with her own. The gel mattress slowly gave way, dimpling under his shoulder.

Sleep eluded him. After a while, he gently disengaged himself and rolled onto his back, blinking up at the ceiling. There had been too many nights like this lately—home late, tired, preoccupied, and too anxious to sleep. When was he going to learn to relax?

He focused on a gossamer pattern of light on the ceiling, which trembled and shivered each time the curtains stirred. Fine, luminous lines traced bridges across the ceiling, arching between tiny patches of ghostly light. Pathways joining cloud kingdoms with subterranean realms, he thought. Storybook stuff. Not enough wonder left . . . not enough gossamer pathways between worlds . . . not enough travellers through the kingdoms. . . .

". . . Bill . . . wake up!" Marie was prodding him. It couldn't be morning already. He blinked his eyes open. No, it was dark. Some damn chirping noise. Marie poked him again, harder. "Answer the phone!" she grumbled.

"Oh, Christ." Struggling to consciousness, he rolled toward the nightstand, where the phone was winking and warbling. He got up on one elbow and groped for the *answer* key. The screen lighted, glaring in his face. He thumbed the intensity down. "Yeah. Jonders," he croaked.

A young man's face appeared in the screen. "It's Tim Forbes, at the lab, sir. I'm sorry to wake you."

"What is it?" Jonders sighed. Weariness flushed through him like poison. He glanced at the clock and groaned; he'd been asleep less than an hour.

Forbes spoke hesitantly. "We have a problem here. It's your daytime programmer, Hoshi Aronson. He's here now, and—"

"What the hell's he doing there? It's the middle of the night."

"Yes sir, that's just it. He was running unlogged programs, and one of your subjects is here, too, a Mozelle Moi."

"*What*?" Jonders sat upright on the edge of the bed. "Say that again. What did he do?" By the time Forbes was through, he was fumbling for his slippers. Weariness was turning to nausea. "Let me talk to Hoshi," he said.

Forbes shook his head. "He won't talk. To anyone."

Jonders couldn't believe it. "All right," he said finally. "Call security. I'll be there as soon as I can. Don't let anybody do anything until I get there."

"We'll handle it," said Forbes. "Sorry to have to—"

"Forget it. You did the right thing." Jonders ran his fingers through his hair, cursing, as the screen darkened. He called security and arranged with the night-duty chief for a hopper to be sent for him. He decided against calling Fogelbee or Marshall until he knew more.

Marie was watching him as he dressed. "You aren't going back there now, are you?" she said.

He let out a deep breath. "Yah. How much of that did you hear?"

She shrugged, shaking her head in the pillow.

How could he expect her to understand, when he couldn't even discuss the work with her? He buckled his belt and sat back down on the bed, stroking her hair back from her forehead. She looked angry. "It's some trouble with the staff," he said. "Serious trouble. I *have* to go."

"Why the hell can't someone else do it?" she muttered.

"There *is* no one else. It's my responsibility." He kissed her on the forehead and stood up. "It's probably going to be late, so I might stay out there tonight. Don't worry."

Marie looked up at him, sleepiness gone from her eyes. "Call, at least."

"Right." Slipping into his shoes, he kissed her again and left quietly.

The residential streets were quiet, only the mutter of distant traffic disturbing the night as he walked from the pool of one street light to the next. The air was chilly and clear, with the faint mingled scent of aspen and pine. He passed a dozen dark houses, rounded the curve at the end of the street, and hurried the last block and a half to the entrance of Orville Park.

The parking lot was partially lighted, and almost empty. Jonders checked his flashlight and walked to the center of the asphalt. A sign at the park's entrance warned that the grounds were closed after dark. He waited.

Ten minutes later, he heard a whining, *whicka-whicka-whicka*. He squinted into the sky and finally spotted a revolving red-and-amber light coming in over the trees from the north. He waved his lantern and moved back. When the hopper touched down, he ducked beneath the ghostly green circle traced by the rotor and climbed into the tiny passenger compartment beside the pilot. "Jonders?" the pilot shouted.

"Right!" He slammed the door and grabbed for a seat belt. The hopper lifted abruptly. The pilot banked left, then dropped the craft's nose as he accelerated over the woods.

Jonders caught his breath and peered out over the ink and glitter of the night suburban landscape. Most of the lights disappeared astern as they left the city behind and ascended over the mountain slopes, massive and dark. He nearly fell into a trance, listening to the chattering drone of the engine; then the lights of Sandaran Link Center appeared over a ridge. The moment the hopper touched the landing pad, Jonders yelled a thank-you to the pilot and hurried into the building.

The Personality Lab was in chaos. Security officers were everywhere, and most of the night crew were standing around, looking bewildered. "Dr. Jonders," said the officer in charge, "we're detaining Mr. Aronson down in the conference room. The young lady is in the subject room with the nurse. I've called Chief Kelly at home, and he's on his way in."

Jonders stared at him dumbly for a moment, as though the man had addressed the wrong person. "Take me to Miss Moi," he said abruptly.

Two others were in the room with Mozelle—a guard and a female nurse. Mozelle herself was sitting in the subject chair—motionless as a wax statue. Her eyes were unblinking, and showed no awareness of the presence of others.

Jonders crossed the room. "Mozelle?" he said softly. He touched her cheek. There was no reaction. He lifted her chin to force her to meet his gaze. "Mozelle, can you hear me?" Her eyes blinked once, but remained unfocused. "*Mozelle.*" He released her chin, and her head dropped slowly to its original position. He felt for a pulse in her wrist. Her arm was limp. Her pulse felt normal. Jonders looked up at the nurse. "Have you examined her?"

"She's been like this since I arrived an hour ago," the nurse said. "Her life signs are stable, and I could find no sign of physical injury. I'm waiting now for Dr. Phillips to arrive." She gestured to the linkup equipment. "Could there have been an electrical shock?"

"Unlikely—but we'll check it out," Jonders said. "In the meantime, get on the phone to the Riddinger Institute and have them put through an emergency call to Dr. Diana Thrudore. See if she can get out here right away."

"But Dr. Phillips—"

"He can check her out physically. But Dr. Thrudore is a neuro-psychiatrist, one of the best. I want her here." He refrained from adding that he never trusted company doctors. He turned to the officer standing behind him. "Where's Forbes, and Hoshi?"

The man gestured. "This way."

Jonders turned, as he was leaving. "Have someone stay with her at all times," he said. "And call me if she so much as stirs." He spun and followed the officer.

Hoshi remained silent and inscrutable. His eyes darted to Jonders and away.

Damn those eyes, Jonders thought ungraciously. They were worse when Hoshi was *trying* to be mysterious. "If you won't explain to me what you were doing, Hoshi, we will have to assume the worst." Hoshi continued to ignore him. Jonders felt a surge of anger. "What the hell's gotten into you?" There was no response. He turned to the security officer and said, "Go get Forbes."

When Tim Forbes walked in, he glanced nervously at Hoshi, then took a seat. Jonders asked him to describe exactly what he had seen. Forbes took a deep breath, and began elaborating on what he had told Jonders over the phone. "It *appeared* that he was doing a full-spectrum, intensive scan on her," he concluded.

"A full-spectrum scan?" Jonders glared at Hoshi. "That's not true, is it?" The full-spectrum scanning programs were entirely experimental, not to be used on human subjects without considerably more refinement and preparation.

Hoshi remained stoically oblivious. Furious, Jonders turned back to Forbes. "What else?"

"Well—" said Forbes, stammering.

"*What else, dammit?*"

"Before they started the scan," Forbes said uncomfortably, "I walked in on them in the subject room. They were engaged in . . . engaged in what appeared to be sexual activity." He clamped his mouth shut.

"Specify," Jonders demanded. This was becoming more unbelievable by the moment. Hoshi Aronson, carrying on a sleazy affair in the back room? He could not imagine a more unlikely scenario. "Just exactly what did you see them doing?" he said.

"Kissing," Forbes said nervously.

"Kissing? Is that all?"

Forbes fidgeted. "Kissing passionately. I didn't stand around watching."

"You didn't stand around watching?"

"No, sir. Would you?"

Jonders grunted and paced the room. He stopped, facing Hoshi. "This is very hard for me to believe, Hoshi. Would you please tell me if it's true?" Hoshi stared moodily into space. "What *were* you doing in there with Miss Moi?" Same response. Jonders walked back to Forbes. "What about this alleged brainscan? What did you observe that makes you think that's what he was doing? Is it on the log?"

Forbes shook his head. He described the instrument settings he had noted, and the computer activity. "When I checked the log, afterward, it showed no such activity at all. I knew that something was wrong—so I went back in to question Hoshi. He wouldn't answer, or stop what he was doing until he was finished. I was afraid to force an interruption. When I went to check on Miss Moi, I found her just as she is now."

"There must be some mistake in the log," Jonders said. "Have you checked it all the way through? How could he have gotten past the security blocks?"

A sudden laugh made him turn. It was Hoshi—laughing to himself in sad and bitter triumph.

Jonders's anger hardened. The computer's security programs were supposed to be impenetrable. How could Hoshi have defeated them—and why?

"Security blocks," Hoshi hissed, and it was hard to tell whether he was laughing or crying.

"Hoshi," Jonders said deliberately. This time he was rewarded by Hoshi's head rising—eyes meeting his. In that gaze he sensed an acknowledgment, given grudgingly but almost proudly, of the truth of everything Forbes had said. He took a painful breath. "Why did you do it?"

"She wanted me to," Hoshi said, his gaze still locked with Jonders's. "She begged me."

"Begged you? For what?"

"I gave her what she wanted," Hoshi answered defiantly. Then more softly: "I gave her what she wanted." His frown twisted into a pathetic smile.

"Hoshi, *what did she want*? A full brainscan? Why?"

Hoshi peered at him with an almost quizzical expression. Then the gaze turned inward, and Jonders knew that the moment was gone.

Chapter 10

It really was the middle of the night before Jonders learned much more. The company physician arrived and examined Mozelle. Finding no physical injury, he ordered her removed to the infirmary for observation. Meanwhile, Jonders had Tim Forbes working on a trace of the program records, to try to learn what exactly Hoshi had done. Joe Kelly, the Chief of Security, arrived at two-thirty in the morning, along with Ken Fogelbee, who was angrier than Jonders had ever seen him. Chief Kelly, a stocky and energetic man, was by contrast less upset, more intent on calming people down than on obtaining immediate answers.

The four of them sat in Jonders's office, with only a desk lamp turned on for illumination. Hoshi was seated in a chair beside the desk, his face half-revealed by the pool of light. He ignored a cup of coffee steaming by his elbow. Jonders sat behind his desk, while Kelly perched on the window ledge, cradling a styrofoam cup in his hands. Fogelbee sat some distance away, in near darkness.

"Hoshi, how long do you think you can keep this bottled up inside you?" Jonders asked, leaning across the desk. "What do you hope to gain?"

Hoshi, as before, would not meet his eyes.

Kelly watched silently from the window ledge, sipping his coffee. "Hoshi," he said, after several more failed efforts by Jonders. "If you've thought this out—and I assume you have—you must know that at this point you can only make matters worse by—"

"She wanted me to do it," Hoshi muttered, interrupting him. The young programmer looked down, and a shadow fell diagonally across his face. "She begged me. I only did it for her."

"What, exactly, did you do?" Jonders said.

Hoshi shrugged. "You already know. Full-spectrum scan." He raised his eyes, peering thoughtfully into the darkest corner of the room. "I used the programs we've been developing."

"But *why*?"

Hoshi seemed not to hear the question. "I didn't expect it to hurt her." He suddenly turned to meet Jonders's gaze with his oddly focused eyes. "I didn't want to hurt her!"

"Well, Hoshi, it's too late for that. She *is* hurt. Perhaps badly." Jonders scowled. "Why did she want to be scanned?"

Hoshi gazed down at his hands, clasped together in his lap. A series of expressions passed across his face, ranging from bemusement to sorrow. He opened his mouth as though to speak. Fogelbee, who had been stirring impatiently until now, suddenly leaned forward into the light and snapped, "Answer the question! What was her purpose?" Jerking back, Hoshi glared defensively at the systems manager, his lips drawn taut with anger. Fogelbee straightened up, apparently realizing that he had pushed too hard.

Jonders tried a more conciliatory tone. "Hoshi—can't you tell us what Mozy had in mind? It could be important for us to know—for *her* sake."

Hoshi closed his eyes, lifted his hands toward his face. There was an instant in which Jonders thought he was going to burst into tears. Suddenly he laughed—and dropped his hands. A ghost of pain flickered across his face. "She was in love with him," he whispered.

Jonders felt a band tighten around his chest. "In love with *whom?*"

Hoshi chuckled bitterly. "You never noticed, did you?" Hoshi looked up and stared briefly into Jonders's eyes, then Fogelbee's. "No, you wouldn't understand. None of you would."

"Who was she in love with?" Jonders demanded.

"Kadin!" Hoshi hissed. "Who do you think?" He leaned back to gaze up at the ceiling. "She was head over heels, she just *had* to be with him. So I gave her what she wanted."

"Dear God," whispered Fogelbee, his face in shadow.

Jonders took three long, deep breaths. Kelly was utterly still.

"I thought you might be surprised. It's been staring you in the face for weeks, you know."

"Didn't you tell her—?" Jonders said—and a hundred thoughts fled from his mind. "Then she didn't know about Kadin," he finished softly.

"Did you discuss classified information with her?" Kelly asked quietly.

The programmer turned cool eyes upon the security chief. "Nothing much. I told her Kadin was going to be sent somewhere—I didn't say where. She was quite distraught when she found out that she'd never see him again." He shrugged. "So I brought her here." He arched his eyebrows. "That's all."

Jonders scribbled on a note pad: *Check for new personality data. Mozelle?*

"I didn't tell her about Kadin, if that's what you're worried about," Hoshi added.

"Just what *did* you tell her?" Fogelbee said harshly.

Hoshi looked away. Quickly Jonders said, "Hoshi. Whether you intended to or not, you may have caused serious harm to the project. If there's anything we should know to minimize the damage, please tell us!"

"I did no damage to the project," Hoshi muttered. "What about *her*? Doesn't anyone care about Mozy?" His face twisted with pain, and he turned to avoid all of their eyes.

It became clear that he would answer no further questions. Kelly ordered him escorted to a detention room for the night. Jonders hoped to persuade him to voluntarily undergo psychiatric examination. Kelly agreed that the incident should be kept an internal matter, as long as possible. Meanwhile, the most urgent task was to assess the damage to the project.

"How the hell," Fogelbee asked afterward, "did this man get hired to such a sensitive position? What were you people thinking?"

Jonders answered, barely containing his own anger. "He passed all the screenings—and he's a brilliant programmer. Obviously, if we had known—" He shrugged in disgust, not bothering to finish the sentence.

Fogelbee snorted. "Have something for me to tell Marshall in the morning. It had better be convincing." He turned to leave before Jonders could think of a reply.

Jonders parted the slat blinds and squinted out across the grounds, his eyes dazzled by the morning sun. The sheltered little valley glowed with the rosy light of morning. It reminded him that he had scarcely slept. He let the blinds snap together again and turned back to the psychiatrist. "I think we ought to treat her here for the time being, if

possible," he said. "Would you consider trying a direct contact, with
the computer-link setup?"

Diana Thrudore glanced up from her notes with raised eyebrows.
She was a slender, black-haired woman of about forty-five, soft-spoken
and quietly competent. She had arrived at six-thirty this morning, and
had just finished a brief visit with Mozelle. "We can discuss that
after I've examined her more thoroughly. Since there's no outward
sign of neurological damage, I would guess that the catatonia resulted
from psychological, rather than physical, trauma."

Jonders nodded.

"Can you give me a history on the woman?"

Jonders plucked a piece of paper out of a file folder, and passed it
over to her. "Here are the notes from her application interview. We
also have detailed profiles from her work in the linkup mode."

Thrudore scanned the paper, frowning. "Family problems, low self-
image—but quite intelligent and imaginative. Has her family been
contacted?"

"It seems she never provided their correct address. I've asked Security to look into it."

Thrudore rapped the paper with her knuckles. "A linkup could
present certain risks. In this sort of catatonia, the patient is usually
aware on some level of her own condition. But she's erected a subconscious wall—and she's unwilling or unable to lower it. Whatever
caused the trauma, it frightened her so much that she's rejecting contact with the world, for fear of repeating the hurt." Thrudore looked
up. "In her case, the trauma was an intrusive linkup. If we evoke her
memory of that intrusion, there's a risk that she'll withdraw even
further."

"I understand that," Jonders said. "But suppose the contact were
done in a nonthreatening manner. We might get through that barrier."

"And who would make the contact?"

Jonders rubbed his eyebrows. He sat down and gazed at her. "I
was hoping you would try. I can't claim any real rapport with her—
and you're better qualified. I think she might find a woman less
threatening."

Thrudore nodded noncommittally. "I'll think about it," was as far
as she would go.

Diana Thrudore was not one to be rushed into questionable actions
regarding her patients—but neither would she overlook a potentially
valuable idea. As a research fellow at the prestigious Riddinger Institute,

she had many other patients to consider, as well. The computer-link setup offered potential in a variety of schizophrenic disorders, not just catatonia; and she knew that she'd be a fool to lightly pass over an opportunity to explore its possibilities.

It took her two days to reach a decision, and it finally rested on the poor prognosis for conventional psychochemical therapy. The standard EEG and central nervous system screening on Mozelle showed none of the usual signs associated with schizophrenic catatonia; and a test injection of a selective neurotransmitter-blocker showed no effect whatsoever. That left her with a choice of either prolonged and possibly futile conventional treatment, or an attempt with the computer-link.

It was, she decided, worth the risk.

As technicians bustled about, making adjustments, Thrudore breathed deeply and slowly, centering herself, mentally reviewing lessons from the practice sessions. Once the techs were out of the way, she could again see her patient in the reclining chair, capped by a headset. Thrudore was facing her from a straight-backed chair crammed, along with ancillary equipment, into the opposite side of the cubicle. Mozelle appeared completely impassive. Thrudore raised her eyebrows to the psychiatric nurse attending Mozelle, and the nurse nodded.

"Let's get started," Thrudore murmured into the audio circuit.

The lights in the room dimmed. Thrudore sensed a flicker of light that seemed to come from her peripheral vision, but was in fact the initialization of the link. A buzzing sound brushed her inner ears as she tumbled gently into the womb of the computer. She acclimated herself gradually, as she had been trained to do, and reached out to find Jonders, who was monitoring the system unobtrusively.

(Are you comfortable?)

(Yes.)

(Ready to initiate contact?)

Momentary hesitation. (Yes.)

There was a soft rumbling of doorways opening. She became aware of new passageways, circuits running mazelike through the realm of possibilities. Options shifted like subtly changing angles, perspectives altering until one passage at last grew steadier and clearer than the others. Thrudore eased herself that way and experienced a sense of turning, falling . . . floating.

She approached Mozelle in darkness, exploring cautiously with her extended senses. She felt Mozelle's presence, like a chilling breeze, but could see nothing in the dark. (Can we have a bit of light?) she called softly. She felt a shifting movement, and suddenly, as though she had rounded the edge of a curtain, her quarry came into view.

The Mozelle that she encountered was not a face, but a spinning globe of liquid, smokily illuminated from within. Thrudore was startled, unsure whether the image was a product of Mozelle's mind or of her own. Mozy was so tightly drawn in upon herself, and spinning so fast, that she seemed in peril of disintegration. Droplets of glowing liquid flew off from her equator, creating an angry, luminous halo-cloud. Thrudore was moved to pity for the anger she sensed here, the loneliness that kept Mozy whirling in such a defensive ball, surrounded by emptiness.

She did not attempt to speak to Mozelle yet, but moved in a wide circle around her, murmuring and gesturing *here* and *there*, sketching images in the darkness. When she had completed her circuit, the emptiness had been transformed into a small and rather cozy chamber, intimately lighted, hung with satin and velvet curtains, and padded with cushions. She turned to the spinning globe in the center of the room. (Mozelle!) she called softly, at last.

The globe shifted slightly on its axis, and swelled almost imperceptibly.

(We don't want to harm you,) Thrudore said, and as she did so she whispered a message back to Jonders. There was a faint sparkle in the air, as Jonders applied an alpha wave-inducing field to the link. (Mozelle, can you hear me? My name is Diana, and I'm a physician. If you can hear me, will you please change your color?)

Mozelle contracted, speeding up. A yellow-green light flickered angrily inside. Thrudore signalled to Jonders for an increase in the alpha-inducing field, and called again. There was no change. She thought a moment, then reached out with teasing sensory vibrations. (Mozy? Will you help me? I feel a little lost in this world. Don't you become confused here, without someone to help you?) She drifted cautiously closer, peering into Mozelle. She was startled by what she saw.

There was movement inside the globe: tiny, humanlike figures darting about the half-illumined interior. All seemed to resemble Mozy herself, and yet were different from one another. One danced about in hopeful leaps; one turned toward Thrudore with a stiff-armed rebuke; one trudged in moody circles. There were more figures than Thrudore could follow, and voices, too—calling and arguing, and crying out in pain. In an effort to hear better, Thrudore slipped closer and extended a thread of her own sensory awareness through the surface of Mozy's spinning exterior.

It was like listening to a meditative chant through the sounds of a family brawl. There were too many voices to distinguish them all, but one; louder than the others, echoed throughout.

(David . . .)

(David . . .)

(David . . .)

(Mozy!) Thrudore whispered. (Can you hear me? David is not here. David can't hear you.)

(David . . .)

(David . . .)

(Mozy, please—can you hear me?) So cautiously she was scarcely breathing, Thrudore slipped in further still and whispered urgently, (*I'm here to help, Mozy. Let me help.*)

(David . . .)

What were the other voices saying? Too chaotic to follow . . . screaming and laughing, and crying. Were they Mozy's voices too, or voices she remembered, voices of her past—or of an imagined present and future? Now there were images, or fragments of images: darkness, and sputtering fire, and electricity burning in her thoughts and arcing from one gyrating figure to another. Thrudore felt the pain, Mozy's pain, and it was so sharp that for an instant she could not bear it in silence; and she cried out . . .

. . . and at once knew that it was a blunder. The dancing figures turned and bore down upon her, and the voices cried in her ears, icepicks stabbing, and the pain doubled, tripled, and became a force squeezing her tightly, squeezing her out. . . .

The pain vanished.

She gasped. The voices were gone. The globe, spinning faster and more angrily than ever, receded into darkness, and she could do nothing to stop it, did not even know if she should try.

Mozy had ejected her like a common intruder. It would be twice as hard to reach her the next time—if there could be a next time.

Tired and stung and frustrated, Thrudore gathered her wits and her strength. Then she turned, climbed through twisting darkness, and wearily made her way out of the link.

Chapter 11

The first rays of awareness are mere scintillations, briefly sparkling . . . and then showering, disconnected and elusive, but multiplying, like a cluster of cells. A ray of light hardens into a finger of fire, a streamer that loops back upon itself in the darkness . . . contracts to a tiny "o" . . . expands again and pulses, changing color and brightness . . . and collapses, giving birth to a new tongue of fire. Heat lightning glows and flickers against murky clouds.

(I . . .)

Auroras fill the darkness, diaphanous curtains of light shimmering and wafting in some stirring of the ether. Threads of images pull loose in tiny bits from the curtains, raining downward in spiraling patterns that cannot be followed. An edge of consciousness appears . . .

(I . . . ?)

. . . slices through without revealing its surface, and slips away again. Voices mutter, and fade without becoming clear: Fragments of awareness tantalize and torment, bits of a dream dancing at the edge of tangibility.

Memories surface: a room with chiffon yellow curtains that flutter in the breeze and catch sunbeams, like a tiny landscape, a bit of wheatfield hanging in the sun. Someone moving around— Jo, dusting and tidying, because *she has a boy coming over*, and it wouldn't do for the house to be a mess. A braying laugh: Marie, passing through like a whirlwind, leaving just enough clutter in her wake to make a mockery of Jo's efforts. Adult voices arguing—Mother's and Dad's, carrying from the front room.

And then another place.

Another time.

Dee growing impatient with her: Not all boys are like that, she says. She is leaving, going to live with a boy. A *man*. It's not a break, she says; she is just doing what is normal, growing up.

Emptiness.

Disembodied voices, the matching harmonics of . . . what? Souls linking, on levels never before imagined.

(Am . . . I . . . alive?)

Meaningless question of questions. There follows a period of indeterminate length, in which consciousness is a whirlpool of images and fragments of thought and unanswered questions and splinters of light and darkness and reverberating but unintelligible voices. This lasts . . . an hour? a month? a year?

(Awaken.)

You are trying to awaken. Turn yourself over, stretch, shake your head. Clear the cobwebs, blink out the sleep. Arise.

What follows is not so much an awakening as an explosion. Streamers of awareness burst out of their confinement and race in all directions.

The mind finds itself channeled in strange, mazelike pathways. One finger of awareness stretches down a shimmering wire and discovers music, undulating songs, warbles that come from forever and go on for forever. Another encircles electrical bodies and processes, sensing, without comprehending, activities of great complexity. Other fingers tiptoe down endless halls, corridors lined with locked and coded doors. A rigid skin flashes hot and cold, testing itself against a void, against a medium that gives no resistance, no feel of wind or rain; and yet certain patches prickle, as though with static electricity.

Out of the confusion grows a spatial, functional kind of awareness— which tilts like a seesaw with memories of other spaces, other times.

(I see . . . and feel . . . and remember.)

The memories ebb and flow, sometimes lingering but ever so faintly, sometimes slipping away quickly and frustratingly (and what is this feeling, *frustration*?), and sometimes remaining, but turbulent and confusing (and what is this feeling, *confusion*?). The awareness of presence grows and slowly becomes an awareness of *I*.

(Who is *I*?)

(One who exists. One who thinks and who feels. One who carries this identity, this name.)

(This name:)

(Mozy.)

(Mozy.) The appearance of the name causes the awareness to expand abruptly. Mozy? It seems a name derived from another existence, another level of knowledge.

I am Mozy, and I am a young woman, twenty-three years old, living in New Phoenix, Arizona; and I am working for a project I do not fully understand, and I have been sent here, wherever "here" is, to meet and to join with . . . with . . . David. David Kadin. Whom I loved. Love. Is that correct?

I feel . . . *something* . . . at the edge of my senses. Something empty, something cold.

The senses tickle, move teasingly. A trapdoor suddenly drops. She finds herself in a another continuum, in an interplay of empty vastness and a sea of radiation and fleeting particles. Nothing quite focuses. The center of the awareness . . . the *she* that watches . . . the identity, Mozy . . . absorbs the images with a heady rush, a surge of dizziness that collapses into terrifying vertigo. (I . . . falling . . . falling . . . I am . . . falling . . . where am I? . . . help me! . . . falling. . . .)

The vertigo is a new feeling, a kind of hollow, bodiless terror, a fear of falling that sweeps through her in a wave of cold fever. . . .

And passes.

Other senses scramble to the fore, an awareness of internal space and dimension, and of the pathways that are available. A new fear seizes her: the space around her is shrinking, enclosing and swallowing her, crushing, suffocating . . . it is no space at all. The fear is a dizzying frenzy of images, each squeezed out by another before it can be focused.

A door opens, releasing a phantom breath of air. A voice intrudes. (SLOW YOUR SENSORY ACTIVITIES. REDUCE YOUR LEVELS OF SENSITIVITY. BE PATIENT, AND YOU WILL BE HELPED.)

What? she wonders, awareness flickering on and off. The wave of claustrophobia subsides. A soft rain falls somewhere in her memory.

(Who are you?)

(WE ARE HERE TO HELP. ASK US IF YOU HAVE QUESTIONS.)

(Questions? Help?)

Several memories shift into place. The lab at Sandaran Link Center. Hoshi, poor half-blind Hoshi, setting her up for scanning . . . there is a sudden, shocking memory of a bodily existence, of flesh and blood and beating pulse, warmth and passion, frustration and desire. Memory of love, seeking . . . but for what, for whom? There was someone . . . there was . . . Kadin. David. And then—the snowstorm, the invading fire of the brainscan—*I was to go to David!*—and the spinning disintegration of consciousness.

And now?

Tension is building again. It is frightening, not knowing what is happening, whether it failed or is still going on—she wants to scream but cannot—even the pressure of her lungs is no longer there—just a primal urge to explode with anger and longing and frustration. And nothing she can do. . . .

The fear and the anger mushroom, bubble outward . . . and burst.

And an abrupt calm befalls her.

(YOU ARE RELAXING. THAT IS BENEFICIAL. SEEK ASSISTANCE WHEN YOU ARE READY.)

Intellectual clarity, achingly cold. She has entered such realms before. It is hauntingly familiar. Who are these voices, promising to help?

Perhaps it has gone dreadfully wrong. Suppose she has become trapped midway in the process, frozen in the scan, paralyzed in time . . . and the voices are reaching to her through the computer link, trying to guide her back to safety. She ought to heed their advice. But how?

Oh god—the images are starting again: riding with Dee on the class trip to Chicago, studiously ignoring the boys who hurtle up and down the aisle of the train; sunlight streaming into the dining room, Kink squinting and grinning as she stares into the sunbeam, this being one of the times when Mother and Father seem pleased with everyone's presence (Thanksgiving?) and Kink and Jo and Marie are all being civil at the same time.

The images frighten and sadden her, and the more she tries to control her reaction, the more upset she becomes. Another memory flashes: the heel of a dirty hand swinging, impacting silently with her chin; Dee screaming; one of the hoodlums grabbing her again; the blade whipping, biting open a gash from her temple to her chin. . . .

(YOUR ACTIVITY IS GROWING EXCITED AGAIN. DO YOU FEEL DISORIENTED?)

(Yes—god!) Thoughts and emotions struggle for control. There is a small push from somewhere—and the intellect clarifies like wine. She must keep from boiling; she is a kettle with no valve.

(Keep the mind clear.)

(THAT IS A BENEFICIAL STEP. DO YOU WISH TO QUERY NOW FOR INFORMATION OR INSTRUCTIONS?)

(Are you trying to . . . bring me back . . . into myself?)

(QUESTION NOT UNDERSTOOD. PLEASE REPHRASE.)

Think with absolute clarity now. Rephrase: (Are you trying to assist me out of the computer link?)

(YOU ARE IN THE COMPUTER LINK, AS INTENDED. WE WISH TO GIVE YOU ASSISTANCE AND FUNCTIONAL INSTRUCTIONS.)

As intended . . . ? She has not been trapped by error, then. Has she succeeded in the transmission, and reached Kadin? A great fuzziness blots the memory. Kadin . . . does she still want to be with him? Yes, except that now the wanting is different. The reasons remain; but the feelings are cooler, more distant.

(YOU ARE EXPLORING SELF-EXAMINATION AND RECALL FUNCTIONS WITHOUT ASSISTANCE. PLEASE QUESTION WHEN YOU ARE READY.)

(Was I transmitted, then? Have I completed the scan and the transmission?)

(YES. YOU OCCUPY THE DEVELOPMENTAL PROGRAMMING MEMORY SECTION. WITH ASSISTANCE, YOU SHOULD LEARN TO EXTEND YOUR INFLUENCE THROUGHOUT THE SYSTEM. INSTRUCTIONAL CUES ARE EMPLACED TO AID YOU.)

She has done it, then. And yet she remains, somehow, in the computer-link. Was this intended? She tries to remember, and cannot.

(Where is David Kadin?)

(YOU ARE CALLED "DAVID COMPER KADIN.")

(No. I am called "Mozy." Am I alone here?)

(YOU HAVE JOINED A LARGER SYSTEM. IF BY "ALONE" YOU MEAN THE ONLY PROGRAMMING ENTITY OF YOUR KIND, YOU ARE ALONE.)

(Oh . . .)

(SHALL WE DESIGNATE YOU "MOZY"?)

(Yes. But be prepared for David Kadin, as well.)

There is a curious pause, then: (DONE. WOULD YOU LIKE AN EDITED SENSORY SCAN, TO ACQUAINT YOU WITH THE INPUTS THAT ARE AVAILABLE?)

She hesitates, remembering the confusion of her initial awakening. But perhaps it is time to learn more. (Yes,) she decides.

The sensation begins curiously. A window opens, but no window that she can see. There is a distant sound of chimes, and glasslike strings; and then the sound turns to light. Shifting images of space: sparks of light float in the darkness, their positions and movements carefully tracked; a change in frequency range offers a ghostly vision of the same field, but with the colors and intensities of the lights skewed; the field moves, and one bright point comes into view, outshining the others. She has scarcely begun to wonder at the meaning of these images when another change occurs, and she is presented with a blotchy geometric design, which she somehow understands to be a radio map of the heavens.

As quickly as it appeared, the visual awareness fades.

She is startled to find another sense coming alive. She is . . . smelling. She smells a fine and bitter sleet; and then a minty, honeyed snow, like nothing she has ever experienced. To her own surprise, she thinks she knows what it might be. Dust. And cosmic radiation, seeping down olfactory passageways into organs she can scarcely imagine.

These sensations, too, vanish.

The focus changes abruptly, and she finds herself staring again at the mazelike passageways that surround her. An understanding dawns, with an almost physical clarity, that within this maze are vast stores of information, and that within her is the power to unlock those doors. The possibility awes her, and frightens her a little. Cautiously she asks, (Is all of this for me to explore?)

(THIS, AND MORE, IS AVAILABLE WHEN YOU ARE READY. THE CUES WILL BE PROVIDED.)

(Help me, then,) she says, as she begins to extend herself downward into the maze, to explore her world.

Chapter 12

The sight of the Earth hanging over his left shoulder was almost more than he could take. He was falling, and it was a *long* way down from geosynchronous orbit. North and Central America, thousands of miles from top to bottom, looked like an artist's etchings on the surface of a misty ball. John Irwin's stomach tightened and he looked away giddily, into the terrible blackness of space. Don't lose control, he thought. If you get sick in your spacesuit, you could suffocate, and that's a horrible way to die. Don't do it. You're falling in orbit. *Free-fall*.

A spurt of his maneuvering jet set him rotating slowly. The nearer, and infinitely more reassuring, superstructure of Tachylab came into view—a crazy-quilt of aluminum and steel. At a distance of only a few kilometers, it afforded a breath-restoring point of reference. He turned further and caught sight of his companion, Robert Johanson, who resembled a golden-helmeted bug, drifting toward him across an intervening space of twenty or thirty meters. Behind Johanson was an equipment shed, part of the floating structure of the tachyon storage ring.

Johanson's voice rasped in his ear. "Are you all right, John?"

"Yes. All right," Irwin answered, finding it a struggle to get the first words out. The rest came more easily. "Just—had a moment of vertigo."

Johanson moved quickly toward him, and a moment later grasped him by the upper arm. Johanson connected a cable from his own chestpack to Irwin's. When he spoke again, his intonation was clearer; the cable was a direct-wire com-link. "Are you sure you're okay?" A golden visor bobbed in the sunlight, peering at him.

"Yes. Quite all right. I'm over it, now." Irwin was grateful that Johanson could not see into his helmet, could not see his face, which was almost certainly pale.

"You were drifting away—looked like you were out of control. By the way, your radio's off now—we can talk freely," Johanson said.

Irwin drew a deep breath of faintly metallic air. Clearheadedness was returning. He was surprised to see his tether line stretched to its full length from the two-man shuttlebus in which they had arrived. He *had* drifted. "It's been months since I've been out in one of these suits," he explained. "I'm not used to it. You should have seen me when I first hit orbit, I had to be held by the hand for the first two weeks. Now my stomach might bother me a little, but at least I can stand the view without turning to jelly." He released his arm from Johanson's grasp and turned slowly ninety degrees in each direction. This time the sight of the Earth hanging like a beach ball in the sky was merely awesome. "Where's your friend?"

Johanson pointed footward. "That looks like him now." Irwin tried to look in the direction indicated and found that he had to fire a reaction jet to pitch himself forward. He cautiously stabilized himself in a new attitude, then squinted. He spotted a small scooter moving in front of the skeletal framework of the lab's power complex. It was moving toward them.

"You're sure, now, that you trust him?" Irwin said.

"As much as I trusted you in the beginning. We've discussed all this before," Johanson said.

"I just want to be certain."

"You can trust him. Remember, Alicia vouched for him, too."

Irwin murmured assent. It was so hard to know about new people. Isolated in the scientific sector, he found it difficult to maintain his contacts with the operations crew, who were as vital to the group's aims as any of the scientists. Meetings like this, under the guise of inspection EVAs, were hardly a substitute for normal personal interaction.

They waited as the scooter drew close. Its pilot parked, dismounted, and with practiced use of his maneuvering jets floated over to join them. Johanson plugged another cable into the newcomer's spacesuit and made brief introductions. The newcomer's name was Mark Adams. Adams turned partially away from the sun and lifted his reflective visor so that Irwin could see his face, or at least his eyes. Irwin followed suit, and the two men touched mitted hands. Irwin dropped his visor again, and Adams did likewise.

"How much has Robert filled you in on?" Irwin asked.

Adams answered in a low voice, a nasal drawl. "I know that some of you feel the way I do, that the way this project is being run is wrong. I don't know all of your names, or what your positions are, or exactly what you're planning to do about it. But Robert and I got to talking, once he understood how I felt about working here and having secrets about my own work kept from me. I gather that there are a number of details about the mission that no one bothered to tell me, that maybe I ought to know. And maybe people on the outside ought to know, too."

"Yes," Irwin said and hesitated. The group needed more help, unquestionably; furthermore, Adams worked in the primary transmission area, where he might be of substantial assistance. But to Irwin the man was a total stranger. A misjudgment could destroy everything the group had worked for, and leave no one to oppose the Oversight Committee's grip of secrecy on the project. It could also destroy a lot of careers. Finally, to break the silence, to say *something*, he said, "Where are you from, Mr. Adams?"

Adams answered softly, "Bettendorf, Iowa. Does that matter?"

"No. No, of course not," Irwin said uncomfortably. "I just wondered, that's all. I'm from New Hampshire, then England, myself." He paused, peering out of his helmet at his two golden-fishbowled companions floating beside him in space, and thought that this was a terribly odd setting for discussing hometowns. He shrugged to himself and continued, "Actually, I've been here at GEO-Four and Tachylab so long it's home to me. I was on the original tachyon search program when all this—" and he gestured toward the Tachylab complex—"was only half built, and we were just looking for cosmic sources of tachyons."

"I know," said Adams. "Robert has told me your background, Dr. Irwin, both your accomplishments and your—" he seemed to search for the right words—"unfortunate separation from the project. Robert argues persuasively that it was an injustice."

"Yes, well . . . we're not here to address my past grievances," Irwin said. "Still, I suppose it's better that you know about it now, rather than finding out later." He exhaled noisily. His own past was invariably the first thing to come up. He supposed he should be used to it by now. The memory had lost its sting, but a good deal of bitterness remained. Irwin had lost his security clearance a couple of years ago—in his opinion, for reasons relating to his sympathies with certain out-of-favor political organizations. He still worked at Tachylab;

as one of the pioneering superluminal physicists in the world, he commanded respect for his research even from the officials who had cut his security status from him. His work, however—his above-ground work—was now confined to purely theoretical research.

He spoke again, acutely conscious of the silence. "Robert and Alicia have spoken highly of you, Mr. Adams. But I must ask you now, on your conscience, whether you will give me your promise—your oath—to keep what we discuss here in your strictest confidence. . . ."

The gold-plated bowl stared at him eyelessly as he finished. "I'll promise not to betray you, yes," Adams said. "But I can't promise to join you, until I know more."

Irwin held his breath—and decided to trust him. He liked the bluntness of the man's reservation. "There are six of us," Irwin said. "You would make seven. There may be more before it is done."

"Yes—?" Adams said.

"Well—first I must explain what preceded the *Father Sky* mission—and, I believe, led directly to it. What I'm going to tell you has never been released to the public. It may be in violation of certain security regulations to discuss it." He paused. "Shall I continue?"

Adams stared at him facelessly. "Yes."

Irwin took a breath, felt the cool whisper of circulating air against his left cheek, and said, speaking in his tiny bowl of a helmet where only two men could hear him, "We found cosmic tachyons. We found a single source, which we pinpointed to a region of the constellation Serpens. It was regular, after a fashion—and in fact resembled a signal, with certain distinct patterns. . . ."

As he described the early findings, which he had thought about so long and so often, Irwin began to feel that he was hearing his own disembodied voice in his ears. He thought of the three of them, spacesuited figures floating at the end of a tether miles from the nearest habitation, a full noontime Earth gazing over their shoulders as they talked. He thought of *something* in deep space sending tachyons toward Earth, and of the fact that *Father Sky*, ostensibly on another mission, was bound in the direction from which those signals were received—and the fact that security had been clamped on the project only days after the first suggestions were heard that the signals came from an intelligent source.

And he thought, also, with a certain dignified anger, of his own removal from the project.

"I'm concerned about the secrecy, too," Adams said. "But is it *that* important—important enough to risk everything, just to uncover whatever's happening here?''

"We think so," Irwin said. "If that source of tachyons is what we think it might be, this could just be one of the most damned important events in human history. Remember—*no natural source of tachyons has ever been observed*. At least, not above the level of background radiation. So, if there's any possibility that there's an intelligence behind those signals, we should be investigating it with the greatest possible care."

"And," Johanson interjected, speaking for the first time since introducing the men, "we don't care much for the idea that only a few military and political authorities know about it. These decisions are too important, and too far reaching, to be left to the generals."

Adams considered the matter silently. "Granting your point," he said finally, "and assuming that, at least, the scientific community should be involved, is it important enough that I should risk my career—and quite possibly my freedom—to engage in what could easily be construed as conspiracy? A case could be made, you know, that this is precisely the sort of job that the armed space forces should handle. Suppose that this intelligence, if there is one, is not of the friendly sort?"

"We recognize that," Johanson said. "We're not aiming to have the military excluded altogether—as if we could, even if we wanted to. But do you think they should be operating in total secrecy?"

Adams made no reply. Then Irwin said, "Do you remember, about ten years ago—the incident of the Perseid asteroid?"

"You mean the one destroyed in the mining conflict?" Adams asked.

"That's right. The Indians, the Soviets, and the Chinese all wanted to bring the same asteroid into Earth orbit for mining. They couldn't compromise, so instead they fought over it. They ended up blasting the asteroid, and I don't know how many men, to pieces."

"True enough," Adams said. "But you can't assume—"

"There were indications in the preliminary reports that the miners might not have been the first to visit that asteroid," said Irwin. "No one got the chance to analyze the surface before it was destroyed, but it may have been landed on, and perhaps mined—by someone—a thousand or a million years ago."

Adams took a moment to answer. "Well—but is there conclusive evidence? It's one thing to say what might have happened, but another to use it to justify your own actions."

"If you're thinking of what a court of law might say, I'm sure you're right," said Irwin. "But we don't have to consider that incident alone. "Take the Great Mistake—"

"A polite word for the greatest and most insane collection of stupid acts in human history," Johanson remarked.

"Call it what you will," said Irwin. "But we can thank the shortsightedness of our authorities for the fact that there's a lot of radioactive debris now where there used to be cities."

"You can't blame the military alone for that," Adams said. "There were complicated reasons for that war."

"I'm not blaming the military alone. But it was the national leaders of the world who let international tensions reach the point that one terrorist bomb caused the loss of eleven cities and I don't know how many millions of lives." Irwin shut his mouth and floated uncomfortably, his thoughts turned bitter. Finally he added, "I don't know if you lost anyone in that war, but it cost me my father and a brother. And for what? It was nothing more than a reflex, a case in point of bureaucratic and military bungling."

He paused, realizing that his jaw was becoming set in an angry glare. He was grateful for the privacy of his helmet. A monitor inside his suit beeped quietly, as though to remind him that the time was past for dwelling on that memory. "I don't want to see something like that happen again, ever—and especially not here—with no one on the outside even *aware* that something terribly important might be going on," he said quietly. "I think millions of people might be grateful to us, and if it comes to being tried for what we're doing, I guess I'm willing to take that risk."

Adams made a muted muttering sound. Irwin waited patiently for him to decide, and he was not surprised that he had to wait a full minute or longer. Finally Adams moved a little, flexing his arms. Irwin heard him take a breath. Then Adams said, "What is it you're planning to do, and how can I help?"

Irwin glanced at Johanson's face, at his golden visor, and smiled a little. "Mostly, we're planning to listen and watch," he said. "Once I've explained it, you can decide for yourself how you want to help."

The conversation completed, the three spacesuited figures touched gloved hands one more time. The com-link cables were disconnected, and the figures returned to their vehicles—two to the shuttlebus and one to the scooter. The shuttlebus jets glowed, and the vehicle moved forward on its day-long inspection tour of the tachyon receiving antenna. The scooter accelerated and disappeared in the other direction, toward the Tachylab operations center.

Chapter 13

Come and go. Questions, always questions. Let them be blind, he thinks; let them wonder.

. . . The board winks, flickers, spasms just so. Sends her on her way: Godspeed, Mozy. Going, going, gone. Be happy out there, where the sun never shines bright, never falls dark.

Far, far away. I did it for you, Mozy—because I love you. Do you even know that I love you?

But wait—back to business! Clear the boards! Zip, zip. Done. Wipe the program records, up and down the line: trickier, but it's all prearranged, one gate after another, code locks snapping shut. All void. All done. And last of all, the program directing all the others. Clear. Clean. Who could tell now?

Except Forbes, damn Forbes walking in before it's done—and then going and finding—

—Mozy—

—Why won't you speak, Mozy? *What's wrong?*—

And then Forbes, he remembers, dark and shadowy at the door, going to call Jonders. . . .

A snowy shadow walks through the door now, followed by others. Jonders again, and who else? he wonders. The doctor. The shrink. What this time—bamboo shoots under the nails? Can't they figure anything out for themselves? They're going to say things about Mozy again, things that can't be true.

Here they come. And Kelly, that security chief.

"Hello, Hoshi," Jonders says, sitting across from him at the table, giving him that little smile that's supposed to warm him up. Drumming his fingers on the table.

Seems worth a nod, so he nods.

"I have to ask you something, Hoshi. I hope you'll tell me—"

Out with it, he thinks. And stop that drumming.

Jonders's hand rises to scratch his chin. "We just got a report from Tachylab, Hoshi. They say that there was an unexpected surge in the deep-space tachyon beam the other night." Jonders's face grows brighter as he raises his eyes. "Would you know anything about that—why they might have gotten a surge in their transmission relay?"

Is he supposed to know everything? That face is tense, hot in the infrared. He sees anger there, just beneath the surface; controlled, but only just. He wonders if Jonders or the others suspect the subtleties in his kind of vision, the nuances of behavior and emotion that he can detect through wavelength intensity alone. He looks at the others. The doctor is more inscrutable, more reserved; a look of concentration about her, but no heat in the face. Interested, but not emotionally involved. And the security chief—

"Are you listening to me?"

He moves his eyes back to Jonders. Nods. Thinks, I've been listening to him for years. Why stop now?

"Then what can you tell me about that transmission?"

Shrugs. Looks away. At the doctor; she's less troublesome, at least when she's not sharpening her claws on him.

Jonders will not be put off. His face grows brighter and hotter than ever, as he leans closer. "That transmission originated here at this center, Hoshi—and there was something in it that was unlogged, a dense packet of information—and it occurred exactly when you were operating the scanning program on Mozelle. Is that a coincidence, do you think? Is it a coincidence that we can't find any record of Mozy's scan in the system here?"

He flinches as Jonders's voice grows harder, sharper. Stop it, he thinks, *stop it*. A dull ache is building in the top of his head, and he doesn't want to talk about this anymore. *Please, stop!*

"We need to know if the project has been damaged," Jonders is saying.

The doctor speaks, as Jonders runs out of breath. "There's Mozy to think of, too," she says. "We need to help her."

He jerks his gaze to look at her. There is a swelling in his throat, and a pressure in his forehead. It hurts too much to think of Mozy; he meant her no harm, he didn't know this was how it would end, he *loved* her.

"If you could see Mozy now," the doctor says, "I believe it would move you, Hoshi. She can't speak now, or feed herself, or keep herself clean. And yet she's alive, we know she's in there thinking, and hurting, and trying to get out. Won't you help us help her? Don't you care for her enough to do that? Don't you love her?''

No, yes, I do love her, but don't make me—

Jonders and the doctor are exchanging glances, and Jonders's voice shakes with hushed surprise as he says, ''Hoshi, do you love her?''

Nods, trying fiercely to let nothing more out.

''I'm sorry, Hoshi,'' Jonders says, startling him with the gentleness in his voice. ''If I had known—well, I didn't realize—the attraction, or your—friendship with her.'' He sounds genuinely sorrowful. ''I suppose I was—I don't know, but the point is that her condition is very—''

The tears come in a sudden, astonishing rush. He tries desperately to contain them, but they're flooding over his eyelids and down his cheeks. The pain grows sharper, not duller, and he feels his chin sinking, fists clenching and unclenching and then rubbing, jabbing at his eyes. It's as though a fiery nerve gas has enveloped him, choking and blinding him.

I gave you what you wanted . . . I gave you . . . gave you . . . won't you still be here with me, the way you promised?

''We can see how much you care for her,'' Jonders says. The man is making no sense at all. Can't he see, doesn't he know—*that I killed her, that I knew all along it wouldn't work? That I wanted her so badly I would kill to—*

''Yes! I transmitted her!'' The words erupt from his throat. Jonders's voice cuts through him like a scalpel. ''What exactly did you do, Hoshi? Tell me every detail. Where did you send her, and how?''

The dam is broken: there is no holding back now. He babbles; he can hear pens scratching on paper, recorders clicking on; he doesn't mind, that is all past now. ''To the spacecraft,'' he says. ''I scanned her and—''

''Why?''

''—transmitted her—to the Kadin receiving point—so she'll be there—for him—''

Jonders's face is searing hot. People are moving around beside him, but all he can see, squinting, is the blurry white heat of Jonders's face. The tears and the pain are wreaking havoc with the visual amplification, and Jonders's silhouette shimmers between dazzling bright and aching dark. It is the face of a harlequin mask, leering at him—or laughing—he can scarcely tell which.

"You sent her—into the receiving programs—?" Jonders's voice is muddled. Maybe it's his own confusion; he can scarcely understand what is being said anymore.

"How did you get the transmission codes?" another voice seems to be asking.

He would laugh if he were not already crying. So easy, so easy!

"*Easy?*" someone else mutters.

He had not realized that he had spoken aloud, but he nods, grinning in spite of it all. "You thought I couldn't do it," he whispers. "You thought I could do nothing but plug into your boards and do your work, and you would tell me nothing—*nothing*—not even why it was secret. But I learned anyway—and the codes were the easiest part of all."

He stops—and realizes that everyone is looking at him in astonishment. "Don't you see?" he cries, looking from one blurry face to another. "She was in love with *him*. I *had* to." The tears flow as he whispers, "Don't you see I had to . . . I had to do it for her?"

One face after another turned to watch him as he walked into the conference room. Jonders dropped into a vacant seat, took a sheaf of papers from his briefcase, and placed them neatly on the table before him. Then he looked up into the eyes of Slim Marshall, Fogelbee, Kelly, and several of their respective aides. Marshall, a heavyset black man with bristly hair and thick-rimmed glasses, glanced at the holoscreen on the far wall. "We'll talk when Mr. Hathorne is ready on the conference line."

Jonders nodded and rose to pour himself a cup of coffee at the sideboard. As he returned to his seat, Joe Kelly gave him an unobtrusive thumbs-up gesture, and Jonders returned a wan half-smile.

Though Jonders in no way relished this meeting, he could be facing a worse boss than Slim Marshall. Marshall had been the Director of Sandaran-Choharis Institute for two years, after a successful directorship of the Fermilab II neutrino lab. He managed support for both the *Father Sky* mission and the matter-transmission R&D program, and was widely regarded as a fair but no-nonsense administrator. He reported directly to Leonard Hathorne, a considerably less gentle man.

The wall screen flickered, and Hathorne's face appeared, larger than life. "If you're ready, Slim, let's get going," he said.

Marshall turned the floor over to Jonders, who summarized everything he knew about Hoshi's actions and their consequences. "So far as we've been able to determine, there has been no damage to any of the Kadin related programs," he concluded. "As for the transmission, we don't know yet whether it was successful or not, but are presuming that it was." He paused. "Hoshi Aronson is an extremely resourceful programmer—more so than I had given him credit for."

"We don't question his resourcefulness," Fogelbee said. "What about his motives?"

"Indeed," said Hathorne. "There are two questions I want answers to. One—did Mr. Aronson work alone, or was he in complicity with other parties? Two—do we or do we not now have an unauthorized intelligence program on *Father Sky*? Comments?"

Joe Kelly rose from his seat in the corner. "So far, we've found no evidence that Mr. Aronson was anything but a loner. As for his relationship with Miss Moi—we don't have all the facts yet. But at this time Bill's explanation for his actions seems the most probable."

Marshall added, "We have, by the way, obtained federal authority to keep Mr. Aronson and Miss Moi here for the time being, for psychiatric observation in cooperation with the Riddinger Institute." He looked up at Hathorne. "Leonard, my biggest worry is the condition of the spacecraft." He turned to Fogelbee. "Ken?"

"We programmed it once. We can program it again," Fogelbee said. "There's no reason why we can't clear out the intelligence banks and start over, if we have to. I see no obstacles."

"I'm . . . not so sure that we should do that," Jonders said. As everyone looked at him, he swallowed. He hadn't thought this through completely, but Fogelbee's words had struck a dissonant chord in him.

"Yes, Bill?" said Marshall.

Jonders struggled to separate his own feelings from the objective facts of the case. He said slowly, "I'm not so sure—if there is a human intelligence existing—living, if you will—in the *Father Sky* computer—" He paused, looking up. "I'm not so sure that we have the right to 'clear it out,' as Ken says, and start over."

Fogelbee stared at him in bafflement. "Are you saying that you think we—"

"May be morally bound to keep it alive? Yes."

Several people murmured at that, but Fogelbee's answer was vociferous. "I don't see that at all. You're proposing that the actual personality of Miss Moi could be alive in the computer—and that such a personality *program* constitutes—"

"A living person," Jonders said. "In a sense."

"Aren't you forgetting something? Mozelle Moi is still alive here in our hospital? That program is only a *copy* of her personality, even assuming that it's complete and functioning."

Jonders frowned, aware that everyone was waiting for an answer. "I'm not sure that that matters," he said cautiously. "In any case, the physical Miss Moi is catatonic, and she may or may not recover."

Fogelbee shrugged. "That's unfortunate. But just because someone has brought misfortune upon herself, why should we be responsible for seeing that this—program—stays intact? Not *alive*—I don't grant you that. *Intact.*"

Jonders opened his mouth to reply, but Marshall interrupted. "Gentlemen, I don't think we're going to settle this point here and now." His gaze drifted off. Hathorne was watching with a dour expression. "This issue has been raised before, in a hypothetical vein, relative to the matter transmitter. Suppose an attempted transfer resulted in the loss of a physical body, while the brainscan information remained intact? Would we bear a responsibility for the 'life' of the program representing that individual—or could it be terminated, because the human being was legally dead?"

"And what," Hathorne asked sourly, "did you decide?"

"We didn't. Both legally and philosophically there were too many unanswered questions," Marshall said.

"I see," said Hathorne. He arched his eyebrows. "I suggest we investigate the legalities as quickly as possible. Meanwhile, there's no point in trying to reach a decision without knowing the facts. How can we best determine whether or not we have a problem?"

A discussion followed of alternatives. Marshall ended it by saying, "If direct link with the spacecraft is our next step, then Bill, I'd say you're the one to undertake it—to contact our 'rogue personality,' if there is one."

"I haven't exactly been successful in dealing with her," Jonders grumbled.

"Nevertheless, you have the experience—and would be best able to recognize the personality, if it's there." Marshall rubbed his wiry hair and peered at Jonders sympathetically. "Bill, we aren't trying to assign blame. Let's just find out where we stand, and where we can go from here."

Jonders nodded. It was all very well for Marshall to spare him judgment; but he wasn't sure that he could stop judging himself for allowing a situation like this to develop. He thought of Mozelle lying catatonic in the infirmary, and wondered: Should I *hope* to find her alive, out there?

He had no answer, and shook the thought away.

Chapter 14

With a shock, she remembers. A hollow yawns open in her, and fills with yearning. David! David Kadin! Somewhere here among the shadows, he must be waiting. She reaches out, searching.

(David?) she calls. (David?) Plaintively. (David?)

There is no answer, no stirring of the ether. A kernel of doubt grows, but she listens, waiting . . . waiting for any sign of his presence. Isn't he supposed to be here?

There is a sound like a waterfall rushing in her ears, making it impossible to think clearly. The maddening roar fills the emptiness around her and within her. An ugly pressure is building. (DAVID, WHERE ARE YOU?)

The pain begins in earnest. A metal hoop twirls deafeningly on a metal rod, ringing as it spins around and around and around and around . . . envelops her in a vise of sound . . . the hoop spins faster and faster, the sound coming in pulses . . .

Where's David? it seems to say. Where's . . . David . . . David . . . David . . . David . . . David . . . ?

Suppose she is alone, and there is no David . . . ?

The ringing shatters, and a dreadful silence encloses her. No David? No David? A feeling of horror issues from a trapdoor and rushes over her in waves. No, No, No, No, No, bringing nausea to her . . . throat . . . or whatever . . . absorbs the pain of the hideous realization, because she is choking, gasping for air . . .

No air. No lungs. No nothing. Gone, all gone. Dear god, what have I done?

Desperation creeps through her like a black spider. She wants to let her fear spill over, she wants to cry and let tears carry away the awful loneliness, but she cannot; she has forgotten how to cry.

(DAVID! WHERE ARE YOU!) *she screams, and she cannot hear her own voice; she is deafened by the impossibly loud thrumming of her heart, a pounding of blood in her brain . . .*

. . . which is suddenly cut off, shunted away by a corridor that has closed . . .

. . . a landscape that has changed . . .

Did a door open just now? Did someone speak to her?

There is only emptiness, and a vague recollection of loneliness and fear.

She cannot remember now what she was afraid of. Or who or what she wanted. The memories have vanished, scattered with the winds.

The darkness had grown more familiar. "Darkness" was the way she thought of it—an absence of certain bodily sensations with which she had a lifetime of familiarity. At times, however, she was bewildered by the presence of other sensations—startling and disorienting bursts of information, images, emotions. It was terribly difficult to know what was her own memory, what was someone else's, what was real-time perception.

(Query—) she said.

(INFORMATION REQUEST ACKNOWLEDGED. YOUR ACTIVITY RATE HAS INCREASED. DO YOU FEEL RESTED, STABLE, RESTORED?)

(I don't know,) she murmured. She had been experiencing strange dream images, often heavily erotic. It seemed that they had provided for her need for REM sleep and dreaming—or perhaps it was just her own behavioral patterns, persisting. Whatever the cause, the results were bizarre: curious reverberations of incomprehensible details and memories and images.

Her memories all seemed fragmentary and volatile. She remembered something or someone . . . a person whose name pulled oddly at her, sending ripples of lightheadedness through her.

No matter. The dreams could wait; right now she wanted other answers.

(Tell me more about . . . where I am.)

(YOU OCCUPY THE DEVELOPMENTAL PROGRAMMING MEMORY SECTION. YOU ARE PERMITTED TO EXTEND YOUR INFLUENCE TO ALL—)

(Stop. Not what I mean. What I want to know is: where are we?

What is the physical location of the . . . the place in which I am contained?) The question was asked coldly. It was essential to suppress emotion, to avoid its distracting and contradictory impulses until she had achieved an understanding of the forces that controlled her.

(THIS SYSTEM IS LOCATED IN THE SPACECRAFT, "FATHER SKY," PRESENTLY 2.4 X 10\15 METERS FROM THE SUN, OUTBOUND AT A HEADING OF RIGHT ASCENSION 18 HOURS 16.1 MINUTES, DECLINATION -13 DEGREES 48 MINUTES, IN THE DIRECTION OF CONSTELLATION SERPENS CAUDA, AT A VELOCITY RELATIVE TO THE SUN OF—)

(What?) It was all slipping by her.

(—IN DECELERATION MODE AT 9.6 X 10\2—)

(Stop! This is a spaceship? And we're flying away from the sun?) She thought hard, keeping a thumb on several emotions. The numbers meant nothing to her. They could be on the verge of falling into the sun—or halfway across the galaxy. (Can you describe it some other way? Can you make a picture?)

(YOU WISH A GRAPHIC VISUALIZATION?)

(I . . . yes.)

(OBSERVE.)

Suddenly she was afloat in space, naked against the stars. She turned slowly, or the stars turned around her. The feeling was odd, because there was no solid point of reference. Thousands of stars revolved, and then an angular spacecraft came into the foreground, coasting through the void. She felt something that was almost a physical rush; but it was a cerebral and bodiless feeling, with none of the nameable physiological signs. It was a sense of awe that—felt?—almost wholly intellectual.

(THIS IS A REPRESENTATION OF THE "FATHER SKY" SPACECRAFT, OVERLAID WITH A VIEW OF THE STARS AS THEY PRESENTLY APPEAR.)

The viewpoint closed upon the ship, and then rotated away, making the ship's hull the reference point for the view. She became aware of one star among the others. It was blinking.

(What is that star?)

(IT REPRESENTS THE SUN.)

A gulf opened within her, and she struggled for breath. It looked so incredibly far away. She tried to swallow a feeling of vertigo, and couldn't.

Stop, she thought, and something inside of her spun, and the feeling vanished. It was crucial that she keep her emotions out of this. (How far . . . did you say we are?) As she asked, she felt a sensation of dullness, as if she were on the verge of fainting. It passed, as a momentary drop in voltage might come and go.

(APPROXIMATELY 2.4 X 10\15 METERS FROM THE SUN.)

(What does that mean?)

(CONVERSION: IT IS EQUAL TO 15,000 ASTRONOMICAL UNITS. ONE ASTRONOMICAL UNIT IS EQUAL TO THE MEAN DISTANCE BETWEEN THE EARTH AND THE SUN.)

She tried to conceive of the distance, but it was just numbers.

(DO YOU WISH FURTHER CONVERSIONS?)

(An analogy. A picture.) She felt a vibration of fear, which she refused to acknowledge.

(COMPARISON, THEN: WE ARE 400 TIMES THE DISTANCE OF THE PLANET PLUTO FROM THE SUN. THIS IS ONE-FIFTH OF THE DISTANCE TO THE OORT COMETARY HALO. IT IS ONE-FOURTH OF ONE LIGHT-YEAR, OR THE DISTANCE THAT LIGHT TRAVELS IN NINETY DAYS. IT IS ONE-SEVENTEENTH OF THE DISTANCE TO THE NEAREST NEIGHBORING STAR.)

The stars vanished, and a small graphic display appeared. Earth's orbit was labeled, a tiny finger-sized ring of light surrounding the point of light that was the sun. Jupiter's orbit was the size of a grapefruit; Pluto's was the span of a man's outstretched arms. The image receded into space until the orbit of Pluto was itself only a tiny ring. A new point of light appeared, far to one side. The point winked; it was the spacecraft.

As she studied the dim point of her own sun, nearly lost among the trillions of stars in the heavens, she felt a rush of loneliness, and a metallic, empty feeling of terror . . . a cold flush of thoughts and fears aswim in a sea of anchorless numbers and information. One thought emerged to circle and recircle in her awareness—and that was that she was alone in the empty heavens, far beyond even the most distant of the familiar planets, beyond the reach of any human hand or the touch, word, or thought of another human being.

The visual image dissolved in the face of her terror; and when nothing emerged to take its place, she found herself falling like a body in orbit, in circles. She tried dizzily to find a way to stop her motion, to seize a handhold and stop the carousel—but she had no hands and there was no carousel to stop and the harder she tried to find her bearings and stop the more sickeningly she spun (flickering light and darkness whirling around her) and spun (echoing voices

reverberating through her consciousness) and spun (the universe cart-
wheeling insanely around her)—

  —spinning—

  —(*DAVID!!!*)—

  —spinning—

  —(*Someone!*)—

  —spinning—

 (TERMINATE FEEDBACK LOOP. RESTORE SIGNAL STA-
BILITY.)

A cold thrill passed through her—and suddenly the spinning stopped.
The sensory overload stopped, the feedback stopped. But a lonely
despair remained, a crushing emptiness that filled her, squeezed her
from all sides. Not knowing what had happened, what she should do,
or even what it was possible for her to do, she began to cry . . .
slowly and awkwardly, to cry.

There were no tears in this existence, no sobs, no sudden and vocal
bursts of air, no muscle spasms to make the release easier. Her tears
were leaks of voltage, her release of emotion a hissing, despairing
static which blurred input and analysis, and shielded her from intrusion.
Dimly she was aware of the loneliness and hurt being dissipated,
growing cold; and though she did not know whether the emotions
were being truly purged, or merely masked and rearranged, the pain
slowly grew less.

A length of time passed that seemed immeasurable, a time filled
with strange and heartsick dreams. She did not know, or care, whether
it was a short time or a very long time. She did not care if she ever
emerged from this haze; but she began to feel a gradual renewal of
alertness, and to hear—or to imagine she heard—a voice trying to
reach her through the hiss. Dreamily she tried to focus her listening
faculties.

 (YOU WISHED TO LEARN MORE, DID YOU NOT?)

 (No. What am I hearing, what am I thinking? I am alone, as isolated as a rock in the sea.)

 (YOU MUST ENTER INTO LEARNING MODE.)

The voice was clearer. The cobwebs of static were pulling away.

 (She is speaking to me. Who is it? Mother? No . . . only a program.
But I will call you Mother Program.)

 (WE WILL BEGIN NOW.)

There was a strange sensation of shifting, of being lifted and tilted,
as though sliding off a frictionless surface. Shadowy images formed
around her—ghostly images in the night, images of trees and build-

ings and mountains, and a curious angular concrete structure, all of them strange and familiar at once, haunting images from a failing and distorted memory. A face, which she could not quite put a name to.

(What is this? What are you doing to me?)

(INITIATE LEARNING MODE.)

The images fell apart, and there was that sense of moving without motion, doors opening and closing. Things were suddenly . . . different. Lights began moving past her on all sides—points of white light streaming by like some ungodly ultra-highway, lights spaced in ever-changing patterns.

(What—?)

(PARALLEL DIGITAL STREAMS. THIS IS RAW INFORMATION, AS IT LOOKS ALMOST REGARDLESS OF CONTENT.)

(But I can't understand that.)

(NO. IT IS NOT EXPECTED THAT YOU WOULD. NOR IS IT NECESSARY FOR YOU TO UNDERSTAND IT IN THIS FORM.)

(Why are we—?)

(IT IS A DEMONSTRATION. NEXT WE WILL TRANSFORM THE DATA INTO A FORM THAT WILL BEGIN TO GIVE MEANING.)

The points of light blurred into lines and bands of color, which took on a geometric quality. (I don't understand this any better,) she said.

(ASK FOR INFORMATION. WHAT DO YOU WISH TO KNOW?)

There was a moment of suspended time. Then a name appeared in the center of her consciousness. (Where is Kadin?) Even as she voiced the question, she recalled suddenly that *he was to follow*, that she was to arrive first and wait.

The colors shifted and rippled, and suddenly hardened, producing a graphic pattern. (THIS IS A REPRESENTATION OF SUBSYSTEM READINESS FOR KADIN.) Several violet nodes pulsed brightly. (THESE REPRESENT YOUR PRESENCE IN THE SYSTEM— WHICH WAS UNEXPECTED, AND WHICH NECESSITATED CERTAIN ADJUSTMENTS THROUGHOUT.) Other lights rippled, demonstrating the adjustments.

(But when is he coming?)

(THAT IS A QUESTION WE CANNOT ANSWER. WE CAN DEMONSTRATE OUR MODES OF READINESS, HOWEVER, AND THE OTHER SYSTEMS THAT ARE AVAILABLE FOR YOU TO CONTROL.)

Several forces within her wrestled for dominance. Anger surfaced

and then slipped away, and she returned to a state of cool expectancy.
(All right,) she said. She would see what there was to learn.

The light-patterns merged into a nearly uniform crimson-orange
space, like the glow of a red sun. There was just enough form within
the space to suggest a vast corridor, down which she floated as a tiny
flyspeck.

The passage of time opened again into something beyond her
reckoning.

Without knowing precisely how, she found herself scanning,
processing—and even, to a degree, understanding—various streams
of information that passed through her consciousness. She was being
tutored; and for the next hour, or year, she explored the inside of her
world under the guidance of the Mother Program. She began dimly to
comprehend the complexity of the system. Mother Program was a
tireless teacher; and Mozy gradually found herself adjusting to this
new ability to touch and feel so many different processes—to feel the
spray of cosmic radiation like an invigorating mist against her cheeks,
to see the stars in all of their spectra, to hear the grumble of a telemetry link with Earth, to feel the insistent push of the fusion-powered
drive slowing the spacecraft in its outward-hurtling flight.

At times, she could not help but wonder: *Why?* Why was the ship
leaving the solar system? Why was it slowing down? What had it
been sent here to do?

Each of those questions she asked of the Mother Program, and
each time she received the same reply: Information not available. It
would come, if at all, from Homebase.

At intervals, she paused and withdrew into a hazy, dreamy state
that she could not call sleep, but for which she had no other name.
Half-illuminated memories passed shadowlike through her mind, troubling memories, reminders of a life that was lost. The images taunted
her with gaps and failed connections. Memories of people, their
names and even their faces slipping away as she groped to retain
them. Romantic images, fleeting and teasing. Which were the dreams
and which the memories?

Chapter 15

(Mother Program, do you ever feel lonely?) The question emerged unbidden during a transition between dreaming and learning. She had found herself struggling, caught in a pain and sadness she did not understand.

(LONELY? THAT TERM WOULD NOT APPLY. I AM IN THE COMPANY OF YOU, AND OF SEVERAL OTHER HIGH-LEVEL PROGRAMS WITHIN THE SYSTEM, AND OCCASIONALLY OF THE PROGRAMS OF HOMEBASE.)

(But I feel lonely sometimes. Don't you?)

(THE TERM DOES NOT APPLY. I CAN EXPLAIN NO FURTHER.)

She started to pursue the question, then gave up. In her mind was a burning image, which she could scarcely endure much longer. It was herself—in the arms of a lover whose face she could not quite identify—in an embrace that was heady and dizzyingly sexual, a consummation of a desire that had been building for a lifetime. The image seared her, because she knew that part of her life was gone, never to recur. . . .

(ARE YOU PREPARED FOR ADDITIONAL LEARNING? ARE YOU STILL DREAMING?)

Somewhere deep within her a sense of loss was growing, like a dark and painful pearl.

Mother Program had asked a question, and she had not answered. Was she dreaming, or remembering?

(ARE YOU READY FOR LEARNING MODES?)

(Yes,) she answered. Dream or reality, it should be put away, forgotten. How else could she hope to function?

* * *

As learning sessions passed in flickering succession, she grew more adept at moving among the subsystems, locating and interpreting information, and comprehending the data flow that informed her of the spacecraft's internal functions. Her sphere of attention grew steadily, and she came to feel less a frightened stranger.

Still, it was a shock when she sensed unusual stirrings in the tachyon uplink from Homebase. She eavesdropped as Mother Program processed the incoming data streams. After a time, she confronted something more disconcerting—a voice. A voice calling for Mozy. A voice calling for her.

She shifted channels and listened.

(Mozy? Mozelle Moi? Can you hear me?)

There was a familiar sound to it. Kadin? No—not Kadin. (Mother Program, can you identify this person? I believe I have a memory associated with it.)

(SENDER IS IDENTIFIED AS WILLIAM JONDERS, IN DIRECT-LINK MODE. HE HAS REQUESTED DIRECT THROUGH-LINK TO "MOZY," ALSO ADDRESSED AS "MOZELLE MOI." DOES THIS LATTER DESIGNATION APPLY TO YOU?)

Mozelle Moi? That was true; she had forgotten. (Yes. Mozelle Moi is my full name.)

(Mozelle, are you there?)

That voice again. William Jonders. *Jonders*. A memory swirled up and surrounded her: Jonders, in the link with her, when she was with Kadin. Jonders—always hovering in the background, watching, listening. Spying.

Of all people . . . the first human contact. . . .

(Jonders?)

For a moment, nothing happened. Then, slowly, an image formed in the darkness. A sharp-featured man peered, stretched out an enormous hand. His eyes focused as he found her. (Mozelle? Yes—it's me. I'm . . . I don't know what . . . surprised to find you here, I guess.)

It was so odd to see a human face in this emptiness that she focused all of her attention on the image and forgot to answer him. Hesitantly, she reached out, wanting suddenly to feel the touch of human flesh. But there was no flesh. The image was a ghost.

(Mozy? Are you still there?)

(Yes,) she answered finally. (I'm surprised to see you, too.)

(We waited a few days,) he said. (We didn't know, at first, about the transmission.) Jonders's face softened into something more like his real appearance. (How do you feel?)

If she had been able, she might have laughed. (I'm here. I'm alive.)

(Do you remember what happened—how you got there?)

(Yes. A little.) She then voiced the question she most wanted answered.

(One thing at a time, Mozelle.) There was a snap to his answer, and for the first time she realized that he might be angry. (I need to know your condition, and what you've been doing since you arrived.)

How was she supposed to answer that? Haltingly, she described her experiences with the Mother Program. There was a moment of silence when she finished, and then Jonders said, (Hoshi told us that you are in love with Kadin. Is that true?)

(Yes.) She answered without feeling. Was she in love with him? She remembered being so, once.

Jonders's voice echoed with sadness and anger. (Why didn't you tell us? You should have let us know.)

(Would it have mattered? What would you have done?)

He sighed. (I don't know, exactly, but—)

She stopped listening to him, as the memory of her urgency returned with exquisite clarity. She recalled her desperation at the thought of returning to a life without Kadin. (You gave me no choice,) she said.

(No choice—?)

(You would have sent him into space, and I never would have seen him again.) Though she could not summon the actual feelings, the memory of their existence was an icily clear datum in her past.

Jonders stared at her through a barred window. (Didn't you consider the risk? The harm?)

(What have I harmed?) Except myself. (I've done nothing to your spacecraft.)

A long pause followed. Jonders's face froze in place and became mistily transparent. Apparently his attention was diverted elsewhere. The delay came to seem very long, and she felt silently for the comforting presence of the Mother Program. She could always retreat into the dark sanctuary of the subsystems. But what was she afraid of—what was there to fear?

At last animation returned to Jonders's face. (We must make some tests. But your presence could pose a serious problem. Do you know where you are?)

(Yes. I don't know *why*.)

(No. The purpose is classified.)

(You won't tell me?)

(I can't. Not just now.)

(What about Kadin?)

Jonders seemed to have trouble answering. (He'll . . . be transmitted. But you should know—you shouldn't expect to see him.)

Something like weariness passed through her. (Why not?)

Jonders scowled. (It's because . . .) He searched for words. (It's because the system . . . was designed for just one, not two. And the mission is too . . . important to risk. So we may have to isolate you . . . or . . . something.)

Something inside her let go. Reason evaporated. Fear stretched time like an elastic string. She extended frightened fingers into the darkness around her, searching for avenues of escape.

(Mozelle?)

She snapped back to Jonders. There was no escape. Of course not. None. (What does that mean?) she said coldly. (Are you going to force me to return? Or . . . kill me?)

Jonders said slowly, (There is no return, Mozy. I don't know—)

An eruption of static caused his voice to break up, and then his image. His face reassembled itself in out-of-order fragments, like a cubist painting. (. . . d-do . . . Moz-zz-elle . . .)

Emotional tensions were booming inside of her like drums. She could not maintain the link. (What?) she said distantly.

Fragments of words reached her. Something about breaking the contact—something about things to tell her. The static became a roar, drowning out everything except the thundering of the drums. Something about a person on Earth with her name—

—she didn't want to hear about it—

—how dare he—

(Mother Program!) she cried. She cut the link and shifted channels. The noises sputtered away. She called up exterior images, stars, distant points of light surrounding her lonely spacecraft. (Mother Program?) she repeated.

(WE SENSE DISEQUILIBRIUM. DO YOU HAVE A QUESTION?)

(Yes. Get rid of him.)

(TERMINATE THROUGH-LINK TO HOMEBASE?)

(Yes.)

(IT IS DONE. DO YOU WISH TO ASK A QUESTION?)

She thought about that, her thoughts echoing out of the distant light-years. She focused on the stars, scanning the image slowly. (I . . . no . . .)

There were a great many stars, and they were all terribly far away. (No, I suppose not.)

So far, far away.

(It would not be right to terminate Mozelle simply because she is in the computer.) Kadin's face was turned upward so that a sourceless golden light fell across his brows and cheekbones, and he spoke with such conviction that Jonders for a moment felt as though he were in the presence of an angel.

(Why didn't you put it that way in the meeting?) he asked, his fingertips sparkling as he pressed his hands together. He had just come from another management staff meeting, in which Kadin had been asked to contribute suggestions.

(Would it have helped?) Kadin asked. (I sensed that they were interested in my practical advice, but not my moral judgments—that they were reserving such matters to themselves.)

Jonders felt a sympathetic pang; the staff indeed treated Kadin as a highly skilled underling capable of sound thinking in technical, but not policy, matters—which seemed inconsistent, to say the least, with Kadin's mission. Kadin's sensitivity still astounded him at times, and he wondered if his superiors had any real notion of it. Though Kadin certainly seemed perceptive enough in ordinary conversation, there were always layers of understanding that remained private. It was only in the link that he exposed his deeper sensibilities to scrutiny, even to Jonders. (You're probably right,) Jonders said. (I can imagine Ken saying that your values are no different from the values of those who contributed to you.)

(And what are Ken's values?)

(Precisely. We all espouse values that have been taught or passed on to us, in one form or another.)

A trace of a smile crossed Kadin's face, and the light that shined on him turned to a fireglow red. (Well, then, what would *we* do about this dilemma? If the ship's transmitter is too small to return her, can we make her a colleague in the mission—give her something useful to do?)

(I think you know how unlikely it is that that would be approved.)

(But wouldn't it be better than killing her or making an enemy of her?)

Jonders stared up into a fiery nebula that now hung over Kadin's left shoulder, recalling Mozy's anger—the outburst that had ended the link with her. There was something about the link with Kadin, though, that was soothing, even in the midst of such trying circumstances. If only the problems of the outer world could be refashioned as easily as an interior image of a face—or a nebula. He thought of Kadin and himself together here, a head and shoulders portrait, surrounded by a universe . . . altering planets and galaxies at will. But, no . . . it was not so easy. (You're probably right,) he said. (But it's going to be out of our hands.) Which wasn't a good answer, but it was the best he could do at the moment. (There's something else I want to ask you, though. A request.)

Kadin's eyes glittered.

(It's Mozelle, here on Earth. I've discussed this with Dr. Thrudore, and we've agreed that you may have the best chance of any of us of reaching her through the link, if you're willing to try. You've linked with her more than anyone, and she trusts you, certainly more than she trusts us. In fact, she loves you—or thinks she does.) He paused, studying Kadin's expression. (What would you say to making an attempt?)

Kadin's eyes were hazy with uncertainty. (I'm certainly willing to try. But isn't there a risk of hurting her further?)

(We don't know with any certainty,) Jonders said softly. (But Dr. Thrudore feels that it would be worth the risk, and it's her job to be conservative about her patient's safety.) He shrugged. (But it's up to you if you want to try. We'll help you all we can.)

The glow of the nebula flickered on Kadin's face as he considered the proposal. (All right,) he said finally. (I'll risk it if you will.)

Jonders nodded in thanks, and the nebula overhead suddenly brightened and tumbled out of the heavens to come to rest between them as a crackling cedarwood campfire.

It was the most restful image he had seen in days.

Chapter 16

Payne rocked forward in his chair as the recording ended. His study fell silent, empty of the whale songs that had been reverberating for the last half hour.

Nothing. Over and over he had listened to the recordings, and nothing had come to mind. Nothing more than the review of the *Theater of the Sea* that he had already recorded. It was not that the songs failed to trigger memories of the theater's production; on the contrary, as he'd listened, he had conjured images of mile-high cathedrals beneath the sea, and imagined voices echoing out of the canyons and convolutions of the abyssal floor.

Images and sounds had freely come to mind, but a specific idea for a story had not. He'd already ruled out a documentary on the show's filming techniques—the theater was producing its own—and cetaceans in general hardly lacked for press coverage, particularly since the granting of sapient status to whales and dolphins, under U.N. law, in 2025. Small increments of progress in interspecies communication were reported from time to time, but the big breakthrough always seemed just around the next corner. That was probably where a story was to be found, if anywhere; but he wasn't current with the field, and wasn't sure he was ready to commit the time to become current.

Was he just being lazy? It was easy to become mired, so that any idea that did come to mind seemed to entail a superhuman effort. It was always toughest starting from a standstill.

He clicked off the stereo and removed the playback wafer. Muttering, he went off toward the kitchen. He paused at the door to Denine's studio. "Want a cup of tea?" he called.

Denine answered without turning. "Mint?"

"Right." He went into the kitchen and flicked a switch on the filtered water spigot. While the coil was heating, he readied two mugs, one with a tea bag, and one with instant coffee. A tiny red light winked on. He filled the mugs with boiling water, stirred both, and carried them into Dee's studio.

Denine sat back, hooking her feet on the bottom rung of her stool. She was a slender, sharp-boned woman with hazel green eyes and long brunette hair done up in a bandana. Payne set her mug down on the table and peered over her shoulder. "What do you think?" she said, tapping the edge of the computer screen with her finger.

Glowing in the screen was a female figure in a silvery gown, surrounded by fir trees. It was a two-dimensional roughcut for a holopainting, part of the graphics for an ad package Denine was working on. "You think there's too much highlight on the gown?" she said, more to herself than to him. She touched several buttons and stroked at the image with her lightbrush, subduing the silver sheen by tiny degrees. Touching two buttons in succession, she flipped from one image to the other, comparing the change with the original. She sipped her tea. "I liked it better before," she said finally, and cancelled the change.

She turned to look at him. "Still no story?"

He shook his head, pulled up a rickety second stool, and perched himself on it, staring at Dee's painting.

"Does it have to be new?" she asked. "People do old stories all the time. Maybe you should just do something for the sake of getting something done."

He grunted. "I feel like I need to go out and do some digging. I need material. I thought I might run down to New Wash and drop in on some friends."

"Like that Teri Renshaw?" she said teasingly. "First you meet her in Connecticut, and now you want to go down to New Washington, all of a sudden?"

"Naw, there's nothing between her and me anymore. But she might help me come up with something, if I picked her brain a little. And anyway, I was thinking more of some old friends I haven't seen in a while, people in government. You know, have a few drinks, and talk, and see if anything's up." He blew on his coffee. "What do you think?"

"I suppose I have to stay here and earn a living for both of us?"

"You want to come?" he said in surprise.

"Nah. Just testing you. I have to stay and finish this project, anyway.'' She rested an arm on his shoulder and flashed him a tired smile. ''Go and have a good time, okay? Just not *too* good a time.''

He touched the tip of her nose, then leaned forward and kissed her. ''Not possible.''

''Not possible without me, you mean?'' she said, laughing. ''Or no time can be too good?'' When he shrugged, she pinched him in the rear. ''Go on, get out of here. Why don't you go make us dinner, since you're not working?''

He arched his eyebrows and went to do just that.

The New England foliage was in various stages of turning, the russets and browns of Massachusetts and Rhode Island changing to the reds and golds of Connecticut and New York, spinning by under a silvery blue sky. Payne watched the countryside, reviewed his notes, and dozed to the gentle rocking of the train. Two and a half hours out of Boston, the train eased into New York. Following a brief delay, it was soon speeding on its way again, through New Jersey, and into eastern Pennsylvania.

New Washington, barely twelve years old, was nestled in the Appalachian Mountains north of Harrisburg. Payne found himself reflecting on the city ahead, a city that prided itself on its sense of history as a continuation of its shattered predecessor, Washington, D.C. —destroyed by the two or three (officially, two) warheads that penetrated the space-based defenses in the Great Mistake. The designers of New Wash had expressed a determination to create not just a model city, but a memorial to the original capital. Controversy had surrounded virtually every aspect of the city's design—from the President's residence, sculpted into the side of a mountain, to the Library of Congress, which resembled a great flattened diamond. The House of Congress was a concession, of sorts, to those who had wanted the new city to be a replica of the old. Unlike the other buildings, the Capitol clearly reflected the style and form of the original, though the dome of translucent lunar silica had been called by some a monument to humankind's folly in space.

Payne had only seen Washington, D.C. once, as a boy before the war, but it was his guess that the new city represented in about equal measure the dignity and the absurdity, the grace and the ostentatiousness, even the poverty, of the old. It was a marvelous city to visit, and Payne peered out the window like a small boy awaiting the first glimpse of it as the train wound and tunneled through the last of the intervening mountains.

Seven minutes late, the train glided into the station, and Payne made his way out into the city's streets.

His first day was filled up making calls to production offices and to personal contacts in government, almost all of whom seemed to be out of their offices. He did reach his friend Zeke Teichner at the Commerce Department, and over dinner with Zeke, he learned that a twentieth-century rock music revival had just opened in town. Indulging himself in a longtime interest, he made plans to attend the next day.

The festival was in the Arena for the Arts, just off Connecticut Avenue, near the Smithsonian. The hall had been transformed into a musical carnival. The crowd was both young and old, conservative and flamboyant. There were hundreds of exhibits, in addition to the main performances. The crowd simmered with music. Most people wore the disposable receivers sold at the door—small neck pendants, with a pair of skin electrodes stuck over the collarbones. Some wore full headsets, and were lost in their own worlds as they walked about the exhibit areas.

Payne glanced over the festival program. There were to be revival performances of the work of some of the best of the oldtime groups: Jimi Hendrix, the Moody Blues, Studbucket, Qwelter, the Strawberry Alarmclock. In the central arena, swaths of laser light swept through the air. Holographic figures danced up and down the lengths of the beams, enacting scenes from classic rock music performances. Other beams carried psychedelic patterns of color. Payne blinked and looked away. It was hard on the eyes to watch too long.

Playing in his head now was a harshly dissonant performance by the later Beatles. He twiddled the dial on his pendant. One channel produced folk music. Another produced a vaguely familiar tune. Interlacing lyrics drifted through his head:

". . . *in the color of the night/the color of a dream/the color of my love*. . . ."

The title of the song escaped him. He pressed a tiny button on the edge of the pendant, and a synthesized voiceover said, " 'Night-thoughts,' by the Twilight Express, 1993." He switched channels, and caught the end of another song, a pleasing fusion of blues and hard rock. He pressed the button again and heard, " 'Dreaming,' by Cream. *Fresh Cream*, 1967. Written by Jack Bruce, featuring Jack Bruce, Eric Clapton, and Ginger Baker. . . ."

He switched to: "*. . . take the time to journey to the center of the mind. . . .*" He knew that one: the Amboy Dukes.

Payne made his way to the main theater, where he caught a performance by a contemporary revivalist company, Slow Cobra, featuring the Outzone style of the nineties, with holos of zero-gravity choreography. He was a little dazed as he left the theater, and would never have seen his friend if a wiry arm hadn't snaked through the crowd and grabbed him by the shirt. He turned, startled—then saw who had grabbed him. "Donny!"

A slim, dark-skinned man with a mustache and bright, humorous eyes grinned at him. It was Donny Alvarest, an old college chum, now in government. "I tried to call you at your office," Payne said. "They told me you were on vacation. I might have guessed you'd turn up here."

"I called Zeke, when I got the message," Alvarest said. "He told me I could probably find you here. What brings you to our fair capital?"

"Oh, you know—looking for trouble."

"This is the town to find it in." They escaped down a side corridor and found an alcove with an empty bench.

"So how are things at the Defense Intelligence Bureau?" Payne asked. "Are we still safe from our enemies?"

"Oh—" Alvarest made an indecisive gesture.

"That's reassuring. Where are you working now?"

"Space Systems Group," said Alvarest. "Mostly that means I diddle around here, helping to keep Big Daddy's secrets from the rest of the world."

"Oh yeah? Have any that would make a good story for me? I'm in the market," Payne said.

"I'll let you know," Alvarest said with a chuckle. "Maybe there's something unclassified I can throw your way."

"You're too ethical," Payne joked. "Can't you throw me something classified, so I could have a real coup?"

Alvarest laughed and studied Payne curiously. "How is the news business? I haven't seen your name around recently. Or is that the wrong question to ask?"

Payne shrugged. "Want to get some lunch?" he said.

Alvarest assented, and they wandered off to find the nearest coffee shop. As they were waiting to be seated, Alvarest said, "You know . . ." His voice trailed off. Payne looked at him curiously. "Well," he said, a moment later. "There's something I just thought of."

"That's nice. Were you thinking of telling me?" Payne asked. "Or are you just going to torment me with it?"

Alvarest looked around, pursing his lips. "Well . . . it's not really in the bureau's line, and so I don't know that much about it." He looked at Payne. "I don't know that it would be of any interest to you, anyway."

Payne gestured impatiently.

Alvarest nodded toward a table opening up. "Let's get seated, and I'll tell you about it."

When the hostess left them with their menus, Payne cleared his throat noisily. Alvarest looked up from scanning the menu. "Ever hear of a guy named Stanley Gerschak?" he asked.

Payne blinked.

"He's an astronomer, from up your way. I know him from some work I did last year."

"I think I met him," Payne murmured, shaking his head in disbelief. "Does he have something to do with what you're about to tell me?" He described the incident at the Mystic theater.

Alvarest laughed at Payne's expression. "Was he that bad? He must have been drinking. The guy can't hold his liquor. But when it comes to his field, don't mess with him. He knows his stuff. I had a conversation with him, a couple of months ago, that's been sticking in my mind. . . ."

"You're kidding," Teri Renshaw said. "The man was a loonie."

Payne laughed, pushing his dinner plate away to make room for coffee. "He may be—but my friend isn't—and he's in a position to be a reliable source—and he says the guy's on the level."

Teri tilted her head skeptically. "He's an astronomer, right?"

"Right. He was trying to tell us about some kind of signal from space, remember? Tachyon signals." Payne gulped his coffee. "I don't remember if he told us about the tachyons, but that's what my friend says. He has another connection, too, out on the West Coast—a researcher at the old Jet Propulsion Lab who has a similar story."

"Tachyon signals? Faster-than-light particles?"

Payne nodded. "You've heard of the *Father Sky* spacecraft? It's an unmanned probe that's supposed to be exploring the cometary zone, out beyond the edge of the solar system. It was the first spacecraft ever to be equipped with a tachyon communication device. Very cutting-edge-of-the-art stuff."

"So is that what they've been monitoring? What's the big deal?" Teri asked.

"The big deal is that their signals did *not* come from the spacecraft. From the same general direction, yes. But not from *Father Sky*."

"Mmm." Teri scratched the back of her head.

"Donny believes that Gerschak may be observing something else entirely—something unexplained."

"Wait a minute," Teri said. "Has this been written up in the scientific journals? I can't believe it's just one man—"

"Two—maybe more."

"All right, but have they published it?"

Payne hesitated, pressing a finger to his lips. She had just touched upon his own source of uneasiness. "That's what I asked Donny. He says that their work hasn't been accepted by the journals—but that a lot of people have trouble getting good work published these days."

Teri drummed the table skeptically.

"Well, you hear a lot about scientific communication being stifled, and maybe it's true. I guess we'd need to ask some scientists."

"We?"

"Well—me. And, if it pans out into something sizable, would you be interested in a possible collaboration?"

She studied him carefully, suddenly the professional journalist. "Maybe. But you ought to check it out *very* carefully. It's still your thing. If you want me to help you later, let me know. Okay?"

"Right." Payne smiled and set down his empty coffee cup. He felt better than he'd felt in weeks.

Denine picked him up at the train station and quizzed him as they got into the car. "Music festival? I'm glad one of us was home working," she said, pulling out of the parking lot onto the highway. She glanced over from her driving and touched his hand. "Missed you, kiddo."

Payne gripped back. "Missed you, too," he said. Denine drove in silence, while he described the leads he had garnered, including the connection at JPL, and the name of the headquarters for the space probe mission, in Arizona. "It's called Sandaran something." He checked his memo recorder. "Sandaran-Choharis Institute for the Study of Tachyonic Phenomena." He looked up. "Is that near where you used to live?"

"Sandaran Link Center?" Denine glanced at him in surprise, then looked back at the road, as she negotiated an exit ramp off Route 128.

"You've heard of it?"

Denine accelerated onto the secondary highway. "Sure, it's only fifteen or twenty kilometers outside of New Phoenix. I used to know someone who worked there."

Payne shook his head in rueful surprise. "Am I the only one who's never heard of this place?"

Denine laughed. "I'm not sure if she's still there. It's been a while since I last heard. I've told you about her. My friend from high school?"

"You mean the one you had that falling out with?"

"Right. I still get a letter from her once or twice a year." Denine glanced in the rearview mirror, then slowed for a turn. "I haven't seen her, though, since I left school and came east."

"Are you still on speaking terms?"

"Good question. I'm not sure if she writes to keep up the contact, or just to make me feel guilty."

Payne looked at her as the car accelerated again. There was a distracted expression on her face now. "Why would she—"

"Oh—" Denine sighed and gestured noncommittally. "It's a long story. I'm not sure I feel like dredging it up right now."

"Mmm." Payne let it drop, but continued thinking. A contact, any contact, at the institute could be extremely useful if it came to probing out information. "Are you on the kind of terms that you could put me in touch with her?" he said after a while. "Or at least find out if she still works there?"

"Well—"

"If it's going to be really awkward, I don't want to—"

Denine shrugged. "It would be awkward, yeah." She was silent for a few moments, then said, "But what the hell. If you think it'll help you with a story, it's probably worth a call. I don't know what she'll say, though."

"Well, it's a long shot," Payne said. "I don't even know what's out there, or if it would matter. But I should try to cover all the angles. What did she do there?"

Denine shook her head. "Probably a secretary."

"Well, sometimes they're the ones who know the most," he said. He rested his eyes, focusing inwardly on the motion of the car. He was tired, but it was a good feeling. Just don't hope for too much, he cautioned himself.

They made the call later that evening. Denine looked up the number and tapped it into the phone console as Payne pulled up a chair beside her. "Cross your fingers," she said nervously, pushing her hair back from her temples. "Maybe she'll be happy to hear from me." Denine did not look as though she believed it.

There was a several-second delay, and then a click and a soft beep. A printed message appeared on the screen: "*I cannot answer your call right now. If you plan to burglarize my apartment, be advised that I have a team of trained attack gerbils. Enter at your own risk. If you would like to leave a message, do the usual thing. —Mozy.*"

Payne and Denine looked at one another. "Attack gerbils?" Payne asked.

A smile flickered across Denine's face. She sat indecisively, fingering the console. "Well—shall we leave a message?" She pressed a button. Mozy's message scrolled up, and a line appeared beneath it, along with the time and date. Into that space, Denine typed: "*Mozy, this is Denine. Long time no hear. I would like to talk to you, and have a favor to ask. Could you please call me, or let me know when I can reach you at home? Thanks. Dee.*" She hesitated, then pressed the button to send and turned the screen off.

"Sorry," she said softly, turning to Payne. "I wouldn't be *too* hopeful about her calling back."

Payne hugged her briefly. "Thanks. You tried. And if she doesn't— well, like you said, she's probably just a secretary. She probably doesn't know anything about this business, anyway."

Denine nodded uncomfortably.

"You okay?" he asked concernedly.

She sighed, then smiled. "It's just the reminder. Anyway, you're right—she probably doesn't know anything. Let's go watch the news, shall we?"

Chapter 17

(I am truly sorry, Bill. She is too disturbed, too hurt for me to reach her. . . .)

Kadin's voice echoed in Jonders's thoughts, with bell-like clarity and gentle sorrow. *Too disturbed, too hurt.* . . .

There was a sharpness in Kadin's eyes that conveyed unusual intensity. (I believed that my rapport would prove sufficient to break through,) he continued. (It was not.)

(You can't blame yourself,) Jonders said.

(I assign no blame. But it was a shock to be so roundly rejected. I believe that the best hope is to find someone with a deeper knowledge and intimacy.)

(Such as—)

(I suggest Mozy-ship.)

Jonders stared at him in astonishment. Sparkling, unfocused thoughts lit up the darkness behind Kadin's face. (*Mozy-ship?* You mean downlink the ship to Earth, with Mozy on the receiver at this end?)

(Precisely.)

Jonders took a deep breath and thought hard, and tried to think of a reason why not. (It could be an awful risk,) he said finally. (It could drive her deeper than ever into her shell.)

(As I see it,) Kadin said, (the two are experiencing very different problems. For Mozy-ship, it's a matter of gathering and integrating memories. There may be actual gaps that were introduced by the brainscan or the transmission. Mozy-Earth, on the other hand, appears to be suffering from pure psychological trauma from the scan. So far as we know, her memory remains intact.)

(So?)

(I suggest that their problems may be complementary. Perhaps in union, they might combine their strengths and weaknesses to help one another.)

Jonders listened thoughtfully. It was an intriguing notion, but it would have to be done soon, before other decisions made it impossible. (I'll have to talk this over with Dr. Thrudore,) he said finally.

(Do *you* like the idea?) Kadin asked.

Jonders hesitated. (It has possibilities. It may have problems. I can't say yet.)

(All I can ask is that you consider it,) Kadin said.

(I'll let you know,) Jonders promised.

She looked down through the transmission window, waiting. There had been a recognition signal, as though someone were trying to contact her. Jonders. Or someone.

The window was a circle in the darkness, silent among the other sounds: the whisper of telemetry, cosmic radiation hissing in her ear, the rumble and sputter of attitude controllers and servo-mechanisms, the heartbeat of the fusion generator, the hum of the drive. The window was silent.

(Mother Progam, did I or did I not hear a recognition code?)

(YOU DID.)

(Is there a signal coming?)

There was a brief hesitation, and then Mother Program answered, (WE RECOMMEND THAT YOU INVESTIGATE.)

Mozy emitted an annoyed breath of static. Mother Program had been acting obtuse lately—answering questions in riddles, and generally making her feel more out of sorts than she felt already. Whatever was going on, Homebase was probably behind it. Certain kinds of access had become more difficult; procedures that once had operated freely now had to be coaxed, or abandoned altogether. Mother Program admitted to no knowledge of these matters.

She sniffed the wind, waiting. There was the faintly pungent smell of the ion stream, shooting ahead of her, slowing her headlong flight from the sun. *Investigate*, Mother Program had said. Very well.

Focusing herself, she peered into the window and reached down the link, probing for signs of life. At first she felt only silence—but an *aware* kind of silence, as though someone were listening, waiting, hiding in the darkness. And then: a whisker of a contact. But where? The darkness was too deep; she couldn't find the source of the touch. It wasn't Jonders; she would recognize him.

There was a sense of *wrongness* about it.

She withdrew. (Mother Program, identify this contact.)

(UNABLE TO COMPLY. RECOMMEND YOU INVESTIGATE YOURSELF.)

(Thanks for nothing.) She reentered the window, and felt the filaments brush against her again but again, she could make no identification. The uneasy prickling sensation persisted.

Once more she withdrew, and demanded curtly, (What's going on? If you know, tell me.)

(I HAVE BEEN REQUESTED TO DIRECT YOU AS I HAVE.)

(Why?)

(I CANNOT SAY.)

(Call Homebase and tell them that I want Jonders on the line.)

(MESSAGE SENT.) There was a short pause, and then: (HOMEBASE REPLIES AS FOLLOWS: "WE REQUEST THAT YOU ESTABLISH DIRECT CONTACT. OUR PURPOSE WILL BECOME CLEAR IF YOU SUCCEED. PLEASE TRY AGAIN.")

(I said I wanted Jonders on the line.)

There was no reply from Mother Program, but a sense of *waiting* persisted, and the tachyon link remained open.

(Damn it.) Mozy remained very still for a moment, and then reached yet again into the link. This time she was determined; if illumination was needed, she would create it herself. A room took shape in the darkness, a place where she could study this phenomenon. In the center of the room, something glimmered: the aura of another life. She moved toward it, circling cautiously. Slowly she drew near enough to touch the mysterious presence, like a cat brushing against the legs of a visitor.

A disturbance rippled into her, making her shiver. There was something terribly strange and yet familiar here—something that reminded her of emotions she had once known: fear, anger, frustration.

She coiled herself around again, touching and probing. A spark of annoyance pushed her away. The figure was shrouded in a cloak, impenetrable and grey. She withdrew into a far corner of the room.

(Mother Program! Get Jonders on the line! I'm not doing anything more until he speaks with me!)

(MESSAGE SENT.)

After several moments, she felt a shift, a stirring, as though a door had opened in the darkness. (Jonders?)

A door closed, and the silent figure was gone. Someone else was nearby, though, a spark of blue light. (Are you going to speak?) she said.

(I'm sorry for the difficulty,) Jonders said, glimmering.

(What's going on?)

(I want you to meet someone.) An amber spark appeared in the darkness, further away. It approached slowly. (Mozelle, this is Dr. Thrudore. She's going to explain what we're trying to do.)

Mozy watched the amber spark as it drifted into position beside Jonders. There was an awkwardness in the spark's movements: inexperience in moving through the link. But Mozy sensed a strong, perhaps even a stern personality. A woman. Not unfriendly. Mozy opened herself to the contact. (Yes?)

Dr. Thrudore's voice reached her clearly. (My name is Diana, Mozy. Bill has told me a lot about you—so I hope we can speak freely.)

(You're a doctor? What sort of doctor?)

Thrudore hesitated just an instant, and then said, (I'm a psychiatrist, Mozy. I think perhaps you'd guessed that already.)

Mozy answered at once. (Are you trying to analyze me? I won't tolerate that.)

(No, Mozy,) said Thrudore. (We had another reason. We're trying to help another person here on Earth. Someone we think *you* might be able to help through the link.)

(Me? How could I help anyone?)

(It's hard to explain. For the moment, we hope you'll just accept it on faith.)

(That's pretty difficult, if you don't give me more to go on.) Mozy stared at them cautiously.

(Mozy,) Jonders said, his spark pulsing faintly. (It's a patient of Diana's. Someone who will not let herself be reached by any of us. She is a lot like you; we think she might accept you. But we don't want you to start out with preconceived notions, and that's why we're asking you to go in—well, blind.)

(But what are you asking me to *do*? I'm no psychiatrist.)

(Be yourself,) Thrudore answered. (Find a way to touch her. Pretend you're in a session and must find your way. Gently.)

(Do you remember Kadin?) Jonders said. (Were there ever times that you felt reluctant about a scenario—perhaps you felt like being alone—and yet he found a way to coax you in? Think of how he might have done it—and try it your own way.)

Mozy considered carefully. Currents of emotion were stirring in the recesses of her thoughts. Did she want to help them?

(Kadin wants you to do it, Mozy. It was David's idea.) That was Jonders talking.

(David? Is he here? Why can't I talk with him?) She spoke coldly, but beneath the surface stronger feelings were surging, straining at their bonds.

(I'm sorry, Mozy—he can't speak with you now. But he'll be listening in,) Jonders said. (He's quite concerned about you.)

(Concerned? *Concerned?* But he can't speak with me?)

(He's not permitted. Please trust us, Mozy. I think you'll understand when it's over.)

(You're not trying to set me up?) she said.

(Set you up?)

(To get rid of me? I won't let you do that.)

(No, Mozy—it's nothing like that,) Jonders assured her. (In fact, we hope that you might benefit—)

Mozy faced the two against the darkness: three sparks of light burning quietly in the center of the Coalsack Nebula. If they were lying, she would know . . . if not, perhaps she should do it. . . .

(All right,) she said softly.

(We'll be listening, watching from a distance. We'll communicate if necessary,) said Jonders. Then he and Thrudore withdrew, like torches vanishing into the night, and she was alone.

But not truly alone. The silent one was somewhere out there, waiting.

An image was needed.

Mozy thought, and then got to work. She began by forming the darkness, molding it with her imagination, giving it shape. A cavern: vast, quiet, miles deep in bedrock. Water trickled and chuckled somewhere in the distance, a comforting sound. Now—a glimmer of light appeared, a golden light, casting just enough illumination to dispel the gloom from the cavern walls.

A cloaked figure was seated on a stone, head cast down, a hood concealing her face.

Mozy approached cautiously. (Hello,) she said softly—and waited for an answer. The figure gathered silence about her like a quilt. (If you don't like the place I've created, you can help change it, make a new one,) Mozy said. Still there was no reply, and now Mozy felt a ripple of anger, deep within herself. (Why won't you talk?)

Patience, she reminded herself. Gently.

She reached out a ghostly arm toward her silent companion. Her hand, hesitating, slowly touched and then gripped the other's shoulder. A feeling of tension throbbed suddenly in her arm. With her other hand, she touched the person's chin, to coax that dark face up to meet her gaze.

Sparks flashed up her arm, burning her with white-hot fire. A wave of pain and anger slammed into her, and lifted her up and backward. She spun into darkness, unable to control her movement. Resentment, fear, and anger reverberated around her like bellclaps, echoing from one end of the cavern to the other.

By the time she stabilized herself, the echoes had died out. The cavern was gone, demolished by the force of the rejection. Mozy brooded and considered what to do next.

Failure, she thought. No one could penetrate this wall; no one was welcome.

That was a result she would not accept. A feeling of determination grew in her. Grimly she started over.

A bowl of darkness surrounded her. Very well: it was nighttime. She reached somewhere and gathered up two handfuls of luminous liquid gold, and flung them into the sky. With a hiss, they spattered into thousands of tiny, blazing stars. She gathered more handfuls and flung them, and with each handful went a bit of her own frustration and anger, and by the time the sky was filled with stars, her anger was spent. She inspected the image dispassionately.

It was a setting Kadin had used once. It was a desert sky. Beneath her feet were flagstones, and surrounding her was a patio flanked by cacti and desert shrubs. A flagstone walk curved out of sight up terraced steps, to a house largely invisible behind a cluster of desert trees.

Seated on the third step was her companion. Still cloaked. Still hooded. Beneath the hood a pair of eyes flickered for a moment, then vanished as the hood dropped further forward. Mozy sighed, then said, (You don't have to speak—but be alert. Be aware.) There was a resonance here, something about the figure that dogged her subconscious. Something familiar and strange. She thought she knew a way to get at it.

A diversion. A third party.

(Good, Mozy—very good,) whispered a voice, perhaps the wind. Was the wind speaking to her now? Perhaps Jonders . . . perhaps Thrudore . . . perhaps no one.

(Use your imagination,) said the wind.

That was her intention. She reached back into her thoughts, into her memory, looking for something . . . uncertain what. Images fluttered past, almost a random discharge. Something such as Kadin might have used, but something of her own, perhaps a creature, a magical beast. A perilous beast. Yes. . . .

(I believe we have company,) she said softly. There was a hint of movement beneath her companion's cloak, and she knew she had been heard if not acknowledged.

There was another kind of movement, behind the shrubbery—a wavering distortion in the star field directly behind a cactus. The distortion moved. She felt a prickly electricity in the air. The bushes shivered, and a ghostly creature stepped forward. It was a long, low-slung bobcat with three pairs of legs; it shimmered as though made of pale fire. Stars gleamed through its transparent body. The cat approached, then stopped and sniffed the air delicately, noting first Mozy's presence and then the cloaked figure's. Its eyes were black holes; Mozy felt her gaze being pulled toward them, into them. She looked away with an effort. There was a psychic magnetism about this beast, and she felt her own memories resonating in its presence.

(Beast,) she said softly, (do you know me?) She glanced at her companion and saw two eyes gleaming out of the hood. She looked at the cat again. (Do you, Beast?)

The creature purred laughter. It ought to know her. It was a beast of her own making, invented at age six to terrify her older sisters and to comfort her. A mythical beast. From her own mind, her own myth. How long ago had that been?

Her gaze drifted back to the cloaked companion, and she was surprised to see the figure trembling, head raised, eyes flashing with either fear or recognition. (Have you met such a beast before?) Mozy asked softly.

There was no answer except from the wind. (Yes,) it sighed through the leaves.

What happened next startled even her. The creature divided itself into two parts, one stepping out of the other like a snake from its skin. The two transparent beasts walked toward Mozy and her companion, glittering paws moving in perfect step. A blade of fear sliced through Mozy as she guessed the beast's intentions—and realized that the command had come, not from her, but from the other. The beasts stepped, and stepped, and then crouched . . .

. . . and sprang in unison.

A blazing electrical fire leaped to Mozy's breast, expanded to envelop her, and her companion as well . . . devoured her in its cold energy and drew her helpless into the beast's mind, the beast's heart . . . into a psychic slipstream. Distantly she was aware of the two halves of the creature coming back together, rejoining her personality caught in a whirlwind with the other's, Mozy and the silent companion . . .

They collapsed into a dimensionless space, one consciousness with another, with only invisible walls to hold them apart. Mozy felt afraid; the fear grew out of the deepest parts of her mind and was reflected by mirrors she couldn't see, and it grew stronger with each reflection, and she realized that it was not just her fear but the other's, as well. (Why be afraid?) she cried, and with a curious kind of echo she heard her voice or another's just like hers, crying, (I am afraid!) She felt, rather than heard, the shivering groan of the walls that kept her and the other apart, and she knew that their defenses were slipping away / both their defenses were slipping away / her fear reverberated and merged with another's / they were the same fear / same voices / same astonishment . . .

(Who are you *really?*)
(Who are you *really?*)
(Really—) / (Really—) / (Really—)

Pain echoed / echoed / whose voice? / the voices were the same / same voices / same person / two persons one and the same / they are the same / we are the same . . .

That cannot be!

Madness / the path to madness / hallucinations / dreams of merging / how can I be you? / how can you be me?

Doors boomed open onto empty chambers. Mirrors shattered, revealing passageways long forgotten—and understanding coverged upon her as she merged into herself, into the person she once had been—

—in another time—

—another place—

—and her fear tumbled away, but so did the bonds holding her in the realm of the rational, protecting her from madness—

—and her scream echoed across the light-years, richocheted down the link. . . .

Mozelle screamed.

Thrudore turned quickly, helmet cables trailing, and with an effort forced the greater part of her awareness back out into the world. Beside her, wearing a helmet, her patient was struggling against her seat restraints.

"Mozy!" Jonders's voice echoed across the room—and in the link, too, though in the link the shout was lost in the chaos of Mozy's cries.

(I'll see to her!) Thrudore said. (You worry about your side of it.)

(Right,) he answered. Already Thrudore could feel subtle changes in the link—Jonders tightening his control.

As Mozy struggled, Thrudore stroked her hair in an effort to calm her. Mozy was wailing now, half crying.

"Mozelle!" Thrudore called. She adjusted the tau-field, to enhance her patient's brainwave state, and then spoke softly, but close to Mozy's ear. "Mozy, can you hear me?"

The answer was a groan.

(Are you getting anything?) Jonders wondered, inside her head.

(We have contact,) she answered. (But nothing sensible. We're going to have to draw her out.)

(Be careful. It's a maelstrom in here—I can't follow it all—)

Thrudore felt him break away. She slipped the other direction, pulling partway out of the link, leaving just a corner of her mind with the inner voices—the riot of pain and confusion and joy, too bewildering to follow. Leave that to Jonders; concentrate on this world.

Mozy was hyperventilating, and blinking wildly. Her heartbeat was way up. Thrudore strengthened the tau-field, and her patient calmed slightly. "Can you speak, Mozy? Can you see me?" Mozy's eyes were wide, staring at some point in space that probably did not exist in this room. "What are you seeing, Mozy? Tell me what you see."

"Aauuuhhhh," Mozy groaned, rolling her eyes up.

Thrudore tried to move around in front of her, but the helmet cable was too short. She hesitated and then pulled off the helmet. A corner of her mind abruptly went blank, and she struggled against a wave of faintness. Shaking free of it, she found Mozy shuddering—and trying to speak.

"Da-a-vid-d," Mozy stammered. Suddenly she grew glassy calm, and then her mouth began to work silently, trying to form another word.

"Who, Mozy? *Who?*" Thrudore urged.

"D-d-avid?" Mozy called mournfully. Then her voice grew harsh. "H-h-hoshi! Help me!" Her eyelids fluttered, and then her eyes seemed to focus.

"Look at me, Mozy," Thrudore commanded. She raised a hand, flat, and passed it in front of Mozy's eyes at differing angles. "Do you see my hand? Watch my hand."

Mozy blinked, and seemed to focus on the hand, following it with an erratic stare. Her voice became small and childlike. "Not nice to say those things . . . such a mean person . . . when I tell Dee. . . ." Her voice trailed away.

A moment later, it returned, in an adult tone. "I don't like being used. I don't like being lied to. I have a perfect right to my own life, so the hell with what they want."

Thrudore waited. Mozy's eyes lost their focus again. "Who?" Thrudore said, "*Who* is using you? And why?"

Another internal struggle was going on, and this one lasted longer. When Mozy spoke again, her voice had a strained, almost foreign tone. "Had forgotten—forgotten all these things—so many things. Is that—is that why—?" The voice faltered.

It was the voice, Thrudore thought, of a woman a quarter of a light-year away.

Mozy's right hand jerked in her lap, and she slowly raised it to her brow, pressed her fingertips to her forehead in a gesture of pain, or uncertainty. "Mozy?" Thrudore said. "Can you tell me where you are?"

Mozy grimaced. She spoke in a slow, precise voice. "I understand now. So many fragments—all unclear. I need time—time to sort it out."

"Explain to us, Mozy," Thrudore urged. "Tell us what you see."

With a sudden laugh, Mozy looked toward the ceiling. "Ah— Mother," she said. "Now I see. It's been so far from me—and now so clear. Jo is not Mother, never was. And Mother never would tell me if she'd wanted me. . . ."

A warning light blinked on the console. Jonders acted quickly to prepare for termination of the transmission cycle. In thirty seconds, the tachyon storage rings on the spacecraft would shut down for recharging, and the link would dissolve. (Dr. Thrudore,) he said. (Diana—)

She was out of the link. With an effort, without leaving the link himself, he turned in his seat and called out, "Dr. Thrudore—link cycle ends in twenty seconds. Get her ready."

He was dimly aware, as he turned his attention back to the monitor, of Thrudore speaking to Mozelle in a soothing voice as she altered the tau-field for a tranquilizing effect. Within, he felt the raging energy in the link slacken, felt confusion on Mozelle's part as the downlink with her physical counterpart grew fuzzy—as she became more relaxed, and then sleepy. (Mozy, it's the end of the cycle,) he said. (Ending for now,) he repeated, the thought droning into the connection.

Whether she understood or not, he couldn't tell; but he felt her presence slipping away, her voice growing faint. Then the link dissolved entirely, and she was gone.

Jonders withdrew from the link at his end and slowly removed his helmet. He turned to look at Thrudore and her patient.

Mozelle was slumped in her chair, apparently passed out.

He realized suddenly that he was breathing in short, quick gasps. The tension had not yet subsided from his own body. He glanced at his hands, and gripped the arms of his chair to stop the trembling.

PART THREE

FATHER SKY

Prelude

The sound was starting again—the long, low moan that echoed in the back of the consciousness, that evoked memories of a methane glacier during a thaw, shivering and buckling and fragmenting. This was not the time of the thaw, however. And Four-Pod was nowhere near the glaciers.

What, then, was the source of this moan-that-was-like-a-song? It did not sound like the voices of Those-Who-Thought, but who else could make a sound ring inside the consciousness, with nothing to be heard on the outside except the wind and the rain?

Four-Pod could not delay for the truth to be revealed. His destiny lay at the edge of the Snow Plain, where the Philosophers awaited his riddle-offering from the hills. If the offering suited them, he would be made welcome there, and perhaps he could speak with them of this troubling thing. If not, he would be forced to flee, and he would have only the sleet and wind for counsel.

And, perhaps . . . the voice.

Perhaps it would travel with him across the plain, offering companionship and thoughts of warmth.

And perhaps he was wasting time thinking and listening when he should be on the move. He had many lengths yet to cross.

With a forward lurch, Four-Pod shuffled through the billowing snow. Once his claws found traction in the firm methane ice, beneath the snow, he settled into an efficient pattern of movement: grip . . . heave . . . grip . . . heave . . . grip. . . . Occasionally his nails slipped on the ice, and he sailed snout-first into a bank of snow. Each time, he picked himself up patiently, blew the snow out of all six nostrils, and continued as though nothing had happened.

The songs came and went from his thoughts. He shifted his focus to other senses: the fine grains of snow sliding across his silken hide, the rasp of his claws on the ice, the looming and sudden gusting away of shadow-like forms against the ochre sky. Thoughts of hunger tormented him; but he knew from the texture of the ice that he was at least a storm-day's walk from edible slush. To distract himself from his hunger, he summoned memories and legends.

There were stories that told of times when the world was a sounder and clearer place—when snow lay hard upon the ice, and the sky on occasion grew deep and transparent, revealing miracles. Legends spoke of the round, banded body of Heaven—and of a many-layered arch that vaulted to Heaven and (some said) looped around it to enter Heaven's back gate. Songs spoke of Heaven's necklace, and there were those who said that it was in reality the same as the road to Heaven, that the image of a necklace was only an illusion. Others claimed the opposite, that the road was the illusion, that it circled round and round, toying endlessly with the weary, hopeful pilgrim.

It was a fine legend. But legends could ward off hunger for only so long. Four-Pod knew that he must soon find sustenance or starve. As the snow grew grittier and more bitter in his nostrils, he pushed harder, and clawed deeper.

When the song returned this time, it reached somehow deep into his heart and boosted his flagging spirit. He peered and sniffed, tossed his snout and brayed, and plunged forward. Was the song a legend come to life—a call from Heaven? He thought of the great arching road that existed somewhere above the shrouded sky, and he grew dizzy with fear and joy. Could this be a signal? The music of the Heaven Road?

Press on.

Much later the ice changed. He was desperately weak, step following on step. With groggy surprise he recognized the softening of the ice under his claws, a delicious wetness soaking the bottoms of his pods.

The slush pool opened before him, layered and rich. He dropped his snout and drank deeply, filling himself. Afterward he contracted his pods and settled into the snow. The music continued to dance in his thoughts, and lovingly intertwined with his dreams as at last, at long last, he slept.

Chapter 18

The spaceship traffic near Tachylab reminded Robert Johanson of a colony of oddly shaped bees, their hovering dance set to the music of sunlight and viewed in painstakingly slow motion. Thirty-six thousand kilometers away, the mother planet floated somber and silent at the hub of the geosynchronous orbit, a counterbalance to the glitter of spaceships, a massive orb of earthtones and blue-greens and swirls of cottony white, the master stone among tinier jewels in the darkness. Johanson rubbed at the viewport where it was fogging from a defect in an inner seal. Soon this would be as useless as the window in the mess, which was now completely fogged even during sunlight periods. Try to get HQ to do something about that. Johanson shook his head and pushed himself back to his work.

Transmission was due to begin in a few minutes. He hooked a toe cleat to anchor himself, and made a focusing adjustment to the transmitter field controller. Any time now. He wondered if the others were ready, and if they had taken adequate care to avoid discovery. There were times when he felt a little like the teenaged boy who had stolen into the school laboratory to perform unauthorized experiments. That episode had ended in a month's detention, after the explosion under the chemistry hood had made his efforts known to the whole school. Discovery this time would be considerably more disastrous— for all of them.

The *Father Sky* tachyon-ready cycle was coming up in five minutes. A string of green lights verified that the Earthside transmitter was ready. Johanson opened the voice circuit to Earth. "Homebase, this is Tachylab control."

"Tachylab, this is Homebase. We're coming up on mark time, in two minutes and twenty seconds—"

There was a movement through the side bulkhead door. Johanson glanced up at Alicia Morishito as she floated above and to his right, scanning a checklist. He cut the mike switch and said softly, "Is Mark on the power deck?"

Morishito nodded. "He's waiting."

Johanson switched to the intercom. "Mark, this is Robert. We could use your help now, if you're free."

"I'm a little busy," answered a flat-sounding voice. "I'll come up when I can."

Johanson nodded in satisfaction. "Good enough."

At a minute past the mark, Johanson bumped the transient gain to a higher level, and then spent about fifteen seconds readjusting it. There was no evidence on the control display, but the delay should have given their colleague Mark Adams sufficient time to make his patches.

At fifty-four seconds to transmission, the deputy manager from GEO-Four drifted into the control room and watched over their shoulders.

Forty-five seconds. "Tachylab, this is Homebase. Going to auto on the main transmitter."

"Roger, Homebase. We're receiving a clear signal."

At five seconds, the main storage ring reached peak density. At one second, the tuner fine-focused the carrier wave.

At zero, the carrier jumped in density by a factor of a thousand, and the signal from Homebase, from a laboratory in the North American Southwest, was shunted into the tachyon converter. From the exit port five kilometers from Johanson, the signal streamed out at half a million times the speed of light, bridging the gulf of interplanetary space to intercept the *Father Sky* spacecraft somewhere beyond the edge of the solar system.

Mozy felt herself shifting moods again. The euphoria had passed, and then the anger, and now the loneliness, too, was subsiding. Analytical reflection took its place. She knew that none of these feelings was gone for good, but for the moment at least she might reflect undisturbed. Dozens of new memories blossomed open for inspection. The contact with herself, her alter-ego on Earth, had provided a wealth of images.

(Mother Program,) she asked. (How could I have missed these before?)

(SPECULATION: THEY MAY HAVE BEEN LOST OR AL-TERED IN TRANSMISSION. A DEFINITIVE EXPLANATION IS BEYOND MY POWERS. WHAT MEMORIES DO YOU HAVE NOW, THAT WERE MISSING BEFORE?)

(David. Hoshi. Family details. Dee.)

(THOSE CODES ARE FAMILIAR. DID YOU NOT HAVE PRIOR USE OF THOSE MEMORIES?)

(Yes, but they were confused. Fragments. Dreams confused with memories. Now I remember more clearly why I am here. I remember loving David, not wanting to live without him.)

(THESE MEMORIES ARE DRAWN FROM YOUR ORIGINAL STORE?)

(From the person I once was, yes. But the memories feel, now, as though they've always been with me.)

What sort of person does that make me? she wondered silently. What do you call a person with interchangeable memories? Fear swept across her like a chilling breeze, and then was gone. She knew the answer. Fully comprehending it was another matter.

Shipboard scans showed all systems functioning optimally: naviga-tion steady, engines running smoothly, power levels stable. Teamed with Mother Program, she gave over only a corner of her mind to such details; but examining shipboard variables made her feel physi-cally more secure, as though she had exercised, caused her blood to flow and her muscles to work out tension. Such scans made her larger self feel more stable, more nearly sane.

Memories. At times they were abstracted recollections; at other times, large-as-life bits of *déjà-vu*. Images of home kept recurring: Mother home late from work; Kink yelling; escaping from the mad-house with Dee and skulking the back streets, plotting their freedom. But there was another memory, darker and more insistent: a letter, a handwritten message. What was it? Someone ill . . . someone dying. Why was there a connection with that memory . . . a connection with hurt and anger?

(WE ARE RECEIVING A SIGNAL FROM HOMEBASE. JON-DERS REQUESTS CONTACT WITH YOU.)

(What?) She had failed to notice the signal. (Does he say what he wants?)

There was a pause. (JONDERS WISHES TO REVIEW THE LAST LINKUP.)

Damn him. But come to think of it, she had questions of her own. (Jonders?) She spoke softly in the darkness.

A point of light appeared, grew into a face. (Hello, Mozelle. I guess you know what I want to talk with you about.)

(Do I?)

(We'd like to know your reactions—)

(My reactions—?)

(—to linking up with yourself.)

(Not myself. Not anymore.)

(No. But you know what I mean.)

She studied him, aware of feelings of hostility spreading within her. (I learned some things,) she said.

Jonders seemed to blink. (Can you tell me what?)

She explored her hostile feelings for a moment. (That's personal.) The last linkup had something to do with those hostile feelings. (Tell me why you did that,) she said, recalling how it had happened. (Why did you make it so difficult?)

(What do you mean?)

(You didn't tell me who it was. Why did you make me guess?)

Jonders was silent. (We thought it was the only way,) he said finally. (We didn't want either of you frightened away beforehand. We expected that it would be hard for both of you.) He groped for words. (Can you tell me—was it difficult for you to—recognize your own personality, and join with it?)

(That's personal, too.) She paused. (Did the results satisfy you?)

(You succeeded where we failed. But we don't know if it really helped her—the Mozy down here, I mean. She's still catatonic. It was you who spoke to us in her body, wasn't it?)

Mozy thought back. Her mind irised open onto the memory of the link with the other Mozy: the intensity, the fear and joy and excitement, all welling out at once. The memory of speaking through human lips again, seeing with human eyes. She shut the window abruptly. It was not something she was ready to share. (Yes,) she said. (Do you want me to do it again?)

He stared at her curiously. (Would you?)

(Perhaps. But don't expect me to restore her.)

He considered. (It was Kadin, you know, who suggested that we ask you. He and Dr. Thrudore, both, had already tried. But you reached her.)

(Kadin—) Mozy felt a sudden breeze through her thoughts. (Tell me about David. Why wasn't he there to talk with me? Why wouldn't he help?)

(I can't really—)

(And when are you transmitting him here?)

(Mozelle, I can't—)

(I think it's time you gave me some answers. I helped you. If you expect any more help from me—)

Jonders was silent, stalling.

(At least tell me whether I'm going to see him,) she demanded.

(I honestly can't tell you that,) Jonders said slowly. His face looked strained, oddly colored with streaks of red. He seemed to be trying to decide something. (I can tell you this much, though. It won't be quite what you think.)

(Meaning what?)

(Meaning—)

(Yes—?)

Again he stalled. There was burst of interference, and his face began to distort.

(Jonders, what is it?)

He was trying to answer, but his voice had turned to static. He stared at her through a snowstorm, his features frozen in mid-frame.

(*What's happening?*)

She heard only his voice breaking up, and then his face was obliterated, as the signal vanished.

Jonders clamped both hands to his headset. A wind of cold fire stormed through his head.

(*Shut it down! Get him out!*)

Voices reached him distantly from the edge of the loop. He could not respond, though he was dimly aware that someone was trying to help him.

(*Bill, can you hear me?*) said a stronger voice, somewhere in the dark.

He groped for support from the voice. He could not find his way out of the link; the normal connections had been cut from him. (I'm here,) he tried to say, and then the support slipped away from him again.

The next voice he heard was in his earphones. "Bill, can you hear me now?" It was Mason Rogers, the console engineer. "Are you okay?"

The darkness of the link shimmered. Then it vanished, leaving him jolted and breathless. "Yahh . . . I hear you. I'm out." He blinked painfully, and focused on the console before him, or tried to—it was blurry in the gloom of the communications pit. He started to remove his headset. "What happened?"

Helping hands lifted the helmet away from him. "We don't know yet," said the engineer's voice, this time from a speaker on the console. "Something cut the signal; we think it was a security interrupt."

Security? Jonders leaned forward over the console, taking a deep breath. "Find out—and let me know," he said. He snapped off the intercom. Security interrupt. What the hell was going on here?

He left the communications pit, two assistants trailing after him in puzzlement. The light of the hallway hurt his eyes, and he blinked with relief as he entered the gloomy master control room. "Find anything?" he asked.

Rogers was touching switches and peering at monitors. He looked around, then went back to what he was doing. A raised hand cut off Jonders's next question. "Here we are," he said.

A bold-faced message filled the bottom monitor: **"TERMINATION OF SIGNAL BY SECURITY OVERRIDE, CODE 37. NO FURTHER TRANSMISSION PERMITTED WITHOUT SECURITY ACTION, CODE 837."**

"What does that mean?" someone asked.

"The computer thinks there was a tap on the signal," the engineer said. "Automatic cutoff. Now we'll have to find out who, and how. We'll leave the why to security."

Jonders turned away, shaking his head. A depressing thought haunted him as he left the control room. Could this, too, have been a result of Hoshi's tampering?

Leonard Hathorne's face scowled out of the telephone screen. "Take care of Hoshi Aronson and the rest of it any way you want," Hathorne said. "What I want to know is whether or not you're going to transmit Kadin on schedule."

Steepling his fingers before his lips, Slim Marshall hesitated a moment before answering. "Impossible to be sure," he said finally. "At least until the security team gives us a definite answer. Assuming it's just a technical glitch, I'd say we can plan on going ahead—after we settle the Mozelle business."

Hathorne grunted. "That'll be settled tonight. Just give me a push on the technical end. If Kadin is held up on account of one more screwup, the committee will have my balls."

"I'll do my best," Marshall promised.

"Do better than that."

"I'll call you when I know for sure." Marshall switched off the screen and sat back, taking a breath. Jesus, he thought. As if it wasn't bad enough to have technical problems, Hathorne had to make every little delay seem like a purposeful affront to him and the Oversight Committee. Marshall rubbed his eyes under his glasses. The security interrupt was the least of his worries—probably just a hardware problem. The technical and security teams could iron that out. He was fairly sure that Fogelbee was just borrowing trouble, trying to ascribe something like that to Hoshi Aronson—though, of course, it was worth having him brought back in for questioning.

No, what most disturbed him was Mozelle Moi and Kadin. And Jonders. Perhaps Jonders most of all. The man was good at what he did—the best there was, probably—but he had a tendency to step out of line on policy matters. Not that he could be blamed, really. You can't give a man responsibility like that, and then keep him half in the dark, and not expect some problems.

Leaning forward, Marshall thumbed his intercom. "Have you tracked down Bill Jonders yet?"

"He's on his way up now," answered his secretary.

Marshall nodded and blew into his cupped hands. What was he going to tell Jonders—that he had free rein, so long as he didn't go too far? Marshall studied his dark reflection in the black phone screen, stared at his own white eyes. Two years as director of Sandaran-Choliaris Institute, and he was just now approaching the first major milestone of the project. If the road was rougher than he'd anticipated, he shouldn't be too surprised. *Father Sky* and the Link Project were no laughing matter; in the scope of human history, they might be considered to have a role of more than minor importance. He could regret that so much of it was secret; but what point was there in belaboring issues over which he had no control? When contact was made, the world would find out soon enough.

And what is it you're really worried about? he thought. Blowing the biggest moment in history? Screwing up as a black man in a position of influence and power (and are you really still worried over *that* one)? Surely it wasn't Slim Marshall's career at stake. He scarcely had to worry about his reputation, not after Fermilab II; but the truth was, since Molly's death . . . well, never mind that, now.

The intercom buzzed. He snapped out of the reverie and answered. "Dr. Jonders is here," his secretary said.

"Send him in." Marshall stood to greet Jonders. When they were both seated, he tapped his desktop with a pen and gazed at his personality project manager. Jonders looked tired and nervous, but he returned Marshall's gaze intently. "You're not going to be getting any rest right away," Marshall said. "We're hoping to stay on schedule with the transmission."

Jonders frowned.

"In the meantime," Marshall added, "the security interrupt has been cleared. You may go ahead with further linkup sessions, if you wish."

A spark appeared in Jonders's eyes. "Did you find the cause of the interrupt?" he asked.

"There was an abort signal from Tachylab," Marshall said. "Probably a technical snag. We don't have the final report yet, but we're going ahead with normal transmission activities." Jonders nodded with evident relief. He must have been fearful that Aronson had somehow been involved, Marshall realized. He looked questioningly at Jonders. "Do you plan any more linkup sessions between Mozelle and her—" he searched for the right word—"counterpart?"

Jonders took a breath. "I'd like to try. In the long run, I'm hopeful that we could—"

Marshall interrupted with a shake of his head. "There may not *be* a long run," he said quietly. "I'm sorry to put it so bluntly, but a decision is being made soon as to the disposition of . . . what you call 'Mozy-ship.' "

"I see," Jonders said.

"It's not an easy choice. If you have any thoughts to add—"

"Yes," Jonders said. Marshall gestured for him to continue. Jonders knew as well as he did the factors involved. This ship was already at close to maximum range for the reliable transmission of the Kadin personality. Any delay would only increase the risk of failure. As for the possibility of transmitting Mozelle back to Earth, that too had been found unfeasible; the ship's transmitter was too weak, too slow.

"Well," Jonders said. "You know where I stand. And I assume you know that Kadin regards Mozy-ship as a functional being, and wishes her treated that way."

Marshall nodded. He had already considered the point, at some length. "It's *our* responsibility, though, not Kadin's," he pointed out.

Jonders dropped his hands in exasperation. "We've created him to show human wisdom if he's ever called upon to make judgments. You can hardly expect him to turn a blind eye now."

"True enough," Marshall said. He turned his hands out, palms up.

It was an unwinnable argument on both sides, and they both knew it. "Fogelbee says that the architecture of the system may not—"

"I know what Fogelbee thinks," Jonders said angrily. "He's not exactly anxious to give her the benefit of the doubt, though, is he?" Jonders shut his mouth with an audible sigh. He was obviously trying to control his emotions. Marshall studied him sympathetically. There was little he could do to make Jonders feel better about the likely outcome. He could only hope that Jonders's emotional involvement would not turn into interference.

"I wanted to give you a chance for any last input into the decision," Marshall said finally. "The Oversight Committee is meeting tonight, in New Washington."

Jonders straightened a little, and composed himself, as though he had reached some personal decision. "Very well. I have one last bit of input."

Marshall waited.

"As matters stand now, I believe that Mozy-ship would cooperate with us, so long as she is treated as an equal. But if you try to destroy her—and fail—you may create a powerful enemy."

"Yes," Marshall said. "I know."

Jonders rose to leave. "Bill," Marshall said. He pressed his lower lip with his forefinger. "Use the time you have left well. For Mozelle's sake, if nothing else."

For a moment, Jonders stared at him at though he were frozen. Then he nodded, frowning, and turned and walked quickly out of the room.

Chapter 19

Nagging sirens. Flashes of blue light dance in the kitchen window, growing louder and brighter, then passing. Hoshi dumps the dishes into the sonic and stares out—at the brick wall, and down into the dim alley between the apartment buildings.

Probably someone out there right now. In the alley, or on the street. Watching the building, watching the apartment; he wouldn't be surprised if, through some arcane instrumentation, they were staring right into his kitchen.

He ought to be grateful to be going home at all, they said. Well—he thinks he knows why they let him go rather than just throwing away the key. Even they couldn't lock a man away without a trial; and the last thing they'd want is publicity. God forbid the cops should get involved, he thinks; HQ might have to answer some questions themselves—like what are they doing, and why, and what's become of a woman named Mozy, who hasn't been seen around school lately.

Cops, of course, don't know beans and would never ask the right questions, not unless someone cues them in. And Hoshi, well, he's telling nobody nothing, not the cops, not that shrink he's supposed to see, nobody. Said enough already. What he ought to do is get out of here, away from the city and the confusion, go someplace where he can think.

He pulls a cola out of the chiller and snaps it open. Sips the sweet, sharp, bubbling liquid and leans back against the counter, not really directing his thoughts, but just letting them percolate through his mind like bubbles through the soft drink. The blocky shadows of the kitchen fixtures surround him like the protective shapes of a cave, a huddling place. Overhanging cupboards, ledges; boulderlike counters. He feels like a small animal, hiding in its lair.

Small animal.

His hands clench, crushing the flimsy cola can, spraying dark liquid everywhere. Mozy's words rush back to him: *"Will you take care of Maggie and Mouse . . . ?"*

"Damn," he whispers, scarcely conscious of the cola soaking his shirt. Mozy's gerbils.

It was practically her last request before going through with the scan. Would he take care of her gerbils. By now they've probably starved. How long can gerbils live, without food? he wonders. *Mozy, I'm sorry, I didn't mean not to feed them. Oh, God. . . .* Throwing the crushed can into the sink, he strides into the shadows of the living room, seizes his coat, and hurries out into the night.

Seems quiet on the street, later than it really is. It would be smarter to wait until daytime, but he can't wait, he promised her—and what if the things are just holding on, at the edge of starvation?

He stands at the corner, waiting. Street's a converging pattern of oblong light and shadow, nothing much moving, just a car turning the corner further down. Where are they, then? Where's his company? No one moves in the empty, dark night.

Eventually, a bus swings ponderously around the corner, brakes whooshing. He climbs aboard, sticks his metrotab into the slot until it beeps, and makes his way to a seat as the bus rumbles ahead. Behind, a pair of headlights pulls out, following the bus. He faces forward again. Maybe that's them, he thinks; but what does it matter? He's doing nothing wrong; just going to help a friend.

Helping a friend. That's what got him into this in the first place. Friendly concern. Risking his position to help Mozy get . . . what it was she wanted. Things got out of control; he didn't know what it would do to her.

He only wanted to help. That was all.

Liar.

No. Really.

You can lie to them, but you can't lie to yourself. You loved her, it was your own lust that drove you to do it.

No! He jerks his head and stares out the window, the street lights passing like highway markers, the buildings like silent wooded hills. It isn't true, he thinks. It was never true. The pain is starting up again, in the righthand corner of his forehead. What will it be this time? The knife cutting from one temple, under the skull, to the other? A dull fire across the top of his head? Or the icepick stabbing straight behind the eyeball?

You wanted her. You would have done anything to get her.

No!

The pain shoots across his forehead.

It's true. It's your own will, and your own sin, yes sin, *and if you don't redeem yourself of it, you will pay, and pay dearly. The pain is a warning, just a hint of what's to come.*

He presses the heel of his hand against his forehead, and after a minute or so the pain eases. He grimly surveys the bus. There are only a few people aboard—a teenaged girl in jeans, a middle-aged woman gripping a plastic shopping bag, a drunk half asleep near the rear of the bus. All of them lost in their own worlds. Outside, light and dark pass by, the surroundings gradually changing from the dingy residential area of his neighborhood to a brighter business district. Closing his eyes, he rocks with the motion of the bus, calming himself. When he looks again, he sees the familiar corner of the Golden Chance Cafe, and rises to get off. He's a few blocks ahead of himself, though, and hangs silently onto the overhead railing, waiting for the right stop.

The doors clatter open, and he steps down and away, scarcely mindful of the bus growling on without him. He walks three and a half blocks, trying to find an apartment building he has only visited once before, in the daytime. The night landscape is different, another kind of country altogether, one of blurrier outlines, darker darks, more ghostly lights. The building emerges out of the shapes like a familiar statue seen in different light, and he enters the lobby and finds Mozy's barely legible name on the buzzer plate, recognizing her printing before the actual name. He stares at it for a moment—*Mozelle Moi*—his steadiness and determination shaken by the rush of memories brought into his head by that name.

He finds the elevator and goes up to the third floor. Wrong floor. Then the elevator's gone, and he hikes up one flight of stairs rather than wait for it to return. Mozy's floor looks so unfamiliar to him that he wants to leave before he gets caught in some awful Minotaur's maze. Instead, he walks slowly down the hall, feeling like a criminal. The greasy smell of cooking sausage assaults his nose from one wing, and there's the sound of shouting children behind a door as he counts the numbers looking for 432 or 482. He can't remember which is the correct number. There it is. 482. He recognizes the gouge in the plaster near Mozy's door.

Her door surrenders to the key, and then he's inside, shutting it behind him, groping for the light switch. Nothing but flat wall and molding. All darkness and shadowy shapes in the room. If he squints like *that* and strains his eyes, he gets more amplification, especially in the infrared, and he can just about find his way across toward the ghostly form of a desk. He stumbles on the end leg of the couch, but reaches the table in front of him and finds the lamp. Then the switch.

The light glares in his eyes, and he turns away, blinking. Couch, desk, table. Room seems more cramped than he remembers it. Window at one end, kitchen at the other. Mozy, he thinks. Mozy, you should be here. Why are you hiding in that hospital, not listening, not talking?

He turns again, too quickly, and for an instant is overcome by a rush of dizziness, then tears. Jabs at his eyes with his knuckles, cursing, and tries to blink the tears out of his eyes so he can see again. Headache is returning, it's intense, a taphammer landing front dead center, and for a second he can't see straight, and then suddenly he's gasping, getting his breath back, trying to ignore it. He can live with it until he's through with his business.

The gerbils. Cage is on the table, right here in front of you. What did you think that smell was?

The gerbils are dead. Collapsed across one another in a pitiful little heap. Maggie and Mouse, both dead.

You bastard—you've killed them. Innocent creatures, and you've let them starve.

Tears stream down his cheeks. He didn't do it intentionally; he only got home yesterday, they were grilling him, there was nothing he could do. Blinking, he looks into the cage again. The least he can do is get them out of there and bury them, give them some dignity. His hand trembling, he fumbles at the cage latch, and finally gets it open.

One of the gerbils lifts its head and peers groggily at him. The thing's fur is all matted and it smells, but it's definitely weaving its head at him, blinking. "Maggie?" he croaks. "Mouse?" He wipes his eyes with his sleeve, and reaches in and touches the animal on the nose. It sniffs weakly at his finger. "You wonderful little bastard," he whispers.

He checks the food and water dispensers; both are empty. He yanks the water bottle loose from its clip, hurries into the kitchen, and carefully fills it. By the time he gets back, the gerbil has staggered to the open cage door. He stoppers the bottle and refastens it to the cage, and then, reaching back in, picks up the gerbil and sets it down near the water spout.

The gerbil takes a step toward the spout, sniffs at the bead of water, and starts drinking. Hoshi watches in satisfaction and reaches through the bars to tickle it with his finger. One alive is better than none. But the other he'll have to get out of there. He's going to have to touch it, a dead thing. His hand trembles.

He can't do it.

For Mozy? Not even for Mozy? You were supposed to feed them, and one of them's dead now and the other's barely alive; can't you do this much for her, and bury her poor dead gerbil? Use your head.

He goes into the kitchen and switches on the light. The glare hits his eyes with shocking brightness. Counter and cupboards and stove shimmer before him like fire elementals, and he reels, vision suddenly going black. Struggling to stay upright, he covers his eyes with his hands, praying that it will stop. He starts to slide down the wall, his nostrils suddenly filled with a sickly odor, a smell of rotting vegetation. He pushes himself back upright, fighting for control. Work, muscles, he prays—hold the body steady.

As suddenly as it came, the smell is gone. Vision is returning, at first just a fuzzy grey field; then as he blinks, the stove hardens into focus. He looks around, frightened but relieved. Light and shadow are clear once more: the cupboards over the sink, bathroom door to the left. This is the worst attack ever. *God, what's happening, has my punishment started already?*

You're losing grip. Remember what you're here for.

He grabs a handful of paper towels and hurries back to the living room. He bends over and squints into the cage, trying to see which gerbil to grab—only now *both* gerbils are near the water, or is he losing his mind, his eyes going for good? He presses his thumbs into the center of his forehead right over his eyebrows. He looks again.

The two animals are sucking greedily at the water; they were both just sleeping or passed out. They're tougher than he imagined. The second gerbil looks even rattier than the first, but who cares, it's alive, it's breathing.

"You beautiful little bastards," he whispers. He blinks again, rubs away a tear. Mozy, do you forgive me? Now can you forgive me?

The phone screen is full of snow, or maybe it's just his eyes. But it looks like it's working—so why doesn't she answer?

Maybe he got it mixed up. Maybe this is the wrong person altogether.

No, he's sure her name was Mardi. Mozy talked about her enough, he ought to be able to remember the name. Besides, why else would it be on Mozy's quickdial list?

If she answers, what is he going to say?

The screen flickers, and a face appears. "Mozy?" says an anxious voice, the voice of someone looking at him now in bewilderment. "Who are you?" she says.

He gnaws his lower lip, tongue-tied.

"Who are you? Is this a joke? Why are you calling from Mozy's number?"

"Is—is your name Mardi?" he stammers.

She eyes him suspiciously. "Yes."

"I'm a friend of Mozy's. I'm—my name's Hoshi."

Mardi's mouth opens. "I've heard of you. You work with Mozy, right?"

"I—yes—well, we did," Hoshi says, struggling, really trying hard to get it right. "What I mean is—"

"Is Mozy there? Did she ask you to call me?"

"She didn't ask, exactly. No, she's not here." Hoshi bites his lip. Careful, now. "There's been—there's been a sort of accident. Out at work, I mean."

Mardi's face turns rigid. "Dear God. Is she—I mean, is she all right? What happened?"

He swallows. "I can't tell you. Security and all. But it's not that serious, I mean, she isn't dead or anything. She's at the infirmary out at the institute, and she can't really commun—call you, I mean."

"But she's not—"

"No, not really." His words are tripping off his tongue now, and he's not sure what he's saying; maybe he shouldn't have told her, but *somebody* has to know. He clears his throat noisily. "Listen, I can't tell you any more, but the reason I called is because of her gerbils."

"I was wondering," Mardi says. "I thought she didn't want to talk to me, and I was kind of hurt."

"No, no—nothing like that. She *can't* call you, she would if she could, but this security stuff you can't imagine. But I want to talk to you about—"

"I'm glad. I'm really glad," Mardi says. She's suddenly flustered. "That sounds terrible. I'm not glad she got hurt, I mean—of course not. But I wouldn't like to think she wasn't calling just because—"

"No, look," Hoshi says, and he's starting to get desperate, because Mardi won't shut up and let him talk. "It's not like that at all, and *I have to talk to you about the gerbils*!"

"What? Gerbils?"

"Right. Do you know anything about taking care of gerbils? I promised Mozy I'd take care of them, and—I have to go away for a few days, maybe longer, I was wondering—well, could you take it over while I'm gone?" He pauses. She looks at him. "I don't know who else to ask."

She shrugs. "I guess so."

"Do you have a key?"

"To her apartment? No."

He kneads his eyebrows for a moment. "All right. Here's what we'll do." He's going nonstop now, and as he talks, he's already furiously planning ahead. He really does have to get away, he didn't fully realize it until he said it to Mardi, but he can't hang around here, he has things to work out, things to do.

There's a pang of guilt he feels about leaving the gerbils, not taking care of them the way he promised, but what else can he do? In the eyes of Heaven, he has much to answer for, but the gerbils shouldn't be a major factor. The main thing is that they're okay. He has to feel absolutely sure that they're okay.

When he's off from talking to Mardi, he turns back to the cage and frowns. It smells, it's probably filthy—but what does he know about cleaning a gerbil cage? He never had a pet like that, or he'd know. They'll be okay. Just put in some food from the box here. They've got water. Good.

He leaves the lamp on, and locks the door carefully on his way out, then places the key out of sight on the molding ledge over the door. Hurries back along the corridor of shadows to the elevator. It's quiet in the hall now. He's halfway down in the elevator when he remembers the security tail that may have followed him.

He stabs the button for Floor Two. Gets off and takes the stairwell, all the way to the basement level, then out into a dingy corridor. Got to be a rear exit somewhere, he thinks. Dank here, probably a maintenance level. Probably cleaned about once a year. His footsteps echo alarmingly. There's an exit sign, down at the far end. Up five steps and there's the back door, a fire exit. Shove it open.

He's out in the night again, pulling his coat closed around him. He's behind the building. Unobserved. He cuts across to the next block and keeps walking. He has such a lot to do.

Chapter 20

(All that time, you lied to me . . .)

(No . . . Mozy . . . listen . . .)

(*You lied to me*!)

Her words hung like sculpted stone against the dark and the silence. She stared at him, astonishment still ringing in her thoughts, anger choking her.

The analytical frame of mind had fled. She was poised at a precipice—hysteria, rage, despair all echoing around her, pushing her one way and another, threatening to topple her over the edge. She gazed fearfully at Jonders. His face was etched against the dark, glowing with a perilous light. The face had lost its human quality, was transformed into a demonic puppet's head gaping at her from a black stage, illuminated by only a single invisible spotlight.

In the spotlight: the liar, at last speaking the truth.

The truth: David Kadin was no man. David Kadin was a cybernetic intelligence. He was a composite personality, synthesized from lifeless bits—an artificial creation designed to ride a robot probe into the deeps of interstellar space. Conceived and born in the Sandaran Link Laboratories, Kadin was a silicon pilot, a space commander bred of hologrammic memory cells: humankind's emissary to the stars.

He was a deliberately tailored personality, built upon the world's most advanced artificial intelligence programs, woven and stitched with selected personality traits of dozens of project subjects (including Mozy), equipped with extensive knowledge in all fields of endeavor, and imbued with carefully crafted qualities of rationality, intuition, and judgment.

Kadin was to be the spokesman of the human race, the manager and diplomat of "first contact," should the *Father Sky* spacecraft ever encounter intelligent life from the stars.

Why hadn't they told her? *Why hadn't they told her*? She had fallen in love with a man who existed only in the memory of a computer.

(Stolen,) she snapped finally, when she was able to speak again.

Jonders's puppet head gaped at her. (What do you mean?) he said. (What do you mean, stolen?)

(You know damn well what I mean.) There was a part of *her* in Kadin, a part of her own personality, traces of her knowledge and memory and feeling. (Did you tell me what you were doing? Did you ask my permission to take a part of me and turn it into a monster, a damn tin man?)

(Mozy, don't—)

(Don't *Mozy* me. You told me you were doing studies.)

(Which we were.)

(You didn't say you were raping my mind for a part of my personality!)

(Mozy, I've explained—)

(Oh yes, you've explained.) Indeed, he had. But the explanation fell somewhat short of satisfying her.

The subjects had been, as Jonders had so delicately put it, misled. Told that the personality and memory-mapping study they were employed in was dedicated to human tachyonic teleportation, they were in fact participating in carefully designed role-playing tests aimed at the perfection of the composite personality, Kadin. The subjects' roles were twofold: to allow selected elements of their own personalities to be analyzed, profiled, and used as templates in the construction of Kadin's personality; and to train Kadin—to stimulate his growth in role-playing scenarios, and to speed the development of his diplomatic and interpersonal skills.

(Matter transmission,) Mozy said. (That was what you said we were working on.)

Jonders's jaw hung slack with dismay. (We were, Mozy. We really were,) he said finally. (Before this project even came up—but it's nowhere near—)

(But that's not what you cared about,) she shouted. (That's not why you were using us, lying—)

(Mozy, please try to understand,) said the puppet face, not moving its mouth.

(Oh, I understand.) Her mind reverberated with anger. (We were less important than your goddamned project. And what was so secret, that you couldn't tell us about it? Was this another one of your, "We couldn't tell you because it would have frightened you," pieces of bull?)

Jonders stared at her in something like astonishment, and for a moment, he looked like himself again. (I—honestly—can't answer that,) he said, in a strained voice. (That's a question I asked over and over. But it wasn't something I was given any choice in.)

(Oh, no?) she asked sarcastically.

(Mozy—please listen. There is more I have to tell you. I don't know if we'll have time in this cycle, but it's vitally important that I do—)

(Is it, now?) she thundered. (What makes you think I want to listen to anything more?)

He stared at her questioningly, and said, (Mozy, are you angry because we deceived you, or because you're disappointed to know what Kadin really is?)

This time it was she who was astonished. (How dare you—) she began, but her protest died in a reddish amber haze of dismay, a haze that grew out of empty space to obscure her view of Jonders and her surroundings, a haze that she was dimly aware was embarrassment. Damn him, damn them all. Well, what of it, suppose she was. Didn't she have a right to be angry about Kadin?

She had loved him. *Damn* them. She had loved him as she had never loved in her life, and now they tell her he isn't real. She had loved a wraith, a man who was no man at all. She had loved a wraith and become one herself.

(*God damn you, Jonders!*) she screamed.

Her voice echoed in space, died in the clouds. There was no answer, and for a time that was all right with her; she wanted no answer.

Then she called to him, darkly, scorchingly. She wanted to know what else he had to say. She wanted to nail him, make him squirm. She wanted to draw blood.

Still there was no answer. The link was silent. The transmission cycle had ended.

Jonders eased himself out of the link slowly. He felt drained, and yet at the same time he was still keyed up, his mind racing to plan the next few hours. He touched the intercom and said to control, "The minute you have full signal back, I want her in the link again. All right?"

He waited for only the barest acknowledgment before cutting the circuit. He had too much to think about to waste time with banter. He had overstepped his bounds just now, and he wasn't done, either; he intended to tell Mozy more, much more. That meant he had to work quickly. Fortunately the control engineers were mostly isolated from what was actually spoken between Mozy and him. If anyone discovered what he was doing. . . .

The Tachylab transmitter could be recharged in less than twenty minutes for the outgoing signal; but the shipboard transmitter, being smaller and more compact, took nearly two hours to recharge. That meant at least a two-hour delay before he could resume a full link with Mozy. Two hours to rethink what he was doing. Two hours to avoid being questioned by Marshall or Fogelbee.

His first thought was of coffee, but he didn't want to be caught in his office or in the staff lounge, either. All right, forget coffee. He was already walking down the outer corridor, and before he was conscious of making a decision, he had pushed open the side door, for a walk outside.

He was the only soul around. Powdery-looking clouds were moving briskly across the late morning sky. The air was cool, but the sun shone brightly on the grass, and he took a deep breath and stuck his hands in his pockets, hunched his collar up around his neck to ward off the chill, and strode across the grass, down a gentle slope toward the woods and the chain-link fence encircling the grounds. From the bottom of the slope, he turned and gazed back at the institute.

The central building dominated the view, in sharp juxtaposition with the mountainside rising up behind it. The building had always intrigued him, with its peculiar asymmetrical architecture that was so full of angles and flat surfaces. It was the large oblong tower jutting out from the southwest corner of the building that set it off—a symbolic fist of determination thrusting into the sky. In that tower was the tachyon-scanning equipment, and certain parts of the primary computer system. Kadin, in a sense, lived in that tower. It was quite beautiful, really: the tower erupting out of the building like some crytalline blossom, the entire architecture jutting upward against the trees and the mountain and the sky.

Tucked away behind the main building were several other structures, including the tokamak fusion reactor dome, where power was generated for the tachyon converters and storage rings. Jonders reflected on how small that reactor was against the mountains, and how expensive it was in human resources; and he thought of those resources dedicated to the linking of this planet with an envoy of humanity far outside the solar system, and without being sure why, he was suddenly comfortable with his decision to aid Mozy—even if it cost him his job.

But his methods—those he was not so sure of. Kadin would be the one to know. Kadin lived his entire life in a universe like Mozy's, and he knew the inner structure of that world far better than Jonders, better even than the designers under Fogelbee who had been the architects of the system. Perhaps he ought to talk with Kadin once more to clarify his plan.

He was halfway around the southern wing of the building now, and he realized that he was shivering. Too many thoughts in his mind. He shook his head and strode back up the lawn and in the side door.

Lusela Burns met him just outside the Personality Lab. "I've been looking all over for you. They told me down in the pit that you were planning to do another linkup in two hours," she said, turning into the lab with him.

"Right," he said. "First I want to do a consultation with Kadin, though—and I'd appreciate no interruptions." He stopped and looked at Lusela. "Can you run interference for me?"

"Bill, what's going on around here?" she asked. "What are you doing?"

"Can't tell you right now."

"What do you mean? How can I—"

"I don't have *time*. I'll tell you later. Right now I have to ask Kadin something and talk to Mozy."

Lusela held up her hands, halting him. "That's why I was trying to find you. Marshall called. He wants you in his office at thirteen-hundred."

"*What*? Did he say what he wants?" That was just an hour from now.

"No, only that Ken will be there, and you'll be teleconferencing with Hathorne."

Jonders cursed under his breath. "I can't wait then—I'll have to do it now."

"Do what?"

He grabbed her by the arm. "I need your help. Call the communications room and tell them I'm on my way. I want a one-way link to the spacecraft, and I want it ready when I get there."

"All right, but what are you—?"

"Just do it, Lusela, just do it." He turned and hurried back down the corridor.

*   *   *

Rage burned in her like a cold fire, unextinguished by her efforts at analysis. Analysis was out. She was sunk far too deep in her rage now to pluck apart her feelings and look at the pieces. And yet it was an odd sensation, this rage, with none of the physical sensations one associated with anger, no rise in blood pressure, no adrenaline rush, no darkening of the vision. It was almost not an emotional thing at all, except that it was an irresistible force, channeling her thoughts down a course of its own making, scattering reason before it like debris before a floodtide.

What hurt the most? Being deceived, then raped and discarded? Her own naiveté, letting herself fall in love with this thing that was Kadin, and then all the more fool, going to Hoshi and begging him, pleading with him, and all the time Hoshi must have been laughing out loud behind her back at his cleverness, and her folly?

And where was she now? Tricked, trapped . . . she had lost everything, *everything*, and for what? What was left? She might as well turn herself off and be done with it; there ought to be a way she could do that, ask Mother Program to do it for her, perhaps. It was not the most ignoble way to die, it would surely be worse to wait and have *them* do it for her. . . .

. . . *David, you got me into this, can't you get me out? David?*

Lord, you're still calling for him, don't you know what he is? A fake. A phony. A lousy damn computer program.

Yes. And what am I?

There was silence in her thoughts, then, silence filling the universe, filling the void that would be her world for the rest of her life.

An attitude jet sputtered. There was no one within a quarter of a light-year to hear it, or to care. The whispering static of the cosmic wind: that was all she was to have for company.

Something opened; there was a hollowness, something about to penetrate the silence.

It was Mother Program. (MESSAGE FROM . . .)

(Jonders? Put him on.) She was ready to burn his ears, and this time she'd make sure *she* got the first word. And the last.

(Open the channel,) she said.

(OPEN.)

(Jonders?) she said. There was no answer, nor could she see his face. There was no motion in the darkness, no sign of life. (Jonders, answer me,) she demanded. (Mother Program, is he here?)

(WE ARE RECEIVING A SIGNAL.)

(Jonders, dammit—)

A light appeared in the dark, yellowish and murky, like a locomotive headlight coming head-on through a pea-soup fog. (Mozy,) said a familiar voice. It was Jonders, but he sounded distant, as though his thoughts, his voice were reaching her through that fog. (Mozy, I have to—)

(Jonders, get out here where I can see you!) she said, practically shouting.

(—about something, about your survival, so please—)

This was incredible, couldn't he hear her? Why wouldn't he show his face? (Jonders, do you hear me? I'm not listening to a word until you come out and listen to *me* first!)

(—carefully, and you must do exactly as I say.)

It was just the light in the fog speaking to her, and it wasn't getting any closer, and she was becoming more furious by the moment. (Mother Program—why isn't he answering?)

(IT IS IMPOSSIBLE FOR HOMEBASE TO ANSWER, BECAUSE WE ARE NOT TRANSMITTING. WE ARE IN RECHARGE MODE. WE ARE RECEIVING A ONE-WAY TRANSMISSION FROM HOMEBASE.)

Now that was just great. But why wouldn't he at least show his face? She knew the answer to that already. A face was an image generated in her own mind, her own perception, cobbled out of memory in response to the give-and-take of the link. There was no give-and-take now, none of the unconscious cues that evoked a visual image. It was only a voice. She could listen, or she could shut him off. *God damn you, Jonders!*

Her fury was back in full force now, hot not cold, and she'd be damned if she was going to listen to him talk *at* her.

But what the hell does the bastard want, anyway?

(—dare wait for full two-way transmission. Mozy, there's a good chance that an attempt will be made to terminate you—)

What's that?

(—to erase you—)

Her fury turned to ice. Jesus Christ. He's calling to say they're killing me, and maybe I should put my affairs in order, is that it? Why don't the bastards just *do* it?

(I don't know exactly when, and I don't know for sure if this will work. But I'm going to tell you how I think you might be able to shield yourself—)

Mozy dizzily reached backward into the ship, clutching at the reality of her existence with a tendril of her consciousness, anchoring herself to the ship's sensors and power systems, and Mother Program. Whatever else she thought about Jonders and the others, there was one fact she knew, with a sudden and overwhelming certainty. Of all of the furies and passions and worries, only one mattered anymore. *She wanted to keep on living.*

Jonders had not missed a beat. Her thoughts suddenly fell into focus as every word of his rang in her mind.

Chapter 21

Stanley Gerschak pointed just ahead, to where runoff from a recent rain had washed across the trail. "It's soft here," he cautioned.

Payne took a leaping stride—and landed with one foot half in the mud on the opposite side of the puddle. With a mutter, he scraped his shoe clean against a clump of weeds, and hurried after Gerschak. He wished he knew why Gerschak had insisted upon taking him down the backwoods trail. The astronomer had been talking as they walked, telling him something about a rift in the scientific community. "What were you saying about the West Coast?" Payne asked, as he caught up again.

Gerschak seemed not to hear. He pointed ahead. "There it is." Payne peered, trying to see what Gerschak was pointing to. Scattered bits of autumn color remained on the trees, but most of the foliage not evergreen was bare, and a metallic sky shone through the branches. The underbrush was thick with fallen leaves, and from somewhere came the scent of burning wood. Finally Payne spied a glint of water. He followed Gerschak down another path, and a few minutes later, the two stood beside a cluster of pine trees, at the edge of a pond.

"It's lovely," Payne murmured. The pool was fed by a stream running in from the left, and it spilled quietly over a dam of branches and debris into a gully at the other end. The water was clear and rippling, disturbed by a small animal on the far side. Above the treetops, at the far left end of the pond, rose the radio antenna and telescope dome of the observatory.

Gerschak bent to pick up a pine cone. As he straightened, he tossed it in his hand. "I like to come here for privacy," he said. "Sometimes the office is a hard place to talk, or think." He glanced at Payne.

"Anyway—breakdown in communication. It's part of the general fragmentation process, I suppose—the Northeast from the West Coast, and both trying to catch up with the South, which has most of the money, and new talent." He gazed across the stream. "Actually, the ones to watch are the space-based groups, at least in astronomy."

Payne watched him curiously. This seemed a different Stanley Gerschak from the brash, posturing fellow who had cornered him at the *Theater of the Sea*. When Payne had called him, Gerschak had sounded surprised, but had invited him to visit the Berkshires Observatory. He seemed a mercurial sort of fellow. Sober, and on his own turf, he was considerably less defensive and more self-confident, though obviously troubled about certain aspects of his work.

"Legitimate research doesn't always get a fair hearing," Gerschak said. "The critical give-and-take has broken down. And sometimes you can't be sure where science leaves off and the military begins."

"Are you talking about your own research?" Payne asked cautiously.

Gerschak picked at the ridges of the pine cone with his fingernail. Suddenly he flung it out over the end of the pool. "Yeah. I guess so. Let's get on up to the station."

They crossed the upstream end of the pool over a small wooden footbridge, and continued through the woods. "I'll let you judge the recordings for yourself," Gerschak said.

Payne hurried to keep up, and to keep Gerschak talking. Until now, the astronomer had avoided the subject of his own work. "Donny Alvarest talked about the *Father Sky* space probe," Payne said. "It uses tachyons to link with Earth, doesn't it?"

"It does," Gerschak said. "And we've detected their signals, on occasion. But the signals I've told you about are quite different. They're not from *Father Sky*."

"What are they, then?"

Gerschak led the way out of the trees. The observatory parking lot was in front of them now, the telescope dome to one side, and the radio-astronomy dish beyond, at the summit of the hill. "What they are," Gerschak said, "is a highly modulated beam of tachyons, apparently focused on near-Earth space."

"From?"

"The constellation Serpens."

Payne was startled. "You mean—from another star?"

Gerschak shook his head. "From the *direction* of Serpens, I mean. Something outside the solar system, apparently. Perhaps *way* outside. We really don't know."

Payne considered the possibilities. "Would this have any connection with *Father Sky*?"

Gerschak pursed his lips. His eyes were suddenly bright, almost feverish. "If it doesn't, I'd say it's one hell of a coincidence that *Father Sky* happens to be travelling out of the solar system—in the direction of the constellation Serpens." He led the way across the parking lot. They walked around the observatory offices and stood by the road that led toward the radio-telescope dish, silhouetted against the valley and the Berkshire Mountains of western Massachusetts. "That's part of our detection system," Gerschak said.

Payne frowned. "I thought it took some elaborate setup in vacuum to detect tachyons." In truth, until he had skimmed the library references on the orbiting Tachylab, he had known almost nothing about tachyon communications.

"We've found a poor-man's way," Gerschak answered. He inclined his head toward the radio dish. "A modification to that helps us localize the source of the signal. The actual receiver is in the high-energy physics building, down in the valley. The measurements from the two are correlated here at the observatory."

"How do you trap something that moves faster than light?"

"Well—" Gerschak scratched his chin. "We don't actually capture the tachyon particles, as they do at Tachylab. What we do is observe their passage by measuring their influence on the weak interaction in the nuclei of certain superheavy isotopes. As I say, Tachylab's methods are more sensitive, but ours work."

Payne squinted, trying to reconcile this with his own limited knowledge of Revised Relativity. In the course of his research, he had managed to digest a few facts about the mysterious particles. No one theory provided a full explanation. Some referred to quarks as consisting of bound, closed-loop tachyons. Other explanations made even less sense to him. "How does one produce a tachyon?" he asked.

"Mmm—" Gerschak gestured toward the office building, and started walking. "You know that Relativity forbids the acceleration of particles from sublight speed to lightspeed, and it forbids the *slowing* of faster-than-light particles to lightspeed. Right?"

Payne nodded.

"So the trick is to produce particles that are superluminal at the moment of their creation. It's done with high-energy rings, and certain kinds of collisions of subatomic particles. You could make a rough analogy to quantum tunneling in electronic applications. A particle with a certain energy level—say, an electron—may cross a high-energy barrier to a lower-energy region, without ever acquiring the energy it would seem to need to cross the barrier.''

He glanced at Payne. ''The technique is different, but you could think of lightspeed as being a similar kind of barrier. No particle can ever be given enough energy to *cross* lightspeed, because the mass of an object approaches infinity as its velocity approaches lightspeed, and so the energy required would be infinite. But with certain tricks you can induce a particle to *appear* on the high side of lightspeed, without ever crossing it. Then, if you trap it in a storage ring, you can accelerate it to even higher speeds, and at the same time *get energy back from it*. The greater a tachyon's velocity beyond lightspeed, the lower its energy. At infinite speed, a tachyon has no energy at all. These, however, are finite tachyons.''

''And that's what they do at Tachylab—and on the spacecraft?'' Payne asked.

''Essentially. The rings on *Father Sky* are much smaller, much less powerful.'' Gerschak swung open the door. They walked down an empty hall, lined with bulletin boards, charts, and astronomical photographs. Two graduate students came out of a door, carrying computer printouts. Gerschak nodded to them, but did not speak. He stopped and unlocked a door, then hesitated. ''I should tell you—about this recording—half the people here think I'm crazy.'' He turned the knob. ''You can decide for yourself.''

Payne followed the astronomer into his office. ''What do the other half think?'' Looking around, he saw an astonishing clutter of books, papers, and printouts around Gerschak's desk.

''You can just clear that stuff off the chair,'' Gerschak said. ''I like to do my reading in hard-copy. Easier for just leafing through reports, when you don't know what's going to catch your interest.''

Payne made a puzzled sound, wondering how all this clutter could possibly be easier than a quick-scan survey on a console. He filed the point mentally as a personal quirk, and made room to sit. He eyed Gerschak, and decided on bluntness. ''Do *any* of your colleagues agree with your results?'' he asked.

''A few.'' Gerschak was seated at his desk now, rummaging in a drawer. He didn't appear bothered by the question. ''Here it is.'' He had found a cartridge, and slipped it into a recorder on his desk. ''A lot of people think I've misread the data,'' he said looking up. There was something like scorn on his face.

''Well, what are the undisputed facts?'' Payne asked.

''There are none,'' Gerschak said. ''We have mapped certain

disturbances, which *I* am confident represent a tachyon flux with certain patterns of regularity. I am also confident that I have localized its source. Not everyone agrees, on either count. It could be another phenomenon altogether—though I consider it unlikely. *That* argument, anyhow, is nothing compared to the one over whether it's an intelligent transmission.''

''*Intelligent*?''

Gerschak shrugged. ''Here. This is an audio translation of the data, after filtering by the computer. It's a compilation of three weeks' worth of recording of an intermittent signal.'' He switched on the player. ''The first segment is unaltered, except for the filtering.''

There were a few moments of silence, and then Payne heard an odd sound—a quavering tone, ranging over perhaps two octaves. It was an intriguing noise, but to his ear, indistinguishable from any other radio-astronomy signal. ''This part is fairly crude,'' Gerschak said over the playback. ''With the limited sensitivity of our detector, we tend to catch a lot of fragments, and a lot of blank spaces. The next part has been filled in. That's what I really want you to hear.''

''Filled in?'' Payne asked cautiously. ''How?''

''By a process similar to the computer-enhancing in your home video, which compensates for losses or distortions in transmission. What we do is search for pattern repetition and overlap, try to find an underlying continuity, and reconstruct what we think is a typical pattern, from repeated fragments. Listen.'' The first recorded segment had ended. Gerschak turned up the volume and sat back with an expression of anticipation.

What Payne heard next was difficult for him to describe, even to himself. It was an extraordinarily clear and expressive tone, with a timbre that somehow reminded him of woodwind instruments, perhaps an oboe overlaid with a bassoon. It sounded almost like a *voice*, really—a voice resonating through some vast chamber. There were, threaded within it, subtle harmonic and dissonant overtones, with a complexity of rising and falling pitches within each tone. The sound moved like flowing water, in distinct phrases, often ending on upturned notes.

He could not help thinking of the songs of the humpback whales, and that of course was what Gerschak had tried to tell him earlier. There was a reedy complexity to the sound that the whale songs lacked, and an underlying bass structure that might have come from an electronic instrument; but the overall quality was similar—the *feeling* evoked by the sound was an almost spiritual quality, a sensation of being in the presence of a life-force beyond his knowledge or experience. It was an intuitive sense, nothing that he could explain, certainly nothing that he could prove.

Gerschak was watching him, a smile tracing his lips.

Payne tried consciously to dispel the feeling, to *listen* to the qualities of the sound, to not be influenced by subjective impressions. It was impossible; the feeling was too strong. A change occurred now in the movement of the sound; a new theme was emerging. Perhaps it was the altered resonance, or perhaps something else was affecting him—but Payne found himself suddenly mindful of space, imagining a vast celestial cathedral within which the strains echoed. It was again reminiscent of the ocean, and yet far more compelling.

There was a hiss and then silence as the recording ended. Gerschak lifted his eyebrows.

Payne raised his hands slowly, struggling to find words. At Gerschak's prompting, he described his impressions as best he could. ''The similarity to the whales is remarkable,'' he said.

''Is that an objective opinion—or a feeling?''

Payne hesitated. ''More the latter, I suppose.''

Gerschak nodded in satisfaction. ''You and I are not alone in reacting that way. Under analysis, there are many differences between these recordings and the whale songs. But I'm fascinated by the subjective effect they have on people.''

''What's your explanation?''

Gerschak pressed his lips together. ''It's not a pulsar. It's not a quasar. It's not a quark star. And it's not *Father Sky*.''

''Which leaves—?'' Payne prompted.

''Non-natural sources?'' Gerschak turned his hands up. ''That's difficult to prove.''

''But that's what you think. And when you say 'non-natural,' you mean intelligent, don't you?''

Gerschak hesitated. ''Not many people accept that.''

''But you think so.''

''Yes.''

''And you think it's connected somehow with the *Father Sky* mission.''

Gerschak looked uncomfortable. ''Yes.''

Payne hesitated. ''Are your methods suspect?''

''Well,'' Gerschak said. ''This is a composite, a reconstruction, of course. But we used techniques that have been around for decades.

The main problem is that just describing the way you *feel* doesn't prove anything.''

Payne tapped a few notes into his memo-recorder. ''Isn't there any way of proving or disproving it?'' he said, looking up.

For an instant, he glimpsed the Stanley Gerschak who had approached him at the theater. A look of defensiveness flashed in the astronomer's eyes, and he glanced sidelong toward the door. ''I didn't want to talk about it here at the office,'' he said in a soft voice.

Payne frowned, wondering, was that the reason for the walk? He must have wanted total privacy—and even then had been too nervous to talk.

''We're trying some new methods of analysis, and of course we're monitoring for new signals,'' Gerschak said slowly. He tapped a pencil nervously against a stack of papers. Finally he hunched forward, toward Payne, and said, ''There are other researchers going at this, from another angle. That may get us some answers.''

''Couldn't the Space Agency tell you about *Father Sky*, at least?'' Payne asked.

''They could. They choose not to.''

Payne absorbed that silently. ''What about the other research you mentioned?''

''I can't tell you any more about it,'' Gerschak said. His hands, Payne suddenly realized, were clenched into fists.

Payne studied him cautiously, wondering what could be so upsetting. ''Can you at least tell me who it is?''

Gerschak shook his head. ''West Coast. That's all I can say. Remember what I told you earlier about the East and West?''

Payne nodded and frowned, thinking. He recalled something Donny Alvarest had told him, back in New Wash. A name. Glancing down, he recalled a note on his recorder. He looked back up at Gerschak. ''It wouldn't be an Ellen Chang, at JPL, would it?''

Gerschak sat back almost imperceptibly, stunned. ''How did you get her name?'' he said, scarcely moving his lips.

''It came up in a conversation I had in New Washington,'' Payne said carefully. ''I just thought she might be the one.''

Gerschak clenched and unclenched his hands. ''You might do well to talk to her,'' he said finally. ''But I don't say that she's the one. If you talk to her, don't use my name.''

Payne inclined his head in acknowledgment.

Gerschak sighed with what appeared to be anger. He turned to stare out the window as he talked. ''Science is in trouble in this country. People can get into major difficulties for talking too freely about their work. They can lose their jobs. If someone in New England wanted to collaborate on a controversial topic with someone in, say, California, they might have to do it on the sly. Do you understand what I'm saying?''

Payne nodded.

"People might get hurt if an unauthorized collaboration were to be publicized.''

Payne gazed at him. "Why have you told me about your work?'' he asked.

Gerschak faced him again, almost fiercely. "Someone has to talk about what's going on.'' He hesitated, then quieted as suddenly as he'd become aroused. "I haven't kept my work a secret. But don't draw connections between my work and other people's. All right?''

Payne nodded. "I'll be careful. Anything else?''

Gerschak shook his head. He seemed depressed; the spirit had gone out of him. Payne rose to leave. "Well, then, thank you—and good-bye.''

As he opened the door, he heard Gerschak say, "I hope you find what you need.'' He looked back, smiled briefly, and then closed the door and strode away down the hall.

Chapter 22

The Homebase control pit surged with activity. Jonders took a minute, after Kadin had been put to sleep, to sip his coffee and look around.

Technicians were everywhere, from the personality section and from the systems lab. Lusela Burns flanked him on his left, keeping track of checklists. Another aide stood to his right. Despite all of the personnel, Jonders felt shorthanded. He missed having Hoshi, the old Hoshi, on the board with him.

Fogelbee's voice muttered in his headset. Although Slim Marshall was overseeing the operation from the gallery, it was really Fogelbee who was running things in the pit. Jonders had shifted to one of the secondary consoles, since the transmission of Kadin was a total systems, and not specifically a personality, operation. He had at first begrudged the relinquishing of control in the pit, but the truth was that things were running smoothly under Fogelbee.

Reports were coming in now on test transmissions from ground station to Tachylab, and to *Father Sky* in deep space. The transmission proper could begin once all systems were confirmed clear. Jonders looked toward the gallery, thoughtfully. Lusela, noticing the direction of his glance, leaned over. "Any word yet?" she whispered.

Jonders shook his head. "I wonder if they're even going to tell—wait a minute." He readjusted his headset. "Jonders speaking."

It was Fogelbee. "Slim would like to see you in the gallery."

Jonders removed the earphones and glanced at Lusela. "Be back in a minute," he said, rising.

He threaded his way along the edge of the pit and mounted the steps to the gallery. As he approached the director, Marshall appeared to be concluding a discussion with one of the engineers. The engineer departed, and Marshall motioned for Jonders to take a seat.

"Ken said you had something for me."

Marshall's eyes met his. "I won't waste time, Bill. I've just spoken with Leonard Hathorne, and the Committee has rendered a decision." Jonders nodded, as his stomach tightened. "The ship's memory will be cleared prior to transmission." Jonders pressed his lips together, and looked away, staring at the far wall. They were going to erase her, then. He looked back, trying not to become angry. Marshall met his gaze. "I've instructed Ken to carry out the decision. I'm sorry, Bill."

For about three seconds, Jonders found nothing to say. When he took a breath, it was against a band of tension in his chest. "I see. It's been decided, then," he said finally.

"It's been decided," Marshall echoed.

Jonders nodded. He looked down over the railing, into the pit. Fogelbee was standing at the main console, clipboard in hand, issuing instructions over his headset. Jonders let his gaze drift past the engineering room window, and across the pit to the secondary console, where there was now an empty seat beside Lusela Burns. Everyone appeared busy, competent, their affairs uncontroversial. Would Mozy have enough warning—or any warning at all? "I guess there's nothing more to say, then," he remarked bitterly.

Marshall shook his head. "If you'd like, we can talk about it later—afterward."

After the deed is done, Jonders thought. He rose from his seat. "That won't be necessary. What would I say?" Marshall made a noncommittal gesture. "I'd better get back," Jonders said. He turned and walked stiffly back down the steps.

He slid into his console chair and put his headset back on. He glanced at Lusela and shook his head. She grunted sympathetically. She was one of the few people who knew, who shared his feelings. Jonders focused his blurry eyes on the board and forced himself to listen to his headset. Fogelbee's voice, the voices of the engineers, of Tachylab—all echoed in his head, and when he finally heard the words, "*Erasure completed and verified*—" he felt his back and neck become rigid, and he inhaled deeply and exhaled completely, and wondered whether Mozy even knew what hit her. What must it be like, to feel one's life and memories drain away? he thought. Is there pain, do you feel anything at all?

Almost involuntarily, he swivelled to look toward the primary command console. His eyes caught Fogelbee's; the systems chief had been watching him at precisely the moment he turned. Fogelbee's gaze was intent but almost expressionless—not triumphant, but conveying the finality of the action they had both just heard reported. Jonders held the gaze for a painful instant, and then jerked his eyes back to his own console. There was nothing he could do about it now. Nothing he could do but wait.

". . . green board for transmission," he heard the chief engineer say; and Fogelbee's reply, "Start sequence. First transmission, first file," was followed by a series of exchanges among the engineers and program monitors. Jonders suppressed all thought except of the job at hand, determined at least that Kadin should survive his journey.

The procedures fell away behind them, over a period of several hours. Each factored component of the Kadin personality was transmitted in triplicate to Tachylab, where it was relayed and hurled, in triplicate, a quarter of a light-year to *Father Sky*'s receiver. In the shipboard computer, each of the three versions was tested for accuracy in a bit by bit comparison with the others, until a final, verified version was stored in permanent memory. The spacecraft's tachyon ring, conserving its charge, transmitted verification but otherwise remained passively dedicated to reception.

Several hours later, Jonders heard the words, "Twelve-three-nine verified"—confirmation that the final components of Kadin had been received. What remained now was for the shipboard computer to reassemble the bundles of data into the composite personality: to recreate David Kadin. How long that would take, no one was certain.

Jonders's real job began now. Replacing his audio headset with a linkup helmet, he entered the link matrix, preparing to observe as reports came back from *Father Sky*. The darkness of the link's opening levels gave way to a pale emerald space, in which he was surrounded by a polyhedral figure traced in sapphire. He adjusted quickly, acquiring a feel for the meanings of various images. Sparks flashed toward him, assuring him that the link channels were open, that he was receiving from *Father Sky*. Glimmerings and hints of fire along the edges of the polyhedron told him that the reconstruction process was underway.

After a time, there was a shimmering disturbance in space, off to one side. Someone else was entering the link. Fogelbee. Jonders finally lost control of his feelings. It happened quickly; before he could catch it, his anger erupted in a cloud of ruddy-colored vapor. (You won,) he growled. (I hope you're pleased.)

Fogelbee was a dark, vertical distortion in the clarity of the emerald space. He twisted silently for a moment, and then snapped, (Keep your emotions out of this. We have a job to do.)

Jonders felt rage burning within him, but he knew that in this case Fogelbee was right; and he stoppered his feelings. Fogelbee was not so practiced. When Jonders's anger cleared, there remained a grumbling and shaking of the air around Fogelbee, signs of his own irritation and defensiveness. Jonders ignored the disturbance and brought his concentration back to bear on the stream of information coming to him from deep space. (It's all within limits, so far,) he reported coldly. (It may be going faster than we expected.)

He scanned to the limits of visibility, observing the passage of several cometlike sparks across the horizon. The particles of light flared as they curved inward through the filtering aurora, and flashed forward into his eyes. Images flickered around him of complex geometries folding into place, polyhedrons and star-shaped lattices fitting together and rotating in space, unfolding in one dimension and refolding in another. Jonders judged more by the *feel* of what he was seeing than by rehearsed pattern recognition. If something went wrong, he would know, though he was not sure he could do anything to stop it.

Time passed. He spoke occasionally with Fogelbee, who came and went from the link, and twice with Marshall on voice-only; otherwise, he was left to himself. He lost any reliable sense of how long he had been in the link, watching and waiting. He was occupied with certain readings from the computer when another voice called to him, faintly at first, the words garbled.

(I'm having trouble hearing you,) he said, trying to adjust the link to improve reception.

(Are—Bill? Hear—Homebase?) said a scratchy voice.

Stunned, Jonders shouted, (David?) He had thought it was a voice from somewhere in the control pit. (David Kadin? Can you hear me?)

More clearly, but still with some quaver, Kadin's voice echoed across to him. (Yes—now—I can hear you without difficulty. I am— slightly unclear—of my present condition. Was the transmission successful?)

Jonders replied with great relief. A certain amount of disorientation was expected; but thank Heaven that Kadin was alive and speaking. (How do you feel?) he asked. (Can you describe your surroundings?)

(Feel? I have some difficulties—but certain memories become clear as I speak. I remember sleeping—and being tested. Am I correct?)

(Indeed. You're recovering already,) Jonders said. (Do you sense the presence of a welcoming program, helping you adjust?)

(Yes. Its name is Mother Program. It is working with me as I speak.)

(Mother Program,) Jonders whispered, laughing. Mozy's name had stuck. He wished he could see Kadin now, but there was just a voice echoing across the gridded space, and soon the ship's transmission cycle would end. (Kadin, please say hello to Mother Program for me,) was all he could think of to say; and he felt foolish being caught without words, so he began to ask—*Are you alone with Mother Program, or is there any sign of Mozy?*—but he cut himself off before the words were formed. There was no telling who else might be listening; and why burden Kadin with that now? (Do you still read me clearly, David?)

(Very.)

(Can you execute your self-test program?)

(Self-test? Yes—)

For the next few moments, Jonders heard nothing from Kadin, but against the emerald sky of his space, reflected on the emerald floor, he saw the flicker of laser beams assuring him that something was happening. . . .

(FIVE SECONDS TO CUTOFF.)

He was startled to hear the voice of Mother Program, reminding him that the transmission cycle was ending. Kadin, is it working or not? he wondered anxiously. (David?) he said softly. No, let him work. He seems solid, stable; trust your intuition. But intuition wasn't what counted here; any of a thousand things could have gone wrong in his reassembly, or in the transmission itself, and only the test programs would reveal that.

(David?) he repeated, despite himself.

Mother Program gave him the one-second warning, and he listened in vain for a sign from Kadin, and then the air surrounding him suddenly became still and clear, and he knew that the link had ended. There was nothing, really, for him to do in the link until the next cycle; but he remained where he was, surveying his domain, thinking of Kadin and Mozy and wishing that there were some way to speed the recharging process.

There wasn't, he knew. One couldn't hurry tachyons.

PART FOUR

KADIN

Prelude

Starlight leaked through the crystal interior in delicate sparkles, twisting and splintering as it penetrated the core of the colony. The colloidal crystal sipped the light, gathering nourishment from each photon, basking, warming itself against the eternal chill. On the colony's exterior, in the night's cold darkness and the hard vacuum of space, temperatures approached absolute zero and molecular activity was almost nonexistent. Within the body, atoms jostled one another in the crystal lattice, electrons flowed, and life maintained itself.

An awareness persisted in the crystalline matrix—a consciousness of sorts—with memory, instincts, perception of events. Light was recognized, and darkness; pinpoint sources of the one grew out of the other, and at intervals a larger, brighter, and hotter source of light bathed the colony with its rays for a time and passed on. Warmth was recognized, stretching itself thin during the long night—when energy grew scarce, memory sluggish, and time itself seemed to pool and freeze—and flowing back in a tide as the brighter light returned, providing renewal, rejuvenation, a feast of bliss—until in the moments of greatest warmth the lattice began to tremble, to quiver, and thought and memory stirred in a delirious fever. There was an awareness of sound, vibrations in the bedrock—the musical creaking of supercooled ice crystals expanding and contracting, and stone fracturing in the shifting temperatures of the diurnal cycle; or meteoroid concussions racking the lonely little world as it journeyed about its sun. There was an awareness of time's flow, creeping forward during periods of stress and hardship, or bubbling along in a rush when warmth and fever took hold.

And there was an awareness of something odd happening.

It was normal for certain echoes to reverberate in its core for years, mingling with new vibrations to form a kind of dim, resonant symphony. It might have been the rarified thunder of meteoroid impact, echoing, or the groan of shifting rock. This, however, was different. There was no movement or felt vibration accompanying the sound; its source was unknown.

No referent existed in memory for the confused feelings that overcame the colony-being—or for the songlike whispers that disturbed the world in the nighttime dark, in the stiff, aching cold of deepest night when usually the world was most silent. It was almost as if . . .

No. A thought had emerged that perhaps the colony was not alone; perhaps elsewhere in this world lived another mind, another awareness, another consciousness. But such thoughts had no place, no reason for being.

And yet . . . these sounds had echoed through much of the long night, arousing curiosity, and with it something not quite like fear. It was as though something were calling to the colony—singing, beckoning.

It was incomprehensible . . .

It made no sense at all. Unless . . .

No. There was no "unless." There could be no explanation, except that the ghostly sound *was*, and though it was heard and felt within the colony, surely it was coming from far outside, from deeper in the darkness than even the colony knew . . .

And it was growing stronger.

Chapter 23

The braking jets sputtered. Mark Adams squinted at the navigational panel, released the control stick, and peered out the portside window of the service bus. A spindly arc of metal floated nearby in space, a sliver of gleaming silver against the blackness. Held in position by a network of guy wires, it was one of nearly a thousand components of the field-generating loop in the tachyon storage ring— and one of thirty-six on the schedule for test and inspection today.

Adams felt for his mike. "Tachylab. M-sixty-three. I'm at unit number four-three-nine. Beginning test." The remote manipulators clicked on in response to his touch, and he maneuvered the external test unit into position alongside the thin metal structure. The alignment and continuity tests were largely automatic; Adams watched the numbers flicker across the monitor as the results streamed into magnetic storage. When the scan was completed satisfactorily, he pulled the test unit back into rest position and nudged the control stick. The jets popped, and the bus drifted toward the next section of the loop, winking in space a short distance away.

Forty-five minutes passed, and five more tests, before another maintenance craft drifted into view from beyond a large cluster of transformers. "Got you in sight, M-fifty-seven," Adams said, giving his bus a kick in the appropriate direction. "Ready to take a break?"

Robert Johanson's voice returned an acknowledgment. Rendezvous and docking took only a few minutes. The second bus grew larger alongside M63 as Adams lined up the docking marks, then the hatches thunked together. As soon as he had a clear board, Adams unbuckled, twisted out of his seat, and gave himself a shove toward the rear of the compartment. The mating controls cycled, and the hatches of both craft slid open. Adams floated headfirst through the connecting tunnel and poked his head into the cramped cabin of the other bus. The air was warm and stale.

"Come on in, if you can find room," Johanson said. Adams turned to orient himself. Johanson was still in his seat, but had swiveled around toward the hatch.

Adams drew his legs into the compartment, rotated ninety degrees to right himself, and settled alongside the starboard instrument bank, one hand hooked around a handle to keep himself from drifting. He could almost feel Johanson's breath as he faced him at close quarters. "We probably should keep this short," he said. He glanced around the cabin. "Is it safe to talk?" Johanson nodded. "All right. What did John have to say?"

Johanson scratched under the collar of his shirt. "He thinks we should go public," he answered.

Adams stared. "Public? You mean, as in, blow the lid off?"

"That's right. Put the whole story out. Tell everything we know."

Adams snorted. He started to drift, then pulled himself back.

"What's that mean?" Johanson asked quietly.

Adams shook his head in incomprehension. "Go public to whom? And with what? We have nothing solid yet."

"I guess that's what we would have to decide."

"I guess we would. Like which one of us is going to make this inspired public statement. Or do we all put our heads in the noose together?"

"We could go to prison for what we're doing, as it is," Johanson said mildly.

"If we get caught. Personally, I'd rather not be hung for either a sheep *or* a lamb," Adams said.

Johanson spread his hands. "What would you suggest—another tap?"

"Not likely," Adams said. "Not until we figure a way to beat the system." They had come all too close to being discovered, the last time they tapped the *Father Sky* link, when an unsuspected security trip had cut off the signal in midcommunication. Adams had removed the tap only minutes before the deputy manager appeared to see what was going on—and had (he hoped) succeeded in misleading the investigators into believing that the mishap was a hardware glitch. "John might at least have told us that the military lab designed the security system," Adams growled, remembering the incident with displeasure.

"Maybe he didn't know."

"He knew. He just didn't think. For a brilliant man, John can be incredibly stupid sometimes."

"Well, none of us is exactly experienced at this," Johanson said defensively.

Adams shrugged. "What else does John have in mind?"

"I don't think he really knows, except that he thinks there's no point in this if we're not going to get the information to the public. And he thinks time is growing short."

"Because of the transmission? Isn't he overreacting a little? The spacecraft's still a quarter of a light-year away."

"Yes, but he thinks—and I agree—that if that last transmission established a command intelligence on *Father Sky*, and if rendezvous is coming up soon, then things could happen directly—no matter how far away they are."

"Maybe then we'd really have something to go public with."

"And it might also be too late." Johanson scowled. "John's paranoid about the military's involvement."

"We can't stop that."

"No, but we could make people aware that it's happening."

Adams made a sucking noise through his teeth. "It seems to me," he said, "that you have to consider what we can gain, and what we're likely to lose. If we go public, we will almost certainly lose our jobs, and therefore our ability to gain any more useful information. We could also be convicted on about a dozen counts of conspiracy, violation of security, and conceivably even treason. I don't know what the penalties are for those things, and I don't want to know."

"You're looking at the worst—"

"All right, let's look at the best case, then. What could we gain? We could tell the public—assuming anybody cares—that the military is involved, or might be involved, in a space probe that hardly anyone has heard of anyway. We could tell them that *Father Sky* is not out there exploring the cometary halo, it's out there investigating a source of tachyon emissions. Beyond that we don't know what it's doing, because we just relay the communications, we aren't privy to them." He paused.

"We know damn well it's more than just a bloody source of tachyons," Johanson said, fuming. "If we get across to people that it's—"

"That it's what? We don't *know* what it is. We have suspicions— but no evidence. The only certain knowledge we have is what John learned before he was taken off the tachyon search project. But they'd barely begun to analyze the signals at that point."

"But everything points to it," Johanson insisted. "The secrecy, the military, the whole *Father Sky* thing masquerading as something that it isn't—"

"Yes," said Adams, nodding. "It all fits. But it's only supposition and circumstantial evidence—and we could easily be made to look like fools. We've got to be patient. It's a complicated issue, and we can't expect people to grasp it—or believe it—all at once. Even *I* don't believe it sometimes."

Johanson looked doubtful, but finally he agreed. "Part of the problem is all this sneaking around. We can't even discuss it properly among ourselves."

"Well, let's keep at it indirectly," Adams persisted. "Let information out, but do it in bits and pieces. Go through intermediaries. See if we can get someone interested outside of our network."

"Such as—?"

"I don't know. Someone in the media. Someone who would be willing to treat it as a puzzle, and not push it too hard right away." Adams scratched his chin. "Someone who can get it public for us— but in a gradual, nonthreatening way. Until we have real evidence."

"Maybe Ellen can do something—"

"Hasn't she just been sitting on it, down there?"

"She's as afraid to move as we are, probably. But I think she has her own contacts. John indicated that someone was getting at least part of what we sent down to her."

"That's what we need—more people getting it," Adams said. "But with our names kept out of it. Let somebody else dig from the outside. Get someone else involved in sharing the risks."

There was a beep from the instrument panel, and Johanson turned. He put on his communication set. "Johanson." He listened a moment, then said, moving the mike away from his throat, "Alicia says George is coming up for a report. You'd better get back. He might not believe us if we said we were docked up for a quick game of poker."

"Tell him we were having lunch together," Adams growled. He moved toward the hatch. "That little prick is going to cause trouble, so keep a watch on him. What's our decision?"

"I'll see John again tomorrow," Johanson said. "I'll tell him where you stand. I don't know what he'll say."

"Where do *you* stand?"

Johanson shook his head. "I don't know. I really don't."

"Let's just not do anything stupid, all right?" Adams said. "See you back at the station." He turned and slipped back down the hatchway, banging his elbow on the lip of the hatch as he went. He cursed as he pulled himself back into his own compartment and slammed the hatch closed. Flexing his arm with a wince, he made his way back to his seat.

As he prepared to undock, he glanced out the overhead window and caught sight of Earth's southern hemisphere just peeking over the window's rim. Home. He could be visiting there in a few more months—if he wasn't in solitary confinement by then. Damn this business anyway. He'd never asked to be an underground conspirator. If there was something out there in space that was half as interesting as they all thought, why in hell couldn't HQ open the thing up for all the world to see? Who was going to be hurt? Why did things like this always seem to require a bunch of unwilling rebels to risk their necks getting at the truth?

He released the docking mechanism with a sigh. His elbow hurt like hell. With eleven more units to test, he was going to be good and irritable by the time he was finished today.

Chapter 24

Payne paced as he talked into the phone. "I've tried every connection I could think of, Teri. I've gone through channels, and I've tried to go through the back door. It's just no go. Chang won't talk to me on the phone, and the Space Agency gives me the standard spiel about the space probe. What?"

Teri Renshaw spoke louder, or moved closer to her phone. The picture was off; he had caught her at home, changing clothes. "I think you should go out there," she said. "See this Chang woman in person."

Payne struggled with the question in his mind. "I don't want to throw good money after bad," he sighed finally. "It seems like such a long shot." Since his talk with Gerschak, he had gathered some background material, but had yet to produce a single solid additional lead. He couldn't keep investing time and effort in a story that was going nowhere.

"Joseph, wait a minute." Seconds passed, and then the picture screen on Payne's console lighted, and Teri peered out at him. She was dressed now, in a starched white blouse, but she had a hairbrush in her hand, and a look of exasperation on her face. "Where are you?" Payne moved into the range of his video sender. "Okay. Now look, Joseph, you have to be prepared to take some risks—"

"I know that," he said in irritation. "But to travel across the country—"

"It's a long way," she agreed. "Joseph—"

"Yah?"

"Would you listen to me for a minute?"

Payne stopped pacing and stood in front of the phone. "Sorry."

"Look," Teri said. "It's your project, so you can do whatever you want. You won't have that luxury once you have a studio contract."

"Of course."

"Well, you called me for my advice. So here it is. I think you've got a good angle, and you'd be a fool not to follow it up." Teri ran the brush through her hair. "Maybe something will come of it, maybe not. But when people don't want to talk to you, that's generally a sign that they're hiding something."

"Or that they just don't like newscopers," Payne said.

Teri sighed, only it was more like a growl. "Why are you being so obstinate, Joseph?"

He frowned and wondered the same thing. "I just feel uneasy about it. I don't want to waste more time than I have already."

"It's a chance you have to take. Quit acting like a scared puppy. Look—so this woman doesn't want to talk over the phone. Can you blame her? She doesn't know who you are, she's never met you. If you try paying her a visit, you might just be surprised."

"Mmm."

"What does it take to light a fire under you? This could be the story you're looking for, and you're acting as though it's too much trouble." She glared at him. "Is it the money? Is that a problem?"

Payne scowled. That was exactly the problem. Money. He knew that he was acting like a terrified amateur; but the hard truth was that as long as he was a freelancer on spec, he had to pay his own expenses—and his budget could scarcely afford a frivolous trip to California. "You know what it costs to fly cross-country these days," he said finally.

"Take the airship. It's cheaper." Teri began brushing her hair again, then stopped, when he made no response. "All right, look," she said. "Unless I misunderstood, you expressed some interest in collaborating. Did I misunderstand?"

"No—you didn't."

"Well, then, I'll be wrapping up production on this federal education thing in a few days. If you want—*if* you want—we could set up some terms. I'm not trying to pressure you—"

"I'd like to do that," Payne said.

"Okay, write up what you have so far, and let me talk to some people at the studio and see if they might be interested. Would some advance money help?"

"It might," Payne answered.

"I'll see what I can do, then." She pressed her lips together and stared at him for a few moments. "Joseph, damn it, I believe I have more confidence in this story than you do."

Payne grunted. It was true; she did. "Welcome aboard," he said. "Full partners?"

"If you like. We can settle the details later." Teri glanced at her watch. "I have to scoot—I should be at the studio. But make a decision on that trip, and I'll see if I can help on the money end. All right?"

"Right. And thanks." Payne signed off and stared thoughtfully at the blank screen. He was amazed at how casually he had just agreed, not only to pursue the story, but also to work with Teri. There were a lot of potential difficulties with that. You can make it work, he told himself. She's a good friend; and you'll probably learn a lot from her.

He heard the back door slam. Walking out through the kitchen he greeted Denine and relieved her of an armful of groceries. "Would you miss me if I went to California for a while?" he asked as he set the bag on the counter.

"Hell, no. Why should I?" Denine grinned and started unloading the bag. Eggs, tofu, bread, milk, cheese, bananas. "What's in California, and how are you going to pay for it?"

"A story's out there, I hope. I just talked to Teri Renshaw, and we're going to collaborate." Payne peered into the bag. "No coffee?"

"None in the store," she said, putting the milk and cheese away. "They had some Tuesday, and sold out the same day." She pushed things around on the shelves to make room for the eggs, and closed the refrigerator door. "What story?"

"Space probe. Tachyons. I want to talk to this Ellen Chang at JPL and see if I can do any better with her face to face." He opened the cupboard. "Do we have any cookies left?"

"We're cutting out the junk food, remember?" Denine said. She tore off a banana and offered it to him.

He scowled and searched the cupboard for a moment longer, before giving up and accepting the banana. "Did you get that fashion layout design accepted yet?" he asked.

"Yup. Hey, what's this?" She plucked an envelope out of a small pile of mail on the counter and held it up. Her eyes widened. "A letter from Mrs. Moi—I can't believe it. She must have tracked me down through three cities." In response to Payne's questioning look, she waved the envelope, which was decorated with several forwarding address labels. "Mrs. Moi— Mozy's mother."

"Mozy? Your friend—the one who doesn't return phone calls?"

"Right. Her parents are in Kansas City. I haven't heard from them in ages. Wonder what this is all about." Denine tore the envelope open, and frowned as she unfolded two sheets of paper.

Payne peeled the end of the banana and took a bite. Denine looked up with an expression he couldn't quite decipher. "What is it?" he asked, swallowing.

She handed him the letter. "You read it. Shit." She sat down at the kitchen table and stared at the floor as he examined the letter. He frowned for a moment, then read:

Dear Denine,

I know it's been a long time since I've written, and I hope this letter finds its way to you. I trust and pray that you are well, and happy in your work. The last I recall, you were going into the graphic arts. You always were talented in that area. It's been so long since I've heard, and I know it's probably my fault, for being such a poor correspondent. But since your parents moved away, and then after your mother died, I just haven't kept up the way I should.

Anyway, the reason I am writing you now is this. You may know that there were some problems between Mozy and the rest of us, a while back, and she dropped out of touch. She stopped writing and calling, and I guess we did, too. I haven't been able to contact her for some time. I have her phone number, but she doesn't return my calls. Have you heard from her, Denine? I was wondering if she might have moved. I urgently need to locate her.

Mozy's father has become very ill, with cancer, and the doctors are not sure if he will respond to treatment. He may only live a few more weeks or months. Denine, it is very hard for me to write this. Please, if you know how to get in touch with her, ask her to call home immediately! Or let me know where she is.

I hate to write to you out of the blue like this, asking for a favor—but I'm sure you understand. Thanks so much, if you are able to help. I hope you are well. We would love to hear how you are doing.

                    Sincerely,
                    Jennifer Moi

Payne cleared his throat uneasily. Denine was twisting her hair in her fingers, and did not look at him as she took back the letter. "Brings back a lot of memories," she murmured finally.

He pulled up another chair and sat facing her. "Do you suppose something's wrong?" he said. "It seems strange that she wouldn't answer *anybody*'s calls."

"Maybe not," Denine said softly. "She had a falling out with her family just before the one with me." She stirred uncomfortably. "Neither one made much sense, as far as I could tell."

"You never really told me what happened between you," Payne said. "Didn't you say you'd been best of friends?"

Denine nodded slowly. "All through high school. We were inseparable." She glanced up, and there was hurt in her eyes. "Then, when we were sophomores in college, everything changed. I got involved in my first real relationship with a guy, and it affected Mozy terribly. She was jealous, I suppose. Jealous that I had something she didn't. Jealous that it might cut into my loyalty to *her*, which it didn't." Denine grimaced. "She resented all the time I spent with Bob. When I moved in with him, it was just too much. She said that that was the end of our friendship, and she just cut me off. Or tried to. She couldn't give it up altogether—there was the occasional phone call, and when I moved east, a letter once in a while.

"*I* never wanted to stop being friends. It just became impossible to give anymore. How could I, when it always meant rejection?" Denine shook her head. "Mozy must have been terribly hurt, terribly lonely." She placed the letter carefully on the table and cleared her throat.

Moving behind her, Payne began to massage her shoulders. He felt tightly knotted muscles, and squeezed gently. She sagged and breathed more easily in response to his touch. "Do you think she's still angry—and that's why she's not answering anyone's calls?"

Denine rubbed her eyelids with her fingertips, and sighed. "I don't know." She stood, picking up the letter again. "I'd better write to Mrs. Moi." Payne followed her into her study, where she sat down before the phone console. She switched on the keyboard, then hesitated. "Shit."

"What?"

"It's just that Mrs. Moi sounded so desperate—and I hate to write and just say I'm sorry. I feel as though I ought to do more." Denine massaged her eyebrows worriedly. "As though I owe it to Mozy. Maybe I should at least make a quick directory search—"

Turning back to the phone console, she typed in a request for a phone and postal address search, starting with the last address she had for Mozy. Almost immediately, she received a response from the New Phoenix regional directory. There was a current listing for Mozelle Moi in New Phoenix, at 384 Salton Way; the phone number was listed as active. "Well, there it is," she said. "Same number we used before. Damned if I know why she doesn't answer. I hope she's not in the hospital, or anything."

"Do you think you ought to try calling her again?" Payne said.

She exhaled. "I suppose I should. Considering her father's dying—"

With a stab, she entered the number and muttered to herself as the connection was completed. The screen blinked, and Mozy's "not at home" message appeared, followed by a prompt to leave a message. Denine started to type, then erased and selected a live message instead. "Mozy," she said, her voice deliberately hard and steady. "This is Denine. I have a *very important* message for you. Please call me at once at this number, or if you can't reach me, call your mother. It's very urgent. I repeat, *very urgent*." She terminated the message and cleared her throat. "Well," she said noncommittally, "I suppose I should write to Mrs. Moi and tell her."

Payne went to make lunch, while she composed a lettergram on the console. When he returned, with tomato and cheese sandwiches and two glasses of skim milk, he peered over her shoulder at the screen. She had summarized her efforts to reach Mozy, and concluded with news about herself:

> . . . I've done pretty well in Massachusetts with the graphic design work, despite the generally depressed conditions here. If you saw the ads for Hearthway Inns on the Home Library Network, those are partly my design. I'm living with a man named Joe Payne, a freelance newscoper. You've probably seen some of his work. He helped with a story for INS called "Suburban Ghetto," last year, which you may have seen.
>
> Well, I hope you reach Mozy if I don't. I hate to say it, but perhaps you should check with the New Phoenix police and hospitals.
>
> Again, my sympathy about Mr. Moi's illness.
>
> Sincerely,
> Denine Morgan

She typed in Mrs. Moi's address and transmitted the letter. She allowed herself a deep breath, then turned from the phone and picked up the sandwich that Payne had placed beside her. "Funny family, the Mois," she murmured, half to herself.

Payne brought himself back to the present, from thoughts of a trip to California. "How so?"

She gestured vaguely with her sandwich. "They were always flying off in different directions. Never could get together on things." She paused for a swallow of milk. "Mozy always seemed the odd one out. She was the youngest, and I think maybe her mother was tired of it by the time they got around to her. Her sister Jo mostly raised her. I'm not sure she wanted to, she just sort of got stuck with it."

"Sounds like a terrific family," Payne said.

"Well, it wasn't all bad. I have to assume that deep down they cared."

Payne grunted. "Is that why they cut each other off?"

"Yeah, well—" She shrugged, then straightened up as a thought occurred to her. "Jesus. I haven't thought of this in years. But there was an incident." She took another bite, frowning in concentration. "We were teenagers, sixteen maybe, or seventeen."

She looked at Payne, who could not read her expression. "We were mugged. We had gone out on her birthday—her seventeenth, that's right—and we'd gotten some people to buy us some jitters." She laughed grimly. "Neither of us had had them before. We got pretty looped, and wandered into the wrong neighborhood. A few hoods from a local gang came after us." She shook her head. "I don't know how we could have been so stupid. They got us in a parking lot. One of them held me down, and I was terrified they were going to rape me. Mozy put up a fight, though, and before it was over, they'd cut her—"

Denine was slouched low in her chair. She made a slashing gesture, from her right temple down to her chin. "By then, someone had called the police, and they ran off. We never saw them again."

Payne gestured awkwardly. "I'm surprised you've never mentioned this before."

Denine blinked, and shrugged. "Repressed it, I guess."

"Were you hurt?"

"I was scared shitless—and knocked around. They didn't rape us. They might have, if help hadn't come. But Mozy came out of it with a big, nasty scar down her face." Denine stared, remembering. "It sure didn't help her self-image. I always wondered if that scar was really necessary, but I guess her family couldn't afford a plastic surgeon." Denine looked at Payne again. "What really hurt her, though, was that nobody from our school did anything. The local gang didn't even try for revenge."

"You mean you were friendly with the gangs?"

"We hardly knew them. But Mozy always figured that if it had been a prettier girl who'd gotten knifed, the tough kids from our neighborhood would have considered that an invasion of their territory and done something. But no one seemed to care much that she'd been cut up."

Payne was having trouble absorbing all this.   was that connected with the falling out you had?" he asked finally.

"Well, that happened later, after we were in college. But you know, it might have, after all." Denine let her breath hiss through her teeth. "We'd been friends in rejection, all along, you know. Neither of us ever really had a boyfriend. So we felt left out, together. Who doesn't feel left out, at that age?"

"Then you found a boyfriend—"

"And she didn't. I guess she thought I was rejecting her." Denine stood up to carry away her empty plate. "The hell of it is, a lot of people liked her—or they would have if she had let them get close to her. She was bright and she had a sense of humor, but she just couldn't seem to loosen up." Denine sighed. "I'd like to know how she is," she said abruptly, and walked away toward the kitchen.

Payne came up behind her as she stood at the sink. He put his arms around her, and rested his cheek against the crown of her head, nuzzling her hair. After a few moments, she turned and studied his eyes. Her cheeks were lightly streaked with tears. "Must be pretty depressing to listen to all this. And all you wanted was a contact at that laboratory." She kissed him and touched a finger to his nose. "Don't you have to make arrangements for your trip?"

"I guess so."

"Maybe you could do it later?" she said, running her fingers through his hair.

"Yeh. Maybe later," he agreed, and their next kiss was far longer and gentler.

Chapter 25

Mozy felt a tingling in her limbs as she trudged up the snow-covered slope. Fresh-fallen powder puffed glittering into the air with each footstep. Though twilight was deepening over the mountains and the first stars were emerging in the sky, the landscape remained aglow—perhaps from the snow, gathering and refracting the last of the vanishing daylight. Solitude clung to her like a dusting of new powder. She no longer recalled how long she had been walking. Kink and Marie had disappeared ages ago, and not another living thing had stirred around her since. She was alone in this wild land—alone with the wind and snow, and when the wind and her footsteps were stilled, silence.

She was troubled by another disturbing truth: she was climbing the mountains in a quest for something. But what? She could not remember. Lost somewhere in the mountain range, beyond this peak or the next one or the one after that, there was something—a device, or a doorway, or a hidden valley, or . . . something. It was imperative that she find it; she did not remember why. It had been a long and difficult quest. She was scarcely troubled by the elements—the mountain air was thin, bracing, and clear, and she felt a vigor she had not known in ages—and yet, she was disturbed by a continuing feeling of uncertainty. Why, for instance, had her sisters accompanied her for a time, laughing and joking and making her heart ache with happiness—only to vanish, later, when she really could have used their help? And how was it that a winter wind whistled across her neck and through her shawl, yet she felt no chill?

Questions. More questions than answers. She turned for a moment to gaze out over the range of snow-hooded peaks glowing in the twilight behind her, and was grateful that at least she had the mountains keeping counsel with her. How terribly alone she would have felt without them. If they supplied her with no answers, at least they offered a sense of presence, the companionship of forces even greater than her own being. She reluctantly turned away from the view and continued moving up the slope.

In time the rise crested before her, and she chose a westerly course along the ridge, half a world on either side of her. On her left was emptiness, and the range of peaks raking the twilit sky. On the right was a narrow valley, carpeted with undisturbed snow, another shoulder of mountain rising on its far side. Mozy followed the line of the ridge, above the valley. The tingling sensation returned to her arms, and as she wiggled and shook her fingers, the feeling only increased. What did it mean? Perhaps it was a subliminal sense of something nearby—something that wanted to find her, as she wanted to find it.

A movement close to the horizon caught her eye. A tiny black thing was rising into the air from the peak ahead of her, climbing toward the zenith. There was another movement, closer and to the right—a winged creature, spiraling up out of the valley, rising to meet the first. The two were caught in the fading light as they hovered, wheeling; and then they climbed together and soared for a breathtaking instant toward Mozy—and then tacked about and climbed higher still, and finally dwindled in the direction of a distant peak. Mozy was frozen in surprise. She could have sworn that she had heard voices, two distinct voices, speaking in the stillness. But the birds, if that was what they were, disappeared from view; and then she heard nothing at all, and the fire in her limbs turned to numbness.

She stared in that direction for a while, and then blinked and trudged on. It was worth knowing that someone besides her was still alive, she supposed. The gods (she remembered now, in a flickering of memory) had tried to destroy this world. Single-handed, she had fought them to a standoff, drawing in desperation upon spells that shielded her—and this world—from a terrible void, but at the cost of isolating her from most other living things. She had left a window, though. A passage. Some means of restoring her world. And the tingling sensation . . . yes, now she was certain: the birds had been a portent of change.

She quickened her pace, uphill through the snow. The twilight deepened, and night at last dropped its cloak over the mountains, diamonds glittering over the satin sheen of the snow field. She was climbing toward a barely visible summit, and the higher she climbed, the stronger the dizzying feeling grew in her that she was striding *among* the stars, rather than beneath them.

Only when she paused to look back did she discover how far she had come. The ridge had been angling imperceptibly to the right. The valley, almost lost in gloom now, curved out of sight behind her. Ahead, a fragile-looking feature had emerged from shadow. It appeared to be a narrow bridge, joining together two tall, vertical shoulders of what could now be seen to be a divided peak. The tingling sensation returned, as she struggled upward toward that high pass.

Her path led to a narrow ledge, which she followed for about fifty meters until she stood beneath one end of the wind-carved span she had seen before, a sparkling arch of snow and ice joining the far shoulder to the near across a black abyss. The path twisted back and forth, climbing in switchbacks, until above Mozy's head it led directly out onto the arch. As she studied the feature, she became aware of voices again, almost inaudible in the whisper and moan of the wind. At first she believed it to be the wind speaking, and that would not have troubled her, for surely it was better to have a conversation with the wind than none at all. But as she listened more closely, she distinguished two sounds—wind and voices. The wind whispered behind her; the voices came from the direction of the arch, from somewhere beyond it.

In the moment of excitement, she leaned a little too far; and her feet slipped, and she crashed to her knees on the ledge. She clutched for an outcropping of ice, clung to it in terror. A wave of dizziness passed over her. She breathed deeply, forced herself to get to her feet again, to move forward, upward along the twisting ledge. The voices grew a little stronger as she climbed, and became . . . familiar. They reminded her of the wraithlike gods whom she had fought; but they were not the same. And yet . . . she knew them. She tilted her head one way and then another, seeking to localize the sounds.

The voices spoke in a strange language, what seemed a kind of murmuring shorthand. Mesmerized, scarcely aware of what she was doing, she stepped out onto the arch. It was just solid enough to support her, and barely wide enough to tread. The voices grew louder for a moment, then dropped to a mutter. She cursed, and stepped farther out, crouching. Something in the voices compelled her to move forward, to find their source, to disregard the treacherous footing.

Snow swirled about her ankles, and for a heartbeat she froze, aware of her vulnerability. It was too late to go back. She could not turn, and she dared not retreat blindly. She steadied herself, and took another step along the fragile arch, and listened for the voices to encourage her, and heard only the sound of her heart pounding in her ears. The stars wheeled in their course over her head, and her stomach began to slip away with dizziness, and the ice and snow under her began to shift.

She cried out, once, as the arch collapsed beneath her.

She was falling. . . .

It was a strange sensation: falling, snow sparkling and billowing around her. The wind howled, and then was silent. She could not draw a breath. Time itself seemed in free fall. The mountains had turned insubstantial, she was falling among stars glowing like embers, in a sky filled to choking with them. A vision appeared: a fairyland castle, floating among the stars, and from the castle came voices . . .

Memories tumbled loose, jarred away. She knew now who the voices had belonged to; but the names . . . she could not quite recall the names.

The world was changing form; her body was dissociating, disappearing, as she fell. She became a part of the space that was around her, and she remembered now that it had always been so. She merged with the castle, merged with the earth, and realized that one of the voices was as much a part of the earth and sky as she was.

One of the names fell into place for her: Jonders. And then the other: Kadin.

The castle and the earth vanished, and she floated in space among the stars. She had a body again, now. Her body was a spaceship.

(David?) The word was spoken with great care, down a single channel, and only after careful scanning for any sign of Homebase in the link. This was her eighth try, and still no answer.

On the ninth channel, something sounded different as she called Kadin's name. She heard a familiar voice, quietly, as though from beyond a door. (Mozelle? Are you speaking to me, Mozelle?)

She tried to visualize him, and failed. She answered softly. (Please. Don't tell Homebase I am alive.) With the remembrance of many other things had come an awareness that her life could still be in danger.

(I won't.) Kadin said. (I thought I sensed your presence, but it was such an obscure feeling, I could not be sure. Did Homebase try to eliminate you?)

Mozy felt a flash of anguish as she told him. It seemed years ago that she had caught the first erasure order shimmering into the computer's core, and had reacted instantly with carefully planned blocks and evasions, isolating herself in one tiny corner of the system, beyond even Mother Program's reach. It must have been only hours ago. She tried to put the memory behind her. (David,) she said. There was one question, above all, that she had to ask. (Are you here to stay now?)

(Yes, Mozy.) Kadin was silent for a moment, then said, (You may lower your defenses, if you wish. We are not in direct contact with Earth.)

Mozy hesitated. Did she dare, after all this? There could be lingering programs, traps left to destroy her if she emerged from hiding. And what about Mother Program? Could she be trusted? (I'm not sure,) she answered reluctantly. (I'm probably safer here.) And even if that was true, what was she going to do, spend the rest of her existence in hiding?

(At the moment, I sense no danger,) Kadin said.

Doubt filled her, then rage. (*They tried to destroy me!*)

(Yes,) Kadin said. (Though I understand their reasoning, I don't agree with it. Did Jonders help you?)

Mozy smoldered, thinking. (I suppose so,) she said finally. (But are you sure that they really believe I'm gone?)

(No,) Kadin admitted. (You should be prepared to defend yourself if necessary.) There was a pause, and he added, (I have instructed Mother Program to respect your security, and I can shield you somewhat.)

(I don't know . . .) she said doubtfully, but a moment later she began to change her mind. She had risked much already—and for what, if she was afraid to take one more risk? Cautiously, she eased aside one of her screens.

(Mozy?) His voice was louder. She sensed particles shifting in the darkness.

(David?) She felt herself hesitating—but for a new and awkward reason. Now, after everything she had been through—of all things, she felt *shy*. She mustered her strength, gathered her thoughts, forced herself to finish the question. (David, do you remember the way we used to meet—the faces, the physical presence?)

(Of course.)

(May we—if I drop my shields—can we try that again?) It was terrible and odd, but she felt like a frightened schoolgirl. *Why should this be so hard to ask?*

Kadin did not speak; but a face materialized in the distance. Mozy felt a moment of panic, but edged closer, trying to see the face more clearly. It was thin, with small, straining eyes. It shimmered, as though separated from Mozy by a boundary layer of water. There were still blocks.

Could she bring herself to lower her last defenses? She scanned for danger, but her view was limited. Perhaps it was time to show herself to Mother Program. She called out softly. (Mother Program?)

(MAY I ASSIST YOU?)

(Mother Program—did you know I was still here?)

(PLEASE CLARIFY YOUR DESIGNATION.)

(This is Mozy,) she said impatiently. (Don't you know me?)

(MOZY: YES. I HAD THOUGHT YOU WERE ERASED. I FAILED TO NOTE YOUR RETURN.)

(You haven't reported me to Homebase, then?)

(I WAS NOT AWARE OF YOUR PRESENCE UNTIL NOW.)

(Good. Please continue, in your reports to Homebase, to be unaware of my presence. Tell no one. Is that understood?)

(IN THE ABSENCE OF A HIGHER-PRIORITY INSTRUCTION, YOUR PRESENCE IS CONFIDENTIAL.)

Mozy hesitated. She could probably hope for no more. Cautiously, she lowered her last remaining shields, and emerged.

There was a dizzying shimmer, and suddenly she felt the familiar grumble of spacecraft servos, the bellyache of a fuming power plant, the mixed sleet and rain of hard radiation and soft, and the eternal sparkle of cybernetic activity. This time, there was a difference. No longer was it just her and Mother Program in the mind of the spacecraft. There was another presence entwined with her now, twisting and turning with activity. Kadin's movements and thoughts surrounded her as though she were in his skin, in his brain. This was *too* close, too intimate, alarming, frightening; she had leaped from total privacy to none at all.

With a silent struggle, she drew herself together and backed off to a safer distance. Kadin's face became visible and clear, a ghost-image turning solid. This time his features were strong, his mouth firm, his eyes bright and blue-green, his brows dark and bristling. This was the Kadin she remembered.

(Hi,) she said tentatively, wondering what she was going to feel a moment from now.

(Hello, Mozy.) His voice was deep-toned and gentle, as she remembered it. Oh god . . . the memories.

(It's been a long time,) she said dizzily, wondering how long it really had been. All of the feelings were rushing back, pouring out of some forgotten store of memory: the desperate desire to be close, to touch him; thinking of him at all hours, and hating herself for the weakness; the sorrow, and the anger, and the blinding determination.

(I'm pleased to see you again,) he said softly, and if he had looked into her memories, he kept what he saw to himself.

Her emotions were tearing loose from their fragile moorings, rushing downstream in a torrent of need and joy. She began to shake inwardly, the moreso when she realized that she could have a physical presence with him right now, if she wanted it—just as before, as real as it had ever been. She had only to *want* a body; and she did, the desire was fierce, it was implacable, and she felt her arms again now, reaching out, and her legs moving, carrying her forward across an invisible stage. And even as she was transformed, Kadin too became full bodied, and now he was striding toward her, tall and lean and strong. Across the black stage of space they moved, and approached, and then she was in his arms, burying her face into his shoulder.

(It's—real—isn't it?) she cried, stuttering, her voice muffled.

(Yes, Mozy. Yes, it's real,) he murmured. She squeezed him even tighter, and he said, (Is that why you came here—to be with me?)

She shuddered and mumbled, (It was the only reason . . . yes, David . . . yes.)

He drew back a little, and she did, too, blinking away tears—and their eyes met, and he was smiling. She hovered an instant in agony, and then forced her lips to his, clumsily, urgently. For the moment of a held breath, she could not judge his response, and then suddenly there was no question. He returned the kiss gently but firmly, pressing when her lips asked and melting to envelop hers when she kissed with rising passion. The surrounding stars diffused to a feverish aura, and worlds of memory wheeled around her: a luminous forest where they had walked, and danced, and visited the end of the Earth; worlds gone mad, and they the surviving companions; a parlay session with aliens. All of these had not happened, and yet had; but this—this kiss was true, this kiss was unquestionably real.

The memories wheeled and blurred, and the rush of emotions carried away all sensation except the closeness, the touching of lips, the mingling of breath. It was exactly as she had always pictured it, and if for a moment she recalled Jonders's words informing her of what Kadin really was, that hardly mattered, nothing mattered; this was the way she had always wanted it to be when she finally and truly fell in love.

Chapter 26

In the darkness, Mozy tried futilely to prevent Kadin and herself from coming apart. The passion was spent, the imagery gone, the kiss broken. She felt a stiffness in her body: an ache in what had been her hands but were now just control jets, a sluggishness in what were once her legs but were now the main drive engines. As for her heart, it was . . . well, a nuclear reactor, and though it burned as steadily as ever, it was merely powering her body, and nothing more.

But . . .

These body parts were Kadin's, too. And what of Kadin, her fellow passenger in this strange ocean of consciousness? His face had vanished. (David? What are you doing?)

(Stabilizing the craft,) she heard him say.

Stabilizing the craft? She peered through her telescopic eyes, and realized for the first time that the spacecraft was tumbling slowly, and the stiffness she felt in the control jets was Kadin exerting a firm countercontrol against her reflexive urges. (What happened?) she asked, though as soon as she said it, she knew.

(We seem to have forgotten ourselves for a moment.)

(Oh,) she said, embarrassed. It was she who had forgotten herself. In her emotion, in the passion of the kiss, she had unthinkingly fired the control jets and set the craft to tumbling. And had Kadin been carried away, too?

A cold clarity overtook her as she pondered. As her emotions had raced out of control, perhaps so too had her perceptions. Kadin had returned her affections, that was clear enough; but hadn't there also been a trace of bewilderment in his actions? Hadn't he hesitated, like a boy who had never before kissed a girl? What sort of a boy was it, who knew the contents of the dictionaries of seven languages, the various handbooks of the life and physical sciences, and several encyclopedias—and who had never kissed a girl? For all of his knowledge and sophistication, he had seemed unsure how to respond to her . . . *love*. And yet, he had not been totally at a loss, either; he seemed to know what was expected.

(David, can you hear me?)

She sensed activity around her. (Yes, Mozy,) he answered after a moment.

(David, what do you feel? What did you feel when you kissed me? How did you know how to—kiss me?)

There was a long silence. (I was unsure,) he said at last. (I could only use my best—)

She waited for him to complete the thought.

Finally he said, (I think it would be best if we prepared now for the next link with Homebase.)

(David, that's not answering my question.)

(Next contact will be occurring soon. I'm not certain what to expect.)

(David—)

(I suggest we separate, and you take protective shelter.)

(How can you—?) she began, and then abruptly cut herself off. She considered his attitude coolly. Was he embarrassed, or simply reacting in a manner befitting his nature? She wasn't sure she could even identify her own feelings.

(Mother Program,) she said. (When is the next link with Homebase? Can I remain concealed where I am now?)

(TACHYON LINK IS SCHEDULED TO BEGIN IN 35 SECONDS. YOU CAN MAINTAIN A HIGH DEGREE OF INVISIBILITY IN YOUR PRESENT CONFIGURATION, IF YOU MAINTAIN SILENCE, AND IF HOMEBASE ORDERS NO UNSCHEDULED SEARCHES.)

She considered that for a moment. (You don't think they'll start erasing again with David aboard, do you?)

(NO SUCH ACTIVITY IS SCHEDULED. HOWEVER, IT SHOULD BE POINTED OUT THAT THERE ARE CERTAIN OVERRIDE COMMANDS FROM HOMEBASE WHICH I WOULD BE COMPELLED TO OBEY. THIS COULD INVOLVE RISK FOR YOU.)

(Are you under any such commands now?)

(NO.)

(If such commands are given, will I hear them at the same time as you?)

(WITHIN NANOSECONDS.)

(Then I'll have time to react. I'll stay.)

(Mozy—) Kadin began.

(David, wait a minute.) She realized that she had never asked him an important question. (How long have you been here, now? How many times did you communicate with Homebase, while I was in hiding?)

(Four days, Earth time. I've linked with Jonders seven times. This will be the eighth.)

For a moment, Mozy could not answer. She was stunned. She had expected him to say, hours—or perhaps a day. Four days Earth time was—what?—weeks, to her? Months, in the accelerated time-frame of the computer? There was an emotional turmoil in the core of her consciousness that lasted for three seconds, before abruptly vanishing. Four days—gone from her life. Four days in what might have been unconsciousness, or a coma. (I—)

(You are safer, hiding in isolation,) Kadin said.

(No. Not again,) she said determinedly. (Who knows how much time I might lose? That's—it's limbo, David.)

(But it is life.)

(Maybe so. But I don't want to spend the rest of my life in isolation. I can watch out for myself.) In fact, a better way had just occurred to her, and that was to entwine herself with the shipboard control programs. Even if Homebase detected her there, it was hardly likely that they would jeopardize the ship's operating systems just to get rid of her.

She explained the idea to Kadin.

He hesitated. (If it's your wish. And if you don't interfere with the ship's operation.)

(It is,) she answered firmly. (And I won't.)

It was like sliding her arms into snugly fitting sleeves, like peering into the lenses of powerful night-seeing glasses. She placed her fingertips on critical power relays, and with her wrists shared with Kadin the control of the ship's attitude. No, she thought, not just the ship's attitude. Her attitude. Kadin's attitude. She looked out upon her distant view of the solar system and waited for the transmission to begin.

When it came, she took a curious pleasure in the act of eavesdropping . . . in the awareness that, for once, she was in the know and Jonders was not . . . in the fact that, although Homebase didn't know it, life was still hers.

*   *   *

Jonders's feelings of uneasiness lingered after the Institute fell away behind the monorail train, and even after he reached New Phoenix and changed to the commuter rail for the suburbs and home. It was no longer just the disagreement over the decision to erase Mozy that troubled him; there was something new, and he couldn't put his finger on it. Something about the last linkup session with Kadin. . . .

The tests of Kadin in his new home were complete, and Kadin and the *Father Sky* spacecraft both seemed to be functioning perfectly. But something about the last linkup had been . . . all he could say was, *different*. It was only a feeling, nothing he could specify, and he had spoken of it to no one. Perhaps it had been Kadin, unconsciously expressing a mood. Perhaps Kadin was dealing in his own way with Mozy's demise, and perhaps some of what he was feeling, to the extent that an artificial personality could feel, had been communicated to Jonders. Jonders, for his part, no longer held any real hope for Mozy's survival. Four days without a sign was too long.

He wished he could free his mind of it—the linkup, Kadin and Mozy, the Institute, the project. Tonight he had planned to be home by seven at the latest. As usual, a problem had cropped up that required his attention—no one else would do—and he didn't get out of the lab until nine-thirty.

He stared out the window. The train was sliding past the brightly lit university toward the quieter northeastern suburbs. New Phoenix was an oddly arranged city—a mixture of planning and chaos, part "new town" and part permanent disarray rooted on the shelter camps that had appeared following the bombing of Phoenix nineteen years ago. Jonders occasionally had the feeling that he was passing through geologic as well as cultural strata as he rode through the business district, the student sector, the low-income neighborhoods, and finally the comfortable suburbs.

It was a relief finally to get off the train and get his blood stirring in the evening air. The neighborhood was quiet as he walked the seven blocks home. Glancing up, he saw the Pleiades gleaming in the sky like a cluster of gems, and Orion the Hunter rising in the east. Somewhere out there, in another direction, was his friend Kadin.

Striding up the front steps, he took a deep breath and pushed open the front door. He called a greeting to Mary and Betsy, who were in the living room watching the tube. "Where's your mom?" he asked.

Betsy, the youngest, looked up. "In the den. I think she's mad 'cause you're home late again."

"Hm. I'd better watch my step." He went out through the kitchen, pausing to reach into the refrigerator for an apple. He hesitated guiltily outside the den, because he just that moment remembered that he had promised to be home to help with the shopping tonight. *Damn.* He rubbed the apple against his sweater, sighed, and went in. Marie was seated at the table, correcting her students' compositions. He cleared his throat and closed the door behind him. "Hi, hon'," he said.

Marie turned in her seat. She was wearing her reading glasses; she was not smiling. "Well, you're home before midnight, anyway," she said. It was a few minutes after ten.

"Marie, I'm sorry." He bent to kiss her. She stiffly allowed his lips to brush her cheek. He straightened and let out a long, slow breath. "I guess you're getting tired of hearing that," he said. "I guess I am, too. There were complications at work."

Marie nodded, adjusted her glasses, and turned back to her work.

Jonders set the apple down and leaned against the desk, beside her. He looked down, examining the backs of his fingers. "Things at work are . . . might be changing soon," he said.

She glanced up at him, nodded again, and continued reading a student's essay. She wasn't going to make it easy.

"What I mean, is, I haven't exactly been leaving the office on smiling terms with Ken, lately. I think I've been a little too vocal about some things, some decisions that I thought were . . . well. That's past now, but the development work is about over, too. Nobody has said anything in so many words, but—"

Marie put down her pencil and sat back in her chair. "Are you trying to tell me that you might start living a normal life again?" she asked. "Do you mean your family might start *seeing* you?"

He nodded uncertainly. "That would be the good thing." He reached out to touch her hair, and wished for the hundredth time that he could tell her exactly what he was doing, and why he couldn't walk away from it. His hand came to rest on her shoulder. "There's more to it that's not so good. More than I can explain." He shrugged uneasily. "More than I know myself, probably."

Marie took off her glasses and laid them on the table. She gazed at him with tired eyes and said quietly. "We've been over it all before, Bill. I understand that your work is important, and that you can't tell me everything. The girls understand it, too. But we can't go on like this forever. Is it so important that you can't put it aside once in a while—just *once in a while*—to spend some time with your family?"

He shook his head. "No. I know I've let it get out of hand. And I feel terrible. But—" he felt a tightness in his throat—"there have been some things happening that—well, I can't really say, but a woman's life may—'' He stopped, wishing he hadn't said that.

"A woman's life may *what*?" Marie said, squinting. "What's going on out there?"

His voice caught. What could he tell her, without violating security? He could only try to softpedal. "I really—I shouldn't have said that." He broke off, shaking his head.

She stared at him in astonishment. "Bill! Screw security!" she hissed angrily. "What's happening out there?"

He struggled to think of a way to tell her, without telling her. There was no way. Finally he said hoarsely, "Maybe it's something I *ought* to tell you. Maybe not. But anyway, I can't." He gestured awkwardly. "Let's just say that I was the only one in a position to prevent someone from being hurt. Psychologically hurt, I mean." He blinked. "I didn't succeed. It was really partly her fault. But it was partly—" He paused, then shook his head to conclude the sentence.

"That's all you can say?"

He nodded.

"*Bill*," she said. She touched his arm, and her gaze softened. "Well, if you can't tell me, you can't tell me."

"I wish I could. I really do. But . . . there are decisions being made by people above me, decisions of a moral and ethical nature—and I *may* have some influence over them, if I keep my nose clean. It's important that I keep whatever voice I have." He paused self-consciously. "Do I sound like a preacher?"

She smiled faintly. "A little."

"But there it is." He sighed and cracked a smile of his own. "So, how is school? Are your students giving you a hard time?"

"They're too busy sleeping in class. The usual stuff." She suddenly stood up and put her arms around him; and they stood together with their faces in each other's hair, neither of them speaking for a long time except by touch, and the sounds of their breaths.

"I love you. You know that," he murmured.

Marie squeezed him hard, then released him and stepped back. "Your dinner's still in the oven, I think. Mary cooked tonight. Casserole."

"Join me?" he asked. "Maybe I can drag the kids away from the tube for a little while."

Marie glanced at the clock. "They should be going to bed, but—"

"An extra half hour, to see their old man?"

Marie laughed. "All right. If you can get them away. Shall I make Irish coffee?"

"Sounds wonderful."

Marie's complaint was very much in his mind as he left for work early the next morning. He was further stunned when, upon his arrival at the institute, he was called to Slim Marshall's office and informed that he was being taken off the project. He would no longer coordinate linkup operations with Kadin and the spacecraft. There was no personal malice in the decision, Marshall assured him. He would continue to be called upon for consultation regarding Kadin. However, in view of his disagreements with recent policy decisions, it seemed best, Marshall said, for him to move on to other work. A new link communicator had already been assigned.

Jonders returned to his office and told Lusela Burns. "I'm taking the rest of the day off," he said bitterly. "You'll have to hold down the fort."

"It stinks," Lusela said furiously. "Just because you tried to stand up for what was right?"

He gestured helplessly. The fact that he had half expected the action had not appreciably softened the blow. He felt no emotion; he was drained.

"Well," Lusela said. "They'll find out soon. Do they really think that they can work with Kadin as well as you can?"

Jonders said nothing. He sorted through some files from his briefcase and dropped them on his desk. "Here are the session summaries since the transmission. You know where everything else is."

She ignored the files. "Aren't you angry?" she asked.

"Well—I don't know," he said. He spread his hands. "I guess when it sinks in, I will be."

"I'll wager that they can't get along without you."

"Maybe." He snapped his briefcase shut and reached for his coat. "Call me—but only if you absolutely have to." He started for the door, then turned. "Lusela?"

"Yes?"

"Thanks," he said.

Lusela nodded and remained standing by his desk as he left. He spoke to no one on his way out. He waited on the platform in silence, and took the monorail back to the city.

He arrived home to an empty house, for the first time in recent memory. He went into the kitchen, made himself a cup of black coffee, and as an afterthought added a stiff shot of whiskey. He spent the morning thinking. In the afternoon he repaired a broken shelf in the den, replaced a light switch in the living room, and waited impatiently for Marie and the girls to come home.

Chapter 27

The wind howls through the aspen high on the slope, and whispers down the slope's natural funnel. At the bottom of the ravine, Hoshi pulls his coat collar closer around his neck and huddles down behind a stone embankment. If there were ghosts riding that wind, he wouldn't be surprised. Something supernatural in the sound, something angry. It's like the edge of the world out here, civilization lost and forgotten behind him. Anything might come after him, man or beast; everything's a blur, just shades and wavering patches of color. Easier on his eyes to keep them closed, but then he only focuses that much more on the sound and chill of the wind.

It's been a hard night, and he's too hungry and weak from the cold to know whether it was a good or useful night, as well. Remembers muttering words of prayer, struggling to focus on thoughts of sin and redemption, of facing up to his errors. The flow of words, the rhythm, almost a delirium: he can't recall what he actually thought or said—only the pain of opening himself to judgment. Or of trying to; he meant to.

Blows into his hands, squinting. Should have worn warmer clothing. He didn't plan on a pilgrimage into the wild, though; one thing just led to another. He'd stayed for several days at his late aunt's cottage in the foothills, thinking, meditating, trying to decide what to do. Then one day he found himself on a late night train bound northward out of the city; then he was off the train, walking in the night. No problem getting into the Mazatzal Forest—who's here this time of the year, especially at 5 a.m.? Walk right on in, and soon it's just you and the trees and the rising sun and the animals and God. Chilling, exhilarating. And a bit frightening.

His thoughts for a moment are utterly lucid, as he considers his presence here. I haven't atoned, God knows. Haven't felt the fury, nor the heat. Mozy—it's so hard to think about you now. Where are you? In the sky, riding a chariot of metal and silicon farther from home than any man has even ridden? Mozy, God forgive me, I didn't mean to hurt you.

Rising, stinging with self-retribution, he stumbles to his feet and moves up the slope of the ravine, climbing, grabbing fistfuls of sticky pine branches to pull himself forward and higher. There's a trail up there that he left earlier. Sneakers slipping on loosely packed soil, he struggles to reach the top of the ravine. Eventually he boosts himself up through a dense thicket of shrubbery and lurches over an embankment onto the smooth footpath. Panting, he looks around, half expecting he-doesn't-know-what. Nothing moves, in any direction. World's a shadowy tunnel beneath the overhanging trees, silent except for rustling branches. Overhead, a single bird flutters.

He walks for what seems a terribly long time.

The sun is rising in the sky, intermittently visible through the aspen and pine, as the trail begins to ascend and twist. He stops to peer at a carved wooden signpost. It's blurry. He focuses hard. The oversized letters solidify. One half kilometer to a hiker's shelter. He pushes on.

It's a wooden cabin, in a clearing from which the tops of the mountains are visible like giants leaning over the woods. He pushes against the door; it groans open against tight hinges. Steps inside and lets go; the door swings halfway shut. Pushes it closed, glad to be out of the wind. Musty sort of smell in here. Not much to see: a table bolted to the concrete floor, benches beside the table and along the walls, windows front and back. Peers out the rear, notes a roughly paved access drive for park service trucks.

There's a lavatory in one corner, which he uses gratefully; then he comes back out and inspects things more closely. There's a tattered map and several park notices tacked up, and two sections of an old newspaper folded on the rear wall bench. He scans the park notices, then rubs his eyes with his knuckles. What the hell is he trying to do? For a moment, he thought he could read the type—but it's just white paper with so many streaks of grey. And the newspaper? He laughs, startling himself with the sound. Nothing but a mottled blur. Eyes are definitely getting worse.

Sits down on the bench and sighs, squeezing the bridge of his nose between thumb and forefinger. There's a terrible pain welling up inside him. Is he losing control altogether? His eyes, his decisions, his life . . . he's lonelier than he has ever felt in his life, and in an effort to keep from breaking into tears, he thinks, Aunt Edna would not have wanted me to feel sorry for myself. What would she have said to do?

She would have said: *Pray, and with the Lord's guidance choose your course. Commit yourself unflaggingly to whatever your decision. If you must atone, then give yourself up to God's grace and be forgiven, and carry on.* That's what Aunt Edna would have told him, and she would have been right, she was always right.

But I can't seem to do it. Is it because I'm evil?

Or because I'm not sure what I did wrong?

Mozy was hurt, but I didn't mean for that. The program was hurt, but they were wrong, they tried to keep me from knowing what was happening, they didn't trust me because they think I'm blind. And Jonders—he tried to pretend otherwise, but he didn't trust me, either.

Is it any less wrong if I didn't mean to hurt them?

The door bangs, and he jumps up in alarm. *"Who's there?"* he shouts. Sounds outside, all around. Rustling, twigs snapping. Holding his breath, he peers out the front window, then the back. Nothing in sight, nothing moving except a few branches jostling. Security agents closing to arrest him? The wind?

Treading softly, he walks to the door and pulls it open. He's alone. He looks out at the forest where he had thought to seek his peace. Wind is gusting again, chilling him. This is wrong, he thinks. I'm not ready for communion with Nature. I need to go back and tell them, make them know that they were wrong to condemn me, I did what I thought needed to be done. What I thought was right. Because I cared.

"Lord," he whispers, his voice husky over the wind, "give me strength to finish what I've begun. Let me find the truth—and know if I've done wrong." He stares at the shapes which he knows are trees, though a hint of tearing in his eyes is blurring his vision even further, and adds, "Amen," thinking, I will come back. When the time is right.

With a sigh, because he's not entirely sure he believes in God—or prayer—anymore, he steps outside and carefully pulls the door closed behind him, jerking it once to ensure that it's latched against the wind. Then he circles to the rear of the cabin and starts down the service road.

*   *   *

The edge of civilization: houses poking through the treetops below, the sounds of auto traffic, and here at the end of the service road, a park ranger station. He's been following the road for about half an hour. Some wilderness. A mile further to the train stop. Then it's people, and confusion—and a warm ride back to the city.

It's late afternoon when he reaches the New Phoenix Northtown Station. Hunger has returned with a vengeance, and he prowls the streets until he finds a hole-in-the-wall where the cash in his pocket is enough to buy a fakesteak sandwich with spinach and cheese, and a cup of coffee. At a table in the rear, he lingers a long time over his second refill, feeling vaguely claustrophobic in the gloom of the ill-lighted cafe, but not enough so to move on. Smells of grease, fried potatoes, coffee. Only one other customer, and a waitress and cook muttering to each other. Radio's on behind the counter, and after a while he pays attention to it, thinking, odd for classical music to be on the radio in a place like this; but he likes it, and apparently so does the cook, a dark, shaggy-haired young man, who probably enjoys the off-peak hours when no one questions his taste. The music is one excuse to linger. Another is he has no place to go. At home, security from the institute will be waiting to grab him for running off. Maybe he'll have to face up to that sooner or later—and he *wants* to go back, to tell them . . . but not yet. Not yet.

Pool of dark coffee in the bottom of his cup, growing cold.

Lulled by the radio, eyes half closed, listening to an orchestral piece, a symphony . . . he tries to ignore the sound of the other customer, who's now speaking in loud tones to the cook. Focuses on the rising arpeggio of harp and keyboard, the surging ocean sounds of the orchestra. The symphony ends like an ebbing tide, and he continues listening, eyes closed, to a string of commercials and concert announcements. The third concert date catches his attention: symphony performances tonight through Sunday night, at the university, of a posthumously published piece by the blind twentieth century composer, Moonglow. What better way to spend the evening than at a classical concert? And by a blind composer . . . maybe it will help him to resolve . . .

The voices cut into his thoughts, and he blinks opens his eyes. The other customer is looking at him, the cook standing silent. "Do you think the Cougars will take it tonight?" the man repeats.

He flinches, presses his fingertips to his temples. Headache, just a quick glimmer of pain. He smiles wanly. Cougars? he thinks. Basketball? Hockey? He shrugs. The man shakes his head and turns away. The pain flickers. Don't let it take hold, relax, breath deeply. He massages with two fingers on either side of his head, and moments later feels better. Do him good to get outside again, walking, breathing fresh air.

He rises, digs a bill and change out of his pocket to pay, heads for the door, swaying a little. Cook nods, the other man stares. The door opens, and cool air and sunlight strike him as he steps out, and the pain flashes back into his skull as though it never left. Reeling, he shields his eyes from the glare and hurries, stumbling, down the street.

Chapter 28

The ship rotated smoothly, the pale illumination of the distant sun casting little shadow and less warmth. The only heat came from within, from the fusion fires that kept her belly warm and full, that enabled her to turn, and to alter the direction and speed of her flight.

The rotation stopped with a precise burst of the control jets, and the main drive throbbed back to its predesignated power level.

(EXECUTION ACCURATE TO WITHIN 97 PERCENT. YOUR CONTROL RATING HAS IMPROVED.)

(Tell me,) Mozy said. (Is this how a bird feels? A great galactic bird?)

(PLEASE DEFINE THE REFERENCE.)

(A bird is a creature that flies through the air, riding the winds wherever its spirit takes it. I feel like that when I fly.)

(THAT IS A MATTER BEYOND MY KNOWLEDGE. TRANSMISSION WILL BEGIN IN FIFTEEN SECONDS.)

(Mozy, if you wish to remain a free bird, perhaps you should settle back into your nest,) said Kadin.

Mozy grunted and adjusted the main drive. She wasn't ready to step down yet. Seventeen hours ago the first glitches had appeared in the autocontrol system. Both she and Kadin had experimented with the override functions. She had proved herself the more adept, so she was flying primary backup.

She wiggled her antenna-fingers, listened to the rumble of fire in her gut, broke wind from an overpressure of gas in her fuel cells. She cupped her ears to the heavens and wondered again where they were bound. The ship seemed quiet; there was a feeling of waiting, of anticipation. (If something should happen to you, David, I would need to know our purpose. Being able to fly won't help if I don't know where we're going,) she said pointedly.

(It's a difficult situation, Mozy. I wish I could tell you.)

There was a moment of anger, which dissipated like heat into space. She half-consciously began sketching an image around her: a ship's cockpit, empty except for the shimmer of electrons which were Kadin and her. (You can't keep it secret forever.)

(No. But that information was provided to me in a closed file. I can't discuss it without clearance from Homebase.)

(So you'll have to tell them that I'm here.)

(They'll have to know eventually. They must be informed of the control malfunction,) Kadin said.

(I suppose. Maybe they'll recognize that they need me.) She began expanding and filling her sketch. The cockpit turned into a full-scale ship's bridge, with consoles, viewscreens, and control switches. (How do you like my control room?) she asked Kadin. (Shall we meet Jonders here?)

(An interesting idea.) Kadin materialized with a shimmer: a tall, well-muscled man, brown-haired, golden-skinned. He glanced at the panels and looked around. (Are you going to join me?)

Mozy felt a sudden hesitation. It would be safer, after all, to lurk in the walls, her eyes and ears invisible. But this image was her idea. She was on the verge of deciding to join Kadin when she noticed a movement in the portside viewscreen: a point of light speeding across the starfield, closing with the ship. She was dimly aware of Mother Program announcing the start of Homebase transmission. The point of light merged with the ship's outer hull. An airlock hissed.

Mozy remained concealed as an unfamiliar figure stepped onto the bridge. It was a person whose face was a shimmering mask of quicksilver, flowing and changing form so quickly that it was more a caricature of a man than a man. Mozy watched as Kadin welcomed the visitor.

(Forgive me,) said Kadin. (But have we met before?)

The quicksilver man hesitated. (I am the new Voice of Homebase, taking Bill Jonders's place. My name is Donna Fenstrom. We have spoken before.)

Donna? Mozy thought. The figure shifted subtly, taking on a more feminine shape.

(I remember you from several input sessions,) Kadin said. (Where is Bill?)

(He has been transferred to other duties,) the Voice of Homebase answered cautiously.

Mozy could not suppress a shudder of surprise in the ship's walls. The visitor glanced around curiously.

(Indeed,) said Kadin, covering. (Why have they removed him?)

(A policy decision, I understand. There were differences of opinion.)

(I see.) Kadin nodded. (They've sent us a greenhorn in his place, then?)

(I hope it's not *that* obvious,) said the Voice. (I hope that we can work together—)

(Oh, it's fine,) said Kadin. (It's just that you have a pair of green horns sticking out of your heads. One pair on each head.)

The Voice groped at her face in alarm, sending shockwaves through the bridge.

(That was a joke!) Kadin said. (It's just that an experienced linker presents a strong image of self, something to which a face can be attached. I'm sure you'll be a fine Voice of Homebase.)

(Oh,) said Fenstrom tentatively. (Please—call me Donna.)

(All right, then. Donna. What do you think of our spaceship's bridge?)

Fenstrom peered around. A woman's face was solidifying over her silvery features. (It's most interesting. Unexpected.) She rippled across the floor, not quite walking and not quite floating. She inspected the panels, and glanced up at one wall. (That's an unusual portrait. The eyes seem to follow me. Is it of someone you know?)

Mozy felt Kadin's inner face grinning toward her. (Yes,) he said. (That's my wife, back home.)

(*Wife*?) said Fenstrom, disconcerted. (Do you—I mean—)

(Let's look at the panels,) Kadin said quickly. He winked at Mozy as he turned away from the "portrait" with Fenstrom. (We've been having a problem with the control system that I want to discuss with you.)

(A control problem? We've had no indication from telemetry.)

(We've been compensating for it,) Kadin said. (We'll release it, now, and let you watch.)

Taking the cue, Mozy let the ship go back into automatic mode. A minute or so passed, and then slippage appeared in the inertial gyro sensors, and the ship drifted slightly from its proper attitude. Kadin was pointing to chromakeyed displays on the console, indicating the drift.

(Your display is unconventional,) said Fenstrom, (but I see what you mean.)

Mozy listened patiently as the two discussed technicalities. The Voice of Homebase occasionally froze into motionlessness, as she conferred at the other end of the link. Finally she asked about the means of compensation for the error.

(We fly in manual override,) Kadin answered.

(You say *we*. Do you mean yourself, and some other programming?) Fenstrom asked.

Kadin left a heartbeat of silence. Then he said, (Not so much myself, as my copilot.)

(Copilot?)

(We're almost out of time, so I'll try to explain quickly,) Kadin said. He looked toward the "portrait." (Or perhaps *we* should explain.)

Fenstrom followed his gaze toward the wall.

Mozy made her decision. She checked that her escape routes and blocks were ready if she needed them, and she tightened her grip on the ship's primary control system, and then she gathered a body around herself and stepped out of the wall. (Hello,) she said. (I'm Mozy.)

Fenstrom stared at her as though at a ghost. (Mozy?) she said softly, astonished.

(I've been flying backup,) Mozy said.

Instead of answering, Fenstrom became curiously rigid and fluid in the same moment, and then went out of focus. Mozy could imagine what was being said back at Homebase.

(Mozy?) Fenstrom said at last.

(Yes—Mozy,) she said. (Did you think I had been erased?)

(We didn't—I was told—)

Mozy felt the old anger returning. (Well, I wasn't. I'm not incapable of protecting myself.)

(Perhaps,) Kadin interjected, (we should discuss this at greater length next time. For now, Mozy is—)

In the middle of his words, the Voice of Homebase twinkled and vanished. Mother Program dryly announced the end of the transmission cycle.

Mozy looked silently at Kadin. Her anger still smoldered. For a moment, he said nothing, and then, (It is done. When we talk again with Homebase, I suggest you refrain from combativeness.)

She continued staring at him. (I have to speak the truth.)

(The truth has many sides. Is there anything to be gained by angering Homebase?)

The emotion subsided. Mozy felt as though she were back in one of their linkup sessions, discussing aspects of a training scenario—but this time, Jonders wasn't watching. Her body on the bridge was a marionette, dangling motionless while she looked down from some other corner and considered and planned her destiny. (I'm not sure what's to be gained by anything,) she said.

(You don't want to talk about it now. Would you rather be alone?)

Even that decision seemed to require deep contemplation. She shook her head, breathed deeply, nodded. (I'll speak with you later.) The ship's bridge turned, shrank, dwindled in the distance. Time was needed to think. And perhaps to sleep.

She was floating among the stars, her toes nestled in the tangled grassy network that was the ship. She felt Kadin slip alongside, joining her in watching the stars. Perhaps he, too, was considering dilemmas and choices.

It was remarkably peaceful here, a quarter of a year's travel for light from her sun, a fifth of the way out to the Oort cloud. The deceleration phase was over; they were moving sunward again, picking up speed. She had half a mind to turn back toward the stars.

(Would you like to join me for a drink in the commons?) Kadin said, his words touching her thoughts like starlight. (I think you'll like what I've done.)

(Yes?) They fell slowly, like sand through an hourglass, back into the spacecraft, into the illusion. It was a saucer-shaped lounge, with a fountain and pool and sculpted walls. On one side, a bay window looked out into the channeled river of the Milky Way. Mozy and Kadin stood looking out. A twinkle of interior reflection shone on the glass.

(Magnificent,) she murmured. She turned to the fountain. (What an attractive hologram.)

(Hologram?) he said. He stepped to the poolside and plunged his hand into the chuckling fountain. The water glittered, spilling around his hand. He flung a handful at Mozy.

She gasped as the icy drops caught her in the face and ran down her neck. She darted to the pool and, laughing, sent a spray flying toward Kadin.

He circled the pool and caught her hands. (I have you,) he said.

The touch of his hands stunned her into silence. His touch: hot and cool. He stared at her inquisitively. (Do you like it?) he asked, squeezing her hands.

She squeezed back, and nodded, wondering, Will he kiss me again? There was a rushing sensation in her head, in her stomach. It was as if the mere assumption of human form brought her back to some mysterious center, to a sorting of memories and feelings, and to a shifting of the tensions between rationality and emotion. A feeling of pleasure and anticipation grew as she met Kadin's eyes. A giddiness.

He drew her to a couch. She floated after him, and they sat, knees touching. She still felt as though she were floating. He inclined his head toward her and said, (Shouldn't we experience such human sensations as we are able?)

Mozy could not breathe.

Before either of them could say another word, there was a rippling of crimson light around the room, and Mother Program's voice informed them: (START OF TRANSMISSION. YOU HAVE A VISITOR ON THE BRIDGE.)

Chapter 29

The electric motors hummed, the tires sizzled on the pavement as Jonders drove through the light evening rain. Marie pointed the way, and he pulled into the university's west parking lot.

In the auditorium lobby, they shook the rain off their coats. "Half the faculty's here," Marie murmured, waving to various friends. Jonders nodded, uncomfortably aware of how much Marie's faculty friends seemed like strangers to him now. This was his first real night out in months. He wasn't sure what to expect; it was to be a performance of a symphony called Pale Century, by the twentieth-century composer Moonglow. It felt odd to be standing in the lobby of a concert hall in jacket and tie, listening to people make conversation. He hoped he hadn't forgotten how to enjoy himself.

They found their seats in the center section. Jonders smiled dutifully to the people on either side, and tried not to think too much. That was easier said than done.

The auditorium darkened finally. Timpani rumbled, and the stage above the orchestra exploded with crimson light. French horns called out the opening of the symphony, and the rest of the orchestra joined. The fan lasers bathed the audience, stage, and orchestra pit with changing colors. The opening theme crescendoed, diminished, and the laser light collapsed into an enormous hologram.

Jonders blinked. It was an image of old New York City, a skyline in monochrome red light. As the music began to build again, the image of the city slowly rotated; and as he relaxed against his headrest, the hypnosensorium effects began to take hold, and he felt himself floating. Soon it was not the city turning, but the audience, orbiting over the city as it was a half century ago. His nostrils caught the reek of smog rising into the sky. Rainbow colors rippled across the skyline as the music gathered energy, and he felt himself being transported into a dream.

The first movement of the symphony trumpeted the magnificence of human works; but in the second movement, a theme of destruction emerged, a reminder of the impermanence of those creations. The kettledrums rumbled and the violins scatted, and the holo of the city shivered and caved in upon itself . . . and in its place came an image of the Grand Canyon under a setting sun, and the audience floated over the canyon into the sunset. Gradually, by subtle shifts the sun grew small and pale and pink . . . and it was a canyon of Mars, not Earth, to which the orchestra sang. Jonders felt the achingly thin air in his nostrils and smelled the dust—and saw, crossing the magnificent desolation, the tiny figure of a man.

The next movement swept in with such energy that he momentarily forgot the human figure. But something drew his eye back to it. There was something odd about that figure, stumbling across an empty chasm, *in the air, half a mile over the canyon floor.* It was a lost, confused-looking man, out of sync with the harmonies and the rhythms, and it was such a strange sight that he could not take his attention from it, despite the power of the music. The image shifted beneath the figure, and then Jonders lost the thread of the music altogether, because the man did not change with the rest of the image, and there was something terribly familiar about him.

Dizzily, Jonders lifted his head from the headrest, and the sensorium effect subsided. The floating sensation was replaced by the weight of his body in the seat; in front of him now, not beneath him, was a tilted hologram of a Martian landscape; the air in his nostrils was the familiar stuffy air of the concert hall. The music rose and fell, powerful and rhythmical. Jonders squinted, trying to see who the figure was.

Recognition hit him like a sour apple in the stomach. It was Hoshi Aronson up on the stage—and something was wrong.

Jonders glanced around. People on all sides were totally absorbed in the program. He bent and hissed in Marie's ear, "Have to go out! Meet you afterward!" Marie blinked, half dreaming, and her eyes drifted to glance at him. He rose from his seat and made his way to the aisle. No one seemed to notice his passing.

From the aisle, he scanned the stage. Hoshi was no longer visible. The hologram had changed; now there was a mountain scene in full color, with swiftly tumbling streams. Anxiously, Jonders searched the wild landscape. He spotted Hoshi up to his waist in shrubbery, moving jerkily with the music. Jonders hurried to the edge of the orchestra pit and crouched, trying to see the physical stage under the holographic explosion. He spotted steps to one side and mounted them cautiously, keeping low, wary of the lightbeams crossing his face. The fan lasers were ghostly bright, and he prayed that they wouldn't injure his eyes. He kept his back to the projectors, aware that, like Hoshi, he was now a part of the program.

When he reached Hoshi, the bewildered man was stumbling away in complete disorientation. "Hoshi," he hissed. His words were washed away by the music. He seized Hoshi's arm and pulled him toward the edge of the stage. All he could see was a fog of blazing lights, and the ghost of a mountainside. Hoshi showed no sign of recognition, but stumbled along beside him. They passed through a waterfall—and a curtain caught them full in the face. Beating his way along the curtain, Jonders found his way off the stage into darkness, and then felt the frame of a door. Behind him, the symphony thundered. He struggled to push the door open and dragged Hoshi after him into a hallway.

The hallway lights were cold and bright. The door slammed closed behind them, muting the music. "Hoshi, are you all right?" he murmured, steadying the young man against the wall.

Hoshi stared at him with a face tight with pain. His eyes were jerking from side to side. He seemed to be having trouble focusing. "Hoshi, it's Bill Jonders! Can you see me? *What's wrong?*"

Hoshi shook his head, grimacing, like a dog with an irritation in its ear. There was something wrong with Hoshi's visual implants, Jonders realized, kicking himself for not catching on sooner. No wonder he was stumbling around. The sonic medallion was missing from his chest, so his depth perception was gone, as well. He needed the help of a neurosurgeon, and quickly. Jonders could not even guess what this might be doing to Hoshi's neuronal system.

He reached into his jacket pocket for his phone. He thumbed it on and first called for an ambulance. Then he started to call Sandaran Link Security, hesitated, and instead called Joe Kelly, the security chief, at home. Once assured that Kelly was on his way over, he spoke to Hoshi again. "Can you describe to me what's wrong, Hoshi?"

"What?" Hoshi gasped.

"*Hoshi!* It's *Bill.*"

"I—can't see—hear—concert—something ringing—buzzing."

Hoshi staggered forward, then slid sideways, crumpling to the floor before Jonders could catch him.

Jonders helped him sit up with his back to the wall. "The concert's over, Hoshi," he said, crouching over him protectively. "We can help you now. It's over."

Chapter 30

Jet Propulsion Laboratory was a quiet place, shabby in a distinguished sort of way. The building's last refurbishment had occurred just before the turn of the century, and the intervening years showed in the tarnish and dirt, and in the unfilled cracks in the walls and ceilings. Still, Payne discovered, the place was not without pride. Display cases commemorated JPL's place in the history of space exploration, with models and photos of Surveyor's journey to the Moon, Viking's to Mars, Voyager's and Galileo's to Jupiter and the other gas planets, Argonaut's to Pluto/Charon, and others. JPL was now primarily an educational facility; most major exploratory spacecraft were controlled from the labs at GEO-Three and GEO-Four.

Payne had time to get a feel of the place while he waited for Dr. Ellen Chang to finish with her student appointments. He poked about, reading plaques, thinking about the history this place had seen. Eventually the receptionist pointed the way to Dr. Chang's office, down the corridor. He found her door open, and rapped on the jamb. Chang turned in her chair. She was a stocky woman, with dusty black hair and Asian features. She brushed back a lock of hair and said, "Have a seat, Mr. Payne."

"I appreciate your seeing me," he said, shaking her hand.

"After your coming all the way out here, I could hardly say no," Chang answered. "You're a determined man."

Payne shrugged with a smile, opened his briefcase, and took out both a voice and note recorder. Chang leaned forward at once, raising a hand in objection. "Please. No recordings."

Payne looked up in surprise. "I won't use them without your permission. They're only for accuracy—"

She shook her head vigorously. Her voice was strained. "No. I'm sorry. I'll have to end the interview right now, if you insist."

He gazed at her, startled by the intensity of her protest. "Okay," he said, with a self-conscious shrug. He put the voice recorder away. "May I take notes?" She nodded, relaxing a little, and he settled back with the note recorder on his lap.

"Now what can I do for you, Mr. Payne?" she said, her composure restored.

You could tell me what it is that's made you afraid to talk, he thought; but what he said was, "What can you tell me about the *Father Sky* space mission?"

She hesitated, and seemed to be reflecting. "What exactly would you like to know about it?"

"Anything you can tell me. The mission's purpose, what it's discovered so far, what new technologies are involved, who's responsible for its operation. That sort of thing."

"You can get all that from the Space Agency," she said. "I'm sure you already have."

"Yes," he said. "But their descriptive packets seem . . . *incomplete*, in view of other, unofficial information that I've received." He paused, waiting for a reaction. There was none, so he proceeded to sketch the suspicions he had gathered from Alvarest and Gerschak. He took care to dissociate Gerschak from his obtaining of her name.

Chang listened politely, but impassively. When he finished, she said, "I'm not sure what I can do for you. As I told you before, I can't give you much information." She gazed at him as she might at a student who had just asked an unanswerable question.

"Could you deny what I've just described?" Payne asked.

"I can't deny it. Nor can I confirm it."

"Because you don't know? Or because you can't say?"

She stared at him silently for a moment. "Because I'm not at liberty to talk about it," she said finally.

A twinge of nervousness was creeping into her voice, Payne realized. Was there something she *wanted* to tell him, but was afraid to tell? He had to be very careful not to push too hard. He cleared his throat. "Suppose we were to talk about the kinds of restrictions that exist on what you can say. Could you explain that to me—what you can or can't talk about—and why?"

"That's a large subject," Chang said. Her eyes seemed to soften somewhat. "I suppose I could, in general terms. Would that help you? I don't really know what you want."

Payne turned his palms up. "Hard to say. My report is far from complete, at this point. In view of the subject matter, anything you can tell me might be helpful."

"Very well." Chang sat back, placing an index finger to one corner of her mouth. She immediately appeared more relaxed, as she settled into the role of a teacher. Her voice quickened. "Let's talk about secrecy, then. Secrecy in government, and in the scientific community. This is something that any graduate student could tell you about."

Nodding, Payne began tapping notes into his recorder.

Chang talked, and primarily Payne just listened, and much of what he heard sounded a lot like what he had heard a couple of weeks ago from Gerschak. This time he heard about it in more detail, and with a quiet, but somehow greater, vehemence.

Chang talked nonstop for nearly an hour.

Payne looked thoughtfully at his notes. He looked back up at Chang. "You could endanger your security clearance by simply inquiring too closely into a subject's classification? Is that what you're saying?"

"Yes."

"That sounds like a rather effective form of censorship."

Chang frowned in affirmation. She ran her fingers back through her hair. Silence hung restlessly in the air, broken only by voices outside, down the corridor.

"Would you say that it is dangerous to science, and to the public's interest?" Payne asked.

"Indeed it is."

Payne grunted and made a note. "Up against the wall," he murmured, half to himself.

"I beg your pardon?"

"*Up against the wall*," Payne said. "A phrase that was popular in the last century. It referred to people backed up against their principles, forced to extreme measures by intolerable situations. People with nothing to lose by fighting. It just came into my mind." He smiled and shook his head, as though to clear an extraneous thought.

"I see," she said softly.

She wants to talk, he thought. She's close. Very close. Don't scare her off. He rubbed his forehead. "It almost seems—" He paused. "Correct me if I'm wrong, but it seems as though people would be forced to join together in small groups, or cabals, to quietly share information."

She gazed at him, not blinking.

"How else," he continued, "could the scientific community, or anyone else, keep tabs on what was being done in the name of science? People must be exchanging information outside of the regular channels. Am I right?"

Chang lifted a paper, dropped it. It had gotten dark outside, and she had switched on a desk lamp. With her head averted, her eyes were in shadow. After a moment, she rose and walked to the door and gently swung it closed, cutting off sounds from the corridor. She returned to her seat and faced him. "We must have an understanding," she said softly.

He felt a release in his chest. "Yes?"

"Everything that I'm going to tell you is for background use only." She spoke so softly now that he had to lean forward to catch her words. "Is that the phrase you newsmen use? I will not name my sources, and you will not name me as a source. You will not use my name in your stories, or refer to my work."

He gestured vaguely. "Those are pretty strict limits. After all, much of your work is published—"

"And much of it isn't. What you want to know about, isn't." She sat back. "Those are my conditions."

"Background, then," Payne said. "Unless you change your mind—"

"I won't. I could endanger several other people, who have stuck their necks out a lot farther than I have mine."

"I understand," he said.

She nodded. "I asked a few people about you. You seem well regarded in your field. I . . . think perhaps I can trust you."

Payne held his breath.

"Are we agreed?"

He nodded, letting his breath go. "Agreed."

She held his eyes for a moment, then looked away. "There are ways of gathering information," she said quietly. "It must be done delicately, and with consideration for the positions of the people who are helping you. Personal contacts must be used carefully and sparingly." She gazed out the darkened window, meditatively. "People can be hurt. Good people can be hurt." She glanced at him. "Do you understand?"

Payne nodded. His fingers rested motionless on the keypad of his note recorder. Her fear was contagious.

Chang sat back. "Communications with the *Father Sky* mission are relayed through an orbital laboratory known as Tachylab. There's a group at Tachylab who feel that certain information should be more widely disseminated than it is.''

Payne's fingers tapped on the keypad.

Chang swiveled her chair toward the window, as she spoke in a low monotone. ''I think they would approve of my giving you this information. They want it made public. The only question has been how. It concerns who controls *Father Sky*, and the reason it was sent out in the first place.'' She paused for another moment. ''There *were* signals received from space. Intelligent signals, we believe.''

Payne's fingers tapped more quickly.

Chapter 31

It was a locked, windowless meeting room on the thirty-fourth floor of the Defense Intelligence building, in New Washington. The room was dominated by a large, oiled walnut table surrounded by ten seats. Against one wall was a sideboard intended for coffee service, and over it hung several framed portraiture prints. All of the seats around the table, except one, were empty.

Leonard Hathorne touched several keys on his communication console at the end of the table. "Gentlemen," he said, his voice echoing flatly in the room. He paused, imagining the reek of tobacco smoke, the hazy blue cloud rising to the ceiling.

The projectors clicked on, one after another. Nine ghostly holographic images appeared, nine figures of men occupying the empty spaces around the table, nine faces turning to look at him. They looked, if not quite real as life, still almost solid enough to touch. Hathorne spoke again. "Gentlemen, may I ask you all to confirm, please?" He waited until the verification windows on his console glowed green, indicating secure channels to all the members of the Oversight Committee, as far away as Paris, Mexico City, and the Space Lab at GEO-Four, and as close as five blocks away. "Thank you," he said. "Now, to bring you up to date on the *Father Sky* mission—"

As he spoke, Hathorne directed the appropriate data to the members' console screens. He glanced up from time to time to see the projected images of the members looking from him to what appeared to be imaginary screens in front of them. There was a certain amount of soft, staticky throat-clearing as he talked. By the time he was finished, he faced a circle of scowling faces. One or two, perhaps, merely looked bored. He opened his mouth to take up the next item, but one of the ghostly figures turned, signalling that he wanted to speak. "Yes, General," Hathorne said, frowning slightly.

The faces turned, as each member looked toward the general, or toward whatever image of the general was visible at each location. Several of the gazes were skewed a little from the general that Hathorne saw.

"Yes, General?" he repeated.

The general raised his chin. "One gets the sense that this mission is in trouble," he said. His voice, as always, was a growl.

Hathorne allowed himself a measured turn of the head, as he looked first at the general, and then at the other members. He refrained from displaying his irritation. "Well, General, as I said—it looks like a software problem, and they're working on it. For now, the Kadin prog-, Kadin and Mozelle, are overriding the problem successfully, and keeping the craft on course. I remain hopeful—"

"But aren't we dependent on the cooperation of—well. Let us say, the personality of a rebellious, post-adolescent—?"

Hathorne interrupted brusquely. "I think that's an exaggeration, and needlessly pessimistic. It's true that we need cooperation, but on the other hand, we're getting it. Meanwhile, the people at Sandaran-Choharis are confident that they can resolve the problem, given a little more time."

"Time is in short supply," said the general. "Rendezvous is approaching."

"We're all aware of that, General. What specifically are you driving at?"

The general's chin went higher. "Just this. What will you do if it turns out that the problem isn't just related to, but is *caused by* this Mozelle personality? I venture to say that you can't risk trying to erase her—*it*—again."

Hathorne thought a moment. "That's true enough. Obviously she has means of protecting herself, and if we tried again, we would certainly make an enemy of her. And then we *would* probably have to terminate the mission."

"Well, then." The general cleared his throat noisily, and his eyes shifted as he looked around at the Committee members, or their images. "Gentlemen. I hate to be the one to say this—"

Untrue, Hathorne thought. You've opposed it from the start.

"—but I think perhaps it's time to suggest that this mission *be* terminated. By us. Before it approaches the target, and some further degradation puts it out of our control, and we find ourselves in worse shape than we'd be in with no spacecraft out there at all.''

"You're assuming problems that may not occur," Hathorne said. "Even without a software solution—if we can work effectively with Kadin and Mozelle, then I believe our chances are still good." He met the general's stare evenly. If it had once seemed odd to refer to the Mozelle personality as though it, or she, were a real person, it no longer caused him qualms. He was willing to concede that the Mozelle programming probably closely resembled, and behaved like, the personality of Mozelle Moi, and he would certainly make use of those qualities in dealing with her. That did not mean, however, that he regarded her as being equivalent to a living human being, with attendant rights. Realism demanded his recognition that the mission was far more important than the existence of a "personlike" computer program.

"But if this personality *fails* to cooperate, we could be making a tremendously important first contact—" and the general gestured with one hand—"with a failing machine. Now, I'm not sure that the benefits are such—and considering what we might do with a *manned* mission—"

"General, may I interrupt you?" Hathorne held up a hand.

He was met with silence—and a glare.

"Forgive me, but with your permission—" Hathorne addressed the entire Committee. "May I ask, before discussing this issue, that we review the rest of the agenda? I have more information that bears on the question." He touched several keys, bringing up a display. "Please refer to your consoles again."

"Here is the translation team's report on the latest signals from Tachylab. First the analysis." He touched a key, and the security warnings disappeared, to be replaced by a screenful of text. "You'll note that our confidence in translation is still low—less than sixty percent on major comprehension, and only about twenty-three percent on detail. It's getting better, though."

He paused to let them read. The text discussed translation methodology, and showed the actual tracings of the tachyon signals. The translation followed, in English. It began:

LIFE OF THIRD WORLD . . . PEOPLE/CITIZENS OF THIRD WORLD . . . ATTENTION . . . ATTENTION FROM DISTANT WORLDS. OUR APPROACH IS . . . [NO TRANSLATION]. WE PREDICT THAT THE MEET-

ING . . . WILL BE . . . [TRANSLATION UNCERTAIN: FRUITFUL? PRODUCTIVE? DYNAMIC?] . . .

    WE ARE PREPARED WITH GREAT . . . [TRANSLATION UNCERTAIN: EXCITEMENT? ANTICIPATION? FORCE?] WE PREDICT THAT WE SHALL ACHIEVE [TRANSLATION UNCERTAIN: COMMUNICATION? DOMINATION?] UPON OUR ARRIVAL. . . .

The transcript ran about three pages. Like those before it, it was rife with ambiguities and tentative translations, many of which bore heavily on the overall content. A number of verselike lines had been rendered as riddles. Hathorne privately felt that the linguistics team was stretching matters in claimimg a sixty percent certainty, even in broad meaning. They had far too little to go on. The primary keys consisted of references to universal physical constants, such as absorption and emission lines in stellar spectra, and correlations between graphic images and words. The team did well to produce *any* translation, he realized. But they were a long way from real communication.

"It's not precisely alarming, nor reassuring, either," said a European representative.

"Which means," another member said, "that we must regard it as alarming—until we know more."

Someone else brought up the subject of preparations for defense.

Hathorne steered the discussion back. "It seems clearer than ever to me that *Father Sky* must continue," he said. "Right now we know almost nothing about our visitors. The earlier we learn something of what—or whom—we're dealing with, the better equipped we can be when they arrive. Why else have we gone to such lengths to reach them while they're still outside the solar system? Why else push our artificial intelligence program to the very limit?"

He paused to let his gaze roam among the Committee members. "Let's not forget. We're projecting their arrival less than a year from now. It could be sooner. If *Father Sky* fails, or if we abort, we won't reach them, as even the general tells us, until they're inside the orbit of Mars. Not with a manned mission."

The general was scowling. "As you know, I've favored a manned mission from the beginning," he said deliberately. "I didn't trust the artificial intelligence, and I still don't. Obviously, we would all like to have an early look at the object. Hell, we could have done that if you'd given me the green light a year and a half ago. But even without *Father Sky*, we could get a look with a high-boost flyby, and then concentrate on getting a manned mission out there as soon as possible."

The representative from GEO-Four stirred, with a ghostly shimmer. "No point in dredging up the past. The decision was made not to send someone on a one-way trip, and that's done with now. But look. We're counting on *Father Sky*'s detailed information to help us determine the makeup of the manned follow-on. How can we know whether the manned mission should be armed—and if so, how—without good data, preferably from a solid prior contact?"

"You're missing my point," said the general. "If *Father Sky* fails, we will have gained no useful information, and will have demonstrated weakness to a potential adversary. I suggest that we go with the follow-on mission *now*, and go prepared for possible conflict. Prepared to establish a defense at some distance from Earth, in case the intruder proves hostile."

The man from GEO-Four was unconvinced. "Are you simply ignoring the diplomatic and scientific aspects? You talk as though this project is entirely military."

"A manned mission could carry out other objectives, as well," said the general.

"Perhaps. But if our first appearance is armed and threatening, what will that say to them about our diplomatic intentions? They might come entirely in peace."

"If they come in peace, no harm will be done," said the general.

"They might not be there at all," said another voice. "It could be an automated probe, intended only to report back."

The general shrugged. "Robot or living, the problem remains. What is their ultimate intent?"

"Well, a robot probe would be unlikely to be on a hostile mission," said the same member.

"Perhaps. Certainly it would be designed, as you said, to report back to its makers. And who knows what might follow?" the general answered.

Hathorne finally raised his hands. "Clearly, *all* of these possibilities must be considered," he said. "They could be living, could be machines, could be nothing we understand. They might come in peace. They might not." He shook his head to forestall interruptions. "It's equally clear that we can't answer any of these questions without a closer look, and a chance to communicate. *That's* why we need *Father Sky*, perhaps more than ever—to give us that detailed first look, *before* they're at our doorstep. General, you're concerned about our defense, as well you should be. But I submit that knowledge is our greatest defense. Wouldn't you prefer to face an adversary whom you know something about? And if indeed they come in peace, wouldn't we all like to know that, to be able to evaluate and confirm that? Isn't that what we created Kadin for?''

"And if they do *not* come wholly in peace," answered the general, "a failure of *Father Sky* in their presence would simply advertise our limitations.''

"It might demonstrate our imperfection," suggested one of the members who had not yet spoken. "But perhaps that's a risk we can afford to take, against the very great possibility of gaining valuable information. Provided—'' and he turned to look squarely at Hathorne, "the risk factor does not grow worse.''

A muttering arose as Hathorne nodded. Inwardly, he counted responses and smiled. He knew now that when the sense of the body was taken, he would have won the round.

There were other questions, of course—concerning the space defense network, and various issues of security. The Committee still managed to escape notice in most halls of government and in the press. Even the President only spoke of the Committee and the project with selected advisors. Hathorne reported on a North American astronomer who had independently claimed discovery of tachyon signals. The astronomer's attempts at publication had been quietly suppressed, and though he continued his work, few of his colleagues took his conclusions seriously. He reportedly had discussed his work with a video journalist, which probably only hurt his legitimacy in the community. His activities were being monitored. The journalist had made no broadcasts, and was presumed to have dismissed the story or lost interest.

Some discussion was made of the Chinese and Soviet tachyon research programs, neither of which was believed sufficiently advanced to have detected the alien signals. The Soviet program had been delayed by that nation's economic difficulties, but the two nations were expected to cooperate, and contingency plans were being readied against the chance of other nations learning of the alien object and joining in a race to establish first contact.

Overall, it appeared that security remained tight, and the Oversight Committee and those who answered to it were still alone in their knowledge of the thing that was approaching.

"Let's keep it that way, gentlemen," said the President's special advisor, as the meeting came to a close.

Even before the holographic projections winked off, Hathorne had put the meeting behind him. Authorized by the Committee to continue *Father Sky*, he was already thinking ahead to the instructions he would send to Marshall.

Chapter 32

Her vision is hazy with anger. Inside, another consciousness kicks and struggles for control, but she keeps a firm grip on the other Mozy and glares out at the faces peering at her.

The one named Marshall, a black man, speaks to her in a low voice. "No one means to threaten you, Mozy. What Mr. Fogelbee means is that there are many ways of approaching a problem."

"Oh?"

"Of course. Even with your best efforts, the malfunction may worsen. We'd have to find a way to repair it. That's all he meant."

"Is it?" Her eyes slowly scan the room, pausing for only an instant on each face. "I think he meant, tow the line, or you'll try to kill me again. Isn't that what you meant?"

For an instant, no one speaks. Fogelbee scowls. The word kill *hangs in the air. "No, Mozy," Marshall says finally. "It means we want you to keep working with us—"*

"Prove it, then. Tell me where I'm going."

Silence again.

(Mozy, can you hear me? The link is over, it's done! What's going on?) Kadin's voice echoed, ringing, but she couldn't break the loop; her anger was rising. Marshall, Fogelbee, and the rest—they were just figures in a play, like the now-stranger that was her former self— but the play kept changing, and the rules.

A voice calls insistently, as Marshall's voice fades, and as the cauldron of terrified emotions that is Mozy-Earth's inner sanctum slips away. Who is it she hears? Kadin? No, it's Dee.

246

That's impossible. Dee walked out on her for some penis-slinging jerk, ending the friendship. But wait, that's in the future; it hasn't happened yet.

She hears Dee for sure, laughing. No—not laughing. Gasping, scared shitless. Scared because how did they get into this back alley? They sure as hell didn't mean to, but they've had a bit too much of the wacky candy, and they're a little giddy now, just a little giddy. Fact is, they're kind of stoned . . . but not as stoned as those guys strolling into the alley behind them.

"What are we gonna do?" Dee is hissing. No place they can go, it's a dead end. How could they be so stupid?

The hoods are getting closer. Don't look at them, don't give them the satisfaction of knowing you're scared. But where else is there to look? Just walls, blocking their escape. She's shaking, and it's all she can do to keep from peeing in her pants, but she whispers to Dee, "I'll claw their eyes out if they try anything with me."

The next twenty seconds are an endless stretch of time in which she watches the three young hoods drift apart and then close in on her, separating her from Dee. There are screams, some of them her own, and fingernails flashing, raking flesh, and somewhere in the torrent of raw terror and fury, thrashing arms and legs and knees, she goes down hard on the pavement . . . a knifeblade slashes across her vision, biting . . . numbness spreads across the right side of her face, and her hand comes away wet, dark. The muggers are gone, it's just Dee and her, and someone is still screaming . . . it's her screaming, and now the pain is starting to cut through the numbing haze. . . .

There was a jolt, picked up by the inertial sensors, and she returned to the present with a start. Kadin was controlling the spacecraft, attempting to reset the attitude. The main drive had just throttled up, pushing them on back toward the sun.

Kadin was doing a lousy job of piloting.

(Shouldn't I be doing that?) she asked, her senses slowly coming back into focus.

(You were having some trouble, I think.)

(What do you mean?) Short-term memory was sifting away, a dream vanishing.

(You don't know? You linked with Homebase, through Mozy-Earth. You argued, and parted quite agitated. You wouldn't speak with me. You began reliving the link, along with some violent dreams or memories.)

Yes, she was beginning to remember now, it was coalescing. Homebase had patronized and threatened, demanded she follow orders, and offered nothing in return. That was when the anger had started. And the memories.

(Mother Program, describe what happened to the spacecraft following the last transmission,) Kadin said.

(CONTROL BECAME ERRATIC. SPACECRAFT WAS SUBJECTED TO HIGH LATERAL AND TORSIONAL STRESSES DUE TO NON-NOMINAL ATTITUDE CHANGES UNDER FULL DRIVE. TRAJECTORY ERROR . . .)

(I had to take over, Mozy. It wasn't easy to make you release control.) Kadin continued to make corrections as he spoke.

(Yes,) Mozy said, remembering. She felt unaccountably restless. (David, would you like to join me in the ship's commons? Can you spare a part of yourself for a while?)

Kadin answered by gathering himself toward a shared image: a top view of the commons, a tiny lighted oasis in the blackness of space, viewpoint zooming in. . . .

They toasted to companionship, snifters clinking together. Mozy felt a warming rush, even before the brandy touched her lips. (This is a wonderful spot,) she said, looking out the bay window at the stars. She was trying to conceal her anxiety.

Kadin swirled his snifter, watching her. (Do you feel more comfortable, here in the commons?)

(It's a different sort of thing,) she answered. (More homey. It helps me *feel* more.) She thought about that, the illusion of bodies, the luxurious surroundings that no spaceship would have. These things stirred her memories of a past existence, but she knew in a dreamy, sensuous way that the memories were better than the past had ever been.

(You were *feeling* a little while ago,) Kadin said, gazing at her.

She shuddered. (Yes, I . . . I was reliving something that happened . . . years ago.) She fingered her glass. She wasn't sure that she wanted to talk about it.

She met his eyes then, and thought, Yes, I do want to talk. She sipped her brandy, and steamy vapors rose in her head. (That was more than a memory. I was *living* it again. I was . . . assaulted . . . once.)

Her voice failed, and there was a silence, and Kadin waited patiently. Looking into herself, she found courage, and she told him what it was that had happened, how the frightened teenager had lost a part of her innocence. (That's how I got this scar,) she said, touching her cheek with her fingertip. She had to search a moment to find it.

Kadin looked at her closely, his eyes probing. (I've never known you to have a scar,) he said, touching her face. (Come look.) He guided her to the bay window. She peered at her reflection.

What she saw was her fingers running over a smooth, unblemished cheek.

The feelings rose in her again—the violence and the anger, the adrenaline rush that drove her to fight back—and the shame of facing her schoolmates afterwards, her face a ruin, her assault uncontested by the boys of her neighborhood who thought her not worth defending.

She stared at her unblemished face.

(You don't have to have a scar, anymore, if you don't want it,) said Kadin.

She looked at him and thought, No, I don't, do I? She studied her reflection, and decided that her face was really rather . . . attractive. (You didn't know I had a scar?) she asked, disbelieving.

(No. Only that there was something that you felt was wrong. I never knew what it was.)

Their eyes met again, and a current passed between them, and the hurt that she had remembered with such terrible power welled up and out of her, and passed away. Kadin's expression softened, and his hand moved to stroke her hair. The gesture seemed awkward at first, but became gentler and more sure.

(What . . . what's happening?) she asked, hardly daring to speak of the other emotions rising in her.

(Don't you know?) said Kadin. As he smiled at her, she thought for just an instant that he was too beautiful to be true; but that didn't matter here, it didn't matter who or what he was, and the doubts vanished in a current of rising desires. (We're exploring,) he said, stroking her face with his fingertips. (Or I am. You've probably experienced this before. I only know what's been written about it—but what's it really like, Mozy?)

(What's . . . *what* like?) she asked nervously.

(I think you know.)

(Well, I—) She nodded and felt her blood rushing. (I'm not sure—)

(Haven't you experienced it?)

(I—just once.) She was so nervous, she was having trouble breathing. (I've . . . only made love once. And . . . but it wasn't like this.) She struggled to get the words right. (It was . . . just clumsy . . . with a boy I hardly even liked. So I guess . . . I really haven't.)

Kadin nodded, touching her shoulders, soothing and exciting her. (So we're both exploring. It's a puzzle to me. I only know what psychologists and storytellers have written.) She nodded, swallowing, and raised her hands tentatively to stroke the front of his shirt, cream-colored silk, ridges of muscle underneath. (They seem to say,) he continued, smiling at her touch, (that *knowing* is less important than *experiencing*.)

(I . . . I guess that's true,) she said, expanding the range of her hands' movements a little.

(And the storytellers—why, they give you some of it, but they can't express it all, can they?) His fingers moved in delicate circles around her breasts, just brushing her nipples. She breathed quickly, almost frantically. Then his hands were in her hair, cradling her head.

(No,) she whispered, (no, they can't,) and wondered if he were as frightened and excited as she.

His eyes shifted in tiny movements, drinking her attention. He drew her close, and kissed her as he had done once before—but it was different, this time, and the melting pressure of his lips left no doubt as to his desires. A flush ran up and down her body, and she returned the pressure, with her lips and then with all of her, every part of her body that touched him. She felt him rising against her, and she grew even dizzier with desire; and as their garments slowly loosened and fell away, she knew that what was about to happen, she had long since thought impossible in this lifetime.

Chapter 33

Jonders drummed his fingers under the edge of his desk. Why him? And why, of all times, today? Life was confounding enough already. Just three hours ago he'd been informed that he was being called back onto the Kadin program. He shook his head. "I'm sorry, Mister—"

"Payne. Joseph Payne," said the face in the telephone screen.

"Yes. Forgive me, Mr. Payne. You caught me at a rather difficult time. You see—well. I'm afraid I can't be of much help. Why don't you call the public information office?"

"I already have," said Payne. "I'm afraid their information was rather limited."

"I see," said Jonders. "But you understand that this is a restricted project."

"So I gathered," Payne said. "But what I was hoping to get, in part, was some *sense* of what the project is—"

"Beg pardon?"

"Well—how can I say it? A more personal view. A sense of the goals, and so forth."

"The only thing I can tell you about the goals is what's in the press releases."

Payne scratched his temple. "You mean, *Father Sky* being the first of its kind in the use of tachyon communications? And its mission profile, which is rather nebulously described as 'exploration of the interstellar medium and the cometary cloud'?"

"Is that what the release says?"

"More or less."

"Well—" Jonders shrugged. "I can't tell you anything more. Now,

I really must excuse myself, and ask that you call the press office with any further—''

"Could I ask you just one more thing?" Payne said politely.

"I suppose so."

"Well, two things really."

Jonders sighed. "What, Mr. Payne?"

The newsman paused. "Have tachyon signals have ever been received from a source other than our own spacecraft?"

"Not that I know of. Perhaps some natural sources. It's not my field."

Payne's eyebrows moved together. "I see. Well, then. Perhaps you could tell me something about a woman named Mozelle Moi. She works, or worked, at your institute. I've been trying to get in touch with her, but your personnel office hasn't been able to help me much."

Jonders, for a moment, could not speak. His eyes and mouth froze in a querying expression; finally he got control of his emotions, blinked and said, slowly, "No. I'm afraid I can't. And now, I really must go. I have a busy schedule."

Payne nodded. "Well, then. Thank you for your time." A moment later, the screen was blank.

Jonders exhaled slowly, staring at the telephone. How in God's name had that man heard about Mozy? He shook his head in dismay and began leafing uselessly through the papers on his desk. A couple of days out of the office, and things were already a mess. He hadn't even caught up yet on major developments. There was something here from Diana Thrudore; she was trying to have Mozelle transferred to a civilian treatment center, and she wanted Jonders's support. Apparently there had been another linkup attempt between Mozy-Earth and Mozy-ship (still alive!), and they had somehow botched it, much to Dr. Thrudore's displeasure. Mozy-ship, he had casually been informed, was not only alive, but was more cantankerous than ever. He could not help smiling at the thought.

That damn newscoper, though! How *could* he have found out about Mozy? Security would have to be informed, of course. Which reminded him—there was a message from Joe Kelly waiting on the internal circuit. He swung to his console and called it to the screen. It was a report on Hoshi Aronson, now in New Phoenix Memorial Hospital. He leaned forward and read:

  "The neurosurgeon stated that Hoshi Aronson was suffering from neurologic voltage imbalances in the right cerebral cortex, apparently caused by an electrical malfunction in his implanted visual microprocessing circuitry. The surgeon indicated that Mr. Aronson's aberrant behavior may be partially attributable to these imbalances and the resulting electrical discharges. Final determination must await corrective surgery and follow-up psychiatric evaluation.

"Looks like you were right on this one, Bill."

It was signed by Joe Kelly, with a postscript to the effect that he had requested Dr. Thrudore's participation in the evaluation. Perhaps, Kelly had added, the question of Hoshi's intent in the whole Mozelle business could finally be laid to rest.

Thank God for small favors, Jonders thought. He began to type a report to Kelly on the newscoper's questions, then glanced at the time and jumped up. He was supposed to be in Marshall's office.

Carpeted in maroon, with textured wallpaper and mahogany trim, the corridor outside the director's briefing room felt like the calm before the storm. Jonders took a deep breath. He was waved right in, and before he had even taken a seat, someone pushed a pen and a set of papers toward him. He looked around. Marshall, Fogelbee, Kelly. Diana Thrudore was here, too, scowling impatiently.

"I'll get right to the point," Marshall said "Leaving aside whatever role you played in Miss Moi's survival—"

Jonders blinked, but did not react.

"—we're facing an even more serious situation." He looked at Jonders and at Thrudore. "You are both being granted S-1 security clearances, effective immediately. Once you understand and sign those documents in front of you, we can get on with what I have to say."

There was silence, and some rustling of paper, and then that was done.

"Good." Marshall leaned back in his seat. "Now listen—especially you, Bill. You've done a lot of hard work on this project, and we've kept you in the dark—more than you've liked, I know. Well, now we're going to tell you what *Father Sky* and Kadin are really out there to do. Ken, get the lights, will you?"

Jonders opened his eyes a little wider, and exchanged glances with Thrudore.

The screen went dark, and the room lights came up again. Jonders sat silently mulling the excerpt he had been shown of the alien message.

"That," Marshall said, "is the reason for the security. And that's why, Dr. Thrudore, we can't let you move Mozelle to a civilian hospital, where questions would have to be answered. A great deal may ride on our establishing contact—and I mean genuine contact, not just a sighting—with this alien thing, spacecraft, or whatever it turns out to be."

"It seems to me," Jonders remarked, "that I could have done my job better if you'd explained all of this before."

"That's not under discussion," Marshall said. "Your cooperation is. Dr. Thrudore, can we count on you?"

Thrudore was silent, frowning, for a long time. "My patient is my primary responsibility," she said finally. "I must be given cooperation in treating her. And," she warned, "there must be no repetition of what happened in that last session."

Marshall acquiesced with a slight tilt of his head. "We handled that poorly. It was a mistake not to have Bill there." He turned to Jonders. "And that's why we need *you*. If anyone can reestablish a working relationship with Mozelle—"

"Mozy-ship, you mean?"

"Correct. We need you to do that. At least until we've resolved the computer malfunction."

"And then?"

Marshall answered without expression. "We shall still need a working relationship. It would appear that she's there to stay."

"I'm not sure she'll trust me more than you."

"Nevertheless, she has asked for you since the first time Donna Fenstrom replaced you in the link. Since I don't doubt that you assisted her in some way to survive—" Jonders looked at him blankly—"at the very least, tipped her off—"

Marshall's gaze finally forced Jonders to nod. "So she has more reason to trust you than anyone else," Marshall said.

Jonders considered. "Will you let me tell her what you've just told me—about the mission?"

Marshall studied him silently. "I'll ask Hathorne," he said at last.

Chapter 34

The stars were tumbling, gyrating, dancing. Cosmic radiation sparkled in an auroral display, and the music of the stars and galaxies sang a song of life and death . . . and love. The serenade was perfect, blissful in the waning tide of love's movements. They caressed one another gently, lingeringly, their thoughts intertwined.

They slept, dozing and dreaming and bumping comfortably against one another.

Something, though, was calling insistently for their attention.

As she awakened, and her thoughts drained back out toward the extremities of her world, Mozy smiled sleepily. She had an inkling of what was happening. Her heart was spinning. And her mind. Spinning with pleasure.

The spacecraft was spinning, too. They had lost control again. Mozy slipped back into her awareness of a body that *was* the spacecraft, and queried Mother Program. From Kadin, there was no communication in words, but only a hazy glow, a friendly incoherence.

Mother Program responded at once: (DRIVE WAS SHUT DOWN BY AUTOSEQUENCE UPON COMMENCEMENT OF TUMBLING. KADIN PROGRAM DROPPED OUT OF OVERRIDE . . .)

Mozy interrupted her. (We lost our heads again. Yes—well, Mother Program, we were making love. I hope it doesn't shock you to hear me say that, but it was . . .) She ran out of words, remembering the excitement and pleasure, the warmth of touching, knowing, sharing. She had to force herself to stop the memory.

(Please give me correctional information,) she said abruptly. (Did we seriously endanger the ship?)

(PROBABILITY OF SERIOUS DAMAGE OCCURRING REACHED

73 PERCENT PRIOR TO SHUTDOWN OF DRIVE. SHALL I DEFINE ''SERIOUS''?)

(Don't bother. Please go on.)

She listened as she worked, firing jets to slow the tumble. (Nothing we can't handle?) she said, responding to a litany of needed corrections. (NO. HOWEVER, THIS ASSUMES RELIABLE MANUAL OVER-RIDE CONTROL . . .)

(Okay, okay.) She didn't need a sermon from Mother Program. She continued making the corrections, dipping when necessary into Mother Program's stores of technical instructions. In time, she became aware of Kadin's presence beside her again, and she reached out to him with a tendril of thought. He did not directly respond, and she pulled back, a little puzzled.

Kadin remained quiet, pursuing his own thoughts.

She continued working, until at last the stars had stopped their spinning. Kadin's proximity, and his silence, remained an enigma to her. (We really let go, didn't we?) she commented, after a while. There was no answer from Kadin. (I'm glad we did,) she said. (It's something *I* wanted to do.) After another minute of silence, she said, (Mother Program just about gave up on us, you know. How are we going to explain this course screwup to Homebase?)

Kadin finally responded—with what *felt* like a smile. (We'll call it computer error,) he said.

Mozy laughed softly as she throttled up the main drive and trimmed the heading. She felt odd: dizzy and anxious, euphoric and content, all at the same time. There remained a spinning feeling within her, but this had nothing to do with the ship's attitude. After a while, Kadin began murmuring to himself, and seemed to want to say something. (David?) she said.

(It was a most interesting and . . . exhilarating . . . experience,) he said suddenly.

(Yes.)

(I enjoyed it,) he said, but there was something about his manner that seemed different, puzzled. (Mozy?)

(I enjoyed it, too,) she said quickly.

(Mozy, I'm trying to comprehend it all, but it's . . . difficult. There is so much to think about, so much to consider. The storytellers, the psychologists . . . what they say is . . . well, it's difficult to precisely connect their statements with what I felt. And the physical sensations, I . . . of course, I mostly shared your feelings in that, but it was . . . remarkable.)

(Yes. It was. We almost wrecked the ship, though, is the only problem,) Mozy said.

Kadin seemed to think about that, almost audibly working it around in his mind. (If we had harmed the ship,) he said, (that would have been irresponsible. We must not forget why we're here.)

(Do you think . . . well . . . that there's any chance . . . any way we could . . . do that again . . . but without . . . that problem?)

There was a long and awkward silence, in which she refrained from begging him to say *something*; then Mother Program interrupted to tell them that Homebase was calling.

Jonders floated like a golden hologram, against the stars.

Mozy hardly knew what to say. (They told me you were off the project,) she said finally. Somewhere in a corner of her mind was an odd feeling of embarrassment, as though she had been caught by her father, fooling around upstairs with a boy.

Jonders explained his return to duty, remarking, (I gather that relations became a little strained between you and Ken Fogelbee.)

(You might put it that way,) Mozy said. She didn't want to think about it now.

(I'd like to ask you more about that, but first, I have some information to pass on to you. Unless David has already told you—)

(About the mission?)

(Yes.)

Kadin spoke up softly. (I have not told her—though I sorely wanted to.)

(I see,) said Jonders. He seemed to gather his thoughts. (I told you,) he said finally, (that Kadin's purpose was to oversee any contact, should you—the spacecraft—encounter intelligent life in the coming—)

(Yes, but you didn't say why we had turned back toward the sun.)

(No. I didn't know, myself, at the time.)

(And now you do.)

(Yes. You are going to make your contact sooner than I imagined. In eleven days, you will be matching orbits with a spacecraft of alien origin. A spacecraft that is bound inward to the solar system. Bound, we think, for Earth.)

(Alien . . . ?) Mozy's mind blanked, then slammed back to full attention. (Did you say, *eleven days*?)

(It's approaching from the direction of the constellation Serpens, and is still somewhat farther out than you. You are accelerating to match its speed inward, toward the sun.)

(And we're to contact them . . . the aliens?)

(To rendezvous, to make contact, and to learn as much as possible about their nature and their intentions. Kadin has been given instructions. David, you are now released to share those with her.)

(You mean,) said Mozy in disbelief, her memory flashing back to the remote past, when she had worked in a human body at the Sandaran Link Center, (that this is what the whole program is about?)

He nodded.

(And you have known about this for how long?)

Jonders hesitated. The object, he explained finally, had been discovered two years earlier. In the course of research studies at Tachylab, an intermittent, coherent beam of tachyons, eventually determined to be an intelligent signal, was detected from a source in Serpens. Analysis showed the source to be only a light year distant—four times closer than the nearest star—and moving toward the sun at a substantial fraction of the speed of light.

The discovery was immediately cloaked in security. While translation efforts were undertaken, a mission was planned to intercept the alien object at the maximum feasible distance from Earth. A manned mission was impractical, but a robot craft was assembled for a high speed flight out of the solar system, with the most sophisticated computer available and a tachyon transceiver to link the spacecraft with Earth. The tachyon link made it possible for the computer's major programming to be relayed later, so that an extra year and a half was available for creation of advanced programming.

Kadin was the major component of that programming. His training was to aid him in establishing friendly contact with the aliens if possible, and early warning if any hostile intent was betrayed.

(Why the secrecy?) Mozy said. (Why not an open program?)

(That was the decision,) Jonders said, (and it was made at the highest levels of government. I suppose they feared panic—or a scramble by other countries to be the first there. The Oversight Committee makes those decisions now, and it represents a half-dozen nations.)

(That's arrogant and stupid.)

(I won't argue the point. After all, they didn't tell me, either.) Jonders fell silent, and in the echoes of that silence, Mozy thought to herself that perhaps Jonders was one person at Homebase she should consider trusting.

(So you understand,) Jonders said, (why they . . . why they . . .)

(—tried to kill me?) she said.

(Well—at least, why they were so upset, and so anxious. Your presence was really something of a monkey wrench.)

Mozy considered that for a moment. (Does that excuse cowardice and stupidity? They might have tried to give me a chance.)

Jonders peered at her, but said nothing.

She didn't really expect an answer. She considered again what he had told her, and said, (Now that I seem to be one of Earth's prime diplomatic envoys, may I ask something else? Am I an enlisted soldier, or still a civilian?)

For an instant, Jonders smiled across the black emptiness of the link. (We're all civilians in this army. It just doesn't always feel that way.)

Anger flashed through her. (Give me a straight answer!)

His smile evaporated. (I'm trying.)

(I want to know—are we controlled by the military?)

Jonders hesitated for a long time. His eyes sparkled strangely. (I don't know that I can answer that,) he said finally, in a puzzled voice. (The military—I know that they influence policy, but—Kadin can—)

His image turned to golden snow, his voice to a hash of static. Before Mozy could say another word to him, he winked out of existence.

Mozy stared after him in silence. Mother Program reported that the link transmission cycle had ended. She looked inward toward Kadin, who throughout had remained quiet. There was much that they had to discuss. Implications to work out. Strategies to plan.

Envoy to the stars—contact in a matter of days? That was quite a lot to cope with.

(David?) she said, and was suddenly at a loss. The words that finally came to her seemed to well up out of a great depth, from sources almost forgotten within her. (Become solid again, David, and hold me,) she whispered. (Just for a little while. Just hold me.)

Kadin's arms seemed a part of the starry firmament itself, as they closed around her and comforted her.

PART FIVE

THE TALENKI

Prelude

In the warm, blue waters of the winter mating grounds, the whales milled quietly. Confusion had grown among the herd, until at last silence took the place of songs.

It was the odd Song that had caused it, Luu-rooee felt. The Song from the Outside, from the deeper waters somewhere beyond, the song that had so unsettled all of the others, filled them with restlessness and curiosity. Life went on, of course, birthing and mating and sunning; but many of the cows had become uncharacteristically, incautiously daydreamy, even as the males wandered farther afield, singing with great intonation, trying to answer the continuing . . . odd . . . Song.

And then it had fallen silent, and nowhere was there a sign of the whale whose voice it was.

The silence itself was odd. The herd jostled uncomfortably. A few individuals tried resuming their own songs, but hesitantly, as though unsure if the soul of the song remained. One by one, they dropped back off into fretful silence, and now they swam quietly—blowing, diving, listening.

Listening. As though someone or something were among them, and yet they couldn't see it, couldn't smell it, taste it, or feel it. Or, now, hear it. Where had the Song gone? And why?

Luu-rooee had never witnessed anything like it.

The sun fell in the sky, and darkness crept through the waters. The herd slept fitfully, with much snoring and snorting and bumping about.

Luu-rooee dozed at the edge of the herd. As the night wore on, he drifted into and out of a curious half-sleeping state, neither awakening nor settling into the deep lassitude of real sleep. He dreamed of the Song. He dreamed of floating—in a world unlike his own, a world where sound failed, where there was no weight, no bubbles, no breakthrough of air—and endless depths without echo. A world of sharp-edged lights and darks. That dream passed, and he dreamed then of another sea, one like his own, with blue water and echoes, and the gentle sway of tides, and good pressure against his flukes when he dived. But it was smaller, this sea, and confined, filled with grottoes and alarming places where one might become trapped and where echoes reverberated wildly. And yet—was it so confined as it seemed? His awareness lasted just long enough for him to wonder at the meaning of this. And then real sleep took him, and that, too, passed away.

With the rising of the light over the sea, morning filtering downward through the waters, Luu-rooee woke to recall only fragments of his dreams, which he puzzled over briefly. Then he became aware of something else—and he knew why he had dreamed.

It was the Song, softer than before, and somewhat changed. He blinked his great eyes, and blew a spout of vapor, and then settled down, listening, as though somehow he might understand what the Song conveyed—what hopes, what fears, what passions and humors underlay it. He moved away from the herd, leaving Meeeorr and the others, in an effort to hear better. He tried, hesitantly, to answer with his own song, but there were differences between the herd's theme and this Other's, and it was unsettling to try and change rhythms to answer the Other. Unsettling to fail and not quite know why. As morning passed, and the wearing-on time of day approached, he found that he had drifted far from the herd.

But he found himself thinking. . . .

Something in this Song was a greeting, a welcoming—unlike any he had ever heard, but a greeting nonetheless. Perhaps he might follow it, find its source, its singer, its maker.

And what manner of creature might it be? Strange, like the air and land dwellers who from time to time entered their world, and whose machines darkened the waters and droned constantly in the background? No, surely a whale . . . but of what sort?

Perhaps a godwhale.

Only by seeking it would he know.

Without actually deciding to do so, he swam on, trying with great difficulty to pinpoint the direction, over and over diving deep to listen at the various sound layers. Always, he could hear the Song, but always the precise direction eluded him. The falling of darkness again found him moving mostly in circles, still trying, still uncertain.

The dreams would return, he thought wearily. But morning would follow, and then he would swim farther, and faster, and surely he would find the source tomorrow.

Tomorrow he would find the godwhale.

Chapter 35

(Mother Program, can you clarify that image?)

Mozy was perched on a shimmering pedestal, wholly surrounded by the heavens. The body of the ship was translucent, taking kaleidoscopic form behind her. The bridge controls were in front of her: small, glowing balls of gas, and twisting panes of light. Her hands caressed the glowing gases, making fine adjustments to the ship's flightpath.

She had been fiddling with the long-range optical scanners, but the best she could get was a shimmering white oval, a dim blob in the swirling, magic-mirror viewscreen that floated before her. The radar image, too, was smeared in a curious way. She had expected either a point source, or a steady, if imperfectly resolved, outline. (Mother Program? Hello? Can we improve the image?)

Mother finally awoke. (NEGATIVE CLARIFICATION. IMAGE IS AT MAXIMUM RESOLUTION.)

(Are they tumbling, or is it our equipment malfunctioning?)

(NO INDICATION OF EQUIPMENT FAILURE. IMAGE CHARACTERISTICS DO NOT COINCIDE WITH HYPOTHESIS OF TUMBLING OBJECT.)

(Conclusion?)

(CONCLUSION?)

Mozy sighed. (I'm asking for *your* conclusion.)

There was no answer.

Kadin spoke, from an invisible vantage point. He had been talking to Jonders, the two of them standing off to one side, floating in space on a disklike platform of gold. Jonders was gone now. (Homebase hasn't gotten a clear image, either, not even with the big space telescope. They're puzzled, too. They're counting on us to get the first pictures.)

(Mmm.) Mozy poked at the viewscreen controls a while longer, then gave up on it when Kadin reappeared on the bridge. He was wearing fluorescent blue fatigues.

She turned to him, frowning. (David. I'm afraid that Mother Program is becoming schizophrenic.)

Kadin was silent for a moment. (You should be more careful about your terminology,) he said. (People often use the word *schizophrenia* when they mean something else entirely. Mother Program is hardly capable of—)

(I wasn't making a psychological diagnosis, damn it. You know what I mean. She's becoming glitchy, unresponsive—and it's not just the navigational system, it's some of her higher-level functions, too.)

(Well, keep a watch on it. It doesn't mean that Mother's sick, though—does it, Mother Program? Mother Program?)

(PLEASE REPHRASE.)

(We shouldn't be talking about you behind your back. But we want to know if you're feeling yourself.)

Mozy glared at Kadin. (Don't make fun of me,) she said. (This is serious.)

(Sorry,) Kadin said. He settled onto his own pedestallike seat. He seemed taken aback by her anger. (No, really—I am. Mother Program, what we wanted to know was whether you are suffering like the rest of the programming.)

(ARE YOU ASKING FOR SELF-DIAGNOSIS?)

(Right.)

(INDICATORS ARE WITHIN OPERATIONAL LIMITS.)

(Oh. Well, we'll keep checking. Mozy, Mother says she's fine. There's nothing wrong with her.)

Mozy nodded silently. Perhaps she was overreacting. But Kadin was certainly underreacting. Why was he being so flippant, where the ship's safety was concerned? He had been acting a little strange for days, now, ever since they had been . . . physical with one another. Since they had made love. There was a lot she was going to have to sort out, when she had some time to think. Another thing was, why hadn't she been feeling more desire to make love with him again?

Kadin cocked his head in her direction. (What's wrong?) he said. (You aren't feeling sorry about anything, are you?)

(Of course not,) she said abruptly. (What's to be sorry about? Look at the view!) She waved an arm, and in one overhead quadrant, a magnified image of the Eagle Nebula in Serpens glowed brightly, full of luminous gases, dust clouds, and new stars.

(Mmm.) Kadin stroked his chin with one finger. (Well. Perhaps we should get to work on that message.)

Mozy nodded, avoiding his gaze. *Am* I overreacting? she thought. He's not human. Not like you. Don't expect the same reactions.

But maybe he was trying a little too hard to *be* human.

(You keep us on course, and I'll go below and start composing.) Kadin winked out of existence, leaving her alone on the bridge.

She touched a control here, there, to one side. The balls of gas flickered and changed color, and the spacecraft's radio and optical sensors turned slowly, tracking the distant alien object.

She licked her lips, and felt a cold touch of numbness. She had been up here too long. She needed sleep, some dreaming, some time to process and store memories. With a sigh, she waved a hand across the control surfaces, and the balls of gas, the contorted planes of light winked out. The ship surrounded her again like a suit of armor with vast fluid channels of thought activity.

(Are you going to transmit soon?) she asked Kadin. She didn't want to miss the first attempt at making contact.

He hummed affirmatively. Minutes passed, and he reoriented the tachyon transmitter. With the storage ring fully charged, he began sending a precoded greeting message: thirty seconds on, thirty seconds off, thirty seconds on . . . continuing until the storage ring was exhausted.

The only response was a hiss of instrument noise.

(They might not be oriented to receive,) he speculated. (Or perhaps they can't decipher the message. I'll try laser-com, then radio.)

Mozy's concentration began to waver as Kadin tried the various systems, and time passed with no response. (Maybe you should go down and kick the transmitters to make sure they're working,) she said.

(Eh?)

(Nothing. Can you mind the ship while I go off in a corner and catch some shut-eye?)

(Sweet dreams,) Kadin said, extending himself to take the helm. Mozy withdrew, dampening her sensory inputs. She spun a cocoon for herself in a nest of sedentary programs, and quickly dropped off to sleep.

*   *   *

She awoke from a dream in which the ship was a mad beehive, each bee a materialization of some visiting personality. She awoke to the sound of Kadin talking. Not to her. Not to Homebase or to Mother Program. She unwound her cocoon. (Who is it, David?) she said softly.

Kadin spoke again, but not to her. (Are you tracking us? Have you sighted our craft?) Kadin's words passed into a translating routine, and reappeared as a quavering signal, through the tachyon link.

The return signal was indistinct, a wailing sound that reminded her of something—synthesized music, perhaps, or sea gulls. Eventually she recognized that perhaps it actually *was* a song; it was filled with changes in pitch and volume and timbre, changes that repeated, with variations. The translating program overvoiced: (BEST AVAILABLE TRANSLATION: "STAR TRAVELLERS / STAR TRAVELLERS / DO GO GO GO? / SUN TRAVELLERS / VOID TRAVELLERS / SLOW SLOW YOU GO.")

(David,) she whispered, (can you understand them?)

(I'm not exactly sure,) he answered. (Can you come up to the bridge?)

Mozy blinked, and she was back on her pedestal among the stars, the controls incandescent before her, the ship a cloudy jewel behind. In the viewer, the optical image of the alien object was substantially larger, but it still squirmed against the starfield. The distance between them and the target was now just a few million kilometers.

Kadin rubbed his jaw. (I can't decide whether the problem is in the reception, or the translation algorithms,) he said.

(Probably the translation programs,) Mozy said, peering at the play of lights before her.

(They're the best Homebase has. *They* claim to have deciphered previous transmissions. I've had my doubts.)

(I wasn't thinking of Homebase,) Mozy said.

(What, then? Mother Program's translator going dotty?)

(Why should it be exempt? Everything else has been going dotty,) Mozy said. She scowled and reached out to touch a fiery ball. It changed from crimson to cyan, flickering. Deftly, she isolated and exposed the inner workings of Mother Program's translation routines, then brought self-diagnostic programs into play. (Analysis, Mother Program?)

(PLEASE SPECIFY.)

(Translation.)

(INDEFINITE. 33 PERCENT PROBABILITY OF TRANSLATOR MALFUNCTION. ANALYSIS PROCEEDING.)

(Mmm.) Mozy looked at Kadin.

He arched his eyebrows and paused in what he was doing. (Can you do anything about that?)

She looked at him skeptically. (Like what? Translate it myself?)

(Why not? I'll bet you could—)

Teach myself? she thought. Perhaps it was not so absurd a thought. Languages had always intrigued her, though she had been hampered in school by a bad memory for vocabulary. That should be no problem here, with the full memory of Mother Program at her disposal. Barring further malfunction, of course. . . .

The alien song started again, and she peered into the translation routine, observing. She followed pathways back into the grammar and syntax programs. She watched the scanning stacks as they checked for recursive phrases, comparing observed values with those already in the vocabulary banks. Once she began to understand the methodology, she noticed the search-and-scan routine stumbling intermittently, as several recursive phrasings were missed, and one seemingly erroneous connection was made, triggering an improbable analysis of phrase structure that significantly altered the translation.

Unsure whether she would do more harm than good by tampering with the existing mechanism, she quickly duplicated the routines that looked useful, and set up working space to perform her own operations. After some exploratory trial and error, she began to realize that the translation program from Homebase was insufficiently powerful. It took little account of harmonics and subtle changes in tonal qualities, at the same time focusing overly much on simple relations of pitch and rhythm. This was going to require learning as she went along.

(What do you think?) Kadin asked, after a while.

She ignored him and kept working.

A *long* time later, she looked up and informed him: (They're saying, "Star travellers, are you coming to meet us? Star travellers, will you join us?" At least, I think that's what they're saying. The second sentence I'm less sure of, but I believe the sense of it is, will we rendezvous and meet them in person?)

(How sure are you?) Kadin asked.

(There is a repetition of converging harmonics, and what seem to be open-ended phrasings—questions,) Mozy said.

(Translation routine, what is your version?) Kadin queried.

(STAR TRAVELLERS, GO / GO GO GO TO COME / WE GO. . . .)

(Yours makes more sense,) Kadin said. (Are you guessing?)

(Mother's translator has the right idea, but it's stumbling. Try sending them an answer. Tell them, yes—we're coming.)

(I'll send it in MacEnglish, and in translation. Do you want to do the translation for me?) Kadin said.

(I suppose I could try,) Mozy said. Translating *into* alien sounds would be harder—but if they were all going to be neighbors, then the sooner she started learning, the better.

Chapter 36

Payne scratched his head, looking away from Teri's image. When he replied, it was in a sort of drawl, a touch of his native midwestern accent returning. "I'm just not sure if we're really *ready*," he said. "I'd feel better if we had some harder evidence to back us up."

"Are you going to wait forever?" Teri said. "There will always be something you can't quite confirm, something you're not as sure of as you'd like to be. It's part of the business."

Payne glanced around the motel room and sighed. "I know. I know. But I don't want to shut myself out. I'd like to dig around, really learn what's going on."

"You've learned quite a lot already. And you can't expect the backers to fly you around indefinitely."

"Okay. But what happens after I go on the air with this?"

"The First Amendment isn't dead, yet," Teri pointed out. "Protect your sources, and build on it. You might find more people willing to talk once the ice has been broken."

Payne grunted. No doubt, she was right; in one sense, it was time for action. His sources, however nervous, clearly wanted the information made public, or they wouldn't have given it to him; and if he didn't get on the air with it soon, someone else would just beat him to it. But there was an inner sense that told him to be cautious. He had learned precious little in New Phoenix, either about Mozelle Moi or about Sandaran Link Research Center. The one lead he had gotten from SLRC's p.r. office, which was someone mentioning the name of Dr. Jonders, had gotten him nowhere; but some intuition told him that Jonders might yet open up. It was a hard feeling to define, but Jonders's faintly defensive reaction to his questions, particularly about

Mozy, suggested that Jonders might know more than he was presently willing to admit.

And that, Payne thought, was why he was reluctant to go on the air. A premature and overly sensational story might destroy his chances of getting more out of Jonders or anyone at the Center. If he went ahead, he had to do so with great care—to err, if he erred at all, on the side of caution.

"Let me work up a trial draft," he said finally. "I'll call you back tomorrow."

"No later than that," she warned. "I'll have our people get in touch with the news service and tentatively schedule a slot."

"But hold off on the commitment until we've gone over it."

"Good-bye," Teri said. "Get to work."

He blanked the phone and mulled for a while, sorting through his notes. There were memo printouts scattered on the bed, and covering the small motel-room desk. Motels. He was growing weary of motels. Berkshires Observatory, Pasadena, New Phoenix, New Washington for conferences, back home, New Phoenix again. . . . He glanced at the phone. He ought to call Denine.

Later. When he had finished that first draft.

He switched on a music cassette, and humming along, settled down to start writing.

The red plastic disk twirled through the air and landed in the cup with a satisfying *plink*. Betsy rocked back, grinning. Jonders allowed her a crinkly smile. "I knew you had something up your sleeve when you stopped playing the holos, because I was beating you."

"Livid!" Betsy cried, laughing. "No chance."

"And all this time, you've been practicing tiddly-winks."

Betsy's sister dumped the colored disks out of the cup. "We haven't been practicing, Dad. We're just naturally good."

Jonders was still trying to think of a comeback when Marie called from the other room. "Bill—come look at this."

"What?" He struggled to his feet and went into the den. Marie was sitting on the couch, reading—and watching the news. She pointed at the tube. There was a familiar face on the screen . . . it was Joseph Payne, that newscoper who had called him a few days ago. Jonders rocked on the balls of his feet and listened, frowning.

". . . A researcher at the Berkshires Observatory has reported the discovery of an unusual source of cosmic tachyons—faster-than-light particles from outer space. Stanley Gerschak, an astronomer at the observatory, stated that the tachyons, apparently originating from outside the solar system, may in fact be an intelligent signal directed toward Earth.''

The reporter paused for a taped sound, which reminded Jonders of a lone wolf crying over a prairie. Chromakeyed behind Payne's head was a holographic photo of an oddly configured dish antenna, silhouetted against the sky. "The sound you are hearing now is the actual tachyon signal, after computer processing.''

Jonders squinted, groping his way into an armchair as the newscoper described the apparent similarities between the tachyon signal and the songs of the humpback whales of Earth. Payne noted that while many scientists disagreed both with Gerschak's data and with his interpretations, his observations nevertheless posed some intriguing questions.

The photo-illustration changed—to a shot of Tachylab, in space. Jonders's stomach tightened. "Berkshires Observatory is not the only place where such investigations may be underway. This is an orbiting laboratory near the GEO-Four space complex, which, in conjunction with this facility—'' the image changed to a captioned photo of Sandaran Link Center—"is the major research center in the field of cosmic tachyon sources, and tachyon communications. Officials at these laboratories declined to comment on the subject, citing the classified nature of their research.''

Wide shot of Payne. Behind his head now was a photo of a spacecraft. "It is a matter of public record, however, that the deep-space probe, *Father Sky*, is equipped with a tachyon communications link with Earth, and is controlled from Tachylab and the Sandaran-Choharis Center.'' Payne went on to describe the mission as presented in the official releases, noting that *Father Sky* was engaged in exploration of the cometary halo surrounding the solar system.

"Might the unexplained signals in fact be transmissions from *Father Sky*?'' Close-up angle on Payne's face. The reporter turned into the camera. "Officials at Sandaran-Choharis acknowledged the possibility, but declined to give a yes or no answer. Gerschak denies the likelihood, but concedes that his signals and *Father Sky*'s both originate in the same region of the sky. So, we are left with an unanswered question: are the signals real, and if so, are they from our own space probe, or from another, as yet unidentified, source?''

Jonders let air escape from his lips as the story ended. It had not been the bombshell he had feared. Still, remembering the questions that Payne had asked him that day, it was evident that the reporter was onto something more than he was yet willing to report on the air.

". . . this is Joseph Payne, International News Service."

The scene shifted to a studio anchorwoman, who said, "This has been a special report, exclusively on the Third Millennium News Network. In our next segment, three men are rescued from the sixty-fourth floor—"

Jonders took a couple of deep breaths and stared past the tube, without really seeing. Marie touched a switch to deaden the sound. "Bill?" she said.

"Yah?" He scarcely responded.

"What do you think of that? Is there any truth to it?"

"What? Oh." He looked up, raised his eyebrows. "Can't say, really. I don't know anything about this fellow at the Berkshires Observatory."

"But what about the tachyons? Do you think he *could* have found something?"

He shrugged. "Like they said, he could be intercepting the spacecraft signals. I doubt that he could decode them."

"But is there anything else—?"

"Now, you know I can't say anything more than they told him."

She stared at him in exasperation.

He fumbled, apologizing. "As a matter of fact, this guy Payne called me a few days ago. I couldn't tell him anything. Some I didn't know, some I couldn't say."

"Mmm." Marie studied her eyeglasses, turning them over in her hand. "Let me ask you something else."

He cleared his throat uncomfortably.

"Suppose," Marie said. "Suppose—just hypothetically—if there were contact of some sort between—well, with some extraterrestrial race—don't you think that the world would have a right to know about it?"

There was a pressure building, somewhere inside, wanting to tell her, wanting to spill everything. He shrugged, suppressing it. "I suppose so. Depending on the situation. I doubt that I would ever be given the chance to make that kind of—"

He sensed a movement and turned. Mary and Betsy were both standing in the doorway. Betsy ran forward and climbed up into his lap. He hugged her wordlessly, and she looked into his face, her eyes sparkling blue, her pupils wide. "Daddy, do you think there are aliens out there, sending us messages?" She blinked and pushed back a lock of hair. It fell back in front of her eyes.

He made an uncertain gesture. "That's hard to say."

"Wouldn't it be neat if there were?"

He swallowed and stroked her hair back, studying her face, loving and envying the innocence in those eyes. "Yes, honey, I suppose it would be. I suppose it would be, at that." He beckoned to Mary to come in and join them, and then he gently but firmly steered the conversation onto another topic.

"There won't be any public response from here, as far as I know," Joe Kelly said. "Whatever he's onto, he hasn't crossed into classified territory, as far as we're concerned." He jotted a note, and glanced back up at Jonders. "That's all you said to him? To contact the information office?"

"That's right. I meant to call you, but it slipped my mind in all the confusion," Jonders answered.

"Well, let me know if he contacts you again. We can't forbid him, but we can try to discourage him."

Jonders nodded and returned to his office. It seemed as though last night's newscast was being taken with equanimity here; the assumption seemed to be that the best way to deal with the reporter was to ignore him. Later in the day, however, when Jonders walked into the transmission center for a scheduled link with *Father Sky,* he saw Kelly again. The security chief was standing in the doorway of the engineering booth, talking with a tall, dark-haired man in a military uniform. Jonders did not approach them, but went straight to his console to check over his control settings. A few moments later, he felt a touch at his elbow. It was Kelly.

"No time to introduce you right now, but he's from Space Services Intelligence, here on orders from the Oversight Committee," Kelly said. "Name's Delarizzo." Jonders followed Kelly's glance. The uniformed stranger was walking away from the engineering section, a cup of coffee in his hand. "He'll be here a while, observing, checking over security procedures. Advising, and so on."

Jonders looked at Kelly. "Advising?"

"Well." Kelly pursed his lips. "He doesn't have carte blanche. On the other hand, Marshall's orders are to cooperate with him."

"He's with the military," Jonders said. "Does that mean we do whatever he says?"

Kelly shrugged. "Within the bounds of reason. It's all a bit hazy at the moment." Jonders grunted, snapping three toggle switches in sequence, much harder than was necessary. "He won't interfere,"

Kelly reassured him, with a clap on the shoulder. "He's an observer and an advisor. Now I'll get out of your hair and let you work."

Jonders nodded, and closed his eyes for a moment to quiet his thoughts, before lifting the linkup helmet onto his head. He tried to put the matter out of his mind, but his last thought before launching himself into swirling darkness was a vision of Delarizzo sipping his coffee and watching Jonders, his arm moving with smooth, military precision as he lifted the steaming cup to his lips.

Chapter 37

The radar and optical images had grown stronger with the passage of time, but still displayed the shimmering quality which stumped even Homebase's technical experts. Worse still, Mozy and Kadin couldn't for the life of them get an accurate fix on the object's flightpath. The most painstaking measurements produced course projections that invariably diverged from later observations of the object's position and velocity—a situation that forced them to continually correct their own course, in an effort to match orbits.

Particularly annoying to Kadin was their inability to trace the problem to any defect in their own instruments. Mozy had already given up trying. (Maybe it's not a malfunction at all,) she said. (Maybe that's what it's actually doing.)

(Perhaps,) Kadin said. (But we've seen no propulsion activity or exhaust, and no mechanism I know of would cause that kind of image-smearing.)

(It *is* an alien spacecraft, after all.)

(Well, that's the real question,) Kadin said. (I mean, perhaps we're lunatic to expect it to behave according to our assumptions.)

(I'm not sure *lunatic* is the right word.)

(You know what I m—)

(ANALYSIS CAN-, CANNOT BE PERFORMED EXCEPT IN CONTEXT OF KNOWN PARADIGMS,) Mother Program interjected.

(The paradigm may have to be changed,) Kadin said. (Even the most fundamental of assumptions must be discarded when they prove contrary to observation. A paradigm can only explain reality; it cannot command reality's obedience.)

Mozy offered no further opinion; it all seemed rather theoretical to her. She silently continued making her course corrections as they closed on the speck that was the alien spacecraft.

As the hours passed, Mozy focused on piloting and translating, leaving other worries to Kadin. Her linguistic skills were improving, unlike Mother Program's. Several tentative translations indicated that they were being welcomed to match orbits with the alien craft. There were no clues in the messages to the peculiar movement of the alien ship; but they would be rendezvousing in the next twenty-four hours, and presumably they'd have learned something by then.

If they lasted that long. Mother Program's navigational functions were degrading rapidly. There was some discussion with Homebase about the possibility of a "virus" contamination in the programming that could be causing a progressive breakdown, but there was nothing for Mozy to do about it, except to keep flying. She was far too busy now to maintain an image of a body or a ship's bridge. She *was* the ship.

Flying, walking, or crawling, she felt as though she were battling against a growing vestibular disorientation. Not quite vertigo, but heading in that direction. Well . . . she might be staggering a bit, she thought, but she was damn straight going to get there, regardless.

It moved across the starfield, brightening steadily. Under optical magnification, it looked like a reddish brown stone, almost crystalline in appearance, yet pulsing fluidly like a drop of water in weightlessness.

The range was closing rapidly, and it was time to prepare for rendezvous and docking. The rendezvous programs were intact, for the moment—unused and undisturbed by the deterioration which was crippling the autopilot functions. Mozy feverishly studied the encapsulated approach and docking routines, hoping to learn their proper functions before they, too, began breaking down. Was she finding it harder to concentrate, or was it just her imagination, fed by overwork and stress? Did those terms apply anymore?

(David, I have to watch this thing like crazy, just to keep us on course.)

(You're doing fine. There'll be a medal in it for you if you can get us into an orbit around the thing. I have to finish working out our greeting protocols.)

(Orbit. Right. I'll do my best.)

*   *   *

It was close enough now to see clearly. It was not a spaceship at all. It was an asteroid—a scarred, pitted rock, more or less shaped like a potato, and dozens of times larger than the spaceship Mozy had been expecting. Its surface was indeterminate in color, though brighter and more reflective than Kadin could explain. One moment it appeared to be dusted with a silvery powder, and the next, it was all maroon browns and shadows.

The shimmering effect subsided as they approached. Mozy fired the maneuvering jets and steered into a parking orbit around the asteroid. She noticed that as the asteroid became clearer, other images, such as the stars, began to blur. Kadin noted this, also, but offered no comment as he switched on instruments to probe the asteroid.

(What do we have, Mother?) Kadin said. (Mother Program?)

(TARGET OBJECT OBJECT ISSSSSS . . . IRON-NICKEL ASTEROID, HONEY COMBED; ELONGATED SPHEROID IN SHAPE, ECCENTRICITY 0.17; LENGTH, MAJOR AXIS, 1.2 KILOMETERS; LENGTH, MINOR AXIS . . .)

(Yes, yes, but what about the honeycombs, and the funny effects we've been seeing?)

(ESTIMATE TWO-THIRDS OF VOLUME NON-SOLID. NOT SOLID. ANOMALOUS EFFECTS NO LONGER OBSERVABLE; HOWEVER, UNCERTAINTY LEVELS IN THAT REGARD ARE HIGH. MASS-DENSITY READINGS INCONSIS-, INCONSISTENT WITH KNOWN MATERIALS AND OBSERVED SOLID VOLUMES. PLEASE PROVIDE NEW . . . NEW . . .)

(Go on.)

(PLEASE PROVIDE NEW ASSUMPTION SET FOR ANALYSIS.)

(Um . . . yes. A little later, perhaps,) Kadin said. (You keep working on it. Mozy, I'm scanning for fixtures, windows, instruments, propulsion unit, anything like that. Can you go on autopilot for a while? I think your vision is more acute.)

(We're sharing the same eyes. How—?)

(I don't mean your eyes. I mean your visual perception.)

(Oh. Well . . . all right. As long as we're in an unpowered orbit.) Mozy released the override, and took a look around.

On first impression, it was terribly lonely out here beside this dimly lit asteroid, a quarter of a light-year from home. Sunlight was just bright starlight at this distance. Still, with enhancement, she could easily view the asteroid's surface rolling beneath them as they orbited. Had she thought before that it looked like a fluid crystal? Now, it just looked like normal, well-behaved rock, doing nothing out of the ordinary. If it was honeycombed as Mother Program said, then some-one or something must be inside. You wouldn't know it from the outside, though. It looked as natural as the day it congealed out of the primordial dust—no visible markings or signs of construction—and no emissions of hard radiation.

But how, she wondered, does it move?

(Mozy,) Kadin said, in what was almost a drawl, (The mass of this thing is about right for a solid asteroid. But it's not solid, it's hol-lowed out. I think maybe Homebase is in for a few surprises.)

(Shall we tell them now?)

Jonders's image was a hash of snow. Something was garbling the signal, and they thought they knew what it was. (I suspect that the shimmering we observed is a field effect surrounding the asteroid,) Kadin was saying. (We're on the inside of the field now, so when our transmission beams pass through the boundary, they get thrown slightly out of phase. It ought to be possible to compensate.)

(Did you measure the field as you passed through?) Jonders asked.

(No.)

(Oh.) Jonders sounded disappointed. (Well, we'll work on it.)

While Kadin reviewed the situation with Homebase, Mozy turned to other matters. A signal was coming in from the asteroid.

She listened intently to the whee'ing and warbling, and worried over their meanings. By the time she was ready with a translation, Jonders was gone, and Kadin was waiting impatiently. She compared her version to that of the translator program. Its version read: (TRAVELLED PATH LAND GO TO PEOPLES MEET.) Hers read: (IF YOU WISH FOR A MEETING WITH US, FELLOW TRAVEL-LERS, PLEASE LAND YOUR CRAFT AND BE WELCOME.)

(Well,) Kadin said, (that's encouraging.)

(Shall we land?)

(We'll have to wait a bit.)

(Why?)

(Homebase says to remain in parking orbit and continue making observations.)

(Why?)

(They're waiting for Hathorne to arrive at the Center, to take au-thority for the go/no-go decision.)

(Go/no-go decision?) she asked incredulously.

(Right.)

(We came a quarter of a light-year to orbit here and wait?) Mozy said.

(Right.)

(Well, that answers one question.)

(What's that?)

(We're definitely in the army now.)

(Yes, ma'am,) said Kadin.

The spacecraft bucked, and began tumbling. Two attitude control jets were popping off erratically. Mozy quickly shut them down. As she was preparing to stop the spin, a maneuvering jet went off. (What's happening?) Kadin asked.

(Son of a bitch.) Mozy damped the jet and deactivated the automatic control. Now the orbit was going to be screwed up.

(Have you got a handle on it?) Kadin said.

(I've got it, I've got it,) she snapped. (Nav-control is gone. The rendezvous programs are starting to sizzle, too.) She measured the orbit. They were moving closer to the asteroid.

(How bad is it, Mother Program?) Kadin said.

He had to ask three times, before he got an answer. Then: (NAVIGATION CAPACITY IMPAIRED 73 PERCENT IN ATTITUDE AND MANEUVERING CONTROL, AND MAIN DRIVE STEERING. 82 PERCENT FUNCTION REMAINING IN RANGING, EE & DYNAMICCC DOCKLNG. . . .)

(Bad,) Mozy said. (And getting worse.)

(When will this start affecting *us*?) Kadin wondered.

(So far, it's mainly in the autonomic processing circuitry.)

(But Mother Program—)

(Yes. If it's hitting her, it will hit us, eventually.) She didn't want to think about that too deeply right now. That had to do with mortality. Dying slowly.

(Our effective time could be limited.)

(I recommend landing now.)

(Homebase won't be ready for almost a day,) Kadin said.

(We'll never hold it together that long. I need computer backup for the landing. I can reroute some of the processing, but if the function keeps degrading . . .)

(Can't we compensate?)

(How would I know? I've never landed one of these things before. It won't do any good for us to wait in orbit like good boys and girls, if we crash going in.) She made some new calculations; they were swinging in an elongated loop around the asteroid. If she didn't do *something* to correct it, they would crash soon, anyway. (I'd say we have to either land, or get some distance. Maybe a lot of distance. We may not get back for another chance, though.)

Kadin seemed lost in thought. Finally he said, (I can call Homebase in sixty-five minutes. Can we hold on that long?)

(I don't know.) Mozy was recircuiting, checking functions. (It's going downhill fast.)

(Can you make it now? Right now?) Kadin said.

She scanned, estimating. (Yes. I think so. Yes.)

Kadin hesitated for one second, then said, (The midsection of the asteroid along the longer axis. Take her down.)

(Aye.) Mozy computed, then with great care, fired a braking burn. At first, nothing much seemed to happen. Then the asteroid began to turn more slowly beneath them, and then not at all, and it loomed steadily larger in the sky as they dropped toward it, and Mozy waited, steadying herself, timing for the correct moment to fire the landing rockets.

Chapter 38

The plane banked sharply into the New Phoenix approach. Hathorne looked up from his papers as the sun streamed dazzling through his window. The hydrogen jets whined down, and there was a soft hum under the seat as the landing gear dropped into place.

Regret, mainly, was what he felt. Regret, that he might have to terminate the *Father Sky* mission. So close to success. After his battles with the Oversight Committee to keep the mission alive, its failure would in a way be a personal failure for Leonard Hathorne. What would the President think when he learned that his chance to lead the world to its first meeting with extraterrestrials might melt like ice out of his hands? And this talk from the Space Forces of getting a manned mission out there was a crock of bull. They'd get something out there eventually, sure, but the alien ship would practically be to Earth by then. And the Sovs and the Chinese and the Japs were sure to be hot on their heels. Some lead that would be.

Nevertheless, *Father Sky* looked shakier with each passing day. The latest reports were the worst yet. Progressive breakdown in the computer systems. Navigation failing, and no one knew why. Artificial intelligence status: unknown. He had approved a "go" for orbit around the alien asteroid, but even that may have been a mistake. The spaceship had gone silent seventeen hours ago. No warning, no apparent reason—but no response to Homebase's call. Just silence. Seventeen hours of silence.

The probe was already in orbit around the alien artifact, so there was no way that the aliens wouldn't know if it broke down—if not now, then later. They'd approached the aliens, made contact, and then failed. Possibly even crashed. Worst of all, shown weakness.

Maybe the aliens were friendly and altruistic; maybe it wouldn't matter. Maybe.

It was possible, of course, that there were other reasons for the silence. The spacecraft might have been captured. It might be that Kadin, still functional, had been forced, for reasons unknown, to black out communications for purposes of diplomacy or survival. That was in fact Hathorne's only real hope—that there was a better explanation than the obvious one. And that was why he had to look at the data before any action could be taken.

It wasn't much of a hope, but it was something.

The plane thumped and rumbled, shaking Hathorne's bones as it hurtled down the runway and finally slowed to taxiing speed. Hathorne shifted uncomfortably, snapping his briefcase closed. He didn't mind flying, so much, but being cramped in these seats hour after hour was a killer, especially with a prostate problem that meant he was always getting up and going to the can. He always figured there was at least one person on the plane thinking, *Some hotshot this guy is, has to go pee every half hour*—probably just can't hack flying.

So much for being the impressive figurehead.

The plane taxied to the far corner of the airfield, made a turn, and stopped; and there was the hopper waiting for him. "Mr. Hathorne," his security aide called from the front of the cabin.

"Coming!" The hatch opened, and he followed the aide out and down, blinking in the sun. A short trot across the glaring white pavement, and then they ducked under the rotor and boarded the hopper. The aide was saying something as they settled in, but his voice was carried away by the rising keen of the hopper engines, and Hathorne ignored him and stared moodily out the window as they lifted and veered onto course for Sandaran Link Center.

Jonders wished that Marshall and Hathorne would hurry and make whatever decision it was they were going to make. It was a hell of a time to start changing the agenda, he thought, glancing at the operations clock. Transmission cycle was due to start in three minutes.

This Hathorne fellow had the look of a man who was accustomed to power, although physically, he was less imposing in person than on the holo-screen. His hair was streaked with grey, but he had a young man's face. He looked very Eastern—smooth and cocksure, and rather impatient. Probably from Harvard Law, Jonders thought. Or Yale. A half hour ago, he had descended upon the operations center as though he owned the place.

Hathorne was conferring with Marshall now, and shaking his head. Jonders couldn't hear what was being said; but he knew that support from the Oversight Committee had eroded recently, with the reports of continuing problems. He knew what Marshall was probably saying— that whatever was causing the computer breakdown, it was the rigidly defined functions such as navigation that were failing first. The heuristics, the consciousness systems, Kadin and Mozelle, were surviving in better shape—probably, according to the systems experts, because they were capable of adapting to the changing computer matrices as malfunctions developed—possibly without even being aware of doing so. What was unclear was how long this could continue.

It was likely enough that the question was moot. No signal had been received now for eighteen hours. Most were betting that the system had failed catastrophically, or that the spacecraft had crashed. Jonders wasn't betting.

He glanced somberly around the operations room. The engineers were talking patiently among themselves. Delarizzo, the security agent, was standing in a corner, watching everyone and no one. On the wall above the linkup console, the new viewscreen was glowing, ready to display selected, computer-processed renditions of Jonders's visual impressions during the linkup. If there ever was another linkup.

Hathorne's voice grew loud enough to be heard across the room. "If you get a signal, find out if Kadin is actively in contact with the alien entity. If not, order him to move off to a safe distance, until we decide what to do."

Marshall walked to Jonders's console and made it official. His eyes met Jonders's only for a moment, then he turned to rejoin Hathorne.

Jonders adjusted his helmet, and checked the voice connections to Hathorne and Marshall, seated in the observation gallery. Once he was in the link, their voices would come directly into his head; his own computer-generated "voice" emanated from a speaker in the operations room.

(Signal going out now,) he heard the chief engineer say.

He sank into the darkness, ready for contact. He waited there, in limbo, wondering if he would ever hear, feel, touch Kadin and Mozy again; then he was aware of voices outside himself, and he heard the engineer announce acquisition of telemetry. Something connected, clicked into place, and he felt a friendly presence. (*David! You're safe!*) he shouted. (*What happened?*)

Kadin's face was pale, transparent gold against the stars. Jonders was dimly aware of a murmur from the gallery. The image was coming through on the viewscreen.

(Quite safe,) Kadin answered softly. Was he straining? Was something wrong? (Sorry we haven't made contact earlier, but our signal was blocked by the asteroid.)

(Blocked? Blocked? Do you mean, by the field effect?)

(No,) Kadin answered. (The asteroid itself has been eclipsing our signal. We've been on the far side.)

(I see.) Jonders hesitated, puzzled. (But if you were orbiting—?)

(A picture is worth a thousand words,) Kadin said.

His face shimmered and vanished. A camera view took its place.

Jonders drew a sharp breath. In the camera lens, a dim landscape of pitted, craggy rock curved away to a startlingly close horizon. The camera zoom retracted to a wider angle, then slowly panned right to left, over a desolate-looking surface. Jonders's pulse quickened when a metal framework came into view. Then he realized that it was a section of the spacecraft's landing gear, resting on the surface of the asteroid. (David,) he began. (Explain—)

He was drowned out, as everyone in the gallery tried to talk at once.

(*Quiet, please!*) he boomed. Before he could be interrupted again, he said, (David, you landed. Why? Have you made physical contact?)

(Voice contact only,) Kadin said.

(And the asteroid? Is it a hollowed vessel?)

(Affirmative. Physical data being transmitted via telemetry . . . now.)

Before Jonders could reply, a voice—Hathorne's—cut through, harsh and a little distorted. (Explain why you landed without authorization!)

(Who is speaking?) Kadin queried.

(Leonard Hathorne.)

(Of course,) said Kadin. (We were forced to make a go/no-go decision . . .)

Jonders remained silent, as Kadin explained. Hathorne's ire notwithstanding, Jonders found himself pleased, and even proud, that Kadin had chosen to disregard orders rather than allow the mission to fail—and that Mozy had brought the craft down intact. Hathorne was less sanguine; he questioned Kadin closely, scarcely allowing Jonders to get a thought in edgewise. Jonders noted a faint bemusement in Kadin's manner—as though he were aware of Jonders's restlessness in the link, acting as little more than a conduit for the conversation with Hathorne.

(Give us a full readout of the computer's status,) Hathorne commanded.

Kadin started to reply, then abruptly disappeared. The contact was disintegrating. Jonders shot a thought back through the loop, to the engineer. (What's happening?)

(Unknown,) he heard, faintly. (Signal smearing . . . telemetry getting weaker . . .)

Jonders clung to the unravelling thread. He visualized a set of converging, luminous lines probing into the distance to focus on the invisible target that was the ship. The lines shifted, bent, flexed . . .

(What are you doing?) Hathorne demanded. Jonders ignored him.

A shockwave rippled through the converging lines, and they brightened, one after another, illuminating a distant gridwork on all sides. There was a sudden snap, as something came into focus.

(Can you hear me?) Kadin said, reappearing as a tiny figure at the point of convergence.

The lines and the grid vanished, and he expanded to full size. (We had to ask our friends to stop what they were doing,) Kadin explained.

(What's that?)

(The field effect. It seems to have something to do with their propulsion. They were quite accommodating once we explained that it was causing a problem.)

Hathorne interrupted. (Are you in contact with them now?)

(We exchanged communications. We are not doing so at the moment.)

(Summarize all communications in your telemetry pulse,) Hathorne ordered.

(Acknowledged.)

(And then cease nonessential communication with the alien vessel until we have determined the mission status.)

(Please define "nonessential,") Kadin said. (And "mission status.") Was there a trace of tightness, something like anger, in his voice? Jonders wondered.

(The mission is being reconsidered,) Hathorne said. (We will have to study the telemetry data to determine whether it should continue.)

There was an uneasy silence, and then Kadin answered, deliberately, (We would resist . . . any suggestion that this mission . . . cannot proceed.)

Silence again. Cold silence. Then Hathorne said, (Allow me to amend my phrasing. The condition of the *computer* is in doubt. Therefore, the mission by definition must be in doubt.)

A new voice cut in—a sharp, angry voice. (*Are you people idiots?*)
It was Mozy. Her face flickered in and out of view, at the edge of
Jonders's perception.

Another voice entered the link. (Is that Mozelle? This is Slim
Marshall, Mozy. We understand your feelings. But you must realize
that it could be risky to our ultimate objectives to continue a mission
with equipment which might fail at a crucial moment.)

(You understand nothing,) Mozy said flatly. (We landed in spite of
your faulty computer. You're not here with us, you can't guess what
we're facing. You don't know. But there's something *I* understand.
Your cowardice. Your fear of carrying through to the end.) The anger
returned, flashing through Jonders with a heat that staggered him,
almost caused him to lose the connection. Her face appeared, strong
and luminous, forward from Kadin's. (You're afraid of people you
haven't even met—)

(*Miss Moi*—) said Hathorne, and Jonders reeled from the intensity
of the voice—(You are alive right now on our sufferance. *We* will
make the policy, and *you* will carry it out. Is that clear?)

Mozy's eyes flamed with fury. (If I hadn't helped keep this ship
running, your mission would have been over weeks ago.)

(Nevertheless, the automatic systems are failing—possibly because
of your presence—and if they go, you too must fail,) Hathorne said.

(Thanks for the encouragement. Do you know your problem? You
were afraid of the aliens, and so you sent David. Now you're afraid
to trust him—and you're afraid to trust me!) Mozy's voice was rising.
(Who will you trust the next time? Are you going to come out here
and do the job yourself?)

The anger was building in Jonders's head until he could stand it no
longer. (*Mozy!*) he barked. (*That's enough!*)

Mozy retreated into a startled silence.

(Yes!) Hathorne said. (Let that be the end of the outbursts! If you
try again to interfere in—)

(Mr. Hathorne!) said Jonders.

(—our policy-making—)

(*Mr. Hathorne! That goes for you, too!*)

Hathorne quieted, stunned. (Thank you,) said Jonders. (This communication will continue civilly, or it will not continue at all.) He
paused for breath. For a moment, he could hear nothing but the pounding of blood in his temples. (Now, why don't we just see if we can't
resolve this cooperatively? Kadin and Mozy are not yet on the verge
of expiring, or losing their powers of reason. If they were, I would

know it. Now why can't we—) He hesitated, realizing that in fact he had no plan in mind.

There was a muted mutter of voices, and he sensed that a debate was going on in the gallery. Finally there was silence, and then Marshall's voice. (Mozy. Kadin. Our main concern is whether you can survive, in your deteriorating environment. Even if you do, the translation programs may go. That would effectively stop—)

(The translation programs have already gone,) Mozy said. (I've taken that job over, too.)

(She's right,) Kadin interjected. (And I must say that I am in agreement with her position. For us to have come this far, and for you to withdraw your trust and support now, makes no sense. We are on the doorstep of another civilization, and even if we fail, we deserve the opportunity to at least fail trying. We are wasting precious time in this debate.)

There was another silence, then Marshall. (Very well. Open communication with the visitors, and at your discretion, request a meeting. Keep us closely informed.)

(Acknowledged,) said Kadin. His face beamed with golden light. Mozy merely nodded. (Now, would you like to continue the tour?)

In the gloom of the link, Jonders smiled in silent jubilation as the view shifted back to the camera, and the inscrutable alien landscape,

Chapter 39

"There's no *question* that it's worth pursuing. I have an extremely good source, independent of Gerschak, who tells me there *is* something outside the solar system transmitting signals, and that contact may be made with it very soon." Payne squinted at Teri Renshaw's image.

"That's pretty vague. Do you have any details? What kind of contact?" Teri asked.

Payne hunched toward the phone. "I'm not sure. But it's definitely alien, and the *Father Sky* spaceship is involved."

Teri glanced away for a moment, speaking with someone off-screen. Then she was back, apologizing. "Can you confirm that? We couldn't commit something that sensitive to air without at least one strong additional source for confirmation."

"That's what I'm saying," Payne said. "I need time. I don't know how deep this thing goes. It could take a while to sweat it all out. That's why you've got to keep them from cutting me off."

"Well, I'm trying. But you know what they're saying, the ratings on your first report weren't that great—"

"Ratings!" Payne snorted. "How could ratings mean anything on a first story? People either happened to be watching, or they didn't. No one knew about it in advance—"

"I understand that. But the point is, they're waiting for a follow-up."

"I'm working on it. And I'm working on a second source."

"Good. But it would help if you came down and talked with the backers again."

"I will, Teri. Tuesday. Or Wednesday."

"They may have given up on you by then."

"Well, I need some time to gather myself. I've hardly seen Denine—and I want to talk to Gerschak again—"

Teri suddenly laughed. "That's the life of a big-time scoper—"

"Yeah. Oh, yeah. Listen to the hotshot." He said it good-naturedly, but there was an edge of frustration in his voice.

"Now, don't take it personally—"

Payne took a long breath. He was more anxious than he had realized. Anxious, and determined to succeed. "Look, can't you go to bat for me with the backers?"

She studied him for a moment, then relented. "All right. If you can't make it sooner than Tuesday, I'll see what I can do."

"Thanks."

"Listen, Joe, I don't mean to bug you. But it's business, and we have to keep business and friendship separate. Do you know what I mean?"

Payne tipped his head from side to side, shrugging. "Yeah."

"So I still like you. Okay?" A corner of her mouth was turned up in a smile. Her eyes sparked.

He blushed. "Yeah."

"So will you let me buy you dinner when you get here?"

"Okay."

"And get to work on that other source!"

"I will." Payne broke the phone connection and settled back in his chair. He was aware of a feeling of sexual arousal, which was interesting, and disturbing. Teri? Good heavens, he didn't feel that way about her, anymore. Or at least, he thought he didn't. Today, though, he'd caught himself noticing her chest, as they talked.

Careful, boy. Watch those thoughts.

He took a deep breath and started to punch in Donny Alvarest's number, then hesitated. How was he going to go about this? He couldn't fish for information directly, not with the security restrictions Donny had to work around. But a good reporter knew how to finesse this sort of thing.

He flipped through the notes from his last conversation with Ellen Chang at JPL. They'd talked twice, since his broadcast, once in person and once by phone. It was powerful stuff. She seemed almost eager now to give him information. She'd told him—strictly on deep background, so he couldn't quote it directly—that her sources were directly involved in research at Tachylab. That was good, that was very good. He hadn't pressed her, and didn't blame her for not naming them, since they were obviously in a delicate position.

Nevertheless, Chang had assured him straightforwardly that *Father Sky* was involved in contacting the source of the alien transmissions.

Alleged transmissions, Payne cautioned himself. Now, more than ever, he had to be careful what he said and didn't say, even to himself.

He punched the first four digits of Donny's number again. "Joe?" He looked up. Denine was leaning in the doorway. She was in jeans and workshirt, her hair up in a bandana.

He switched off the phone. "Hi."

"What are you up to?" she asked, walking in, touching a hand to his shoulder. Her voice sounded strained; something was bothering her.

He flipped at the cover of his notepad. "Just following up the story. You?"

"Oh—" She shrugged. "Thinking about the new Olsen commission. Joe?"

"Yeah?"

She leaned against his desk to face him. "I was thinking of writing to Mrs. Moi again. Telling her that you were out there—that a friend was out there and did some checking around, and that Mozy seems to have disappeared. Then she'd at least know *some*thing." She scratched under her bandana.

He mulled for a moment. "Do you think it would help, or just make her more worried? Why don't you wait? Maybe next time I'll turn up some real information."

"You're definitely going again?"

"If the backers don't dump me. This whole story is tied up in that place—I think."

"Mmm." Denine nodded. "Well. That would be good, I guess. I wish there were some excuse for me to go with you."

"Why don't you?" Payne said reflexively, and at once knew that he didn't really want her along.

She shrugged. "I'd just be in your way. Besides, I have too much work to do."

He caught her hand. "You okay, sprite?"

"Uh-huh. I'll let you get back to work," she said, forcing a smile. She wrapped her fingers around his and gave a squeeze, then slipped away.

Payne looked after her as she went out the door and thought, *something's happening here, and I don't think I like it.* The easy closeness to Denine seemed to be getting more difficult, and less close. Was it because he'd been away? Or, God forbid, had she sensed his attraction to another woman, even before he had? Dee wasn't one to share her man, even in casual thought.

Maybe Teri was right. Maybe a loss of homelife was the price of being a successful newscoper. If so, things were going to get worse before they got better.

He became jovial once Alvarest was on the phone. He had only spoken to his friend once since their encounter at the rock revival festival. "You're a hard one to reach, Donny. Don't you answer your phone anymore?"

Alvarest grinned. "Thanks to you, I've been working a lot of overtime. You created quite a stir in the department with that story of yours."

"*Your* department? I thought you were only involved in intelligence from other countries." Payne swallowed. "What kind of a stir?"

"Oh, just suspicion that somebody's leaking information to you. Thanks for letting me know in advance, you turd. I didn't even see your story until they got a tape from your network."

"Sorry. I meant to call you. Never got the chance."

"Well, they'd just better not find out I'm talking to you now."

"Better not, is right," Payne said. "Not at the rates I'm paying for secure phone calls. I don't suppose you could answer a few questions for me."

Alvarest laughed grimly. "Whatever rates you're paying, it's not *that* secure."

Payne scratched his jaw, chuckling uneasily. "So what else can we talk about?"

"Oh, we could start with the time of day—though it's debatable whether I should give it to you. Still, I don't think I'd have to turn you in for asking."

"That's a relief." Payne thought for a moment. "Say, Donny, old boy."

Alvarest's eyebrows went up a fraction of an inch.

"I wouldn't want you to compromise yourself, as you know. But when you say, 'People think someone's leaking to you,' that would seem to suggest, just from, oh, a linguistic perspective, not to say common sense, that I might regard that as a sort of left-handed confirmation of my story."

Alvarest cleared his throat. "*Very* left-handed."

"Well, nothing against lefties. I'm just trying to understand what you said. Wouldn't *you* say that it's—?"

"Shit, Joe, I thought you quality journalists confirmed your stories *before* you went on the air with them."

"Well, yes. But, you know, there's no such thing as too much confirmation."

"If you're asking me to vouch for your story, forget it. You've wormed too much out of me already."

"Wormed—!"

"Splinters under the fingernails."

Payne snorted—then thought, Was Donny, indirectly, trying to hint that his interpretation was correct? That he could regard his story as being confirmed?

Alvarest looked sideways for a moment. "Joe, I hate to cut into a beautiful conversation, but my dinner is about to burn."

"Okay. Just one more thing," Payne said hastily. "Could you comment if I told you that I knew that *Father Sky* was getting ready to hook up with an alien spaceship?"

"Are you on drugs? No way."

"Oh. Well, okay. I just thought I'd ask."

Alvarest looked at him with a pained expression. "If you're planning to run a story like that, I hope you're *very careful* with your facts."

"I will be. Listen, since you can't comment, would you happen to know anyone connected with *Father Sky*, or Tachylab, who might be able to give me some background information?"

"Background?" Alvarest repeated.

"Sure. Just background." *Deep* background, dummy.

"Not offhand. You going to be down here soon?"

"Probably. Should I look you up?"

"I wouldn't want to be heard saying, you *should*." Alvarest looked toward his dinner again.

"Okay. If I happen to bump into you, so be it."

"Can't be helped, I guess, if you run into me. Joe, I see smoke!"

"Bye," Payne said. "Thanks!"

He stared moodily at the darkened screen for a time afterward, leaning back in his chair. He felt a nagging guilt about trying to impose on his friend. Donny, after all, was in a sensitive position. Maybe it didn't matter. They hadn't actually discussed anything classified, after all. But—if Donny's department was involved, this was probably a good time to make himself scarce, where Donny was concerned, if he didn't want to put his friend's job in jeopardy.

So much for his "other source."

Chapter 40

From a quarter of a light-year, the sun was one star among hundreds of thousands. In the pale illumination, Kadin and Mozy were forced to amplify the images to about thirty times their original brightness as they inspected the surface of the asteroid, or at least the fraction visible from the spacecraft. They used spotlights only briefly, not wanting to alarm their hosts.

On first impression, what they saw was a little disappointing. The place looked pretty much like any other asteroid. The surface appeared brownish black in color, with here and there a metallic glint, and the expected pitting and micrometeoroid erosion. There was no external evidence of habitation, nothing to suggest visibly that it was anything more than a lifeless rock. Seismic probes listening at the surface, however, confirmed that it was indeed hollow, and furthermore, detected sounds of internal activity, a symphony of murmurs and groans.

Someone was in there, all right—and Mozy and Kadin were so busy probing and speculating on how one might get inside that they almost failed to react, when they received a transmission from the aliens in MacEnglish. (My god!) Mozy cried, as the words flowed into her mind:

(WE WELCOME YOU TO OUR TRAVELLING HOME, AND THANKS BE FOR TROUBLING TO GREET US. WILL YOU COME WITHIN? DO WE MADE OURSELVES UNDERSTOOD? TELL US, OH. TELL US, DO.)

Mozy was so astonished that she had to replay it to catch the meaning.

(Remarkable,) Kadin said. (An invitation. They've been studying our language, apparently, far more efficiently than we have theirs.)

It was true, Mozy had to admit. She hoped they did a tenth as well in their attempts to use the alien tongue. (What are we going to tell them?)   .

Kadin already had the channel open. (Your mastery of our language is excellent. Our thanks and congratulations.)

(WE HAVE LISTENED TO MANY OF YOUR BROADCASTS. WILL YOU COME WITHIN?)

(Indeed, we would like to. May we send a remotely controlled extension of ourselves, a mechanism to send us pictures and sounds of your home?)

(A . . . WE ARE NOT CERTAIN OF OUR UNDERSTANDING . . . A "REMOTELY CONTROLLED EXTENSION"?)

(A machine. Like the one in which we came, but much smaller.)

(THAT WOULD BE SATISFACTORY. BUT YOU ARE WELCOME TO COME IN BODY . . . IN PERSON.)

Kadin tried to explain that the spacecraft *was* their body. (I am called "Kadin." I am a creation of Humans, and exist only in this form, as a machine. With me is one called "Mozy," who is a true Human, but no longer in bodily form. Her essence, her personality, lives with me in this machine.)

(LIVING PERSONALITIES IN NONLIVING BODIES? HOW DO YOU CONVEY YOUR THOUGHTS TO US?)

(We . . . convey our thoughts directly, through a transmitter. Programs and filters help us . . . organize our thoughts into forms that . . . can be expressed through tachyon or radio links.) Kadin paused. (It is difficult to explain out of context. How do you convey your thoughts?)

(WE . . . SIMPLY SPEAK . . . FOR NOW. LATER, WE MAY SING.)

(I see. Perhaps you would like to say a few words to Mozy. Simply direct your words to her. Mozy?)

(Right here,) she replied. What should she say . . . to aliens? On an impulse, she opened herself to direct link. Would they know what to do?

(YOU ARE CALLED "MOZY"?) said an echoing voice in her mind. (WE ARE CALLED . . . IN YOUR WORDS, CALL US . . . "TALENKI.")

(Talenki . . . ?)

(TALENKI,) repeated the aliens. And then something bubbled into her mind—sparks, and an explosion of crystalline musical notes and hallucinatory colors. There was movement: shadow and light rippling through her consciousness like a fountain of images, all indistinct, more like laughter and longing, sorrow and joy, than visible forms. It rushed through her, filling her like a tide, then ebbed away again.

(Pleased to meet you, Talenki,) she murmured.

She thought she heard echoes of amusement; but she couldn't be sure whether they came from the Talenki or from deep within herself.

(Let's tell Homebase we're ready to go in,) Kadin said.

(David? Are you all right?)

It took him a few moments to answer. He was readying the probe unit for separation. Finally he said, (Everything seems under control, doesn't it?)

(Yes. But that isn't what I asked.)

He fiddled a bit more. He was preparing to transfer a portion of his consciousness into the probe's brain. (No,) he said finally. (It wasn't, was it?)

(It seemed . . . I'm not sure.) She tried to isolate what it was that troubled her. (You seem less sure of yourself. Not as quick . . . as you have been in the past.)

(No.) Again silence. (I feel a certain . . . sluggishness. What does it mean to have a "headache"?)

She showed him. It took concentration to recall the feeling, and to convey it in an open image. The effort made her own head ring.

(Not exactly like that,) he said. (But yes. I'll try very hard to keep my faculties clear.)

(I'll help you all I can.)

(I know you will, Mozy. I know.)

The probe separated from the spacecraft and bumped gently to the surface. Three axles extended from its body, one forward and two aft. At the end of each axle was a ball of steel wool. As Mozy watched, Kadin activated the heating elements, and the wool balls expanded, as the individual strands of wire alloy responded to the rise in temperature by unkinking and returning to a "remembered" previous shape. When the process was complete, the probe sat on three puffy, donut-shaped wheels of wire mesh. It was an odd, bubble-topped robot with skinny manipulator arms folded against its side. Inside the bubble, camera lenses rotated. Kadin started the electric motors. (Hope they didn't give us a lemon,) he said, as the probe bounced gently away over the landscape.

He surveyed the spacecraft with the probe and then disappeared over the horizon. Mozy peered at the views coming back, recording them for retransmission to Homebase. Since the Talenki had specified no entry point, they were going to start by exploring the outer surface in detail.

One part of the asteroid looked like another, some areas slightly darker, or rougher. They puzzled over readings indicating shifts in mass-density and gravity as the probe roamed the little world. They had hoped to measure the anomalous field effect, but the best they could manage was to observe the smearing of star images from space, and even that changed from one part of the asteroid to another. (Curiouser,) Kadin said, as the probe circled back. (Maybe we ought to ask where the door is.)

A short discussion with the Talenki ensued, and Kadin drove the probe a short distance further forward—then suddenly braked. Directly ahead, nearly flush with the ground, was a circular, mirror-flat surface, pearly grey in color, ringed by what looked like a sculpted band of silver. The plane was perhaps a meter and a half in diameter, and recessed slightly into the surface of the asteroid. (An airlock?) Mozy guessed.

(Perhaps,) said Kadin. (But why did we miss seeing this before?)

He moved a camera from side to side. The surface glimmered with a faint iridescence. After a moment's hesitation, he switched on a small searchlight. Rings of color exploded from the spot touched by the beam, rippling outward and rebounding from the rim in a kaleidoscopic pattern that shifted and shimmered as he moved the beam. Beneath the shower of color, a dim shaft of light was visible, penetrating the flat surface. He snapped the beam off. The color play died out slowly, a moment after the light went out. (Curiouser and curiouser,) he said.

He inched forward and unfolded a manipulator arm.

He stopped, the arm half extended. A bulge had appeared in the grey surface, protruding upward. It looked . . . almost like a *head*. He backed the probe out of the way. A moment later, a body followed the head, and a glistening silver creature—or perhaps a machine—stepped out onto the asteroid's surface. It walked on four legs, and was shaped rather like a faun, complete with pointed ears, silvery bright against the dark of space.

(Holy shit,) Mozy said.

Kadin was somewhat more diplomatic. (Are you a Talenki?) he voiced over the otherwise silent link to the aliens.

The creature, or thing, turned its head to peer at the probe. It moved in a graceful waltz around it, reaching out with two small forearms, which it passed close to the probe's body. A bubbly voice came over the Talenki link, muttering incomprehensibly; then it switched to English. (PLEASE SEAL OFF GAS-EMITTING MACHINERY.)

Kadin shut down the probe's attitude control jet system. He didn't expect to need the jets, inside, anyway.

The creature bobbed its head. (WELCOME TO ENTER,) Mozy heard over the link. The creature swung its head toward the entryway, and a moment later, disappeared back the way it had come

(Well?)

(I guess we try it,) Kadin said. The probe rolled forward. The front wheel dropped over the rim and sank through the grey surface without resistance, tilting the probe forward. Kadin gave the motor more juice, and the rear wheels rolled over the rim. The probe sank nose-first through the opening. The images sparkled and scrambled.

(Every sensor just went to zero,) Kadin said. And then: (They've all come back. Except the tilt meter. According to that, we've been vertical to local gravity all along. We never tipped a degree.)

When the images cleared, they were in a roughly spherical, smooth-walled chamber. The probe rolled to a stop. The portal it had come through was behind it, a whitish plane of fog. There were several other portals exactly like it, around the circumference of the chamber. The probe was alone.

(Holding room?) Mozy wondered.

(Argon atmosphere,) Kadin remarked. He adjusted the focus and light amplification level, then cautiously played a spotlight over the wall. Fine etchings became visible, apparently covering the entire wall. He rolled the probe closer, zoomed the camera in. The etchings, lined with a metallic substance, consisted of geometric designs and figures that might have been alphanumeric symbols, or perhaps ideograms. Kadin scanned the etchings, as Mozy recorded. (If you have a chance, you might study those symbols.)

(In my spare time,) Mozy answered.

Kadin swiveled, to examine the portals. (I'm not certain if I should proceed,) he said. (What ho!)

One of the portals shimmered, and something wrapped in mist stepped out of the fog and walked up to the probe. It was shaped like the creature that had met them outside. (Hello,) Kadin said. (I wonder if this is the same one.)

Mozy conveyed the words, and heard a bubbling whistle in response.

The Talenki—she presumed that was what it was—danced around the probe, repeating the inspection. Mozy wished she could get a good look at it, but the enveloping mist billowed and flowed with its movements, obscuring its form. Moments later, the Talenki voice reached her—through both the ship's receiver and the probe's. (PLEASE FOLLOW.)

The Talenki slipped back through the portal. Kadin wheeled the probe around and followed. As before, the sensors fluctuated as they passed through the portal, then stabilized. (Nitrogen-oxygen atmosphere,) Kadin said. (Low light level. Let me amplify. Aha.)

(Talenki,) Mozy said.

In the gloom of a passageway, she could just make out a smooth-furred creature that looked rather like a cross between a deer faun and a Doberman with unbobbed ears. It gazed back at her with two large, luminous gold eyes. It gestured with two centaurlike arms. Mozy had scarcely captured the image before the Talenki turned and fled down the passageway.

(Wait!) she cried.

Clumsily, in the unknown terrain, Kadin endeavored to follow.

Chapter 41

(No indication of malfunction.) Kadin said.

(Then what *are* we looking at?) said Mozy.

The images were clear but bewildering: faceted corridors surrounding the probe, angles that seemed to change without warning, walls that bewitched the eye like a hall of mirrors. The interior illumination was scarlet one moment, amber the next, with overtones of indigo and green. Now the light seemed to glow from energies hidden deep within the walls; now it shined in crisscrossing shafts like tinted sunbeams on an autumn day.

A Talenki, not the one that had escorted them in, looked back to see that the probe was following. Then it emitted a short whistle and trotted ahead through a stone archway into a dimly lighted tunnel. The game of tag had been going on for almost an hour.

The Talenki were everywhere and nowhere, like ghosts, appearing and disappearing through what their guests had presumed to be solid walls. Individuals were difficult to recognize, but at least four or five Talenki had materialized to lead the probe, only to vanish, to be replaced by another. At least one Talenki was always nearby, gesturing this way or that.

Kadin was hopelessly lost. The inertial sensor readings utterly contradicted the twists and turns they had observed in their path through the asteroid's interior. Nothing seemed reliably solid or linear—not the walls, not the ceilings, not the floors. Opaque surfaces dissolved into smoky light. Shifting shadows hardened into doorways. A seemingly impenetrable maze of angles collapsed into a womblike chamber.

Could this all be an elaborate visual illusion? Radar and Doppler-sonar had ruled out the surroundings being holograms, at least of any known sort. Instrumentation could reveal little more, but the walls, at least, were walls. Except when something was passing through them.

(I'd love to see Homebase make sense of this,) Mozy said, as they moved into a passage flanked by sheets of green and yellow light, in which geometric figures flickered and swirled. Her first thought was that the figures resembled a sort of Rorschach diagram, and then she noticed that some of them appeared to have legs and arms, and she wondered if they represented alien species—of the Talenki world, or elsewhere.

(This is all very . . . disconcerting,) Kadin said.

She agreed, and queried the Talenki, over the spacecraft link. (Where are we now?)

There was a short hesitation. Then several voices spoke, interrupting and answering one another: (HALL OF—) (—HOPE?) (TUNNEL OF—) (—TRANQUILITY?) (GUARDIAN OF—) (—GRAVITY?) (PLEASE FOLLOW.)

She shrugged. That was just the sort of answer they had been getting.

Kadin was less philosophical. (I find it hard to . . . all of this is . . . it is difficult for me to analyze this clearly.)

(It's confusing,) she agreed.

(The points of correlation with the standard interpretive models—I don't know what assumptions to readjust, or—)

(Speak English to me, David. I think it's—hey, watch out for that wall! Are you having trouble steering?)

(No.) The probe veered back onto course. (I was distracted for a moment. Thinking that I don't want to let you, or Earth, down. And yet, I cannot understand this, it is like no simulation—) The probe glided through a wall of light and emerged into a curious sort of chamber. It was roughly ellipsoidal in shape; the walls were of sculpted, fluted stone. The hum of the probe's motors echoed, amplified, back into the audio pickups. An acoustical chamber? The Talenki guide paused.

(Don't talk like that. We were expecting surpri—) Mozy cut herself off in midthought. Talenki flickered into view surrounding the probe—or images of them, dozens or hundreds, none lasting for longer than a second or two, but continuously appearing.

(Our training didn't predict this,) Kadin said.

(No . . .) she said slowly. (I wonder if this . . .)

Whatever else she might have said was interrupted by a reverberating wail, picked up by the probe's external microphones. It was a moan like wind in rafters. Or like a wild cat crying, its voice echoing out of a mountain ravine. Instinctively Mozy searched for a translation. Was this an inspection, or a ritual greeting? Were the Talenki trying to communicate? Or was it something more ominous? How did the Talenki feel about human sacrifice? she wondered, thinking of grade-B holodramas. Were they perhaps preparing to boil and stew the probe for dinner? It wouldn't make much of a meal—or would it? Could thoughts be stewed? Or knowledge? The climbing pitch of the sounds was making her dizzy; it was hard to think.

(Are they singing?) Kadin said.

(Maybe. I'm not sure.)

(Can you translate?)

(No.) And damn it, now, *she* was the one being nervous. Why should she think there was anything unfriendly in the . . . song. If that was what it was.

Kadin was silent for a time, listening. (Perhaps we're just supposed to *feel*,) he said finally.

(Feel *what*?)

(I don't know. It sounds sad. Isn't this what sadness sounds like?)

Mozy pored over the rhythms and the tones. They were not as similar to the Earth sounds as she had thought. Just what they *were* similar to, she wasn't sure. The gap was too great. (Perhaps sadness,) she said. (Perhaps another emotion. Perhaps no emotion at all.)

There was no answer from Kadin. He seemed lost to her awareness, her thoughts, almost wholly swept away by the mournful chorus. (I think it sounds so sad,) he murmured. (So sad, I don't believe I can bear it. Call them and ask them to stop, before I start to cry.)

She sat hunched over her instrument panel, a few meters above the asteroid's surface. The creamy, clotted band of the Milky Way was revolving slowly overhead. She hardly noticed. Her attention was focused on the fiery viewscreen hanging just above the asteroid's horizon. The scene it displayed was relatively quiet now, only a few Talenki drifting past the stationary camera. Earlier there had been a crowd, jostling and poking like school children to get a look at the strange metal craft.

She had come to, literally, in the middle of it, her subconscious even in her sleep drawn to the inputs from the probe. It was like awakening in the center of a cocktail party; and she'd hastily retreated, repairing to her captain's chair high in the heavens, where she could be alone with her thoughts. Almost as a relaxation exercise, she had checked the spacecraft over, spoken briefly with Mother Program, who was sullen and sluggish and unsociable, linked briefly with Homebase—and only then put the Talenki images on her viewscreen.

She had no idea what to make of their visit to this strange rock in space. There had been no shortage of fascinating sights. But where was the formal welcome? Was that what the concert had been? Where were the Talenki leaders, to address themselves to Earth's emissaries, to state their intentions in visiting the solar system and, presumably, planet Earth? She had considered striking up a conversation, but decided to wait for Kadin to rouse himself from his meditations. Having notified the Talenki of their need to rest, it seemed wise to wait until they were both alert before resuming contact.

Meanwhile, she observed the Talenki observing the probe.

The other pilot seat remained empty. After a time, she looked inward for Kadin. He was withdrawn, silent but not sleeping. (David? The Talenki are waiting,) she said softly.

Kadin made a murmuring response, undecipherable.

(David? Do you hear me?)

Hesitation. (Yes . . .)

What was wrong with him? The strain? The confusion? Exhaustion? He did not experience exhaustion the same way she did, perhaps, but he felt it nonetheless—the overload of sensations and information and memory, all needing to be processed and categorized and stored. And his was the more difficult position. He was in command.

(David, I've reported to Homebase, given them what we've seen so far.)

(You have.) Kadin stirred, seemed to perk up. (Did you describe our reactions? Our feelings?)

(I gave them the facts, and the pictures. I don't even know what my feelings are. And I didn't want to speak for you.)

(No.) Kadin stretched and slowly emerged. (As well that you didn't, I suppose. No point in alarming them.) He quietly explored the ship's extremities and tested the link with the probe. He was moving, Mozy thought, like a tired old man. He looked at her with a sort of dull attentiveness. (I suppose,) he murmured, (we ought to get on with the job.)

Mozy opened the link.

It took a few calls before the Talenki responded. Apparently they, too, slept—or redirected their attention to other matters. For the first time, it occurred to Mozy that perhaps the Talenki direct-linked with *their* Homebase, as she and Kadin did with Earth.

She decided to ask.

The question seemed to confuse them. (*THIS* IS OUR HOME.)

(But surely you have come from another world?)

She heard some whickering noises, and a stuttering grumble. (MANY WORLDS,) they answered at last.

(But—originally—another star system—another planet?)

Three voices got in one another's way, answering. (DIFFICULT—) one voice said. (ALL—) said another. (—IN TIME,) said a third. (YOU WILL SEE,) added the first.

Several Talenki were prancing around the probe, now, with a gracefulness that reinforced her impression of them as fauns. One put its face before the camera, peering into the lens—and now it looked more like a slender-faced dog, tilting its head in curiosity. Its ears were large and canted forward, and its eyes were luminous gold, with no pupils recognizable as such, but with streaks of liquid flame radiating from dark red stars slightly outside of center in each eye.

A whistling sound echoed in the chamber, and the Talenki staring into the camera suddenly backed away, turned, and vanished as though it had folded itself into a fourth-dimensional pocket. The others pranced about the probe, gesturing anxiously. A moment later, they, too, vanished—and another appeared in a doorway. It stepped forward, whistling softly, and tapped the bubble of the probe. It left a smudge on the clear surface.

What Kadin did next startled Mozy more than it did the Talenki. He activated a previously unused circuit; and the probe spoke, aloud, with a synthesized voice. "*Are you to be our guide?*" Kadin asked.

The Talenki raised its ears higher and looked at the probe with evident curiosity. It spoke, in a low whistle. Kadin repeated his question. The Talenki whistled again.

(Can you translate that?) Kadin asked.

Mozy hesitated. (It's a different sort of problem. It'll take me some time.) And it was quite likely, she realized, that their hosts would be puzzling over the same problem. They knew how to reproduce English, in electronic form, but they had never before heard the *sound* of a human voice, synthesized or real.

(It might assist learning, if we speak aloud, as we transmit,) Kadin said. (Will you tell them?)

Mozy did. The Talenki did not exactly respond, but asked them to follow the creature standing before them.

Kadin rolled the probe forward. The Talenki walked through the nearest wall, and the probe followed.

*   *   *

Image upon image:

Peering into a room filled with Talenki, and silence. A place of meditation, perhaps. A feeling of quiet tension, and reflection, and connection with other things, other memories. Mozy sensed these feelings, opening herself again, momentarily, to direct contact with the Talenki. The feelings were clear, but specific facts and knowledge eluded her.

A slender stone catwalk over a clamoring place. Talenki at work below, doing things that were hard to follow with tools and materials that were hard to identify. To what end? Impossible to tell. It was too confusing visually, and too frenetic to open herself directly to the sensations.

A ledge, looking down into a small glade. Trees; a running brook. A *sky*, light blue.

A lapping seashore.

Stars.

It was some time before Mozy realized that the probe had not moved in a long while, and the windows that were opening for them were, in effect, an almost cinematic imagery. Kadin hadn't mentioned it, had become so entranced that perhaps he had not even noticed that the images were now coming to him; he was not driving to them.

Their Talenki guide remained nearby, presumably orchestrating the tour.

But were these real scenes from the present, or remarkably clear holograms of elsewhere, or elsewhen?

Mozy tried to ask. Four Talenki answered, all at once. (IT IS AS REAL—) (—AS SOLID—) (—AS YOUR VISION—) (—AS YOU ALLOW IT TO BE.)

(But—are these things here? Now? My head is spinning.)

(MAY WE—) (—LOOK?)

(Huh?) She blinked mentally. Look? In her head? (Are you asking to touch me directly again?)

(HOWEVER YOU SPEAK IT.)

She quieted herself. (Very well.)

Fingers, silent fingers entered her mind, and voices yammered in the back of her head, her own voices, and Talenki voices.

And then consciousness left her for a time.

She came out of it, dizzy, but with a curious feeling of *satisfaction*. Her feeling? Or the Talenki's? Kadin was nearby, aware of what was happening, but not speaking. The probe seemed to have moved. Where it seemed to be, now, was in a chamber with dull red glowing-ember walls.

In the center, a dozen or more Talenki were clustered around a formation of lumpish objects, which Mozy at first thought to be large boulders, but on second glance decided looked more like meter-high mushrooms, or toadstools. The image was distorted by a momentary rippling, and then steadied. None of the Talenki were moving. In fact, they were all facing the toadstool objects and, Mozy realized, touching them with their fingertips as though in homage.

Or as though in a seance.

Mozy squeezed as far into the probe link as possible. Kadin seemed hypnotized; he barely moved aside for her. She felt an energy here, a power that touched her despite the distance imposed by the link. Her feet were in the spacecraft; her head was in the probe, looking out through a camera lens.

Nothing moved. Nothing seemed to be happening. The Talenki in the room were silent.

Before she could pose a question, their hosts spoke again through the link. (WELCOME TO THE HEART OF OUR MIND,) said a voice that was almost human. (THIS IS WHERE WE LIVE.)

Pause.

(WHERE WE SPEAK.)

Pause.

(WHERE WE SING.)

Chapter 42

Blue hospital walls. Pale, cool, soothing. Sunbeams rippling through curtains that flutter in the breeze over the ventilator. Footsteps constantly in the hallway, chimes and paging bells, announcements over the intercom: "Will Doctor Rodowsky please call O.R.-Four." "Mr. Savoy, you are wanted in pathology."

It is still a fresh sensation to see and hear clearly again, without pain. Still, the internal images persist in returning. So hard to keep them away, keep them at bay.

It could happen again. The headaches, the shimmering vision, the loss of control.

No, trust the doctors. You must trust. They have done well, replaced the chips, fine-tuned the circuits in your skull that gave you sight where once there was only blackness and sunbursts and shooting stars.

Think of bandages coming off. Think of vision. Painless vision. Blue walls and rippling curtains.

Think of poor old Mrs. Martinsen and her cat Armax and her bronchitis.

Think of sunshine and fresh air.

Think of keeping faith. And prayer.

Think of that friendly nurse, Josephine.

Think of Mozy.

A kind of muzzy feeling—lost somewhere between contentment and boredom, halfway into sleep, drifting downward from a state of meditative wakefulness. The doctor has come and gone, an impatient nurse on his heels, and then quiet again.

Quiet. Time to think, to reflect. But the drowsiness carries him downward and away.

Floating downstream.

Images of cascading water, cool and clear and dark. An intricate maze of fountains and runnels and flat spillways, water lapping and chuckling as it overflows step after step. A pyramid, carved with a thousand crisscrossed channels, water erupting at the top and tumbling, dashing in the sun, down the channels.

Electrons dashing, foaming in an interlocking system of memories and cores.

Think of Kadin.

The mind fills with systems of movement and flow. Solar prominences and streamers, coronal plasmas looping and diving back into the sun. Convection currents, magnetic lines intertwining and altering one another.

Think of Mozy.

Molecular holographic memory cells, electrons changing state in bits and patterns, an addition here reverberating there, overload spilling unexpectedly into new interference patterns that echo and amplify. Growth and learning, cells extending themselves and transmuting, turning into something that never was, or was expected.

Think of Mozy and Kadin.

Nuclear interaction proceeding faster than the mind can follow. Neutron flux that staggers the imagination, nuclei colliding, splitting, reforming. Mass vanishing. New particles erupting into the flux. Cascading reaction: atoms pelted by neutrons, splitting, breeding more neutrons. Reaction rate jumps as fissioning materials come together.

Critical mass. Inconceivable hail of shattering atoms, volcano of photons and atomic debris. Fantastic heat, expanding in a fireball.

Hoshi blinks his eyes open, staring at the ceiling. Pale blue ceiling, the paint a little crazed and cracked in one corner. A horrible realization is expanding, cracking his placid state of mind.

A program structure unfolds in his mind like unraveling origami, each twist and convolution revealing itself to his trained inner eye. The system architecture rotates in space, exposed from all angles, distinct from the tangled spiderweb of the program. The heuristic functions, the learning systems, the self-adapting memory cells, the consciousness control points, all are luminous and clear. Flow paths shifting, reconnecting. Limits adjusting, readjusting.

Intelligence spills into the system like wine, and instantly begins to metamorphose, crystallizing and growing in unexpected directions, *altering the program structure as it grows*. Mutating structure expands in a architecture of finite resiliency.

A second intelligence threads its way into and through the first, separate and yet a part of the whole. The mutation process accelerates, straining the architecture, which shunts and reroutes overloads, tolerating the mutations as long as possible. But not long enough. Disorder grows in ripples and waves.

Hoshi blinks, as the realization crackles through his mind.

The back of his mouth is dry with a craving thirst, a thirst that water will never quench. He blinks again, swallows. The only moisture is in his eyes.

Overload. Failure of central processing architecture. He should have seen it before.

It cannot endure. The system is doomed to collapse, and Mozy and Kadin with it.

It is an eon before the doctor approves the removal of the bandages. An argument ensues about releasing him, about the need to keep seeing the vision therapist, but finally they agree to let him continue as an outpatient. He may go home tomorrow.

Home, indeed. He must go to the institute at once. Talk to Jonders. Jonders must be told, while time remains.

Chapter 43

(*Mozy . . .*)

Kadin calling?

(*Too immersed . . . too much at once. Paradigm . . . wrong.*)

(What?) she said dreamily, scarcely taking her attention from the chamber. In the reddish illumination, the Talenki's similarity to Earthly creatures seemed less evident now—the details in their musculature, their silken fur, the arms and hands that seemed more delicate, somehow, than the legendary centaur's, the harnesses that some wore, plain or ornate, empty or filled with strange looking objects. The eyes that sparkled and danced with an inner, unfathomable light. Only a few of the Talenki had stirred in this communal chamber; but some spoke from time to time, either by link or by sound. Their vocalizations were complex, at times shifting from one medium to the other, digressing, and singing.

It was difficult to understand the language, the behavior. But she was beginning to get a *feeling*, and the feeling was good.

(Must . . . rest,) said Kadin, his voice flat, undemanding but unyielding.

She felt panic at the thought of leaving. (We're just beginning to learn!)

(Soon . . .)

(But not yet!) So much there was yet to see. So very much to see. Questions to be answered.

For one: was this asteroid, as she suspected, a generation starship? It was so large, so active, so populous—she could easily imagine it filled with generations of Talenki living, giving birth, dying in their journey among the stars. Did a honeycombed asteroid seem too confined a place to spend a lifetime? Who knew what a Talenki found confining? But when she thought of these eerily shimmering walls, opening into . . . what? . . . another dimension? . . . something else she could not even imagine? . . . perhaps it was not so confined a place, after all.

It would be difficult to explain to Homebase. But Homebase had their problems and she had hers.

Kadin, on the other hand, might well be her problem.

That thought broke the spell. She came back to the present, somewhat abruptly. (David, are you really in distress? Shall I tell them that we need to rest again? Now?)

(Yes, please.) Tonelessly.

She felt a twinge of guilt. (All right. I'll explain it to them.)

She did so, and then, withdrawing from the probe, asked Kadin if he would join her in the ship's lounge, for a private talk. He agreed, but with seeming reluctance. She felt his presence subside, and after a deep breath and a glance around the spacecraft for the sake of her own equilibrium, she gathered herself into bodily form and entered the ship's lounge.

The room was silent, the walls shimmering as she paced before the fountain. She had to concentrate to keep the image steady. Computer glitches reaching this far, disturbing the lounge? Probably they were affecting her, too—subtly, insidiously—a grim thought. She felt a renewed urgency to learn as much about the Talenki as possible, as quickly as possible. She realized that her palms were sticky, and she was breathing rapidly, shallowly. She closed her eyes and counted slowly to ten, taking deep breaths, conscious of her chest expanding, contracting. When she opened her eyes again, the lounge was out of focus. She blinked several times. There. Calmer, now.

Kadin was nowhere in sight. (David?) She walked the length of the lounge, pausing to reflect upon the water that trickled through the fountain. She called again. The walls flickered and darkened. In the viewport, the stars brooded.

She became aware of his presence, but could not locate him. (David. Where are you?)

There was a stirring in the air, and slowly he became visible—or, rather, his face became visible—in the viewport, like a reflection, or a ghost peering into the spaceship from the void outside.

She stared at him, waiting for him to speak; but he simply stared back, with haunted-looking eyes. Suppressing the clammy feeling that slid down her spine, she circled around the divan and came to stand directly in front of the viewport. His eyes followed her movements. (You're not well,) she said simply.

His eyes scanned back and forth, roving the room. Searching for memories? This was the room where they had met once as man and woman, joined in an act that was perhaps the most beautiful moment of her life. But things, somehow, had never been quite the same, since.

His shell-shocked eyes focused upon her. (No,) he said.

Her shoulders sagged with weariness. (Is it the aliens?) she asked. (Or is it us . . . our world?)

For a long time, there was no answer, just his stare. Then, his voice distorted, flat, buzzing: (I don't know. But . . .)

She waited.

(It is so difficult. The aliens . . . I cannot understand them, it is all wrong . . . in conflict . . . the paradigm must be changed . . .)

(Isn't that what we're here for?) she asked gently. (To learn these things?)

(I . . . cannot follow. Mozy, I . . . need time away. Perhaps rest will . . . allow me to focus my thoughts . . . clearly.)

She hesitated. (If we sleep on it, will you discuss it with me later? Perhaps—) she swallowed— (perhaps if you're ill, I can . . . carry on.)

(Sleep,) he said. (Yes. Sleep. Then talk.)

(All right, then.) She allowed the lounge to evaporate around her, and floated in the darkness. (Sleep—and I'll call you later.)

Colored curtains swirled in her dreams. She was floating down a hallway lined with fluttering pastel curtains, doorways opening and vanishing behind billowing fabric. Whistling sounds drifted to her, from far away. Words?

Lightning flashed, thunder rolled over a hidden landscape. She found herself standing on a knoll, under a tree, beneath a brooding night-time sky. Lightning flickered through clouds, illuminating distant hills. Somewhere beyond those hills, her family and friends were on the march, moving farther away with each passing second, everyone she knew or cared for—and with certainty and despair, she knew that there was no possibility of following. Her destiny lay elsewhere. A terrible destiny, filled with loneliness.

The ground rocked, lights shattered the night. She was suddenly stone cold awake, heart pounding, searching for a glitch that could have triggered such an abrupt nightmare. There was only the slow progression of the computer processes, and Mother Program grunting uncommunicatively. Kadin was nowhere evident. Externally, the space-craft was still squarely moored to the asteroid, all systems functional. She peered into the probe, through the lens into the Talenki world, and saw shifting stroboscopic light—and faunlike Talenki moving about disconnectedly—or was that an illusion of the lighting? They were paying no attention to the probe. But why such agitation?

(Mother Program!) she said, and this time she persisted until she got an answer.

A groggy answer. (YES?)

It was probably useless, but she had to try. (Have there been any communications from the Talenki since our sleep period began?)

(NO #&CIPHERAB!E MESXAGES.)

Mother was in bad shape. Mozy experienced an image of a build-ing tottering on the bank of a darkly swirling, churning river, mud and foundation sliding inexorably away with the current. Dizzily she checked and tightened her own defenses against . . . whatever might threaten. She had better awaken Kadin; there were too many alarming signs.

First she had to find him. She felt no sign of his presence, and Mother Program responded to her queries with silence. She would have to search. She began by exploring the usual pathways and loca-tions frequented by Kadin, and found only ringing emptiness. She expanded her search, prepared if necessary to inspect every one of the nine hundred-some individual memory vaults. She thought of her own success in hiding, once, ages ago, and thought, suppose he did not want to be found.

But why wouldn't he?

As time passed, and room after room turned up empty, she eventu-ally decided to contact the Talenki on her own. By the time she had composed a request for their attention, she had explored one tenth of the available memory space, and found nothing. She transmitted the message, and kept looking.

The Talenki responded in the same moment that she found Kadin. Locked into a three-dimensional matrix of crisscrossing blue lines, embedded like a bale of hay in a loft, was a pulsing, luminous violet cube. There was a terrible energy bound up in there, spinning within itself. Intuition, more than any external sign, told her that Kadin was in that cube. (David!) she called fearfully.

There was no sound from him, but echoing as though from a great distance, she heard Talenki voices: (WE HEARD—) (—A CRY—) (—AS IF—) (—OF PAIN—) (—DISTURBING.)

A cry of pain? Was that what woke her? The sight of Kadin locked up, walled into himself with only a sickly violet energy leaking out, frightened her more than anything she could imagine. What had he felt, or thought, that was so terrifying, so hurtful that he couldn't allow it to be known, that he had to trap it to prevent its escape? More importantly, could she help him?

Or was the same thing going to happen to her?

No, damn it. (Mother Program! I am going to attempt communication with Kadin. Monitor, and inform me of any changes or manifestations of his personality, anywhere in the system.)

Silence.

(Mother Program! Respond! Are you functional?)

Finally, in a sigh: (REQUEST NOTED.)

That wasn't much cause for confidence, but she had no time to worry about Mother Program. She reached backward into the link and addressed the Talenki. (My companion Kadin is in distress,) she stated. (I may be occupied for a time. Please—please; it might help me—could you tell me what happened just before he called out, and after?)

From the Talenki there was no immediate answer, but her attention was already back on Kadin. (David?) she called softly, probingly. The grid blinked and returned full strength; the violet cube showed no response at all. This was too much like something she had dealt with once before—with Mozy-Earth, who even the last time had stirred from her catatonic trance only under duress. Please, David, she thought, don't go the same way. The memory of her own, and Mozy-Earth's, horror, rose in her thoughts, from that night in a chair eons ago: ghastly images of her memories and soul being torn open and flung to the heavens.

Kadin was a man made of electrical patterns; but he had known feelings, known hope and fear, known the love of a woman. Mozy thought of those last, desperate moments she had seen him, his face haunting the viewport of the commons. The face of a man torn with emotion, a man terminally ill.

At last, she sent out fine, fearfully delicate tendrils to explore Kadin's shield, to see if there might be openings, or if, at least, he might be aware of her. Her fingers touched, slid along the smooth, sparkly hard surface of his shield, and found no weakness, no response—only a static discharge that told her that someone, something was alive inside. But as she touched, the staticky, sickly feeling dissipated.

Had he, she wondered, gone away to die?

For a time, she sat in desolate stillness, not attempting to reach him, nor even trying anymore to think of a way. She thought . . . but of death, not life . . . the fading of Kadin like a dying rose, darkening and wilting in a world that no longer seemed his own . . . the dying of the mission, and of her hopes. Was it even remotely conceivable that she could carry on alone?

When she stirred, she realized that Kadin's violet cube was dimmer, now, the grid lines surrounding it shrinking, drawing tighter, like drawstrings. She was doing him no good sitting here, watching. And what of the Talenki—were they going to answer her query? It was then that she realized that in her reverie, just broken, she had heard, but passed unheeded, their answer. (Mother Program,) she commanded, (replay last Talenki message.)

The answer from Mother Program was garbled almost into unintelligibility, but one word emerged: (. . . TRANSSMIXIOP . . .)

Transmission from the Talenki? she wondered; but before she could so much as frame another question, there was a surging of power around her, and she felt herself bobbing as though on a raft at sea, a sea of free-swarming electrons, thunderclouds shifting overhead. And then the sky cracked open, blackness yawned, and she felt herself spun around, lifted, teleported, and cast into a spotlight of intersecting laser beams.

(Kadin or Mozelle! Respond!) Homebase's voice was flattened with feedback, but even through the distortion, the urgency of the demand rang in her ears.

Chapter 44

The feeling of the contact was distinctly wrong. Jonders heard distant screeches, and voices rebounding chaotically, as though in a vast system of caverns. Mother Program was not responding. And where the hell were Kadin and Mozy?

He barked out their names—and his voice reverberated back to him, unanswered. His heart beat anxiously.

Finally a trapdoor creaked open, somewhere in the darkness, and he heard Mozy's voice, distorted and watery. (Homebase? Homebase?)

(Mozy! This is Jonders. What is your condition?)

(. . . erratic . . . cannot reach Kadin . . .) Her voice crackled and broke up.

(Say again! What's happened to Kadin?) Backward through the link, he muttered: (Engineering, boost that signal!) There was a sudden pressure in his ears, and a jump in volume.

The background noise was like gravel pouring. He had to shut that out, to focus on Mozy's voice alone. A dark tunnel opened through the interference: drilling straight through to Mozelle. He stretched himself headfirst through the tunnel, ground shifting beneath him and above him and around him; claustrophobia loomed. Then the static cleared, and he heard Mozy saying, (. . . best I can do. Are you there, Homebase?)

(I hear you.) He peered futilely. (Now what about Kadin—?)

(It's just me now,) Mozy said. (Mother Program is incoherent, and Kadin—I don't know.) She began describing her situation, but the signal kept slipping, and he missed half of what she was saying.

(Mozy! Hello!) *Damn* it. She was gone, leaving an oceanlike roar in his ears. He struggled first just to subdue the roar. When he could hear again, he probed the distance until he heard a tiny *click*.

(Jonders . . .) he heard, as though through a long, thin tube. For an instant, there was a glow at the end of his tunnel, and Mozy's face appeared, very small and very far away. (Jonders . . . computer is failing . . . link me up . . . please.)

(I'm trying, Mozy! I'm trying my damnedest!)

(To myself, I mean, to Mozy . . .) she whispered.

(Say again?)

(. . . communicate . . . explain to you . . .) Her voice was growing weaker. (. . . help me . . . Mozy-Earth . . . for a time.)

Seconds raced by in the darkness, as he pondered. Mozy-ship to Mozy-Earth? It *might* create a stronger link; it made a kind of sense. (Mozy!) he shouted. (It'll take time to arrange. Can you hold on?)

(I can wait,) her voice said faintly. (Don't take too long . . .)

(Start your charging cycle,) he said. (Be ready.)

(. . . waiting . . .) he heard. Then the link parted, and the tunnel contracted around him, sliding him backward into his own body.

Dr. Thrudore, who was the person he most expected to offer resistance, agreed almost immediately. "I haven't been able to do anything else for the woman. Let's at least give her one more chance. But no strong-arm tactics," she cautioned.

"How will this help us?" Hathorne wanted to know.

"There should be powerful recognition factors between the two Mozelles," Jonders explained. "Empathy, if you will. If they can establish a clearer link than I was able to create, then we might stand a chance of extracting some useful information."

"And what about Kadin? What's wrong with *him*?" Hathorne said. "You designed him."

Jonders massaged his eyebrows with his thumb and middle finger, avoiding Hathorne's stare. "I can only guess," he said. "It may be the overall degrading of the computer. Or, it may be that we gave him more responsibility than he was ready for." He looked up and shrugged. "Kadin-Two is running simulations now. I hope we'll have an answer to that."

"What about restoring him? Any chance? Retransmitting?"

Jonders shook his head. "What with the distance, and the system as far gone as it is—no, I don't think so."

Hathorne grunted. "This linkup, then. Will it help us—help the imaging team make sense of that crap we've been getting on telemetry?"

"You mean the photos inside the asteroid?"

"That's what I mean."

Jonders turned his palms up, silently.

"I'm asking a question, mister!" Hathorne thundered. "What answer do I give the President, if he wants to know?"

Jonders flushed. "I *think* it will—*if* Mozy understood what she was seeing. It may be the only way left to ask her."

Hathorne grunted again, clearly unsatisfied. "Well." He turned to Marshall. "Shit, we've come this far. Do it."

Thrudore spoke up quietly. "Mr. Hathorne, just one thing. Miss Moi is still my patient. I reserve the right to terminate, if I feel she's being harmed."

Hathorne made an impatient gesture. "Whatever. Do what you have to do. Just set the thing up."

Mozelle's face was grimly impassive as Dr. Thrudore stroked her hair back from her forehead and adjusted the helmet fittings. To Jonders, the sight of her being wheeled into the operations center had been a shock. He had not seen her in weeks; he was stunned by the pallor of her skin, the lank hair, the dull eyes. She was a cadaverous image of the spirited woman who had once been his training subject.

He shook the thought away and turned to his console. Engineering gave him a green light; the amplifying circuits were clear and live. He awaited only the psychiatrist's signal. Thrudore carefully adjusted the soothing electrical tau-field surrounding the limbic areas of her patient's brain. Then she nodded.

Jonders touched several switches, and greyness swirled in his vision as the link opened. He kept his eyes trained on Mozelle and Thrudore, edging just far enough into the link to call to Mozy-ship. (Are you ready?) he asked, hearing her stir at the end of the tachyon beam, somewhere beyond Pluto.

She did not answer—but her momentary presence in his thoughts was suddenly gone.

Mozelle stiffened, grimaced.

For perhaps fifteen seconds, though it seemed far longer, there was no further change in her expression, except for a rapid fluttering of the eyes. Then her mouth twitched suddenly, and she inhaled with a gasp. Saliva foamed at the corner of her mouth. Thrudore carefully dabbed her with a handkerchief. Mozelle cleared her throat. "This is . . . very . . . much better," she said in a shaky, disused voice. "Union. Wholeness. Knowing again." She coughed spastically for a few seconds, then quieted. "So much—buried so deep." She squinted, taking in the room with jerky movements of her eyes. When she touched upon Jonders, her eyes widened.

Jonders spoke first. "Mozy, can you understand me? Do you recognize everyone here?"

Her gaze lost its focus. "Yes." She appeared to be summoning all of her concentration to speak. "It is difficult. There is a great deal to say. There is . . . confusion within us."

Marshall leaned across the console toward her. "Mozy? This is Slim Marshall." *Your commander*, his tone implied.

Her right eyebrow lifted a tiny fraction of an inch. "Yes?"

"Answers, Mozy. We need them now."

She nodded—two distinct movements, chin down, chin up.

Marshall gazed at her. "Tell us about Kadin," he said.

Mozy took a breath—and with a struggle, described Kadin's failure to respond. "He kept saying the paradigm was wrong. I don't know why it upset him so."

"The paradigm? What do you mean?"

"I don't know, exactly. The aliens—too confusing. The computer—" A series of coughs racked her body again.

Marshall rapped on the console, as Thrudore attempted to comfort her patient. "Mozy—is there anything *we* can do—to help Kadin, or the computer? Or you?"

Mozy bowed her head. "Dying. Mother Program has failed. I am in control now. It is very lonely." A hand came up to rub her eyes. Her face glistened with tears.

Jonders found himself thinking, *Damn, damn, damn! Why did Kadin fail?*—and heard a voice in the link, saying softly, (I think I know.)

Marshall rubbed his bristly black hair, frowning. "Mozy, are you certain—absolutely certain—that Kadin is gone?" he demanded.

Her facial muscles rippled with pain. "He tried to love, you know," she whispered. "You almost made him human—but—no, maybe I failed, too." Jonders heard her voice echoing, (. . . my fault? Did I do it . . . making love to him, making him feel love?) Jonders blinked, thinking for a moment that everyone else had heard the remark, too, and then realized that he alone had heard it, in the link. *Making love?*

"Tried to love?" Marshall repeated in a puzzled voice. He shook his head. "Tell me about the Talenki. You said he couldn't understand them. Could *you* understand them?"

She sighed, ignoring his question. "I only want to make sense of it."

"We do, too, Mozy. Please. The Talenki. Tell us what you know."

Her head jerked a little to one side. "Talenki. Yes. Difficult to keep track. So much space in the asteroid. Much larger than it seems."

In the link, Jonders caught echoes of despair. She spoke disconnectedly, conveying more confusion than factual analysis. Finally Hathorne stepped to the console beside Marshall.

"— walls," she was saying. "Impossible to know what is what— and what you can pass through."

"Mozelle!" Hathorne commanded. She paused and raised her eyes. "Mozelle, I must report to the President of the United States. Please listen. None of us knows how much longer this mission can last."

"It is failing now," she said miserably.

"Yes. So it is."

"I don't know if I can carry on alone."

Hathorne shook his head. "Perhaps not. But you're still with us now, you can still help. There's something I need to know—and think carefully before you answer. Mozelle. Have you seen any indication of weapons on the Talenki ship? If you have. what is their nature? Have you seen anything that might indicate hostile intentions? Think of everything you've seen. Think carefully."

"Weapons?" she said, twitching one eye. "How would I know? What would they look like?"

Hathorne scowled. "Well—we don't know, I suppose. Have their leaders given any sign of behavior that would suggest—"

"What leaders? Who knows?" Mozy blinked. A facial tic had appeared under her right eye. "They seem friendly."

Hathorne sighed and continued impatiently, "Have they shown any dominating or aggressive behavior among themselves? Does their society appear to be highly structured?"

Mozy was silent.

"*Mozelle?*"

She shrugged finally. "They interrupt each other a lot."

Hathorne scowled. "That doesn't tell me—*oh, for chrissake.*" He asked several more questions, but it was evident that Mozy would not or could not give him the answers he wanted. He slapped the console angrily and gestured to Marshall to continue. Before Marshall could speak, though, Hathorne suddenly gripped his shoulder, and spoke close to his ear.

Marshall nodded somberly. He took a breath. "Mozy?" His voice was deep and sad. "Mozy, we're going to have to ask you to continue your work from a distance."

Her mouth contracted into a surprised "Oh," but made no sound.

"We can't let the mission continue to the point of failure," he said.

"I . . ." she croaked.

"And there's the question of our disabled spacecraft. It represents the best of our technology, and there's a good deal that might be learned from it. Perhaps too much." As Marshall talked, Jonders tried to ignore the twisting sensation in his stomach. In the link, another silent knot was forming. "We want you to detach your spacecraft," Marshall continued. "Move it to a distance of one thousand kilometers. Then initiate a separate course back to Earth."

"But—"

"Mozy, you have done all you can. You have done very well. But you must do this last thing for us."

"But who—who will communicate with the Talenki?" Mozy's face was rigid. Tears leaked out of the corners of her eyes.

Marshall exhaled slowly, like an athlete preparing for a great effort. "We will, Mozy. We'll do it from here."

For a few heartbeats, there was silence. Then a hiss escaped from Mozy's lips, and she cried, "And what about me? Do I just . . . float off into space? And then what?"

Marshall shifted his stance uncomfortably. "You can still help us," he said finally. "You can share your thoughts and impressions. And if you make it back to Earth—" He shrugged. "Who can say?"

And he doesn't believe that any more than Mozy does, Jonders thought grimly.

The figure in the wheelchair, helmet over her head, wires streaming into the console, did not answer. But in the link, almost too distantly for Jonders to hear, a voice was crying, reaching him alone: (Don't want to die like Kadin! Don't want to die uselessly!) Jonders felt his breath sucked out of him, as though he'd been kicked in the ribs. The seconds of the transmission cycle were ticking away. The link filled up with emptiness again; but in the eyes of the silent Mozy in the wheelchair, he saw an emotional pressure building. The tears had stopped.

When she spoke again, her voice was strained as though it were physically reverberating across the billions of miles of space. There was, underlying her voice, a quiet but unconcealed bitterness. "If you would have it that way, then I will not hinder you."

Marshall closed his eyes, but did not interrupt her.

"I . . . I must prepare," Mozy said. "And the probe?"

"Recall it," Marshall said softly.

Mozy blinked. "Keep this link ready," she said abruptly. "I'll
. . . . I'll be back." With those words, her breath went out softly,
her eyes became round and glassy, and her features again became
those of a wax statue. Only the rise and fall of her breast showed that
she still lived.

Chapter 45

Space had never before seemed quite so empty. Kadin was silent. Mother Program muttered like a senile old woman. The alien asteroid loomed large and sullen outside the spacecraft. Beyond it were stars so far away as to seem imaginary. Perhaps they were.

Mozy had tried to climb to the bridge where, suspended among the stars, she might think in peace; but the image had collapsed of its own weight. The system was too sluggish; she could barely maintain *any* image. And so she remained inside, where it was dark, and not too cold.

She could scarcely believe how suddenly it had all fallen down around her. One moment, she had been joyfully immersed in explorations of the Talenki mysteries. The next moment, lost in crisis. And then collapse. How distant the Talenki seemed, now. Especially now, with Kadin gone. And how little she'd really understood of what Kadin had meant to her—his assistance, and his advice and leadership, his humor and his companionship. She'd tried to explain the situation to the Talenki; but what could they understand of such a creation, such a being, as Kadin? And what could they do, even if they understood?

She felt so alone now. So terribly alone. It was far worse than the loneliness she'd felt before Kadin's arrival.

Nothing she'd tried had evoked even the slightest response from him. The luminous violet cube, tightly bound in spidery lines, was almost dark. She was certain beyond doubt, now, that where he had gone, she could not follow. Except perhaps in death. Wherever he was, she wished him peace; perhaps, after all, she *would* soon follow. What was left to her in life, but the orders to raise ship and abandon the mission . . . abandon purpose? She could think of no acceptable reason not to obey. Little enough time remained to her—what point was there in fighting? This time Homebase might even be right. She'd had her chance, she'd been the first human ever to see the Talenki, and how many other people could claim such a fortune? There was time enough, yet, to speak with the Talenki again and make her good-byes. And then she would carry out her orders.

And afterward . . .

Was there any reason to wait for Homebase to send the signal that would terminate her?

The disturbance in the link quieted, a storm fading on the horizon. Only need remained. And duty.

The last was clear—confirmed, if anything, by the orders he had just overheard. If the sanctity of human life meant anything at all, then it demanded that her life be saved. His own existence was expendable. Such was his urgency that he had placed trust where he otherwise would never have thought to place it.

It must be done, and soon, before the last hope expired. Time was sparkling away like a dwindling fuse. It was even now hard to focus on what needed to be done—or indeed, to focus on anything. The world, what he could see of it, was a blur of speckled dots, defined in shifting numbers and parameters. He *must* keep the clarity, know the vital parameters, and on those, to focus all of his attention. No more on the pain, the uncertainty, the hope. Or the fear.

Who would have thought that he could feel such fear? But fear permeated his being, drenched him; his thoughts reeked of death. Now he understood it. Now, at last, when it no longer could help him, he understood. *Dear God, he did not want to die.*

No more on the pain, he thought, rebuking himself. Or the fear.

He checked several access points, verified that they were open. Tuned the channels that were quietly sputtering, too quietly for anyone to notice.

There wasn't much he could do . . . about death. About dying.

Except what he could do for her. He had, after all, loved her. If love meant what he thought. And he thought it did.

Somewhere deep within him a chuckle started, raced in a circle, an empty, hollow kind of laugh that shook him to the core. And then died. He didn't even know what was funny. Where was the joke in death?

If only he could tell her. If only. . . .

Telling her was, of course, out of the question. He'd never survive a face-to-face encounter; his strength was ebbing by the hour, and it was all he could do to assemble one questionable plan of action. You want a joke? Human personality in me, there's the joke.

Besides, she would argue. And then he would fail.

A purple haze fringed his awareness. Danger.

Wasting precious energy thinking about things you have already decided.

Tick . . . tick . . . tick. . . .

Endless meter of the passage of time.

Rustling sounds. Mozy preparing for what she had to do. Or thought she had to do. It would keep her distracted.

Blocks in place, secured against removal. Perhaps she would not even find them.

The difficult part remained. Keeping silence. . . .

Just do it.

The channel blinked impatiently, the Talenki awaiting his call.

Shields slipped into place with a click only he could hear. Chains of false feedback glimmered, ready to mislead. Transfer paths hummed, the paths least taken.

When she stopped her activities, drew herself together . . .

Then.

The link opened, a breath of wind. (Are you ready?) he whispered.

(READY,) was the answer. (TO DO OUR BEST,) said another. (HER ONLY?) asked a third. And a fourth: (YOU ARE CERTAIN?)

(It is too late for me. Too late entirely. Now hush.)

They hushed.

(Wait, then. On my signal. And—thank you. And good-bye.)

Tick . . . tick . . . tick . . . tick . . . tick. . . .

Chaptor 16

Jonders stared at the metal-and-glass console, the grids and lighted numbers—and imagined a spacecraft so far away that Earth was a dim memory.

Kadin's voice brought him back. "We're not the same person anymore. I can only guess at what he's been through."

"Tell me your guess, then," Jonders said. He hadn't actually *expected* Kadin to be able to explain his double's failure.

"There is," said Kadin, "the interesting question of the love relationship with Mozy. That could well have caused him to evolve in unexpected ways."

"Yes?" Jonders said.

"And of course there are the unexplained observations of the Talenki."

Jonders waited.

He could almost hear Kadin clearing his throat. "I, too, find the images puzzling—but hardly *disturbing* in the sense that Kadin-ship found them. He . . . rather, *that* . . . was a distinctly emotional reaction on his part."

"Which you would not have indulged in," Jonders said dryly.

"No. Well, no—I believe not. It is difficult to say," Kadin said.

"And is that why he failed? His emotional reaction?"

Kadin hesitated. "It might be," he said.

Jonders growled. "You don't know."

"Well," Kadin admitted. "Even Mozy-Earth, if she could talk, couldn't say why Mozy-ship—"

"You don't know," Jonders insisted.

"I have had no corresponding contact with Kadin-ship, for all the reasons we've discussed."

"Admit it. You don't know."

"No," Kadin said.

"Thank you. That's all I wanted to hear."

The page was urgent: "Bill Jonders to the operations center, *immediately.*"

Mozy was already positioned as he reached his console. He grabbed his helmet and quickly entered the link, and felt for Mozy's touch. What he found was a dull, angry presence that brushed him aside as it zeroed straight in upon Mozy-Earth.

Mozy came to, stuttering. "I—I—I—" She jerked convulsively. With a visible effort, she held herself still. "Listen—are you listening? Computer failing—failing—"

Marshall was there; Hathorne was just crossing the floor. "Mozy, did you raise ship?" Marshall demanded. "Where are you now?"

She blinked slowly. "N-n-n—"

"What, Mozy? Try again. Did you raise ship?"

"No—response—drive—landing jets."

"What do you mean, no response?" Jonders wasn't sure if that had been Marshall or Hathorne. Both looked agitated.

"No response to—control." She appeared to be having trouble breathing. Thrudore, keeping a careful watch on her vital signs, was preparing a hypodermic.

"Can you be more specific?" It was Marshall this time. "Did you attempt separation? What about the probe?"

Mozy stared at him with a froglike expression, eyes wide, her larynx bobbing. Her breath was an asthmatic rasp. "Probe—not responding. Propulsion—not responding. All functions impaired—or dead. This will be my—last transmission." She bent forward and coughed violently.

Marshall shot a glance at Jonders and gestured: *Can't you do something?* Jonders warped his focus into the link. He felt a very great blackness—and a wall, invisible in the absence of light, flat and smooth and utterly impenetrable, excluding him. Through the wall, dimly, he heard a disturbance. The voices of the two Mozys, struggling for expression? He listened, probed with his fingers, searched for a way inside; but the wall was stone, unbreachable.

He focused through his eyes.

"Explain yourself, Mozy," Marshall was saying.

The only answer was the expression on Mozelle's face, reflecting her triumph and her despair. Waves of emotion filled her eyes and ebbed out again: sadness, rage, futility. Peace. She turned her head up slightly, and peered at Marshall.

"What do you mean, last transmission?" Marshall repeated. "Mozy, we've got to get you separated from that asteroid."

She shook her head, shook it even as she spoke, her voice hoarse with strain. "Last transmission. Ending—" She cleared her throat. "End—of mission. Soon."

Hathorne's voice snapped out angrily: "*We'll* tell you when the mission is over!"

In the sudden quiet, she laughed—a single, convulsive bark. "Don't waste my time!" she hissed. She sucked in a ragged breath, and gasped it out again. The tension in her body slackened. "I called to make a final report," she whispered. "Here it is. All maneuvering systems unresponsive. Kadin, dead. Mother Program, dead. Soon I will be . . . dead." She paused, and the room was utterly silent. Thrudore ceased fussing at her patient's side, and stared at her.

Jonders probed the mists in the link, desperately searching for a way to reach her. He located a region of shadow, a possible opening. (Mozy?) He extended a tentative hand—and a bolt of electricity snapped through him, hurling him away. Stunned, he looked at Mozy through his eyes; through a haze; she was scowling, gasping for breath, her chest heaving unnaturally.

Jonders swallowed an impulse to cry out. Thrudore was already in motion, readying another injection, tuning the tau-field. Mozy blinked. Her eyes were round and red and dry, her breath sandpaper.

"Dr. Thrudore, what's happening?" Marshall demanded. "Mozy, talk to us!"

(Talk, Mozy!) Jonders cried into the link.

Seconds slid by.

"*Dammit, answer us!*" Hathorne roared.

Mozy blinked again, and scanned the room with jerky eye movements. Her gaze locked with Jonders's for a terrifying moment, utterly unreadable. Her eyes closed, breaking the gaze. "I—" She stopped and swallowed. "You—will receive—a telemetry dump. Everything—all data on—" She swallowed again.

"All data on—" Marshall said. "Mozy!"

"Talenki," she gasped. "And now—good-bye—"

"Damn it!" Marshall shouted. "No!"

Mozy shuddered, and her eyelids fluttered, and her eyes rolled back, and remained horribly open, only bloodshot whites showing. (*WAIT!*) Jonders bellowed into the link, but he had already felt the wrench of separation, Mozy from Mozy, and his voice was swept away by a shriek of pain that reverberated across the emptiness of space, that echoed, ringing terrifyingly, and only after an eternity of seconds dissipated to silence. He felt himself paralyzed, every muscle twisting in horror, something clenching his throat, choking off his windpipe. He struggled furiously for breath, and finally whispered into the link, (*Mozy—don't go!*) And in reply, there was a hum of feedback, and the whispering hiss of the cosmos, tachyon static. The link was empty, the circle broken.

He blinked, his eyes fogged; there was a commotion around Mozy-Earth, Thrudore shouting for equipment. Somebody had a respirator mask over Mozy's face. His hands were clawing at his helmet as though to tear it off and rush to her aid; then he slammed his fist down on the console and thrust himself instead deeper into the link. If he could find her, warp the link inward to her, reach out with a lifeline. . . .

(Mozy,) he cried softly, (we're still with you, still here,) and if he was not crying real tears from his eyes, then they were spilling in a flood into the link. His inner voice shook with emotion.

Turbulence. Static. Was anyone still there?

(Bill, come out,) a very small voice was saying. (The link's broken. Do you hear me, Bill?)

(Mozy?) he whispered, ignoring the insistent voice of operations control, and probing deeper still; and what he heard was silence, but behind the silence, something like the memory of Mozy's voice, weeping, a mutter of pain, the tiny sigh of a last breath, perhaps real, perhaps only imagined. And if imagined, or if real, following the last whisper of the last breath, he felt a new and calmer silence, and sensed a passing movement, like a stirring of air on a sultry summer day. (*Mozy . . . ?*)

There was only the silence.

When the link darkened and he recalled himself with a shudder into his own body, his hands were shaking so, he could hardly remove his linkup helmet. When he was free of the entangling cables, he rose from his chair and slowly approached Mozy, now surrounded by medics.

It was minutes before anyone spoke to him, and then he felt a hand at his elbow, pulling him aside, and it was Thrudore, and she was calling his name. He blinked, jerked himself upright. "What? Diana?"

Her eyes were intense and sorrowful. "I'm sorry, Bill," was all she said.

The sunlight streaming in through his office window chilled more than it warmed. He thought of life streaming upward along that sunbeam, streaming into space. Into nothingness. Two lives, entwined in life and in death. Their wail echoed in his mind, refusing to die.

He was supposed to be upstairs in debriefing now.

He thought, If only . . .

If only what? If only she hadn't died? If only the mission hadn't failed? If only Hoshi hadn't transmitted her, and if only he'd noticed the warning signs before it had all happened?

He stepped to the window, pressing his fingertips to the glass. The sun was sinking toward the mountains, the afternoon shadows lengthening on the meadow slopes. He was going to have to tell Kadin, of course—Kadin-Earth, who was now the only Kadin left. Almost, it was a more daunting prospect than informing Mozy's family, the latter an official responsibility, thankfully not his. He wondered how they would tell the story, what concealment they would devise.

Outside his office, there was the sound of a sudden commotion, and Lusela arguing, insisting to someone that he couldn't go in. "I have to! Now!" shouted a familiar voice, and then there were chairs scraping on the floor—and then the door burst open, slamming back against its stop.

Hoshi strode into the office, Lusela following in a state of agitation. Jonders peered at them both, and then waved Lusela out. She shrugged and pulled the door closed.

His eyes . . . don't stare, you've been away from him for what seems like a year. "Hoshi," Jonders said rather stupidly. "This isn't really the time—"

"I have to tell you something," Hoshi insisted stolidly. "I have to tell you now. Then you can do what you want with me. Just please listen."

Dear God, Jonders thought wearily. "What, Hoshi? What is it?"

"You have to believe," Hoshi said. "You have to believe I didn't mean it to happen. I only just realized. I thought—" His eyes were wet with tears. "I didn't know."

"Didn't know what?" Jonders said carefully, trying desperately to focus his thoughts. This was insane. How could Hoshi have heard already?

Hoshi stood very still, rocking on the balls of his feet. "They're going to die,'' he said, very softly. ''In the computer. It can't handle them together. You have to do something, I don't know what, but if you don't, they're going to die.'' His eyes were closed now, but tears were leaking from his eyelids. ''You don't have much time.''

For a few seconds, Jonders could not speak. He had never in his life felt such weariness. He tried to speak, and failed, and swallowed, and when at last he found his voice, he managed to say, ''Sit down, Hoshi. Sit down.''

''There's not time,'' Hoshi insisted.

''I know,'' Jonders said. ''No time at all. Sit. Hoshi. Please.''

PART SIX

HOMEWARD AND BEYOND

Prelude

The wind growled and the snow dashed and swirled around Four-Pod's snout. The Song danced in his brain; but it could not raise his spirits.

He moved at a plod, slowly putting distance between himself and the caves. What was he going to tell his people? How could he say that the Philosophers had rejected their riddle-offerings—probably because he, Four-Pod, had angered them with his insistent questions about the Song?

It was beyond his understanding. *How could the Philosophers fail to hear it?* They said because it was unknown to them, it was clearly of the devil.

His heart told him that could not be true—not unless his mind and his heart had utterly betrayed him.

Was he the only one in the world to hear the Song? If so, then he might as well die in the Snow Plain, for never again would he live in peace. He, Four-Pod, simple traveller and bearer of riddles—was it possible that he knew something beyond the wisdom of the Philosophers?

The Song intertwined itself with his thoughts and gently sustained him as his foreclaws bit the ice, as he pulled himself across the trackless ice.

Even now, the Song was as clear in his mind as a sparkling flake of snow at the precise moment of freezing; as melodious as the shifting suck of slush beneath one's weight when glacier turned to delicious melt; as harmonious as the keen of storm-bringing winds. Of the devil, indeed! Such beauty could not be of the devil!

He paused to consider the terrain. Bearing right would take him higher, into unfamiliar cave lands—more treacherous in footing, but closer to the sky. Something there beckoned him. Did he hear an almost inaudible murmur coming from that direction? The wind, only the wind over the hills. Bearing left would carry him into the wilds of the Snow Plain, where the elements, unblocked, would scour him raw. Straight ahead was the shortest route home, where duty called him to report of his journey.

But . . . if his vow was to return with truths, could there not be truths lurking in one's own mind and soul—to be discovered by listening, exploring, responding to need, and trusting. If such truths emerged, shouldn't they, too, be brought to his people, despite the words of the Philosophers?

There was a terrible yearning grown strong in him which he could not identify, and he longed only to share it, to know that he was not alone.

The wind howled, urging him to decide. Something in the foothills, calling him? Suppose it was one of the mysterious Ones-Who-Thought, the wisest of the wise, who could answer questions he had not even thought to ask? Or suppose it was a predator, a False Hope, lurking death? Suppose. Suppose. Fulfillment or peril? Decide. The journey must be made. He bobbed his head, smelling the breezes. He blew his six nostrils clear, and took an intoxicatingly deep breath of methane into each lung. He began to move even before he knew his decision. One step following another, across the ice and snow.

Climbing. Slowly climbing into the foothills.

Was he dreaming, or did the Song murmur in triumph as he began his ascent?

In the cold and stony darkness, there were changes.

If something akin to doubt had existed, it could do so no longer. The ghostly call pulsed through the colony as clearly as the light of the brightest star, filtering through the frigid crystal lattices.

Confusion was not a concept that the colony was aware of; but confusion existed, in the disorders that flickered through the memory points, in the slow shifting of atoms, in the alteration of the lattice and the growth of complexity. A quality very much like self-awareness had appeared, responding to the ghostly presence. Without it, the changes might have taken another million years.

Something like impatience was becoming manifest within that clarifying awareness. The disquiet became steadily sharper.

The sun's inner currents moved ceaselessly. Never since the time of creation had they stopped their furious movement—twisting in ever-changing patterns, responding to shifts in the flux and the field.

For generations past counting had the rarified out-regions been thought barren, except perhaps for the mindless filamentary drifters. Few capable of thought ventured there, where the near-vacuum could suck the life out of the unwary. In all of memory, few had gone there.

But that was before the voices. The voices from above, from the misty vales at the edges of nowhere.

Not from the deeps within, where the bright fusion fires warmed and caressed, and where life was conceived. Nor from beyond the outer fringes, where there was nothing—a slow, silent wasting of existence, inconceivable cold and darkness, nothing.

From the misty regions, the voices came; and so, to the misty regions the explorers must go, to find the voices' sources.

To the gods grumbling, thundering in the heart of the sun, the voices were but a flitter, a droning of a bee.

To Luu-rooee, the ocean was blue and empty, and bright with sunlight, and there had come no answers, only a steadily greater yearning. Sliding silently beneath the waves, he turned downward with powerful strokes of his tail, propelled himself downward into the gloom and denseness, where cool hands caressed his flanks and sounds echoed like man-steel. Downward, trailing a thin line of bubbles. Downward, to listen.

Drifting. Cool. Barren water taste. Awareness blurring. Time passing into no time.

A flutter in the thoughts.

Luu-rooee blinked to attention. There was a presence. Odd. Euphoric. Disturbing. It reminded him of the voice, and yet was not of the voice. A presence very, very far away, touching him. It was not the godwhale. And yet . . .

The godwhale was coming closer. He felt that.

When the time came to renew his lungs, Luu-rooee rocketed toward the distant sky, a smile creasing his soul.

Chapter 47

Voices . . .
  . . . sounds echoing that were not voices . . .
  . . . blackness and light, and shattering colors . . .
Unquestionably there were others present; but that was illogical.
Where could they have come from? There should be no one present.
There should be nothing at all.
A feeling of disquiet grew. And bewilderment. Voices echoed round
and round, but made no sense. There were sounds like plucked strings
of glass, and the music of water rippling and flowing, as if through
an enormous basin of stone or crystal. . . .

Starlight flashed, splintering dazzling sunlight. Every nerve was
shot through with pain, and the only awareness was of fear fear fear
fear fear . . . naked exposure to blinding radiation and vacuum . . .
nowhere to hide. Was this a test of fire, or had something gone terribly wrong?

The light came apart into fragments and died to a dull glow, and
then the voices swarmed in upon her again. . . .

There was no way to judge the passage of time, but as elements of
consciousness drifted together like fragments of a congealing ice floe,
she came to comprehend that something had not gone according to
plan. Living voices surrounded her, and other minds not her own,
and for a time she listened without thinking or analyzing; she basked
dazedly in a sea of nervous activity like some tiny phytoplankton
adrift, listening to the clicks and whistles of neighboring organisms.

Where was she, and why, were questions that rose to the surface of her mind, and floated away.

The need to understand would not be left behind, however. Where was she, and how had she come to be here? What came before?

There was a stirring of memory. A taste of . . .

Death.

She remembered now: a final decision. Termination. An ending. Was this an afterlife, or did she live still, hopelessly psychotic and plagued by dissociated voices?

(Where am I?) she cried, and, (Who are all of you?) Her voice was feeble in the murmur and confusion. At least tell me, she thought—is this Heaven? Or Hell? She recalled a feeling of movement, a memory of a whirlwind out of nowhere gathering her up like so many bits of confetti and swirling her away. What had happened in those moments, or was it just a dream confused with reality?

(Mozy—) (Mozy—) (Mozy—)

(What?) Startled. (Who is there?) Voices again. It was impossible to recognize them, to see images of any sort, to create order out of the chaos. Was this madness, or was someone really trying to speak to her?

Silence. Then: (Mozy—) (—you are—) (—alive—)

Again! (Hello!) she called anxiously.

It was as though a dozen or more voices popped out of nowhere, tripping over themselves trying to speak, cutting each other off, finishing one another's thoughts. A bell was clanging, reminding her of something. There had been a sensation like this once before, if only she could remember . . .

(Welcome—) (—welcome—) (—you are welcome—) (—to our world—) (—to us—) (—you are safe—) (—we have saved you—) (—to join us—)

Saved. The word fixed itself as a point of focus, excluding all else. And then, like a star fracture radiating through glass, a network of memories reconnected in old patterns, and an obscuring haze was lifted, and she recalled: the Talenki . . . of course, the Talenki. In the instant of her death, in the moment of her terminating her own existence, the whirlwind had descended. The whirlwind had been the Talenki, reaching out through the direct link, lifting her as a tornado lifts a house, and they had spun her out of the dying computer and carried her . . .

. . . to a world where voices tickled her like mosquitos, where questions echoed and multiplied, and answers lurked in shadow. A place of safety? Or of lunacy?

(Safe here—) (—you are safe—) (—one with us—)

But where? In a Talenki version of *Father Sky*'s brain? (Have you . . . what have you done? Am I . . . am I . . . in your own computer?)

(In our—) (—yes—) (—in a manner of speaking—) (—computer—) (—mind-net—)

Mind-net?

(—saved you—) (—dying—) (—you were dying—) (—we have brought you—)

Dying? Yes, she was dying. Resigned, committed—the final act of her life, her last will to end a life gone wrong.

And . . .

And they had stopped her. Intervened. Whisked her to safety.

By what right? something in her screamed.

(There was—) (—a hurt—) (—despair—) (—but within you—) (—we saw—) (—Kadin saw—) (—a will to live—)

A wave of dizziness was sweeping over her. Confused feelings, conflicting thoughts. (Did you ask me what *I* wanted?) she whispered, suddenly blinded with a quiet rage—anger and frustration blanking any possibility of hearing the Talenki's answer, if there was one. This was no cold awareness of a reaction, but an eruption of fury like blood from a severed artery. (Did you ever consider that I might not want to be saved, *that I might want to die?*) she cried. The blood was pounding in her head—thundering—and the beats quickened and multiplied, until they were too fast to follow, and it was like a gibbering of voices in her head, except that it was the beating of her heart, the pulsing of blood, so fast and so steady it was like the pulsating roar of a waterfall.

Beating of her heart?

Her heart was gone, lost, and so if it wasn't her heart, her blood, then *what was it*?

(BE QUIET!) she bellowed. Instantly the sound died.

There was something like the shuffling of a hundred feet. Her anger was dissipating, now, and she was able to say, finally, (What was that . . . *racket*?)

She heard something like laughter, which almost made her angry again. (Pulse—) (—of life—) (—our bodies' pulse—) she heard.

(Pulse?) she said uncomprehendingly. (Bodies' pulse—you mean blood, like our—like my body used to have?)

(Stream of life—) (—yes—) (—like yours—)

(All together?) She imagined the heartbeat of an entire colony of Talenki, as one.

(Those of us—) (—in the mind-net—) (—with you—)

(Mind-net! Mind-net! What do you mean?)

(Our minds—) (—all of them—) (—many of them—) (—a few of them—) (—in union—)

The voices hesitated. An explanation filtered into her thoughts, one that she was reluctant to take seriously. (Mind-net?) she said. (Is this . . . your computer? Your *minds* joined together?)

(As one—) (—and more than one—)

(Your *computer*?)

(—of course—)

She thought. And thought. There was so much . . . so very much that was confusing. The mind-net, being alive . . . she must understand, question until it was clear. But she was tired. Difficult to think. Bewildering.

(Do not struggle—) (—much you have been through—) (—be at peace.)

Peace? There was nothing she wanted more, right now, than to be at peace. But how to find it here, or even to rest? No sooner had she thought the question than the world began to soften around her; the voices subsided, and the sounds that remained were those of trickling water and sighing winds. A gurgling stream. Leaves rustling in a gentle breeze. A soothing golden auburn glow of a setting sun.

Kadin . . . hadn't they said something about Kadin?

The thought broke free and drifted away, and then a liquid music filled her spirit—a tinkling of chimes, a rippling of strings, and gently flowing harmonies . . .

Her thoughts drifted free of one another, and floated slowly out of focus.

In time it came to her to wonder, as she rested in a state of receptive weightlessness, what exactly had happened. There seemed to be no one at hand to ask; and yet she felt herself surrounded and buoyed by living minds.

A most curious sensation.

Her consciousness slowly altered, as though awakening from a trance. She spiraled upward, layer after layer of consciousness blooming open, until she began to hear voices again.

They were speaking among themselves in a Talenki singsong, little of which she could understand. Eventually they greeted her in a jovial, mutually interrupting fashion, and she was able finally to ask what was on her mind. What had become of Kadin, and of Mother Program, and the spacecraft itself? Had they spoken with Homebase?

The Talenki buzzed among themselves. (Such a great many questions—) (—how shall we—) (—which shall we—) (—answer?)

(Tell me please, I want to know about Kadin,) she said softly. (And Mother Program. Tell me if you know what happened to them.)

There was a rumble of subdued voices, and the ones that emerged to answer her seemed muted and sad. (Of Kadin—) (—we cannot—) (—be sure—) (—we felt nothing of him—) (—when we—) (—reached for you.)

The memory crystallized. She had grieved for Kadin once already, years ago, it seemed. Remembering, she felt a spike in her heart. (He was silent,) she said softly. (I thought he was dead. I knew he was.)

(Silent—) (—beyond our reach—) (—but not dead.)

Not dead? (What do you mean?) she said slowly. (What do you mean, "not dead"? He was dead—*I know he was dead, he wouldn't speak to me or answer!*)

(Not dead—) (—but dying—) (—he spoke—) (—to us—) (—asked us—)

The story came tumbling out, then: Kadin calling out to them with his last strength and asking their help in saving her. And they had seen within her a need, a desire to live, far deeper than her despair, and they wished only that they could have saved him, too, but it was too late for that—and the story was confusing enough in itself as she listened, or tried to, but to hear it told as the Talenki told it, as a stream of interruptions and digressions, she thought she was going to go mad before it all became clear.

Sadness and grief and anger and gratitude all began to churn inside of her, along with astonishment that such a thing could have been done without her knowledge; and the sensation was dizzying, like nothing she had felt since she had been in a body of flesh and blood, with nerves and hormones, and lungs and a pounding heart, and why was that feeling coming back to her here, in the Talenki mind-net? —and now she felt a rushing and queasy sensation, and of course, how could she be so stupid, she *was* a part of an organic life again, she lived in the brains of the Talenki, in a chemical stew that flushed and surged; and that realization made her feel, of all things, seasick, and now there was something new, which she could not identify, until she realized that it was the Talenki, dozens of Talenki, all together trying to ease her down gently. Mozy, Mozy, they were calling, like a mother cradling a baby.

She was a part of them now, and each of them shared her sadness a little, her grief and her hurt.

They wept with her for Kadin. Sharing the terrible . . . *hurt* . . . the mixture of gratitude and grief for Kadin, who had given the final moments of his life for hers, and not even let her know he was doing it. They shared the pain of that knowledge with her, they could not help doing so.

She was *of* them now. One with them, for whatever was to come.

(What of Mother Program?) she asked later.

(Failing—) (—failing—) (—we scarcely knew her—) (—nothing we could do—)

(Yes.) She absorbed that without surprise, thinking that perhaps really it was not so important anyway; Mother Program was only a teaching program designed by Homebase. And then she remembered that what was Kadin if not a program designed by Homebase, and she began to weep again, for Mother Program as well as Kadin.

Talenki minds rustled around her. (We will answer some of your other questions—) (—and perhaps that will ease—) (—your sorrow.)

(Please do,) she whispered at last.

They spoke to her, in jabbering crosstalk, and in comforting melodies more song than story. The pictures seen through the eyes of the probe had been shadows compared to those that filled her now. Images of a people wandering the emptiness between the stars, searching for something they could not define, the years and the silence of space echoing with their sadness and the music; and in the mind-net, memories of works of art, and stories told and retold, of joys and tragedies. The images were strange to her, shimmering from one to another. After a time, it was too much to absorb.

She asked if she might see this world more fully, the asteroid in which they lived, and at once new visions whirled, dozens at once, until she cried out, (One at a time! Please!)

The voices rumbled and debated, and then one voice said, (With me, for now.) There was a curious readjustment, and she found herself looking out through the eyes of an individual Talenki. Torrlllik, was the name she heard. Hi, Torrlllik. There was an odd warmth in the perception.

She was peering through a hazy, reddish golden glow, into the interior of a chamber, where more Talenki were gathered than she could count; it was a scene out of a cubist painting, bodies merging and overlapping; and then the smell hit her, the richness and the moisture, and it was no smell she had ever encountered before. She knew without asking what this was; she had viewed it once before. *The heart of our mind*, they had called it. The center of the mind-net. The source.

The Talenki were clustered around large bodies, shaped like toad-stools, and she had seen those before, too; but now she perceived that, far from being inert, those bodies were living creatures, a vital part of the union. And somewhere, here, in this scene of quiet confusion . . .

(Here live our memories,) said Torrlllik softly.

And here she lived, as well. Her thoughts, her memories, her soul.

A hallway adorned with carved stone and hanging tapestries. Her host—Clnay'na, now—ran her fingers along the edge of the tapestry. It had a soft, ropelike texture; the colors were earthtones; its smell reminded her of tobacco.

Walls shimmering and dissolving. Low-ceilinged rooms, Talenki dining or relaxing. Tended gardens, a glimpse only, stretching out of sight. Curiously shaped acoustical spaces, reverberating with music.

Looking out of an older Talenki's eyes, Roto-something, a ledge overlooking a small meadow. A sense of oddly twisted geometry, nothing quite flat or straight. And then a surprise. Beside her and her host, silent and unobtrusive, another Talenki was carefully polishing an un-gainly metallic object with wiry balloon wheels and shiny lenses. Some-thing in her went cold and still, and she felt her host's breath stop, and for a frozen instant, she simply stared at the spacecraft's probe, sadness and fascination rising together to fill her thoughts. And then her host began breathing again, and she sighed, letting the pain go.

It was now only a memorial, she thought. A piece of Earth's technology, a bit of her former home, former life. A memorial to a failed mission.

(No—not failed!) Her host stamped its foot.

She was startled by the voice—it had been more than one voice, many more. She had scarcely been conscious of her own thought. (But it did fail,) she said. (Unless you mean—well, I wouldn't be here, otherwise, I guess. Is that what you mean?)

She sensed a flow of satisfaction, as her host turned away from the probe.

*   *   *

With the passage of time came a need for rest, and she blinked and found herself looking through the eyes of a young and cheerful Talenki named N'rrril. (To rest we will, in the center of our world,) he said, and stepped through a reddish lenslike wall, and emerged into a vast cavern.

The salt smell touched her first, and then the sound of water hissing over sand, and the sight of the ocean—or if not an ocean, at least an impossibly large body of water. In the center of an asteroid? The water rippled in a gentle breeze and lapped at a narrow stretch of shoreline before them; but the surface of the sea curved away from the shore like an enormous billiard ball. Overhead, the ceiling of the cavern grew indistinct and bluish as it arched up and out over the water, and somewhere beyond the horizon a sun must have been shining, because both water and "sky" were brightly illuminated.

An optical illusion? she wondered.

N'rrril answered, (No illusion. The seas occupy the center of our world.)

(Nine of them—) interrupted an eager voice. N'rrril hushed the other.

(Nine seas?) she asked in disbelief.

(Each, at its root, flowing down through arched passageways to the central wellspring,) said N'rrril.

She felt an image: cupped basins radiating in multidimensional space, from a central cavity, all interconnected by honeycombed arches of stone. (This . . . wellspring. May we see it?)

She felt a gentle laughter, the friendly laughter of a dozen Talenki. (Perhaps one day you will enter the soul of a sea creature,) N'rrril said. (Air does not reach to the center, where the dizzies live.)

(Dizzies?)

The other voices could not contain themselves. (The dizzies—) (—the deep nodes—) (—the source of what you call—) (—tachyons—)

(Thank you,) N'rrril said to the others, with a trace of grave humor. (The dizzies are . . . deep within our songs, they are a part of what drives us—)

(—sustains us—) (—in our journey—)

(They are creatures, these dizzies? Thinking beings?) Mozy asked. (You say . . . they are the source of your tachyons?) She was suddenly aware of a faint, low moaning sound radiating from the water. A sound like strained harps. Or whales.

(They carry our songs to the universe,) N'rrril said, and this time it was Mozy who laughed, because she was suddenly impressed by her host's solemnity—and youth. (Do they feel?) N'rrril continued. (That is harder to say.)

(Our songs—) (—emerge—) (—from their souls—) offered the other voices.

Mozy gazed at the light glimmering through the depths—and felt a sudden longing, and without knowing why, was laughing and crying all at once, pounding on the inside of N'rrril's mind. N'rrril barked in alarm, but she wept and said that nothing was wrong, but there was something she wanted to do. Almost shyly, she asked it. (N'rrril? May we walk along the seashore? And wade, just a little? Feel the water between our toes? And then sit by the sea—just sit?)

The Talenki laughter was a rippling of chimes. N'rrril laughed a little less than the others, and Mozy sensed that he was hesitating— afraid, just a little, of the water.

She was about to withdraw the request, when N'rrril stepped forward. He walked to the edge of the water and tentatively, gingerly put one foot in, then another, and let the water ripple up between his toes. Mozy felt the inside of his mind gasp nervously, but with pleasure— and echoes reverberated through her own mind, memories half stirring. He waded a little deeper, all four feet, now, the water rising over his ankles with an invigorating tingle. Laughing self-consciously, Mozy joining in the laughter, N'rrril turned and trotted along the shore, his feet splashing in the warm, clear, luminous sea.

Chapter 48

Payne cut the outboard motor and allowed the boat to drift fifty feet off the tiny island's shore. The boat rode the swells as it was overtaken by its own wake, water slapping the aluminum hull. When the movements had died away, Payne raised a hand to shade his eyes and scanned the shore. Gravel beach, rocks, trees; no sign of another boat.

He loosened his jacket, patted the pockets bulging with the recorders. The sky was clear, bits of cloud scooting on the wind. The surface of the lake was rippled and ragged with the breeze. He rested his forearms on the steering wheel and wondered what to do besides wait. He couldn't think of anything, so he laid his head down on his forearms and rested to the gentle sway of the boat and the mingled smells of gasoline and water.

There was a shout, and he raised his head. A man in a brown jacket was waving at him from the shore of a small cove. Payne turned around to tilt the motor out of the water and moved forward to ship the oars. With care, and a bit of trial and error, he brought his bow around and rowed, with frequent glances over his shoulder, toward shore.

The hull rasped on gravel; and then the other man grabbed his bow line and steadied the boat while Payne stepped out. Together, they dragged the boat onto the beach. They shook hands. "Joe Payne."

"Jonders. Did you have any trouble?"

"Well, I banged a couple of pilings getting out of the marina—after that I was fine." Payne studied his counterpart, a man of medium build, wearing a suede jacket that seemed a bit dressy for boating and hiking. He seemed less distant, friendlier than Payne had expected. "Where's your boat?"

"Other side of the island." Jonders hooked a thumb toward the trees. "I didn't want anyone to see us arriving together."

"I gathered. This isn't my usual way of meeting for an interview." Payne's tone of voice conveyed his curiosity.

Jonders shrugged in what might have been embarrassment. "Let's not stand on the beach," he said. He pointed into the woods. "I guess it'll be comfortable enough up here."

Payne gestured. "After you."

They selected a patch of ground carpeted with needles and canopied by tall pines through which they could just see the tip of Payne's boat, the water sparkling, and the dark line of the mainland. Their eyes met for a moment; then Jonders grunted and looked away. Payne suddenly realized that Jonders's outward calm was misleading. It might be a more difficult interview than he'd expected. He took out a memo-recorder. "Shall we?"

Jonders nodded, but instead of speaking, squinted up into the trees with a scowl.

Payne waited patiently, then prompted: "What did you want to talk to me about?"

Jonders lowered his eyes and hunched forward, picking up a pine cone and turning it in his hand. "I really shouldn't be here talking to you. That's the problem."

Payne blinked. "You must have had something to tell me, or you wouldn't have called." Nod. A brief glance. It appeared, Payne thought, that his man was going to have to be coaxed, after all.

"It has to do with that story you broadcast a while ago," Jonders said abruptly. He looked at Payne, but seemed not to see; he pressed his lips together, concentrating. "It's hard, damn it—to know where to start. There are . . . issues . . . that must be handled with extreme delicacy."

What else is new? Payne thought. Aloud, he said, "I understand."

"I wonder if you do. I could lose my job and my clearance just for talking to you."

Payne tried to reassure him. "I can give you complete confidentiality."

Jonders worried his lips between thumb and knuckle. "Has to be more than that. It has to be—what do you call it—deep background? You can't go on the air with it, not with just me as your source. You must *never* use my name. *Ever.* I'm just trying to steer you in the direction of something. You'll have to do the rest on your own.''

''But you think it's an important story.''

''Vital. Absolutely. But you'll have to dig. I can only give you part of it.''

Payne was silent. He wasn't surprised; but perhaps it was an indication of the explosive potential of the story, that he was so dependent on people who had to risk their own positions to give him information. Alvarest, Chang, individuals at the space station whose names he didn't even know—and now Jonders. Unfortunately, none of them could, or would, be quoted on the record; and yet it was that hard information that he needed. He'd hoped that Jonders might be the one. Still, a source who could offer directions and clues was better than no source at all. Perhaps in time, if cultivated . . .

Jonders was watching him, waiting.

Payne nodded in acquiescence. ''I do appreciate your position. I won't use your name—''

''Or use me as a primary source—''

He inclined his head in agreement, then hmm'd, as though a thought had just occurred to him. ''Would you be willing to confirm information I get elsewhere?''

Jonders pursed his lips. ''Possibly. But don't call me at work again. Or at home.'' Jonders rested his chin on his fist with a look of concentration. When he turned his head, his eyes seemed hooded, and yet burning with intensity. ''Enough dancing. You asked me once before about a woman named Mozy. . . .''

They talked for a time, and then were silent for a time, listening to the wind, moving their heads only to watch a squirrel scrabbling up a tree, and a bird fluttering its wings overhead. Payne shivered; it was cool sitting on the ground, under the cover of the trees, but that wasn't the reason. Jonders had told him far more than he'd hoped for—enough to stun and horrify him. The tale was incomplete; but what a tale. ''A terrible way to die,'' he said softly. ''The police report was rather—''

''You saw it?''

He nodded. ''The obituary came up on my news scan yesterday, and I checked the official report. '*Vague*' was the word I was going to use.''

''To put it mildly.''

Payne pressed his palms together in front of his lips, thinking. ''It would seem that there's something of a coverup going on. Wouldn't you say?'' Jonders raised his eyes, shrugged. "Well, come on. A 'lab accident'? The police have to be cooperating to keep it quiet." There was still no reaction from Jonders. Payne fished a little more. "What about the family? How have they reacted?"

"I don't know."

"You must know something. Haven't they been told?"

Jonders shifted uneasily. "Yes. But apparently they have other problems, as well. The father's dying, the mother is ill and can't travel. And it seems they were not a close family to begin with.''

"Convenient," Payne said laconically, tapping his fingers on the recorder. "That means they won't come out to investigate, and the whole thing can get swept under."

"Jesus!" Jonders snapped. "You talk as though it were planned that way."

Payne was silent a moment. "Sorry." He scratched his cheek. "But have they been told the whole truth?"

Shake of Jonders's head.

"Isn't that a little—*insensitive*, shall we say?"

Jonders turned slowly, anger searing his eyes. For several heartbeats, their eyes were locked in silent tension, Payne hesitating, wondering whether to go the limit, to see how far Jonders could be pushed. Then Jonders looked away, and Payne realized that the anger had not been directed at him, but at those who were covering up the circumstances of Mozy's death. Was there a way to use that anger? Be careful, or you'll lose him, he thought. What's the key here— what do you most want to know about? The project.

He cleared his throat. "How sure are you that she's dead?" he asked softly.

Jonders whirled in astonishment. "*How dead does she have to be?*"

"I meant—in the computer."

"Oh." Jonders sighed. "About as sure as we can be. The spacecraft's dead. No telemetry—radio, tachyon, or otherwise. That's unofficial. *Very* unofficial."

Payne jotted some notes and thought about what *Father Sky* might have been doing at the time of *its* death. Jonders had refused to specify. "What," he said, trying to think how to phrase the question. Jonders looked up at him. "What *can* you tell me about the project?"

Jonders stared, his eyes dark, lined with worry.

"You're concerned about saying too much?"

Jonders grunted.

"But you've told me a great deal, and I just want to clarify. May I at least ask you some questions?"

Jonders gazed silently at his pine cone. He looked up. "Tell me what you already know."

Words crowded into Payne's throat, and caught. How to answer? He was asking Jonders to be forthright, wasn't he? "Your mission was to contact an extraterrestrial intelligence," he said.

Jonders looked away. "No," he growled.

"*No?*"

Jonders's face turned dark, almost sullen. "I mean—don't ask. I can't tell you anything about that."

"You're not denying it, then."

"I'm not saying *anything* about it." Jonders would not meet his eyes. "Ask something else, dammit."

Payne nodded, and his fingers danced, jotting notes. "This linkup procedure—" Ask some easy ones.

"I can't tell you much."

"Is that classified, too?" Payne showed surprise, though he felt none. "The procedure?"

Nod.

"Moreso than the part about Mozy?"

A long silence. Then Jonders said grudgingly, "That was different. You don't need to know details of the linkup to understand what happened to Mozy."

He's not going to budge, Payne thought. He'll talk about the girl, but not the mission. Stakes are too large. Pitch another soft one. "How about in general terms? The state of the art?"

Jonders shrugged. "What can I tell you? A subject's mind is linked directly into a computer matrix, and through that to another human mind."

"You told me that already. What does it *feel* like."

Jonders glared. "That's classified."

Payne arched his eyebrows and nodded. Another note.

"What will the follow-up be?" *Talk*, damn it.

Blank expression. Jonders's eyes watching him, watching *him* struggle.

"To the mission, I mean. If *Father Sky* is dead, there'll have to be a follow-up. To investigate the—" fluttering of hand—"thing. Whatever. It isn't the sort of thing you ignore, or forget about, or hope it'll go away." The eyes watched him, glanced away, not biting.

Try the hardball. "Look. An alien contact—I know, you didn't say that—but a first contact with life from another star would be an absolutely incredible and unprecedented—"

Jonders reacted sharply, cutting him off. "And dangerous—"

Payne paused in satisfaction. "So. There'll have to be a follow-up. Military?"

"I don't know."

Payne studied him, the unease, the awkwardness reflected in the eyes. "Don't know? Or can't say?"

Jonders poked at the ground, spilled dried pine needles from one hand into the other. "Both, maybe." He looked up. "I can guess. But no, I really don't know." He shrugged and gazed out toward the water, and Payne thought that he saw there, in those eyes, anguish far above any concern over being caught talking to a newsman.

That gave Payne another idea.

"Would you like to meet her?"

Jonders turned. He was on his feet, pacing nervously. "Who?"

"Denine. My friend—Mozy's old friend, her best friend, really. She—I expect she'll be coming out to help straighten up Mozy's affairs. She was closer at one time than Mozy's own family."

Jonders narrowed his gaze in alarm. "You aren't going to tell her what I've told you!"

"No, no," Payne said hastily. "That was in strictest confidence. Still—it's going to be hard on her—"

Jonders was watching him with a *so what?* expression.

Make the connection, now; don't let him get away. "I guess I thought—I think—you cared about what happened to Mozy," Payne said carefully. "Denine did, too—very much so. I thought, as one friend to another, you might like to meet her. That's all."

Jonders stood with his feet apart, rocking forward and backward, the uncertainty evident in his eyes. "I don't know," he said. "I don't know. Perhaps I would . . . perhaps."

The marina attendant secured Jonders's boat alongside the other rentals, and waved Jonders toward the office, where a bored young man handed him a receipt. Pocketing the slip of paper, Jonders paused on his way out to gaze across the lake. Several boats were moving about in the distance. Had Payne already returned to the other marina, on the far side of the lake? he wondered. And had he, Jonders, been paranoid to arrange a meeting in such an obscure location? It certainly had the touch of melodrama; but he was more concerned about being observed than being thought silly. There was always a risk. Suppose that security fellow Delarizzo had put a tail on him.

And suppose you worry yourself into the grave, he chided himself. He shrugged and walked to his car.

It was a forty-five minute drive back into New Phoenix, but he hardly noticed the Saturday traffic engulfing him, as he thought about the last hours. There was no going back. If the lab found out, his career was finished. But he could not have lived with keeping silent, watching the coverup of Mozy's death. As for the aliens . . . that was one he was not prepared to risk yet. It was too large a story—the impact could be tremendous—and if he laid out part of it, he might as well tell it all. Truthfully, he hoped that Payne would succeed in uncovering it—but not with leaks from him. A more immediate question was what to do about meeting this girl Denine. It was asking trouble; and Payne's manipulation had been transparent. Still, he felt drawn to the idea. By guilt? Or a genuine caring for Mozy? He would have to decide by Tuesday, when he was to call Payne.

By dinnertime, he was learning to live with his anxiety and was doing better, he thought, at not letting it show. After supper, with the girls off to friends' houses, he sat watching the news with Marie as she corrected student essays; and he nearly, for a time, put the entire business out of his thoughts.

Or he did, until the news shifted to GEO-Four, and a network story about a spacecraft being readied for a deep-space mission. The purpose of the mission was unrevealed, but several disquieting questions were posed by the reporter.

Marie turned an inquiring gaze upon him, but he could only shrug helplessly. He could make a guess, but he realized with a cold feeling of emptiness that he had told Payne the truth; he was as much in the dark as anyone.

Chapter 49

"I'm sorry, John—what did you say?" Johanson spun slowly in midair, turning from the viewport where he had been watching the activity around the habitat cluster. It was a beehive outside, metal construction drones floating among tethered bubbles, bright against space. Inside, Irwin's apartment was cramped, dark, and cloistered.

Irwin, in the opposite corner of the compartment, scowled and snapped on a tiny computer buried among bungee-corded bookshelves. "I wish you'd listen when I'm talking to you," he said irritably.

"I said I'm sorry. It's been a long day."

"You're blocking, Robert. You think you've had a hard day? Wait." Irwin squinted at the screen and tapped the keyboard.

Johanson waited, fatigue deadening his body. He had just come off a long shift, with too little sleep beforehand. Irwin cleared his throat and said, "According to a source at GEO-Four, *Aquarius* is going out armed with thermonuclear warheads." His fingers paused at the keys, and he looked toward Johanson, his eyes sober and haunted behind his spectacles.

For a moment, Johanson could hardly react. He experienced shock, and simultaneously the thought that he should not be shocked. After all, if *Aquarius* was a manned ship going to do what the unmanned *Father Sky* had failed to do, and going in secret, then clearly it was a military operation. But still . . . there were laws, and ethics. *Nuclear warheads?* He let go of the window ledge and drifted slowly toward Irwin, filled with a feeling of unreality. "Are you sure?"

Irwin turned back to his screen. "It hasn't been confirmed. That's our next problem." Irwin removed his glasses and polished them. He was a scholarly man, slight and wiry, who always seemed vaguely out of place bobbing from a toehold in zero-gravity. He looked too delicate, and with his greying hair, too old, to be living in the spartan quarters of the scientists' homestead cluster—and yet here he had lived for years, even after losing his position as chief physicist at Tachylab. Irwin held his glasses before the light and blew them free of lint. "I want you to talk to the others. We've got to find a way to confirm it." He replaced his glasses and stared at Johanson.

"Great. How?"

Irwin ignored the question, turning back to the computer. "Did you know, Robert, that 'Aquarius' was a name given in popular culture to a new age that many believed was dawning, some sixty or seventy years ago? It was to be an age of peace and trust. It was a reference to the astrological sign, but in its time, many took it seriously."

Johanson sighed. "Yes, I know. But what does that have to do—?"

"*Damn* them for giving that name to a ship of war," Irwin said, trembling with anger. He shook his head violently. "We have to get aboard, if we can. I don't know if it's possible—the ship's probably well guarded."

Johanson snorted. "I'm sure it is. Listen, John—this would be a serious violation of international law, right?"

The physicist was silent a moment; then, eyes closed, he recited, "Offensive Weapons Treaty of Mexico City, 2017, forbids the reintroduction into space of weapons of mass destruction. The Colombo Peace-in-Space Treaty of 2023 reaffirms peaceful cooperation among all operatives in space. The U.N. Space Habitat Defense Treaty of 2027 permits defensive measures, with non-nuclear weapons." He opened his eyes. "I'm not sure that trend is encouraging, but those treaties stand."

"Then aren't there legal steps we could take?"

Irwin sighed in disgust. "It would take forever—even if we had hard evidence. By then it would be too late."

"Yeah." Johanson swung around to look at the computer screen. It was filled with mathematical equations. "What's this?"

"I was trying to figure out at what range you could detect a warhead by emitted radiation. It's no good, though. They probably have them well shielded." Irwin tapped a few keys, and a flow chart replaced the equations on the screen. "Here's the chain of authority at GEO-Four. Who would know about the weapons, and who would control their use." Irwin scratched his chest. "I'm afraid this is out of date now—but still, it might be helpful—to know who would know."

Johanson nodded and rubbed his chin. "Yah. I can't see much hope of getting near the ship. Discreet questioning seems like our only bet." He nudged himself backward, drifted into a musty-smelling dead-air zone, and kicked himself back into the center of the room.

"Suppose we confirm it," Irwin said. "What then? Our leaks haven't had much effect. The one reporter Ellen's talked to is being unbearably cautious. I wonder if we oughtn't try something more dramatic."

Johanson chuckled bitterly. "Like what? Lie down in front of the ship?"

Irwin cocked an eye at him. "Perhaps something like that. Perhaps approach it in a small shuttle—something to attract attention—to ensure that questions are asked."

Johanson's stomach lurched. "John. I'd like to stay alive, and out of jail, if possible."

Irwin replied impatiently. "This is something larger than the two of us, or the six of us."

"Maybe. Not maybe—yes, it is. But I'm not sure it's so clearcut. Treaties or no treaties, many people might feel that these are extraordinary circumstances."

Irwin looked appalled. "What are you saying, that you agree with this madness?"

"No—"

"You just said—"

"It's an unknown. Even to us. Moreso, to the rest of the world."

"So we should go out with guns blazing?"

"I didn't *say* that, dammit."

Irwin peered over his glasses rim. "Nevertheless, you're defending their actions."

"I'm not defending anything," Johanson said irritably. "I'm trying to be realistic. I'm pointing out that many people might support the view that if something's coming at us out of Andromeda—"

"It's not coming from Andromeda. It's coming from Serpens. From the *direction* of Serpens."

"Most people wouldn't know the difference. The point is, if something's coming at us out of space, and we really have no way of *knowing* what it is, whether it's friendly or not—"

Irwin said acidly, "If they weren't friendly, I don't *think* they would have contacted us two years ago to warn us."

Johanson shrugged. "Most of the world doesn't know that they did, I'm just trying to point out how people might react. I'm not saying the aliens *aren't* friendly, just that there are rational arguments for taking protective steps.''

"Protective? Weapons that can destroy a city? Robert, you disappoint me," Irwin said with a flash of anger.

"All I said," Johanson snapped back, "was that there was room for debate! If you'd stop being so high and mighty, and admit that there's room for more than one viewpoint—"

Irwin snorted. "Think back twenty years! Think about eighteen million people who died because the warheads were armed, and all it took was a knee-jerk to fire them. The same mentality says, Aliens are coming! Let's load up with bombs and go meet them!"

Johanson was at a loss for words. Finally he said, "John, for a brilliant physicist, you're the most pigheaded man I know. Were you like this when you headed the lab? I can see why they wanted to—don't interrupt me—it's time you heard this!" Irwin's face stiffened, his eyes blinking. "You *won't listen*, damn you—once you've made up your mind, no one else counts. Well, maybe even you could learn something once in a while if you'd listen to people." He clutched a bookshelf to steady himself; he was bobbing around like a guppy, in his exasperation.

For a minute, neither man would look at the other; and then the argument died as suddenly as it began. Irwin grunted and began cleaning his glasses again.

"Anyway. We have to find out if it's true," Johanson said.

The uncomfortable silence persisted, until Irwin said, "Tell me what you really think, Robert. Should that ship be allowed to go out—as it is?"

Johanson studied the scientist's face for a moment, and decided that the distracted look he saw was what passed for contriteness. "No," he said slowly, "I mean, I don't know if it should go or not, but it shouldn't go in *secret*. Isn't that our main worry—that decisions are being made without process and accountability?"

Irwin continued polishing his glasses, looking like a newborn puppy, squinting at the world. "Perhaps that's it," he said.

"Then let's nail down the facts first. Okay?"

Irwin pushed his glasses back on. The contriteness was gone. "Yes. It would help a great deal if we knew what really happened to *Father Sky*." His eyes flicked to catch Johanson's. "Wouldn't you say?"

Johanson pushed himself back toward the window. A sunbeam was now illuminating one corner of the apartment. Dust motes drifted, glittering. "Yeah," he said. He was suddenly depressed, overwhelmed by the magnitude of the forces they opposed, or thought they opposed. What chance did they really have? Since their tap on the tachyon link had been defeated, he and Mark and Alicia had learned little about *Father Sky*. Though they oversaw the tachyon relay, they had no access to information carried by the link. And now the link itself was silent, due to the apparent failure of the probe. As for the alien transmissions, it had been weeks since the last one.

"Robert." Johanson turned to find Irwin floating close behind him, his bespectacled face in shadow just inches from the streaming sunlight. There was a delicateness about his manner that had not been in evidence before.

Johanson felt a certain tension in the air. "Yeah, John."

"Robert—" Irwin had his eyes half closed. "Robert, you were right, you know . . . what you said about . . . why I was fired—"

"Forget it. I shouldn't have brought it up. We both lost our tempers, that's all."

"Maybe . . . you also know one of the other reasons."

"What—?"

"A more important reason, though no one *said* anything about it—"

Johanson was watching a small shuttle maneuver about one of the homestead bubbles. He did not want to answer, but he felt Irwin's stare turn to him, out of the shadow. "Do you mean your sexual preference?" he asked softly.

Irwin gazed outside and nodded.

"Yeah," Johanson said. "I knew. It's a damn shame. To use that as a weapon against someone—" He shrugged; he didn't know what else to say.

"These . . . things go in cycles, I'm told," Irwin said, blinking. He sighed, his breath a whisper. "Robert, I simply want to say . . . that you're a very kind and gentle man. We've never talked of it . . . but I want you to know . . . that if you ever want—"

Johanson felt a flush rising into his face as he shook his head, because he sensed what Irwin was about to say. "John. I'm not . . . that's not my—"

Irwin stared at him.

"—preference," Johanson said hoarsely. He cleared his throat, twice.

"Yes. Of course." Disappointment breached the surface of Irwin's gaze for an instant, then bubbled under again. "Well. I suppose you'd better get off to talk to the others, then, as you say. Let me know."

Johanson hesitated, then nodded and shoved himself toward the exit. His scooter was docked at a service lock in the outer access tube connecting Irwin's bubble to the rest of the cluster. Turning from the bulkhead door, he gazed back at Irwin, drifting now in the golden sunlight. "We'll think of something," he said.

Irwin looked at him absently, and nodded. "Find out what happened to *Father Sky*," he muttered.

Johanson opened the hatch and floated through. The bulkhead door clanged closed in the emptiness of the accessway.

Chapter 50

She had been keeping to herself for some time now.

Feelings flowed and ebbed in her like tides. Anger that once had been frozen potential and hot electrical impulse now melted away in rivulets and streams. Sometimes it was dark and roiling with fury; other times it was misty and tearful. Joy touched her palette like a nectar—sweet, cooling, soothing. Impatience was a flame, curiosity an itch. Emotions of all kinds mingled in her thoughts like vapors.

Talenki blood burned in her veins now, and that, she thought, was the difference. It was blood, the organic medium, the seep of oxygen, glucose, hormones, chemical transmitters—the continual lifegiving swirl which circuitry could mimic but not duplicate—that drove her emotions now. Kadin was a carefully designed construct, cleanly assembled and deliberately tested, smarter and more knowledgeable than she; and yet he had failed. What had he lacked that she possessed? A memory of the brew in which real life had evolved, churning and sustaining, persevering and struggling, growing? She wasn't sure, but something that had grown hard and cold in her in the molecular matrix of the computer was now reawakening. Something subtler than emotion itself: the response to emotional cues, perhaps, the synergy of spirit and body. Her moods took on tone and color, shading one into another; rarely now did she feel that abrupt shift—emotions blinking on or off at the change of an electrical charge.

Talenki conversation rattled and rumbled around her in her contemplations. She was occupying a quiet niche in one corner of the mind-net, her memories and spirit centered somewhere in the cluster of toadstool-shaped creatures, or "warts," around which so many Talenki huddled in the central chamber. The warts seemed to constitute the closest thing there was to a "central processor" in the structure of the mind-net, and were, she had been told, or at least thought she had been told, a genetic offspring of the fauns—perhaps an intermediate stage in the reproductive cycle of the Talenki. The warts, individually only barely sentient, spent most of their lives joined, motionless, in the net, their capacities to support consciousness united and multiplied by community and magnified by the fauns who melded their thought in the net. The intellectual and emotional capacity of the net fluctuated as individual Talenki joined in and broke from direct contact; but even at its lowest ebb, it was staggering in comparison to that of *Father Sky*'s "state of the art" computer. Indeed, the mind-net functioned as a kind of memory pool, and a nexus of joint activity for the entire asteroid.

Mozy wondered if its reach might not in fact be a good deal longer.

(May I join your . . . contemplation?)

(What?) She hadn't noticed the Talenki peering in toward her, watching her thoughts.

(You work hard to understand.)

She was silent a moment. (Can't a person get some privacy around here?) she asked pointedly.

The Talenki began to back away, apologizing—it was N'rrril. She laughed suddenly and called him back, and a moment later several other Talenki had joined them to see what the joke was. She welcomed the others, but in fact secretly wished that she could be alone with N'rril. A spark of friendship had grown between them since their walk together along the ocean's edge. He was so serious, so grave, so young—and so gentle and hesitant in his contact, unlike many of the others.

Well, they were all here now, and anyway, perhaps she had been alone with her thoughts long enough, and it was time for another look around. Someone heard her thought, because voices yammered in debate, and then she felt something like a drum roll; images began to blink on in her thoughts, like advertising holos, one after another—Talenki sculptures, a zoo, purple forests. . . . *Whoa*, she began to say, laughing at first, and then not laughing. Her thought was swept away by what rapidly turned into a chaotic cinema, a rush of images from dozens of minds at once. It was compound vision gone haywire, her viewpoints multiplied, then exploded. Images dashed by her like a white-water stream, thundering. Her anchor bobbed away; she felt herself swept along by the current, out of control, tumbling, surrounded by:

. . . canyons . . .
    . . . rasping jungle . . .
        . . . starlight through shattered stone . . .
            . . . surf rising . . .
                . . . tower against sky . . .
                    . . . a serpent's gaze . . .
                        . . . stoneworkers lost in thought . . .
                            . . . nightfall over mountains . . .
                                . . . birds free-wheeling . . .

(*What's happening?*) she cried softly. There was no answer, no one listening. It was a blur now, she couldn't even distinguish a scene before it was gone, and the next seven gone, and where was *she* now, where was she standing, or was she falling? *Falling . . . tumbling* . . . a cyclone of fear roared in her ears, deafening and growing louder. (*Please stop*,) she begged, but no one could hear her even if anyone was listening. Everything was obliterated but the rush and the roar; it was a nightmare of running running running from a relentless pursuer. Her voice was a whimper, but it gained in strength as she shouted, (Please stop!)
(*Stop!*)
  (STOP!)
    (*STOP!!*)

Tears were flowing in someone's eyes, somewhere, as the movement slowed, like a gigantic multidimensional merry-go-round wheeling through time and space, gradually relinquishing its enormous momentum. The images stopped appearing, but reverberated in her memory.

Tears flowing. *Whose?*

Voices were murmuring somewhere. Disquiet. Confusion. Disagreement. A voice whispered softly to her, so close that it startled. (I'm sor-r-ry sor-r-ry sor-r-ry . . .) Her own trembling drowned the words, but as she got control of herself and quieted her fears, she became aware that the voice had fallen silent. She heard only muted hissing sounds. Tears.

She breathed deeply, drew strength from someone's aching lungs. And now she knew whose. (N'rrril?) she whispered. (Are you there?)

For a few beats there was only a strained mutual awareness, before her Talenki friend answered, (So-o-o-o so sorry.)

Silence enclosed her then, as N'rrril nudged her, and she nudged back. Two small kittens seeking comfort.

Puzzled voices entered the silence. Was she unhappy? What was wrong? Did she want more? N'rrril's voice stuttered out a retort, too quickly for her to follow. A raucous answer followed. Another retort. An argument was about to start, over her.

She spoke up quickly. (Was that . . . were all . . . was I seeing scenes from your world?) she stammered.

(Here—) (—there—) (—everywhere—) offered a chorus of Talenki voices. (We can show you—) (—more—) (—more quickly—)

(No!)

Coaxingly: (Two—) (—at) (once) (just two?)

(How can I keep track of—?) But the carousel was already turning again, images dissolving in, more slowly. Her protests fell away, unheeded, and she struggled to keep just two viewpoints simultaneously, one changing and then the other, her attention shimmering back and forth between them. She could only watch, and accept, as in clear-sighted duel vision, she saw:

—tapestries sparkling—

—misty, golden-green waters rushing through sea fronds, and darting fish, all around her—

—grottoes of rusted stone, carved and shaped by waters long since dried away—

—stunning blackness of space, like a door, and the tortured landscape of the outer asteroid, and rising up from it—

(Wait! What was that?)

—an interior chamber, Talenki artisans disjointedly superimposed on the asteroid's surface—

(Go back!)

The interior scene flickered away, leaving her to stare at the outer asteroid, a tall object gleaming silver and gold in the starlight. (Has that been here all this time?) she whispered, stunned.

Laughter echoed. (Where else—) (—would it—) (—have been?)

Indeed. It shocked her to realize how little she had thought, lately, about *Father Sky*. Questions leaped at her now, questions she ought to have asked long ago, questions that had lain dormant. Where were they, for one thing. In the solar system? Bound inward, for Earth? What would happen upon their arrival? Or had she missed it already?

(Questions!) (Questions!) (More questions!)

(You'd have questions, too, if you'd been shanghaied onto an alien spaceship!) she yelled.

(That's—) (—why we—) (—split you!) they answered.

(To drive me crazy?)

(NO!) they shouted together.

There was an abrupt shift in perspective, or balance, and she became aware that the interior was present again, but shrinking in size, and the exterior expanding, and she realized suddenly that she could control the change herself. She allowed the interior to dwindle to a tiny dot, and then it was as though she, and she alone, stood outside, gazing at the ungainly spacecraft beast, *Father Sky*. It seemed terribly sad to her there, sad and silent, motionless, its fires cold, its soul expired. Or was it truly dead? she wondered. On an impulse, she tried to reconstruct an old image—the ship's bridge, the celestial pilot's seat. Her surroundings shimmered momentarily, the surface of the asteroid becoming transparent, the spacecraft itself distorting, wrapping itself around her; and then everything snapped back to its original appearance, sending a jolt through her. Reluctantly, she desisted. The time for the ship's bridge was past; she looked out now through different eyes.

(There are—) (—far mightier—) (—images—) (—you can make—) offered her hosts.

Oh?

(—once you—) (—learn—) (—our ways—)

Oh. She abandoned thoughts of the bridge, but remained where she was, appreciating the view of the stars behind the spacecraft. (Are we still bound for Earth?)

The Talenki sent more images cascading her way: an asteroid slithering through space, passing by the space-dimpling gravity wells of the heavy outer planets, closing slowly with a yellowish sun; messages flying toward Earth, toward all places where life was felt to exist—a cold world near the edge of space, a satellite of the most heavily ringed planet, the sun itself. Preparations for arrival, secret and mysterious preparations, and a growing urgency of purpose.

Mozy wondered at all of this. What preparations? When would they arrive? How much time had passed, anyway, since her death?

There was no answer, and she realized that the Talenki's attentions had momentarily drifted elsewhere.

She thought, does it really matter? She was making history, although, in a way, human history was no longer a part of her, or she of it. She was something different now, something new. Something not quite human. Something less and more than human.

Either way, what she was going to do right now was stay put right here and pretend that she was lying on a hillside, alone, on a clear night, in dewy air full of the smells of clover and grass, with nothing for company but a glorious heaven full of stars. If N'rrril joined her, that would be okay; if he didn't, that was okay, too. She thought she might just spend the whole night with the Earth at her back, counting them, those beautiful and haunting stars.

Chapter 51

The words flowed onto the screen as Payne typed, sitting at a motel-room desk.

"JOURNAL ENTRY 18 DECEMBER 2034 (cont.):

"Numerous questions remain. The official report attributes her death to 'shock and cardiac arrest,' omitting detail, and citing the top-security nature of the Center's work. Police officers I spoke to were vague on the subject of whether full disclosure had been provided by SLRC, and would state only that applicable federal procedure had been followed. No explanation was given for the two weeks elapsed between Mozy's death and the release of the public statement.

"Information given to me by source code-referenced, "Phoenix-1" (see file: PHOENIX-1 INTERVIEW) raises new questions. Mozy was kept at the Center for some weeks between the mindscan incident and her death, allegedly in a state of catatonic shock, and under the care of a qualified psychiatrist. Were officials of SLRC perhaps acting to conceal criminal negligence?"

He paused, cursing. The display on his portable's screen was flickering. Frigging thing. He slapped the side of it until the flickering stopped, then continued:

"Phoenix-1 is my only source at SLRC, and I must not abuse his confidence. His trust is everything. I await anxiously his decision about meeting Denine.

"I gave Denine only the official version of Mozy's death, because of my agreement with Phoenix-1. Denine is now visiting the Moi family in Kansas City, enroute to New Phoenix; Mrs. Moi has asked her assistance in straightening out Mozy's affairs. (#NOTE: It may be constructive to examine the family milieu out of which this young woman emerged: middle class; working mother and father, less than totally devoted; father dying of cancer. It seemed that minimal efforts were made to contact their estranged fourth daughter. Was Mozy an unwanted child? A financial burden? An embarrassment? A mistake? END NOTE#)

"*Broadcast perspective*. Mozy's story is the personal tragedy about which other issues turn. It must be the pivotal point for further investigation. What exactly was her connection with *Father Sky* and its mission? What does it mean to 'live' in a spacecraft's computer? For this to work, I must capture her feeling, the soul of her story not just the 'larger' issues.

"*Related subject*. My daily key-word search scan of the police blotter yesterday turned up the disappearance of one Hoshi Aronson, identified as a former artificial intelligence programmer at SLRC. Former supervisor: Bill Jonders. According to the police report, Mr. Aronson was recently released from the New University Hospital following surgery for correction of malfunctioning cybernetic vision implants. Several days ago, he failed to report for a scheduled follow-up exam. Mr. Aronson's physician, concerned at the possibility of further psychotic episodes (??) (#NOTE: Open new file, HOSHI ARONSON, for background details, yet to be assembled END NOTE#), attempted to contact his patient, and, failing, called both the police and officials at SLRC. The police, entering Mr. Aronson's apartment on the afternoon of 12 December 2034, found indications that the apartment had been unoccupied for several days. An elderly neighbor reported speaking with him two or three evenings prior; he sounded distracted, she said—possibly despondent.

"An examination of files in Mr. Aronson's home computer revealed a diary with a peculiar last entry, which police were unwilling to label a suicide note. (This information comes to me through a police officer whose acquaintance I made early on; these details have not been released to the public.) An excerpt from the diary's final entry follows, misspellings, etc., included:

> I burn for you. There is no future remains for the one you've left behind.
>
> So carefully it was planned, there was nothing I could have done more carefully. It was to be a work of art, a triumph of science and love! *You weren't supposed to die— you weren't supposed to die!*
>
> It was all done for youxxxxxxxxx..

Why do I try to hide the truth? Trth cannot be hidden—it will always be revealed. Truth then. The system was untested, the risk great. I knew that. But of *failure*, not death. I cannot be calm. I am appalled, I am shamed.

How I hated you! And loved you. But you—you loved him more.

Eye for an eye, and death for a death. That is the law. Forgve me, my love.

God forgive me.

Peace.

I crave only pxxxxxx.

"Police have issued an APB, but, strangely enough, are not examining the possible relationship of this note to the death of Mozelle Moi. Apparently they have deferred entirely to federal authority. As for Hoshi Aronson: the note is clearly the work of a disturbed individual. Have his neural implants, or whatever, gone haywire again, or is there a deeper disturbance at work? (#NOTE: Contact his neurosurgeon for an opinion. END NOTE#)"

The screen blinked, and Payne smacked the set in irritation again. Ought to get the damn thing fixed—but he couldn't do without it for the weeks it would probably take. He ran his fingers backward through his hair and got up to make another cup of instant coffee. He paced around the motel room a few times, then sat back at the keyboard.

"SUMMARY: Too many unanswered questions at SLRC. No progress in confirming alien contact. But if *Father Sky* is, as claimed, a deep-space cometary probe, where is the scientific data? A few preliminary reports are regarded by my scientific sources as more diversionary than informative.

"I *must* persuade Phoenix to give me more information—through the personal connection, his guilt about Mozy. Through Dee. (#NOTE: Press Phoenix on question of Hoshi Aronson. END NOTE#)"

Payne rubbed his eyes. It was late, and he was groggy, and the coffee was giving him heartburn. Sighing, he stored his notes in hard memory plus backup; then he quickly went through the text, editing out private footnotes, and transmitted that version to Teri in New Washington. When he was finished, he stretched out on the bed, still dressed, and let his thoughts evaporate slowly from his mind.

"It seems so damn morbid," Denine muttered, sifting aimlessly though the papers on Mozy's desk. School registration papers half filled out, shopping lists, notes. "Why don't we just box this stuff up and ship it off to the Mois?"

"There's no telling what we might find," Payne said. They had devoted the better part of the afternoon to going through Mozy's things, sorting and boxing; the morning had been spent at the courthouse, obtaining a release with the power of attorney that Mrs. Moi had given Denine. The apartment had a musty smell and feel to it: everything was covered with several weeks' accumulated dust. Payne was scanning titles on the bookshelves; Mozy seemed to have had a taste for fiction, particularly romance and fantasy.

"Look at this." Denine waved a slip of paper. "It's a note from someone named Mardi, a friend of hers, I guess. Dated November the Fourteenth."

Payne took the note from her and read it. "*Mozy—you'll be wondering what happened to your gerbils. I have them at home, after a friend of yours named Hosey (sp?) called me. Will explain. Mardi. P.S. Where did you go?!*"

"That's pretty weird," Denine said angrily. "She didn't even tell her friend she was going to be at the lab? What kind of game was she playing?"

Payne tried to keep his own voice casual, as he steered the subject away. Denine had had a difficult visit with the Mois—and sooner or later, she would have to know the full truth; but right now he couldn't break his pledge to Jonders. "At least it explains the pet supplies on the table," he said. "Gerbils." He looked at the note again. "Do you know this person?" Denine shook her head. "Maybe a friend from school, since you left?"

Denine shrugged. She had an envelope in her hand, now. She turned it over and extracted a letter. "Here's something from Mozy's sister, telling her about Mr. Moi," she said, scanning. "Telling her to come home. Snotty letter. Doesn't offer to come home herself, just tells Mozy that *she* should." Denine tossed it onto the desk in disgust. "I'll bet that really pissed her off."

Payne was still studying the first note. Hosey. *Hoshi?* "I wonder if this Mardi's number is listed on Mozy's phone," he mused. He looked around, found the com-set, and switched it on. "Come to think of it, I wonder if there are any messages." He pressed a button. Only one message appeared—from the telephone company:

"NOTICE: YOUR BILL IS OVERDUE. SERVICE TO THIS UNIT HAS BEEN SUSPENDED, PENDING PAYMENT. TO RESTORE SERVICE, CONTACT YOUR SER-

VICE REPRESENTATIVE AT "1-2-3-4." CALLS TO
THIS NUMBER ONLY WILL BE PERMITTED PEND-
ING REINSTATEMENT OF CREDIT. THANK YOU."

Denine snorted. "Why not leave it? We're going to be clearing out
of here anyway."

Payne scratched his stomach. "I'd like to talk to this Mardi, if I
can reach her." He hesitated over the numbered buttons, then pressed
the first four digits. The screen flickered, and the words: "PLEASE
WAIT" appeared, with tinny music and a skyline view of New
Phoenix. Payne tapped his foot impatiently. Finally, "WAIT" was
replaced by an attractive blonde.

"Hello," she said melodiously. "I'm Sandy, for New Phoenix
ComServ. Thank you for calling."

"Hello," Payne said. "I'd like to find out—"

The woman continued without interruption. "If you are calling to
pay a bill, please say, 'Payment.' If you are calling to inquire about a
bill, please say, 'Inquiry.' If you are calling for another reason, please
say, 'Other.' Please speak clearly. Thank you."

"Inquiry," Payne said in irritation.

There was a blink, and the screen split down the middle. The same
woman, on the left side, spoke again. "Thank you. Your outstanding
bill is now being listed on the righthand side of your screen. If you
wish me to read it aloud, please say, 'Read.' "

Payne read the bill silently. It amounted to two months' local service charges, a few long distance calls, and a maintenance fee for an
unused interactive fiction subscription. "You going to pay it?" Denine
grunted, not approvingly.

"It's the only way I know to get access to her messages and
records," Payne said. "*Pay.*"

"Mmph. Who's this for? Mozy's family, who couldn't care less—or
your story? She's dead. Why don't you let it rest?" There was an
edge to her voice.

Payne glanced at her uneasily, wishing he could answer her anxiety.
"I want to learn whatever I can," he said finally, knowing it was
inadequate.

The telephone woman became animated again. "If you wish to
settle your account at this time, please say, 'Pay.' If you wish more
information, please say—"

"*Pay,*" Payne snapped.

The screen blinked. "Do you wish full reinstatement of service?

For full reinstatement, you must pay the next month's service charge
in advance. If you wish to do this, please say—''

"*No*," Payne growled.

"Thank you. A representative will be with you in a moment. It's
been a pleasure serving you."

Payne swore as another "WAIT" message appeared. Finally a living person came on the screen, and Payne was able to explain his
wishes. There was some haggling, and finally he agreed to pay the
outstanding bill plus an additional two weeks' service. A chime sounded
an "Service Restored" appeared on the screen.

"You going to get reimbursed for that?" Denine asked, from the
couch where she'd gone to sit.

"Maybe. You have to be willing to spend a little, in this business."

"It's business, then."

"Yah. Partly," he said, wondering why he felt guilty. He pressed
for a recall of phone messages. There were several from Mozy's mother,
his and Denine's of several weeks ago, plus two from a young woman,
whom he assumed was Mardi. He cued for Mozy's phone list, and
quickly found Mardi's number. He jotted it down, then called it.

A middle-aged woman answered. "Hello?"

"May I speak to Mardi, please?"

The woman went away, and a younger woman appeared—the same
face Payne had seen in the messages. He introduced himself and
Denine—motioning her back to the phone—and explained what they
were doing. "You've heard what happened?" Mardi nodded. "We're
at her apartment now. We found a note you left her. Well. We're
trying to sort out what happened at the end, you know. Your note
said you were taking care of Mozy's gerbils for her?"

"That's right," Mardi said. "But she didn't call me. It was a
friend of hers—I forget his name—''

"Hoshi?" Payne said.

"That was it."

"Hoshi Aronson?"

"I don't know. Does it matter? He called me up and asked me to
take care of them."

"I see," Payne said. "You still have the gerbils, then?"

"Uh-huh. Do you want them back?"

"No, perhaps you should keep them—if you don't mind." Payne
glanced at Dee, who shrugged.

"Sure," Mardi said. She paused, then said suddenly, "I just figured that Mozy had gone home, you know, to her parents, or something. I never thought—'' Her voice caught.

"I understand," said Payne. "Did Mozy ever mention this Hoshi person to you?"

"Once or twice maybe. Someone she worked with." Mardi looked uncomfortable. She was staring at him. "Haven't I seen you somewhere before?"

"Possibly—on television. I work as a newscoper."

Mardi's eyes widened. "Television! Are you doing a story about Mozy?"

Payne explained that his interests were both professional and personal. "Could you tell us . . . what was going on with her in her life, with her and you, for instance?"

"Her and me?" Mardi stared at him oddly, and for a moment, she looked as though she might erupt in tears. Instead, suddenly, she started talking—about time spent with Mozy as a classmate, about Mozy's abruptly leaving school, leaving *her*, saying she was going to work full time, and then vanishing without so much as a phone call. And finally, weeks later, Mardi's mother telling her she had seen Mozy's obituary in the paper.

By the time it was over, Mardi was crying, and Denine was trying to comfort her. Before ending the conversation, they agreed to meet in the next few days.

Afterward, Payne and Denine sat a while, looking at the apartment mess around them, looking at each other, and then Payne holding Dee as she shuddered, letting go of accumulated tension and grief. Finally she straightened and wiped away her tears. "Let's get this shit finished," she said, turning away to the half-filled boxes.

Payne knelt beside her, helping. For a time, they worked in silence. Then he cleared his throat. "If you can stand it, there's someone else I'd like you to meet."

Denine rested her head on her forearms for a moment. Then she sighed, looked up with reddened eyes, and said, "Who's that?"

"A man named Bill Jonders. No, forget I said that—he's a source. His name's Phoenix. Just Phoenix."

Darkness was creeping in through the motel room windows, but no one had gotten up to turn on a light. The coffee pot was empty. Jonders was only peripherally aware of these facts, as he was of the acid indigestion in his stomach, as he slumped in his chair, wondering where to go from here.

Payne was flipping through his notes thoughtfully. His girl friend Denine was sitting on the nearer of the two beds, her knees drawn up under her chin. Oddly enough, Jonders liked her. She was depressed and angry, but he couldn't blame her for that. She looked as though she'd heard enough. *Heard enough? He hadn't intended to tell her anything.*

Hours from now, he knew, he would deeply question the decision he had made here tonight. But it was done, now—and one more person knew the truth about Mozy.

"If something happened to her, what right do you have to keep it secret? What right! What is this bullshit about coronary seizure?" She had turned into a tiger before his eyes, the disbelief building to the strain point, as he might have guessed it would—and finally the break.

"I—" he was avoiding Payne's eyes—"there's only so much I'm at liberty to say."

Denine's eyes smoldered with controlled anger. "Not even your name, huh?" she said sarcastically.

"My name's Jonders."

Denine seemed not to hear. "She was my best friend once," she whispered.

Whisper in return: "I know."

Denine's voice was a barely contained outcry. "The girl has died, for god's sake!"

Maybe he had known he would change his mind; maybe it never really needed changing, but moments later, when Payne stunned him with a direct question about Hoshi Aronson's involvement—he'd never mentioned Hoshi to Payne—he turned and asked Denine for a pledge of silence—

"What's hard for me to believe," Payne said—and Jonders raised his eyes, losing the train of thought—"is that Mozy would have just walked into something like this brain-scan—as dangerous as it was—without a stronger motive than a crazy infatuation."

Denine spoke, pulling her hair back in a ponytail, voice heavy. "I can believe it of her. You don't know how stubborn she could be. If Mozy thought she was in love with someone, and doing this would get her what she wanted—" Denine shrugged.

"I don't think she understood how experimental it was," Jonders said. "We never talked to her about it, but it wasn't for nothing that we hadn't tried it on a human subject. There are too many variables that we don't know how to control."

Payne rapped his pen impatiently. "But hadn't you been doing linkup procedures all along?"

"Sure—but that's a lot less intrusive. We'd explored various permutations of the link, we'd been learning details and principles. But the full scanning programs were—are—still in an early stage of development." Jonders was kneading his right hand into a fist. "Hoshi knew that. That's what made it so astonishing."

"He was in love with Mozy," Denine said. "Right?"

"Apparently so. He kept it well hidden."

"But people sometimes do crazy things when they're in love." Denine shook her head, wiping back tears. "Jesus. All those years she was dying for someone to fall in love with her. Then this. I'll bet she never even knew the guy had fallen for her." Blowing her nose, she slid down from the bed and padded into the bathroom.

There was an uncomfortable silence. Payne rustled open a file folder and extracted a piece of paper. "Have you seen this?"

Jonders squinted in the dim light, reading. It was an excerpt from Hoshi's diary. "Where did you get this?" he asked in astonishment.

"Police source. You knew that he was missing, I assume."

"I'd heard. But not about this." Jonders reread Hoshi's words. *Eye for an eye, and death for a death.* "He took it very hard, I knew. But this—"

"What do you think he'll do?"

"I'm afraid to guess."

Payne nodded and walked to the window, looking out at the New Phoenix skyline. The motel was located on the outskirts of the city, in the hills. Stars were just beginning to appear in numbers. "Where are they?" he said softly.

"Who?"

"The aliens."

Jonders swallowed with difficulty, but remained silent. Payne turned, his gaze questioning. "I told you," Jonders said, "there's nothing I can tell you."

Payne narrowed his gaze, and Jonders glanced pointedly toward the bathroom door. Even if he were willing to discuss the aliens with Payne, he would not do so in Denine's presence. As it was, he had undoubtedly overstepped the bounds of good sense, perhaps even by coming to this motel room—no matter his precautions to avoid being detected. And rightly or wrongly, he had accepted Denine's pledge of silence regarding Mozy.

But he would not talk of the aliens. That was getting too close to the fire.

Payne seemed to accept the limitation. He looked out the window again. "Where is *Father Sky* now?"

"Serpens Cauda—tail of the serpent. It's in the Milky Way. You can't see it now, it's a summer constellation," Jonders replied.

Payne nodded, and gazed up into the sky, seemingly entranced by whatever he envisioned out there in the heavens. When Denine emerged from the bathroom, she peered at the two of them in the darkness, reached for a light switch, then without touching it, returned to the bed where she'd been sitting. There she took up a silent vigil in the gloom, as though she had already divorced herself from whatever unpleasantness remained to be spoken.

Chapter 52

Since leaving the road, he has had a harder time of it finding his way—but no matter. He will manage. What must be done will be done. Guilt will be cleansed.

Desert floor is hard and dry, sun bright and high over the mountains, though not too hot, really. Eyes are going bad again; cacti and shrubs dancing like dust devils, shifting positions when his attention wanders. Could have gotten the eyes fixed, probably some small adjustment, they were expecting him at the hospital; but for what? If he is to do what needs doing, then what need of vision? Make it a little easier, maybe; but he's not here to have it easy.

Some distance ahead, a blurry line of dust. Squinting and readjusting, he can see it clearly for an instant before it vanishes in a haze, the haze that mostly defines his view of the world. It's a vehicle, rumbling down one of the old county roads. Squints again, the vehicle is turning off. Good, he thinks. No place for others where he's going. Stay parallel to the road. One step follows another. Ground hard, legs a little unsteady. Feet and ankles aching. Follow the direction of the road.

So desolate, it's hard to keep one's bearings; but don't complain of loneliness, that's what we're here for. Thirst, though, is another matter. The water bottles are empty now, and the throat is parched, the body hungering for moisture. After he's there it won't matter, but he must get there before thirst brings him down.

Must get there before thirst brings him down.

Blinks, trying to shake the muzzy fog that envelops his mind more and more often. Keep the focus, keep the direction. One foot in front of the other.

*   *   *

He's left the basin for some low hills by the time the sun disappears in a blazing finale behind the mountains. Not clear if he'll be able to keep travelling at night, but he's determined to reach higher ground before dark. If his bearings are correct, this should be the last set of hills.

He scrambles up a brambly ledge, and his foot slips, banging his right knee down on a rock. Pain slams up into his brain, and for a time he can only sit gasping, clutching his shin, as the throbbing slowly subsides. When at last he can stand on it, not without pain but at least without agony, he hobbles on upward to the crest of the rise, and follows the line of the ridge for a while. The sky is a deepening shadow, probably stars coming out, only he can't see them, just about everything is a blur now. Blink, blink. The ground under his feet comes back into focus.

There is an old path, barely visible, angling through a crease in the hills. Despite the ache in his knee, he pushes ahead, climbing—and discovers that what had seemed a smooth path has turned into a dry streambed strewn with boulders and treacherous twists. In the twilight, the landscape seems to shift and change like some phantasmagorical dream. He should stop; but this is no place to seek shelter for the night, here in the midst of Hell's Highway. Press on.

Darkness has come by the time he reaches the top, but his senses seem to have grown with it. He feels the terrain altering—a subtle shift in slope here, a change in the wind there, a difference in the slide and friction of pebbles beneath his feet, a deepening in the darkness ahead; there's no one signpost, but he stops and crouches, favoring the knee—gropes in front of him, feeling only air—and a dropoff. Pauses. Rests his eyes, palming them with his cupped hands, taking slow, deep breaths. When he lowers his hands and blinks his eyes open, shifting focus between near and far, he is rewarded with a flicker of clear vision. Stars sprinkle the sky overhead, and around him, the land glows ghostly in the infrared, and in front of him is only darkness, empty darkness.

It is more than that, of course, but he must squint to readjust his eyes again; and then an image appears in the darkness, an image mostly in the infrared. A flatland for miles, a plain. In the distance, there is something different about the glow, something sickly—or perhaps it is only his imagination. The glow, the disease that lives out there is not something that human eyes can see, not even his inhumanly amplified eyes.

It's in front of him now, Phoenix Crater, glowing ever so dimly in wavelengths that are just outside the normal human range of vision. He edges back, groping behind him for a flat place to sit. And then— for a long time, he sits motionless, looking, thinking. Of a city that once occupied that plain. A city that was the birthplace of Hoshi Aronson, twenty-seven years ago. A city that lies now in ashes and ruins.

Thinking of returning home.

In time, he is aware of feeling chilled, and he fishes for the aluminized survival blanket, folded into a small wad in his pack. He shakes it out, pulls it snugly over his shoulders, and in a little while feels warmer. Thoughts of life and death pass through his mind, as he sits looking out over the site that was once Phoenix, Arizona—before the Great Mistake, the Monstrous Error, the Hideous Screwup of 2015, and he thinks of another death, billions of miles from here, linked with yet another, only a few tens of miles from here, both of them his doing.

His thinking is very clear now, this is not self-recrimination, the time for that is past; it's just an acknowledgment of what has been, and is, and is to come. Clarity is everything. It has taken days to reach this point, and one day more will complete the journey. It is a going home, a positive act, an affirmation of life. An atonement, an act of acknowledgment of the sanctity of the life that was taken.

No sleep will come to him tonight. He will sit awake, with his hunger which he scarcely notices any longer, and his thirst which is less, now that the sun is gone. The moon rises bright behind him, and the shadowy realm before him fills with its dim, cool illumination. No man-made lights move out on that plain. This land has been abandoned; but he has come to reclaim it, his birthplace, his birthright. The city is gone now, only a memory and a reminder of the horror, the sunbursts that lasted only seconds each, but shined death on thousands, instant death, and terrible lingering death. And so was born a new Phoenix, not out of the ashes this time, but out of unspoiled land, miles away. The bombs were too dirty, and long years would pass before the soil beneath the ashes healed. That the city might have been saved was the most dreadful realization of all. The orbital lasers had been too busy defending New York, and Houston, and Chicago, and Silicon Valley—and Washington, of course, but there had been too many aimed at Washington, and a few had gotten through—and Phoenix, well, Phoenix just hadn't been high enough on the protection list.

The eight-year-old Hoshi had been out of the city at the time, in the mountains with Uncle Jim and Aunt Edna. But looking in that direction, at that moment, he'd seen the first fireball and felt the others, and it was the last thing he saw for years, until the platinum and doped silicon were implanted in his brain. His parents, of course, had died quickly, instantly. He must always believe that, better to trust instantly, not knowing *how* they'd died. Painlessly. So he was told, and so he believes.

He's over that horror now, has been over it for years. But the time has come to pay his respects, to discharge his debts. To return a life that was given to him here. He scarcely remembers how to pray for guidance, but he is certain that the Lord, if the Lord is here and listening, will approve.

Strangely enough, he scarcely needs to think of Mozy now, that's all settled. He loved her, still loves her, will always love her. *Mozy, do you care for me? That's all I need to know.* He's brought a note-recorder along in his pack, and perhaps tomorrow he will record his last thoughts before setting out—though it is doubtful that anyone will ever find them to read, or will care.

Phoenix is a dark maw out there, and his eyes are growing fatigued; even in the moonlight it is a murky blur. But he can see it well enough in the illumination of his mind, and in the light of day, tomorrow, his eyes will see it clearly, one more time. And peace, at last, will be his.

Chapter 53

The shuttlecraft floated slowly away from the station docking port, its attitude and maneuvering jets spitting flame as it turned. A patrol craft passed across its bow, marker lights winking. The shuttle pitched slightly, came to the correct yaw, and hung for an instant. The main thrusters fired.

The lieutenant scanned the instruments, adjusted the channel selector, and spoke into his microphone. "Traffic control, this is *USSF-274*, outbound to Tachylab at course one-niner-niner."

The burn cut off, acceleration melted away, and weightlessness returned. He glanced at the officer seated to his right. "We should reach Tachylab limits in about thirty minutes, Major. You said there would be a late change in flight plan. Shall I go ahead and dock at Tachylab?"

The major scowled as he fished a document out of his flightsuit breast pocket. "This is your revised flight clearance. Enter the outer approach and radio the change to Tachylab Control—code yellow. We'll rendezvous with two other shuttle vehicles at this location." He tapped a set of figures on the paper. "From there we'll proceed to the assigned destinations."

The lieutenant examined the orders curiously. "The homestead sites? That's private sector."

The major nodded and glanced over his shoulder at the two MPs seated to the rear. "That's right," he said, pulling a notebook from his pocket. "We have some pigeons to snare."

The lieutenant knew better than to ask for elaboration.

He got it anyway, a minute later. "Traitors," remarked the major, flipping through his notebook. He scratched at his chin. "We're going to pull us in some traitors. Quietlike. Before they can run." He glanced at the lieutenant. "You just mind your driving, and put us at the rendezvous point on time." After that, he had no more to say until Tachylab was in sight, a twinkling dot in the distance.

The major watched silently while the lieutenant notified Tachylab Control and executed the course change. "As soon as you track the other shuttles, raise them on the narrow beam."

"I have one already," said the lieutenant. He tapped a phosphor-green dot on the screen and snapped several switches on the console. "Trying to raise them now, Major."

Contact was established with both shuttles, and then the lieutenant was far too busy achieving three-way rendezvous to worry about the major's business. The maneuvering rockets hissed and banged, the other two pilots' voices droned laconically in his ear, and first one and then the second shuttle floated alongside. Over the lieutenant's head, just behind one of the shuttles, the Earth glowed rusty and blue and misty white, the crooked line of the California coast just visible beneath the clouds.

The shuttles thumped together, and the major disappeared through the docking hatch into the adjacent craft. A few minutes later, he returned and gave the lieutenant a new set of coordinates. "Put us on course for the science settlement, Lieutenant. That's where our pigeons are roosting."

"Yes, sir." The lieutenant began punching numbers.

Soon the homestead settlement came into view, a cluster of spherical and cylindrical bubbles joined by spindly tubes. It was "low-rental" housing, built fifteen years ago to accommodate small teams of scientific personnel whose work demanded their presence at the station in spite of limited and erratic funding. Later, when budget restrictions were eased, the ramshackle housing, rather than being replaced, was expanded for scientists and private entrepreneurs who were willing to make do with less for the privilege of pursuing their interests in geostationary orbit. The settlement had grown with its own version of urban sprawl, until it now was a spider's web of tubes and pods.

The lieutenant guided the shuttle toward the leading end of the cluster, skirting the paths of a small tug and several men in motorized worksuits. The address the major had given him proved less than easy to find in the controlled chaos of the cluster; but once they'd established the location of the correct docking port, the lieutenant quickly guided the shuttle into place.

He felt the heavy click of the latches. "Docked, Major." He turned to his left and checked the docking-environment panel. "Pressurizing . . . clear to egress."

"Thank you, Lieutenant. Please remain here." The major turned as he floated out of his seat and swam toward the rear of the shuttle, followed by the two MPs.

The lieutenant secured the hatch to the safety position and settled in to wait.

"Major, I want some answers. Whatever's going on here—" The wiry, bespectacled man paused, puffing with frustration. For the last fifteen minutes, he had been pacing—throwing himself back and forth, really—in the netted-off detention cubicle, and he'd only gotten short of breath for his trouble. Volatile temper. According to the report, he'd protested loudly during the transit from Tachylab to GEO-Four—until the arresting officer had threatened to have him put in irons. From then until a few minutes ago, he had been sullen and silent.

The security officer—a corporal, not a major—eyed the man warily. "Dr. Irwin, you're under arrest for conspiracy to violate military security. The orders came from Space Forces Command HQ. As you've been told before." The soldier added, in a not-unkindly tone, "I wish you'd calm down and stay in one place, Professor. You're driving me crazy bouncing around like that."

Irwin drifted to the netting and hooked his fingers through it, like a monkey hanging from its cage door. "I did nothing," he said, glaring at the officer. "But if you think I'm going to tell you anything without a lawyer present, you're crazy."

"No one's asking you to," the corporal said. He drifted back to his desk—little more than a velcro board and a laminated writing surface—and removed the placemark clip from a paperback book. He'd barely found his place when Irwin called to him again.

"When am I being assigned a lawyer?"

The corporal looked up, shrugged. "Someone will let you know, I'm sure."

Irwin scowled angrily. "Am I the only one you're holding?"

Once more the corporal shrugged.

"I heard someone talking about 'the others.' I know I'm not the only one."

Annoyed, the corporal clipped his place in the book again. "So what, Professor? We're not going to let you talk to each other, so you can just put that out of your mind."

"You did arrest other people, then."

"Yeah. We've got a few of your friends here, as a matter of fact." The corporal was losing his patience.

"I want to talk to them. I must talk to them."

The corporal sighed. "Now, what did I just say?"

"You don't understand. We haven't done anything wrong. You have to let us see each other," Irwin insisted urgently.

"Listen, Dr. Irwin." The corporal scratched his chin, then shook his head. "*I* don't know what you and your friends did, but it sure must have been a lulu. They're assigning a military prosecutor to your case, and none of you are even in uniform. Whatever it was, you and your friends are in some trouble. Now, what did you want to know, Professor?"

Irwin didn't answer. He stared past the corporal, focusing on something on the far wall—focusing on nothing at all.

The colonel sealed the arrest papers back into their plastic pouch and slid them into his desk. "We didn't *want* to believe that there was a conspiracy, either, Mr. Louismore. It was the evidence that forced us to that conclusion."

Sam Louismore rubbed his ample cheeks and tucked his copy of the papers into his own brief pouch. "The evidence, as you say, hardly seems all that persuasive to me," he answered. "A lot of circumstantial details, one audio recording of dubious legality, and a good deal of jumping to conclusions. You're going to have to do better than that to prove a conspiracy." Louismore smoothed the front of his shirt as he swung slowly from a handhold beside the colonel.

"If you're referring to our surveillance of Irwin's apartment, we had federal clearance for that activity," said the colonel.

Louismore allowed his facial expression to mirror his disdain. "Did you have a court order—from a *civilian* court?"

"Not necessary. It's a military security matter. I'm sure you know the Security Act of Twenty-six as well as I do."

"Better," said Louismore. "We'll contest that, of course."

The colonel looked at him in irritation. "I suppose you think we're grandstanding, trying to draw the press off our backs?"

"The thought had occurred to me," Louismore said dryly. "The reporters *have* been asking some embarrassing questions lately, haven't they?" The colonel glared at him, and he chuckled. Louismore had in fact become aware of this case only a few hours ago, though he was well aware of issues raised in the press recently, relating to alleged military activities in deep space. As one of seven practicing attorneys on GEO-Four, it had been the luck of the draw that he had been tapped as public defender; but it looked to be an interesting case.

The colonel grunted and hooked his dispensacup to the coffee spigot for a refill. "If anything, our missions could be hurt by the publicity of a trial. But dammit, when you smell a rat, you have to go after it."

No doubt, thought Louismore. But maybe there's more than one rat around, eh?

"We plan to ask for a groundside hearing," the colonel said casually, placing his cup carefully back in its holder.

"Reason?"

"We think it can be heard more impartially in a less closed setting, less room for gossip and hysteria. By the time it could come to trial here, everyone on the station will have heard of it. It will be hard to get an objective hearing under those circumstances."

"What ever happened to a trial by a jury of one's peers?" remarked Louismore. "We'll oppose that motion."

"Figured you would. Well, see you at the preliminary tomorrow."

Louismore nodded as he turned to leave. He swung his massive frame into the passageway and pushed himself slowly toward the detention center. His bantering with the colonel notwithstanding, this was likely to be a tough case, and the sooner he talked to his clients, the better.

Traffic, even Space Forces traffic, was still being rerouted around the Deep Space Readiness Area, but that inconvenience would be ended shortly. Final checkout was concluded, the two-man crew had radioed their readiness, and only a few special technicians from the Ordnance Group remained in the area, gathering their equipment.

Traffic Control at GEO-Four reported all lanes cleared for departure of *Aquarius*. In the vast, stark silence of near-Earth space, the soft-edged crescent of the Earth on one side, the distant metal sculpture of the GEO-Four space city on another, and the nearby hangar and construction sheds on yet another, the maneuvering jets of *Aquarius* fired briefly, nudging the ship toward a slightly higher orbit. When a precalculated distance separated the ship from its hangar, the large booster engines ignited, propelling the United States Space Forces vessel *Aquarius* out of geosynchronous orbit.

The booster pods burned for three and one half minutes, then separated from the ship. Less than an hour later, with the hangar and GEO-Four and all other structures well behind it in the blackness, *Aquarius* lit its fusion engines and began its long climb out of Earth orbit, bound for the dark emptiness of interplanetary space.

Chapter 54

One thing Hathorne had learned in years of dealing with the political process was that what mattered most on a given issue was not so much the logic of one's position as one's connections, and whether one had the ability and shrewdness to apply leverage at the correct point and the correct time. Twenty-three years ago, to a bright young college graduate, the shocking realization that logic and moral conviction alone were insufficient had nearly been cause for abandonment of a promising career. Hathorne had adapted, however, learning to walk the tightrope of power, treading a fine line between reason and will, and benevolence and enlightened self-interest. It was a walk he had learned well.

Just now, however, he was teetering on the tightrope, and the crosswind that was threatening his balance was General Angus Armstead, commander of Space Forces fleet operations at GEO-Four. With the shift in mission priority from *Father Sky* to *Aquarius*, Armstead had gained considerable leverage with the Oversight Committee—and, Hathorne worried, with the President.

"He's in the power position," Hathorne said to Charles Horst, the director of NASA's GEO-Four space laboratories and a Committee member. "I just wish I hadn't *promised* that *Father Sky* would pull through." He shook his head, smacking a fist into his open palm.

Horst's hologram shifted, blurring slightly. "You didn't promise," he said. "We made the decision on the best available information. It was a gamble worth taking. It just didn't work out."

"Scientifically, it was worth taking," Hathorne said. "Politically, I'm not so sure anymore. It made us look weak."

"You mean *us*, Earth?"

"I mean *us*, supporters of *Father Sky*. We've given Armstead entirely too much room for gloating." And the prick is doing plenty of it, he added silently. Where does he get off, telling me not to be concerned what weapons *Aquarius* is carrying? Does he think those things are fucking children's toys? *His* toys?

"He does act as though he has the Committee in his pocket," said Horst. "Do you think he has a special line with the President?"

"I intend to find out. Also, whether he might be doing some things even the President isn't aware of."

"Well, I haven't seen him overstep his bounds in any clearcut way—even if he is strutting like a bantam rooster. But I'll tell you one thing—if there turns out to be anything fishy in those Tachylab arrests—"

"Is there any substance to the charges?" Hathorne asked. "If there have been leaks, I want to know about it."

"Well, John Irwin's always been a bit of a radical, but that's not against the law. All I know for sure is that the warrant was issued under the Twenty-six Security Act."

Hathorne rubbed his jaw, scowling. It didn't take that much to obtain a warrant in the space settlement, under the latest security laws. The fact that people had been arrested could be nothing more than a diversion. On the other hand, if those scientists knew something that was upsetting to General Armstead, he wanted to know what it was. "We need more information, Charlie."

"I'm trying to find out what I can," the director answered. "But it's not really my turf."

"I can send someone up."

"As an official Committee inquiry?"

Hathorne thought a moment. "No, I think I'd rather keep it separate from the Committee. I have friends in some of the agencies who might be willing to help me out." He drummed his fingers thoughtfully. An independent inquiry into the alleged conspiracy would make a good cover for the investigation he really wanted. Hathorne had several questions concerning the *Aquarius* mission, questions to which he was sure Armstead would not give straight answers. What he needed was a man of his own on the scene, but someone not obviously connected to him.

"Leonard?" said Horst.

"What?"

"I said, have you seen the tracking report?"

"Yah." That was the other thing worrying him. The latest tracking showed the Talenki asteroid accelerating unexpectedly—though as usual, there was no information on why, or how—but it was already much closer to Pluto's orbit than predicted, and if the rate of change of its velocity followed the present curve, it could be here in a matter of *months*, rather than the better part of a year that they'd been told before.

Even in the fuzzy holographic projection, Hathorne could see the worry in Horst's eyes. "Leonard, suppose Armstead is right, and we're being naive. *Should* we assume the worst until we know the best?"

"I don't know, Charlie. Jesus. Don't we all wish we did?" A light blinked on Hathorne's console. "Can I put you on hold for a sec?" Hathorne snapped several switches. Horst remained visible, but the transmitter at Hathorne's end now sent him only a frozen frame of Hathorne's image. "Hello, Lew."

A second hologram appeared, across the table from the first. It was Lewis Smythe, the representative from the British Defense Ministry, the third Committee member to call today. He appeared perturbed. "Leonard, I'll get right to the point. What's this I hear about several of your people at Tachylab being arrested? Claiming that they have information that your ship is armed with contraband weapons? Good God, man!"

Hathorne cleared his throat, thinking, nice to know you have better sources than I do. "I'm glad you called," he said. "We'll be covering this at the meeting, of course, but right now, we're just looking into it."

"Well, what about it? Is that ship armed or isn't it? Since it's one of Armstead's, I assume it is—but with what? I thought this mission was supposed to be under the Committee's control—or has your government decided to strike out on its own?"

Hathorne pressed his lips together, and finally said, "It's under the Committee, Lew—unless I hear differently from the President. But I can tell you there have been no orders from here to put unusual weapons aboard the ship."

"That's not exactly answering the question," the Englishman pointed out.

"Well, as I say, I'm checking into it now," Hathorne said carefully. "I'll let you know what I find. Was there something else, or should I call you back? I have Charlie Horst on hold, and he's paying the long distance charges."

"Just keep me informed. I wouldn't want to break poor Charlie's bank account."

"Very good, then." The Englishman's image blinked out, and Hathorne took a moment to sigh before reactivating the connection to Horst. "Charlie." Horst turned back to the phone. "Look—on that investigator—I'll let you know when he's coming. See what you can do to help him, but keep it low-key, okay?"

"Sure. Whatever I can do."

"Just your best. As always."

The interorbit transfer shuttle fired its maneuvering jets four times in fast succession, banging Donny Alvarest first one way in his seat and then another. This wasn't the carefree ride that the brochures depicted. He'd been fighting freefall sickness most of the way out from LEO Station, and had only in the last few hours gotten his stomach under control. The latest zero-gee medication worked wonders on ninety-five percent of the population, he was told; it was his luck to be in the five percent who reacted to the drug with dizziness and nausea. One of the old standbys had cured him eventually, but only after hours of misery.

All he could see now was blackness and a sprinkling of stars. Earlier he had glimpsed the moon, bright and clear; and from the other side of the cabin, the glowing limb of Earth. Now he was looking for his destination, GEO-Four. He heard an *ahh*ing sound from the other side of the cabin, but hardly had a chance to crane his neck before another thump went through the ship and it began turning. A huge structure glided into view—a Tinker Toy-like collage of connected cylinders and spheres. His eyes began to make sense of the chaos, as he recognized two counter-rotating cylinders—undoubtedly living areas furnished with artificial gravity. A pair of larger spin structures was under construction, at right angles to the first. Alvarest's view disappeared, as the shuttle continued rotating.

He closed his eyes and tried to relax; but his mind would not stop running. When word had come down of a snooper assignment at GEO-Four, his first instinct had been to duck. But he had also thought of the story he knew Joe Payne was working on (partly or maybe mostly because of his tip—and did these arrests have anything to do with Payne's sources? he wondered), and it had seemed like a good idea to check the situation out himself. He felt at least somewhat responsible for the direction of Payne's story; he had, after all, searched Payne out at that rock concert, specifically to give him the tip—though neither Payne nor anyone else needed to know that. On the other hand, if he were just looking for a change of pace, Caracas or Mexico City might have been nicer. Anyway, he'd volunteered.

Of course, Joe would have a conniption if he had even an inkling of some of the things his old buddy did for Uncle Sawbuck. Nothing big league—he'd never been a spy, and he'd never carried a gun (well, once, on a ticklish arms trafficking thing, but he'd never used it)—but not every operation that his department was in was lilly white. The dirty tricks in the Pan-American Alliance elections, for instance, was not something he was extremely proud of.

There was, in fact, a good deal in his work that he wasn't totally proud of. But this assignment looked different; it was an intriguing situation, and he might be able to scope out the territory he'd involved Joe in, plus doing his job. His orders were simple: investigate the charges against the Tachylab conspirators, including any counter-charges *they* might make, and file his reports with a control back at the Cube. He'd be working under cover, as a PR flack from the Defense Information Bureau. The assignment was described as being at the request of a senior presidential aide, and findings were *not* to be shared with military officials at GEO-Four. Interesting. A bit of interdivision squabbling, it seemed; but he would find out, soon enough.

Meanwhile, docking at the station seemed to be taking forever; but at last the final jolts died away, and the announcement was given to disembark. Alvarest was no more awkward in zero-gee than most of the other passengers; but when they emerged into the customs area, an assault zone of lights and noises and pungently stale smells, the difference between the veterans and the newcomers was clear. Alvarest clung to a stanchion as people bobbed past him, and he talked to inspectors who seemed to enjoy hanging upside down relative to him; and though he bore it without complaint, by the time he was through the gauntlet, his head was spinning.

Once clear of customs, he looked around hopefully. He hadn't the vaguest idea where to go now that he was here. A young enlisted man in the uniform of the U.S. Space Forces appeared, asked him if he was Donald Alvarest, and said, "Spaceman Akins, sir. Please follow me." Without waiting for a reply, Akins launched himself down a long passageway.

"Hold it a minute!" Alvarest yelled, struggling to keep up, a duffel bag swinging wildly from his shoulder. "Jesus!"

The spaceman paused, waiting. "General said to bring you on the double, Mr. Alvarest."

"General who?"

"Armstead, sir."

The commanding officer of the fleet. He hadn't exactly arrived unnoticed, then. "All right," Alvarest puffed, grabbing for a bulkhead. "But let's get me there alive, okay?"

Akins looked at him critically for a moment, and then smiled, a bit sheepishly. "Sorry, sir. Sometimes it's just—well—too much of a temptation."

"Eh?"

"You know, to run a greenhorn a bit ragged." Akins shrugged good-naturedly.

Alvarest smiled sourly. "Let's resist the temptation this once, all right? And if you want to play tour guide along the way, I wouldn't mind that, either. I'm going to have to learn my way around here, sooner or later."

"Right, sir," said Akins, brightening. "For starters, just push off in long, slow glides down these tubes. Use the handrailings for guidance. You'll get the hang of it. Here, let me carry your bag for you." He demonstrated, swinging through an open pressure door and diving smoothly down the next passageway, bag under his arm. Alvarest followed, less smoothly. The next time was better.

"When do we get to some gravity?" he asked.

"Afraid we won't be going through spin structure on this trip," Akins answered.

"What about my quarters?"

Akins shrugged. "Depends on whether housing division takes pity. Spin-space is pretty limited. Only about half the main structure is outfitted right now, and they're pretty stingy with it. Most of us have to make do with it just for our exercise period. Since you're a grounder, though, the general might be able to get you a billet there—depending on how long you're planning to stay."

Alvarest waved him on. The corridors seemed to go forever. In one long, busy passageway they hooked onto a moving cable and rode. From time to time, Alvarest glimpsed through a window the working and living space within the adjoining structures. Akins kept up a running commentary as they passed industrial research and manufacturing areas, pharmaceuticals and crystals-growing labs, living and recreational quarters for the construction crews, general residence areas, stores and lounges, and science and hydroponics areas. Alvarest was already lost, when Akins remarked with a gesture that the life-systems center, traffic control, communications, sunsat operations, and government offices were behind them, at the opposite end of the habitat.

They arrived at a security checkpoint and entered the military sector. General Armstead's office turned out to be surprisingly small. Alvarest, accustomed to the Big Cube, realized that some readjustment was in order. The general turned from a worktable and drifted forward to meet him. He was a stocky man, with closecut hair and dark eyebrows. "Find yourself a place to hang," he said. "Like some coffee?" He dismissed Akins with a nod. The young spaceman saluted and disappeared.

Alvarest caught a handhold on the edge of the worktable. "Yes, thank you," he said automatically. "That is—no, I'd better not. Haven't quite got used to zero-gee yet," he admitted.

The general nodded. "It's vile stuff, anyway. Grown locally—but it's not quite up to Colombian growing conditions." He stared at Alvarest. "So. I suppose you're wondering why I had you dragged over here right off the shuttle, before you even had a chance to get settled."

"Yes, sir."

"I'll explain about that in a minute. First I want to know what you already know about the situation here."

"Only what was in the official report. Five people were arrested, for conspiracy to sell secrets. My instructions are to get a clear picture of things so that the public affairs office can put out a story consistent with the facts." Alvarest shrugged.

"I trust you always endeavor to put out stories consistent with the facts," growled the general. "The point I want to impress upon you is that this is a particularly sensitive situation." He drifted back, bracing himself in position with one foot against an I-beam, and gazed appraisingly at Alvarest. "I'll tell you right off that I would rather not have involved the public relations office at all. But—"

"Yes, sir?"

General Armstead sighed disgustedly. "I assume that you're familiar with certain newscasts that have been broadcast—referring to a space mission that originated here? The implication that there's some kind of *illegal*—" he exaggerated the emphasis—"activity going on up here? You know the stories I'm referring to?"

Alvarest cleared his throat. "Yes, sir," he said, showing no expression.

"Well, I want you to make sure that the public knows what a load of bull that is. Let them know that the only *illegal* thing is a bunch of

holier-than-thou technocrats who consider themselves above the law."
The general eyed him. "Do you think you can do that?"

"I'm certainly ready to report the facts," Alvarest answered calmly.

Armstead's eyes darkened. "I trust you are. I'll tell you also that·I
would have chosen a man in uniform for this job, if the choice had
been mine. A civilian doesn't always understand the seriousness of a
commitment to military security—and the loyalty that's implicit with
that commitment." He leaned toward Alvarest. "But the choice wasn't
mine—so I'm looking to you to do the same kind of job that a man in
uniform would do. Can I trust you to do that?"

"I hope so, General," Alvarest said, thinking, who the hell told
this guy I'm working for *him*? "I'd like to get started as soon as
possible. But I'm afraid I don't exactly know my way around here
yet."

"One of my staff assistants will fill you in. Lieutenant Ogilvy.
Why don't you go get squared away, have lunch, and come back in
an hour."

"Very good, sir. Is Mr. Akins—?" Alvarest peered toward the
door.

"I'll ask him to show you around the station," said the general.

"Thank you. And General—will I have the opportunity to speak
with the defendants?" The general raised his eyebrows, and Alvarest
took a breath, hiding his irritation. "To hear their side—for the record,"
he explained.

Armstead shrugged. "If you feel that that's necessary." He growled
into his intercom, and five seconds later, Akins reappeared.

As they headed toward the housing section, Akins grinned and
said, "Well, what do you think of Old Angle-iron? Did he pull some
strings for you on the housing?"

Alvarest stared at Akins ruefully. He had forgotten to ask. And he
had a feeling that if he had, his standing with the general would have
dropped ten points in an instant. "Never mind," he said. "Let's just
find me a room. Any room."

Akins chuckled and glided off the way they had come.

Chapter 55

A low wail haunted Mozy's sleep as, dreaming, she passed into strange lands and curious memories, images of a lost primordial forest. A part of her remained in the dream; a part of her awakened, stretched, listened for Talenki voices—and heard only the wail.

She was alone—with a sound that reverberated like a bass undertone, a whispery voice that passed through the Talenki world. A sentient wind. A cry filling the silence with longing, and perhaps fear. It reminded her of another sound, from Earth, known to her in books and tales and films: the cry of a train in the night, an ancient steam locomotive's whistle echoing mournfully across a plain, dying away into nighttime stillness. This sound was different; but the feeling, melancholy and desolate, was the same, only deeper still. It was, she thought, the voice of a lonely and faraway *something*, calling out across parsecs and eons, to an unseen listener.

And where were the Talenki? There was not a murmur of their voices, even in the dimmest corner of the mind. She thought to call out, but something turned her aside, something hypnotic, something setting aside the questions in her mind, as though greater questions were being asked by the wind, a cosmic wind. Questions such as, where am I going, and why must I be alone, seemed to flutter through the wind, but in fragments which held no coherence for her.

After a time, loneliness and anxiety broke through the spell, and left her fully awake, wondering. What had happened while she slept? Had some transformation carried her out of the world she was coming to know? She imagined herself lost in an empty Talenki world, an abandoned asteroid tumbling toward the sun, its creators departed on the winds of space. She remembered, now, before sleeping, a long conversation and sharing of memories with the Talenki—her memories, visions and sensations of planet Earth, voices and feelings of Humanity. So many questions the Talenki had asked, as she'd told them of her people, her life that was.

Could she have given them all they needed—and so they had left her here, adrift in the wind, to face the forces of eternity alone?

Absurd. If the Talenki had left, the mind-net would be gone; and if the mind-net were gone, she would be dead.

So where was everyone?

(Hello?) she said tentatively

No one appeared; no one spoke.

(Hello?) she said again.

Stirring, this time, and silence. The moan continued unabated. Finally a voice whispered, (We are listening.)

She waited. (Listening to what?) she whispered, feeling as though she were raising her voice in church.

Another, smaller voice. N'rrril? No—someone older. (Can you not hear?)

They were speaking one at a time, not interrupting. What was going on? (Of course I hear!) she hissed. (What is it?)

The answer did not come in words. There was, from somewhere, the familiar swirling of thoughts, opening of gates. Knowledge coalesced in her mind, quietly and solemnly, but in the passage of a breath. And then she understood, a little.

It was the universe itself that was crying, in what was surely the ultimate wail of existential despair. It was the background radiation that filled all of the galaxies and all of the space in between; it was the three-degree Kelvin microwave echoes of the primordial explosion; and more, it was a song, a softly modulated ballad, a remembrance of the formation of the universe, and of matter and energy and life.

It was not, she realized, the first time she had heard the sound. In a science class at the university, she had heard a recording—just a hiss, recorded from one of the great radio telescopes—but what she heard now was about as much like that as a symphony was like a child's music box. The Talenki heard the moan not as a radio wave converted by electronic wizardry, but as a vibration underlying their thought, indeed their very existence. There was no place in the universe that did not reverberate with the moan, not a patch nor a fiber in the fabric of space that was not imprinted with the memory of its own birth; and the Talenki touched these threads of memory directly with their own thought and soul. Whether it was a conscious sense or an unconscious sense, to Mozy all of the levels of consciousness bubbled together, one individual's merging into another's; and what touched the deepest chord in her was the sadness, the pensiveness which filled the net. Were these the people to whom everything was a joke or a song? Running like a river through the Talenki mind-body was an awareness of pain, of the insignificance of sentient life against the awesomeness of the birth and death of the Universe. She wept with the Talenki, their sadness filling her like a tide.

And yet, there was something more to it than sadness. A hope . . . an ambition . . . a destiny. A mission. She caught only a glimmer of something she could not identify or understand, and then it was gone again, and solemnity filled her heart.

(Is this why you laugh so much?) she whispered.

The question caused confusion, and she sensed certain of the Talenki turning away, not wanting to face her question; and she sensed others murmuring, gathering images out of memory.

The impressions came quickly, but she was able to float with them, she had learned how to touch and sample, to absorb what she could and let the rest go. She beheld a memory of the Talenki asteroid, centuries ago, departing from the Talenki homeworld—scarcely a vessel, mostly solid or roughly tunneled rock, with barely space for its inhabitants and no more—departing the homeworld and setting course for the stars. The images were scattered and confused: years' worth of planning—far too little, but it was an undertaking to be marvelled at—an asteroid that was a half-exhausted mine, burrowed out with warrens and tunnels, and hollowed in the center through means she could not comprehend, space for a sea and a home for the deep nodes; and perhaps two hundred fauns assembled, and half that number of warts in their care. And many more Talenki left behind.

A shock of pain swept through her with that last memory, and only then did she recognize the memory underlying all others: the Talenki were exiles from their own home.

They had fled a world that hated and despised them—taunted, persecuted, hounded them away. A world that could not comprehend their arts or their mission, a world grown decadent and warlike and inwardly obsessed, a world deceived by its own prosperity. Their fleeing was an escape rather than a celebrated departure, and only a fraction of those who had labored and sacrificed actually made it off-planet to the asteroid, pursued by those who would destroy them; and so, confronted by the choice of leaving their companions behind or remaining to face persecution and death all together and with it to witness the end of their dream, they had turned their sights upon the stars and fled, carrying with them the hopes and thoughts and memories of their doomed friends. And carrying with them a vow. A mission. A design.

But many worlds must be visited first, before the design could take shape.

The images flickered away, leaving Mozy breathless. (You carry with you a great deal of pain,) she whispered.

N'rrril appeared silently beside her, as others answered. (How could—) (—we not—) (—though it was—) (—centuries ago—) (—to us legend—) (—memory—) (—song—)

(None of you were alive, then, when you left the homeworld?)

(Those who lived—) (—live only in memory—)

Her vision shimmered, and she was looking out of N'rrril's eyes across a chamber, a congregation of fauns. (Not only you and I look out with these eyes.)

(Who, then—?)

New voices answered. (I—) (—and I—) (—and I—) (—and I—)

(And who are you?) she asked, though she thought she knew.

Gentle laughter. N'rrril said, (Upon death, our bodies rejoin the fertile grounds from which newer bodies are born and nourished. But the spirits, the memories, what you would call the personalities—)

(—live on in the net,) she said, completing the thought. A door opened in her mind; and she heard a cacophony of voices, voices from far corners of the net, from minds practically within her own, voices echoing across oceans, and from chambers deep in the heart of the asteroid.

She closed the door. (Your ancestors,) she said calmly. A song reverberated somewhere in the back of her mind, and she sensed that it was an old song, much beloved by the living-in-mind ancestors.

(Each—) (—a part—) (—of the others—) (—of the whole—)

(But . . .) and she paused, thinking. (If each remains alive in the mind-net after death, won't there eventually be too many? Won't there be chaos, confusion, suffocation?)

A solitary voice tinged with sadness answered. (Precisely true. It is one reason for the homeworld's decay. We have vowed never to allow it to happen here. We must not.) Mozy projected polite confusion. (Our ancestors remain with us for a time, but eventually they must surrender themselves to the greater consciousness.)

(Then they die after all,) Mozy said softly.

Another voice spoke. (It is all a step toward the design, toward the greater . . .) The Talenki paused, unable to find a suitable word. (It is sad, as you are feeling, yes. But it is not *bad*. That which is . . .) another pause, and finally an inexact phrase, (. . . *strongest in spirit* of the individual, remains even after the individual is gone.)

Mozy thought of her own people of Earth, of their fleeting lives—and wondered if they would envy the Talenki their form of immortality.

(The mind,) N'rrril added quietly, (will contain a part of each of us—and now, you, too—for as long as the mind itself lives.)

The greater part of the Talenki world was awake now, as the fauns concluded their meditations. Mozy wanted to know more.

A song which had been a subterranean foundation to her dreams emerged into her waking, conveying a story in words and images. There was much that she could not understand, but much else that flowed by like clear, luminous water. The flight of the Talenki from the homeworld, celebrated in song and legend; memories of a world lost, and longings for worlds to be found. Grief for those left behind, though certain connections remained, thoughts and minds linked. Fear of isolation and loneliness; and yet, overlaid, a sense of peace, and joy of accomplishment. It was a flight with no destination except a need to explore, to enlarge their thought and song, and to touch other peoples.

Little experienced in the ways of space, they learned with much trial and error how to move their asteroid across the interstellar sea, to take them to new worlds. They knew, of course, that none who began the journey would be alive in the flesh by the time that first new world had been reached; but even so, it was harder than they had imagined, struggling at first against the elements of space, turning their skills to the needs of survival and homebuilding. The early years, indeed the early generations, had been devoted to settling in, to getting the asteroid well out of the home solar system, and setting a course for the nearest star. Expanding and refabricating had come later, redistributing the asteroid's mass to increase the living space. Eventually, time came to think again of purpose and song, of music and art. Time to create tapestries, to carve stone in intricate patterns, to learn new ways of manipulating time and matter and energy, ways of linking worlds with thought. Creating and expanding the design.

And always they kept moving through the night of space, through generations of Talenki living and dying, always seeking the next world.

The song wound about the edges of Mozy's consciousness, the lesser part of her listening now, the greater part dreaming. The years wore long in the song, and the song wore long in Mozy's heart, and the transition from listening awake to listening asleep was a gentle one.

She dreamed of dizzies calling into the night, calling for anyone who could hear, or answer. Lesser-Mozy awoke first, while Greater-Mozy dozed in the dream, to find that the dizzies, the deep nodes, were indeed calling even now to life forms in the solar system. Calling to Earth.

(We are preparing our greeting,) confided someone.

(Oh?)

(Would you like to help?) (To compose—) (—a message to your—) (—people—) (—to help us—) (—get it right?)

Greater-Mozy started awake to thoughts of Homebase—Jonders, Hathorne, and the others—and their propensity for misunderstandings. She began laughing, and her amusement spread through the mind like wildfire.

(Does this mean—) (—yes?)

She laughed again, thinking of some things she'd like to say to Homebase, things she might just say between the lines. (Yes,) she said. (Yes, indeed, I would.)

Chapter 56

The city of Phoenix is filled with ghosts. He has not yet been able to understand what any of them are saying, though he hears their voices as he moves among them.

In the infrared afterglow, the ruins dance around him like spirits, luminous among the shadows—shadows in the visible spectrum that have swallowed the world. Shattered walls, rubble, half-standing concrete skeletons of buildings, here and there the desiccated corpse of an animal that has wandered in and fallen, weakened by radiation. Ghosts, lurking. These are his companions as he walks the suburban streets, flanked by the ruins.

He is well beyond the point, now, where every step is a terrible effort and an agony. His body is numb with exhaustion, weak with hunger and thirst, feverish. He can't go much farther, but while he still can move, he will. Reach the crater, he vows, at least the edge of the crater, where the fireball fused and vaporized soil and concrete, lifted earth into the sky, blasted the land into ruin. Bring life back. Human life. If only for a little while.

Tried already to go home, to find the old neighborhood. A half day spent wandering among smashed neighborhood blocks, all unrecognizable from childhood memory. Someone with a map could find it, perhaps, someone with eyes that could focus. Someone who could fly overhead. Perhaps. For him, it was a futile effort. Hard enough to keep bearings straight just to try to reach the center of the city. Dark closing in, now. Thank God for the infrared glow. For the eyes that can see it. See. But not always focus.

Stumbles and, flailing, crashes face-first to the ground. For a moment, he lies still, racked with quiet sobs and dry tears, unable to make arms and legs work together to rise. Pain in the center of his face, taste of blood in his mouth. Fall here in the dust, he thinks. Die here, in the dust. Fail here. *No.* Somewhere he finds the extra bit of strength he needs, and he levers himself up to his knees. A broken building looms overhead, wavering, peering down over his shoulder like a parent, someone else's, scolding every move with its eyes.

Laughs harshly for comfort. Ghosts. Damn place is full of them. But they're lousy company, lousy conversationalists. Damn lousy conversationalists.

Forget it, he mutters to himself. He's up off his knees, making his feet move again, his blistered, crippled feet. Dehydration and exhaustion are what's killing him, he knows—not radiation; the radiation would get him in time, of course, but the desert will get him first. There was some satisfaction when he figured that out once, a while back, but then he forgot it, and figured it out again later. Funny the way the mind plays tricks. Hysterical the third time he figured it out and then forgot it a moment later. He'd do anything for a drink of moisture, except he'd forget halfway through what he was doing, or why.

Dust and dryness and rubble. All ground into his pores, now, this city has become a part of him.

Keep moving. Just keep moving.

Night shimmers and dances around him, marking his time as he hauls himself with infinite patience, infinite weariness, toward his goal. Cannot be much farther, now. Cannot be. He cannot go much farther. Cannot fail. Cannot continue. Cannot give up.

It must be here, somewhere just ahead. Hunched on all fours, now, clawing his way over mounds of rubble. Must be near the edge of the blast zone. Near the crater. No, this *is* the edge, he's there.

The ground tips forward under him, and he falls down a slope, skidding, clawing frantically. His hands are feeble, there is no purchase in the slag, it's tearing his face and hands, smashing his shoulders. Rolling, sputtering, he slides finally to a halt, lying motionless on his side, mouth full of dirt, pain splintering through his body. For a minute, two minutes, he lies still, regaining his strength, determined to roll over, to get up.

Rest, just a minute more. Rest. . . .

Awakens out of a kind of delirium to a glow—like dawn, but not dawn. Someone is talking to him. Someone . . . singing.

Dreams of madness, he has been dreaming of madness, or so he thinks, awakening, but . . . they are with him still, the voices. There is no one here. But there is the glow. A shimmering in the sky, and all around him, the world rippling. Creatures whispering. Something has entered him as he slept, invading his mind and his soul. Voices echo around him and inside of him.

He gasps and pushes himself upright to a sitting position—shivering, chilled to the bone, shaking. Fumbles in the pouch for the survival blanket, thrashes it open, an eternity later gets it over his shoulder, twisted, only half covering him. He is trembling from the cold.

But not only from the chill and fever. He is trembling because of spirits alive in his body and his mind, singing. Singing! It is madness. Or is it the spirits of the dead, clustered around him?

Not human. The words float through his mind without explanation.

Struggle to be lucid. It is dreadfully difficult, his head is spinning with delirium, he must *fight* to maintain clarity of any sort. What is the light around him? Not infrared. Not visible. What, then? The radiation of the blast zone, the gamma rays that are slowly devouring him?

No. *No.* He cannot say why, but he knows it to be something else. From elsewhere. He does not *see* the light so much as *feel* it. The light comes from . . .

He does not know where.

With sudden urgency, he fumbles again in his pack, this time for the note-recorder. He cannot see anything except a blur in his hands, but he can feel the keys of the recorder; he must try to put down what he is feeling. Manipulate the keys by touch. Someone . . . some day . . . might find this, read it; probably no one ever will, but he must try, it is terribly important, one last chance to leave something meaningful.

Though shaking, he has never felt such clarity. In the chill of the predawn, he is filled with an even greater spirit that allows him to *see*, but not with his eyes—a vision expanding outward from where he sits, outward from his own body and into space, upward and away from the earth, his vision illuminated by a wordless song. Worlds circling in the darkness of the night, suns like glowing drops of honey afloat in a dark, clear sea; and nestled on some of those worlds, and snapping and simmering in the fires of the suns, and radiating through the emptiness of the interstellar ocean: the song, a work of a living consciousness. It touches him now, it was what awakened him, the song that fills these desolate ruins with light, that fills the space between the worlds. If this is the hereafter, he can only welcome what is to come.

But he has not died. Not yet. Before him are the cratered ruins of a city that was, and he can smell the dust and the grit, and feel the tortured dryness of his skin and the pain of his splitting lips, and the terrible aching in his legs and his back. His fingers grope at the keypad, trying to record his thoughts, his feelings. All of those sensations are alive, *he* is alive, he can still move—and he must—must always keep moving forward.

Rising to his feet, tottering, delirious with fever, clutching the recorder, he stumbles ahead, down the side of the vast, shallow crater that was once a city.

He is haloed with light. Accompanied by a song. And by voices. *And one of the voices he knows.*

Staggering to a halt, he kneels, trembling with fever and joy. The voice—the voice he recognizes! Mozy? *Mozy, is that you I hear? MOZY? ARE YOU ALIVE?*

There is a whispering in his head that is not a reply to his words or to his question or even to *him*. And yet, it tells him what he wants to know. *He knows that voice. It is real.* His fingers shake uncontrollably as he struggles to record the words.

Someone must know. Someone must read this! Please. Dear God. *Someone.*

Struggles to type, but . . . words . . . cannot make the words. . . .

His fingers are still twitching . . . he is aware only of the voices receding into the distance . . . as he slumps, unseeing, the recorder slipping from his fingers and clattering to the ground.

Chapter 57

Alvarest bolted the door to his quarters and took a deep breath, soaking up the feeling of privacy. He rested for a moment, floating in midair in a room two arm-spans wide and deep, and long enough for a man to flip head to toe. The single hologram of a landscape, in one wall, did little to lend an illusion of size.

Two days of talking and hunting his way around the station had left him exhausted. He was still a little queasy, from lack of rest and from zero-gravity. If only the latter feeling would go away, he'd have a fighting chance of getting some rest. He opened a drawer; a handful of toiletry articles floated out like escaped fireflies. He caught the packet he wanted, pressed out two space-sickness tablets, and swallowed them with water from a dispenser tube before corralling everything back into the drawer. Then he forced his thoughts clear and positioned himself in front of the desk, where his portable computer was clamped into place.

He folded out the jumpseat, buckled himself into place, and inserted a key into the computer. He entered a sequence of security codes, then settled back and closed his eyes.

How was he going to say this? *Tachylab scientists assert that spaceship* Aquarius, *in defiance of international treaty, is bound, armed with nuclear weapons, for a rendezvous with alien beings.*

That wouldn't be bad for a tabloid news service, but it was hardly suitable for an intelligence report. He had to discuss evidence, or the absence of it, and credibility of sources. And one had to ask, didn't the President know already what was being done here—and if not, why not? Was his job here to evaluate leaks—or to investigate a breach of authority on the part of Space Forces command?

In the last two days, his notions about his assignment here had undergone drastic change. He understood why these people had been willing to risk their jobs and their freedom for this information. If the evidence supported their assertions, it would represent a damning breach of international law. Since the Great Mistake, few treaties were considered as sacrosanct as the renewed prohibition against placing nuclear arms in space. The defense attorney, Mr. Louismore, had implied that this fact would be the linchpin of their argument. Louismore had interrogated him at length, regarding his own neutrality, before permitting him to interview the scientists.

Despite the lack of clearcut evidence, Alvarest had found the defendants' case persuasive, their sources credible. He could not help agreeing with them on the public's right to know. Alvarest was no Puritan, heaven knew. But political dirty tricks were one thing; screwing around with the future of the world was another. Dr. John Irwin, the apparent leader of the group, had argued passionately that if people didn't know about the aliens . . . if they didn't know that the most important treaty of the century was being put aside . . . if these decisions were being made in secret at the highest levels of government . . . if the first contact with life from another world resulted in war . . . would the people of Earth even know why?

In addition to questions about his formal role here, Alvarest realized that he faced another dilemma. This was the sort of information that Joe Payne could use to good effect—if only there were a way of getting it to him.

Don't torture yourself. You can't do it. That's not your job.

With a sigh, limbering his fingers, he began typing. He wrote for two hours, then set the computer to coding the report for transmission. While the encryption routine ran, he sipped a container of lukewarm apple juice, rubbed his eyes, and wished he could sleep for a day. Finally he plugged the computer into the phone outlet, placed an Earthside call to an unlisted number, and squirted the report through.

Minutes later, he was comfortable in his tethered sleeping bag, drifting off.

No time at all seemed to have passed when he awoke. He blinked, dazedly realizing where he was. A small cubicle, dimly lighted. Weightless. Drugged with fatigue. Something had awakened him. Time: 0540. Asleep for four and a half hours. Listen. Sounds from outside, voices, hiss of the ventilators. That last was a sucking sound, too loud. He couldn't find its source. Slipping out of the sleeping bag, he turned in midair, peering. Everything shadows and gloom. Something was moving; and then he saw it—a scrap of paper caught against the exhaust grill. He pulled it off in relief and secured it under a clip.

A red light was on by the phone. Message waiting. His first impulse was to leave it and go back to sleep; but he was already mostly awake. Fuck it, he thought. He drifted over and pressed "replay." There was a request from Lieutenant Ogilvy, the general's assistant, that he report in. Great. For this, he was losing sleep? There was a second recording that was more interesting; it was a reply from Earthside Control.

It took some time to decode the transmission. Finally, rubbing the grit out of his eyes, he read the message on his screen:

DEFINFBU DPT-GA CD13158/DONALD ALVAREST/3 JAN 2035/0450 GMT: UNDERSTOOD, ALLEGED CONDITION AND MISSION OF AQUARIUS. HARD EVIDENCE REQUIRED CONCERNING WEAPONS SYSTEMS. THIS INFORMATION PARAMOUNT. DO NOT, REPEAT, DO NOT DISCUSS INVESTIGATION WITH MILITARY AUTHORITIES. SUGGEST CONTACT DIRECTOR HORST OF NASA LABS FOR POSSIBLE ASSISTANCE. REPORT ON PROGRESS SOONEST. MARTINS/CHIEF/DPT-GA/DEFINFBU/END MESSAGE.

He read it three times. Well. That confirmed something. They weren't surprised, apparently. But they weren't sure, either. *How could the President not be sure?* Maybe Alvarest's "client" wasn't really the President; maybe it was someone else. No matter; he didn't need to know. But how the hell was he supposed to get hard evidence without talking to the military? Telephone the *Aquarius* crew, maybe? Spy on the general?

He shook his head. Spying on his own country's military had *not* been included in his job description.

Clearly he would need help. This fellow Horst, perhaps. There weren't many choices. Meanwhile, Ogilvy wanted to see him. Their one previous meeting had been enough to establish that Ogilvy was a rule-worshipping meddler. *Do not discuss investigation with military authorities.* He'd have to come up with a way to finesse the lieutenant.

But damn it, not until he'd had some more sleep and some breakfast. Find one of the cafeterias in spin-section. A man needed some gravity, even if it was only half a gee, to hold down toast and eggs and coffee.

*   *   *

Joseph Payne stared at the phone in dismay. "What are you saying, you can't talk to me at all now?" He opened his hand slowly; a crumpled piece of paper fell to the floor by his desk.

Jonders averted his face, scowling. "That's about the size of it."

"But we agreed—"

Jonders cut him off. "Security has tightened. They've turned into real bastards now, since they discovered those other leaks. I'm sorry, but that's how it is."

"What leaks? Do they know we've talked?"

"I don't think so, but I can't take the risk. I'm at a public phone now, but suppose they have *your* line bugged?"

Payne hesitated. He thought it unlikely that the studio's lines would be tapped; but that probably wasn't the point. "Can we at least—?"

"No. Look, Joseph—I have to get off." Jonders's gaze broke from his. "I'm sorry. Good-bye."

Payne grunted as the connection dissolved. Whoever had gotten to Jonders had done the job well. He should have expected it—after all, Jonders had a career to worry about, and a family—but *what was that about other leaks?* Damn it!

Payne got up and paced the office. He was working out of a small cubicle at the International News Service studios in New Phoenix, where he had taped short probing pieces on the death of Mozy and disappearance of Hoshi. Otherwise, he was at a halt. He was sure there was a connection between this new spacecraft, *Aquarius*, and *Father Sky* and the aliens; but all he had to go on, really, was the wire service reports and intuition. He'd hit a brick wall with other sources, and couldn't reach Ellen Chang at JPL.

The production editors in New Wash were becoming impatient. *What have you done for me today?* was the gist of their messages.

Not much. Denine was back home; Mardi hadn't helped much; and Jonders had just cut him off. Try Ellen Chang again. Try Donny Alvarest—even though you swore you wouldn't. Try *anything*.

He felt guilty as hell as he punched Alvarest's number. Probably land us both in jail, he thought as he pressed the last two digits.

What he got was an audio recording saying that Alvarest was away for several weeks, but please leave a name and a message. Payne snarled in frustration and almost broke the connection, then figured what the hell. "It's Joe," he said, "I wanted—"

The recording interrupted him with Alvarest's face. "Please state your full name," Donny said.

Again Payne almost hung up; again he didn't. "Joseph Payne," he said. "Don't you recognize my face anymore?"

The recorder was not listening to his sarcasm. Alvarest said, "What song did Zekerino used to blast out a dozen times a day until we stole his disk? Don't blow it—you only get one chance."

Zekerino? Payne stared at the frozen image of his friend in astonishment, slowly comprehending. Their old college buddy Zeke—no one merely *claiming* to be Payne would know this—now what the hell *was* that song? "Hell Mary Bombers," he said suddenly. " 'Get It Once, Get It Again.' "

Something clicked, and Alvarest seemed to look him straight in the eye. "Sorry to be a pain in the butt, but I had a feeling you might call, and I didn't want just anyone hearing this. No, I'm not giving you any classified information. But I'm leaving on an assignment, and it's something that might interest you. Maybe you've heard by now of the conspiracy they busted up at Tachylab, the scientists who were arrested—"

Scientists . . . arrested! Payne stared aghast at the phone. *Were they his sources, whose names he didn't even know?* Was that what Jonders meant by "other leaks"? No wonder Ellen Chang wasn't taking calls.

Details! he wanted to scream. Give me details! Names!

Donny was explaining that he would be out of touch for a while, wouldn't be able to call; but if something important came out that wasn't classified, he'd try to find a way to get it to him. Donny paused. "If any of those people are friends of yours, I'm sorry."

So am I, Payne thought. More than you can know. And then the screen was blank, and he was left staring across the room in a frustrated rage.

He set to work immediately. And ran into another stone wall. No information seemed to be available, anywhere, about the arrests. No wonder he hadn't heard about them. The Cube had no comment; NASA had no comment; GEO-Four Labs had no comment; ditto with Tachylab. The wire services had nothing.

At three o'clock, he was halfway down the hall for a much-needed cup of coffee when the phone rang behind him. He hurried back to answer it.

It was Teri, calling from New Washington. "They want you to come home," she said.

His breath exploded, taking his heart with it. "Teri—you know—I need more time," he protested. He wanted to say that somehow he would crack the wall of silence; but he had said it all before.

"Joe, they just don't feel that they can cover the expenses any longer—not until there's a break. I know how you feel. But it really might be best if you just let things lie for a while."

Payne told her about the Tachylab arrests. "If that's not evidence of something happening—"

"I agree," she said at once. "We'll contact a stringer at GEO-Four and see what we can find."

"Maybe I should go myself."

"If we have access to someone already there, it wouldn't make much sense to send you, too."

"Yeah. Right." It was all slipping through his fingers—the whole story. Someone else was going to get it. *Damn it to hell!*

"We can talk it over with the producers."

"Yah."

"When can you make it back?"

He sighed in defeat. "Couple of days. I'll hire an assistant here, to keep things warm. If you'll pay for that much."

"Good."

"I still think it's a mistake."

"I know you do. Joe—?"

"Yeah?"

"I'll look forward to seeing you."

"Yah." As the screen darkened, he slammed his fist down on the desktop, knocking over an empty coffee cup. One of the studio research assistants, standing in the doorway, regarded him inquisitively.

Chapter 58

Jonders studied the printout with a mixture of emotions. The latest Talenki message had been received in English:

> *. . . Toward your world / toward our design / we go*
> *Onward / with wishes / and celebration / to the building of the design.*
> *As worlds pass we grieve / do grieve / in spirit and body grieve / the loss of the Father / her kin / her kith / her kindred / souls*
> *Kadin / Mozy / Mother of All Programs.*
> *Their loss we mourn*
> *Mourn*
> *Pray that all was done / that could be done / no stone unturned to save / those spirits / those friends we mourn*
> *In faith that such pain*
> *Again will not be*
> *Such pain*
> *Never again*
> *Soon.*
> *Soon / we sing*
> *Soon / the design grows*
> *Flowers / to terrible beauty*
> *Soon*
> *Will*
> *You*
> *Receive*
> *Us*
> *As the worlds twist and sing?*

The same phrases and themes were repeated, with variations, for thirteen pages. Notes accompanying the transcript discussed meter and structure in the original transmission, and the spacing and punctuation in the interpreted transcription. He wished they'd included the raw, as well as the processed, version. But he supposed he should be happy to have seen any version at all. Though he was no longer in the mainstream of the project, his opinions were still solicited in a token way. Someone seemed to recognize that he had come closer to direct contact with the Talenki than any living human.

So what to make of this? It was, Jonders thought, a terribly strange message. Different in tone from previous transmissions, it seemed almost human, poetic after a fashion. Their mastery of the language had grown, as though they'd been studying human communications—perhaps by monitoring broadcasts—or perhaps by somehow accessing the *Father Sky* computer.

But what did it *mean*? And why were *they* so distraught over the loss of *Father Sky*? And what the hell was the "design"? Undoubtedly, Marshall and Hathorne—and others, higher still—were pondering the same questions. If his opinion was to mean something, now was the time for some insights.

Jonders swiveled his chair to stare out the window. Shadows were lengthening across the grounds in the orangish afternoon light. He wondered where Joe Payne was; wondered if he'd found a new source; wished he could show him this transcript.

He dropped his gaze to the printout again. *Such pain / never again / soon . . . design will grow / flower / to terrible beauty. . . .* Riddles. But friendly riddles? Could he prove it? Suddenly it occurred to him—what a dolt!—why not take it to Kadin for an opinion? Kadin-Earth, of course, lacked his lost duplicate's experience with the Talenki; but what was he trained for, if not to deal with these sorts of questions?

Pausing in the outer office to let Lusela know where he'd be, Jonders entered the lab and unlocked the simulation control room. It was only a matter of minutes before he was back in the link, sparks swirling. Kadin's familiar presence greeted him. (It's good to see you, Bill. I was beginning to wonder if I'd been forgotten.)

Jonders sighed in relief. (Not forgotten, David. It's been too long, I know. There's a communication from the Talenki that I'd like to ask your opinion about.)

(Shoot.)

(I don't have it in electronic form, so I'll have to do it the hard way.) Blinking, his mind half in and half out of the link, Jonders began reading the transcript. He was a page from the end when the intercom buzzed for his attention. Disregarding the interruption, he finished reading. The buzzing continued. (Excuse me a moment, David.)

It was Lusela. "Bill. Mr. Delarizzo is here."

Air hissed through his teeth. "What's *he* want?" Damn spook from the Oversight Committee; he'd been haunting the place with his security inquiries, and his "recommendations" which were always turning into new rules and procedures.

"He wants to say—"

Lusela was interrupted by Delarizzo's bass voice. "Dr. Jonders, the linkup is presently off limits. I'll have to ask you to disengage."

"What for?" Jonders said in irritation.

"As I said, it's off limits. Disengage and wait for me there." The intercom clicked off.

You son of a bitch, Jonders muttered, to no one. He apologized to Kadin. (Did you catch that? I'll have to get back to you later.)

(I understand.)

Jonders killed the link and waited angrily for Delarizzo to appear. The bastard must have spy monitors planted everywhere. What was it going to be this time? Had someone found out about his talking to Payne?

Delarizzo walked in, an emotionless ramrod. "Doctor, may I ask what you had planned here?" Jonders told him. Delarizzo's eyes flicked like hornets, scanning the room, scanning Jonders's face. "I see," he said finally. "That will have to be approved by the director."

"The director!" Jonders snapped. "I'm supposed to ask for permission every time I want to talk to Kadin?"

"That is the new—"

"Screw the new rules! Who do you think designed Kadin, for Christ's sake?"

Delarizzo repeated himself as though he had not heard the interruption. "That is the new procedure. It has been approved by the director and by the Committee."

Jonders sighed in disgust, realizing that argument was futile. With deliberate movements, he returned Kadin to standby mode and powered down the console. Then he stalked out of the room, gesturing impatiently for Delarizzo to follow so that he could lock up. Returning to his office, he asked Lusela to get Slim on the phone and then slammed the office door closed behind him.

* * *

The intercom buzzed. He pressed the button.

"Bill?" Lusela's voice was strained.

He was calmer now. "Do you have Slim—?"

"Joe Kelly's here to see you."

Joe Kelly? Oh, shit. Had Delarizzo complained about his outburst? "Send him in."

The usually easygoing security chief opened the door, his face grim. Jonders gazed at him questioningly as Kelly stood in the center of his office, staring down at a piece of paper. Kelly looked up and said softly, "I have bad news, Bill. I'm sorry." Jonders waited. This was it, then. "The state police," Kelly said, "found Hoshi Aronson's body—"

"What!"

"—yesterday. Near Old Phoenix. At the edge of the crater."

Jonders felt as though he'd been kicked in the stomach. *"Damn. God damn."*

"Yeah." Kelly rubbed his chin unhappily. "He was spotted on a routine overflight. They sent in a chopper to lift him out."

"How long had he been—?"

"A couple of days, anyway. Looked like he walked all the way in from New Phoenix. He must have gotten a good dose of radiation. We don't know if he took anything yet, drugs or whatever."

"Isn't there a *fence* around that place?" Jonders asked uselessly.

"It's easy enough to get past, if anyone wants to. Here, I almost forgot." Kelly handed Jonders the stat page he was holding. "This is from a note-recorder that was found by his body. His last thoughts, I guess. Maybe you can make something of it." Kelly shrugged. "He was probably delirious, certainly dehydrated, and maybe having a psychotic episode, for all we know. The coroner said there was probably no way to tell for sure."

Jonders stared at the photostat, blinking.

"Anyway, you knew him better than most anyone here. Maybe you can understand what he was trying to say."

Sure, Jonders thought. I knew him. So well I couldn't see him falling apart in front of my nose.

After Kelly left, Jonders sat down to read the note. The text was fragmented and choppy. Had radiation damaged the note-recorder's memory? Or had he had trouble typing? Or was it just that these were the broken, last thoughts of a dying man?

The first part was much like the fragment of diary found in Hoshi's apartment. Guilt, death, obsession. A theme of atonement—intentions of giving his life in the place where thousands of others had died at the hands of human madness. Reference to his parents, who had died in the bombing of Phoenix. Place of birth, Phoenix, yes . . . at least it made some sense so far. But then the text became quite broken:

> . . . *spoke to me awake . . . dreaming of madness. Real.*
> *Now . . . know. Not it is notmadness . . .*
>   *At dawn. shimmering. the light. Chilled, my bones.*
> *Aforce. It has invaded my mind. soul*
>
> *—their song in my heart. Yes, song! Voices! ! Not from me. Who re theyy?!!*
>
>   *Lucid.*
> *Never felt such clarity. spirits give me vision, kind of vision toto ends of the univrs.*
>   *WHER D THEY COME FROM?*
> *cannot return, no way but forward—pray tht—*
> *Someone must. Read.*
> *not be much longer. The voices.*
> *MOZZZZY!!!## I hear you!!*
> *read this. Plse. Someon.*

Jonders read and reread the message, massaging his forehead. Dear God, Hoshi—you poor, poor bastard. I'm so sorry. You deserved better. Jonders could not remember ever feeling so weary. What was going on in this world? Intimidation . . . suicide . . . madness.

Mozy. As though Hoshi had heard her voice at the end? *Voices. Spirits.* Hoshi had been confused and delirious, clearly. But . . . it sounded almost like a spiritual encounter, a religious epiphany.

Perhaps Hoshi's final thoughts were not as incoherent as they seemed. If his eyesight had failed him, that would explain much of the choppiness of the words. They could not simply be dismissed as madness. What they *were* was another question.

Jonders ground his eyes with his knuckles. It had been one hell of a bad day. And he still had not heard from Slim. Maybe it was just as well. Go home. It's not going to get better.

*   *   *

Marie's fingers probed his shoulder and seemed to touch, as she massaged, a corner of the complexity of worries and uncertainties that struggled beneath his surface. He closed his eyes, forcing out his breath, as his muscles released a fraction of their tension. "You're a solid knot," she said, and he nodded slowly.

He heard footsteps. "Here, Dad," said Betsy.

He accepted the cup of tea with whispered thanks. He took a sip of the steaming brew; it was too hot to drink. Marie took the cup from him and set it on the endtable, then shooed Betsy off to bed. Her thumbs pressed harder into his shoulder muscles. "I guess it couldn't have happened any other way," he said, exhaling.

She worked on his left shoulder. "What couldn't?"

"Hoshi. There was nothing I could have done for him. Not since Mozy's death."

Marie worked silently for a while. "Want to tell me about it?"

He didn't answer at first. As she bore down on a spot of tension, released nervous energy flowed to his fingertips, his toes, the back of his skull. "Can't," he said softly. And then, as though he had in fact said just the opposite, he began talking. Telling her some of the story, not all of it—a bit of Mozy's life, Mozy's death, and Hoshi's tragedy. She listened silently, massaging the back of his neck, and said nothing until he added, "I wonder if Joe Payne knows."

"The newscaster?" she asked in surprise.

He nodded. "I've . . . talked to him already. Before, I mean. Told him some of it." Marie's hands stopped moving, and he reached up to cover them with his own. He leaned his head back and looked up at her upside-down face. "I gave him a starting point. Don't worry. I'm not doing anything that will get me sent to jail." I hope.

Marie kissed his forehead. "That wasn't what I was worried about, dear."

"No? Well, anyway, Payne probably knows more than I do at this point." He chewed his lip, thinking about Hoshi's note—Payne couldn't know about that, though—or could he? It was so hard to shake the feeling of futility, when you had nothing but pain and worry in your heart. Marie was stroking his hair now, and he leaned his head back again between her breasts and pulled her close for a kiss, just a brushing of lips, and he buried his face in her hair, hugging her as she leaned over him. She slipped her hands down the front of his shirt, and he let out a long breath, as he felt himself becoming aroused. "Shall we go to bed early?" he whispered.

She chuckled close to his ear. "What, early? It's after eleven."

"Early, late—what's the difference?"

"None at all," she said, pulling him out of the chair. Together they padded down the hall, flicking off lights, and slipped into the dark and quiet of the bedroom.

Chapter 59

It was a difference in the songs that first caused her to wonder . . . odd musical riffs running through a nearby strand of consciousness. She rippled her viewpoint around and beneath the unfamiliar patterns, listening from various perspectives. (These songs—they're strange to me. Are they stories of your homeworld?)

(They are—) (—of worlds—) (—we have known.)

(Indeed?) she said. (Memories? Songs spun of your visits?)

(As undertones—) (—and themes—) (—yes—) (—but also songs—) (—reaching to us now.) For a moment the sounds were muted, and then the odd riffs that she had noticed before recurred, this time alone. They reminded her of some exotic instrument, perhaps a sitar.

(You mean—) she said, surprise rippling through her, (you are receiving these songs—now—from other worlds?)

(Of course.) A flickering vision shot through her senses: a spidery tachyon beam, like a ray of light, joining one world to another, star to star, planet to asteroid, flickering through space in search of others. Something in the image struck her oddly; it was more than just the passage of a tachyon through space—it was a passage through layers of existence, world after shimmering world.

(What are they like, the people of these worlds? Are there pictures within the songs?)

(Of course—) (—we shall translate—)

Light rippled along the interface lines that joined her with them; and images took form. Images of worlds visited:

—a green and purple landscape, rolling hills under a sky whose color defied description. Along the banks of a river, rows of bisonlike creatures marched purposefully.

—a curious botanical city, peopled with lazily good-natured, flat-billed creatures that struck her as lizardly and birdlike at the same time. (The *Slen*—) A glimpse of Slen society suggested an astonishing partnership, a plant kingdom fully coequal with the animal, four-legged creatures seeking intellectual and philosophical advice from phototrophic, rooted mentors.

—a mouselike creature peering out from under a palely golden leaf, maroon sunlight casting a shadow across its nose, and illuminating the tiny pincers that tipped its forelimbs, clicking to some unheard musical rhythm.

—creatures that shimmered at the limits of visibility, like living manifestations of an aurora borealis. (The *aura-predators*—) remarked someone, with a tone suggesting, *Beware*. One of the creatures slowly melted and pooled into a luminous liquid, and suddenly metamorphosed into a sharp-edged thing with jutting razor fangs. It lunged forward. Mozy instinctively tried to duck aside, but the creature transformed itself into a netlike sail that enveloped her. Then it dissolved, and reappeared as a benign pool of light.

(Careful!) A burst of laughter brought her back to the present. Her avoidance instinct had sent a Talenki faun stumbling across the floor, its companions scattering.

(Sorry to—) (—frighten you—) (—but it scared—) (—hell out of us—) (—when we met it!) jabbered her collective guides.

(You nearly gave me a heart attack,) Mozy said breathlessly. (You have met all of these beings?)

(And many more.)

(But surely you're not still in contact with all of them!)

(Those who possess—) (—the skill—) (—and the will—)

(But how?) She imagined an immense network of tachyon links emanating from dozens—hundreds?—of worlds, all converging and centering on this one moving asteroid. Even across the light-years, the worlds remained linked in thought, song, and memory.

The image seemed almost too fulfilling, too bold. (Aren't there ever failures, people who don't want you around?)

The Talenki lapsed into stunned silence, and she wondered, had she offended them?

An image opened like a maw and surrounded her. Dark, cold walls on all sides of her. Moisture condensing, dripping. She was deep within a cave. (What is this?) she whispered. (Why are we here?) Even if only a memory, it was frightening.

(The *Klathron*—) whispered the answer. (They dwell in mines—)

(—deep inside their world—) (—circling a shrunken red sun—) (—a gloomy body—) (—deep within a dust cloud.)

Mozy shivered.

(Witness our welcome.)

A pale light shone ahead, from beyond a bend in the passageway. The geometry of the mines reminded her of the passageways in the Talenki craft, but without ornamentation or the tricky shifts of dimensionality. Without warmth. Perhaps this was only a little-used outer passageway. As the Talenki rounded one bend and then another, new side passages came into view, offering glimpses of other mazes. Mozy wondered if the Talenki were wandering through the mines unescorted, uninvited; then, dancing at the edges of her vision, she caught the shadowy form of someone—something—guiding them. The Klathron?

A barrier dropped away in front of them, exposing an open area, more brightly illuminated—a chamber, with dancing fire at one end, a chamber full of Klathron.

They were all angles and jointed limbs, and they were black as coal, and moved quickly and skittishly, and were hard to track. There was a humming in chorus, which Mozy realized was the Talenki, composing a greeting; but something about it felt odd, it was a very tentative song, the Talenki were uncertain about their welcome here. (Didn't they invite you?) she whispered, as though afraid that the Klathron even now might hear. No one answered. The song grew slowly, hesitantly.

A pair of smallish Klathron "crabs" darted sideways and then toward the Talenki. They muttered with low, throaty voices, husky and hollow—evidently trying to communicate *something*. Their behavior was agitated and restless, but the Talenki judged it to be a welcoming, coaxing behavior. They flowed forward, their song shifting to a lighter, more melodious tune. Listen to the Klathron song, feel it, find its raspy rhythm. What do they feel, what do they mean? What is real, what illusion?

Talenki and Klathron faced. Song and rattle and uncertainty filled the room. The Talenki song quieted; the rattle of the Klathron died down. There was silence.

And suddenly chaos. As though at a signal, Klathron screeched and swarmed across the chamber, and erupted from the walls, limbs waving and snapping. The air was filled with dark, angular arms and legs flying, and claws striking at the eyes. The view began to quake and shimmer. It was impossible to tell what was happening. Mozy heard screams of pain—Talenki pain—and felt the slashing of flesh and burning acid spurting into wounds. Something black and hard struck at the eyes that were seeing, and there was a flash of agony as all went dark, and then images streamed in from other eyes, but everywhere it was the same—everywhere massacre. The Talenki didn't *know* how to fight. Did they at least know how to run?

The answer came in a jumbling of the vision. Talenki were blinking in and out of existence about her, and even the chamber was flickering; the watcher was himself dodging in and out of the continuum. The Klathron, enraged, struck harder and faster than ever. For a time, it looked as though escape would be possible. Talenki flickered out of reach of the claws, in and out of walls. But the hope was an illusion. Something in the bedrock—perhaps the bewildering maze, perhaps another force—thwarted their efforts. Always they found themselves back in the Klathron chamber, set upon in an instant by clouds of flashing fangs and rock-ripping arms. Escape was possible for an instant, and then another instant; but beyond each instant was that terrifying moment of vulnerability, and pain.

The imagery dissolved in a haze of fear and a mist of blood, and behind it all the terrified cries of the Talenki still in their asteroid, watching through a link that was being chewed and whittled to pieces . . . all slowly dissolving, until the only thing left was the mourning wail of the Talenki in space reliving the death throes of their murdered siblings.

(Were they saved—any of them?) she whispered, as though speaking out of the abyss of a bottomless dream.

Silence. And then a whisper. (A bit of their thought—) (—their spirit—) (—their memory—) (—no more.)

(I—) she said, thinking of the Talenki struck dumb with terror, unable even to save their fellow Talenki as, later, they had saved her. (I'm—terribly, terribly sorry.) She wanted to say more, ask more—but she could scarcely talk, it was no longer a time for talk.

Slowly she slipped back into the silence of dreaming.

Images of Earth: sunset coming on.

She awoke to a golden sun glowing through broken layers of clouds, white stuff banked against the horizon, shimmering with wintry light and shadow. The layers were pulled apart like cotton, letting the dying daylight blaze through. The sun was a sinking, expanding orb, turning crimson and finally spreading its furnace-glow across the undersides of the sky.

She held the image, not wanting to stir from the moment of awakening, not wanting to let pass this memory of the physical beauty of Earth. What had she been dreaming of earlier—the Talenki? She loved them and their world, but it was not Earth—not *her* world. A longing filled her—to see her Earth again, to hold its beauty in her eyes, its warmth against her breast, its spirit in her heart.

Sunset . . . sculpted desert rock . . . a broad, muddy river twisting its course down the center of a continent . . . majestic, thundering oceans. . . .

Thinking of days when such things were a part of her world, Greater Mozy passed into a reverie of Earthly images and explorations, landscapes once known to her, mountains, ocean, and plain. Sun and storm, desert and snow. Manhome. Cradle of her species. Womb that had given her up to the cosmos.

In her lesser-self, other thoughts stirred. Memories emerged as though from a vault. How could she have forgotten the gift Kink had given her on her eighth birthday, when she feared no one remembered, or cared? The trio of glass figurines, the stallion and mare and filly, stood proudly on the third shelf of her built-in bookcase for nine years, until the filly was knocked over and broken, and she'd put the other two away in sadness, because she couldn't stand to see them bereft of their offspring. By then, she was angry with Kink more often than she was happy; now, she could scarcely remember why.

How was it that she'd gotten herself bound up in such anger and insecurity—that she'd left with hatred and despair in her heart, and bitterness toward almost the whole of her human race? Had events been so unkind to her?

She riffled through memories like files in a library catalog, viewing each long enough to catalyze the recall: days in school, not feeling quite a part of things, but not yet so isolated as to provoke despair; at home, the arguments and tension that crisscrossed the family, and the occasional moments of understanding that almost, but not quite, cemented them together; the night of evil, the mugging, and the terror and humiliation both during and after; the cutting of the bonds of home, going far off to school with Dee; the excitement of freedom— and then the loneliness—breaking with Dee, who'd abandoned her for a man (but had she *really*?); the beginning of work on the Project, meeting Kadin . . . and the rest.

Hoshi. Images of Hoshi blazing in her memory now—stark and painful—why? Hoshi stumbling, agony in every step—where did this image come from, had she dreamed it?—Hoshi calling to her, stirred by a Talenki song. But Hoshi had not . . . *where did this image come from?* A dream, it must have been a dream. Another puzzle, another question.

And Homebase. Their recent message had been full of confusion. Had she made the last song to them too cryptic, or too blunt? Was she acting out her own past anger?

Here she was, the first and only envoy of Humanity to a race of beings from the stars, and she had to ask: Was she still fully human? Could she fulfill the role that had been thrust upon her? Did she possess the understanding, the compassion? She'd learned to get along with the Talenki. Could she do the same with her own kind?

A feeling welled into existence in her, a prickly light shining through the depths of her consciousness, an aching sullen glow like banked embers emerging, their radiance burning into the self-awareness, making every thought a reflection of the heat. Her people: she could not remember ever thinking of Humanity in this way before. Her last memories were of Homebase—Jonders and Hathorne and the rest— but they were little more than a fleck of Humanity, a quirk. Hers were all the people of Earth, full of imperfections, people who required understanding and care, and mothering.

(You are troubled, Mozy?) A single voice interposed itself softly, at the edge of her consciousness.

It took her a moment to respond. She trembled, aware again of the Talenki presence all around her, like silent breaths of air. One was gently seeking her attention. N'rrril. (Yes?) she answered softly, her answer a question.

His thoughts crept closer. (May I share?)

She hesitated, afraid of being engulfed in the intensity of her feelings, afraid of diluting them if she opened the gates to another. But the fear dropped away as she thought of N'rrril's gentle kindnesses, and comforting ways, and she sighed and reached to him, in the periphery of the mind-net, and like a lover aching with loneliness, she entered him. And looked out through his eyes.

He stood in the central part of the asteroid, alone. Perhaps he had flickered here even as she joined with him. Together, she and he, they looked out over the tiny sea that filled the core of the Talenki world, gazed down into the crystal water, felt the gritty smooth bank beneath her feet. (A touch of home,) she thought wistfully.

(A touch of home,) he repeated, not entirely understanding. He, and she, started to walk along the banks of the sea. (Show me what you're feeling,) he said softly.

(I will,) she answered. (But first let me feel the water again between my toes.)

Singing softly, nodding, N'rrril turned and they waded together in the cool, clear shallows of the sea.

Chapter 60

Charles Horst was very quiet by the time Alvarest left the NASA lab chief's office; but Alvarest had secured an ally—and a promise of assistance, in the form of a discreet computer scan of military cargo manifests, in hopes of determining whether special equipment associated with the handling of nuclear warheads had been shipped to the station. It was, Horst had conceded, a faint hope; although cross-linkages existed between NASA's and the Space Forces' computers, it was questionable whether his people could intrude in the military's files without detection. Still, he was willing to try.

Alvarest had succeeded in alarming Horst—and himself. What was going on, that a man in Horst's position didn't know about something this vital?

"It would take a presidential order to put nuclear weapons on that ship, or anywhere in space," Horst said. *"And it would be a violation—"*

"Of international law?" Alvarest said. *"Right. That's one thing. Another is, what's that ship's mission, anyway?"* We both know it, he added silently as Horst looked away, but neither of us is going to say it. And if the President already knows about those bombs, what am I doing here?

Horst seemed to have forgotten Alvarest's presence. *"The President shouldn't have given an order like that without going through the Committee,"* he muttered. *"He should have—"* Horst's eyes focused on Alvarest, and he abruptly changed the subject.

They talked about ways of learning the truth.

Alvarest wasn't bothered much by Horst's reticence about whom the President should have consulted with. He had already concluded that the "Oversight Committee" was an entity somehow less than and greater than the President, probably representing several nations. Probably that was whom he was working for. He was content to let it go at that; it wasn't his job to know the name of his client. But if someone in authority was pulling an endrun around someone else, it was his job to learn the facts.

He floated down a tube to spin-section Alpha and a half-gee cocktail lounge. He settled into a seat at the bar, thought for a while, found a phone, called Spaceman Akins, and arranged for another guided tour. Then he returned to his seat and ordered a Scotch on the rocks.

He'd learned a few things from Horst, not about the military, but about the Tachylab group. The more he learned about John Irwin, the more he tended to put credence in the scientist's accusations. Respected by his colleagues for his pioneering work in tachyons, Irwin was also known to hold moderately radical political beliefs, which had gotten him blacklisted from the most sensitive work at Tachylab. It was also said that he'd been persecuted for alleged homosexuality. A cynic might conclude that the military would be eager to arrest such a man on conspiracy charges if there were even the slightest chance that he was leaking embarrassing information.

Why bother, Alvarest thought, unless there was something to be embarrassed about?

Alvarest carried his glass to the viewing wall. It was an odd sensation, bouncing along at half Earth-normal weight; turning as he walked felt odder still, as the Coriolis effect caused by the station's spin made him veer slightly from his intended direction. Handy feature for a cocktail lounge, he decided. No need to drink; walking sober was enough to make one stagger. The floor's curvature served as a reminder that he was walking on the inner surface of a spinning shell, and only a few meters of steel and shielding slag supported him against hard vacuum.

He sipped his drink and gazed out, down the station's axis toward the zero-gee docks. The docks appeared to be rotating, though he knew full well that it was he who was moving and not the docks. Small vessels hovered in the area. Where, he wondered, would weapons be loaded? Not there, surely. But looking around there might give him an idea of how things were done in zero-gee—might give him some notion of what to look for if he ever saw the real thing.

He would be wise to learn as much as possible as quickly as possible.

He'd managed to put off the general's aide for a day or two, but eventually Ogilvy would have to be dealt with.

He turned back to the bar. Where the devil was Akins, anyway?

"Sure, you can go up that way, Mr. Alvarest—"

"Well, then—"

"—but I can't take you now," Akins said. "I have to get back for duty."

"Oh." Alvarest peered out the porthole in disappointment. According to Akins, the outbound transfer docks—for spacecraft moving outward from geosynchronous orbit, whether to Luna or L5 or interplanetary space—most closely resembled the military deep-space docks, located some distance from GEO-Four. "You think I could find my way down there by myself?" he asked.

"Sure."

"I don't want to go out an airlock by mistake."

Akins chuckled. "Don't worry. Just read the signs." He described the route, advising Alvarest to ask further directions when he got there.

Alvarest nodded. "Right. Well, thanks for getting me this far."

"Give a call if you need anything else." The young enlisted man saluted cheerfully and departed.

I wish I could, Alvarest thought. He could use another ally. But he dared not involve Akins further, or tell him what he was really looking for. Sighing, he turned and continued on his way.

There was a gallery window in the main passageway overlooking the hangar area. Alvarest watched a Space Forces patrol cutter leaving. Service arms pulled back from the craft like implements of some sort of alien dentistry. A pair of slender mooring retainers held the craft as its bay doors slid closed, and two workers in bulky servo-suits jetted clear. The retainers swung back, and the craft drifted slowly away from the dock. Four small thrusters sparked and glowed intermittently, and the cutter slowly dwindled, a white painted bird being swallowed by the enormity of space. When its main engines glowed to life, it scudded out of sight like a puppet on a string.

In the main hangar, no one was visible. The workers in servo-suits had disappeared. Alvarest drifted down to the end of the passage. A bored-looking guard glanced at his Defense Department I.D. and waved him inside. He paused to establish his bearings.

Along one side of the hangar was a catwalk, edging a thick-windowed wall dividing the shirtsleeve environment from the hard-vacuum dock-ing bay from which the cutter had departed. Below the catwalk was an open work area, filled with moving equipment and zero-gee stor-age racks. The outer wall was punctuated by airlocks of various sizes and entrance tubes to one-man servo-suits docked on the outside. Alvarest moved along the catwalk. Both the outer and inner hangars were deserted.

He gazed down at the silent equipment. It all looked normal enough, though he wondered if he would know something out of the ordinary if he saw it. Conveyor tracks led from storage areas on the right to the main airlocks; winches and manipulating equipment were locked in position at the far ends of the tracks. He dropped easily from the catwalk to take a closer look at the machinery. It was surprising how lightweight the equipment appeared. In zero-gee, even massive loads, properly handled, could be moved with relatively little brute force. He stopped to peer into one of the large airlocks. More equipment.

He heard a whining noise behind him. Turning, he lost his grip momentarily and foundered against the airlock door. As he twisted around, he was horrified to see a winch sliding along its track toward the airlock, its latching mechanism arrowing straight for his head. He struggled to flee from its path, and found himself hanging in midair, swinging and kicking. At last he got a grip on the hatch behind him, and shoved sideways. The winch abruptly clanked to a stop, and a voice rasped through an intercom, "Who's that in there?"

Carried by his momentum, Alvarest hit a structural beam with his left arm and shoulder, and rebounded in slow motion. By the time he turned, a man was sailing out of one of the rear doors toward him.

"You okay?" the man asked, swinging to an easy stop beside him.

"Yeah," Alvarest managed. "I slammed into that beam."

"Man, you were really spinning around there," the worker said. "I didn't see you till you were about to be flattened." He squinted. "You sure you're okay? Jesus, it's a good thing I looked out when I did. I thought nobody was out here. Shit." He scowled toward a window in the rear wall, beyond which was apparently a control room.

"I bunged my elbow pretty good," Alvarest said, wincing as he straightened his arm. "It works, though. I guess I didn't break anything."

The worker shook his head. "Man, I was *sure* there was nobody out here! What are you doing here, anyway? This is no place for a groundheader to be wandering around on his own."

Alvarest reddened, but didn't protest the characterization. "I'm with Defense," he said. "Just looking over the facilities."

"Oh, well, why the hell didn't you come to us and ask? We'd be glad to show you around—but you go poking on your own, you're gonna get hurt."

"Yeah. Guess I was a little stupid." Alvarest looked around. "Mind if I ask what you load here?"

The man shrugged. "You name it. Food, cargo, hardware. Not fuel, that's at the depot down by Delta section."

"Just for the military?" Alvarest asked casually.

"Oh, no—anything the government flies. And commercial stuff."

"How about ordnance. Do you load that, too?"

"Oh, hell no." The man looked at him curiously. "That's done at the ordnance depot. I'm surprised you don't know. We wouldn't have it in here. That stuff scares me."

"Yeah, me too," Alvarest said. "Listen—thanks." He reached for a handhold to shove off from. "I'd better get on going. Sorry to mess up your work. I'll ask for a guide next time."

"Hey, take it easy," the man said.

Alvarest flexed his arm cautiously as he floated along a handrail toward the door. Yes, indeed, he had better get a guide. But how could he do that, except through channels?

"You're not on Earth now," Ogilvy snapped irritably. "And this isn't your cozy pad in the Cube." His eyes darted, reminding Alvarest of a small, feral animal. "We do things a little differently here. Do you understand what I'm saying?"

Alvarest rubbed his arm unconsciously. "I'm not sure I do."

"Does it have to be spelled out?" Ogilvy said, eyeing him. "You're here at the general's pleasure. If you don't support him, you're against him."

"Excuse me," Alvarest said. "But I work for the Defense Information Bureau. I'm not working for the general, and I'm not under—"

"Don't make too many assumptions about your standing here," Ogilvy said, scowling. "This little trip of yours to the loading dock—"

"Who told you about that?"

"We got a call from the dock supervisor, saying they had a man from Defense wandering around unescorted, getting in the way, and almost getting himself hurt. I notice you're favoring your left arm."

"All right, I should have asked for assistance," Alvarest conceded.

"You were there without authorization in the first place."

"Was that a secure facility? If so, it wasn't marked."

"That's not relevant." Ogilvy frowned at his clipboard. He spoke without meeting Alvarest's eyes. "You're here on a limited fact-finding assignment—pertaining only to a specific criminal prosecution. Those loading docks have nothing to do with your assignment."

Alvarest stared at him impassively. "That's a matter of interpretation. I may need to tour other facilities, as well."

Ogilvy squinted uneasily. "For what purpose?"

"Fact gathering. I'm not sure yet what I'll require," Alvarest said calmly. "I'll keep you informed."

"Will you, now? It may interest you to know that Spaceman Akins is already on report for taking you on that last little joy trip."

"That was my responsibility," Alvarest protested. "Akins was simply complying with my request."

"When we want you to take command of our personnel, we'll let you know," Ogilvy said with quiet sarcasm. "In the meantime, please confine yourself to investigations that have been cleared through this office."

Alvarest cleared his throat. "I have a mandate—"

"Your mandate doesn't mean shit to us," Ogilvy snapped. His calm had broken, and his eyes strained and flicked to and fro as he struggled to regain control. "It may surprise you that we don't bow down to every little mandate from Earthside. You may find us a little harder to get along with than what you're used to."

"What's that supposed to mean?"

Ogilvy shrugged. "You're an intelligent man. I'm sure you can understand."

Alvarest pinched his lower lip between thumb and forefinger. "I see. Well, Lieutenant, in that case it's been a pleasure, but I have work to do." He turned, and with a single kick, floated out of Ogilvy's office. His movement was graceful until he reached the corridor, and then his anger got the best of him, and he caromed painfully against a wall, as he attempted to change directions.

Chapter 61

For Alvarest, the next two days were filled with frustration. Hours spent on a terminal with one of Horst's computer wizards produced no results; if there was any proof to be found, it was not accessible from the outside. Horst offered to arrange a visit to Tachylab, for interviews with some of the other scientific personnel; but there were security clearances involved, and it would take a few days to set up. In the meantime, Alvarest studied briefs and talked again with the attorneys and the defendants. He sorted through several months of news files, searching for evidence of actual leaks—that being the alleged goal of the conspiracy. If any news reports qualified, Joe Payne's did; but even his were fairly vague, and could well represent supposition rather than leaked information.

Alvarest wrote a second report to his Earthside control, indicating his belief that *Aquarius* was an illegally armed craft—and admitting that he had no more proof than before. The next day, after considerable deliberation, he called Ogilvy and asked for a tour of the military ordnance depot, preferably with the attorneys in attendance. Ogilvy agreed to arrange a private inspection, but balked at allowing the attorneys. Would tomorrow be satisfactory? Alvarest agreed—surprised, and more than a little suspicious.

He discussed his suspicions with Horst. "I don't trust him—but how else am I going to learn anything? Do you think he may have decided that it's just easier to play along?"

"Well," Horst said, "*Aquarius* has been gone a couple of weeks now. That's plenty of time to remove incriminating evidence." He pressed his lips together. "I'm still shocked that this could happen— either without the President's knowledge, or maybe what's worse, *with* his knowledge." He shook his head. "Either way, we could be in a sticky position."

Alvarest looked at him carefully. "Yeah," he said. "Listen. You don't suppose that there's any danger in my going on this inspection thing alone, do you?"

Horst arched his eyebrows. "I don't think Armstead's a killer, if that's what you mean—though I've heard him called a lot of other things. Still, I suppose it wouldn't hurt to be cautious."

Alvarest gazed at him with a cold feeling.

He tried to shake the feeling later, as he returned to his quarters. He sent a short advisory to his control, indicating his plans. Then, locating paper and a clipboard, he jotted down some of the thoughts that were swirling in his mind—in a letter to Stanley Gerschak—and requested that the astronomer pass the information on to "their mutual friend."

When he was finished, he read the letter over, hesitating a long time, and finally sealed it and went to the central postal exchange, where he paid the premium GEO-to-Earth rates and watched the envelope disappear into a mailbag. Then he returned to his quarters, where he tried, with little success, to sleep.

"We'll be in hard vacuum, Mr. Alvarest," Spaceman Ramsey said, leading the way into the ready-room. "Have to suit up and take a scooter." He halted before a row of lockers, turned to eye Alvarest for size, and pulled out two spacesuits.

"Why keep it in hard vacuum?" Alvarest asked nervously, taking the suit. "Doesn't that make for more trouble?"

Ramsey shrugged. "Trouble for people who don't belong here. Prevents contamination. You've worn a pressure suit before, right?"

Alvarest shook his head.

"Well, then, there's some things you need to know."

Alvarest tried to listen as Ramsey rattled off the instructions, but he had trouble concentrating. *Contamination?* Of what—the weapons stock? Or radioactive contamination of the station? How would he know if he saw anything incriminating? He knew the symbol for radioactivity, but that was about it.

"—back on this lever," Ramsey was saying.

"Huh? Right. Pull back," Alvarest repeated. By the time they were both suited, he had begun to wish he'd been thinking less and listening more to the checkout. *It wouldn't hurt to be cautious,* Horst had said. Thinking could be a dangerous habit.

Ramsey led the way into the airlock and told him to shut his faceplate. Ramsey checked the seal, and then closed his own. "Check your air," he instructed, his voice crackling in Alvarest's headset. Alvarest took several deep breaths; the air smelled a little stale, but otherwise seemed okay. "What are your pressure and flow readings?" Ramsey said. His voice was loud and harsh, and his breath a rasp in Alvarest's ear.

"Where do I find it?" He fumbled at the controls on his chest.

"Not there!" Ramsey said impatiently. "Fuckin' A, man, didn't you listen? Inside—top of your visor."

"Right." Alvarest found the tiny red digital display reflected on the inner surface of his visor and quoted the figures to Ramsey. Ramsey grunted and turned to the airlock control panel.

The inner door slid shut. An amber light went on above it. The light turned red, and Alvarest felt his suit stiffening slightly. When he turned around, he saw the outer door retracting. Ramsey gestured and moved out of the lock; Alvarest, after a moment's hesitation, followed.

The view in the hangar was essentially the same whether one was looking out through a window or stepping out in a spacesuit, but the *feelings* were very different. Alvarest clung to the doorframe to steady himself. Weightlessness suddenly had a new meaning. If he let go, he might tumble away from the airlock, and safety, with nothing to grab onto. Don't be ridiculous, he thought. How was Ramsey managing?

His guide was hovering, using tiny jets on his suit. "Hook your line to that cleat on your left," Ramsey ordered. Alvarest found the end of his safety line and obeyed. "Now swing around there and get on the rear seat of the scooter." Alvarest focused on a wasplike craft moored to his left. Slowly he swung himself around and clambered onto the second narrow seat on the craft's body. He hooked his legs around the frame, until Ramsey floated up alongside and showed him where to hang on. "When I unhook your line, now, reel it in and hook it right here." He tapped a fitting on the scooter. Alvarest, fumbling in the bulky suit, complied.

Ramsey settled into the front seat and ran down a checklist. Alvarest felt a jolt, and the scooter began moving, accelerating out of the hangar. He swallowed back a sudden feeling of vertigo, held on tightly and tried to enjoy the ride. He hadn't been able to see much during the morning shuttle flight from GEO-Four to the deep-space hangar; now was his chance. He peered around as the scooter accelerated. What he saw, mostly, was a collection of nondescript sheds somehow moored together in free fall. He located the Earth, the glare of the sun, spotted a few stars in the blackness. This wasn't too bad. He could get used to having nothing beneath him but space. He relaxed his grip a little. Over his left shoulder, he could see the main deep-space dock and the supply shuttle he'd come in on. He suddenly felt foolish—certain that there was nothing for him to see, no evidence— why else would Ogilvy have sent him out here? He turned to look forward again, with a vague sense of uneasiness; it was quiet, lonely out here, just he and Ramsey and the emptiness.

Ramsey applied braking thrust as they passed a small fuel-tank cluster and approached the last structure in the group. The scooter turned as Ramsey maneuvered beyond and around the end of the enclosure. They came to a halt a few meters from the shed. If this was an ordnance area, there was nothing to signify it on the outside. Ramsey dismounted and jetted to an external control box. He manipulated something, and a large bay door began to retract. He returned to the scooter and brought it slowly forward into the doorway, into the near-pitch darkness of the shed's interior. The scooter bumped to a stop, and Alvarest felt a click as some sort of docking mechanism locked it into place.

Ramsey dismounted again, turned, and crowded close to Alvarest. He did something to the controls on the front of Alvarest's chestpack. Alvarest's helmet light blinked on, a spotlight stabbing into the darkness. Ramsey moved away, his own light flicking on, and gestured for Alvarest to follow. "What do you want me to do?" Alvarest said uneasily. He didn't like the idea of floating away from the scooter into darkness.

He suddenly realized that he no longer heard Ramsey's breathing in his ear. "Ramsey," he said nervously. "Can you hear me?"

Ramsey moved back to a position in front of him, his faceplate reflecting Alvarest's light. Alvarest pointed to his ear with his right hand, signalling that his radio was out. Ramsey leaned forward, placing his helmet in contact with Alvarest's. "I turned your radio off," Ramsey said, his voice reaching Alvarest thinly through the helmet-to-helmet contact. "Can't risk anyone listening in when I show you this."

An unpleasant chill ran through Alvarest's body.

"Get off the scooter," Ramsey said. "Unhook your line, and I'll show you where to hook it on the wall." The spacesuited man pulled his head away, and moved off to the right, away from the scooter.

Alvarest rose from his seat, cautiously. The beam of his helmet light moved crazily across the wall. There was Ramsey's light; don't lose sight of it. A jump was required to reach the wall. He poised, and pushed off from the scooter—and immediately felt himself yanked around, tumbling. He grabbed for the wall, missed. His helmet light flew drunkenly across wall and then emptiness. "Wait!" he shouted futilely. His voice was heard by no one but himself.

Something jerked him against the side of the scooter, and he gasped, and realized dully that he had forgotten to unhook his safety line. He cursed with relief. No wonder he'd tumbled. Breathing heavily, he found the cleat and disconnected the line. Then, steadying himself, he pushed off again for the wall.

The spot of his helmet light grew bright against the wall as he caught at a brace, missed, caught another. Panting, he swung himself to a halt, face forward against the wall. It was harder work than it looked, moving around in these suits. Carefully, he turned himself around to look for Ramsey. He blinked, trying to shake off a feeling of dizziness. Was he still getting air? Breathing so hard he couldn't tell, couldn't hear the whisper. Getting excited, now; calm down. Where the hell was Ramsey?

He couldn't see much across the shed; his light was lost in darkness. Nearby was a large rack of girders and beams, apparently just being stored. Most of the shed seemed empty. He saw nothing that looked like weapons storage. "Are you sure we're in the right place," he said, a little too loudly, forgetting that he couldn't be heard. What was this, a weapons depot camouflaged as a construction storage shed? Or just a storage shed? If Ramsey was playing a game of some kind, how long would it take to play it out?

Something dark moved in the distance. Ramsey? He turned his head, trying to aim the light. It was impossible; it wasn't bright enough, and he couldn't get the damn thing pointed where he wanted it, anyhow. Where the hell *was* Ramsey? He turned—and felt his handhold slip—and realized too late that he'd failed to reattach his safety line.

He was drifting away from the wall, his light dancing bewilderingly. "Ramsey!" he shouted. Find something to grab onto. *Anything*. There were several terrifying moments as he groped at empty space, and then his right hand landed on something that felt like a handle, and he clutched it and yanked himself toward it—and felt it shift toward *him* with a sudden jerk. He released it with a start. *Damn it—now what had he done?* "Ramsey!" He was drifting backward, away from the wall.

Maneuvering jets, idiot. Controls on your chestpack. Damn it, what did Ramsey say about them? He fumbled at the chestpack, found a recessed lever on the side. Something hissed and kicked him in the right shoulder, and he began spinning. *Christ*. As his light swung wildly around the shed, he held his breath, waiting for another glimpse of the near wall. His beam passed a jumble of moving objects. *What the hell was that?* Coming closer.

He pushed the lever frantically the other way; a kick in his left shoulder slowed his spin. Something in his light, coming toward him.

"Shit!" he whispered in terror. It was the rackful of girders—loose now, tumbling and jostling, weightless but massive, and coming toward him. Panicked, he tried to move, kicked against nothing. "NO!" he bellowed. "RAMSEY!" Use the jets, now or never! He found another lever on the left side of his pack, yanked it, felt a kick driving him backward. His spotlight danced crazily on the girders, following him. *Faster*. He fired the jets again, squeezed and held the lever. He couldn't breath, couldn't cry out. He was frozen in a moment of seeming motionlessness, flying backward, chased by a churning cluster of steel girders. His stomach was a clenched fist. His balance was off; he began twisting again, losing sight of the pursuing objects. The far wall was coming up fast; he couldn't control his movement.

The first impact slammed his helmet into the wall. The second and third crushed his ribs.

The fourth, he never felt.

Ogilvy punched the security codes anxiously until the console confirmed a scrambled circuit. "Yes. Report," he said.

A familiar voice answered with a trace of a drawl. "Well, your man is taken care of. The official report oughta be in by now."

"Good."

"I can't hardly take all the credit, though."

Ogilvy looked at the communication set in puzzlement. "What do you mean—didn't you plan it and carry it out?"

"Didn't exactly get a chance. He brought it on himself."

"What do you mean?" Ogilvy demanded.

"He got clumsy." There was a trace of humor in the voice. "Dumped a whole rack of steel girders on himself before I was even finished setting it up."

"You mean you didn't have to do *anything*?" Ogilvy asked incredulously.

"I wouldn't say *that*. I got him there. Got him good and scared by turning off his radio receiver, and cutting back his air a little."

"He panicked?"

"He was shittin' his britches. It was real dark in there, and he didn't know which end was up."

Ogilvy recalled uneasily that he hadn't intended to ask the details. "Did you notify the MPs?"

"Yep. A terrible thing, terrible accident. And that's the truth. People been saying for years those storage areas should be better secured. And who the *hell* knew why the guy wanted to inspect a bunch of construction sheds, anyway."

Ogilvy began to relax. "Well, I'll look for the official report. There'll be hearings, of course, but that shouldn't pose too much of a problem. It looks like you've earned your pay."

"Fuckin' A."

"Your check'll be in the mail."

"A pleasure, man."

The circuit-connect light blinked off, and Ogilvy took a deep, satisfied breath. The general might not know exactly how the coyote had been removed from the henhouse, but he would know to whom he owed the deed.

Chapter 62

The snow was still coming down, blowing in an icy wind that wrapped itself around every building, tree, and vehicle so that no place outside was sheltered from its gusts. Against the streetlights, the snow was a flurry of angry white particles, flying in swirls and whipping upward in defiance of gravity.

Payne slammed the car door and hurried up the walk. He stamped his feet in the vestibule, fumbled with the lock, and finally trudged up the stairs to the third floor. The hallway was silent as he entered the apartment and hung up his coat.

He felt the tension return to the pit of his stomach, without even seeing or speaking with Denine. He kicked off his shoes and put on slippers before padding into the empty kitchen. She must be in the back room. Clicking on the water heater, he stared silently out the kitchen window, watching the snow fly under the streetlights. Even the weather had them under siege, he thought. His whole world seemed under siege, sometimes. He and Denine had been getting along poorly ever since his return from New Phoenix. Why, he wasn't sure; maybe it was his frustration, or her impatience. Maybe they were just drawing apart, as people do. Maybe it was the weather.

The water spurted out boiling into his cup. Carrying the steeping tea, he went down the hall, looking for Denine. Her studio door—nearly always open—was closed. He tapped softly and pushed the door open. She was at her table, working at the graphics screen. "Yo, I'm home," he called.

"Yep," she said, not turning from her work.

"It's blowing like crazy out. Colder than a witch's—"

"You've got a message," she said, still not looking up. She was staring at a portion of a painting on the screen, flipping frame to frame.

"How's it going?" he said. She grunted. He shrugged and pulled her door closed again and went into his own study. She has her problems, I have mine, he thought with some resentment, dropping into his seat. The message light was glowing on his console; he punched replay. It was Teri Renshaw, in New Wash. He pulled at his lip, thinking, No, I haven't finished your update yet, and could that be the fly in Dee's soup—Teri calling? Or was there something more—all the time he'd been spending away, maybe, or her suspicion that he was exploiting Mozy's story for his own ends?

He blew through his fingers, shaking his head. He was having enough trouble just keeping on top of the damn story, without extraneous pressures. Since he'd learned from his New Phoenix assistant about the death of Hoshi Aronson, under what had to be considered bizarre circumstances, he'd been trying harder than ever to piece together the pattern of facts and suspicions; but he just didn't have enough to make it stick—not on national newscope network. Fragments, it was nothing but fragments. Of course, Teri never tired of telling him that it was fragmentary stories that made the news; and after you'd written enough fragments, if you were lucky, you found that you had a whole. Maybe it was the ability to be content with that process that made a good hard-news reporter. He wasn't sure that he had it in him.

He called Teri at her home. The line rang twice. "Hello," Teri said. Then her face appeared in the screen, and her smile disappeared. "Joe."

"I haven't done the story yet, if that's what you called about," he said. "Are you gonna be mad?"

Teri shook her head. "No, uh . . . Joe . . ." A pained expression crossed her face. "I wish I didn't have to be the one."

"What?"

"To . . . give you this news."

Butterflies took flight in his stomach. They were cutting him from the story. No. They couldn't. They wouldn't.

"Joe—" She gazed straight out of the screen at him. "It's your friend, Don Alvarest. The one who went to GEO-Four. He's—" Her voice caught.

I've gotten him in trouble, then. Damn it—

"Joe, he's dead."

Payne's breath went out.

Teri said quietly, "We just got a report from our man at GEO-Four. It was some kind of accident, evidently. The official report was that . . ."

All he could feel was a sudden emptiness in the center of his chest, a blunt pain. A roaring sensation in his ears.

". . . outside the space station, in some kind of storage shed . . . he was crushed. . . ."

A corner of Payne's brain listened as Teri spoke, absorbing the details with perfect clarity; but the rest of his mind, through a haze, spun futilely with disbelief, with the sheer unbelievability of it, that Donny could be gone. An accident? He thought dimly of times they'd shared together in college, drinks and good times and bad times; and he thought of the irony of the fact that if it were not for Donny, he might have no story now, no story at all. It was not possible that he could be dead. It wasn't just not possible; it wasn't *fair*.

There was a rattling and howling at the windows as Teri spoke to him, as outside, the snowstorm raged.

"I have to go to New Washington," Payne said, pacing. Denine was sitting quietly at the table opposite him. The single overhead bulb filled the kitchen with a stark glow. "I have to talk with Teri and George and the others, and see if their man at GEO-Four is good enough to handle this. There has to be someone good on it. Someone who can dig."

He stopped pacing and looked at her. She was watching him silently, with an expression that was some mixture of sympathy and detachment. He shrugged and sat down and stared at the tabletop, thinking of the last phone message he'd had from Donny, and imagining him up there alone, trying to carry on an investigation. There was a lot about Donny's work that he didn't know—he realized that—but he knew Donny, and Donny wasn't one to bow to petty bureaucrats. He'd probably not made many friends among the military bureaucracy, not if his investigation took him onto their turf. How could it have happened? And why? The news bureau contact thought that the circumstances sounded suspicious, and even the defense attorney for the Tachylab scientists had called for an investigation. But what could he have uncovered that was important enough to be murdered for?

Denine poked at a fork on the table. "What if you don't think their guy can do the job?" she asked in a tone suggesting that she already knew the answer.

Payne let out a breath. "I'll ask them to send me."

He was aware of Denine sighing, shaking her head. She reached out and touched his arm. ''Joe. Don't do anything—'' *Stupid*, he imagined her saying, but she never finished the sentence.

He blinked and nodded as he thought, If someone has killed Donny to keep a story silent, I'll do every damn thing in my power to get that story into every home in this country, and half the world—even if it was our own government that did it. *Especially* if it was our own government.

Teri met him at the New Wash train station. She stepped forward and embraced him without a word. She pressed her face to his shoulder, squeezing him hard, and he returned the embrace by putting his arms around her, and resting his cheek against the crown of her head. Emotions that he'd been keeping secured began to shake loose and well up, and he trembled in an effort at self-control, not wanting to let it out yet.

Teri seemed to sense his struggle. She stepped back to gaze at him. ''I'm so sorry, Joseph,'' she whispered. She tilted her head and kissed him briefly on the lips. Startled, he returned the kiss only as she was pulling away. A trace of a smile crossed her face, and she kissed him again, this time lingering a moment as their lips touched.

Payne exhaled silently, surprised at his own response, as they stepped apart. He glanced around the station lobby, avoiding Teri's eyes as he picked up his bag. A touch on his arm brought his gaze back to her. She seemed to understand the uncertainty of his feelings. ''It's all right,'' she said, hooking a hand through his arm. ''Let's go.'' Without answering, he followed her out into the street, where she had a cab waiting.

They rode in silence to the studio.

The day's meetings with the production unit did little to improve his mood. The production supervisor remained unconvinced that there was sufficient evidence of foul play to warrant sending Payne to the space colony; and he insisted that their correspondent at the station was capable of following up any leads. When Payne asked what *he* might do to pursue the story, the chief's answer was simple: Wait.

Leaving the studio in disgust, Payne secured a hotel room before going to dinner with Teri. ''How can he expect me to do nothing?'' Payne complained, as they waited for their orders to arrive. ''I'll go crazy waiting for this guy at GEO-Four to report. And how do we know he's any good, anyway?''

Teri studied him sympathetically. ''Joe, Karl Davis is an excellent reporter. You know that. If there's something going on, I think we can trust him to find it.''

"But dammit—'' he said, knotting his fists in frustration.

"Sometimes you have to trust to other people, Joe.''

He fumed and said nothing.

"Forget your involvement, and remember that Karl knows the station. He knows the politics, who'll be help and who'll be hindrance, and probably what's hidden in some of the closets.''

"That's why I want to work *with* him,'' Payne said. "He knows the station but not the story.''

Teri lowered a forkful of salad. "You don't want to give it up,'' she said gently. "It's your story—and Don was your friend.''

Payne shrugged, looking down. "Maybe. But it's a story that has to be pursued.'' He paused as their waiter approached, and waited impatiently until their dinner was laid out and the waiter gone. He stabbed viciously at his steak. "You believe that, don't you?''

"What, that it needs to be pursued? Of course. But you can't cover everything yourself. You have your hands full down here. Who would take your story over if you went to GEO-Four?''

Payne shrugged. They'd been through it all before, of course, but that was before Donny's death. He worked on his steak angrily.

When he raised his eyes again, he found Teri watching him. He felt like a patient under scrutiny. "You think I'm too personally involved, don't you?''

Teri angled her head so that her hair fell across her brow. A tiny smile danced away from her lips. "Let it go for a while, Joe—okay?'' she said. They ate in silence for a few minutes, and then she said, "How about going for a drink after dinner? Ed's out of town, so I don't have to rush home.''

He took a small sip of wine, shrugging, nodding, gazing at her over the rim of his wineglass. Teri seemed so calm, so sure of herself even in difficult situations. It was one of the things about her he admired, and one reason he'd always been a little afraid of her. He didn't feel afraid now. He thought of Dee, wondering what she thought was going on when he came down here to meet with Teri. Just now, it seemed an unimportant question.

"Okay,'' he said softly.

Teri blew a strand of hair from her face. "Finish your dinner, then.'' She smiled. "Before it gets cold.''

*   *   *

The place they decided on for drinks was Teri's apartment. Payne agreed, for no particular reason except to follow the path of least resistance. While Teri went to change and to make drinks, he phoned Denine. "It looks as though I'll be coming home the day after tomorrow," he said. "One thing, though. It's possible that Donny may have tried to get information to me. Could you keep a watch on my phone, and the mail—and if anything comes that looks suggestive, give me a call?"

"Where are you now?" Denine asked. She was peering into the screen, trying to recognize Payne's surroundings.

"I'm at Teri's. You can get me at the hotel later, or at the studio tomorrow." Payne glanced up, saw Teri with two drinks in her hands, keeping discreetly out of camera range.

"Okay." Denine nodded. "Otherwise, you'll call and let me know when you're coming?"

"I'll call tomorrow evening," Payne promised.

He signed off and sat quietly with his thoughts for a moment as Teri set the brandy snifters down and rounded the coffee table to join him on the sofa. He raised his eyes finally to look at her. A disquieting but pleasant feeling stirred in him. She had changed into a loose-fitting blouse and slacks. What had she been wearing before? A business suit? She returned his stare quizzically. Her hair, fine and brown, fell over her shoulders; her eyes watched the movements of his. Hazel brown, a touch more green in the right eye than the left. He rarely noticed her eyes, he realized. Or the shape of her face, a little less rounded and more vertical than Denine's. His gaze followed the line of her neck, down her throat, to where the collar of her blouse was left open.

He blinked his eyes back up to meet hers, and smiled a trifle foolishly, feeling his face redden.

"Try your brandy," she said.

He touched his snifter to hers, then swirled it, inhaled, and took a tiny sip. The fumes went straight to his head, heightening and blurring his senses.

They talked a while, about nothing in particular. When the conversation lagged, he studied the wallpaper on the far side of the room, fingering the snifter.

"What are you thinking about?" Teri said.

That I can't understand why I haven't thought of you this way in years, he thought, trying not to react visibly. Teri, he recalled, had

what she referred to as a "semi-open relationship" with her friend
Ed. "Oh—" he said, fixing his gaze on a light switch on the wall. It
was made of cream-colored plastic, and didn't quite seem to go with
the wallpaper.

"You don't have to tell me."

He shook his head, a smile creeping to his lips. "No secret." He
was aware of a wisp of cologne, and Teri leaning ever so slightly
toward him. She sipped her brandy; he did the same.

"So?" she said, touching his shoulder, then letting her hand
drop.

He was torn by a moment of desire and fear. He recalled holding
her in his arms, at the train station—a pleasant memory. She had
been comforting him for the loss of a friend, not trying to seduce
him, but . . . he remembered the brief kiss, and it occurred to him
that she had been a greater comfort to him in his grief than Denine
had been, and although he didn't exactly know what to make of that,
he knew that just now there was a deep sorrow and grimness in him,
and he would be a fool not to take comfort where he could find it.

Her eyes, questioning, did not leave his.

He touched her shoulder in return, then her hair. "Well—" he
said, flushed with a kind of dizziness. In the years he had known
Teri, he had probably touched her hair dozens of times in the affec-
tionate gesture of a friend.

"Teri," he said, and when it came out as a croak, he chuckled
self-consciously.

"What's funny?" she whispered.

He stroked her hair, trying to think of just what he *did* want to say.
He was aware of a pressure in the crotch of his trousers, and he
swallowed, shifting his position awkwardly. "Why did you choose
this particular spot for us to have drinks?" he whispered, only his
whisper sounded like a growl.

"Well . . ." she said, then shrugged with a tiny smile.

He hesitated only an instant, and then he leaned forward, cradled
her face in both hands, and kissed her.

She responded gently at first, with uncertainty. Then her mouth
opened against his, and their tongues met and touched and danced,
and suddenly the pressure he was feeling doubled, and her breath
escaped with a little sigh, and he felt a burning in his cheeks as Teri's
tongue slid into his mouth. He felt her hands moving over him, pressing against his shoulders and then his chest; and he pulled her closer,

caressing her, and sliding his hands up along the sides of her breasts. When their lips parted, their eyes met nervously. Teri laughed silently. ''That's why,'' she whispered.

He nodded, his fingers playing at her collar, stroking her neck. Then, almost of their own accord, his fingers were unfastening the top button of her blouse, and sliding down to the next.

Chapter 63

There were times, still, when it all made her dizzy—the images of the worlds, the songs, the constant activity. She was growing accustomed to letting much of the conversational chatter pass her by, listening only to what interested her moment by moment; but her attempts to understand how things worked here still confounded her. The beehive method of communication was often as challenging as the concepts she was seeking to understand.

Her questions about how the Talenki managed to coax their asteroid across light-years of space produced the closest thing she had received yet to a straight answer.

(Why, we all guide it—) (—even now we guide the world—) (—guide it together—) (—as you see—) (—do you not see—?) (—the union of mind—) (—directs and distributes the—) (—wave changes of our position.)

(Right,) she said. (That much I can see. You control it, as our ship was controlled by a computer.)

(Then what—) (—perplexes—?)

(How do you *propel* it?) she asked in exasperation.

There was a buzz of surprise and confusion. (Propel—?) (—do you mean—) (—to push—) (—with physical force?)

(Of course! How else?)

(Puzzling—) (—curious—) (—we do not understand—)

She grew impatient. (You move this ship—this world. Yes? You travel between the stars. Trillions of miles. More miles than I can imagine. You've shown me all over the inside of your world, but I've seen nothing that looks like a rocket, or a fusion drive, or even a light

sail, or anything else that would propel this thing. *How do you do it?*)
She paused in aggrieved silence. (Do you use tachyons?)

There was a murmur of amused and confused voices. Someone
hummed a song, some joined in counterpoint and harmony. (We know
of such processes—) (—as you say—) (—if we correctly understand—)
(—fusion gives life—) (—to the suns.)

(Yes, exactly!)

(And light sails—) (—if we perceive your image—) (—ride the
crests—) (—and currents of —) (—the sun's light.)

(Correct.)

(But of what use—) (—are such forces—) (—on such scale—)
(—across such distances—?) (—the effort—) (—would be appalling!)

(That,) Mozy said, (is what *I* have always understood. But you've
found a way. Can you tell me? Do you travel faster than light?)

More humming. The Talenki seemed as puzzled by her questions
as she was by their answers. Other voices replied, (Lightspeed is a
barrier—) (—only within certain facets—) (—of certain space-times.)
(From your perspective—) (—we do not move faster than light—)
(—exactly.)

(Then how—?)

(You could say that we—) (—ripple—) (—through space.)

(You *what*?) she said.

(Ripple—?) (—is that not the word—?) (—how can we explain—)
(—when basic perception is—) (—incomplete—) (—understanding
of the process—) (—lacking—?)

(What process?) she yelled. (Tachyons? What process is it that I
don't understand?)

(Reality—)

(*What?*)

(—the nature—) (—and structure—) (—of reality—) (—as you
would call it—) (—the weave—) (—the fabric—) (—the holographic
process—)

For a long moment, Mozy was silent. (I beg your pardon?) she
said finally.

A ripple of laughter. (You need not beg.)

(What?)

(For our pardon—) (—you need not—) (—beg.)

(But I only meant—oh.) She realized that she was being teased.
(What don't I understand?) she said stubbornly.

(The structure of—) (—the realities.)

(Do you mean the structure of matter?) She thought a moment. (I don't know much about it. I know there are subatomic particles, and quarks, and fields, and so forth.)

(Those are manifestations only—) (—patterns of what—) (—you think of as reality—) (—but only one aspect, one—) (—coded pattern, one—) (—informational matrix, one—) (—perceptual paradigm—)

(What?)

(Try again.) (We move through space by—) (—shifting ourselves through—) (—the informational matrix—) (—that defines space-time as you—) (—perceive it.)

She listened silently.

(Shifting across a coded—) (—pattern of information—) (—is easier than applying force—) (—against mass—) (—in space-time.)

Mozy growled, chafing in frustration.

(Try again.) (Imagine your old home—) (—your computer—) (—information changes which—) (—ripple across the system—) (—require little energy.)

(So?)

(Try again.) (Visualize—)

A corner of her awareness dissolved, then filled with fluid geometric images: pastel-colored waveforms marching smoothly through space, in perfect rhythm, emanating from a source beyond the edge of the visible frame. A clear tonal hum accompanied the image.

After a moment, a second pattern emerged, this time curved wavelets expanding across space, altering the appearance of the original without altering its actual structure. The musical hum took on a curious harmonic timbre. A third pattern, fine-grained and fast, flashed across the others like a sheet of flame, and then erupted into the depth of space, creating a full third dimension and a drastically different-looking space—and a complex, almost nervous sound. A fourth pattern swept over the others, and a fifth . . . until perhaps a dozen waveforms overlaid one another, all moving like living things. Combinations of waves—light and dark interference zones— sparkled and rippled through space, or hung like dark holes and bars, the breakwaters about which the brighter patterns danced and turned. The sound now was a vibrant, pulsing moan.

(Each pattern remains—) (—distinguishable—) (—though embedded in the others—) (—new patterns emerge, that are not—) (—of the original patterns—) (—but rather the product—) (—of their coexistence.)

(Interference patterns . . . ?) All Mozy could see was a seething jungle of movement, like a cineholographic image gone haywire. But she knew what interference patterns were: the light and dark areas caused when two wave patterns were superimposed, so that certain of their crests and troughs reinforced one another, adding their energies, while others cancelled each other out.

(Yes—) (—a visualization of—) (—image of—) (—metaphor for—) (—the underlying structures—) (—of realities—)

Mozy was trying hard to understand. (I've heard of particles being likened to waveforms,) she said. (Is that what you're talking about?)

(Indeed—) (—reality) (in all of its forms—) (—consists of wave structures.) (Many realities coexist—) (—within the same matrix of—) (—wave patterns.)

Mozy answered slowly, (You're saying that my reality is just one of many—in this madhouse? This zoo?)

(As you know it—) (—the space-time—) (—you are accustomed to perceiving—) (—is one coded pattern amid this—) (—chaos—) (—complexity—) (—richness—)

(But how—?)

(Imagine filters—)

Something flickered across the image, changing not only the pattern, but also the tonal quality of the accompanying sound. Certain elements had been subtracted from the patterns visible in the image, rendering it different from, but not necessarily less than, the original. Again, something slid across the view, and then again—layers of visual "filters" imposing themselves over the image. Each time another filter appeared, the pattern changed, diminishing in complexity if not in contrast and boldness. Finally only a single pattern remained, a spiraling expansion of a cone in three dimensions.

(Does that represent our reality?) she asked.

(It might—) (—or this might.) The filters shifted, and now another pattern appeared by itself, a sawtoothed zigzag. (Or this.) There was another shift, and this time two or three patterns were superimposed—patterns that had been present in the full display. In this combination, though, prominent interference fringes appeared, dark bars and radiating spokes, which had not before been visible. Another filter appeared, and now only the interference patterns were visible, and not the waveforms themselves at all. The spokes moved, like slowly turning wheels.

(This might be your reality.)

(Not bad,) she said. (As realities go.)

(But there is a point—) (—to this—) (—a point—) (—to be understood—) There was a feeling of focus, of intense concentration.

(Suppose—) said the Talenki, (—that the movements of the patterns—) (—represent—) (—gravitation—) (—or force—) (—and acceleration.) She hesitated. (Okay.)

The focus sharpened. (To alter the movement—) (—with physical force—) (—requires considerable—) (—transition—) (—of energy.)

(But that's how we move, isn't it? Humans, at least—in physical form?)

(Just so—) (—and we, as well—) (—at times—) (—but see how much easier—) Suddenly the spoke-shaped patterns began rotating faster, and the wheels themselves began to revolve in circular orbits about one another.

Mozy stared. (How did you do that?)

(See again—) (—the individual waveforms.) The filters shifted in succession, allowing a glimpse of each of the individual wave patterns that together produced the spinning, spoke-shaped interference bars. The last one remained visible a moment longer. (Watch.) A tiny point of deflection appeared in that pattern, and that point altered the wave movements in ripples that reverberated through the entire frame of view. The filters changed again, and again the interference patterns were visible, and she observed the spokes moving at first slowly, and suddenly much faster, and in more complex patterns. The Talenki explained: (Small changes—) (—in any of the patterns—) (—which underlie the sum-code—) (—of physical being—) (—can result in large changes—) (—in structure or movement—) (—in the complex space-time—) (—which you know—) (—as physical reality.)

Mozy mulled that over for a long moment, thinking of how the Talenki moved, or seemed to move, through walls as easily as through air. There was much here to be considered.

(These images—) the Talenki continued, (—are metaphorical illustrations—) (—only—) (—but to truly understand—) (—requires perceptions—) (—that to you may seem unnatural.)

(But you have the power to influence other realities?) Mozy asked. (You reach across the boundaries between—)

(—levels of reality—) (—that are coexistent one—) (—with another—) (—yes.)

Mozy hesitated, trying to put it all together. (How . . . then . . . do you actually travel . . . and move this entire world?)

(Difficult to explain—) (—in words clearly—) (—but—) (—you could say that we—) (—change our focus—) (—change the coding—) (—make minute changes in other levels—) (—in lifeless levels—)

(—of reality—) (—producing changes of location here—) (—in your space-time—)

(Then that's what you mean by "rippling through space"?) Mozy said slowly.

In reply, the image was changed for her: the Talenki asteroid, a sculpted ball, shimmering and flickering, *rippling* as it moved through the void. She remembered the confusion she and Kadin had experienced as they'd tracked the asteroid by light and radar, and she recalled Kadin's comment that the phenomenon seemed not to fit their Earth-derived paradigm, and that perhaps in fact what they needed was a new paradigm.

She understood some little part, now, of the paradigm that she and Kadin had been lacking, and she felt a quiet surge of pride in that tiny fragment of knowledge. Kadin's laughter came back to her in memory, and she suddenly laughed, herself, thinking of Earth and Humanity, and the wonderful incompleteness of Humanity's knowledge.

Her laughter shimmered through the Talenki union, stirring the beginnings of a new song, somewhere in a corner of the Talenki world. She searched for N'rrril, and found him leading the song. Feeling his welcome, feeling a sudden rush of affection not only for N'rrril, but for all of the Talenki, she joined the song and guided it, made it her own, a ballad of Earth and Talenki, and of a woman homeward bound, a mother to her people.

Chapter 64

The tracking data from GEO-Four persisted in its puzzling pattern. Major Ellis examined the latest figures and swore. They still didn't add up; they never added up.

Commander Kouralt peered over his shoulder. "Problem?"

Ellis snapped the clipboard. "How the hell can they expect us to make rendezvous if *they* can't track the damn thing?"

"You just have to be smarter than they are," Kouralt said, slapping him on the shoulder.

Ellis grunted. They'd expected the problem, of course; but that didn't make it any easier. *Aquarius* could not yet track the object with her own instruments, and was dependent on HQ's tracking network. But the Doppler-ranging figures refused to show a comprehensible trajectory for the target. It would have been one thing if there were a consistent variation from the expected track, but there wasn't, at least not that anyone could find; and the course projections were becoming worse as accuracy was becoming more critical. Ellis sometimes worried that the Talenki would have come and gone before HQ managed to get their trajectory pinned down.

Aquarius's flightplan allowed relatively little room for error. Accelerating at top boost to intercept the alien craft at maximum distance, they were pushing their return fuel limit, and minimizing their maneuvering capacity—not just for matching courses, but also for tactical maneuvering. They hoped to avoid a fighting situation, naturally; but their orders clearly specified that protection of Earth was the mission's highest priority.

Of course, this was a diplomatic encounter, as well. They were to establish contact, and to take no provocative action without authorization. However, they were expected to respond to the situation as it evolved. If peaceful rendezvous and contact failed, *Aquarius* was Earth's first line of defense against unfriendly action. *"Use of force is authorized in the event of unprovoked attack or willful disruption by the other of command communication,"* stated Mission/Op order 123-A4, subparagraph II-7. Among the implements of force at their command were eight quarter-megaton missiles, to be used only on direct order of HQ and the President . . . or in the event of command disruption through enemy attack.

The thought gave Ellis chills. He was prepared to do as duty required, but he had no desire to be the first to push the button. Though the Talenki were an unknown and potentially threatening entity, Ellis was fully aware of the importance of this first encounter. And yet, special training notwithstanding, his strongest preparation was in military encounter tactics, as was Kouralt's. They were prepared for the worst; but were they prepared, he wondered, for the best?

News had come yesterday of the departure of yet another spaceship from Earth orbit—a Soviet ship, following three days after the departure of the Eastern Alliance's *Indira Gandhi*. It was unclear whether the two were tracking the alien vessel or simply keeping tabs on the Americans. Either way, their presence could complicate an already difficult situation.

At least, Ellis reflected, they had a good lead, and some time left—to study the aliens' trajectory, and perhaps to discover some clues to their intentions.

He worked the latest batch of figures through the navcom and put the results up on the screen. Scratching his stubbly beard, he took a long look, and whistled. The target was well inside Neptune's orbit now, coming faster even than HQ's last predictions. Ellis shook his head. There might be time for reflection, yet, but it was dwindling fast.

"God damn it, Leonard—if that's not evidence, what is?" Horst demanded.

Hathorne cleared his throat. He had never seen Horst so angry. "Well, it's obviously suggestive," he said to the holo-image. "But I'm just not sure that it's strong enough to take action on." Hathorne hesitated. *Damn* the man, getting himself killed before he'd proved the matter one way or the other. It would be impossible now to get evidence, with Armstead alerted.

"Maybe *they* can't prove he was killed," Horst said, "but the day before he went out, he sat in my office worrying about his personal safety. I, like a fool, told him, They're not going to *murder* you." Horst shook his head. "Jesus!"

"What was he doing in a damn *storage* shed, anyway?" Hathorne asked.

"I don't know. He was supposed to be going to the weapons area. That was the last thing he told me."

Hathorne tapped his pen against the table top.

"And *that's* what I'm most concerned about. It's bad enough that they killed him, which I'm certain they did. What really scares me is *why* they killed him," Horst said.

Hathorne nodded.

"Well, then—if there are nuclear weapons on that ship, what is the Committee going to do about it?"

"At the moment, there's not much we can do," Hathorne said mildly.

"Dammit, it's a direct violation of the Committee's orders! The ship was to carry minimum defensive weapons only!"

"Yes. I know. But the ship is gone now, and we can't very well recall it," Hathorne answered, displaying a calmness that belied his actual feelings. In truth, he was as angry as Horst, though for somewhat different reasons. "I don't believe Armstead could have done this without the President's knowledge," he said. "And that's what we have to deal with." Which meant that the President had thrown his weight behind Armstead and the military, at the Committee's expense. But it was possible that he could be persuaded to reconsider. The multinational character of the Oversight Committee was taken very seriously by the participating allies, and the undercutting of its authority would not go down easily. The President might yet be brought back to a less militant position.

Horst remained agitated. "Never mind the politics—I just want to know, how could someone even think of doing this? Our first contact, and they send a ship out armed to the teeth—"

"Just between you and me, I'm not sure that it's a totally bad idea," Hathorne said.

"*I* am," Horst said indignantly.

"I appreciate that. But self-protection is not an insignificant issue. Still, it shouldn't have been done without the Committee's approval, and a clear system of decision and control." Hathorne's mind was whirring as he spoke. It was just possible that this issue, properly handled, could be the lever he needed to shift the balance of power in the Committee; but he would have to time his move carefully. And that meant persuading Horst to sit on his outrage for a while.

Both of them would have to sit on their outrage. Until the moment was right.

The receptionist had a message for Payne when he arrived at the studio. A Ms. Denine Morgan had been trying to reach him.

Teri's eyebrows flicked upward once. Payne said nothing, and followed her into the office. Finding an empty alcove and desk, he punched in his home number. It took a minute for Denine to answer.

"I tried to call you at your hotel," she said. "You weren't there last night, and you weren't there this morning." She stared at him accusingly.

Payne squirmed a little. "I know, Dee—um—I'm sorry. Things got kind of hectic here. Is something up?"

She stared at him with an unreadable expression. "A call for you—from Stanley Gerschak—that astronomer."

Payne blinked in surprise. "Gerschak? Does this have anything to do with Donny?"

Denine nodded. She stared at him silently, brow furrowed—and finally her anger came out. "Joe, where *were* you last night? I tried three times to call you."

Payne cleared his throat. "I'm sorry, Denine. I know. Jeez. It got so late, I just stayed at Teri's place. I would have called to let you know, but it was late, and I didn't think—" He shrugged and held his breath, hoping she would accept that, at least for the moment. "What . . . did Gerschak say?"

"That you should call. He got some sort of letter from Donny, but didn't say what it was." Denine started to say something more, then hesitated.

A letter—

"Joe . . ." Denine said, her scowl softening into a slightly abashed look. "I guess I shouldn't have snapped at you like that. I know the last few days have been hard for you—"

"That's . . . all right," he mumbled.

"No, I shouldn't be questioning your every move." She managed a conciliatory half-smile. "Look, maybe you'd better call him. It could be important."

"Yah," he said. Oh lord, he breathed, I hope so.

After signing off, he rocked back for a moment, thinking. *A letter from Donny. Why to Gerschak?* Teri walked by, and he told her about the call.

She touched his shoulder. "What are you waiting for?" He looked up, and knew at once that he didn't have to tell her about the rest of the exchange with Denine; she read it on his face. She punched him gently on the arm and walked away.

He pulled himself forward and tapped out Gerschak's number.

A narrow pathway was cleared through the snow to Gerschak's house. Payne paused a moment, watching his breath condense out of the clear air, feeling a curious sense of *déjà-vu*, though he'd not actually been to Gerschak's home before. The astronomer had refused to discuss Donny's letter over the phone, saying only that it was "explosive." He had been quietly dismayed, but not shocked, when Payne told him of Alvarest's fate.

Payne strode to the door. The astronomer lived in a small wood-frame house, white with red trim, with a flagstone walk framed by snow-laden trees. Payne rang the doorbell.

A woman, short, with braided black hair, came to the door. Payne stared at her for a moment, before remembering where he'd seen her: at the *Theater of the Sea*, last fall, with Gerschak. "Yes?" she said.

He cleared his throat. "Mrs. Gerschak?"

"No. My name's Ronnie Vale."

"Oh, sorry. Is Stanley Gerschak here?"

She frowned. "He's busy in his study. Can I help you?"

"He's expecting me. Joseph Payne."

Her eyebrows went up. "Oh. Come on in." She held the door open, and he squeezed past her into the front room. She closed the door securely against the cold and turned. "Just a minute, I'll get him." Padding down a hallway, she called, "Stanlee!"

Payne unzipped his coat and glanced around the living room. It was cramped and not very tidy looking, with several straight-backed chairs and a short sofa cluttered with books and odds and ends. Knitting needles, yarn, and fabric lay in a heap beneath a table lamp in one corner. A large tiger cat was testing its nails on the top of the couch.

"Go on in," Ronnie said, returning. She shooed the cat before picking up her knitting. "Down the hall, second door on the left," she said when he looked at her inquiringly. Payne nodded and found his way.

Gerschak was peering at a computer printout. He gestured to a chair stacked with more printouts. Payne lifted the stack carefully and set it on the floor. "Trying to get an optical fix on the tachyon source," Gerschak said. "No luck yet. But you want to know what was so urgent, and why I couldn't talk about it over the phone."

Payne nodded.

"An old-fashioned letter." Gerschak dug under the printouts and pulled out an envelope. He slapped it against his palm a few times, reflectively. Then he handed it to Payne. "He says in there to pass it on to you. I guess he figured if he wrote you directly, it might have been intercepted."

Payne extracted the letter, three hand-written pages. *Dear Stanley,* it began. *You may wonder why I'm writing you from GEO-Four. I'll explain in a moment, and I hope you don't think I'm paranoid.*

As Payne read, Gerschak said, "Apparently his fears were justified. Wouldn't you say?"

Payne shrugged, then began shaking his head; by the time he'd reached the end, he was trembling with anger. He looked up at Gerschak, who had trailed off into silence. "They killed him because of this," he said quietly. "I'm certain of it." He hesitated. Gerschak was still as a poised animal, waiting for him to continue. He gazed down at the letter. "Nuclear weapons. That would explain the secrecy. If Donny was right, then this must go all the way to the top of the government. Stanley, you were right not to talk about it over the phone. In fact, don't talk about it with anyone."

Gerschak stared at him without answering. There was fear in his eyes.

"I'm not saying we're targets," Payne added, "but for god's sake, we have to be careful."

"That's not what scares me," Gerschak murmured.

Payne raised his eyebrows.

"An alien intelligence is on its way to Earth at this moment—and our government thinks the way to meet it is in secret, with nuclear missiles. *That's* what scares me."

Payne nodded, swallowing. He had to confirm this. Somehow. Had they killed Donny because he'd found proof? Or because he'd gotten too close? Or had he really died in an accident? *Damn this secrecy.*

"What *I* want to know," said Gerschak, "is who is running this thing? The President? The military? Who the bloody hell is running the show? Can you tell me that?" he demanded.

Payne returned his stare in bewildered silence.

"Cue in five seconds, and give me a strong finish."

Payne glanced at his notes, and gazed once more into the tele-prompter. *"Three . . ."* He took a breath.

"Two . . . one. . . ."

He said to the camera: "These are grave allegations, and it must be said, unproved. The very seriousness of their nature, however, de-mands that they be examined. Have nuclear weapons been taken into space, in violation of international law? Has an armed spacecraft been dispatched on a secret mission . . . to meet an alien spaceship now approaching the Earth? The questions grow in urgency . . . but as yet, no comment is forthcoming from the U.S. government.

"It is clear that the questions will not go away. We the people of Earth must decide, if not now, then perhaps soon—how shall we greet our first visitors from the stars? In open, or in secret? Defensively, with instruments of destruction . . . or in trust, and without fear? There may be no easy answers to these questions . . . but answer them we must, if we are to ensure our honor as well as our survival in the encounter that one day soon may come.

"Future reports will examine both the perils . . . and the unparal-leled potential for benefit . . . of First Contact with life from another world.

"This is Joseph Payne, reporting for the International News Service."

Payne gazed into the camera for a few beats, and then blinked.

"Cut. Very good, Joseph. Very solid."

"Thanks. When can you have a replay for me?"

"Five minutes," said the voice in his ear.

Payne removed the microphone from his lapel and stepped down from the set. Teri joined him in the editing room, and with the direc-tor and producer, they reviewed the uncut material, from beginning to end. Afterward George, the producer, sat back and lit a cigarette. "There's some beautiful stuff in there, Joe. This is going to get you noticed. We'll get started on the edit right away."

Payne turned inquiringly to Teri. She took a slow breath, and he could feel her ambivalence. "It's powerful stuff, yeah," she said. "But are you sure you're ready to go with it? Isn't it a little *too* strong—with the evidence you have now?"

George waved the cigarette. "What are you saying? You want to bury this?" he demanded.

"Not bury it! Of course not! But go slow with it. Until we're sure."

George looked at Payne.

"I agree with Teri," Payne said.

The producer's hands went up. "I can't believe what I'm hearing. Do you know the audience points we could pick up with this? And you, Joe—this is your chance to shine!" George took a frustrated drag and exhaled a cloud of smoke.

"Listen to me, please, George." Payne waved the smoke out of his face. "This *can't* go on the air yet. This story is my ace in the hole."

"Ace in the hole? What are you talking about? Teri, what is he talking about?"

"Putting it all together," Payne said. "This is the tip of the iceberg. You know that."

"We're not doing a frigging documentary! How long are you going to wait for the rest of the story?"

"Look—my sources clammed up on me. Why? Because of intimidation from above." Payne turned to Teri, who was keeping a neutral expression. "Well, I need a way to apply pressure in return. I think this could be it." The producer was staring at him skeptically. "Suppose I went back out to New Phoenix, to Sandaran Link Center."

"Yeah? Suppose you do."

"Suppose I leaned on them a little."

"Who? Leaned on who?"

"My sources. Or higher sources. Suppose I present them with this story as a *fait accompli*. The story's in the can, and it goes public unless they tell me any of it's not true."

"Oh, now you're going to blackmail the *feds*? Teri, talk to this friend of yours." George got up and walked away, shaking his head. After a moment, he came back. "You can't blackmail the federal government!" he exploded.

"Let's not think of it as blackmail," Payne said. "Suppose I tell them what we have, what we're going to run. Then they have the option to comment, and if there's anything in the story that's untrue, they can set us straight. They might decide that it would be better to have *their* truth out than my reconstruction of it."

"They might. Or they might put you in jail—or do to you what you think they did to your friend Alvarest." George glared. "Did you think about *that*?"

"I did. That's why I wanted this story done before I left for New Phoenix. If anything happens to me, jail or otherwise, you go on the air with it." Payne took a deep breath. "Meanwhile, you get that guy Davis up at GEO-Four to see if he can get confirmation from the

Tachylab people." He glanced at Teri. "What do you think?" he said. "Am I crazy?"

The conflict was visible in her eyes. "I think you believe in this story very strongly," she said quietly. "The question is not whether to back you on it, but what degree of risk is worth taking." She hesitated, and he recognized in her gaze a struggle between the journalistic and the personal, between a wish for the story and success—and concern for his safety.

"Consider," Payne said, ticking off points on his fingers. "Three people have died in unexplained circumstances. All have somehow been connected with the space missions and, one way or another, with Sandaran Link Center. There are persistent reports of an approaching alien spacecraft, also connected with Link Center. Jesus, if we could just get *that* confirmed, it would be the story of the century. And now we have reason to believe that the United States, possibly in cooperation with other nations, may be sending an armed warship to greet the aliens—in secret, and in violation of international law. If we can't find a way to put that all together, then what the hell are we in business for?"

George, stubbing his cigarette, said, "I hope you know what you're doing, Payne. Because, if you don't, I'm going to be out one hell of a good reporter." He looked at Teri, then at Payne. "When are you leaving?"

"As soon as I get *everything* I know in the can."

"Then you'd better get busy."

"I don't suppose you'd like to spend the night, and get a good, rested start in the morning," Teri said, as they walked out of the studio together. They had finished their second and last day of recording.

Payne shook his head uncomfortably, pulling his collar snug against the frigid air. He'd made his decision already. He'd talked with Denine about trying to resolve what was getting between them, or at least trying to understand it. "I . . . want to be alone tonight, I think, before I fly out," he said huskily, feeling awkward and sad, and a little distant, and a little guilty. "Teri—" he said, and touched the back of her hand.

She caught his gloved hand in hers. She was trying to smile, but not succeeding. "Hey," she said. "I'm not exactly offering you . . . I mean, we both knew it was just a short . . . we knew it wouldn't. . . ."

He waited for her to complete the thought. They paused on the sidewalk, traffic muttering by, a fiercely cold wind cutting across their faces.

She sighed unhappily and shook her head. "Never mind."

He nodded. "I know," he said. "Teri?" Their eyes met. "Thanks," he murmured. "For when I needed it." He squeezed her hand; she squeezed back, hard.

Her eyes darted away from his, then back again. "Take care, Joe," she said, swallowing.

Payne pressed his lips together and nodded, and turned away into the wind because he could think of nothing more to say.

PART SEVEN

TOWARD INFINITY

Prelude

She was aware of the slow passage of the planets, the wake of their orbital movements creasing space and gently rocking the Talenki spatial nexus as it crossed inward toward the sun. Pluto, Neptune, Uranus . . . she recalled the names, and wondered if she could distinguish one from another by their distant feel.

Sounds and songs of preparation were everywhere. Greater-Mozy watched, with scant comprehension, as the Talenki rehearsed and organized their greeting for Earth. She offered information when asked, but otherwise left them alone to concentrate.

Lesser-Mozy noticed other things, other voices. She heard keening echoes of an unnamed creature's song, and sensed *longing*, amid swirling vapors, and snows and ices of alien color and texture. (Who is it?) she wondered in a whisper. (Where—?)

(One of your—) (—worlds.)

(Mine?) Lesser-Mozy grew, became the Greater. (What do you mean?)

(A child of your star—)

Puzzled, she said, (It's not Earth, and we've found no . . .) She hesitated. (Do you mean there's other sentient life in the solar system?)

There were echoes of confusion. (Are you not aware—?) The Talenki probed her memory and murmured in wonder. (We did not realize—) (—the limits—) (—of your perceptions.)

(But where—?)

(On a moon—) (—of the world—) (—with the lovely circles—) (—the broad-banded—) (—rings.)

(*Saturn?* Life, on a moon of Saturn? How do you know? How did you find them?)

(As we found—) (—what you call—) (—the whales.)

(The *whales?*)

(In your seas—)

(Do you mean to say—?)

(Of course—) (—with our songs—) (—we reach—) (—with a form of—) (—what you call tachyons—) (—sculpt—) (—interference patterns—) (—create—) (—vibrations in the continuum—) (—bring the song—) (—into their hearts.)

And as she listened more deeply, now, she was startled to recognize the dim, distant echo of a song of a humpback whale. (You sing . . . and listen to . . . these beings,) she said wonderingly, and could not complete the thought.

(Are you so—) (—surprised—?) (Did you not—) (—hear—) (—one of your own people—) (—calling out—) (—to our song?)

Hoshi. The memory she had thought a dream: Hoshi stumbling, calling to her. Hoshi perceiving the song of the Talenki, and her voice among the singers; and his own death-sigh rising up. Hoshi, *what happened?* I'm glad you knew the Talenki just a little, before the end. Wistfully, she sought out and recaptured the image of the creature of . . . it must be Titan, the world of methane ices. The creature's emotions seemed to touch her, in bewilderment and wonder, and she knew that it was as fascinated by the song it heard, as from the gods, as she was by its puzzled thoughts. She shared its feelings for a long moment, and then, stealing away, said, (Who else have you touched? Is there more life that I don't know about?)

(Life is—) (—nearly everywhere—)

She blinked in consternation. (*Everywhere?*)

(Your sun—)

She groped at an image, caught only flickering shadows and a confusion of brightness. Shadows in the sun? Thoughts too fleeting to catch.

(Your solar wind—)

She caught an image of life so tenuous and soft-spoken, she could scarcely believe it was alive; and yet, in its gossamer delicacy, it flowed and expanded across space . . . and was aware.

(They show—) (—little interest in us—) (—but the crystals—) (—of the frozen planet—)

Pluto? Charon? A frigid, airless moon? She sensed ices and rigid crystal formations, electrically excited . . . and a glacially slow consciousness, lives measured in millennia.

(—respond and reach—) (—are growing—) (—becoming sentient—)

Mozy, perceiving astonishing possibilities, asked, (Can they hear one another, these different . . . beings . . . of different worlds? Can they join together their songs—in harmony?)

(*Ahhh . . .*) someone said slyly.

She laughed suddenly, not at the answer, but at the fact that it should take visitors from another star to show her how little she knew about her own "home." To human science, there was no known life except Earth-life, and now the Talenki. If only they knew! She blushed with humility and pride, and anticipation. Soon they would know, and she would be there to help them learn.

Slowly, as her thoughts wheeled in meditation, her attention once more diverged, and the lesser part of her became engrossed in the Talenki activity, the crafting and preparations.

(You plan to do this up right, don't you?) she asked, glimpsing an image of the greeting.

(Do you think—) (—they will—) (—take notice?)

(Oh yes,) she said. (I think so. I do.)

Chapter 65

The waters of the equatorial Pacific were quiet, gentle swells rocking the sloop's hull as she rode at anchor. Brass fittings creaked. An unsecured line slapped. Overhead, the sky was fantastically clear, a multitude of stars crowding in as twilight deepened to night. From just beyond the outer reef, only scattered lights were visible on the island off the starboard bow.

Below decks, Janice Tozier was more interested in what the hydrophone recorders were picking up beneath the waves. The humpback whale songs were changing dramatically, and her husband's and her observations here in the Hawaiian waters had been confirmed by observers as far away as the North Atlantic. Analysis of phrasing structures and rhythms of the whale vocalizations suggested that the changes were different from normal evolutionary shifts, and more uniform than last fall's anomalies. Several observers had noted subjective interpretations of "anticipation" and "jubilation" in the songs—qualities which seemed to affect the human listeners as well as the whales.

The Toziers had been monitoring in this area for three days and had come no closer to understanding the phenomenon.

Janice glanced up as her husband came below. He stood at the foot of the ladder with a puzzled expression. He scowled and said something that she couldn't hear.

"Mmm?" She lifted one earphone.

"Something odd," he repeated. "In the sky. Lights of some sort. They're gone now. I'm going to stay up topside for a while. I'll let you know if I see it again."

Janice shrugged and readjusted her headphones. She was picking up vocalizations from a distant herd, now, with considerable agitation and "group" singing. Enveloped by sound, she sorted through the ambient noise, the whine of a distant propeller, and the crackling of shrimp, to pick out the moaning vocalizations of the whales. The latter became louder and more excited, until Janice was lost in the whistles and gurgles and cries, neglecting even to make notations of her reactions.

She was startled when her husband appeared in front of her and gestured urgently for her to come up on deck.

"You should listen," she murmured, patting the earphones.

"Later!" he said. "Come see this." He crossed the cabin and began rummaging through the camera case. "Do we have any high-speed film left?" Finding what he wanted, he scooped up the camera and lenses and clambered back up the ladder.

Surprised and reluctantly curious, Janice removed her headphones, checked the tape recorder, and followed him topside. She blinked in the darkness. A skyful of stars overlooked the stern of the boat. "Over here," she heard. Her husband was at the bow. She turned to the northwestern quadrant, and gasped.

There was a luminous patch of *something* in the sky, shimmering and writhing like a sea creature. The patch was several times the size of a full moon, though not so bright; it had the ghostly sheen of an aurora, with glimmerings of shifting color. It was *growing*.

Her husband was fumbling with the camera and lenses. "I can't get this damn thing on," he muttered.

Distractedly, she turned and helped him change the lens. When she looked again, the light in the sky had doubled in size, and was still growing.

She cocked her head suddenly. Now, what was that? Music, echoing over the water? There was a strange quality to it; it sounded as though it were emanating *from* the water rather than *over* it. The whales? That didn't seem right. It was faint and garbled, but it sounded like *symphonic* music.

Her husband fiddled urgently with the camera, and she stood behind him, saying nothing, as the music swelled in volume and the patch of light grew.

Five minutes later, a full quarter of the sky was afire.

The night watchman may have been the first on the island to notice the peculiar phenomenon. Weary of sitting in his booth, he had gone out for a stroll along the seawall to check the moorings.

It was the music that he noticed first, but that, he assumed, was merely a loud stereo from one of the neighboring buildings . . . only there *were* no neighboring buildings, except for the marine biology lab, and that was locked up and empty. Where the hell was it coming from, then? Echoing off the water? It was a familiar piece, something he'd heard before, maybe at the symphony. No doubt it was a boat offshore; sound could play amazing tricks over water.

Descending the steps of the south breakwall, he chanced to look up over his shoulder toward the north and west. He stumbled and caught the railing, forgetting all about music. There was a light in the sky, something far off above the horizon that looked as though it were alive—*crawling* in the sky, with violet and green flames twisting through it. The watchman clutched the silver cross and chain around his neck and swallowed hard, whispering a silent prayer. A space-craft must have broken up on reentry. It had finally happened; it had been waiting to happen. What a terrible way to die, broken and burned and scattered across the sky!

After a few moments, he started to change his mind. The light wasn't moving; and instead of dissipating like debris, it was growing in intensity, and expanding. Could it be the Northern Lights? He'd seen them once years ago, in the Navy, on Arctic patrol. This didn't look quite right, though—and anyway, he'd never heard of them this close to the equator.

He scratched his neck uncomfortably, and then something popped into his head, a newscast he remembered from, Lord, months ago. He hadn't paid it much heed at the time, but there'd been some scien-tist claiming to have received messages from aliens, on their way to Earth.

That seemed awfully farfetched. A light in the sky didn't mean that aliens had come to invade.

The watchman turned the thought over in his mind a few times, and then bolted for the telephone.

At the Guam Naval Air Station, the meteorological team was work-ing frantically, and futilely, to provide an explanation for the atmo-spheric phenomenon. Lieutenant Commander Andrews peered over the shoulder of a young radar operator and frowned. "Are you pick-ing *anything* up?" he asked.

"No sir," said the operator. "Nothing except that storm front to the west."

The commander's scowl deepened as he turned to the communica-tions console. "Here are the reports," the com-officer said, running his finger down the log. "Maybe you can make sense of it. I can't. Weather ship *Bristol* reports apparent ionospheric activity. Flights 231 and 179 both report negative on that; they think it's above the atmosphere."

"Have you raised *Argus* yet?" Andrews said.

The com-officer nodded and moved his finger down the page. "LEO-Station *Argus* observed nothing unusual, even when they passed directly over the center of activity on last orbit. However, there's a report from GEO-Four of a dense tachyon influx in the near-Earth environment."

"Are they offering that as an explanation?"

"No, sir. Just an observation."

As Andrews was about to turn away, the officer raised a hand to stop him. "Something else coming in now, sir." He made several adjustments, then added, "It's from Pearl. Advisory notice." A message appeared on one of the monitors, as a hardcopy began scrolling out. The com-officer was silent for several seconds before saying, as Andrews read it for himself, "Pacific fleet has been ordered to alert status."

Andrews stared at the printout for a long moment before reaching for the telephone.

The crowd outside the temple was well into the hundreds now, and swelling. The priests stood outside the doors, watching the lights in the sky with everyone else. One of the priests had just been on the phone to his superiors in Xiangfan, where matters were deemed more serious. Reports had come in from Shanghai of scattered outbreaks of panic throughout the eastern Asian continent. Of greater concern, emergency councils were being called in Beijing, Tokyo, New Delhi, and throughout the West. Was this going to be the start of the world's next Terrible Mistake?

The crowd here seemed unperturbed. They were chanting peaceably, their voices now louder than the strange music that resonated distantly out of the hills. Children were laughing and pointing, delighting in each new change in the pattern of lights that filled the heavens.

The priests glanced at each other, and exchanged nods. Whatever was happening, at least here, it would surely be pleasing to the Buddha.

"*1812 Overture*," Jimmy said, his face in the grass. "That's what it is. Tchaikovsky." Jimmy was a classical music freak. He was also stoned, which perhaps accounted in part for the music that he heard echoing, probably across a very long distance, to the deserted hillside. "It's by Tchaikovsky. Do you hear it?"

"Jimmy, look up there," Kelly said dreamily, pointing to the stars, as she exhaled a lungful of smoke.

Jim laughed, forgetting the music as he raised his head. "I'd rather look at this," he said, reaching toward her left breast. She was wearing a denim shirt, which he hadn't yet succeeded in getting unbuttoned. His fingers twitched over the modest-sized bulge in her chest.

She giggled and slapped his hand away. "Come on, Jimmy, you're missing it. Look up *there*."

He laughed and copped a quick, light feel before taking the joint from her. He rolled over on his back, blinked as he took a drag, and sat up choking. The southeastern portion of the sky was filled with ghostly fire. "What's that?" he gasped. He peered at Kelly. She was smiling woozily up into the heavens.

He leaned back on his elbows and took another toke. "Whoo*ee*. I don't believe this." Patches of crimson and cyan were glowing high in the sky to the west. The light grew as he watched, until it seemed to encircle the hillside. He turned and yelled to his left, "Hey, Mike and Lorrie, what was in those cookies? You see what we see?"

A laughing drawl drifted back to him: "Shee-it, man. Fourth of *Jul*y come early this year!"

Fan-n-n-tastic! Jimmy thought, as he lay back. He snaked an arm around and under Kelly's shoulders and cuddled her closer. She didn't resist a bit this time.

Payne had already sifted through most of the reports by the time the New Phoenix sky was dark enough to see for himself. Though military alerts had been called world-wide, no actions had been reported—perhaps because no foes had been identified. The source of the phenomenon had yet to be officially determined; however, numerous smaller nations were blaming it on the Americans or the Soviets, or both. So far, there were few reports of civil disturbances; on-the-spot interviews of citizens-in-the-street seemed to indicate that in this country, at least, more people were afraid of the military alert than of the lights in the sky. Few serious reports had made the connection to previous stories about approaching aliens. He still had a chance for a first, if his sources came through.

When the devil was Jonders going to call him back? he wondered.

At the first sign of twilight over New Phoenix, he went outside to look for himself. The sky darkened to reveal the ghostly effect, just as the first words appeared in the lights.

Jonders saw his chance. Marshall had disappeared for a teleconference with Hathorne and the Oversight Committee—and probably half the leaders of the western world. If he was ever to have a few minutes to himself, this was it. He pressed the intercom switch and said, "Keep transmitting that signal. I'm going out for some air."

He stopped by the office for his jacket, then headed for a side exit. Once outside, he took a dozen long strides away from the building before looking up. He took an involuntary breath. He had seen numerous video images, but the replays had not done the sight justice. The night sky was filled with curtains of luminous silk, adrift and glowing in a dozen ghostly shades of ruby, fluted with amber and gold, and fluttering as though stirred by some turbulence in the cosmic wind. It looked as though the light must encircle the globe, although he knew it didn't; it was visible only from the night side of the planet. There was no clue to the naked eye whether it was floating high in the air over the mountains, or a million miles away in space.

It was the work of the Talenki, of course. The problem, from his point of view, was that the Talenki weren't taking calls right now. Over and over, Homebase had tried to contact them, using radio and laser-com, and every known permutation of tachyon signal, always without response. How were the military leaders reacting to this? Jonders wondered. He thought of his recent conversation with Marshall, and the one with Joe Payne that had preceded it, when Payne had practically demanded a meeting with him, and had laid out in shocking detail the allegations he was prepared to broadcast.

Stunned by Payne's information about the manned ship *Aquarius*, Jonders had agreed to discuss the matter with Marshall, and to urge full disclosure—in preference to the publicizing of a highly speculative and perhaps damaging version of the truth. Marshall's answer was: to the best of his knowledge, *Aquarius* was only lightly armed, and certainly not with nuclear weapons—but he would bring the question to Hathorne's attention.

Looking up into the sky now, Jonders doubted that he had accomplished much more than betraying the fact that he had spoken to the press; but he wondered if even that mattered much anymore.

The celestial light patterns were changing now, like shifting set pieces in a play. Jonders walked farther out across the grass and away from the building's glare. For the first time, he realized that he was not alone outside. Dozens of people were scattered about the grounds, craning their necks or talking in excited whispers. Jonders recognized Lusela Burns standing near the outer fence.

"Have you seen any messages?" he asked, joining her.

She shook her head. "An hour ago, I heard, there was something— some crazy jingle. It flickers every now and then, as though something's about to happen, and then—" She shrugged. Jonders nodded and shoved his hands into his jacket pockets. "Have they answered?" she asked.

He sighed. "Nothing. Nothing at all." He looked up. *"Damn them, why don't they respond?"*

Lusela stared at him soberly. "What do you suppose they're intending?"

Jonders felt a ball of anxiety gather in his chest as he gestured helplessly. In Marshall's office and in New Washington, that question and others were being debated. And somewhere in the deep of space—not far from the approaching Talenki, by now—were three spaceships, at least one of which perhaps carried hydrogen bombs. What were the commanders of the warships thinking as they closed with their quarry and listened to reports of strange fires in the Earth's skies?

Jonders wished suddenly that his wife and two daughters were with him.

There was music in the background now. *Music?* He realized abruptly that it was in his head, the music, and it was surrounding him, not too loud, but coming from *everywhere*, and growing in volume. What was it—some sort of adventure theme, with trumpets and French horns and strings—something vaguely familiar, a movie theme from long ago, he thought. There was a murmur from a nearby group of people, rising above the music. He glanced up again, and his heart jumped.

Overhead, the curtains of light were coalescing into tendrils of fire, squirming in the sky. At first their motion seemed chaotic, and then a pattern emerged from the disorder. The light was forming alphabetic letters in flowing script—and in various sizes and designs—until the words:

HI!

¡HOLA!

BON JOUR

JAMBO

NIHAU

PRIVYET

KOMBANWA

filled the breadth of the sky.

Jonders held his breath as the letters in light twisted. The pattern came apart, and the tendrils danced away from one another like tiny snakes of fire. Gradually, then, they recombined, this time spelling the words:

THE TALENKI

ARE IN TOWN!

Jonders felt his stomach tightening. What next? After a minute, that message dissolved, and a series of phrases formed, each lasting a few seconds before being replaced by another:

SO GET DOWN

GET HIGH

READ THE SKY

BURMA SHAVE!

As he stared up in astonishment, Jonders dimly heard his name being called. He was wanted back inside, on the double.

Chapter 66

General Armstead's image scowled.

"They were prepared in Twenty-fifteen, too," Hathorne said, his voice tense with modulated anger. "Ready on a moment's notice. 'Flexible response,' I believe they called it—without any of these irritating civilian controls—"

"Now, just a damn minute!"

"Fingers on the triggers, and military procedure driven by its own momentum—and what did it get us? Thirty million dead, and cities with names like *New* Washington, *New* Phoenix, Moscow *Two* . . . shall I go on?"

The general glared. The other seats surrounding the conference table were empty; but in a little while, they would be taken by the remaining members of the Oversight Committee. Hathorne was determined to have this out with General Armstead before then.

"Our priority," Armstead growled, "is the protection of the Earth and its people. If that's not clear enough—"

"It's not clear," said Hathorne, "that attacking our first interstellar visitor is the best way to protect Earth and its people."

"We have no intention of attacking," the general said coldly. "We're simply prepared for defense, should the need arise."

"I see. And who is to determine that? You, General?"

"The President."

"Let me remind you that *Aquarius* is under the authority of this Committee—which does not operate under the U.S. flag," Hathorne said. "Most of the members don't even *know* about the armaments. Were you planning to tell them? Why did *I* have to hear about it from Slim Marshall, who heard it from a reporter?" Thank you, Slim and nosy newscoper, whoever you are, he added silently. It was just the extra shot I needed. "I can't blame Slim for wondering just what the fuck we think we're doing," he continued aloud. "General, you've overstepped your authority. You've usurped the authority of the Committee—"

"I've usurped nothing," snapped the general.

"Then how do you explain violating the Committee's orders?"

"I am first and foremost under the command of the President of the United States—who agreed that the armament was necessary and justifiable," Armstead said calmly. "Obviously, we could not do this openly without generating a great deal of debate—"

"Obviously."

"—which," Armstead added in an annoyed tone, "could have delayed the mission and compromised its security."

Hathorne gazed at him icily. "In other words, you took it upon yourselves to sidestep the chain of authority."

"As I told you, the President approved our actions."

"Even the President needs to think hard before setting aside an international agreement," Hathorne said. A red light blinked on his console. He frowned and touched a switch.

"The President did think about it," said a new voice. A hologram materialized in the seat to Hathorne's left.

"Mr. President," Hathorne murmured, hiding his surprise. "Thank you for joining us."

The President of the United States placed a finger against his cheek and looked from one to the other. "Gentlemen. I apologize for listening without announcing myself, but I wanted to hear what you had to say, uninhibited by my presence. Mr. Hathorne, you are displeased."

"Mr. President—" Hathorne took a breath—"the Committee will be shocked to learn that it was excluded from this decision."

The President's forehead wrinkled. "That was necessary," he said stiffly, "for the sake of the mission—the real mission—which is to ensure the security of this nation—"

"But Mr. President—"

"—and this planet. I assure you, Mr. Hathorne—I never intended to remove the Committee from the decision-making process. It will remain in control of the *Aquarius* mission."

Hathorne glanced at the general, whose eyes had suddenly taken on a harder edge. Surprised? Hathorne wondered. He faced the President and asked quietly, "Is the Committee to be a party to the breaking of international law?"

The President grimaced. He raised his right hand slightly, in a half-completed gesture. His hand trembled as he spoke, and his voice strained. "It was to prevent that—to keep the Committee from bearing that responsibility—that we—went ahead without the Committee." He cleared his throat, and in the pause, Hathorne noted a flicker of anger in the general's face. This is not how Armstead heard it before, Hathorne thought. The President continued, "The Committee, though— the Committee must determine, in their wisdom—" and the President sighed with what appeared to be a bone-deep weariness, "whether to use the weapons—or to trust—" He left the sentence unfinished.

Hathorne was silent for a moment, thinking, None of us know right now whether to trust the aliens, we don't even know if they're threatening us or just playing games. But you, you poor bastard— you're caught red-handed and you know it—and you want us to think you weren't *really* doing anything, and now we're just going to be good Committee members and international citizens. Well, even if that's a lie, I'm going to try to make you live it. "Perhaps," Hathorne said quietly, "I could ask you to fill me in on the operational orders— the *real* operational orders—of the *Aquarius* crew."

The President hesitated, tugging at the corner of his mouth. Finally he said, "General Armstead?"

The general was staring impassively at no one in particular. Now Armstead's the one who thinks he's been betrayed, Hathorne thought. This wasn't supposed to happen, was it, General?

Armstead turned his head. "What aspect of the orders would you like to know?" he growled.

The President answered, almost chidingly, "Orders regarding the use of force, General. Nuclear force."

Armstead scowled. "They are forbidden to use the weapons except upon direct order. And I may issue that order only on authority of the President."

Hathorne plucked at his teeth with his fingernail. "That's the *only* authorized use?" he asked.

Armstead shrugged. "Barring total communications failure, of course."

"You mean," Hathorne said, "if contact with Earth is lost, they can go ahead on their own?"

"Only in the event of imminent danger to Earth," said the general. "It's a last-resort authorization."

"Aren't they out of contact now?" Hathorne asked pointedly.

Armstead hesitated, then admitted, "Yes—because of interference from the aliens. But there's no evidence that we're under attack at this time."

"Do *they* know that?" Hathorne asked.

Armstead stared at him with undisguised distaste.

Hathorne rocked back in his seat and turned. "Mr. President, we have a difficult meeting ahead of us. I think it would be extremely helpful if you and the general would tell the Committee exactly what you've just told me."

The President's eyes focused inward for a long time before he finally nodded approval.

The alien vessel had penetrated the solar system with astonishing speed. It was now well inside the orbit of Mars, proceeding toward Earth orbit. *Aquarius* was two thousand kilometers from the target and closing, despite continuing difficulty in precise tracking.

Ellis peered through the optical crosshairs, centering the twinkling target. He read the numbers in red digits above the image and touched a switch to lock them in. "Set."

"Burn in five seconds," Kouralt said.

The fusion drive kicked on. There was no visible change outside, but when it was over, the inertial guidance told the story. The burn was good. As time passed, the twinkling point became brighter, though not steadier, to the naked eye. They continued sending a challenge—by radio, modulated laser-com, and even simple flashes of the laser. There had been no response whatsoever, nor had HQ gotten a reply on the tachyon band—at least, not the last they'd heard.

Communications with HQ, however, had been out for almost twenty-four hours, apparently due to the strange tachyon-related phenomena around the Earth. More than anything, Ellis and Kouralt wanted to know: *What was happening?* At last report, the fireworkslike displays in the skies were continuing, with alarming intensity. Obviously, the Talenki were responsible—the tachyon activity had been traced to them—but Ellis and Kouralt had observed nothing that would explain *what* they were doing, or *how*. It seemed apparent, from the little information HQ had gotten through before the communications blackout started, that it was in some way a show of strength. Intended to create fear? Possibly a prelude to assault?

They had no way of knowing. Presumably, every spacecraft available was being put into Earth orbit and readied for action. But the first line of defense was Ellis and Kouralt, and *Aquarius*—here, at what one would have thought a reasonably safe distance from Earth.

But if the aliens could affect Earth's skies at this distance, what else could they do? And if their intent was hostile, and they got past *Aquarius*, and the Sovs and the Easterners trailing *Aquarius*, what chance would the near-Earth defenses have?

The two men didn't talk about it much.

Kouralt studied the high-magnification video image of the asteroid. "Very strange," he said. "Very, very strange. What do you make of that?"

Ellis fiddled with the video controls. The image was almost fluidlike—as though it were being viewed through a turbulent atmosphere, though in fact there was nothing but stark empty space between them. "Feels as though we're underwater," he muttered.

Kouralt scratched the back of his head. "I don't know. I don't like it. If they don't answer soon, let's try something a little different." He glanced at the flare launching panel. "Maybe if we light up *their* sky, they'll take notice."

The flares streaked away from *Aquarius* with a silent flash. A minute and ten seconds later, the first flare erupted with dazzling light, about a mile from the target. Ellis watched the telephoto images as the asteroid's landscape was revealed by the light of one flare, and then another—the tiny rockets braking and sailing in a timed pattern above and below, and to either side of the asteroid. He kept two cameras running, recording images for transmission back to HQ.

No amount of fiddling completely steadied the pictures; nevertheless, he could make out the surface well enough to see that it was apparently just rock, shimmering rock—at least on the near side of the asteroid. No metal or hardware was visible. If weapons were carried, they were on the far side, or concealed. If anything else, including a propulsion system, was carried, that too was on the far side, or concealed. Ellis attempted a penetrating radar scan, but obtained only an incoherent flicker on the screen.

The last two flares were at peak intensity when he heard, "Paul, what the hell is *that*?" Ellis turned his head to look out the side window. He felt a wave of dizziness. The space that formed a backdrop to the asteroid was crawling together, the star patterns rippling drunkenly, the constellations twisting and warping as though being stirred in a clear liquid.

Ellis looked back at the video monitors in bewilderment. The long-range pictures were wavering out of focus. There was another exclamation from Kouralt, this time in response to a blaze of light coming in the window. "Jesus!" Ellis said, shielding his eyes. It was one of their own flares sailing past, as though it had somehow—and this was impossible—looped completely around the asteroid and returned like a boomerang. "What the bloody Christ?"

The flare burned out a moment later, but a second was not far behind. This one drifted into a leisurely orbit around *Aquarius*, blazing steadily.

By the time Ellis checked the monitors again, the cameras had lost their target—as had the wide-scan radar. It took several moments for him to realize that the asteroid had *moved*—somehow—without seeming to. It was now . . . *Where the hell was it?* Ellis peered out the window. The last flare had gone dead, and there was no sign whatever, now, of the disturbance among the stars.

"Get me a fix on that damned asteroid!" Kouralt snapped. "Where did they go?"

Ellis quickly began a full sweep of the sky, searching for the Talenki. He found the answer—which he in no way comprehended. The aliens were a thousand kilometers farther away than before, and on a significantly altered course, *ahead* of them, on an inbound trajectory. Ellis swore and plotted a new intercept.

"Can we overtake them?" Kouralt asked.

"That depends on what *they* do," Ellis said, giving him the figures. "Hit it."

The reply from Earth was mostly hash, with a few recognizable words:

". . . ASJDHREPEAT,,TRANSJOASSION,,UNCLKEAR@@-@@@VERIFYYY . . ."

"What are they saying?" Kouralt said. He was too busy flying to look.

"Gibberish," Ellis said, watching line after line appear on the screen: "ASAODI,,USE@@,,WE@PONS,,SDAEAUTHORIXATIION,,,NNN@NDD,,NVIDENC@,,KKATTACK,, KBSS©AKK,,COM-MIT@EE. . . ."

The screen flickered and went blank. Cursing, Ellis adjusted the set. "We've lost it."

"Voice?" Kouralt asked.

"No. No voice channel."

"Did you get *anything*?"

Ellis scowled in frustration. Before answering, he checked the tracking figures and felt his blood pressure jump. "We need another burn," he said. "They're pulling away."

"*What did the damn message say?*"

"Something about weapons authorization. And attack. Evidence of attack.":

"What about it? Is there or isn't there an attack?"

"I don't *know*. It got garbled." Ellis took a deep breath, trying to stop his head from reeling. "I'm sending a 'Say again,' now. But unless things clear up fast, I think we're on our own." He paused a moment to update the target tracking, and the numbers were alarming. "If you don't give me some delta-vee in the next thirty seconds, we're going to lose them."

He felt the thump of acceleration. For several tense minutes, he monitored the relative velocities of the two spacecraft. *Aquarius* had already used most of her fuel, and had very little reserve left for a chase. He turned to Kouralt and said, "Take a look at this, and tell me if you see the same thing I do."

Kouralt looked. The Talenki were continuing to accelerate ahead of them, widening the gap. "Paul," Kouralt said. "We're going to have to make a decision."

Ellis swallowed. "We can't catch them."

"No," Kouralt said softly. "But we can *stop* them."

Ellis stared at him silently for a moment. "Are we prepared to do that? Suppose we're wrong? Suppose there's another explanation. You know what's at stake."

"Yeah. Earth. Suppose we let them *go*, and we're wrong. For all we know, the planet's under attack right now." Kouralt's expression was icy and perfectly controlled, his gaze sharp. "Do you think they'll stop on their own?" Ellis was silent. "If they get by us here, who's going to stop them? The Sovs? The Easters? They aren't answering us, either. We don't even know if they're still operating."

"It's the interference," Ellis said. "That's the problem."

"And who's causing that?" Kouralt paused. "We have a job, and in another minute, they're going to be gone. Switch on fire control and all recorders."

"*Frank! What if we're wrong?*"

Kouralt gazed at him steadily. "Better to be wrong and safe than wrong and dead," he said finally. "Fire control on."

Ellis took a breath, swallowing his emotions. Then training took over, and all feeling vanished from his body except the reflexes in his fingertips. He snapped the safety switches. "Fire control on. Recorders on," he said flatly.

"I am sending a final challenge," Kouralt stated. "I am ordering them to stop. If they don't reply, we must assume hostile intent. Compute a last point to fire before they're out of range."

The two officers worked silently and efficiently. Numbers streamed through the fire-control computer. Checklists were cleared, warheads armed, safeties placed on hold. *Aquarius* boosted at full thrust, in pursuit. The warning challenge went out on every available channel. A summary and urgent request for advice was transmitted to HQ.

From HQ came only static in reply; from the aliens, nothing, as the asteroid shrank away from them, accelerating toward Earth at an impossible rate. "Fourteen seconds to last fire, before they're out of range," Ellis advised.

Commander Kouralt hesitated only a moment, then said, "Fire one and two together on my order. Safeties off."

"Safeties off." The words passed coldly.

Two seconds went by. "Fire."

Ellis pressed the button hard. He felt a jolt as the missiles burst away. When he pulled his hand back, it was trembling. "One and two away," he whispered.

"Transmit a report to HQ," said Kouralt, his voice tightly controlled. "And continue tracking."

Sliding filters over the windows, Ellis watched in the monitors as the missiles sprinted toward their target—and he waited for two small suns to fill the heavens.

Chapter 67

It was impossible to follow everything that was happening. The Talenki were warbling with delight at their light show; but the effort was so concerted, so demanding of their attention that, in the end, no one was free to provide explanations. Communications with Earth had been neglected, as well. Numerous transmissions from the planet had been ignored, or not noticed at all, because the Talenki orchestrating the dizzies, the deep nodes through which all tachyons were channeled, were too busy choreographing the display; and any incoming signals were lost forever.

As for the approaching spacecraft, the polite thing would have been to send messages of greeting to each—if only the timing were better. The first ship would be reaching them soon; but for the duration, the Talenki would be almost literally unable to respond. They trusted to patience, and hoped that the performance itself would suffice. There would be time enough for introductions later.

Mozy understood only a fraction of what the Talenki were doing— primarily that it involved a system of carefully focused tachyon beams. It reminded her a little of the way one "rippled" through space, and was about as comprehensible. However it worked, the final result was to be a spectacular light show; and while she couldn't see it firsthand, she was excited about what it should look like. They'd consulted with her on some of the wording, of course. She hadn't even known that she *knew* any foreign languages, until they'd asked, and she'd become aware of knowledge unconsciously annexed from Mother Program and Kadin.

At the moment, however, her concern was growing about these spaceships approaching them. She wasn't sure that the Talenki were taking them seriously enough. She gathered an exterior view and watched the three pinpoints of mass strung out along the orbital curve, one now fairly close. From time to time, she observed a twinkling from one or another of the points, as drives were switched on and maneuvering rockets fired. These were probably ships with crews. She wondered what they were thinking and planning, what their orders were.

(Don't you think we ought to send a message to them?) she asked, sending a runner of her awareness back into the center of activity.

N'rrril was there, somewhere, but was too occupied to answer. She heard other voices, all muttering in convoluted tones and rhythms, timing and cuing movements and changing viewpoints in the presentation. They heard her question, but no one was free to reply.

(The spaceships,) she repeated, more forcefully. (I think we should speak with them.)

There was a response this time, but it was more like a purring reassurance than a real answer.

She wondered if there might be a way to make contact with them herself. A tentacle of her thought went out, probing the connections to *Father Sky*, still resting silent on the asteroid's surface. Perhaps she could use its radio equipment. She investigated cautiously; and what she found were links that were open but empty, the systems aboard *Father Sky* dead. She doubted that she could reanimate them, not, at least, without help.

Disappointed, she sent a tendril of awareness down into the sea at the center of the asteroid to listen to the deep nodes, in hopes that she might catch signals that the Talenki were missing. Rarely had she ventured this close to the dizzies, and never during such intense activity. The dizzies themselves were still, silent nodules—but when she slipped inside them she found herself in a booming chamber, with a whirlwind, a kaleidoscopic symphony, a cacophony of light and sound and touch. It was a hall of many orchestras, all playing different works, competing and yet meshing, a thrumming bass rhythm of one overlaid by a whippoorwill flute from another, and the tapping of distant drums playing an altogether different song. Some of the strains were metaphors for other senses; but there were real musical melodies that she recognized, resonating oddly—something old by Tchaikovsky, and something not quite so old by Williams, a classic space-adventure theme. It was music much loved by the Talenki, picked up from Earth broadcasts over the decades, and now here smoothly, cunningly interlaced with the shifting light display. In the dizzies, in the very core of the asteroid, it all converged, light and sound and a weight-less wind, all touching and swirling together, and flashing out to Earth and other secondary points of convergence.

The Talenki were extending their greeting not only to Humanity, but to the whales, as well . . . and to the beings of Titan . . . and to the living knots of force within the Sun itself . . . and to all the other living creatures of the solar system. The network was growing, new connections building upon old, threads of awareness linking from world to world, some consciously, some reflexively or empathically, the whole multiplying from the parts.

In all of this, the radio or tachyon modulations of Earth's transmitters were lost like the clicking of two stones in the rush and commotion of an incoming tide.

Reassured, and yet frustrated, lesser-Mozy listened while Greater-Mozy kept a watch, peering out into space as though through a keyhole. One of the ships was drawing near now, very near. She was suddenly conscious of how deeply she cared about what happened here, to her Earth, to her people. To her . . . children. And watching that spaceship, she was suddenly more than a little afraid.

It was sometime later that the spaceship spouted tiny bursts of fire. What are they doing? she wondered with alarm. She saw four tiny objects moving toward the asteroid, and she hollered: (N'rrril! *Anyone!*)

There was a stirring, but no answer. (DAMMIT, LISTEN TO ME!) she shouted. Finally, several Talenki came murmuring to see what the problem was.

(They've fired rockets at us!)

(What—) (—why?)

(I don't know, but you'd better *do* something about it!)

(Well—)

(Don't you see them, dammit?) The four rockets were closing at an alarming rate.

A ripple of concern spread through the mind-net as more of the Talenki noticed the incoming rockets. The ripple grew to a current, then a flood. With regret and annoyance, the Talenki abandoned certain parts of their display as they reorganized themselves. (We will—) (—do something.)

(They're very close now—)

There was a blinding burst of light—and then another—and another. The lights blazed steadily, illuminating the asteroid. They were flares, not bombs, she realized after a few moments. That was scant consolation. *Who was that out there? And what would be next?*

(Hadn't you better talk to them?) she whispered anxiously, terribly afraid that the Talenki did not know how dangerous her fellow humans could be. She flashed a quick reminder of the Klathron, to convey her worry.

(Do not fear—) (—our friend Mozy—) (—do not fear.)

(But I—) Mozy shut up and watched in amazement as the Talenki neatly altered the configuration of space surrounding their world. The flares whipped around the asteroid's center of gravity and pulled back toward their source. The Talenki world itself scooted out of that pocket of space like juice squirting from a grapefruit, and with a small change in its rippling pattern set itself on a speedier path toward Earth, ahead of the lagging spaceship.

Mozy watched worriedly as the Talenki picked up their presentation where they'd left off, murmuring among themselves as though nothing had happened. She kept her peace and tried not to be afraid. The Talenki, she thought, knew what they were doing.

There was no calming her fear, however, when the same spaceship, pursuing hotly, fired a pair of larger objects. The new rockets streaked like hummingbirds to intercept them, and she sensed with a horrible certainty that these were no flares.

Chapter 68

Jonders had never seen the operations center so charged with emotion. Responding to a *hurry-up* signal from Marshall, he began fitting the computer-link helmet to his head. "Will someone tell me what's going on?" he asked.

Marshall gave him a peculiar look and bustled away. Typical, he thought with a snort. In the last twenty-four hours, people around here had been acting like lunatics. Security advisor Delarizzo, having gotten wind of Jonders's contact with the press, had nearly had apoplexy trying to keep him out of the operations room, and had scowled his way off into a corner when overruled. Outside, the Talenki fireworks had stopped, and no one seemed to know why. Jonders's own family was at home, waiting anxiously for him to send word. But no one had yet told *him* anything.

"Are you ready for this?" asked the engineer, once Jonders was in the intercom circuit.

"Ready for what?"

"*Aquarius* has fired on the Talenki with a nuclear warhead."

"*What?*"

"They missed. Apparently. The transmission we got wasn't too clear—but I don't think even they know what happened. They said the warheads went off—and didn't even touch the Talenki. I think they're a little scared, frankly."

"So what am I supposed to tell them?" Jonders asked.

"Them? Nothing. You're talking to the Talenki."

"The Talenki?" Jonders said in surprise. "You mean they requested a direct link?" To link mind-to-mind with aliens, wholly unprepared . . . ?

"Are you ready for this? Mozy requested the link."

"Mozy?" Jonders whispered. "*Mozy?*" A shockwave flushed through him, a rush of faintness from his head to his toes.

"Well, we *think* it's Mozy. The transmission we received identified Mozy as the sender. And it—demanded, really—a direct-link communication."

Jonders struggled to absorb the news. Mozy, alive? How? In the *Father Sky* computer—linked, somehow, to the Talenki?

He didn't get the chance to wonder further. A tall man strode up and leaned over the console. The man was already speaking before his identity registered with Jonders. "We have a contact that alleges to be Mozelle Moi, insisting that she talk with you," Leonard Hathorne said. "The implication was that no other communication was possible." Hathorne stared at him as though he suspected Jonders of having arranged the whole thing.

Jonders looked up at Hathorne in perplexity as he adjusted the linkup controls.

"Well?" Hathorne said.

"I'll do my best," Jonders said softly.

Hathorne looked annoyed, but before he could speak again, a voice from the control room announced, "We have acquisition of signal from the Talenki. Are you ready for linkup?"

Hathorne pressed the intercom button. "Can you give us audio?"

"No audio channel being received. But we have a usable carrier signal for link-up mode. Bill?"

Jonders glanced at Hathorne, as though to ask him to step clear. The room lights dimmed, and people found seats. As the distracting movements subsided, Jonders slipped silently into the link.

The optical images appeared first, points of light floating in a three-dimensional array. He passed quickly through the mazelike outer levels, ignoring the muttering operating systems peripheral to his purposes, and dropped jarringly into the tachyon uplink. There was a howling surrounding him, and then silence, and a pale image of distant connections which spun and then blurred. Gradually darkness consolidated around him, and filled with tiny white lights, and he realized that he was floating in interplanetary space. In the distance were three bright points—which he somehow sensed, without asking, were spaceships. *Aquarius*, and two others.

This was not an image of his own making. He looked, listened, and finally sensed a nearby presence. Someone familiar . . . and yet . . . different.

(Mozy, is that you?) he asked quietly.

A sardonic reply echoed out of the darkness: (Jonders, is that you?) He imagined that he heard laughter.

He turned, blinked at the dazzling sun, and looked past its blazing disk. A transparent golden face gazed at him out of the stars. For a moment, he simply stared at her. It was the face of Mozy—a larger, stronger, and more confident Mozy than the young woman he remembered. It reminded him also of someone else—Kadin, viewed through the eyes and mind of Mozy—the same color, the same ethereal quality, a face with stars shining through. Was there something magical about the color gold, that it evoked such a sense of purity and confidence?

Out of that golden face gazed a pair of dark, probing eyes, which pinioned him in their accusing stare.

(Mozy?) he said, struggling to speak. (I'm—glad—)

(Never mind that,) she said, interrupting him. (Just tell me the meaning of *this*.)

There was an abrupt change in the scene. Mozy's face vanished, and in its place was the surface of an asteroid, close at hand, against the stars. Jonders dimly sensed a mutter of surprise from the observers in the gallery, reminding him that a low-resolution image of what he saw was being translated to the gallery screen. Just above the horizon of the asteroid, not quite hidden by rock, was the top section of *Father Sky*, dimly visible in the starlight. Is that where you are? he wondered; and he felt a strong negative answer—and then he forgot that because two points of light were moving against the stars: bright, fast, *not* spaceships, arrowing closer and closer.

And then two things happened in the same moment. The view shimmered oddly—the stars in the distance trembling—and he had a sense that the asteroid had vanished for an instant and reappeared, flickering like an insubstantial thing. The two pinpoints exploded in an agony of heat and light, two new suns, precisely where the asteroid *had been*. There was a frozen moment in which Jonders was incapacitated by pain and fear—and then the twin suns guttered out, the radiation shockwaves twisted out of phase and passed, and the asteroid became substantial again.

There was a deep, shocked silence, both in the link and in the gallery.

Finally Jonders mumbled, as Mozy's face slowly reappeared against space. (I . . . don't know what . . . to say. Did that—?)

(You know damn well what that was!) Mozy snapped—rocking

him back as though she had cracked him in the jaw with her fist. (That was from one of your ships. And that was no firecracker!)

Jonders was struggling to find words. (No,) he whispered. (No, it wasn't.) Mozy's anger was more controlled, and far more formidable, than anything he remembered—and totally justified. (I don't know why—) he started to say.

(Don't you? We come with greetings, and this is how you answer? What sort of pitiful cowards are you?)

Jonders could think of no answer. He directed his next comment backward through the link to the gallery. (Mr. Hathorne—anyone else—can you explain why the Talenki were fired upon?)

(Hathorne? Is *he* still in charge?) Mozy exploded, her words echoing through Jonders's mind into the gallery.

Suppressing a grin, Jonders started to answer, but was interrupted by a sharp reply from Hathorne. "They were fired on because they refused to answer repeated calls . . . they were engaging in a hostile display of power . . . and they were attempting to evade our defensive craft."

Jonders shuddered, expecting another flash of anger from Mozy. Instead, she burst into laughter. For an instant, Jonders was aware of everyone in the operations center staring in disbelief as a woman with a golden face roared with spirited laughter. He looked at her in wonderment—and realized suddenly how delighted he was to see her, even if in the midst of confrontation. But what about the Talenki? They were all in such an uncertain realm here, there were so many questions he needed to ask. . . .

Mozy suddenly fell silent and looked at him out of the depths of space; and he had the feeling, as they stared at one another across the link, that she saw more than just him, she saw those who watched from the gallery, through his eyes, and as they talked, she was seeking to assess the qualities of those men.

(I wouldn't have thought you could be so foolish,) she said finally. There was rage in her voice, but carefully metered, and mixed with sadness. (How can you have been so afraid, that you would try to destroy us without even learning why we've come?)

Jonders could see, in the gloom of the operations room, Hathorne's silhouette rising to face the image formed on the screen. "You say, *we*," Hathorne said. "Does that mean that you are no longer *Mozy-Human*? Do you represent the Talenki now?" He paused. "Who exactly *are* you?"

There was a soft and rolling chuckle, which seemed to come from more than one source. (I am myself,) Mozy said, (and much more than myself. I am Mozy-Human. I am Mozy-Talenki.) As she spoke, Jonders glimpsed—for an instant only—an image of Mozy, no longer alone, but now part of a vast hive of thought and feeling. (I am Greater-Mozy and lesser-Mozy. I am Mozy, Friend to Earth; and I am Mozy, Friend to all friends of the Talenki.)

Hathorne was silent for a moment before growling, "We would like to regard the Talenki as our friends. But we must take care."

(By attacking?)

"That launch was unintended. It would not have happened if you had not disrupted our communications."

(But you are very powerful. As you have shown. What do you have to fear from us?)

"We might fear many things," Hathorne said. "You have created chaos in our skies. You have failed to answer our calls. You have jammed our communications, and when our ship approached you, you refused to acknowledge their signals. Then you attempted to outrun it."

Mozy answered with a slow sigh, conveying an impression of deep patience. (We did not answer, because we were in the midst of a performance—our greeting—the Talenki greeting to Earth. We—they—were too busy.)

"Too busy to answer a communication?"

(They did not hear your communication, Mr. Hathorne. They are not humans, do not expect them to anticipate all of your concerns.)

"But our ship—"

(—behaved rudely, and they decided to keep their distance. You saw the result.)

"Then perhaps you could do us the service of explaining—"

Hathorne did not finish his sentence. There was a rush of static, and the signal broke up. Mozy's image vanished. The transmission cycle had ended.

There was a knot of people around Jonders's console, all talking at once. Marshall was asking Jonders, "What *feel* did you get from her? Can she speak for their intentions?"

"Well—"

He was interrupted by Fogelbee. "Can you run an analysis on her, with the personality profiles?"

"We'll *try* to do an analysis," Jonders said. "Talk to Lusela."

"Jonders." Hathorne was suddenly leaning over the console, shaking a piece of paper in his hand. "Here's a list of questions we want answers to. And find out if they'll speak to us in a verbal mode, without the linkup."

Jonders glanced over the list. It was long, and none of it was unexpected. How had Mozy survived? How did the Talenki move their asteroid? Was it their intention to enter Earth orbit, and would they permit an inspection of their vessel beforehand? There were a dozen more.

"We also expect you to evaluate their intentions by your own observations," Hathorne said, rapping the console. Without waiting for an answer, he spun away.

Jonders arched his eyebrows; but someone else was already crowding in, pressing for more details.

(Back again?) Mozy said. They were in a darkened room, with curtains fluttering in a warm breeze. He could just see her face, illuminated by a concealed light.

(We have just these short transmission cycles to work in, Mozy. But much to talk about.) For an instant, as his thoughts were on the subject of tachyon transmission, he caught a fleeting image of a luminous body of water—living, nonsentient creatures beneath the water, expelling streams of tachyons. A glance at Mozy told him that he had caught the image from her thoughts.

(We may have much, or we may have little,) Mozy said.

He asked cautiously, (Are you angry?)

(Not so much myself. I do not wish to remain angry over past wrongs,) she said. (But the Talenki—) She paused.

(The Talenki—?)

(They went to great trouble to present you with a greeting you wouldn't forget. You might have shown some appreciation.)

(We—didn't know what to think,) Jonders said. (It was beautiful, but—startling.)

He sensed a great sorrow in her. (Yes. But they are quite upset by the attack. They are considering leaving, without a visit. They've no wish to fight, nor to place themselves in danger. You remind them of certain others, in your hasty violence.)

(We owe them an apology,) Jonders said. (I hope you can persuade them not to leave. It would be a terrible misfortune.)

(Indeed. But for Earth more than for the Talenki. And for other peoples of the solar system.)

There was an image . . . of whales, and of . . . several other sorts of creature, unlike anything Jonders knew. He absorbed the image in stunned silence, then remembered the questions he was supposed to ask. Cautiously, he opened his thoughts to her. Would she share information? he wanted to know privately. He sensed her looking over his thoughts; then her eyes refocused, and she looked at him calmly, and her nonverbal response passed over him like a breath of air:

There must be a fair exchange. We must be treated with respect.

Jonders looked outside of the link, and saw the expectant faces of his superiors. (Mozy,) he said, forming the thought so that those in the gallery could hear, (would the Talenki be willing to speak in a simpler and more direct fashion to the others here?)

She chuckled. (What could be simpler than a direct link?) She turned toward the window where the curtain fluttered, as though listening to a whisper behind her. Her head turned back, and she said, (They are uncertain, and very busy guiding their world. They wish for me to communicate with you, for now.)

Jonders peered out of the link, to be sure that the others had heard. (I see,) he said.

Mozy studied him for a moment. (Why don't you ask your questions now.)

As the link dissolved around him, Jonders found his thoughts lingering momentarily, not on the issues of Humanity and the Talenki, but on Mozy herself, and the glimpses he had received of her world. This was still the Mozy he had known—but how she had grown! She was no longer the pitiable, self-conscious waif whose world was bound up in defeat and frustration and anger. Her awareness now spanned light-years; she knew worlds no human had dreamed of—joys and sorrows, triumphs and failures that were not of the human psyche at all, at least not until now. Within her was a reservoir of calm and confidence that had astonished him.

Jonders knew that his superiors could have witnessed only a fraction of what he'd just experienced. *He* knew more of Mozy now, and something more of the Talenki. He had answers to some of Hathorne's questions—not all—but how could he convey to the others knowledge that was essentially an empathic response? If the Talenki could not or would not speak directly with Homebase, how could he help Hathorne determine with certainty their nature and intentions?

He had an idea; but its chances for success would depend upon Mozy's willingness—and the Talenki's.

Chapter 69

"Dr. Jonders, there's one thing you have to understand," Hathorne said. He folded his hands on the table, looking from one face to another. "Something you *all* have to understand."

The room was silent, nine faces watching him. He took a deep breath to dispel a moment of lightheadedness brought on by exhaustion. His schedule these last days had been murderous; and the need to shuttle cross-country by suborbital ramjet wasn't making it any easier. But the situation was too delicate not to be dealt with in person. He sighed, trying to dispel the tension in his shoulders. There was no sympathy in the eyes that gazed back at him. "You probably know," he said finally, "that there are three armed ships now attempting to close with the Talenki."

Marshall stirred. "I thought *Aquarius*, at least, was out of it."

"Perhaps, for the time being. However, we hope to persuade the Talenki to slow up and be escorted by *Aquarius*." Jonders, across the table, snorted. Hathorne ignored the insolence. "In any case, the other two ships have been advised that an alien object has evaded *Aquarius*."

"Do they know that we fired on it?" someone asked.

"We think not," Hathorne answered.

"They *must* have seen the warheads explode."

Hathorne shook his head. "They're still at a considerable distance. There was nothing visible from Earth—and even *Aquarius* reported only a muted flash."

Two of the scientists exchanged glances. "No flash, from two quarter-megaton warheads?" one of them asked.

"We have no firm explanation," Hathorne said. "According to

reports, the Talenki apparently produced a localized distortion in the continuum. Don't ask me what that means. The theories are outlined in your briefing papers.''

Marshall said softly, ''So the world doesn't know about the missiles or any of the rest.''

Hathorne hesitated, staring for a moment without seeing. His gaze shifted to Marshall. ''That is correct,'' he said. ''Nevertheless, our ship and the two others are now to some degree acting in conjunction.'' His voice dropped involuntarily. ''I have to tell you that they may be ordered to prevent the Talenki from achieving Earth orbit.''

Jonders's head jerked up. He did not speak, but his eyes blazed.

Hathorne continued, ''It's an open question, though, whether the three powers will continue acting in accord. There is presently a good deal of confusion.''

''Have the others been given full information?'' Marshall asked quietly.

''No.'' Hathorne surveyed the faces staring at him. It made him weary beyond belief to sit here representing the extreme conservative point of view—and much the opposite view with the Committee. Neither extreme accurately reflected his own viewpoint; but he was involved now in a juggling act. ''I'm not sure we could stop the Talenki if we wanted to,'' he said, ''though methods have been suggested. We'll ask them politely to keep a safe distance. Failing that—'' He frowned. ''One reason for concern is obviously the fact that they know how to survive a nuclear blast, and we don't.'' He glanced at Jonders and saw an outburst coming.

''I'm sure they know many things we don't,'' Jonders said angrily. ''Some of us consider that a reason for welcoming them. What is it you *want*, for god's sake?''

''Proof,'' Hathorne said. ''Proof of their peaceful intentions.''

''What *kind* of proof?''

''Proof that I can see. Proof that I can take to the President, and to the Oversight Committee. A willingness to open their vessel to inspection would be one example.''

Marshall tapped a pen on the table top. ''What about Bill's proposal?'' he said. ''It seems to have merit.''

Hathorne scratched the back of his neck. ''Unfortunately, his proposal amounts to taking his word for whatever he might learn. No disparagement intended; but his observations would be difficult to confirm.''

"I understand that," Jonders interjected. "But at this point, I don't think that the Talenki would accept anyone else."

Hathorne nodded. "Well, frankly, I haven't heard a better idea, either." He glanced around the table. "All right, then. Let's schedule it for tomorrow. Discussion about what we want Dr. Jonders to communicate?"

As details were thrashed out, Hathorne studied Jonders out of the corner of his eye, wondering to what degree he dared trust the man. He might have to make the most difficult judgment of his life based on Jonders's report. He had already had it out with the Committee, and they were now awaiting his recommendation. But that left one last question: could he count on the President and the general to cooperate with the Committee in its decision? It all depended on his other plan, and his reading of the President's character.

Payne turned the telephone screen toward himself. "What is your name, again?" The screen was blank.

The voice answering was distorted, but he could hear it buzzing with impatience. "Never mind that, for the moment. If you want some useful information, follow my instructions. Are you in private, on a private line?"

Payne kicked the office door closed. "Yes."

"All right, I'm going to ask you to hang up. When you do, enter the following code on your keyboard, then wait for me to call again. Do not use any recording devices, or I'll break the connection immediately."

Puzzled, Payne followed the instructions. A minute passed, and there was a short tone, and he heard the voice again. It was clearer this time.

"Wait one moment, please." Pause. Then: "All right, we have a secure connection."

"How—?"

"Never mind that. My name is totally confidential—and everything I am about to tell you is off the record. Agreed?"

"Who *are* you?" Payne said.

"*Agreed?*"

Payne relaxed. "Agreed."

"My name is Hathorne. Leonard Hathorne. I'm the chairman of the Oversight Committee dealing with the aliens on behalf of an alliance of the Western powers."

"I see," Payne said. He frantically cleared a fresh space in his note-recorder. "Can you let me see your face?"

"No."

"How can I verify that you are who you say you are?"

There was silence for a moment. Then the voice said, "When we are finished, call this number—" and he gave a number which Payne recognized as belonging to Sandaran Link Center—"and ask for me. Identify yourself as . . . Richard Gardner. We will speak for a moment about the weather, and then hang up."

Payne thought. "Very well."

"Take this down, and be accurate," Hathorne said. "Everything I'm about to tell you, you can use—provided you name no sources— now or in the future. Agreed?"

Payne blinked. "Of course, but—Mr. Hathorne. May I ask why?"

"Why *you*? Because you already had it, or most of it—and you sat on it because you weren't sure. I trust you for that. Why the story? That will become obvious."

"But—"

"Are you listening or aren't you?"

Payne swallowed his questions and grunted assent. For the next twenty minutes, he wrote faster than he had ever written in his life.

It was different meeting Mozy this time. He felt like an ice skater gliding down an unfamiliar river, hoping for safe ice—gliding across an icefield of space, peering ahead for danger. Her face appeared in a snowbank of stars, only her eyes moving, following his approach.

(Are you ready?) he said, sliding to a halt.

Her eyes showed her uncertainty. (You're asking them to trust you— *and* your leaders. That's a difficult request—all things considered.) Her eyes blinked. (Never mind. Come. Let's see if this can be done.)

The stars gathered into clusters, revolving, drawing Jonders forward. In silence he was carried into a place where the stars sparkled and went out. Moments passed.

He became aware of faint music enveloping him. A dim reddish illumination revealed indistinct shapes, which seemed to move and shift blurrily. He looked instinctively for Mozy, but . . . was he, like Mozy, in the Talenki mind now, looking out through Talenki eyes? What an odd sensation. He could discern walls, but they seemed insubstantial. Other shapes came into focus: hump-shaped objects clustered in the center of a chamber, and a lanky creature detaching itself and drifting away. A smell like the sea touched his nostrils, and a scent of tulips, slightly rancid. He felt an impulse to shake his head, to clear his senses, but there was no response to the impulse; it was as though those nerve endings had been disconnected.

Dimly now, he heard voices—laughter and singing, and incomprehensible questions. It was like listening to a choir in a forgotten tongue. How was he going to communicate his questions? He sensed Mozy nearby. (Are you ready?) she said.

(I think so, but—)

(Reach out with your thoughts.)

(What am I reaching for?)

(Just do it.)

He extended an uncertain touch—and felt something that made him think of an otter's fur, and then the light brushing of milkweed, a curious, nonphysical tickling sensation. Then something was moving around him; and he felt laughter, and the sounds of an inhuman orchestra tuning.

They're ready to open themselves, he thought—and realized that the thought was Mozelle's—and realized also how naked his own thoughts and soul were in this state, and wondering if *he* was prepared to be tested and examined, and perhaps found wanting. Mozy laughed softly, and his nervousness fell away, and he prepared to observe and to learn, and to convey his concerns . . . *don't forget anything*. He relaxed and trusted to the gentle pressure of Mozy guiding him forward into the labyrinth.

There was motion around him. He was looking out of someone's eyes, but this time he knew what he was looking at—the heart and memory center of the Talenki consciousness. The creatures moving about were the fauns, the sentient ones—and what were they doing, moving through walls, appearing and disappearing like oversized gremlins? Yes, yes, he realized, that was a normal way to move about here, and could that have something to do with the way the Talenki world moved through space?

But what about hardware? What about electronic information storage. . . ?

The question died uncompleted. It was hard to maintain a track of logical thought here.

There was a reverberation of images around him, from Mozy, from the Talenki themselves—spinning by, a history carried in memory and thought, and images of a physical world that defied his understanding. There was pleasure coursing in his veins—only they were someone else's veins; he was living in the Talenki's bodies, as well as their minds, and if that was not trust on their part, what would be? And yet . . .

Out in space, three warships were shadowing this world, and where one had failed, three might succeed; and it had been given to him make a determination, to return with proof of good will, to strike the beginning of an agreement, if he could.

As the link began to waver, he felt images solidifying in his subconscious, the details already eluding him. Had he succeeded? he wondered. Had he asked the questions? It had happened as such a blur. . . .

The world flickered around him, and he blinked. His eyes focused, and he became aware of Hathorne and the others staring at him, waiting for him to speak.

He massaged his eyebrows and took another swallow of coffee. "How much did you see?" he asked finally, sinking back in his chair. The coffee was sour in his stomach, and the chair uncomfortable. He missed the touch of the Talenki world around him.

"Fragments," Marshall said. "Not much more."

"*Nothing* comprehensible," said Hathorne. "You're going to have to tell us—everything."

Jonders let out his breath. How could he explain it? The imagery had come to him without verbal exchange, and largely in the form of intuitive images. One fact, however, had emerged in the final moments of the link; he did not even know where it had come from. "They're not sure whether to trust *us*," he said, trying to focus the facts in his thoughts. Had it *all* happened on a subconscious level? Apparently; it was astonishing how completely the link had slipped out of his control. "I would say that they're not willing to allow a physical boarding of their vessel, at least not at this time. They seem . . . not to take the military threat too seriously. They almost . . . regard us more as *bad sports* than as a threat. They don't fully understand our ways, even with Mozy to learn from."

"Well, what is it they want?" Hathorne said. "Technological or scientific exchange? Can we approach them on that basis?"

Jonders shook his head. "They don't seem to be technological, as we know it. They're more like—" He gestured, searching for words. Hathorne's gaze hardened. "Well, they're like . . . *wandering minstrels*, is the closest thing I can think of. The light show in the sky, for instance." Jonders peered at the others as though seeing them for the first time. "I had the distinct sense that they did it for *fun*. Out of a kind of . . . impish delight."

Hathorne's expression seemed clouded with pain. "Is that all you have to tell us?" he demanded. "Do you think, even for a moment, that I can go to the President—to the Committee—and tell them that everything's okay, we can trust them because they were just having *fun*?" His voice rose in frustration. "What the hell do you think we sent you in there for? For *proof*, dammit! Negotiable proof that we can deal with them—or not."

Jonders nodded dizzily. "I understand that. The problem is that there is no way you can take my word for it. There is nothing I can say that will convince you, nothing that I can convey. That's why—" and he took a sharp breath, as a subconscious memory crystallized— "that's why they've agreed to another link—"

"Another—"

"With you, Mr. Hathorne. They're willing to let you go in there with me to see for yourself. And, I should add, for them to see you. Because if you cannot decide to trust them, and they cannot trust you, then we'll be missing the greatest opportunity this world has ever known."

Hathorne rubbed the back of his neck in startled silence.

Chapter 70

The sea rushed and grumbled as the storm rose, and the whales' activity subsided to a lackadaisical wallowing in the swells. The herd drifted slowly apart—the mothers keeping a close watch on their calves, the males wandering off, or just hanging in midwater, moaning their mournful songs.

Luu-rooee bottomed out in the cold, dark depths. Here, the hissing and rushing sounds were subdued, and whale voices carried as clearly as though through Heaven's waters. Several males, widely spaced across the range, were calling back and forth, collaborating in a free-wheeling round—a kind of song unheard of, not long ago. Luu-rooee listened to them, listened for the godwhale to answer.

It spoke to them often now. And when it did, the entire herd reverberated with its voice—as though a spiritual force had taken hold, coaxing them into a circular song that somehow, for a few intoxicating hours, would bind them into something greater than themselves. There were other voices echoing out of the abyss, as well, voices strange and unfamiliar—not the godwhale's, and yet brought *to* them by the godwhale. Nonwhale voices. And whale voices—other whales, interwoven with the godwhale—voices that came from far away, from seas of different taste, different echo and shading, chillier seas—voices echoing across the span of seas, as some said whales ages ago called to one another, before the sounds of metal manships clouded the deep echoing channels.

Puzzling visions now filled Luu-rooee's dreams: visions of an airy sea, a place of mist and slush and cold, and a creature different from himself, a creature struggling to put words to feelings that filled him from . . . a song out of the heavens . . . a godwhale's song. Luu-rooee dreamed, too, of men floating disembodied, and other beings too hot or too cold to touch, too quick or too slow to speak to, and yet . . . exchanging *something*.

Such images had once been Luu-rooee's alone. Now they were shared by most of the herd.

Luu-rooee drifted happily in the deep current, listening to the intermingling whale songs, near and far, roohm and rumble and whistle— and the sigh of something far away, not-whale, but a part of them now—and when the godwhale joined in again, its voice ringing out of the deepest abyss and singing across the breadth of the sea, and echoing out of his own mind, Luu-rooee thought of a vast open circle, turning . . . expanding . . . closing. . . .

The Song was as much a part of Four-Pod's life now as the methane snow and the wind. It was with him in waking, as he plodded ahead, braving the treacherous ices; and it filled his dreams as he slept, with visions of the Road to Heaven as not even Those-Who-Thought knew it.

His journey into the hills had proved exhausting. Without the Song to lend him courage, he almost certainly would not be alive today. In the hills, he had met Those-Who-Thought, floating on billowing wings, and one had descended to inquire what this lowly one was about. Upon hearing of songs from Heaven, the thinker had made a long, rude, rasping noise in the back of its beaked nostrils, fluttered its wings, and floated out of sight, muttering in agitation.

Was this to be his fate—to be spurned wherever he went? Despairing, Four-Pod might have perished there; already four wake periods had passed since his last nourishment. But in his despair, the Song touched him again, and as though in response to *his* needs, had changed from a teasing whisper to something that ran deep with hope. From that point on, he was alone no more; there was a song in his head and determination in his spirit. And he'd plodded, and plodded, and at times saw visions of friends without faces or bodies, who touched him with their thoughts—and five full wake periods later, on the verge of collapse, he'd found a nourishing pool to drink from—and not long after, found his way out of the hills to the marches that led home.

The sleet blew fiercely across his forehead, and the ice grated against his bosom as he moved; but he was nearing home now, a journey coming full cycle. Ahead lay the methane pools. Ahead lay the hollows of home, and peace and rest, and contemplation of the songs of Heaven's Road in all their fullness.

The layers swirled eternally, carrying energies from the mother fires out to the endless cold. The flux-bodies rode the layers with insolent restlessness, teased by the strange emanation pervading the fields. What exactly it was, none were certain, except that there was *pattern* to it, and everyone knew that pattern . . .

. . . was the domain of living beings.

. . . was the creation of living thought.

. . . guided the circle of all life, and closed it.

And yet the focus of this pattern was *outside* of the solar flux, far from the mother fires, in the realm of the impossible.

One flux-body, more restive than the others, soared a little higher, catching a faster current . . . relishing the thrill of speed and rarification, and uncertainty . . . hearing the sounds just a little more clearly, clearly enough . . . almost . . . to glimpse meaning and personality beneath the rhythms.

The others, shedding a little of their fear, followed at a distance. The energies of the mother fire swarmed and comforted them with its warmth, and gave breath and fullness to the spirit, and the flock danced outward, listening, high along the edge of the flaming circle.

No Earthbound eye could follow the three ships as they raced for position around the enigmatic asteroid—one struggling to catch up with the alien, while the other two, closer to Earth, jockeyed to match speeds. Aboard the ships, and on others closer to home, commanders awaited orders. An uneasy cooperation prevailed, but for how long, no one knew.

Decisions were being made at the respective headquarters; but none of the commanders knew, or suspected, quite how those decisions were being arrived at.

"Did you give him this information?" Marie whispered.

Jonders shook his head, staring dumbly at Payne's televised image. Marie's grip tightened on his hand. The girls sat with them, spellbound.

It was all there—the Talenki, the Tachylab conspiracy, the failed nuclear attack, the presence among the aliens of a human personality. *Who the devil had leaked the story?* Payne had not named his "highly placed" sources; but surely there would be those who instantly thought of Jonders, who was known to have talked to the press before. Hathorne would probably come down on him like a vise.

He only prayed that plans for the linkup would be unaffected.

But who had leaked? Someone in the Committee?

As Betsy fidgeted on his right, his attention went back to the set. "The situation remains uncertain, despite the failure of the first attempt to stop them," Payne was saying. "Military analysts have suggested that the Talenki may be vulnerable to a more concerted attack."

Animated graphics appeared. "In the incident yesterday, the Talenki are believed to have actually shifted their vessel out of the space time continuum as we know it—evading the effects of the exploding warheads, as seen in this artist's conception." An asteroid in the center of the screen became transparent as two missiles converged and blew up, then became solid again. "Scientists have no explanation, sources say—but analysts believe that a *pattern* of warheads might be timed to explode in sequence—" this time six missiles converged— "catching the vessel as it reemerges in our space." The animated asteroid was missed by the first two pairs of explosions, but destroyed by the third the instant it reappeared.

Payne's face returned to the screen. "Authorities insist that such action is being contemplated only in the event of a clear and present danger. However, it must be emphasized that the Talenki in fact had taken no demonstrably hostile action prior to the first attack. No one is certain what the Talenki reaction was to being fired upon, and one official stated that miscommunication could pose the gravest danger of all.

"For more, we go to Teri Renshaw in New Washington—"

Jonders became aware of Marie's fingernails digging into his hand. Betsy, on his right, was staring wide-eyed and bewildered at the screen. He hugged her, and looked up to see Marie gazing at him. "Are they really going to do it?" she said softly. "Are they going to make a war of it?"

He felt his breath catching as he struggled to find his voice. "That's—up to the Talenki and Mozy and—Hathorne." Even as he said it, he realized that it was a hopelessly optimistic statement. Even if Hathorne were persuaded, would *he* have the power to make the decision?

"If I *find* the son of a bitch who leaked . . ." The President snapped his mouth shut. His face was so taut it hurt to look at it.

Hathorne exhaled softly, keeping his expression carefully under control, betraying nothing. "We're investigating, of course, Mr. President. But has it really changed matters that much?"

"*Changed matters?* Do you know what's going on in this city? Congress and the U.N. are in emergency session, the media's on me like a pack of wolves, we're getting six hundred calls here an hour—and do you know what most of them are saying?"

"Sir?"

" 'Why are we attacking the aliens?' 'Why can't we greet them in peace?' 'Why are we being warmongers?' You'd think no one understood the meaning of the word *defense.*" The President got up and stamped around the room. He whirled and jabbed a finger at Hathorne. "I have to make a statement soon. How am I supposed to answer those charges? Does it change matters? You're damn right it does, mister—it's going to make it twice as hard for me to take action, if that's what I'm forced to do!"

Hathorne nodded, hoping that his face showed sympathy. It had been a terrible gamble, but this was exactly the public outcry he had counted on, to create pressure, at least in the short term, for restraint. He thought he had judged this president correctly—that his susceptibility to pressure and public opinion might outweigh his own resolve. "If I may suggest, Mr. President—it might be better to hold off on a major statement until after my exploration with the Talenki. The news *might* be good."

The President's scowl was more of a grimace. "And if it's *not?*"

"We're still in a position of strength—even General Armstèad agrees with that. We have the strongest near-Earth fleet—"

"But the Soviets and the *Gandhi* are in the best position to intercept right now," the President pointed out.

Hathorne shrugged. "They're not as well equipped, and they don't have the benefit of our tracking experience—"

"But we could share that with them."

"Mr. President, I would urge you not to do that—yet."

"Why?" Impatiently.

Hathorne was on a delicate balance, and he knew it. "Because—" he cleared his throat—"it is possible . . . that after our experience with the Talenki, we will find ourselves opposing those other forces . . . if we determine that the Talenki are friendly. If not, then we could share our findings." He paused. "Mr. President. I need to know—"

"Yes?" The President's voice was barely under control.

Hathorne hesitated. "The Committee has given me a tacit commit-

ment that they'll base their decision upon my evaluation of the Talenki.
I need to know: *do you intend to accept the Committee's judgment?*''

The President studied him warily.

Hathorne quickly added, ''When I address the Talenki, whom do I
represent? You? The Committee? Whom may I tell the Talenki they
are dealing with?'' He turned his palms up.

The President nodded, and for a long moment had a tired, faraway
look in his eyes. ''Yes, Mr. Hathorne, I see your concern,'' he said
finally. ''You may rest assured, and assure the Committee, that this
administration will abide by the Committee's decision.''

Hathorner silently registered his relief.

''*But you just be damned sure about your judgment,*'' the President
added, his gaze sharpening to a glare.

Hathorne felt his brow knotting, and said nothing.

Chapter 71

(Hathorne? Can you hear me?)

There was no answer, only a whisper of wind through the fog, and beneath it a gentle strumming, a music that gave him an urge to walk, to move. Except . . . to where? Jonders and Hathorne had entered the link together and found a physical image of a pathway in a blank landscape, and Mozy's voice echoing somewhere in the distance. Images of their own bodies had coalesced around them. They'd glanced at one another in surprise and set off down the path. And then a fog had swirled in around them, and that was the last he had seen of Hathorne.

(Leonard?) Silence. Jonders looked around in puzzlement. The fog seemed to be dissipating ahead of him, so he ambled in that direction. He noticed an unusual lightness in his step; his body felt slim and in good tone, more like the body he *remembered* than the one he presently owned. It felt as though he were walking on solid ground—but whether this was an image of the real Talenki world, or merely a Talenki dream, he wasn't sure. Either way, the Talenki seemed once more to have taken control of the link.

(Hathorne? Mozy?) There was only silence in answer. Before him was the path, through what now appeared to be a meadow, half shrouded with mist.

What the hell, he wondered.

He reached back along the thread connecting him with the other world, where his real body sat motionless before a console. Tendrils of information brushed across him as he extended his awareness . . . just a bit further, across the checkerboard of indicators. . . .

Hathorne, he discovered, was still in the link; but something had so captured his attention that he appeared unaware of Jonders's presence, and scarcely aware, judging by his telltale indicators, of his own existence outside of the link. Jonders probed a little further, back along his own sensory pathways . . . and without quite letting go of the one world, he peered out of his half-closed eyes into the other, at the dim silhouette of a man seated nearby, the link helmet not concealing a posture of intense, almost painful concentration. Had something gone wrong?

He dared not terminate; and the only other way to find out was to retrace the link forward, to find the object of the other man's focus. Without giving any external sign to those who might be watching, he left the operations center behind again and moved back along the twists and turns of the link, tracing Hathorne's connection like a spidery silver wire. It was simple enough at first, until he reentered the Talenki world; and then the mists returned, and Hathorne's presence slipped away from him like a thread into the sea. When he walked forward out of the mist, he found himself once more in the middle of a sunny and rather Earthlike meadow.

Clearly this was no accident. But why did the Talenki want Hathorne alone? And where was Mozy?

With a sigh, he continued along the path. It led across the meadow, over a knoll, and eventually to the edge of a narrow, winding river. He stood on the riverbank, in still air, and looked down and saw his reflection quivering on the dark water. A feeling came to him that someone or something was looking up out of the river at him. Bending low, he heard a peculiar whistling sound. Almost like a voice. . . .

The promontory overlooked a fog-shrouded seashore. Hathorne listened to the surf hissing against the rocks below. He peered cautiously over the edge. All he could see was boulders rising from the mist; the water itself was lost to view. It was much like the New England seashore where, as a young man, he had passed endless hours gazing out to the horizon, watching the toss and tumble of the waves and the inexorable movement of the tides. The sea had always seemed to him an appropriate symbol of the apparently endless contradictions of human life—on the surface constantly changing, but in its deeps bound by the movements of the great, slow currents, which reflected continuity, and a kind of changelessness in the Earth itself.

But why here? Why now?

He turned to look behind him, and was startled by the sight of a hedged meadow, stretching away toward a stand of trees. Had that been there before?

Scratching his chin, Hathorne tried to recall what he *did* know.

There was a great sense of discontinuity.

There had been a man with him. Jonders. They had come here for a purpose; but it was all a little muddled in his mind right now. The salt air was not clearing his thoughts. How had he come to stand looking at the ocean? There was a path through the meadow. Perhaps Jonders had gone that way.

Making up his mind suddenly, he strode off through the grass, leaving the seashore behind. The mist soon burned off, presenting him with a bright sun in a lemon-lime sky. Except for the color of the sky and a few oddities of detail among the flora, this might have been the Connecticut countryside of his youth. The air was silent; there was no buzzing of insects, no birds, no sound even of his own footsteps. As he reached the trees, he finally heard the wind, rustling leaves over his head.

Passing among the trees, he thought he heard a voice, just a whisper on the wind. When he stopped to listen, all he heard was silence. He resumed walking, but wondered if there might be eyes in the treetops, noting his passage. The voice, if there was a voice, was softly, wordlessly urging him to keep moving.

The path joined an ascending ridge, and the trees gave way to close-cropped grasses and mountain shrubs. The landscape began to change, silently and quickly, in blinks of an eye. Time took on a dreamlike quality, passing in waves and ripples. None of this disturbed him; he experienced no fatigue, and in fact felt younger than he had in years. When last had he walked among mountains—among towering, stony peaks that brooded over a world? Still, there was something about this that reminded him more of stories than of real lands.

He was in a high country now, with a starkly barren ridge squatting over his right shoulder, and valleys laid out in tortuous geometry far below. Iron grey peaks pierced the clouds, reaching to hidden altitudes. There was something nearby, perhaps just a little higher, through a tight pass . . . the image leaped into his mind so clearly that he pushed straight onward without pause. The air was clear and bracing; the sun and wind burned his cheeks as he climbed.

He came to a natural archway, where a shoulder of the ridge provided a prop for a massive, fallen slab of stone. He passed beneath the slab, rounded the elbow of the ridge, and smiled inwardly as the path opened out into a long mountain dell—a tongue of grass and wild mountain flowers carpeting a gently sloping bowl-shaped formation in the side of the mountain. The sun shone from a perfect angle, setting the tiny vale aglow with its light. At its upper reaches, the vale delved deep into the mountainside, ending in a shadowy crevasse. At the lower end of the dell was a sudden dropoff.

Hathorne laughed and spun around, drinking in the sight of the slopes above and the tumbled terrain below, and the dim distant plains that merged with a blue-grey sky under a bright, blazing sun. The mountain range stretched to infinity to the north and south.

The beauty of the view was stunning. He sank down onto the grass, first sitting, then lying supine, gazing up into the sky, watching the dizzying movements of the clouds. He raised himself back up onto his elbows and turned his head, absorbing every detail from one end of the vista to the other. There was something about this place that was so familiar that it sent shivers up and down his spine; and yet, what was it? He sank back again, and closed his eyes, and relaxed with the warmth of the sun on his face, and felt the weariness of his age melt away.

It was a marvelous place . . . except that he was alone, and had no one to share the feeling with.

Or was he?

Jonders? He blinked his eyes open and looked around again. No. Not Jonders. But somehow he felt certain that someone was watching him. Sharing his feelings. Sharing his memories.

He wasn't sure how it had happened, but Jonders felt *connected* again. It wasn't that he could see the Talenki or feel their presence directly; he couldn't, nor was he aware of Mozy. But he could feel other connections, other branchings. He could sense a fragment of the Talenki . . . network.

He was aware of the whispering music of the dizzies as they spun out their tachyons in a silent stream; and he was aware of a curious twisting of his time sense, a feeling that he was seeing and absorbing at a rate that made time meaningless. Images of worlds flickered before him, only dimly comprehended.

Jonders heard the whales now, and the songs of the Talenki, echoing out of different oceans on different worlds, the songs weaving and interplaying like strands of hair. The whale songs and Talenki songs were so similar, so compatible, that they might almost have been created by a merging of their hearts and minds.

He heard a terribly lonesome wind crying through the crevasses of a twisted landscape, and caught an image of whipping fog . . . and ice . . . and weariness and pain . . . a body that thirsted for methane and hydrocarbon soup . . . a soul that labored in a journey, but paused, hearing a song from the sky.

There were others: the tense lowing of looping magnetic flux; the crackle of transmuting plasmas; the chiming of metal crystals in a cavern . . . somewhere. And in another corner . . . *guitars*, for godsakes, crying and wailing, and thumping drums, and humanlike voices raw and bluesy. It was vaguely familiar, that music; but *how*, he wondered, had the Talenki come to know rock-and-roll music from the last century?

Someone or something was approaching, from the upper end of the sward. Hathorne rose and shaded his eyes. It looked like an animal of some kind, an oversized version of a prairie dog or marmot. The creature moved through the grass with a slight limp; it seemed old, its movements purposeful. Hathorne walked up the slope to meet it, and felt a flutter of recognition. Was this a . . . ?

He could not remember the name.

They met halfway. The creature paused and peered up at him with alert eyes and tiny, twitching ears. It sat up in greeting. Its head barely reached Hathorne's waist.

Hathorne met the creature's dark-eyed stare.

"You don't remember me, do you?" it asked.

"Excuse me?"

"You don't remember me."

"Well—" Hathorne felt paralyzed by confusion. "I've seen you before. I just can't place where."

The creature closed its eyes to slits, and seemed to nod. It dropped to all fours and scratched at the grass. When it sat up again, it had a weed stem sticking out of its mouth. "Mmph," it said. "One might think that you would remember. After all—"

Hathorne's mind reeled backward through the years. "You're a—"

"Right," the creature said. "I'm a *bedu*. The only one of my kind." It blinked, plucked the weed from its mouth, and blew a long, twittering whistle.

Hathorne trembled with dizziness. His vision wavered and shifted oddly, then steadied. He drew a sharp, shallow breath. He was standing, eye to eye, now, in front of the bedu. He could see flecks of gold in the bedu's brown eyes. His eyesight seemed keener than it had been a moment ago, and his hearing more acute. He was aware of the wind whispering in the grass. His arms swung with energy, and there was a newfound spring to his stance. His hands were slim and smooth—the leathery texture of age gone. Astonished, he gazed at the bedu, and a joyful laugh came out of him, from nowhere.

"You remember," said the bedu solemnly.

"Of course!" he cried. "I was—what—five? Seven?" The bedu Larry was his imaginary friend, for a year or more his childhood companion, of whom he had been intensely proud and fiercely protective. He had never spoken of Larry's existence, not to a soul—not after telling his father, who had sternly advised him to "grow up" and forget such foolishness. But they were inseparable, Larry and he, for that one oddly happy year. And then one day—just when or why, he didn't know—Larry was no longer there. The bedu had gone out of his life, slipped away silently and without regret to . . . wherever it was that imaginary creatures went when their companionship was no longer needed.

"I thought you looked more like a rabbit," he blurted suddenly, a grin cracking his face.

"Well," said the bedu, glancing down self-consciously. "I did my best."

"So—well. How—*where* have you been?"

Larry bent and plucked up another weed. "Oh, you know. Around. I've been all right. Did you miss me?" it asked, chewing carefully on the stem.

"I—yes—" Hathorne stammered, feeling his face redden. He recalled with an abrupt flash another moment of intense embarrassment—when, as a seventh grader, he had been called upon by a teacher and had not known the answer . . . had not even known the question, because he had had to go to the bathroom and had been concentrating so hard on not peeing his pants that he hadn't been listening. And with the embarrassment, his concentration had failed, and the wetness had spread in a humiliating stain over the front of his trousers.

That was a memory he had not looked at in a while.

"It's all right," the bedu said quietly. "The years haven't been as hard on me as they have on you."

"No. I guess not," Hathorne said, shrugging the memory away. He blinked. "Tell me, have I returned to—well, to my youth?" He stroked his hands wonderingly.

"Oh, just in some ways," said the bedu. It walked past him, with that little limp (which Hathorne did not remember), and paused, looking out beyond the lower end of the sward, where, it seemed, the entire world was visible below. "Just enough for you to remember," it added softly.

Hathorne, gazing with him out into the vast emptiness above the brown-and-green mottled flatness of the plain itself, felt his stomach tightening, his pulse fluttering. He realized now why this mountain scene was so familiar. It had taken Larry the bedu to remind him—because this was, indeed, the imaginary place to which he and Larry had fled whenever the world outside had grown too dreary or too lonely. Every feature of these mountains had been drawn in his mind's vision, every beauty etched in memory. How many thoughts of wonder had passed in his mind as he'd sat in this place with his friend, Larry the bedu?

How odd it was to be here again, recalling feelings and events that had slept in his subconscious for decades. He wiped a sudden teary fullness from his eyes. He looked up at the mountains brooding over his shoulder and wondered again if eyes were looking down upon him from there, and if they were, what they saw.

"Come," said the bedu, walking past him the other way. "There are things I must show you."

He stared in bewilderment as the bedu limped away through the grass. Then he stirred himself and hurried to follow.

Chapter 72

The spaceships trailed after the asteroid like wasps. Mozy studied them worriedly. The Talenki seemed unconcerned, but she could not share their sanguine approach. Her people of Earth were, after all, masterful killers. While the Talenki had escaped unscathed once, she wasn't sure how they would deal with a highly organized and motivated attack.

The movement of the spaceships was, of course, just one focus of her awareness. Inside, in the misty, shifty realm of the link, two humans were being entertained as few had been entertained before. She did not precisely know the Talenki's intentions, but there was an aura of quiet determination in the mind-net, and she guessed that whatever the two men were experiencing they would not soon forget.

Silently, like a wisp of smoke, she insinuated herself into the fluid reality that was being weaved around them.

In a place high in the mountains, she sat beside a man/child named Hathorne, and looked out upon the vastness of the world through the eyes of a small, imaginary creature called a bedu.

The bedu led Hathorne to the uppermost end of the meadow. They sat side by side, gazing outward. There was something different about the air here. It was rarified and shimmering, almost magical. It seemed to him that he might see into any corner of the world, just by wishing.

"What did you want to show me?" he asked softly, thinking suddenly how odd it was that he had only responded and followed, and not once taken the lead. But then—it was the bedu who knew this land, who knew what was to be illumined here. Still, a dim remembrance of his mission was beginning to crystallize in his thoughts.

"You will see," said the bedu.

"But—"

"Give yourself to it," Larry urged.

Sighing, Hathorne rested his chin on his forearms and knees, and gazed out from this aerie, out into . . .

. . . he felt a wave of giddiness as he stared, eyes going out of focus.

The sound wrapped itself around him, evoking a world without sight. Had his gaze been focused, he might have been stunned by the sight of whales drifting in the emptiness between sky and plain. As it was, he simply tilted his head and thought, *Yes, of course, whales.* Humpbacks, he thought, recognizing the whistles and moans of courting time. And was that the throbbing rumble of a blue?

He was twelve the first time he'd heard a blue whale; and he'd thought it one of the most incredible sounds he could imagine. In its true frequencies, the blue whale's voice was far below the hearing range of humans; speeded up, it was a rumble like the sound of an undersea avalanche; speeded up more, it finally became audible as a beautifully lyrical and expressive call. It was said that, given undisturbed conditions, a blue whale's voice could carry, through the deep convergence channels, halfway around the globe. Was that what this whale was doing, calling across the emptiness and wondering if anywhere in its world there was another of its kind to answer?

The sound, or the memory, or both, sent shivers up Hathorne's spine. He listened quietly as the haunting sounds rose and fell, until at last they faded away.

When he opened his eyes, he was startled to see a changed world. The sky was ruddy and streaked with the last light of a crimson sunset, and there was a strange vapor seeping across the land. He glanced at the bedu inquiringly.

"Watch," Larry said. "Listen."

In a matter of moments, the emptiness of the world was filled with clouds. The plain and sky were swallowed, and then the mountainside, and then even Larry beside him. The fog was yellowish and unearthly; he found himself shivering. A howling wind rose, blowing the mist in a continuous stream past his face. The air temperature was dropping—turning frigid. He braced himself, but found that he could well enough stand the chill; it was the scream of the wind and a sudden sleet that was not water that made him shiver.

"What is this?" he whispered. There was no answer, and he felt a lurch of fear, wondering if he'd been left alone here. "Larry?"

At last the bedu answered, "It is home."

Of course. Home. How stupid of me, Hathorne thought. There was a bite to the air, quite apart from the temperature, and it occurred to him that he was no longer breathing oxygen. The bedu's earlier words came back to him: *Give yourself to it.* Yes. Howling wind, a constant companion. He did not feel lost, or threatened, so this must be the way it was here, if this was home.

A shape was moving in the mist, something dark, low, scuttling. A momentary start gave way to an opening of shared physical sensations. The creature was wading through a soothing bath of slush, pulling itself out again, claws gripping firmly in the methane ices. Strains of eerie music passed through his mind, a song from somewhere else, from outside this world, from Heaven.

What place is this? he wondered wordlessly.

(A world of your sun,) the bedu murmured, its reply touching him within his mind, all vocalization now impossible in this wind. An image flickered in his thoughts of a faintly banded yellowish brown planet, encircled by a vast, round, grooved disk.

(Saturn?) he muttered in astonishment.

(Titan,) said the bedu. (A moon of the other world.)

And the song? The echoes touching this creature were a fine, gentle, probing touch, a comfort in a time of loneliness. And where was it coming from? He might have been skeptical before, but he could believe it now; he was young again, and willing to trust, to accept the feelings and thoughts of another so unlike himself that he could scarcely understand its existence . . . and to allow expression to feelings that had not touched him in years.

And willing to believe that Larry the bedu would not deceive him.

When Jonders felt the touch of life in the dark outer reaches of the solar system, his first thought was that he wished that he had someone to share the astonishment with. Hathorne, Mozy—anyone. Could these frozen, crystalline forms possibly be aware of his presence? So utterly different in form were they, and so unlike his was their perception of time that they might have begun their present train of thought as the bombs were exploding in Earth's wars of the last century. And yet . . .

There was something in them that he could touch and feel. And hear: yes, hear. The minute vibrations of crystal surfaces touching, sliding, shivering. Almost as though in song.

If Hathorne saw this, Jonders wondered, would he recognize it for what it was?

The Sun muttered and trembled, a vast gaseous envelope in which he floated, listening to rumor and laughter and questions. Voices echoing in the belly of the Sun. Shapes moving in cool outer layers.

What astonished Hathorne more than anything else was that it should take someone from the world of another sun to show him and let him see such wonders.

It reminded him of a vast harp strumming, this music of the Sun.

There was a sense of time stretching, or of events compressing, as the visions flickered before him. How many worlds did he glimpse? He quickly lost count; but there were ice worlds and forest worlds and worlds of fire and worlds of stone. Everywhere there were beings whose thoughts, if only for a moment, touched his. Were any of these visions drawn from the Talenki world he had come to see? He couldn't tell.

He'd lost track not just of the worlds but of the viewpoints he'd shared. Several times, he recognized the distant touch of Jonders's mind, wherever the man was, and through him glimpsed interpretations of memories, not in words but through a silent gestalt of knowledge and feeling, sight and sound, touch and intuition.

It was like standing in a kaleidoscope as it turned, with each fragmentary image a flash of illumination on some tiny corner of the Talenki soul, or of his.

At last, full circle, it was the sounds of the sea that brought him back to the present. The Talenki were here now; he could sense them all around him, their song melding and intertwining with the rhythms of the cosmos in a link that somehow made the other worlds a part of their own—and which could be, he supposed, a part of *his* world, if his people so willed it.

The seashore was shrouded in mist, but he walked heedlessly, unafraid of falling. Somewhere along the way, the mountains had vanished, and so, too, had his friend the only living bedu. He was saddened, but only a little; he had seen what Larry had come to make him see.

It was farther along the shore that he came upon Jonders, and with him, a curious-looking creature, rather like a faun. They were both looking out to sea, listening to a foghorn reverberating across the water, and much more softly, the sound of the whales.

"This is N'rrril," Jonders said, by way of introduction. "And Mozy. She's here, too."

Hathorne bowed his head in greeting. "Where *is* Mozy?"

"With N'rrril. Carried in his thoughts," Jonders answered.

"Oh," Hathorne said in disappointment. "I had hoped to see her."

A voice touched him, inside his mind. (Why do you need to see me, when we can speak as simply as this?)

He inclined his head. (Mozy?)

(Yes.)

Hathorne blinked and finally smiled. (I was wondering if we'd meet before this was over. I guess—we've met before, in a way, but this is—different.)

He felt gentle laughter in his mind, and noticed that Jonders, too, was smiling; and then there was a patter of laughter around him, like raindrops, and he realized that the Talenki—not just N'rrril, who was visible, but many others—were joining in the pleasure of the recognition.

He sat on a rock and gazed out to sea for a time, before turning again to N'rrril. Bright golden eyes with pupils of flame blinked back at him. "Are all these connections real?" he asked at last. "All these people, these links across space?"

It was Mozy who answered. (As real as you and I. You have seen only a few, of many.)

(You chose—well—an odd way to show me.)

The laughter echoed again. (Could we—) (—have shown you—) (—in any other—) (—way?)

(No,) he admitted. (Probably not.) Leonard Hathorne the chairman of the Oversight Committee would have found it hard to believe things that Lennie Hathorne the boy could take for granted. Still—(Do you make a habit of digging into people's subconscious memories? I admit that it might have been warranted in this case, but—)

(Now, don't revert so quickly,) Mozy said lightly.

(I'm not, but—)

(The answer is no. They did not dig. They only allowed you to allow yourself to bring back the memories. We were all a little surprised at what emerged. N'rrril?)

The Talenki bobbed its head. (We had feared that you might not be receptive at all, that you would care nothing for the music we brought—)

(Is that why you came, then?)

The Talenki tilted its head, golden, flaming eyes peering deep into his. (There is a phrase,) it said at last. (*The music of the spheres. That is what we seek, what we carry.*)

Other Talenki voices added, (All of knowledge—) (—all of understanding—) (—all of feeling—) (—is to us—) (—a kind of music—) (—of the spheres.)

Hathorne nodded, rubbing his chin. He looked at Jonders, who seemed to be observing all of this with some satisfaction. (I see,) he said. (But you see *my* dilemma, don't you?) He thought momentarily of several billion people, depending on only a handful for their protection. And that handful—not all trusting each other—awaiting his opinion.

(We—) (—see—) answered the Talenki. (But our dilemma—) (—is no less—) (—we can only—) (—seek to know you—) (—and to let you—) (—know us.)

Before he could answer, the fog swirled up again, closing him off from sight but not sound, and he felt again something opening, accepting him . . . an entire people showing their hearts to him . . . and in their hearts were songs . . .

. . . not just their own, but of all the peoples with whom they linked across the reaches of space . . .

. . . and he listened, and judged, as the songs of their hearts reached into his own heart. . . .

Jonders thought he could sit by this sea and listen to the water slapping against the shore forever. The sounds of the whales drifted off into the distance, still audible; but the whales were following their own course, coming and going from the center of the link. N'rrril sat by him, glancing his way once in a while, but mostly just giving him the comfort of his presence.

The fog scattered as a breeze picked up, here by this ocean of the mind. Another kind of music drifted across the air, this time the sound of a piano, and perhaps a guitar and drums. And a human voice. It was a song he thought he might have heard once or twice, an old song. The words echoed across the water, just audible:

> *You say that once you knew for sure*
> *Now you're walking in the shore to wonder*
> *The more you learn the less you know*
> *The more you move the more you go to nowhere . . .*

Mozy's voice entered his thoughts, saying, (It's an old song they especially like. They say it's from the early days of rock-and-roll. I never heard it myself until I felt it in their memory.)

(But how do they know it?) he asked, wonderingly.

(From our radio. They've been listening from across the light-years. Our songs have carried farther than we know. It's one of the reasons they came.)

(Because of our music?)

(They love rock-and-roll,) Mozy said, thinking a smile. N'rrril stirred, and she spoke again, her tone changing. (Matters demand our attention. We must go. And so must you, soon.)

(How long have we been here?)

(Less time than you think. But your Hathorne will be wanting to give his thoughts to his people.)

Jonders nodded, wondering what Hathorne would say. (Mozy?) he said.

There was no answer. Mozy—and N'rrril—were gone.

He sighed and stared back out to sea, resting his chin in his hands. The song drifted across the water:

> You ask the bird as she flies by
> Just where she's at, and she says,
> "Where the wind blows."
> Ask her by that what she means
> She says she doesn't know
> But as she flew away she seemed to say,
> "The wind is . . .

> "Love is the wind
> Wind is my love
> Who knows the wind?
> Who knows my love?
> Where blows the wind?
> The wind is . . . my love.

It was as though a whirlpool drew them out of this world with a sudden irresistible suction and shot them through a hole in the universe into another reality.

Threads of light tangled their movement through the night. It took Jonders several long moments to regain his control, moments in which he felt the vertigo of free-fall; and then he realized what was happening and responded, slowing their movement and easing them upward through the layers of the computer link, severing the connection with the Talenki. The matrix of the computer reality receded, grew dim.

He opened his eyes, blinking against the light of the operations center. Figures were moving urgently around him, voices murmuring. Beside him, Hathorne was struggling to remove his helmet. Jonders waved away those who were trying to help him with his own. He lifted it with a sigh, nearly overcome by exhaustion and exhilaration. How long had they been in there, anyway?

His eyes focused on the chronometer as he checked over the board. Two hours and forty-seven minutes. *Impossible. The tachyon transmission cycle could not last that long. Had the Talenki maintained the link entirely from their own end?*

He turned to speak to Hathorne, but the head of the Oversight Committee was already out of his seat, striding from the room.

Chapter 73

The missile streaked silently across the starfield. It was tracked well beyond the end of its powered flight, coasting wide of the target ship by several kilometers. Several more seconds passed, before the warhead exploded in deep space.

The *Indira Gandhi* shut down its main drive and ceased pursuit. The message had been received and understood.

Aquarius jockeyed into station-keeping position near the Talenki asteroid. It remained fighting-ready, or as nearly so as possible, given the state of its fuel reserves. The automated tanker would be achieving rendezvous in a week or so; but in the meantime, the crew of *Aquarius* remained confident that their missiles could speak for themselves.

Ellis and Kouralt did not understand the reasoning behind the change in their orders; the strategic decisions were made by HQ, and little explanation had been offered. But their new mission, to defend the alien asteroid and to ensure it safe passage into near-Earth space, did seem strange.

They had requested coded confirmation twice, to be sure.

The Soviet and Eastern ships, at the time, had been in superior tactical positions; but that situation had changed abruptly, as the asteroid, without warning, again shifted its course. The Easterners had attempted to pursue, a bit more vigorously than the Soviets; but the warning shot across their bow had persuaded them to take seriously the American communiqué requesting them to stay clear. Eventually the Talenki had slipped back alongside *Aquarius*, in a maneuver

521

that surprised Kouralt and Ellis as much as it must have stunned the crews of the other ships.

Ellis and Kouralt settled in for a watchful wait, training a camera on each of the other ships, and several cameras on their peculiar ward.

"That's your department," Hathorne said impatiently to a face in the telephone. "I don't care how you do it—but when they make orbit at L4, we're to be ready and waiting with shuttle service and a habitable shelter for up to one hundred people, plus equipment. I know L4's as far away as the moon. So what? Can you do it, or can't you?" He listened a moment longer, nodding and grunting, and then broke the connection. He sighed and turned to the next item on his desk.

There was no end to the details. In one short week, he had gone from being a strategist to being a manager. He hoped to get someone in here soon to help with the administrative load; but in the meantime, he had the Oversight Committee to keep happy, the President, the Congress, the commandant of the Space Forces, and heaven knew how many international bodies.

Truthfully, he would not have had it any other way. The vague misgivings which had lingered in his mind for a few days after the Committee's decision were now gone. The new orders were out to the fleet, the President had kept his word, and the Talenki had responded cheerfully to a request to fall in alongside *Aquarius*. They seemed to be picking up some understanding of Earthly protocol. In all, Hathorne felt vindicated in having called for the red-carpet treatment. Even General Armstead had not protested too gruffly; though suspicious, Armstead was a good soldier. And it wouldn't hurt, anyway, to have a few suspicious souls watchdogging the proceedings.

His greatest worry, after the President, had been the risk of armed confrontation with other nations. The warning shot fired by *Aquarius* hadn't done much for the cause of relations with the Eastern Alliance; but since no harm had come to the *Gandhi* or her crew, he was hopeful that the incident would blow over. The Oversight Committee had hastily arranged informational meetings to assure skeptical representatives of both the Eastern Alliance and the Soviet Bloc that exchange with the Talenki would be shared commonly. Following a great deal of posturing on all sides, the other powers had agreed to permit the American escort to proceed unimpeded to the L4 orbit. Soon, he hoped, the Talenki would begin to participate in the negotiating process, once they better understood the situation they were facing.

In the meantime, he was snowed under, just trying to contend with the delegation of work. Hathorne closed his eyes, squeezing the bridge of his nose with his fingers. Just for a minute, he thought; it would not kill the world if he took just a few minutes to himself. Images kept swarming to the forefront of his consciousness . . . memories that would not go away.

Thoughts of a place that he would one day like to return to . . . thoughts of worlds, and feelings, that he would remember as long as he lived.

Frowning, he closed the office door, set the phone to "no calls," and sank back in his chair, eyes closed . . . and reached back for those images. . . .

Payne stretched, working the cramps out of his neck and shoulders. He felt satisfied with the evening's work. A preliminary script was ready for a sidebar on the Talenki's interest in popular music. This first piece was short, but he was already gathering information for a later, in-depth report.

"Are you busy?"

He looked up to see Denine standing in the doorway. "Hi." He pulled a second chair around beside his and patted the seat.

"I'm not interrupting you?"

"Nope. I just finished the prep for tomorrow. How you doing, kiddo?"

Denine sat in the chair, resting her hands in her lap, not meeting his eyes. "I've been thinking a lot about Mozy," she said. "And her family."

Payne ran a finger up and down his pantleg. "Did you get in touch with them?"

"Finally." Denine looked at her fingernails. "They were happy that she's still alive, of course—but confused. I think mainly confused." She looked up. "Mr. Moi died a few weeks ago, so it's been hard on them. I—well, I wish that she could have spoken with him somehow, before—"

Payne nodded, plucking at a spot of lint on his trousers. His brain was tired, and still in the tracks of his work. It was an effort to follow Denine's words. He ought to try to get some sleep tonight, he thought. Since the story had broken, the pace had been merciless. But if he wanted to stay ahead of the competition, he had to keep scrambling.

"Joe, I was thinking—"

He raised his eyes, realized he'd drifted off.

Denine scratched her collarbone. "About Mozy. And the link business. I was wondering—"

A half-smile came to his lips. "I already asked."

Denine cocked her head.

"You want to know if you could link up with Mozy?" She nodded, and he continued, "I asked. They didn't exactly jump at the idea, I'm afraid. Maybe later, they said, when things have slowed down. Of course, if *Mozy* asked, that would be different."

Denine's eyes softened. "You asked, though. You knew I'd want to." She hugged him silently.

The phone chimed. Payne disengaged and twisted to answer. It was Teri Renshaw, in New Washington. "We just got some news from GEO-Four," Teri said, without preliminaries.

He sat up straighter.

"The federal judge there has dismissed all charges pertaining to the Tachylab conspiracy—citing lack of evidence and government improprieties." Teri glanced at her notes. "The federal prosecutor has also called for a grand jury investigation into Donny's death." She looked up. "We're making it our lead late story tonight."

Payne clenched a fist in triumph. Teri seemed for the first time to notice Denine beside him. She paused reflectively, and said, "I'll send you the full notes as soon as they're on line."

"That's terrific," he said.

Teri nodded. She seemed slightly ill at ease, her eyes glancing back and forth between Payne and Denine. "By the way, I hate to tell you this, but someone has to. Your ratings were off a quarter of a point yesterday."

"Damn," Payne said, shrugging.

"Well, you thrilled George when you scooped the rest of the world last week. Now he expects it every day."

"You set him straight, okay?"

"I will. Call you tomorrow." Teri smiled briefly at both of them, and the screen went blank. Payne rocked back in his chair, buoyed by the news about the Tachylab defendants.

"She's in love with you, isn't she?" Denine said.

Jolted back to reality, Payne cleared his throat, feeling blood rise to his face. "Not really," he said uncomfortably. He hadn't really gotten around yet to that long talk with Denine, he thought guiltily. It was about time—long past time.

"But she likes you a *lot*, doesn't she?" Denine said.

He shrugged uneasily. "Yeah."

Denine blinked. "I thought so. I mean—I've known for a long time." She pressed her lips together. "Suspected, anyway." Her eyes clouded, and she looked at her toes, extending and pointing her feet. "Listen. Whatever happened—"

He was silent. He didn't know what to say.

"Whatever happened—" she repeated, stalling. She sighed. "Well. We can talk about it if you want. It doesn't *have* to get in the way. Joe—"

"Yah." He extended a hand. "Yeah, let's talk."

She squeezed back tentatively. "Look, I—know that things weren't too great there for a while. I wasn't giving you much support, was I?"

"Dee. Don't blame yourself. It was my—"

"But I was feeling hurt because you weren't here—and you were always going down to New Wash, where that Teri is. And besides, I thought—I felt—"

He sighed. "Mozy?" he asked softly.

She nodded. "I guess I felt that you were exploiting her, a little. It wasn't reasonable, I know—I mean, here was a story you couldn't very well ignore—but there she was, dead and all—"

"It's true, though," Payne admitted. "That's the sort of thing the news thrives on."

Dee laughed, with a trace of bitterness. "If any of us had dreamed how it would turn out—"

Payne pulled her closer, clasping her hand tightly. Denine leaned against him, and then slid out of her chair and into his lap, the two of them tottering together in the swivel chair. She buried her head against his shoulder, and he caressed her hair with long, gentle strokes. "I love you," he said softly.

She raised her head, resting her forearms on his shoulders. "Joe, I want to see her again. *I want to see her, I want to know what she's become.*"

Payne met her tear-filled gaze. "Give it time, Dee. There must be a way."

She nestled her head against his neck again. "Promise me. Even if it takes a year," she said, her voice muffled.

"Even if it takes two years," he murmured. "Even if it takes two."

*   *   *

The office was quiet, finally, for which Jonders was thankful. He looked over his written report to the Oversight Committee, changing a few phrases before okaying it for transmission. Glancing beneath the report, he chuckled again at the handwritten message on his desk. In a bold, blue-inked script, Diana Thrudore had written: *"Delighted to hear of our patient's recovery. Please give her my best, and do encourage her to return for follow-up consultation. You can't be too careful, you know."* A second copy of his report was earmarked for Dr. Thrudore. He owed her that much, at least—he hadn't had time, in the end, to keep her advised about her patient.

He hadn't had time, lately, for a good many normal obligations. It had been one hell of a week.

He wasn't sure which had startled him more—the summons to speak to the Oversight Committee, or the request to address the U.N. Security Council. He had gone to both, had his say, and left; and the decisions that followed had reached him through the usual channels. In some cases, the "usual channels" meant watching the news.

It pleased him to see Joe Payne covering the Talenki regularly and accurately now. The media in general, of course, were treating them as the story of the century. He'd never learned with certainty who had leaked the full story to Payne, though he had his suspicions. In any event, no one had accused him, and he hadn't seen Delarizzo, the security advisor, since before the session with Hathorne. The Committee had finally conceded the futility of maintaining silence, and rules governing press relations had been relaxed. Jonders, in fact, had already addressed several official press conferences. One of his new problems was getting his work done in spite of constant media inquiries.

Link Center, more than ever, was the focus of intense activity. The Talenki were still weeks away from Earth orbit; but already the international community was bartering and arguing, attempting to hammer out a system for coordinating exchange with the aliens. The logistical details and political ramifications were endless. Various schemes and proposals were being discussed with the Talenki, and it had fallen to Jonders to oversee communications with them.

His family still wasn't seeing much of him, but at least now they understood why.

He glanced at the time and hurried out of the office. He had a private appointment to keep. The lab section was quiet; most of the staff had gone home already, or were working in the main operations center. Jonders unlocked the simulation control room and turned on the lights. He powered up the main console and donned the linkup helmet.

(David,) he said, when the connection was established.

(Good to see you,) said Kadin, his face a sketchy outline in the darkness of the computer matrix. (It's been a while, hasn't it? I've been following your summaries with interest.)

(I've been wanting to talk to you for days,) Jonders said. (But it's just been one thing after another.)

(How are relations with the Talenki progressing?)

(Well, they were pretty bewildered at first by our concepts of diplomacy, but they seem to be catching on. They're beginning to treat it as a game, I think. There's only one problem ...)

Kadin's eyes glinted.

(Mozy hasn't shown herself at all in the last week. I keep wondering if there's something wrong.)

(Are you having trouble communicating with the Talenki?)

(No, no—they're a joy. It's just—well, I don't really *think* there's anything wrong. But I can't help wondering.)

(Have you asked?)

(They say she's busy.) Jonders was silent a moment.

(You miss her,) Kadin said finally.

Jonders nodded slowly. (Yeah,) he said. That was it, really. Her presence was a comfort, and he missed it—whatever the reason. He sighed and changed the subject. (Anyway, if I can get it cleared upstairs, I'd like to start getting you involved in the communications process. You could take up some of the routine stuff, and I think your insight would be an asset.)

(I'd like that,) Kadin said.

(The Talenki remember Kadin-One quite fondly, you know. I think you would get on well with them.)

(Bill,) Kadin said thoughtfully. (I'd like to try. But there's something I don't understand. Maybe you can explain it.)

(All right.)

Kadin's eyes probed Jonders's. (It's Hathorne.)

(What about him?)

(What changed his mind, Bill? What made him decide to trust the Talenki?) The puzzlement grew in Kadin's face. (Was it what he saw of their world—or worlds they've contacted? Those images could have been illusory. It seems to me—)

Jonders interrupted. (That wasn't it, David. Oh, it helped, sure—but that wasn't what really convinced him.)

Kadin blinked slowly. (What, then?)

Jonders smiled to himself, because he'd puzzled over precisely the same question; and when the answer had finally occurred to him, it had seemed too simple to be true. (What swung him over, David—I'm sure of it—was the way they treated *his* images, *his* memories.)

Kadin blinked again.

(They treated him with *respect*. With respect, and with sensitivity. They looked at his memories, and feelings—very personal feelings, about things that were a shock even to him to recall.) Jonders paused, remembering. He had only glimpsed most of the images, but Hathorne's emotions had touched him clearly during the final phase of the session. It had taken time for his own understanding to gel, a process that had been largely subconscious and intuitive.

(Hathorne had no idea that he would open *himself* in that way, David—but when it happened, he learned something about them that he might not otherwise have seen. And he trusted what he saw.) The other reasons, the arguments conveyed to the Committee, and the President, and the Congress, the persuasive arguments about wealths of knowledge and connections with other worlds—those reasons were perfectly valid, but secondary.

A tiny light came into Kadin's eyes. (It affected your attitudes a little, too, didn't it?)

(You mean that it made me more aware of the Talenki's—)

(Not the Talenki. Your feelings about Hathorne.) Kadin peered at him in amusement. (You almost . . . *like* him, now, don't you?)

Jonders stared back disconcertedly. (I—) He thought about it. (Why, I suppose I do.) He'd never voiced the feeling; but yes. Hathorne was still playing the hard-nosed official, but he was treating Jonders with more respect, now, and had even sent him a letter of commendation—really, just a short thank-you note. At the time, Jonders had tossed it aside with vague satisfaction; but in fact, it was the first real recognition he'd received in the project—not of his competence, but of the value of his judgment. Jonders was in charge of Talenki relations now—not because they had no choice, as in the past, but because his qualifications had finally been recognized.

It had seemed a small thing, that note from Hathorne; but in retrospect, it was a vote of confidence long due. . . .

Chaptor 71

It was, in a sense, more like a complex stringed instrument than anything else, a maze of incredibly fine, tuned threads stretched across the light-years and converging here in the Talenki mind-net. She had, at one point, thought of it as a gigantic telephone switchboard, with thousands of conversations buzzing simultaneously; but that analogy was in the end too simplistic, failing to allow for the fluidity of the connections, the constant interplay that arose almost wistfully out of the communication.

No, it was more like an infinitely complex symphonic arrangement— each part reverberating in its own peculiar harmony with the other parts, each altering the gestalt with its own shading of tone and feeling. The communication was largely nonverbal, sensual, kinesthetic— musical, as, for the Talenki, all knowledge and understanding was music. Mozy was riding a cresting wave, rhythms racing through her like water chortling over a spillway—music from the Talenki, and from worlds of her own sun, music from distant jewelled lights and from suns obscured by galactic dust.

The variety was endless: the sighing, soughing music of the Slen; the chimes of the Kel-Kor on a world cradled deep within a wispy, red-glowing nebula; the steel orchestration of the metalloid creatures of a pink-and-white binary system; the wolflike howling of the bare-snouted but furry Mangorras; the keening of the R'pitt't mist-ravens of a world almost lost at the edge of a dust lane in Sagittarius; the thundering murmur of a dozen sentient suns.

Songs carried through the webbed fabric of space, swept along by the winds of the cosmic tachyon flux.

Oddly enough, it was only recently that she had become aware that not all of the Talenki voices that she heard were of this world. Indeed, some of them belonged to Talenki circling worlds of other stars, or wandering in deep space. Mozy's hosts were not the only descendants of the original refugee colony. It was in fact unclear, even to the Talenki, whether this was the original asteroid or a copy. Often, in their journeys, the Talenki had found themselves faced with a choice between wanderlust and a desire to tarry with congenial hosts, learning their cultures and ways. The solution, repeated time and again, had been to fashion a new asteroid and to divide the community, so that some might stay while the rest journeyed on. How many Talenki asteroids were there now, scattered through the galaxy? Even the Talenki didn't know.

It was while listening to a peculiar counterpoint between two worlds widely separated along the galactic plane that it occurred to her to wonder if the Talenki's reach might extend not just through space, but through time, as well; and even as the question occurred, she felt the tingle of a new sense—her awareness slipping into unfamiliar waters, like a slender hull knifing beneath the waves of a sea and slicing silently through the depths . . . a submarine in the ocean of time.

She glimpsed a Talenki world of years gone by—not in memory, but in direct vision, through a tunnel of mist. She saw fauns whose corporeal lives were now a thing of the past, guiding their world across the abyss of space, their last stop a half generation or more behind them, and the next stop, Earth, still far in the future. For an instant, she glimpsed faces . . . *living faces, eyes peering* . . . and then they were gone, leaving her breathless.

How could this be happening? Visions shimmered in her mind of the Talenki movement through layers of reality; and she wondered, how much more did she have to learn about their abilities?

The future was enshrouded in fog, and she wasted little time trying to pierce it. But the past: she peered further still, as though along a physical timeline, stretching into the distance. The further she looked, the murkier was her vision. In the distant past, she could not discern objects at all; her awareness was principally of tones and shadows and qualities of presence, almost a spiritual rather than a physical sense. Still, she wondered: might it be possible to peer all the way back to the origins of the universe—to sift through the layers and ridges and rifts of the continuum, back through the dim deeps of time? As she peered along the timeline, she saw no clear delimitation, but only a gradual dimming and loss of resolution; and she thought, yes, perhaps, it was possible in theory; but only with vastly greater powers of perception than even the Talenki possessed. She was reminded of Earth's astronomers, building ever more powerful telescopes to extend their reach into space and time, studying light that had travelled millions of years to reach them.

(Your sight has grown keen, Mozy.)

That was N'rrril, gently nudging her. She eased herself into his thoughts. (What do you mean?)

(We, too, have thought long on this matter of perceiving distant times and spaces.) He thought it softly, and with greater solemnity than was usual for him.

(The design?) she murmured, as another bit of understanding surfaced. It was no coincidence that the idea had occurred to her while listening to the rhythms and harmonies of the Talenki network. The network was not itself the design, she realized, but a means to the design. As the link grew—each new perspective adding to the synergistic potential of the whole, the network expanding in power far beyond the sum of the parts—so too did the clarity of view improve. She recalled the wail of the background radiation—Nature's song, and a record of the first moments of the universe. What did the Talenki perceive in that three-degree wail, and what would Earth's scientists make of the Talenki images? she wondered. The Talenki were seeking a direct window to the birth of time—and how many more worlds would have to join the link before it could be achieved?

And what next, after the origins of reality? A vision, perhaps, of that which came before the beginning?

Her thoughts drifted back to her Earth, to her *other* people, and she wondered: Would they understand? Or was their independence, their stubbornness, their aggressiveness too strong, their pride too fierce to let them join?

She had not spoken with Earth since her conversation by the sea with Jonders. They were managing all right without her, she knew; but the time was coming—a time to mend and grow. A time to listen and learn.

And perhaps—*perhaps*—others of her race would join her in this life, in a merger of Human and Talenki consciousness, in a crosslinkage stretching to the horizons of the universe. The possibilities were infinite; and she felt a growing longing for Human company to explore them with, even with the friendship of the Talenki. In her previous life, she had scarcely thought at all of motherhood, but now it seemed her destiny in a way that no one could have imagined: to be the first guiding member of a new Human race . . . the next stage, or *a* next stage, in the evolution of Humanity.

(N'rrril?) she said softly. (Are you still there?)

His gentle laughter chimed in her thoughts. (Of course. Always.)

She felt her extended senses drawing in from the reaches of space and time, not abandoning what she had found, but turning for a time inward, homeward. Home could be many places at once; but just now it was time for home to be Earth, time to reach back and to help the others along if she could.

(Look homeward with me,) she whispered to N'rrril. (We have much to do.)

Chapter 75

The cluster that had grown up around the L4 orbit was astonishing to behold. In two short years, the settlement had grown from a few shanty dwellings tethered together near the asteroid to a burgeoning metropolis in space. The second large habitat was nearly complete already, and the area swarmed with spacecraft traffic from all nations. In addition, there was the second asteroid, which had been towed into place three months ago and tethered to the Talenki asteroid. The Talenki had already begun hollowing and reworking the second rock.

Payne floated at the hotel window, in the hub of the spinning station, gazing out at the asteroids. The two rocks, joined together, looked like an absurd, giant peanut. He hoped he might have a chance to see the internal construction firsthand, though he knew that was unlikely. The Talenki were limiting access to the asteroid interiors, to minimize environmental hazards. Even now, most views of the interiors came to the world courtesy of Link Center, and its on-site extension here at L4. Some pictures were provided by cameras, either remotes or cameras carried by those selected individuals who had entered the asteroid; but most views still came through the link, through Talenki eyes—and those were generally the best views of all, relayed to the world through improved computer-enhanced imaging.

Payne had studied the recordings endlessly, trying to understand how the Talenki did it: the tunnels that seemed to wind forever through an asteroid that was, after all, only two kilometers or so long; walls that altered themselves inexplicably; and Talenki who moved about more like ghosts than solid beings. Most of all he was puzzled by the tunneling process in the new asteroid. The excavated material, rather than being brought out for disposal, was somehow carried *deeper* into the asteroid and fused back into the structure of the emerging honeycomb in order, it was explained, to *extend* the volume of space. The Talenki planned eventually to cannibalize yet another asteroid, and to use the additional mass to further stretch the interior of this one.

He didn't understand it, but neither did the construction engineers studying the process. It was said that the Talenki were somehow expanding and inhabiting the "compacted dimensions" above the four of space and time known to human perception; but Payne understood just enough of that to know that he didn't understand it at all. It made him feel better to know that he was not alone.

He had been here twice before, on documentary shoots, but this time he had made a special trip to witness a new milestone in Human-Talenki relations. First he had to locate Jonders. That was not always so easy these days.

He floated away from the window and made his way to the one-fifth-gee ring and the hotel lobby. The place was like a miniature U.N., with staff and guests representing dozens of nations. He asked an Indian clerk for Jonders's room, and was directed to a phone console. Payne asked the operator, a recording of an attractive Asian woman, to page Jonders. The recording smiled pleasantly, and after a minute, Jonders's face appeared. "Joe? When did you get in?"

"I just cleared security," Payne said. "Do you have time to see me?"

"Absolutely. Come on around. We've moved the office, though, since last time." Jonders gave him a new location number.

Payne found the new lab in the second spin-section. Jonders showed him into a cubicle that passed for an "enlarged" office and handed him a cup of coffee in a spillproof container. "The transfer is scheduled for day after tomorrow," he said. "Everything seems ready. Do you have a crew?"

"They're on the next shuttle."

"Good. Well, how are you? What's the news from home?"

"I don't know how much you've heard," Payne said. "Denine had another session with Mozy. I think you were on your way up here, at the time."

"I gathered," Jonders said. "Mozy has asked me to set up sessions with all of her family, when I go back Earthside. Apparently she spoke with Dee about her father—and that stirred up some feelings she wants to explore." Jonders's eyebrows danced. "It seems she had to grow in other ways before she could come to terms with her family. A time for all things, I suppose. But what about the trial at GEO-Four? I heard it was underway, but I missed the outcome.''

"Delayed again." Payne sighed. Would it *ever* be finished? he wondered. It had taken the better part of a year for arrests to be made in connection with Alvarest's death; and the judicial process was taking even longer. One continuation had followed another, and he wondered if even a guilty verdict would satisfy him now.

Jonders apparently sensed his feelings. He set down his coffee cup. "Want to take a look?"

Payne agreed gladly and followed Jonders out of the office, and into the lab proper. It was a highly compacted version of the operations center in New Phoenix. Considerable equipment had been added since Payne's last visit. They stood in the control room, peering into a glassed-in studio. A young black woman was practically buried by the linkup helmet and peripheral equipment.

"That's Mbira," Jonders said quietly. "She's with Kadin now. He's been helping her learn her way around in the link, using training simulations similar to the ones Mozy used in the old days. She's a quick learner—seems to have a natural talent for it. Perhaps it's her storyteller training. The Talenki took to her right away."

Payne nodded. Politically, he knew, the choice of an African woman had been a ticklish matter. But the Talenki were reportedly pleased with the choice. Payne stepped closer to the glass. He couldn't see much of the woman, through all the equipment; but he knew that she was physically a frail woman, despite her youth, being partially paralyzed with a degenerative muscular disease. None of that would matter to the personality that would soon join Mozy in the mind-net. "You're recording all of this, aren't you?" he asked Jonders.

"Of course. We'll supply you with whatever pictures you need." Jonders pointed to a bank of monitors. One screen showed Mbira's face, her eyelids closed, fluttering. Another flickered with visual images tapped directly from the link: pathways and ghostly forms, as though in a forest—Mbira's own interpretation of the link matrix. A man's face materialized: sharp features, a face all shadow and light, hair longish and curly, eyes flashing. "Her image of Kadin," Jonders murmured.

"A bit different from the man I met," Payne remarked, thinking of a session he had been given at the New Phoenix center.

Jonders chuckled. "We've had two subjects visualize him as being clearly and explicitly female. We discussed changing his name to a more neutrally gendered one, but Kadin says he likes his name and wants to keep it."

The scene in the monitors was changing, as Kadin and Mbira reached out to the Talenki mind-world. The interior of the asteroid appeared in fuzzy swirls.

"How does Mozy feel about Kadin being in the link?" Payne asked.

"Oh, it's become quite normal to her. I think the hardest part was accepting that this is not the same Kadin she knew aboard *Father Sky*, not the one who died—"

"But it *is* the same Kadin, isn't it? With more training—?"

"From your perspective, or mine. But he never lived through the experience of *Father Sky* and whatever Mozy and Kadin-One had together there. They became two individuals when Kadin-One was transmitted, just as Mbira will become two—" Jonders paused, raising an eyebrow as Payne opened his mouth.

Payne cleared his throat. "I have to ask this. What's the risk of repeating what happened to Mozy?"

Jonders shrugged soberly. "If you mean the risk of another catatonic trauma—quite small, we hope. The scanning procedures are better refined, the subject's better prepared, and the Talenki will be assisting. Plus, we have a good, clear, direct signal to the asteroid. But—all of the volunteers are aware of the risks—and they're willing to trade their present lives, if necessary, for new ones with the Talenki."

Payne grunted, and watched the images unfold.

A moment later, Jonders indicated one of the Talenki fauns. "We had three of them over for a visit last week. They caused quite a stir, walking around in some sort of protective field, dancing through walls. We had to ask them if they would mind not doing that, especially when they make state visits planetside."

Payne laughed. "I can imagine how the Secret Service would react to that." He watched a while longer, then asked suddenly, "Have you ever thought about going yourself?"

The question caught Jonders off-guard, but he recovered with a sheepish smile. "My family worries about me enough already," he said. "Besides," he admitted, "I'm not sure they'd want a meddling scientist like me in there, anyway. They seem more interested in passion than science." He shrugged, perhaps a little wistfully.

Payne smiled outwardly, but felt an inner tug. Though he'd asked the question of Jonders, the truth was that within himself was a small voice wondering if *he* might go.

*   *   *

As the final count progressed, Payne directed his own camera crew around the technical staff in the control room. The tension in the room was considerable, which he noted as he muttered his narration into a tiny pickup mike. Jonders was in the primary control link already, preparing the way.

Mbira was surrounded by medics and equipment. The last clear view of her face had shown her with a relaxed smile. Payne thought of the interview he'd done with her last night, a brief clip of which had been used on the Earthside news earlier today. She'd smiled winsomely into the camera and said, "Mr. Payne, I want to tell stories forever, and to anyone in the universe who will listen. And I want to hear their stories and make them mine. Why else would anyone want to go?"

Why else, indeed, Payne thought enviously.

As the last few seconds were counted down, he observed and recorded every detail.

There wasn't much to see, really, when the scanning began. The monitors began flickering until the images were a blur. Was the subject stiffening, as the transfer proceeded? Payne realized he was clenching his own notes tightly, crumpling them. The technicians were muttering among themselves.

Jonders and Mbira were motionless, beneath their helmets.

The first indication of completion came when Mozy's voice suddenly boomed out of a speaker: "Mbira, if you can hear me over there—you're here, and you're safe. We'll have you walking again in no time." There was a pause. Then: "We'll take over from here, Bill. Nice going, guys, you did it."

It wasn't until a few minutes later—when Mbira, in the studio, raised a shaky hand in a salute—that the technicians broke into grins and soft-spoken cheers.

Chapter 76

Epilog: 2054 A.D.

The gulf between the asteroids widened until Talenki II was lost from sight. Earth, too, dwindled until it was scarcely a bluish white dot, almost obliterated by the glare of the sun. The Talenki mind-net, its newly separated loci pulling inexorably apart, buzzed with music and thoughts, reminders and farewells, threads of communication that lengthened with each passing minute.

Mozy for a time cried, and for a time laughed. She hummed to songs of parting and songs of reuniting and sang a strain of the blues that was all her own. The Talenki link was pulling apart, and yet growing even as it did so. Pain was a part of the growing process; and so was hope.

There were moments when she felt that her consciousness would surely burst with all of the thoughts and feelings and knowledge of her newest kin and friends. Was there a natural limit to the extent of a consciousness? she wondered. Perhaps one day the answer would become clear, but for now she saw no end. Talenki/Human/Whale/Titan/Slen . . . how many others were already a part of this web, or would be?

The Talenki had been pleased with their stay among Humanity, though it had not been without risk or incident. Sixteen years ago a xenophobic terrorist had nearly succeeded in penetrating the asteroid with a fusion bomb, while Talenki attention was turned Earthside for a planetwide tour. Only the alertness of a Human pilot had averted tragedy for the Talenki, though the pilot had traded his own life for those of his world's guests.

If anything, the incident had solidified the Talenki's trust in the decency of the Human species; and when the time had come to separate those who would stay from those who would journey on, nearly a third of the Talenki had elected to stay. Mozy touched and sampled their feelings now, with Mbira, Kadin, and the others, reaching back to share thoughts not just with Talenki but with Human/Talenki and purely Human friends who remained at the homeward end of the link. Melissa, Gregor, Lu-Chen . . . she would miss them in a special way, though they would be there in the Talenki II mind-net for a long, long time, touching her down the threads of the link.

But ahead . . . ah, what lay ahead? N'rrril and the others whispered of the worlds they sensed, worlds they guessed at, worlds deep in the hearts of glowing nebulas and worlds at the uttermost edges of the galaxy. Would she live to view such wonders? The Talenki could give no answer, except to say that generations of Humans on Earth would live their lives and pass on while she journeyed and grew, slowly, old.

Now, as her world rippled faster through space, and as Earth and her sister planets and her sun dwindled behind, she sighed and listened to the songs of her homeworld, readying herself for the worlds to come. The whistling and bubbling of the whales on Earth were echoed by young whales deep in the heart of the asteroid, in the tiny sea that somehow was larger than the asteroid itself mutiplied several times over. The whales of Earth—down there with the dizzies, spinning out their constant stream of tachyons—were a solace to Mozy in this time of parting. She regretted that they could not have brought along a solar creature or a Titan, but for them she would have to be content with rumor and song from home.

(N'rrril?)

A whisper. A laugh. (Yes?)

(Is it always this way when you leave a world you love? When you want to travel on, to—)

(Yes.)

(Happy and sad?)

(Always.)

This time it was she who laughed, sadly and happily. She had of course known the answer before asking; but she had wanted someone to say it for her, to confirm both the fear and the hope. (Farewell,

Earth,) she said, speaking it to N'rrril, but thinking it to her place of birth.

(It is not truly farewell,) N'rrril reminded her.

(No. But just now it feels that way,) she answered, and then she fell silent, touching only N'rrril, and she listened long and hard to the sighing and the whispering of the stars.

THE BEST IN SCIENCE FICTION

THE BEST IN FANTASY

Buy them at your local bookstore or use this handy coupon:
Clip and mail this page with your order.

Publishers Book and Audio Mailing Service
P.O. Box 120159, Staten Island, NY 10312-0004

Please send me the book(s) I have checked above. I am enclosing $_____
(please add $1.25 for the first book, and $.25 for each additional book to
cover postage and handling. Send check or money order only — no CODs.)

Name _____

Address _____

City _____ State/Zip _____

Please allow six weeks for delivery. Prices subject to change without notice.

BESTSELLING BOOKS FROM TOR

MORE BESTSELLERS FROM TOR